PLAGUE

(Book Two of The Search)

Philip J. Cook

Published in 2012 by FeedARead Publishing

First Edition

British Library C.I.P.

A CIP catalogue record for this title is available from the British Library.

Dedications

Kath, my long-suffering wife, who still cannot understand why I spend so much time on my computer.

Debbie, Dean, Hayley and Samantha, my children who have spent their lives wondering who the hell I am.

My grandchildren, Charlene, Nathan, Liam, Matthew, Kieron and the latest, my beautiful little Constance, all of whom just let me get on with it, as long as I'm there when they need me.

For their support, my sons-in-law, Leslie, Simon and Christopher.

And for all my friends, too numerous to mention by name, who have cajoled, advised and ridiculed me over the years.

PART ONE

OUTBREAK

And his God spoke:

'The pestilence precedes you.
Hurry, let it not be wasted.
Reap all the souls for Purgatory.
Search for the key.
The key must be found!
Kill the boy!'

One

The ceremonial chamber in the vast, roughly circular cavern, deep within the bowels of the volcano on Sanctity, was filled with dense, black smog. On the cold, grey stone benches around the walls, lay hundreds of corpses, the floor surrounding the altar in the centre of the arena, strewn with more.

The aftermath of the battle hammered the eyes, for it was not only the cadavers of monks which lay where they had fallen. Intermingled with the white robed figures were smaller, black bodies dressed only in loin cloths and ragged dresses of calico. These were the remains of the courageous and desperate slaves killed in the conflict. But interspersed with all the human remains were even smaller bodies, these were animals covered in sleek black fur—the rats that Thaddeus, wizard of understanding, had called on for assistance.

But nearly all the bodies had one thing in common. All bore the marks of their hideous, violent deaths. They lay uncaring of the horror the sight evoked, for there was an abundance of bits and pieces of flesh scattered across the chamber.

There was one body in particular, though, that lay slumped over at the foot of the altar. It had been decapitated, its grey flesh drained of every last sickening morsel of blood. Leash, the vampyrus, had sucked completely dry of blood, Zorzecai, the demon master, before escaping through the dungeons.

The fog, sublimating from the cold, black rock of the basin floor at one end of the altar, continued its noisy, violent motion. The disgusting smells, permeating the site of the deaths of Tragen, wizard mentor, more than a hundred slaves, the Abbot of Sanctity and Zorzecai, was of flesh already turning putrid, the noise that of confusion and insanity and threat.

Moving within the cavern were deformed and dismembered souls, nothing at all do with the recent battle. They were the ensnared souls of old, their shapes insubstantial, gliding through the swirling miasma. Colliding with each other, each encounter led to some further form of savagery, which only increased their pain and disfigurement. Yet each maiming was not enough to bring on annihilation as a little later the souls underwent a bizarre, unnatural renewal, a never-ending vicious circle of mental anguish, physical pain, near oblivion—and a healing of all but the mind.

The insubstantial dead souls of the humans trapped within the Darkness could neither see, nor feel a living soul. Unlike the abhorrent creatures that accompanied them. These were the demons bred in Purgatory with the express purpose of tormenting those dead souls previously herded by the collectors. And no two were alike. Tall and reed thin, squat and toad-like some had sharp outlines, others flowing together their bodies merging and then re-appearing as a totally different demon. The foul beings with an offensive caricature of a body, could feel both the living and the dead. And they all had two aims—one to slay the living, the other to torment the dead souls thereby harvested.

The interminable surge of the Darkness, curling and roiling from the basin and into the freedom of the cavern, resulted in an inordinate compression of the mists. There was not enough space in which to exist, so its rate of flow slowed for a while, but not for long. Inevitably the Darkness found escape from the cavern, mostly through the small aperture in the rockfall – made by Leash – which led into the bleak dungeons. It whistled through the gap into the cells like steam through a spout and emerged at the sewer's outfall.

But this rate of diffusion of the fog was still not enough to circumvent congestion. The Darkness needed to find escape elsewhere, the dispersal of the black mist was not swift enough to allow the demons ingress. They could not get through the gateway in the basin to dig at the fabric of the chamber, to enlarge the hole in the rockfall, or clear the doorway into the chapel at the other end. And so the Darkness searched the walls and the roof and squeezed itself into all manner of crevices and indentations and cracks.

But it was the floor of the cavern which it found more conducive to its hunt; the greater part consisted of stone slabs laid on compacted earth. And as with all such floors deep underground, it was subject to small earth movement. Here and there, edges of the flat stones rose or dipped, leaving soil runnels and small fissures in the hard, igneous clay beneath. It was in these chinks and crannies that the Darkness found its way into the burrows and tunnels running under the stones. It escaped deeper into the island as it trickled through the granules of the soil and seeped through the larger gravel and rocks.

To survive the frightening influence of the black rock, Sanctity's myriad rodents had dug very deep underground. But not deep enough—the menacing black mists found escape through their runs and tunnels.

And the small animals and insects promptly found themselves the prey as they were instantly within reach of the creeping Darkness. The black rats – called upon by Thaddeus to aid the wizards in their bitter battle – having enlarged the entranceways to their nests, fled the acrid smog. But the fog caught up with them – and the rodents' fleas – and it infected the jumping, biting insects. The rats, the mice, the voles and all manner of other subterranean life forms bolted in all directions, panic taking some deeper underground to die of starvation and suffocation. Others sought different routes to the upper world.

And the Darkness followed these last, gleefully.

The desperate rodents, plagued by the pestilential fleas, had no thoughts but flight, some primeval instinct telling them they would die if they remained on the island. The rats escaped on boats, accompanying the newly liberated denizens of Sanctity. For there were others living on the island besides the soulless monks and slaves, these were the sailors and fishermen of the port, the farmers, the dockworkers and the slave traders. They were all desperate to escape the island madness. And the fugitive rats, and their biting fleas, landed on other islands with the humans they had infected on the way. These rats were fast movers, used to the wharfs and the salt water, the grime and the refuse of a busy port. Some had already found safe havens on vessels that departed Sanctity's shores before the Grim slipped its moorings for Griffin Island.

A few of the stronger, larger rats climbed the hawsers securing the wizards' ship to the jetty and the fleas carrying the evil pestis travelled with them—as did something else.

What no survivor had noticed when fleeing the cavern was the thing that preceded the Darkness. A diabolical freak appeared out of the rock and climbed surreptitiously the low banks of the basin. A shape-shifter with a devious, demonic intelligence, it took a swift look around the cavern and quickly decided to take the form of a rat. But, although it had fully succeeded in transforming into the rodent shape, it unknowingly had a feature that distinguished it from all other rats— a white stripe running down its back. But it didn't interfere in any way with it hiding amongst the other rats as they escaped.

It was the first to hitch a ride on the Grim.

Two

The Grim, fleeing the devastating nightmare following behind, sailed the calm ocean serenely the weather-stained canvas on three of its five masts billowing full. Its two broken masts, their stumps cut cleanly by the bo'sun, were standing shoulder-high, mute reminders of the terrible storm that had struck the largest warship in the known world. The weather, fragrant, soft and warm, denied the evilness abroad in the world. The gentle motion of the dismasted ship proceeding east on its return to Griffin Island, calmed raw nerves, easing eyes recently subjected to terrible scenes of violence. But nothing at all could alleviate the horrendous memories, the smell of the carnage or the foul acts of viciousness they had been forced to perpetrate against unfeeling people—the walking dead, their bodies empty of souls now ensnared within the Darkness by pure evil. Emotions were in turmoil, everyone unable to acknowledge or understand the dreadful pain of the last few days.

Along the narrow, dark passage that ran between the berths set aside for passengers, in the small cabin that up to now had been shared by Tragen and his apprentice, Anders' friends kept vigil over the deeply traumatized Aidan. The young wizard, who found himself unexpectedly the leader among his four friends, lay in a deep sleep. His companions, Thaddeus, Augusta and Beatrix in the living world, and Anders in the Afterlife were in accord. All were petrified to leave the young man's side in case he succumbed to the power in his mentor's, Lord Tragen's, staff and again ended up in the Darkness. The Darkness – they trembled at just hearing it mentioned – was the vile weapon of an unknown God…a God who wanted them all dead, their souls entrapped in Purgatory for his amusement.

The dread of that almost certainty lay heavily on their shoulders. If Aidan's soul was again thrust involuntarily from his body by Tragen's staff then they would all have to follow him. Where Aidan's soul went so would Augusta, Beatrix and Thaddeus. And this time Anders would insist on entering the black mists of the Darkness to aid their search. And the consequences of the dead Ander's decision, the risk to the murdered boy's soul would be insurmountable. Anders could not enter the Darkness and return for it never relinquished gladly a soul that had passed from Life.

The only one it had released was Thaddeus' mother, Bettina Portolan. She had been killed by a demon whilst protecting her unborn child. At his birth she had been instrumental in keeping Thaddeus' soul safe from the One behind the Darkness. Her dead soul had been rescued from the black mists by Aidan and his friends and she was now residing in Paradise after fifteen years of caring for her son.

Aidan, short and slight, his shoulder-length black hair plastered across his forehead, lay sweating on the lower of the two bunks, grief and exhaustion had sent him, hopefully, into a healing sleep.

Thaddeus, taller than his friends and overweight, stood over him and cocked his head listening for signs of distress. He heard only Aidan's breathing, deep and regular.

Beatrix, her shoulder length blonde hair falling over her pretty face, sat on the bed holding Aidan's hand, showing the worry clearly in her dark, ever-changing eyes reflecting her moods. She alone of all of them, enabled by her powers for creating light, had clearly seen Lord Tragen – bathed in incandescent radiance in his cage – disappearing into the black rock. No brightness could ever dazzle or blind Beatrix, though she knew it not, yet. She had perceived the aged wizard struggling to halt the power in his staff, and witnessed him failing.

Now she was mortally afraid for the safety of Aidan, the young man who had passed on his magical abilities to her. A young man she was very fond of, her affection growing without her realizing it.

Thaddeus, staring out of the cabin's porthole at the calm ocean just inches from his nose, reading Beattie's thoughts, felt her fear. 'Perhaps you worry too soon, Beattie. It may not happen this time; he seems to be sleeping peacefully now.'

'He was sleeping the last time his soul was forced into the Darkness, when he found you there,' Augusta snapped. Tapping her chin worriedly and brushing her long black hair out of her eyes, she sat hunched over in the only chair, helplessly gazing at the boy she loved.

'We thought it was a nightmare,' Beatrix said into the silence following her princess' retort. She released Aidan's limp hand. Brushing her hair from her pale and haggard face she turned and stared at the back of the newly ennobled Prince Griffin. 'Why should it be different this time, Thaddeus? We all know what happened every time Tragen used that…that staff of his,' she paused, chewing her bottom lip she continued. 'Aidan either had some sort of vision or ended up in either Limbo or the Darkness.'

'From what you saw, Tragen was trying to halt the power, not use it. There's a difference…it might not send Aidan here, this time,' Anders, looking remarkably as he did in Life – another with long hair, this time blond, broad-shouldered and tall, he wore the habitual britches and tunic – interrupted from the wall of colours. He was doing his best to ease everyone's mind, including his own.

'But Tragen is imprisoned in the middle of a magic that's powerful beyond belief, and he is holding his staff. If you're wrong and it happens this time, I think Aidan will go so far into the Darkness we'll never find him,' said Beatrix.

'Then we'll go in and search until we do find him,' said Augusta, again snapping, her nerves raw with worry.

'By the Gods, you don't know what you're saying! Haven't you been listening to us tell you of the horrors in there?' Thaddeus countered, white-faced, knowing her words stated the inevitable.

They'd have to enter the Darkness. They could never leave Aidan alone in that place to spend eternity evading the demons, knowing that in the end he'd succumb to the roving herdsmen, as everyone always did. They loved him, he was their friend—their leader. They could never allow that fate to befall him.

'When we do follow him, you will do as I say.' Thaddeus picked his words carefully; he did not want to frighten the girls but knew he inevitably would. But trying to find a balance between caution and the terrible reality of the demonic habitat was extremely difficult.

'In the mists of the Darkness roam beings that will give you nightmares for the rest of your life. The wraiths…the poor dead souls trapped within it, can't harm us physically, but they can hurt us mentally. You'll all have to learn to switch your minds off, protect them from the horror—and you'll have to learn quickly.

'Zorzecai is not the only herdsman; there are many collectors of Purgatory equally as terrible.' Zorzecai was the evil demon, who had killed Dyfrig, the Abbot of Sanctity, and presided over the sacrifices of slaves and felons to his God. He was also the one who had consigned Lord Tragen to suffocate within the black rock. Thaddeus continued, his voice trembling as he endeavoured to block out the memories of the sacrificial chamber beneath Sanctity. 'There are other demons as well, all just as dangerous because they act purely on instinct, their nature telling them to kill whenever they meet life. And they don't care if they die attacking you, for many will be reborn…renewed by the One behind the Darkness. We will need to avoid them all. If we stop and fight, then others will be attracted to the scene and we'll be overwhelmed by an unending number. The God controls thousands upon thousands of demons. 'So…I will lead us in the Darkness and you will obey me without question or we'll never come back out.' He resumed staring out the porthole.

'*You agree with Beattie then, Thaddeus. You think it likely Aidan will end up there?*' Anders asked.

And the young man, who knew more of the Darkness than he did of Life, hung his head frightened out of his wits. He knew that when Aidan recovered, nothing would dissuade him from entering the black fog to seek Tragen. Thaddeus' legs nearly gave way at the thought—the terror turning his limbs to jelly.

Hopper, the huge First Mate of the Grim, trod the salt-scarred boards of the quarterdeck counting the knots in each plank as he passed over them. He reached fourteen before lifting his head. He looked across at an even larger man, a man with the nickname of the Bear, the ship's master Hugo Locklear. The captain of the Grim stood, his shoulders atypically slumped, at the starboard rail his back to everyone.

Hopper was struggling to come to terms with the previous night's harrowing events. But the more he dwelt on the unbelievable experiences he'd learned of, the more he tried to make sense of what he'd seen and heard himself, the more confused he became. And he hadn't even been present at the worst of the action. Fear is an emotion that very rarely troubled the veteran seaman, but now he was terrified. And because the sensation was new, aberrant to his normal self-assured nature, he was lost. He needed direction to find his way back to some sort of customary behaviour. The only one who could possibly supply this support was his friend and master.

'Captain,' he called quietly, not wanting to disturb the uncharacteristic silence shared by the other occupants of the quarterdeck. 'Captain, what are your intentions for when we arrive at Griffin?'

Locklear, his shoulders still hunched, continued to stare out over the calm ocean for a moment longer. Considering his second in command's query his eyes were inevitably drawn to his right. Looking aft, past the poop deck and over the stern, he studied the muddy, black fog spiralling above Sanctity. Its source, the sewer outfall below the monastery, was now concealed by distance and evil.

13

'By the Gods, Hopper, I wish I knew,' he tugged viciously at his beard and stared at his hands, noticing with surprise the black hairs he had inadvertently pulled from his face. 'The boy, Aidan, is he sleeping or is he in a coma?' he asked of no one in particular.

It was Mazumbai, the chief of the Brakwannans – those people taken as slaves by Dyfrig years before and now freed from captivity with the help of the ship's passengers – who answered. 'I left the young wizards in their cabin not fifteen minutes since. Aidan, the Wizard of Life and Death is sleeping I believe, although it is a sleep nigh on to death. He is not comatose but his body and mind are in desperate straits. He needs to put behind him the appalling effects of last night's trauma.' He paused a moment remembering the events, wishing he also could shut them out. 'His recovery will depend on how soon he can assimilate the knowledge of his mentor's death and his own actions prior to it. It will not be easy for him.'

'It will not be easy for any of us. We are all at the end of our tether, my friend, all desperate to put last night's memories behind us,' said Lodovico Portolan, the clan chief of the lowland Griffin islanders. Before succeeding to the title on the death of his brother, Paul, Lodovico had been the harbourmaster, the Seneschal of Griffin. 'Marcus, as soon as we land your first task is to ensure the safe passage of Leonid through Griffin Town.' Marcus Janne was his militia commander, Leonid the Green People's emissary from Bylani, the underground kingdom beneath Griffin Island. 'He must be away to Bylani immediately…I just hope they have everything prepared for the influx of refugees.'

'Aye, we should be able to get most of our people away on boats, though,' Marcus replied, his voice saying one thing, his mind dwelling on the recent past. Distracted, he was another who couldn't get Zorzecai out of his mind.

'We will hopefully. But we also have to find accommodation for the Montetors on those same boats,' Lodovico stated in a voice unexpectedly full of amazement. 'We are one people now, the Portolans and the Montetors…we are Griffins, and as such our task is to protect all in our islands.'

'An enormously difficult undertaking, my friend,' interrupted Bazyli Montetor, the clan chief of the highland Griffin islanders. 'It's going to be an uphill struggle to persuade our two clans to work together after all this time. It's not going to happen overnight,' he sighed. 'For all intents and purposes we have been at war for twenty years, hatred and distrust has become endemic among us. People cannot change at a whim.' Bazyli stroked his face where but a day before a dreadful scar had existed.

'Then, perhaps, Prince Griffin can help heal those wounds.' Lodovico all at once beamed at everyone, using his son's new title for the first time made him inordinately proud. But then, his smile faltering at the thought, could the young man inexperienced of living, possibly succeed with a people he had never been aware of ever meeting? Moreover, they were a people who had always thought of him as a brainless buffoon.

And there was another dilemma to be faced eventually, one of equal complexity. Wizards were distrusted throughout the civilized world, their mysticism frightening, their good works often misunderstood. Would the islanders agree to a magician ruling them? It had never been possible anywhere else in the world that anyone knew of.

Hugo Locklear was in shock, mourning the loss of his greatest and oldest friend, Tragen, to an impossible enemy. 'Hopper,' he said, gazing at his first mate, 'with Lord Tragen's death the responsibility for the immediate safety of Princess Augusta falls on my shoulders and therefore, on yours also. We must formulate a course of action bearing that in mind,' he paused. 'But devising the proper plan is going to be extremely difficult. There are so many considerations to take into account, notwithstanding the girl's own inclinations,' he grimaced. 'No strategy that we can come up with will be followed without her co-operation and that will not be easy to obtain, especially as she is also a wizard.'

'I agree,' Hopper smiled ruefully, 'if she doesn't like what we decide then she will probably countermand our orders…or just simply ignore them.'

Hugo continued to tug at his beard absent-mindedly. 'Well, our first destination will obviously be Griffin Island to disembark our friends here,' he indicated the rulers of Griffin Island standing, watching and listening. 'And the Brakwannans, we are all decided upon, must be shipped home as soon as possible…for the sake of their sanity, if naught else.'

'Thank you, Captain; it would indeed be a blessing. But may I say that Brakwanna will welcome any refugees that land on our shores.' Mazumbai smiled quickly. 'Any aid we can supply will be gladly proffered.'

'Thank you, Mazumbai. I expect many of our people to indeed sail that far south when we inform them of your hospitality. But you must, of course, ascertain the situation in your homeland first. There are bound to be problems facing you...your country has been without its rightful ruler for some years now.' Lodovico Portolan stared at the very courageous, honourable chieftain, the truth of his words reflecting in the black man's, momentarily thoughtful, eyes.

'We will all need to spend time recovering, especially the youngsters,' said Bazyli Montetor. 'All of us together will need to plan our future policy. For now I believe rest is the priority. It is too soon after this terror to think straight. Although speed is also of the essence, I suppose...we cannot linger for long while the Darkness flows free.'

Bazyli Montetor continued his watch at the larboard rail. Again he was unable to halt his incessant caressing of his non-existent scar, or cease recalling the euphoria of its disappearance—or the despair of his captivity. And the knowledge that his twin sister, Ariana, and her husband, Paul Portolan, had died as sacrifices at the hands of Zorzecai was utterly devastating, his grief almost unbearable.

Closing his eyes, Bazyli tried to block from his mind the many memories of the sacrificial chamber. But there was one he could not, its meaning a complete mystery. The Abbot of Sanctity's death at the hands of his master, Zorzecai, was inexplicable. Lodovico gazed down into the waist of the ship at the unwitting cause of the hateful cleric's death, Leonid of the Green People, sitting quietly with his back resting against the stump of the broken mainmast. And he wondered.

Leonid, also attempting to unravel the same enigma, was re-examining Zorzecai's frightened statement—for fear there was in the demon's ranting. "Plans are always disrupted in the presence of a Green Man", Zorzecai had screamed. There must be something in it, Leonid thought, after all that was the reason for the mad abbot's demise. Could that also be the reason they survived? He sat pondering his future looking up at a sun he had seen for the first time only a few days before. Now the Green People would have to fulfil their part of the prophecy far earlier than they had expected.

But what did it mean when the evil one had implied that the Green People were dangerous—were they also dangerous to their friends? Leonid continued to brood, but not deeply...he was too busy savouring the free air above ground.

Up on the quarterdeck Lodovico's thoughts turned to that of the young man sleeping deeply on his bunk below. Whenever he thought of Aidan he felt a lump catch in his throat and tears well behind his eyes threatening to fall. For his gratitude knew no bounds where the boy was concerned. But he still could not grasp the totally incomprehensible phenomenon of three young, full of life souls, passing into the afterlife and there meeting the soul of a friend who had died days earlier. And then their ultimate miracle—the rescuing of his son's lost soul wandering within the Darkness.

Lodovico, chewing his lower lip, stared unseeing at the receding island of Sanctity as his thoughts inevitably returned to that which followed the abbot's murder, the true nightmare. The prisoners had been ritually disembowelled in a sacrificial ceremony designed to inflict as much pain as possible for the God desired it. Thankfully Aidan had been prevented from committing suicide in the same way, but in a most unexpected manner.

Leash, second helmsman of the Grim, murderer of Anders, was also host to a vampyrus. And he had killed Zorzecai.

But why had Leash killed the herdsman? There was no doubt that in so doing, Leash had saved the life of the young apprentice wizard. But why had he done so when he had admitted striving for weeks to kill Aidan?

In the early hours of the following morning, Aidan opened his eyes. At first nothing registered with him, not the sight of Beatrix sitting at his feet her head nodding, not Augusta her eyes closed as white as a sheet sitting in the chair, or Thaddeus quietly pacing the floor. The gentle pressure of Beatrix's fingers in his hand was the first thing he felt and instinctively he returned it.

Beatrix jumped; the pressure of his fingers startling her. She looked over at Aidan's ravaged face, his skin pale, and eyes sunken deep and dark. 'Welcome back,' she smiled tentatively, 'how are you feeling?'

Augusta roused and immediately fell to her knees and kissed him. 'Aidan, I'm so sorry, so very sorry,' she said, tears streaming down her face. 'We've been so worried for you, we thought you'd end up in the…' Augusta suddenly released him; her untoward reaction to his waking had surprised her. She was not supposed to show affection in public, her parents would be shocked and Cornelia, her lady-in-waiting, livid. She blushed to the roots of her shoulder length black hair when she recalled that she had kissed him even more fervently in the dungeons, and that had been in front of everyone.

Thaddeus, not noticing her confusion, interrupted quickly not wanting the Darkness mentioned yet. 'We've sailed for Griffin, Aidan. When you're feeling better we'll tell you what's happened.'

'And what we are all going to do about it,' said Beatrix equally shocked with Augusta. She'd abruptly realized she was envious of her mistress.

Gazing into space she recalled how it had been between her and Anders, the relationship slow and tentative at first, her nerves tingling every time she saw him, touched him. And then there was the blossoming of their love over the too short days of the voyage home. She remembered the comfort of her hand in his, his arm around her shoulders and his quick smile whenever they caught each other's eye, which they did often – their first kiss as he lay dying. She nearly burst into tears there and then.

Seeing Augusta and Aidan together, she was taken aback at her totally unexpected jealousy. She knew it was wrong and, flustered, she tried to turn away, but her eyes inevitably returned to watch them. Nevertheless, the strange constriction in her chest would not disappear and she had the overwhelming urge to shove Augusta from the young man lying on the bed. So she did the only thing she could. She glared at them both, her feelings utterly confusing.

Aidan stared up at Augusta and lifting his hand he stroked her face tenderly. Smiling into her eyes he wished she'd kiss him again; he liked the taste of those lips. Saying nothing for a while, he sighed and then, looking around at Beatrix and Thaddeus, with his eyes glistening he recalled all of the terrible events of the last days.

'Anders...Anders are you there? Can you hear me?' He called the boy who, up until this voyage, was his only friend. Anders was sitting at the wall of colours – the panorama displaying all Life – in Limbo.

'Aye, Aidan,' the ghostly boy answered slowly, ceasing his whittling, dreading the next question.

'Did he...I mean, is he there...in the Darkness?'

'Oh, Aidan,' said Augusta grasping his hand tightly, breaking her heart.

'Anders, answer me...is he alive in the Darkness...or is he dead in there?'

'He's dead, I think, Aidan,' his voice shook. *'I saw him enter the fog...and I've searched as close as I dare. I can't see any evidence of his lifeline, but I may be wrong...I'm sorry.'*

Aidan stared upwards at the bottom of the bunk two feet above his head. His brain not taking in what was before his eyes, he saw only the dark and terrifying mists of the Darkness, and its horribly maimed inhabitants.

'Will he survive, Thaddeus, will he…if he's dead?' He turned his drawn, frightened face and looked at his newest friend standing with his back against the bulkhead staring at his feet. 'Will Tragen survive in there?'

'Tragen was no ordinary man, Aidan,' Thaddeus drew a deep breath, not wishing to impart false hope, but believing there was room for doubt. 'He was a very powerful wizard and I've been thinking…the One may have now made a crucial mistake that he'll not easily overcome.'

The heir to the Griffin Isles paused and stepped away from the bulkhead; walking over to his friend he bent over Aidan. With his arm resting on the upper bunk he stared into his friend's misery-filled eyes. 'He may have needed Tragen's magic to form the rift…to allow the Darkness to move out of the Afterlife and into this world. But he's now also got Tragen's immensely powerful magic in his world. I don't think he realizes that Tragen's magic will have an unexpected impact in his realm. What he hasn't foreseen is that it won't cease to exist for quite a while, if ever. He has no idea of the fantastic force he holds captive, for it can't be controlled by anyone other than Tragen. If the magic is ever loosed from that cage it may well cause horrendous havoc in the Darkness.'

Prince Griffin stared at his friend, knowing his next words would ignite optimism; he just hoped his conclusions were correct. 'I don't believe Tragen is dead. I think his magic will protect him for as long as it can sustain itself…I may be wrong but I don't believe so.'
Aidan sat up swiftly, the expected reaction alight in his eyes. 'Why? What makes you think that?'

The two girls held their breath as Anders pressed his ear to the wall of colours determined not to miss a word.

'He carried his staff with him. It wasn't broken, was it, Beatrix?' and seeing her shake her head he continued. 'It holds part of his soul—that part within his staff is still alive and it will cling to Tragen. As I've never heard of a soul that is partly dead, or partly alive then Tragen must still be living, and the staff will travel with him! He'll always have his magic wherever the One behind the Darkness

19

takes him—that magic protects both his soul in the Afterlife and his body buried somewhere in the depths of that rock.'

Aidan and the girls were silent for a moment studying his words. 'Are you saying that Tragen will still be able to use his magic even though he's dead…or maybe not dead?' asked Augusta.

For the first time excitement entered Anders' voice. He ceased again his eternal whittling and thrust the misericorde deep into the ground in front of him, not noticing that the hilt had partially entered the wall.

'Of course! Don't forget, I'm using the magic that Aidan gave me, that's how I read this wall and talk to you.'

The wall of colours, the boundary between the living world and Limbo, thrummed with life. If they'd read Elder Findar – the long dead leader of the Green People, the recipient of the prophecy – correctly, it was Anders' task to understand the vast panoply…a terribly difficult task. The wall itself was a picture, a representation of all those living in Life. The continually moving shapes and colours almost indistinguishable as, more often than not, they merged into a kaleidoscope of constantly changing shades.

Elder Findar's prophecy stated that Anders was the "all seeing" one. But every time Anders thought of those words, the more he worried. It was his mission to interpret the wall, help them all to find the shadow's bane. What if he made a mistake, what if his readings were even slightly awry—where might that lead his friends? But he knew that each time he looked at the wall, searched it, he was using magic – and his skill with labyrinths that his mother had taught him – to interpret his viewings. And he loved both abilities. He thanked Aidan from the bottom of his heart for the life-changing gift of magic…and his mother for her prescience in teaching him how to solve mazes.

Aidan's hope rekindled at Anders' words. 'But I have to be certain. I'll have to find him. I have to search the Darkness.'

'We will all search it, not just you,' said Beatrix.

Aidan looked at his friends, a lump in his throat, fighting back fresh tears. 'You understand, then?'

'Of course we do. And you know we'll never let you go alone,' stated Augusta bluntly.

He smiled his thanks, relief palpable in his face; he knew if he entered that place alone he'd never keep his sanity. If he went unaccompanied, the madness would claim him and he'd never leave.

He breathed deeply finding his fear abated a little by the love of his friends.

'How long do we have before the staff's magic dies? Has anyone any idea?' Aidan asked.

There was silence until Beatrix broke in. 'When I watched him disappear through the floor the magic was still building in the staff. I had the impression it would go on increasing, that it was nowhere near its full potential. Of course I don't know for certain, but I do know there was a whole lot more power in the staff to come,' she paused. 'I don't believe it'll stop growing for ages yet and then it might take equally as long before it dies—if it can die, that is.'

'Thank the Gods for that,' Aidan sighed with relief. 'Later then, I must get my strength back first,' and then his voice trembled. 'I must find him, speak to him; perhaps…perhaps he can explain why…why I now believe…' he swallowed and looked away. 'There are so many questions.' He blinked the tears from his eyes and grasped Augusta's and Beatrix's hands again. 'If I had killed the herdsman when I had the chance…' his voice trailed away, uttering words he'd never have allowed to pass his lips only a day before. He had railed against anyone wanting to kill, believing earnestly that harming another's soul damaged your own.

'Oh, Aidan,' Beatrix said comforting him, 'you couldn't have, don't you remember? Zorzecai said that magic couldn't harm him.'

'You can't attempt the search until you're all somewhere safe anyway, you'll need someone to watch over your bodies. You've no idea how long you'll be here…it may be days,' said Anders. *'And you have to be very careful; you can't be outside of your bodies for too long.'*

'Why not?' Augusta asked, she didn't like the sound of that.

'Your body deteriorates the longer you are out of it. It will be more difficult to return if it is harmed, and if you delay too long your body will begin to decompose.'

'But Thaddeus was out of his body for fifteen years, his body as healthy as if he'd never left it…even if it was overweight.' She glanced at him quickly, hoping he wasn't offended. His weight was a problem because he had never been able to exercise, had never been able to do anything for himself whilst separated from his soul. 'How do you explain that?' Augusta asked, feeling sick.

'I don't know, but it should never have been. His body should have died years ago,' Anders replied.

Thaddeus didn't know what to say to that and he stared at his friends, stunned. And then he thought of the horror ahead, of actually returning to the nightmare he'd lived for years, he was petrified. But why hadn't his body succumbed to natural death? How many more questions were there going to be before all this ended.

'We should be back on Griffin sometime tomorrow. Anders is right, Cornelia and Mistress Barbat can care for us,' Beatrix said, deliberately blocking out Anders' last words. Mistress Alessa Barbat had been Thaddeus' nurse from the day of his birth and had cared for him all the years his soul and body were apart. In doing so, she and her betrothed, Marcus Janne, had come to look on Thaddeus as their own son. The look of bewilderment on Thaddeus' face was disturbing. Was someone else involved in all this, someone yet to be revealed? Perhaps it was the Lady in the Light, the spectre Anders had met in Paradise and who had returned him to Limbo to help them fight the Darkness. Had she put Thaddeus' soul in danger and then protected his body?

'But there is another thing I have to do as well,' Aidan said.

'What?' Augusta asked as Aidan suddenly clutched her hand tighter.

'My master was right, he said all along I'd know when I was ready—I feel it! The tree calls me...I must seek my own staff, my apprenticeship is finished,' he paused, his cheeks again damp. 'I'm going to sleep again now,' and at her gasp he looked at Beatrix and smiled. 'No, don't worry, I won't be going anywhere without you, I...I need my friends. At least I understand that much,' he turned over on his side and faced the bulkhead. He was asleep again in moments.

Three

Constructed in the nethermost regions of time, on the highest hilltop to the north of the wetlands and visible from the road for leagues about, the Guild's home was encircled by a shoulder-high, stone wall separating it from the densely wooded lower slopes. The tall Tower spiralled skywards, a drab splinter pointing at the moon…an ancient black finger at the sun. It dominated the skyline overlooking Jasper, a town that sprawled amid the freshwater swamplands in southern Drakka. The massive edifice brooded as it watched travellers approaching.

But those same travellers, catching their first glimpse of the Tower, were immediately assailed with a dread dismay and they instinctively averted their eyes. Nevertheless, the distress awakened by that first glance left wayfarers depressed and anxious, their recovery only possible when shelter from its baleful influence had been reached. The damp, black granite walls of the huge structure hid an immense interior; twenty floors stretched above ground and just as many rooted beneath the earth's surface. Each floor consisted of a labyrinth of rooms, niches, corridors, secret passageways and staircases—within and between its walls.

The majority of the floors were occupied by very powerful sorcerers who designed their little kingdoms to suit their individual needs. Some were alchemists, others necromancers, a few dealt in healing but not of the normal kind. Yet the vast majority followed the black arts, too numerous to be acknowledged by sane people. The secretive, oppressive sorcerers ruled the Tower's servants and guards with an iron fist, inflexible in imposing an unbendable discipline. But they all owed allegiance to their master, the Magus.

However, there was one notable exception to this rigidness. An ancient oriental monk-turned-sorcerer, Chong-An by name. He was a good-natured man who quite often found himself out of his depth in consorting with his amoral colleagues—and quite often was also the butt of their contempt. But, though he had an easy-going nature, even he shared a common attribute with others of the Brethren. Each was inherently mistrustful of his or her neighbours to such an extent that he or she allowed no infringement of privacy, whether it was of a personal or a professional nature. And many a violation ended in execution.

The third floor above ground level was one of the few used by all members of the Guild. Its walls bore the tallest windows in the Tower for it housed the largest library in the known world, boasting a copy of nearly every book of importance ever written—or so the Guild thought.

Chong-An knew different. The annals on the Guild's shelves, gathering the dust of centuries, had been his life for the last hundred or so years. But he knew of another place that held other tomes with ancient knowledge that the Guild would quite happily kill to obtain.

He had recently returned from an expedition in the Drikander, way to the north of Jasper. It was a densely-wooded region of central Drakka, abutting the Great Forest in the east. The Drikander was home to the Grekkos, barbarous tribal peoples who waged a sporadic war amongst themselves and against all those outsiders they came in contact with— except for the black sorcerers. But though many Guild members used its hidden highways, the tribes harboured an acute fear of them, a feeling shared by the vast majority of peoples in the empire. But for some reason known only to them, the Grekko tribesmen welcomed the Master of the Guild of the Brethren of Wisdom, the Magus Brenin.

Chong-An, an adept, had retrieved an ages-old parchment from amongst a hoard of arcane documents. He had discovered them in a long forgotten library hidden behind a disintegrating, centuries-old spell of illusion, in an underground chamber long concealed by dense undergrowth within the Drikander. He had detected the spell because he practised the highly secret art of Illusion to a very great degree of refinement. To his surprise the fragile roll of papyrus contained the original drawings for the building of the Tower. He, of course, told no-one else of his findings and had replaced the old protective illusion with a new one of his own design.

The soundness of the drawings, though, required verification and this he was busily testing by following another of the obscure passageways outlined in the faded sketches. This was his seventh investigation in as many days. But today the plans had brought him again to Brother Drudwynn's apartments on the floor immediately beneath those of Brenin's at the top of the Tower. This surprised Chong-An as the dark and dusty passageway he'd followed the day before had also brought him to these same rooms. This particular passageway within the walls had been altered, its direction changed, for the deviation did not show in the original drawings.

Thinking back to that previous visit he shuddered for he'd accidentally upset a strange mixture of yellowish-green liquid in Drudwynn's laboratory. It had splashed over him and the floor. Later, Chong had realized the mixture had removed the yellow pigmentation from a patch of skin on his arm and he had been questioned by Drudwynn who had the eyes of a hawk. His explanation had seemed to satisfy Brenin's deputy and Chong had vowed never to enter that apartment again. Drudwynn scared the life out of him, for the deputy emulated his master in his implementation of viciousness and in his research of the powers of degradation.

But like a fool Chong's inherent inquisitiveness got the better of him and he again entered Drudwynn's apartment, this time through an old sliding panel almost unworkable because of the grime and silt of years. It creaked – not loud – but enough to set Chong's teeth on edge as he squeezed his rotund shape through the small gap. He'd only been in what appeared to be an old storage cupboard for a few moments when he heard voices approach, the soft gurgle of wine being poured into goblets and two occupants settle in the deeply upholstered chairs the other side of the door. Chong had himself tried those same chairs the day before and had almost fallen asleep. If Drudwynn had a weakness it was in his love of comfort and good wine. Many a man shared the same, but the deputy was manic in his pursuit of luxury and had stolen and killed to attain his needs.

And Chong-An no longer needed proof of the old adage "eavesdroppers never hear good of themselves".

'You think the Slipper's not to be trusted?'

Chong-An shook like a leaf and abruptly broke into a sweat when he recognized the voice speaking his nickname. Brenin was the only magus in the world, ten times perhaps a hundred times more powerful than any other wizard. There had only ever been one before him and that had been eons ago. Chong, exploring the archives when he'd first come to the Tower, had discovered a fair amount about him. That magus had been defeated in a war with the white wizards and their allies a thousand years or more before.

Chong was well known for his unusual fetish. Whenever and wherever he went on his journeys he always returned with new footwear. His colleagues thought it hilarious and delighted in their sarcastic comments. The truth was that Chong suffered abominably with arthritis in his feet and was continually seeking comfortable slippers to alleviate the chronic pain.

Chong considered fleeing the cupboard immediately but suspected that the closing panel would probably be heard by the master sorcerer. He breathed slowly and shallowly afraid to move, his mind in turmoil wondering why they distrusted him. But as the conversation continued his knees trembled uncontrollably. He thanked the Gods for his new soft shoes…his steps would never be heard if he was forced to run.

'I have commanded that he remain in the Tower for the foreseeable future. He is to make no more journeys abroad unless authorized by me,' answered Brother Drudwynn pouring more wine. 'He is spending far too much time in the Drikander gathering sticks and stones and whatever for his auguries. But I want to be sure his prying has not harmed us before I kill him.'

'Do away with him immediately you have obtained all his knowledge!'

'I will, but I have work for him at present. His manner irritates me painfully and he is an unmitigated nuisance, but his outstanding abilities as an augur are worth some risk,' he snorted derisively. 'They are the only reason he is not already dead.'

'Be wary! If holding off gives him time to discover word of my plans and he speaks of them to others…I will kill you both!' Brenin rasped.

Drudwynn quailed, the smugness draining away. He was even more afraid of Brenin than Chong-An was, having worked with the magus for countless years and seen him at his vilest. Sweating, he changed the subject.

'The other business, Master, any news?' Drudwynn asked, lowering his voice.

Chong-An no longer cared about closing the secret panel. He prepared to bolt from the room at the earliest opportunity but his curiosity won again on hearing the deputy's query, Why had the man practically whispered the question when there were only the two present in the room?

'The search proceeds apace so I am assured, but it seems the Locust is lost somewhere in the Great Forest. Nevertheless, Cumbria's minions are close—he cannot escape them for long.'

'And the Fly?'

Chong-An – in the midst of brushing a stray spider from his face – all but choked in alarm. In all of his auguring for Drudwynn the oriental had never once mentioned the "Fly". He could not; the consequences were too bleak if the prying Guild ever apprehended the man.

The name had cropped up innumerable times in his travels, the last occasion in the annals of the Drikander library where he had discovered more of the prophecy he had been investigating on and off for years. But how on earth did the leaders of the Guild know of him? Did they know the Fly's identity? He licked his lips with a dry tongue. There were three siblings referred to in the prophecy. The document implied all carried the codenames of fauna that flew. The second and third codename had unluckily been partially obliterated – along with other relevant information – by age and mildew. He had been able to translate from the old language only one name—the "Fly".

What was the first name these two had mentioned…the "Locust"? Could he be one of the other two? It did seem a hell of a coincidence he should be mentioned in the same conversation as the "Fly". And the Locust was of supreme importance to Cumbria. Chong-An grimaced, he had come across Cumbria, the Abbot of Sentinel, the dark leader of monks, several times over the years. A hateful man now appointed Chancellor of Mantovar, a very unexpected and curious appointment of Prince Cedric's.

'The Fly is near…I sense him though I cannot see him. You have set sentries?'

'I have, at this very moment they are patrolling the hill. When night falls they will take cover nearer the perimeter wall. If he attempts to penetrate the Tower he will be taken!'

'You had better be right…he must be caught, it is imperative I have his knowledge.' Brenin supped his wine musing on the consequences to his plans if the agent managed to infiltrate his sanctum.

'No, I cannot afford the luxury of another problem at this time. The more I think on it, the more I believe there is a danger our unpredictable Chong may encounter the Fly. There is too much at stake, we take unnecessary chances with the oriental. Conclude your business with him over the next few days and then bring him to me. I will interrogate our so-called colleague from the East. Your distrust is infectious.'

And Chong-An fled. Panic-stricken, he swiftly created a spell of illusion to hide the open panel as he went. He hoped it would remain in place for a few days more, long enough for him to escape the Tower.

He hid in his beloved library for the remainder of the day, quaking in his new pearl-beaded slippers, thinking on what the future held. He was now in grave peril. He kicked himself mentally, he should never have got involved with the Guild in the first place, should have heeded its evil reputation. Deputy Drudwynn had never troubled to hide his dislike of him and Chong had crossed him many times—too many times he now realized. Brooding, a cold shiver running down his spine, he knew he'd never be able to hide anything from the magus— the black magician could strip a person's mind in the blink of an eye.

Chong-An sighed and looked along the central aisle of the many stacks of crammed shelves. Gazing longingly at countless unread parchments and books, he decided that in the morning he had no option but to leave with the treasures untouched.

He made the decision to return to the Drikander as soon as possible now and follow up on the unearthed references to the Fly and the others. He'd only examined the documents cursorily; he'd been short of time. Nevertheless, he had promised himself he'd return when he'd ascertained the authenticity of the Tower builders' plans. When he'd come across them at the back of a high shelf almost buried behind a cloud of cobwebs, he had grinned. To actually have knowledge of the Tower that his leaders did not, appealed to his vanity. But searching the passages was no longer important.

The little he'd managed to read in the old prophecy – the language archaic – had led him to believe it was essential to bring together all three mentioned. Dispirited at the thought, he was doubtful of even identifying their codenames correctly, let alone identifying each of the men. He had known of the existence of the Fly for years, but however much he'd examined and explored documents of all ages, he had yet to discover the identity of the man. He had not realized the urgency until now.

And then a horrible thought arose, again he broke into a sweat. If he succeeded in the task of bringing them all together, wouldn't it precipitate the catastrophe? For the auguries stated unequivocally that all three, once united, would immediately join with others to battle the Shadow.

That same evening the Tower was ablaze with light, the walls concealing a hive of nocturnal activity as necromancers went about their furtive undertakings. It was a few hours past sundown and a full moon peeked above the horizon in the darkened blue skies. The thin, swirling, malodorous daytime mists, lifting off the mires surrounding the town, diminished when the sun disappeared, although the ever present stench sometimes sickly-sweet, often acrid and stinging, lingered. It was hot and muggy, the night temperatures dropping only slightly at this time of year…it was the middle of summer.

On the topmost floor of the Guild's Tower, immediately beneath its steeply sloping circular roof, was a laboratory. Its walls were screened by a shambles of dusty shelves holding a vast array of objects ranging from scrolls and tomes to jars of liquids and powders. On a long table against the north quadrant stood other unusual items, large and small, most of them unsightly and smelling abominably. Many were obscene caricatures of exotic swamp flora and fauna, some living and others that should not have been.

Brenin, a thin man of middle height, almost skeletal in appearance, with high cheekbones stretching taut the semi-translucent skin of his face, was dressed in a stained red robe, the cowl lowered. He stood unmoving, his back to the only window, his wispy grey-haired head bowed amongst the strange and obnoxious odours, the smells an accidental danger for him. The magus had a disability that often gave him problems when he worked on potions—he had lost his sense of smell when an earlier experiment had gone disastrously wrong. Now, when he worked on poisonous vapours, he was forced to wear a face mask and he used a servant as an early warning system. When the lackey showed signs of suffering or, as had happened on many an occasion, when the underling dropped dead, Brenin ceased work and opened the window.

Breathing shallowly, the magus placed his long slender hands either side of the sparkling, black granite scrying bowl on the table top before him. Careful not to disturb its contents he caressed the rim of the dish; it felt soapy to his touch.

His hands were scrawny, the skin almost transparent, blue veins bulging across the backs. His long fingers – discoloured by the various chemicals he experimented with – were a magnet for the eyes of companions. Completely devoid of nails, the digits ended in perfectly rounded stumps as if they had suffered amputation, the procedure leaving no scarring. They had not undergone surgery of course, Brenin had a fixation—he abhorred fingernails. He found them ugly, usually extremely dirty, sometimes irritatingly overlong, more often ragged or bitten to the quick. The magus had invented a spell to remove his own nails and a few others in the Guild had followed his example. He held the sycophants in contempt, though they knew it not, for his plans required their assistance, not their survival.

Brenin removed his hands from the bowl, kneading his swollen knuckles to relieve the pain of arthritis, the discomfort excruciating. He was not a healer. He distrusted healers, even those in his own order—perhaps those more so. The practitioners of the medical arts usually needed to explore within a patient's head, his mind to heal any affliction—he was not going to allow anyone entrance to his.

It was a nuisance having to contact the man by scrying, but he had no other option if he wished to speak with his accomplice. The man was leagues upon leagues away in the north—in the country that was the home and inheritance Brenin's family had been wrongly denied, exiled centuries before. The only other method of speaking at any distance, the ancient art of mindmelding, was unachievable; the other party too far away.

Brenin rolled back the charred, voluminous sleeves of his plain robe and resumed his stance at the bowl. This time as he stroked the rim he stared purposefully into the clear water held within the dish. The surface remained perfectly motionless for moments and then, without warning, bubbled for a moment and then settled to a milky-white when the magus spoke a name. A middle-aged face appeared in the cloudy solution, its visage devoid of all hair below a scalp that had never grown any.

The magus thought the man resembled his nail-less thumb and indeed, in a very rare moment of puerile behaviour, he had once drawn two eyes, a nose and a very thin mouth on the ball of the thumb on his left hand. Brenin smiled, recalling he had then ground the likeness into the top of the table in front of him. He hoped to do so in reality when his plans succeeded.

The man was the Abbot of Sentinel and his abbey, once dedicated to Tarria, Goddess of Healing and Mercy, was on an island of the same name in the mouth of the River Mantovar. He had a cruel face below his bald head, a perpetual sneer and a deep seated arrogance that was only bested by the magus. Aged about sixty years, centuries younger than the Brethren's leader, tall and lean, Abbot

Cumbria returned Brenin's gaze. For a moment there was silence until Cumbria's mouth twisted into what passed as a smile.

Brenin waited patiently for him to speak, expecting to hear of the capture of the Locust. He was jolted from his distraction at the abbot's first words.

'It has begun,' Cumbria said, failing utterly to keep the elation from his voice, 'the Divide has been breached.'

The air in the laboratory seemed to thicken, Brenin's chest constricted, afraid to speak in case he changed the meaning of the words he'd waited so long to hear.

'Where, man, where?' he demanded huskily.

'Sanctity!'

Brenin, sharing the abbot's euphoria, allowed his harsh exterior to slip for a moment and he grinned cruelly through his short grey beard. He recalled the Abbot of Sanctity, had met him several times. He thought him a contemptible little man, hadn't liked him at all. But he tolerated him; he'd required the abbot to accomplish his aims.

'He was adamant he was further along than any of us thought … I didn't believe him I thought he was boasting,' said Brenin.

Then he reflected on what he, himself, had already been capable of. Unknown to any of his co-conspirators he had received a gift, a pendant, from the Ekolo. They were a dark, supernatural people who defied death and resided in the in-between worlds secreted in the Scissor Mountains on the border with the Drikander. It was a talisman in the shape of a pyramid with two horns at its apex—with its help he had ensnared a demon. He had put that demon in place years ago and it still remained unknown to those it watched. His own source of intelligence among those he needed to defeat.

But he had also been gifted with a second talisman, a smaller pendant. This he was ordered to pass on to the Abbot of Sentinel so that it could aid him in his task. Brenin knew of this undertaking and waited impatiently for the abbot to complete it. Nevertheless, the fact that Cumbria had such an artefact made Brenin cautious in his dealings with the man. He didn't know all that the small pendant was capable of.

Brenin's expression returned to its normal unreadable appearance. He was irritated at allowing his self-control to lapse, or keep the excitement from his voice. It would not happen again.

Sanctity must have been very fortunate, he thought, even though Dyfrig had a ready supply of sacrifices in his slaves. The abbot must have discovered a greater source of energy to have completed the task this early.

'What does he say? How did he manage so soon? Did he have problems?'

A shadow flitted briefly across Cumbria's eyes. 'I do not know. For some reason I have lost contact with him…he does not acknowledge the scry. But I have espied the Darkness, it flows free, my friend—free!'

The magus paused and chewed his tongue at the impudence of the man assuming friendship. But then he thought of all the possibilities that had now opened up, all things were now probable.

'Whatever, the Darkness is here at last! Perhaps it is having a detrimental effect on communications. The next stage must be implemented immediately, though it is far earlier than we expected. Still, we must be in place ready to act when its existence becomes known on these shores. Have you any idea how long it will take to get here?'

'No! The cloud appears smaller than we envisaged its drift slower. Mayhap the rift is constricted. If it is, then we will have to wait until the breach is enlarged, as it undoubtedly will be ere long. However, I will keep a close watch, I may determine the reason.'

'Have you discovered yet how it will affect those it engulfs?'

'All I know is that it will instigate panic and exterminate in the same manner as it does in the afterlife.'

Brenin raised his eyebrows at the abbot's faux pas and struggled to keep the mockery from his voice, failing badly. 'My dear Cumbria, how can it slay in the afterlife? Everyone there is already dead. Or are you about to tell me there are people alive on the other side?'

'You know what I mean, sorcerer!' The Abbot of Sentinel snapped, his face resuming its sneering.

'And will it destroy all those who are likely to oppose us? Will it be able to identify its enemies—our enemies?'

'Yes, we have been assured. The numbers of peasants fleeing the islands will likely be greater than we anticipated because of the slow speed of drift of the Darkness, of course, but we need not worry overmuch about them. In fact the increased numbers will escalate the terror and that will be highly beneficial. The storm off the coast of Mantovar still blows mightily and it will force the refugees' migration towards you in Drakka. They will serve your purpose; your success will now be achieved sooner than you think. My own, of course, was accomplished months ago.' Cumbria smirked.

'Yes, I will seek out my agent on the emperor's council immediately and alert my allies at the same time.' Brenin fumed at the man's implied superiority and he warned. 'But you forget, it is only your political aims that have been achieved—there is still the other.'

Cumbria had no idea of the depth of Brenin's dislike and hatred of him; if he had Cumbria would have fled years ago. For the abbot's one success had been engineered by the magus, the man's present position of power in Mantovar an integral part of Brenin's plans.

'I will leave at once for the Drikander and then go on to Abferkarn. Our time is here, my dear Abbot,' Brenin's tone conciliatory now, his needs requiring the ongoing co-operation of the monk, at least in the short term. 'Nothing can halt us now.'

With that final remark, the magus removed his hands from the scrying bowl abruptly breaking communication. And Cumbria's manic face disappeared from the room.

Four

Clinging to the sharply inclined slate roof and overhanging the single window to the laboratory, a small, wiry, black-haired man lifted his head from a gap in the casement through which he had overheard every word spoken. Bewildered by the conversation and full of unanswered questions, he pushed himself backwards from the roof's edge. Dressed all in black, his face smeared with soot, he was indistinguishable against the backdrop of the dark Tower. He was very careful not to stand upright in case he was outlined against the moon. He was also quieter than a feather falling on grass. He had been trained by masters in the art of camouflage and clandestine movement, skills essential to stay alive in his highly perilous occupation. If Magus Brenin's guards had detected him on his way to the Tower, he would have died and died very slowly, divulging all the information held in his head.

His long training had also instilled the capacity for immense patience and he waited for all movement to die away within the building, all lights to be extinguished on his chosen route. In the early hours of the morning, under a lowering moon, he made his way to the ground. On his hands he wore gloves covered in tiny, flexible, concave-shaped suckers manufactured from vegetable matter mixed with magic by a very knowledgeable hedge-witch. On his feet were slippers bearing the same. These he used to descend the sheer walls of the Tower, taking infinite care to release the suction of each glove and slipper silently with each move he made across the stones.

It was nearly sunup before he finally reached the kitchen garden. Standing on the soft earth he leant back against the wall of the Tower and studied the surroundings for sign of movement. Espying none, he escaped rapidly across the intervening cleared ground and climbed the encircling wall. He passed the two sentries he had silenced and immobilized on his arrival. Elstan smiled…someone was going to suffer when their gagged and bound bodies were discovered.

Reaching safety in nearby woods, he removed the tools of his trade from his hands and feet and packed them in a black canvas bag he'd hidden previously beneath a nearby bramble. Retrieving his boots from the same bag, he put them on his tired feet and, picking a handful of the large succulent blackberries, he munched them as he moved off.

Jasper was a dilapidated town, home mainly to wetland dwellers, their livelihood deriving from the harvesting of papyrus sedge, marsh-fishing and the hunting of vicious alligators. It was also a stopping off place for itinerants riding in dusty coaches or on horseback, and for the majority who walked along the Great North Road.

The road split the town into two more or less equal halves and was the main arterial highway leading eventually to Abferkarn, the capital city of Drakka. But in the town of Jasper there were numerous smaller roads leading off it into the dismal suburbs. Many of these were narrow, dingy alleyways that most people avoided. The dark lanes sufficed as temporary homes for the many distressed drunks who were incapable of finding their families. They had either fallen down in a stupor to sleep in the gutters, or were there because they'd been attacked and robbed of what little coin remained to them.

The eastern half of the town was maintained in a fairly affluent state of repair. Here the citizens were the more prosperous trades' people and town bureaucrats enjoying a higher quality of life than those living in the west.

Across the road the shoddier suburbs of Jasper were home to the indigent industry. In the backstreets were lacklustre workshops for the pressing of the reedy papyrus plants. Here also were the many small fisheries, the catch mainly tilapia and the common snapping turtles, providing the basic culinary needs of the poverty-stricken townsfolk.

In the southwest corner of Jasper was Sedge, a jumble of streets, alligator sheds, ramshackle houses and taverns catering to the reptile hunters. These were tough, always violent, very earthy men, a large majority of whom had been maimed in some way or other by their very fast prey.

Farming around Jasper was non-existent; there was no arable land among the vast tracts of bog. The additional staples of most people's diet, flour and potatoes, were brought in from the north, salt, sugar and sundry spices purchased off traders up from the hot south. There was a thriving haulage business in Jasper, a monopoly in the hands of a few and overseen by the criminal fraternity.

But it didn't matter who they were, rich or poor, adult or child, criminal or law-abiding, only those who were coerced into trading with its occupants, or employed as domestics within its bowels, ever went near the Tower. Those that did were paid well and men and women grew rich—if they managed to live long enough.

Hurrying into the outskirts of the town Elstan made his way to his lodgings deep in Sedge. Arriving at the rear of a three-storey timber building in great need of repair, Elstan pushed to one side the green scum floating on the surface of a nearby water vat and washed the soot from his face and hands. Drying his face on his sleeves he climbed up onto the tumbledown privy leaning against the outside wall of the kitchen, and thence through an open window into his room on the top floor. Before settling to rest he checked the wedges he had jammed into the doorframe to keep the room secure from overnight revellers and thieves.

He lowered his backside slowly onto the grubby woollen blanket of his bed, the old straw of the lumpy mattress emitting a foul reek as it took his weight. His nose puckered against the smell and then ignored it…he'd slept in worse places. Leaning back against the rough timbered wall at the head of the bed he kicked off his boots and stretched out his legs in front of him, wriggling his toes he relished the feel of cooler air on his bare feet.

Taking out his well-worn pipe from his tunic, he filled the bowl from his old black leather tobacco pouch, a present given him by his dead wife many years before. Puffing gently, he relaxed as he had been taught. Starting in his toes, he consciously released the tension in each of his muscles as he worked his way up his body. He then faced his greatest difficulty, easing his anxiety. It was getting harder to do the older he got, questions forever racing through his head.

Brenin intended leaving the Tower to consult his agent on the emperor's council. Would it be possible to follow him and finally ascertain the identity of the spy? What was the "Darkness"? Elstan bit down hard on the stem of his pipe…what on earth was it supposed to do? It was obviously some sort of weapon and would be used to kill all those who did not support the Guild. But there were many, many of those. How was the Darkness going to slay thousands? You'd need an army for that. He sighed, whatever it was it boded ill for the empire.

But one thing he'd learned for sure—the Abbot of Sentinel had planned his accession to the role of chancellor with the full cooperation and aid of Magus Brenin. So what was their final objective? And what was the other thing Cumbria had to do?

He groaned and stretched languidly, it was also taking longer these days to assemble his thoughts in any sort of logical order…he was not a young man any more. But moments later, having made the decision to make for Abferkarn and await the magus in the city, he ignored the din, the smell of stale ale wafting up from the tavern on the ground floor and the stench from the privy outside. Burying the last night's deeds deep in his subconscious, Elstan fell into a dreamless sleep.

But his presence on the Tower had not gone unnoticed and his pride would have been badly affected if he'd known of it.

Chong-An, had watched closely as Elstan first ascended and then hours later descended the walls and he had followed the intruder, also without being seen, to the tavern.

Chong's main skill lay in predicting future patterns, the ability that made him Drudwynn's indispensable augury. But he did not pass on everything he learned to his employer. One of the predictions kept from the deputy had indicated an incident such as this. Chong had spent most of his evenings for the last few months outside the Tower, watching and waiting for the interloper. And despite the threats he'd overheard earlier in the day he had been determined to spend one last night on watch.

The mystic arts of the East had led Chong-An as a boy to this most complex branch of magic and it had not taken long for his tutors to realize that the boy from a backwater farming village had great potential, albeit flawed. It was centuries before Chong-An became accustomed to the fact that not all predictions came to pass in the manner that he foresaw. Years of study and practical experience had taught him that the future was not set in stone. It could be changed depending on decisions made under a vast number of variables—and that a great deal of what was to come was hidden within the folds of time.

Chong came to study at the Tower because of the extensive fund of knowledge held within its library. He might have suffered great difficulty in attaining the position of librarian – the Guild did not usually engage those who were defective in the full arts – but his unusually accurate predictions had travelled before him. His reputation had attracted the attention of the deputy and the Brethren had recruited him as a fringe member.

His instinct bade him conceal his expertise in the art of Illusion.

His own future, though, was hidden from him. But he was insatiably curious of the world and its many wonders and it was his earnest wish to influence forthcoming events. He wanted to alter the future, knock it off its present course, for if he failed the auguries spelt out sure disaster.

Staring up at the tavern window he grimaced. Having discovered the intruder he could now move forward. It was even more imperative that he seek further answers in the underground library. But this unknown man spying on the Guild gave rise to many questions that needed satisfying. Hopefully they would lead to many options that Chong could pursue.

It crossed his mind fleetingly that he could inform Magus Brenin of the intruder. But if he did, matters would inevitably be taken out of his hands—the man would be subjected to torture and killed. Nonetheless, it might show Brother Drudwynn that Chong could be trusted and maybe the threat of Brenin's interrogation would be lifted. But Chong shrugged, he knew this was highly unlikely. Whatever Chong did, the magus would never change his mind. He was set on gleaning all information from his librarian's mind.

Chong could kill the prowler himself quite easily, of course, but it would be pointless – rendering his sleepless nights on watch a waste of time – he'd never discover anything of the man. Again, he could question the trespasser; there were many means of extracting information, but what then? Depending on the intelligence extracted, he could release the man to continue his purpose, remove the man's memory and instil one of his own making or wait and tag along for a while, maybe manipulate events at a later date.

Chong nibbled at the nail on his thumb and cogitated in the darkness. He owed no allegiance to the Brethren any longer, in fact he'd thought of departing long before this, but the library had held him, its eternal allure never ceasing.

But the conversation he'd overheard that morning had brought matters to a head. Brenin and Drudwynn would kill him and have no second thoughts—many times those invited to the top floor had never been seen again. It was vital he leave the Tower before being interrogated, before becoming another of the disappearing guests.

Chong had at last made up his mind and reluctantly decided to depart immediately. He'd make for the hoard of documents still hidden in the Drikander. And examine further the confusing material on the others the three codenamed people must join with in the final battle.

But Chong was glad now that he had given in to the compulsion to await the arrival of this stranger. He'd been hoping desperately to meet the man before setting off on his mission. This uninvited guest both intrigued and worried him, for he'd always had the overwhelming urge to take the intruder with him. And now, knowing the man was the Fly, it was vital they accompany each other for the foreseeable future. Could he persuade the man? After all he must have knowledge of the other two—the prophecy implied they were brothers.

He smiled, the Gods were undoubtedly watching over him. For wasn't it fortuitous the interloper arriving this night, his final night as an associate of the Brethren.

Brother Chong-An made the fateful decision to stay his hand, wait a while longer, follow the Fly and see what ensued, unintentionally exercising the influence on future events that he craved.

He closed his eyes and cast his mind into the darkened room above him and espied the object of his musings fast asleep in bed. The adept was exhilarated at the possibilities evolving.

'Well, my friend, what extraordinary events are we going to experience together, I wonder?'

Chong-An returned speedily to his chambers and hurriedly gathered a few possessions for the long journey. He didn't need much – mainly unguents for his feet and knees – packing them carefully into a canvas shoulder bag. Whilst he was occupied thus, he discovered an unusual increase in the activity in the Tower. His anxiety grew on discovering the magus was setting out on a journey. Would he want to interrogate his librarian before leaving? The possibility of Brother Drudwynn sending for him served to give further impetus to his hasty departure.

Arriving back within the woods behind the tavern, Chong had a quick peek at the recumbent Fly and, utilizing his gift of illusion, created a spell that could last for hours when not on the move. There was no actual physical change in his body as he settled himself to sleep on soft rushes between a fairly dry log and the rough bark of a white willow tree, but he blended against the background of the wetlands as if he was invisible.

Five

The mountains stood impossibly high and bitterly cold, the peaks disappearing into fluffy, grey, snow-laden clouds. Below, drifting had given rise to a falsely attractive terrain, the snow obscuring narrow paths, small hills and deep treacherous crevasses alike.

The blizzard, inadvertently called into being by the magic created by Ryn, in his need to rescue his friends from the trolls, had ended. In its place an icy, yet invigorating, wind blew across a scene that was mesmerizing in its clarity. Snow, crisp and dry, blanketed the landscape in high mounds, deep vales and sloping, virgin plateaux. Huge, ice-covered, black rocks sleek and shining, most with knife-sharp edges, others moulded by the weather into fantastical shapes, stood proud amongst the whiteness. The occasional snow gum and Sitka spruce dotted the landscape, their long shadows and loneliness somehow adding to the pleasing vista. The only sounds within the mountains were the gentle moaning of the wind whistling through the peaks and narrow gorges, and from their steps breaking through the thin crust of new fallen snow to find an insecure purchase on old hard-packed snow beneath.

The fugitives were traversing country that had not seen a human footprint for hundreds of years; it was a cold country of extremes.

They had left the cave that had nearly become their tomb as soon as Shadra regained his strength, earlier that morning. Ryn, his vast wings fixed in place, coasting overhead, had wanted to carry him, but the four foot high, green-skinned forest elf had wished to walk alongside his tall, fascinating cousins. Roidan, liosalfar, the man-size pure white elf of the mountains, dressed in white ermine, was leading the procession. Anselm, the human minstrel and Mantovarian spy, walked behind him, and bringing up the rear was the other tall elf, Xelnor. Both liosalfars constantly alert, on their guard searching the glaring landscape for signs of the Cragga, their enemy.

Ryn, a Wandering Albatross of the Giant Albatross family, was overcome with emotion. Exhilarated, he was in his element flying in new air currents high above the vast range of the Scissor Mountains that formed the boundary between eastern Mantovar and the western border of the Great Desert. He'd always loved exploring new territory, often disappearing for months at a stretch flying in places as diverse as the tropics far to the south, and the very cold wastelands of the far north. But thinking of the snow deserts of the frozen tundra at the top of the world all of a sudden made him shudder. There was a rugged, broken region there that had wafted terror and he'd kept well away from it.

But his pleasure now was not wholly genuine; he was deliberately suppressing a feeling of threat. It was not the same feeling of gut-rotting evil as in the northern wastes, yet there was something very unpleasant here that he could not define. And it got worse the higher into the mountains his companions climbed. Wherever his small black eyes fell he saw an immeasurable landscape of mountain peaks and deep gorges. He had never seen so many, being a seabird he was used to an expanse of wild, untameable ocean dotted with the occasional volcanic island. But here the mountain peaks had taken the place of the islands and they poked up through an ocean of snow.

With mixed feelings he stared down at his friends plodding along an unseen path, they were safe, at least for the moment. Nonetheless his anxiety was growing the nearer they came to Alfhime. Speculating on the nature of this mysterious Cragga and the reason for the liosalfars' fear, his thoughts drew no conclusions, as their questions had drawn no answers from their rescuers. But the day was wonderful, the mountains beautiful and the winds…the winds were so magical his mind drifted away from his concerns and he soared through the skies in utter bliss.

Later, however, his thoughts returned to those below. One thought in particular made him smile. He had never before had friends and the wonder of it would be with him forever. The small forest elf had been the first, the human following shortly afterwards. And then Ryn squawked fearfully, recalling the three of them had nearly lost their lives in that cave. Suffering hypothermia, though they knew not the name of it, the two liosalfars had discovered them and had brought them back from the edge of death.

Now Roidan was leading them to Alfhime, the liosalfar's legendary home, a stronghold deep amongst the highest peaks of the Scissor Mountains. But to get there they had a long and arduous journey before them, following paths only Roidan and Xelnor could see.

'Shadra,' mindmelded Ryn, flying low overhead, *'remind Anselm of his promise to teach me to sing! Perhaps my first ballad will be the story of this journey.'*

'No-one would believe it,' laughed Shadra, his mirth boiling over, driving him to skip over the snowy hillocks. 'Liosalfar…Alfhime…'

'Schrat?' Anselm, smiling all over his face not quite believing that his mission to find the Garda, the guardians of a legend, had succeeded, called Shadra by the ancient name for forest elf that the liosalfar had first used. 'And what won't we believe?' Having no mindmelding skills, Anselm had only heard one side of the conversation.

'Please, cousin,' said Roidan interrupting quietly, putting his finger to his lips, 'do not make loud noises here. This is not only avalanche country but also the Cragga's.'

'Oh! Sorry!' Shadra paused and looked around uneasily. The long, pure white slopes took on a new meaning; there were hidden dangers amongst the splendour. 'Tell me, Roidan,' the green elf asked equally quietly a moment later, 'how far is Alfhime?'

'Another day, yet, we should arrive at noon tomorrow.'

'We aren't going to sleep out here, are we?' Anselm asked, dreading the prospect. It would be freezing in the mountains once the sun had gone down. And although he and Shadra had been assured that the potion administered them, besides reviving their spirits, would also protect them from the cold, he didn't know how long the effects of the potion would last.

'There is shelter ahead, what you would call a guard-post, to us they are listening stations.' He didn't say what they were listening for. 'There are other liosalfar patrolling these mountains and we occasionally gather in these places to converse, pass on knowledge face to face.'

'We'll meet others? How many of you are there? Why have you hidden yourselves away? Why…'

'Wait, cousin,' Roidan said with an air of distracted impatience, 'so many questions! All will be answered in time, if needs be.'

'Does that mean some won't be, Shadra?' Ryn flying overhead had heard everything. The magic gifted by Aidan seemed to have no end—his hearing had also been enhanced far beyond normal.

Shadra gazed up at his friend playing amongst the thermals. *'I wonder…something is not right! But quiet now they may overhear our mindmeld.'*

'I don't think they can. Haven't you noticed? I don't believe they can mindmeld.'

'Don't be silly, of course they can, they have magic…all elves mindmeld!'

'Try it, then,' and when Shadra hesitated Ryn continued. *'They hide their magic as well.'*

And anxiety gnawed at him—for Ryn was correct.

The Cragga, lying in the ice beneath the surface of the snow on which they walked, listened and was puzzled. While their boots trampled her she wondered why she had not yet killed them all, for she could have quite easily. All she needed to do was open a crevasse beneath their feet and they'd plunge to oblivion. But their deaths would only give momentary satisfaction; transitory revenge for no positive outcome could come of it. Besides, she didn't like killing indiscriminately, although she had many deaths on her conscience.

She was confused by her feelings. The strangers were of such a disparate nature, a schrat, a human and a bird…she pondered on why they were together and so obviously friends. Elves had hidden from humans for centuries, ever since the dragons had disappeared—and the humans had been blamed for that though she knew different. And a bird, a magical bird of enormous size, where on earth had he come from, and why!

Without warning, from the depths of her memories, she recalled another large bird and its companions—surely it could not be happening again?

And yet Roidan was helping them…the liosalfars' leader would not like that.

Flowing beneath the path they walked on, she tried to digest their conversation, detecting unease in the schrat and in the bird, a disquiet that would eventually be shared with the human. And she knew the reason, for their companions would soon bring them face to face with a danger that not even the liosalfar could guess at.

Sometimes she had sympathy for the tall, pale-skinned elves; they had no idea what was leading them. Nevertheless, their intractable demeanour drove her to fury; their blindness, to helpless frustration. But they had made their decision years before their new leader had come along, her enmity could not be blamed on him, though he upheld the injustice.

But these three strangers intrigued her; she felt an irresistible attraction to one of them though she did not know which. If she'd had shoulders then, she would have hunched them, bowing her head as well. She'd despaired for so long, having tried persuasion, begging, pleading and even gone on her knees before the tall elves—all to no avail. The liosalfar just didn't want to know.

So she had been left with no option but to fight them. In the beginning it had been hard they had used magic to defend themselves. But so had she, a different kind. But they had fought each other to a stalemate. And then he had come. Twenty years earlier he had tricked her and entered Alfhime closing the door behind him, leaving her devastated and the liosalfar in mortal danger, though they knew it not.

But now, studying these three friends and burying her memories, she felt a resurgence of optimism. She had not felt hope for such a long time she almost didn't recognize it. But when it hit her, when it filled her heart, she found she could not kill any of them.

She accompanied them unseen and unheard.

They plodded on along the invisible track, climbing higher into the blinding, white peaks. Anselm, though, slowed his pace, he was suffering headaches. Shadra, looking back and up at his friend, noticed his eyes closing.

'What is it, Anselm? What's wrong?'

'He has the beginnings of snow-glare…he will be unable to see before long. We need to lead him. Keep your eyes closed, we will care for you,' said Roidan, edginess barely hidden in his tone.

'Oh! Hang on a minute, I can help him now.' Shadra rummaged in his bottomless purse and came up with a shade for the minstrel's eyes, and a potion which Anselm drank to relieve the pain in his head.

'I have heard of the schrat's purse, cousin. Is it true you can hide a pony in its depths?' Roidan asked quite seriously, not taking his eyes from Shadra's bag.

'Don't be stu…' and then peering up at the earnest look on Roidan's face, he stopped, not wishing to offend. 'What other stories have you heard about it?'

'Many, some fantastical…but is it true?'

'Maybe…maybe later I will reveal more of its secrets—if needs be,' and he stared at his tall cousin wondering how anyone could believe he'd have a horse in his bag…it'd be too heavy to carry! Were the liosalfar as intelligent as they appeared? Or…he stopped conjecturing, he wasn't quite sure what he thought.

Roidan did not miss the point. 'When we have told you ours, is that it?' And he returned irritably to the path before him. He was getting more anxious and abstracted as the day progressed, his initial affability receding rapidly.

'Ryn,' Shadra mindmelded, *'did you let on back in the cave that you had magic?'*

'I don't think so. Why?'

'That feeling I mentioned earlier, that something is not quite right…it's growing. I may be wrong but until I'm certain keep your magic and your fingers secret.'

'You will have to warn Anselm,' said Ryn perturbed.

'I shall find an opportunity before long.'

They continued on, the tall pale elf walking confidently leading the short green elf with the tall human minstrel floundering behind. Xelnor, meanwhile, was dropping farther to the rear, worry lines creasing his forehead, allowing the distance to grow between him and the others. He seemed to spend most of his time walking backwards, peering along the track they had passed over.

Floating in amongst the air currents above, his wings locked for cruising, the giant albatross became very subdued. Everything had appeared as sweet as a shrimp at first, he thought, now the influence of the shark was making itself felt.

Hours later – just after Shadra had passed on his feelings to Anselm – at the top of a long rise they walked around a sheer cliff stretching many feet above their heads, and came to a rift in the rock wall. At the mouth of the narrow opening another liosalfar waited, his skin the same in colour as Roidan's, but he was a full foot shorter. He was dressed in a white jerkin with baggy britches tucked into the tops of white boots, his long white hair tied back at the nape beneath a white cap that hugged his head. Like his fellow liosalfar, he carried a crossbow on his back and a sheaf of bolts at his waist; he also had a slingshot stuck into his belt alongside a bulky leather pouch. The whole of his appearance made him invisible against a backdrop of snow. But at this moment he was outlined against black stone.

The third liosalfar stared at the strangers seemingly more surprised at the sight of Shadra than the human and the giant bird. Anselm could have sworn he saw fear flicker across the sentry's eyes.

'Well, Roidan, this moot will certainly be lively,' he raised his eyes and squinted against the sun, staring above at Ryn. 'Is that bird really with you?' and when Shadra and Anselm nodded, he went on. 'Then what do you intend doing with your feathered companion? He is too big to enter here,' he said brusquely.

'Ryn, you will need to find shelter elsewhere,' Roidan ordered when the albatross came to rest on the top of the cliff. He wondered if the bird could comprehend his words, he seemed to understand those of Shadra well enough. 'This tunnel is far too small to admit you as you see. Can you find safety elsewhere? I wish I could help you, but…' Roidan, his tone anything but caring, cast a look lower down the slope catching the eye of Xelnor. Making up his mind he turned a troubled gaze on Shadra. 'Can he understand? It is of the utmost importance that he does.'

'Yes, he is a very intelligent fr…bird,' Shadra replied, his anxiety increasing, for some reason he again felt it best to hide their true relationship.

'Ryn…please, as you search keep in mind there are enemies in these mountains. I would not like the Cragga to find this station.'

The Cragga, beneath his feet smiling her contempt, almost laughed aloud at his intolerable smugness. She knew the site of all the listening stations throughout the mountains. She'd had years to locate them.

'Do not worry, Roidan, I am very discreet.' Ryn mindmelding to ascertain the merit of his suspicions received no reply. It served to confirm their earlier fears. The liosalfar could not mindmeld.

'Will you be all right, Shadra?' Ryn asked.

Shadra looked at Anselm, his glance asking for silence, and saw his own trepidation mirrored in his friend's eyes. Anselm was as equally suspicious of the new circumstances as he was.

'Allow me to introduce Qillan,' Roidan said.

Qillan nodded his face impassive; he took Roidan to one side. Believing he was far enough away not to be overheard he whispered in Roidan's ear.

'Are you sure we should be taking the schrat with us? You know the prophecy; the law states quite categorically that no schrat is ever to enter Alfhime!'

'What do you propose we do…murder him here and now? Or refuse him entry and leave him to die out here? I for one will not go along with either option…I have no stomach for such treachery to our own people!'

'The Magician will be extremely unhappy,' Qillan said his face grave.

'No more than me! But as it's his law…he can do the slaying!' With that Roidan broke off the conversation.

Qillan grunted and turned to the fugitives; he bowed his greeting and then led the way quickly into the rift, visibility decreasing rapidly the deeper they proceeded into the mountainside.

Ryn, sitting quietly on the cliff top had overheard every word and he passed it on to Shadra as the forest elf stood at the opening.

'I think you make a mistake going with them, Shadra,' he said very alarmed.

'I don't see what else we can do; there is nowhere else we can go,'

'I can carry the two of you down the mountain!'

'And kill yourself like you nearly did before. Besides, I told you the mountains are calling me and I believe it is in Alfhime I am wanted.' He looked up at his avian friend and smiled reassuringly. *'I do have my magic to protect us…do not worry,'* and then he glanced into the cliff entrance after Qillan. *'But wait here, we may be back quicker than I think if I am wrong…and when we do appear we may be running.'*

With that parting remark, Shadra grabbed Anselm and they walked out of sight of the very frightened bird.

The Cragga wondered if she should allow them leave to enter Alfhime, she knew the likely outcome. But she couldn't warn them without betraying her presence and causing panic amongst the liosalfar. And like their captors, the strangers probably wouldn't believe her either. Unable to make up her mind she watched their backs disappearing into the cliff.

Anselm, unaware of Roidan's conversation with Qillan, became alarmed at the pace of the elves and the length of the passageway; he stumbled and banged his knee against the rock wall.

'Whoa, please slow down will you, how you manage I don't know, but we humans can't see in the dark.'

'Oh, sorry, Anselm, I forgot your eyes were failing you…here,' and Shadra retrieved a small torch from his bottomless purse. Handing the bound and tarred bunch of twigs to the minstrel, the schrat also removed flint and match from the same place. Igniting the torch with a flourish, Shadra replaced the flint and moved on without as much as a bye or leave.

Anselm stared after his friend not knowing quite what to say, almost coming to believe that, maybe, there was a pony somewhere deep in the bottom of the elf's pouch. But the glimpse he'd had, in the striking of the flint, of Qillan's face made him nervous. The liosalfar's look conveyed avarice as he stared longingly at Shadra's purse.

The tunnel was narrow, the roof high, and it seemed to go on forever twisting and turning in a random manner along its length. There were no side passages, just one cold, dark and narrow entryway leading eventually into a high, wide and warm cavern lit by torches in sconces around the walls. In the centre of the floor was a large circular rock, flat on the top. On this was spread gravel, the stones glowing red, giving off a radiant heat. The rock was ringed by larger stones on which had been placed pots and pans. A mouth-watering aroma rose from the large iron pot hanging to one side of it—the gravel itself was used for cooking.

Around the walls were bundles of supplies, mainly packages of food, some standing open. Short stabbing spears were standing in cones, blades uppermost in easy reach and packs of clothing and bedding were arranged neatly in rows. In one spot against the wall was a pile of waterproof leather sacks, one was open and contained white pellets, more of the gravel used for cooking and heating. Everything gave the impression that all could be retrieved speedily if an alarm was raised.

There were three other liosalfar within, all eating from wooden bowls and drinking mulled wine. They were unsurprised at the entry of the human, Qillan having warned them earlier of Roidan's approach with his unusual companion. But Qillan had missed seeing the small forest elf. They all stared at Shadra, their mouths dropping, all thought of food gone from their minds.

The schrat stood before them, fidgeting at their silence. 'Good evening, cousins. My name is Shadramintamablinski of the Great Forest,' and he bowed courteously. I thank you greatly for rescuing us. This…' and he turned to indicate the human, 'is Anselm, a minstrel from the city of Mantovar.'

Anselm in turn bowed, puzzled at why the elf had not introduced him as an agent of the Chancellor of Mantovar. From the moment Shadra had told him of his and Ryn's fears the jubilation he had felt at their recovery diminished swiftly. He didn't know the reason, but his instincts were warning him—and his instincts had never let him down yet.

But, whatever, the liosalfar also had concerns and Anselm suspected it was more than this mysterious Cragga. From the way Roidan's manner was shifting, becoming more abrupt and suspicious, and the way the others kept glancing at their cousin, what really bothered the mountain elves was Shadra.

Nevertheless, whether their rescuers liked it or not Anselm had been given a mission to gain their aid. The liosalfar leadership would have to be approached with his request sooner rather than later. Anselm brooded, there was threat here and he surreptitiously loosened the misericorde that was strapped beneath his armpit, a knife that no-one yet suspected he had. The mountain elves had taken his overt display of weaponry as the only arsenal he possessed, or they were cleverly hiding their knowledge of it. He shrugged, deciding to go along with his friend, he remained silent.

'Please, forgive our bad manners,' said the only mountain elf showing any colour, it was a red scarf hanging loosely around his neck. All three elves rose and laid their bowls aside. 'I am Zilbor, these are Wellen and Crystal.'

The three returned the bows of the two guests and it was only then that Anselm realized that the third liosalfar was a female, her looks quite extraordinarily beautiful. She smiled quickly at the minstrel's obvious admiration.

'Come, please be seated,' Crystal said pointing at spare places against the packs. 'Make yourselves at home, Wellen will get you soup and bread and Zilbor, I'm sure, will be delighted to furnish you with his magnificent wine. When you have rested, then perhaps you will satisfy our curiosity,' and she smiled again, this time thinly and nervously as she adjusted her slingshot in her belt into a more comfortable position.

Avoiding Shadra's eyes she went on. 'The schrat are legendary peoples!'

Six

Deep in the bilges of the Grim, hiding on the keel, the shape-shifter stirred. It still had the appearance of a rat and it swam slowly through the murky water climbing unseen into the main hold where it again found a place to hide, this time behind the bales and crates. It felt comfortable in darkness and settled against the hull of the ship to await nightfall before investigating the upper deck.

But it was soon disturbed when someone unexpectedly slid the hatch cover to one side. It squinted in the unexpected shaft of light streaming into the hold and watched as a heavyset sailor descended the ladder.

Unused to the light it, nevertheless, listened to the strange new world above. It had never before heard seagulls screeching as they searched for titbits thrown overboard, or the sound of the wind whistling through the tight rigging, or the occasional voice of a living human shouting above. But then again it did twitch its nose in disgust at the stench of fresh air…and it smiled as it followed the progress of the man down the ladder. It waited for sustenance.

It did not attack immediately, never having encountered live humans before, it studied the big man searching in a crate. It took stock of the man's size and shape, it smelled the rank sweat glistening on the sailor's skin and its ears perked up when it heard the man's breath wheezing in his throat.

The shape-shifter padded silently in the narrow passages between the bales utilising every dark spot, every place of shade, until it arrived directly behind the man. It halted and turned its head from side to side not yet comfortable with the constricted movement of the rat's neck; in its usual form it had no such limitation. It tweaked its whiskers, its nose irritated again by the breeze flowing through the hold. It sneezed.

The man, hearing it, straightened and turned with something in his hands. The shape-shifter knew not nor cared what it was, but it stilled, its tiny black eyes staring up at the man returning its gaze. The moment didn't last long before the man grimaced and kicked out, his foot connecting with the shape-shifter's rat body. It flew through the air and thudded against a bale of wooden planks. Normally the impact would have broken the back of the rat, but this was no ordinary rodent.

Landing on its tiny paws it snarled at the sailor and reacted in a manner that terrified the man.

The shape-shifter began to grow, maintaining the shape of a rat it ballooned to a gigantic size until its head was at a level with the man's waist, but it didn't stop there. It paused as if taking breath and then continued to grow even larger.

The sailor, his eyes popping, stood paralyzed, his terror stifling his scream before it left his mouth.

The rat continued to grow until its size jammed it between the crates, inhaling deeply the rat's chest thrust the cargo aside as if it were feathers.

The man continued to stare hypnotized at the mindboggling sight. His eyes were all that moved and they were drawn inexorably to stare into the rat's open maw. His senses only returned the instant the rat took his head into its mouth. By then the scream was obliterated in the gullet of the shape-shifter—his body was not long following.

The shape-shifter resumed the normal size of a black rat and licked its lips. It again settled to wait for nightfall…and another human.

Seven

Elstan had remarkable recuperative powers. He may well have spent most of the night clinging to a high sloping roof and climbing up and down sheer walls, but you wouldn't have thought it. He rose fully rested from his bed, just before nine in the morning, some five hours after turning in. Over the years he had developed the habit of catnapping, short periods of sleep taken often were sufficient for his needs. As was his custom when this close to his employer's enemies, he had slept fully clothed, the need for caution and the possibility of a swift flight always uppermost in his mind. He had not survived this long through being careless; his life had been in jeopardy too often in the past.

He trod barefoot across the dirty wooden boards of the small room, the soles of his feet hard enough to withstand the splinters and the grime, and peered out of the filthy window into the backyard of the tavern. He studied the scene microscopically from his vantage point behind a broken shutter. Hidden from all but one watcher, he was satisfied that the only movement came from the tavern's cook, a scruffy little man entering the lean-to privy below his room. Elstan gazed at the closed door abstractedly for a moment before lifting his eyes and peering farther afield. He stared over the broken fence forming the boundary wall separating the yard from the swamp encroaching at the rear of the tavern. One day, in the not too distant future, the tavern itself would be swallowed up by the mire, its memory lingering in the minds of no-one.

Nothing moved within the stand of box elder, the male trees resplendent with dense red tassels. All was quiet…too quiet, he thought. At this time of day there should have been the incessant chirping of crickets, the rustle of undergrowth as the vole and the larger mallard wandered in and out foraging for food, keeping wary eyes open for the occasional insomniac alligator. Only yesterday he had espied a little grebe trilling happily as it swam between the legs of a grey heron croaking and retching as it called to its mate. This morning there was nothing, not even the relentless, hovering clouds of midges that usually infested the place.

He stared hard, his eyes narrowing, the sun only now peeping over the high mountain range. He searched for a reason for the lack of life in the thicket, finding none made him nervous. He could not see Chong-An, the culprit, staring up at him from beneath the drooping green clusters of a lone female box elder growing to one side. The oriental was hidden within his illusion.

The early morning was again hot and humid promising a sweltering heat later in the day. It never varied in the wetlands. The sun lifted thin tendrils of mist off the choked waterways meandering haphazardly beneath willow and sallow. The slight breeze wafting softly over the rotting vegetation brought with it its familiar mix of smells. The stench encompassed the sickly sweet aroma of blooded carrion killed during the night by nocturnal predators.

Elstan turned from the window and inspected the room, ignoring the snores rattling the thin wooden walls, late night revellers still in a drunken stupor in the room next door. He found nothing untoward, no signs of anyone's unwelcome presence whilst he'd been sleeping. He picked up his meagre but essential belongings from the floor and off the three legged table propped against the wall alongside the bed…once there had been four legs. He packed everything into his canvas shoulder bag. With one last look around, he slung his baldric over his shoulder and strapped to it his sword in its worn scabbard. He armed himself with a variety of long and short knives intrinsic to his profession. The last, his misericorde, he removed from its sheath beneath his left armpit and checked its edge, satisfied he replaced the weapon he never went to sleep without holding.

He removed the pegs from the doorjamb and crept softly into the passage and down the back stairs, the dilapidated treads creaking loudly even though he stepped lightly alongside the wall. Halting at the kitchen, he debated for a moment whether to obtain food from the scruffy cook scratching his backside at the table. But needs be, he went ahead and purchased bread, cheese and a large slab of the previous day's fish pie hoping it was still edible. He didn't intend stopping to eat until the late afternoon.

He exited the tavern through the back door and crossed the yard, walking through and over the detritus of the hostelry, leaving through a broken gate hanging by one hinge. Turning left he slung the canvas bag over his shoulder and made his way around the corner heading to the town centre to pick up the road north.

If he'd but known it, he passed almost close enough to touch the seated and excited figure of Brother Chong-An still hiding beneath the box elder, six feet away.

Chong-An gave Elstan a lead of a hundred yards and then stepped from cover and the shelter of the illusion. Dressed in the everyday clothes of a swamp dweller – dirty brown britches, ragged tunic – and with a cloak tied to the top of the bag carried on his back, he held his staff in one hand and walked after his quarry with a spring in his step. He smiled; his life was at last becoming interesting again, if not exactly safe. He had no qualms, only relief, at leaving the Tower, although he fully intended keeping a sharp lookout for Brother Drudwynn and the guards he was sure to send in pursuit.

Chong-An was always optimistic at the start of his journeys. The road ahead held so many options and differing fortunes. If he took it into his head to take the next turning on the left instead of the one on the right, it would inevitably take him to a variety of different circumstances. If he walked on and waited at a crossroads he'd find something else that he would not have seen if he hadn't stopped. Chong-An loved the uncertainty of his travels even if he'd planned the route well in advance.

But, of course, there was a fundamental dissimilarity in this journey. This time his route depended on the choices the man ahead made, an intriguing and exhilarating prospect. It was a happy coincidence that the interloper was going north, the direction in which he, Chong, wished to go. But he'd always been a firm believer that coincidences had a purpose…although he was not sure what they were. For once he had no notion of the immediate future as he mingled with other itinerants travelling towards the Drikander.

Throughout the rest of the morning and into the middle of the afternoon, the short, flabby, ancient oriental man followed the small, wiry, middle-aged occidental. The traffic on the Great North Road lessened only slightly when they left the town limits. Chong-An smiled. The "great" in the road's name didn't only apply because of the measureless extent of the ancient highway. It was also because of the "great" numbers of people always to be found walking somewhere along its length. There was an old saying that everyone in the empire, at some time in their lives, walked a section of the road.

The travellers were many and varied, peasants looking for work in the larger towns of Drakka, these keeping company in threes and fours, very rarely more. An occasional family trundled along dragging or pushing a rickety old handcart holding all their worldly possessions, refugees from the poverty of Jasper heading towards the even greater penury of the larger cities, dwindling hope driving them on.

The richer denizens rode with self-assurance noticeably absent from the body language of the downtrodden majority. Not only their horses set them apart but also their clothes, these being of the finest cotton and silk imported from the south. The dyers had worked their arts into brilliant colours, dazzlingly bright in the light of day and the lanterns of night. The costumiers had worked wonders creating ever more flamboyant styles of pleated sleeves and ruched necks, tight leggings and leather boots, the latter sometimes of excessive length.

The hoity-toity, Chong-An called them. He derided the upper classes, lumping them all together as parasites on the backs of the poor working peasants. But he seemed to forget that the educated classes passed on their knowledge down the line to the betterment of those same peasants, even if the knowledge was learned in a haphazard fashion.

And, of course, there were the even rarer Drakkan military patrols policing the freeway, an inadequate force attempting an impossible job.

Many leagues farther north of Jasper, prior to traversing the passes and paths of the Drikander, most of these travellers would band together for mutual protection. The poorer itinerants, desperately hoping to be allowed to join the convoys, though, were resigned to the fact that they would have to part with unaffordable coin to pay the armed mercenaries. They plodded along despairing. The only other alternative for these pitiable people was a journey around the vast forest lands which would take months, an inconceivable trek; they would never survive the plains, rivers and mountains…or the bandits.

Bands of Grekkos – from the many tribes inhabiting the densely wooded hills and vales of the Drikander – warded the Great North Road as it wound its way through their territory. The Drikander was a bulge on the western edge of the Great Forest, the vast woodlands that stretched northwards to the Frozen Wastes, south to surround Qula and eastwards over the massive range of the Scissor Mountains.

The tribesmen were a law unto themselves, demanding a toll from each traveller for safe passage. But quite often the tribes vied with each other and tolls had to be paid to more than one chieftain. The Drakkan military were powerless within the region. The emperor had admitted, on more than one occasion, that the whole might of Drakka and Mantovar would still never remove the menace of the savage, heathen tribesmen in their wild, inhospitable, but strangely lovely country.

The Great North Road itself went more or less in a straight line until it approached the hills twenty leagues north of Jasper. Here it wound west around the Wolfshead promontory, a high forested hill shaped like its namesake, before continuing on.

Nestled below the nose of the Wolfshead, alongside the river Wry flowing southward to feed the wetlands was the Vixen's Haven. A large roadside hostelry, it was reached by leaving the road temporarily and crossing a wide bridge over the fast moving river where it flowed through a narrow culvert. The inn was very popular with rich and poor alike as it marked the northern end of the easiest stretch of road between Jasper and Mulkie's Cross.

A well-cared for tavern, the Vixen's Haven was a two storey building in an L-shape with stables behind. The ground floor of the short leg of the "L" held the bar and kitchen. The long leg and the entire upper floor held accommodation for those travellers heading north who were willing to pay exorbitant sums for the last comfort for a hundred leagues or more.

That afternoon Elstan ambled up to the front door and, while taking the bag from his back and stretching his worn shoulders as if weary, he looked behind and covertly studied those people walking up the road. Satisfied, he entered the long bar, crowded at this time of day as people's thoughts were turning to resting for the night.

He settled himself at a small empty table adjacent to the kitchen at the rear of the smoke-filled, dim room, it still being too early to light the lanterns. Placing his sword, in its scuffed black scabbard, on the old scarred table top in front of him, he removed the thin bladed misericorde from his armpit. Stabbing it into the top of the wooden table, the dagger quivered momentarily at his right hand. The occupants of the tables nearby shifted imperceptibly at sight of the weaponry so close at hand. But as no threat was made against them, they resumed their eating and drinking and ignored him. Elstan sat with his back to the wall facing the doorway, watching all those who came in after his arrival.

He ordered food and ale and waited, it never ceasing to amaze him the large number of people always on the road. Those walking north were making for the same place as he, the gathering point of the convoys in the substantial town of Mulkie's Cross. It was a town that had grown considerably over the years to service the immense bridge over the Wry at the southern edge of the Drikander.

Chong-An had never been so relieved in all his life as when he saw his quarry enter the Vixen, he hoped, for the night. He stumbled with fatigue and pain as he stepped up onto the two-step porch before the doors. He moaned and looked down at the sorry state of his feet. Three of his toes were skinned and bleeding, the very inappropriate slippers he wore had rubbed his feet raw. The luxury footwear, designed to comfort his sore feet during a full day's study in the library, were now somewhat the worse for wear. He had forgotten they were still on his feet in his excitement and haste to escape the Tower. The uppers were soft with decorative lines of pure white pearls, the bottoms thin and light, unfortunately not made for walking long distances on rough roads. His legs were killing him, burning mightily, he preferred toothache.

He had grown rather lazy in his old age and very rarely walked any great distance. Riding in an open carriage or coach and four gave him the comfort his old bones required. He was not a fit man and the battering his knees and feet had just undergone had exacerbated the inflammation in the membranes of his heels—each one felt as if it was on fire, his insteps agony as his arches dropped. His lower back ached, his lumber muscles spasming relentlessly, slowing him, forcing him to take short rests leaning on his staff. He did this more often as the day wore on. He tried lifting his feet from the hard surface of the road to ease the pain in his heels, but this only served to increase the pain in his insteps. For the removal of the ground's support made the joints in his feet hurt even more.

He'd suffered years with slipped vertebrae in the base of his spine and healers had on many occasions set in motion the repair of the bones and cartilage. But no physician, though they be practitioners of the magic arts, could work miracles. They initiated the healing and then expected the patient to follow their instructions to reach a healthy conclusion. Unfortunately, back pain required movement of the spine to relieve the malady. Chong-An would follow the instructions for a few days, carry out the exercises as required. But then his eye would catch an item in a book and he would sit hunched over for hours at a table reading—his back would seize up again and the remedy would just peter out.

He had no stamina at his age, so he said, for prolonged exercise and never saw the sense in deliberately working up a sweat. He was often heard to utter, as he reclined with his feet up resting on a stool, a goblet of the finest brandy in one hand a tobacco pipe in the other, that there were more fitness freaks inside the infirmary than outside.

But now he was starving as well as hurting, his empty, rather portly belly rumbled audibly. He was used to three square meals taken at exactly the same hour each day and with an abundance of food on his platter. These meals were also supplemented with snacks taken at regular intervals between the set meals. Travelling by coach he always managed to follow his habitual diet, but walking for hours on end on an open road meant his eating regimen went by the board.

He shook his head in desperation, setting out this morning he'd forgotten all this. Exhilaration at discovering the fruits of his foretelling had been correct – and the agonizing threat of Brenin's interrogation – had made him hasten. But fear had made him forgetful also, because he had soon realized that his slippers were totally inadequate for the journey. He had been too afraid to return to his rooms to retrieve his boots. He was a firm believer in sod's law. It was a fact beyond any doubt that if he'd gone back into the Tower, Drudwynn would have apprehended him.

His breakfast, this morning, had consisted of several chicken drumsticks, a great wedge of extra matured blue cheese along with half a large loaf of bread. He'd eaten all of it as he trudged along, the whole lot washed down with a medium sized flask of homemade rice wine, his speciality.

But being hungry he had made the mistake of saving nothing for his lunch. He was expecting the man he was following to halt long before this, for there were always purveyors of food, hot and cold, on the road. But he had forgotten that there were always long queues of moneyed peoples in front of these wagons. Delaying to purchase the succulent meat pies risked him losing his quarry, for he could never rush to catch him up, not with his feet. So he swallowed bravely and walked on past.

He was sorry now, though, for his hunger, his aches and his introspection led to irritability and it was this perhaps that led to his momentary carelessness.

He walked through the door into the bar, looked around the room for somewhere to sit and straightway made eye contact with the man he was pursuing. A silly blunder he realized immediately, especially when Elstan beckoned him over and pointed to the bench opposite him at the table.

Chong-An contemplated for a moment on whether he should ignore the call, look behind and pretend mistaken identity. But it would have been futile, the look in the man's eye told him there was no doubt—he'd been found out. He wended his way through the packed tables; the smell of the cooking wafting from the kitchen, ensuring he salivated well before he reached his destination.

Pushing past diners and bar staff alike he stood silently before his quarry. Perceiving no alternative and no immediate threat, he accepted Elstan's offer of a seat. He drew out the bench on his side of the table, dropped his bag on the floor beside him and placed his staff on the table to lie parallel with the sword. He sat bemused as a platter of the most delicious roast pork, green beans and turnip was pushed towards him by his grim faced host, along with a jug brimming with mouth-watering, steaming gravy, Elstan having ordered it prior to his follower's entrance. A harassed barmaid pushed her way over to them and placed two foaming tankards of ale on the table, careful not to touch the sword, the staff or the dagger. The warning implied by the thin misericorde was not missed by Chong-An.

The oriental sorcerer, unable to prevent a groan of relief, dragged his aching feet from his slippers and gingerly flexed his sore toes in the hot, still air beneath the table. Resting them gently on the hard, ale-wet, dirty floor, he removed his small eating knife from his belt. Using the wooden spoon supplied with the food, he gave no further thoughts to the unexpectedly early encounter with the man who held such a fascination for him. He thankfully gave in to satisfying the overwhelming pangs of hunger before his belly shook the table.

Half an hour of non-stop eating later, when both men had sated their hunger in silence, Chong-An looked across the table at his host, took a large swig of ale, belched and wiped his greasy mouth on a large kerchief that he pulled from a pocket in his dirty britches.

'How long did it take you to realize I was there?' Chong-An asked. Retrieving a toothpick from the pouch on his belt, he ignored the very cold expression on Elstan's face. Feeling the underlying threat of violence in the man he was not unduly troubled despite the overt display of weaponry on the table. Did the man not understand the menace of a wizard's staff, he wondered.

'Well before we left the outer limits of Jasper,' Elstan stated softly, not batting an eyelid.

'My, and I thought I was being so clever. Was I that obvious?'

'Not really, you were indistinguishable from the others on the road, at first. You blended in well, but then you made a fundamental error, a blunder that a member of the gentry would make having no need of them … you threw the chicken bones away.'

'What's wrong with that?' Chong-An asked. He had settled on employing his skills of illusion in the normal everyday manner that the un-magical community would use. He dressed the same as everyone else, walked and talked like the others on the road. He'd chosen the mode because illusory magic called for an inordinate amount of energy and was very difficult to maintain over long periods, especially when on the move amongst a crowd of other folk. It seemed that his subterfuge had worked well…up to a point. But how had his breakfast led to his discovery? And then he kicked himself for being so stupid.

'No self-respecting poor traveller, as you appear to be on this road, would have discarded such a morsel. The bones would have been hoarded to make soup…food might very well be scarce ahead. Then I noticed your limp seemed to get worse and, despite the obvious pain, you hardly stopped to rest. Do you recall me speeding up a couple of leagues back?'

'Yes, you nearly killed me!'

'It was a test…I wanted to check my theory. When you also increased your pace I knew I was right, especially when you passed the food hawkers without stopping. You made me curious so I slowed again. Why was a man so obviously under serious stress doing his damndest to stay with me? Judging by your footwear, I'm not a bit surprised now about your pain, any normal person would be. What on earth possessed you to wear such things? Didn't you think of boots?' Elstan cocked his eyebrow; a small smile creased his mouth, though no humour reached his eyes.

'I could not chance losing you by returning to change them. But you are perfectly correct, I am desperately sorry that I'd not thought of the need when I set out,' he flexed his toes again, they'd stiffened up and he felt another blister burn as it burst.

'You could have slipped into the Tower as we passed,' Elstan said, taking a toothpick from his own belt and employing it manfully on his own well-kept teeth, enjoying his follower's discomfiture.

The adept, startled, sat up straighter on the creaking chair. He studied the man opposite without saying a word. He may be inept at hiding from a trained observer, as Elstan obviously was, but there was no way it could have been evident that Chong-An was a sorcerer—a denizen of the Tower. Elstan stared at him icily, all pretence of camaraderie disappearing fast.

'I have had many a cutthroat and beggar follow me hoping for rich pickings. All they got for their trouble was a slit gizzard. I have had the occasional run in with a wizard, each time they failed to best me or detain me for long. But let us get one thing straight between us before you say anything more. I would rather trust the vilest bandit than even the most inept wizard. Why do you follow me, Librarian?'

Chong-An tensed, careful not to show it, the change in the man's manner had slightly unnerved him. He stared hard and long at the small man opposite him. He took note of the man's manifest strength, his blatant confidence—his lack of wasted movement, the near proximity of the dagger to his hand. And he knew that this man was not boasting of his prowess but warning he was not an easy opponent.

But none of it seriously worried Chong-An and he resumed cleaning the last of the pork from between two molars. He had ways of killing against which this man could never defend himself. Methods he had studied and practised over many long years. He had, for a long time, resided at an oriental assassin's training school and had learned many of their tricks of the trade of murder. If this man assumed that he could only use magic to slay him perhaps he would surprise him by using the normal un-magical methods of the Orient. At the very least it would be amusing, thought Chong-An. He lifted his goblet and finished his ale, waving his arm across the room to the barmaid for refills before answering.

'I, also, have a certain distrust of sorcerers, not that I expect you to believe that as yet. But be aware that I watched you ascend and descend the Tower and did not take you into custody, although I could have easily then and on numerous occasions since. But I am not here to threaten your liberty or your life, in any way. I follow you because you intrigue me and I know not why, although I am a Seer of the First Order. Would it trouble you to tell me your name? I am Chong-An of Cuomo Province in the Orient.' He slowed his breathing in anticipation of at last discovering the name of the Fly.

Elstan stared at him, would it harm to say? If this sorcerer was truthful, if he was as curious as he admitted, then there was no way he was going to be shaken off easily. Sorcerers had many ways to keep track of him. He thought over the many unpleasant encounters he'd had with the Brethren. He'd never beaten any of them in open confrontation; he'd always had to resort to subterfuge. Every last one of them had been a veritable nuisance to escape.

He did not have the time to wrangle with this man or spend an inordinate amount of time throwing him off his trail. He needed to be on his way quickly, without interference. But it didn't look as if he was going to get away this time unless the man succumbed to his glib tongue. An unlikely event in the circumstances, although he'd often been told that he could charm the hind legs off a donkey.

'My name is Elstan of Miskim, Librarian. If you are wondering how I know you, I have had you pointed out to me by the Tower's servants.'

Chong-An's hair on the back of his neck suddenly rose. He knew of the town and of the strange travellers called there, each of them returning home bewildered, having succumbed to an unknown urge to visit the frontier post, none of them knowing why. Chong, though, thought he might know the reason. Is that where this man is bound, is he going home…is now the time for my search to take me there?

He sighed, he couldn't go there straightaway, first he had to visit the Drikander and secure the all-important documents. But could he possibly find a way to persuade Elstan to accompany him to the land of the tribesmen? And then, equally as important, induce him to travel on together to his home in Miskim.

Putting his toothpick away he went on to question Elstan, desperately hoping for answers that could explain years of complex research. But he was equally anxious that Elstan should not know of his apprehension.

'Miskim is that not a town in the north? You have the accent of a man of Mantovar so it must be. Am I correct?'

'It is a frontier town in the foothills of the Scissor Mountains, north of the city of Mantovar, yes,' Elstan paused and copied Chong by replacing his own toothpick, but this time the toothpick was pushed into a small sheath attached to the front of a dagger on his belt. 'It is a town whose only claim to fame is that it has the highest crime rate in the duchy…and a hell of a lot of foreign visitors who maintain that rate. It is a place far remote from here. How do you know of it?'

'I read a lot,' said the wizard off-handed, his heart missed a beat beginning to tremble with excitement. He knew now that his instincts had not led him astray—this man could lead him to that which was of the utmost importance. But there were other things he needed to know before he could even attempt to persuade the man to his purpose.

'Why are you this far south…and so interested in the Brethren?'

But at that moment the main door opened with a bang and all noise dwindled and ceased altogether. The sudden raising of tension in the room could be cut with a knife.

Chong-An turned his head slowly to seek the reason for the disruption and, with an impulsive jerk, returned to staring at Elstan. His face drained of colour and he immediately vanished into thin air. But before the startled Elstan could react and give the game away by drawing attention to them, Chong whispered, his words appearing to come from the air over the table.

'Do not panic…don't say a word or the both of us are dead!' the oriental warned. 'Grab my bag and follow me through the kitchen.'

Eight

Augusta, dishevelled, weary and not caring enough to hide it, approached Locklear on his quarterdeck. Leonid, in the act of climbing up from the waist of the ship, joined the Portolan, the Montetor, Chief Mazumbai and Marcus Janne in studying her. Before anyone could speak the Green Man abruptly bent down and rubbed a red spot on his ankle.

'What is it, Leonid?' Augusta frowned at his violent scratching.

'Oh, no worry, Highness, I seem to have suffered a bite that's all. Aidan…he's come around, he's all right?'

She dismissed Leonid's fierce kneading; insect bites were quite common, nothing for concern. 'Yes, my Lord Aidan has awakened and…'

'Of course,' Locklear sighed deeply at the initial use of the young wizard's honorific. 'With Lord Tragen's death Aidan carries his mantle, now.'

'The poor lad…I hope he's ready to accept such an exalted position,' Lodovico said worriedly.

'He may be young in years, Excellency,' replied Augusta. 'But in experience of life and of magical power he is way beyond us. Aidan has now become an extremely wealthy man and will, in future, command tremendous influence, so, he must be accorded his dues. But not for the reason you all assume.'

'What do you mean…we assume?' asked Bazyli Montetor frowning. 'I for one do not understand, surely the death of his guardian is a good enough reason for his elevation?'

'I'm sorry, but you have reached conclusions without knowing all of what has passed,' she said.

'Highness?' Lodovico coaxed.

'Your son, Excellency, believes Lord Tragen may still be alive.'

'But…how is that possible? He disappeared within the mists…you all witnessed it.' Locklear stared at his princess, disbelief on his face, but hope in his eyes.

'Lady Beatrix,' and at their collective indrawn breath she continued. 'Lady Beatrix – for she also has earned that elevation now that she is an extremely powerful wizard in her own right – can see within a light that is too brilliant for normal sighted people. She watched Lord Tragen enveloped in magic as he sank through the rock. From what she told us, Thaddeus believes Tragen is still protected by the power in his unbroken staff.' She paused and stared out over the ocean, misery tugging her mouth to one side.

'Aidan takes the honorific because his apprenticeship has come to an end. He feels his staff calling him, he…he has grown to adulthood rather quickly over these last days,' she uttered quietly.

'As have you all, Highness,' Mazumbai inclined his head.

'What are Lord Aidan's intentions?' Lodovico held his breath, fearing her answer for he knew that Thaddeus' fate was in the balance, tied up with whatever decisions these friends of his made. For Aidan, at present, was undoubtedly his son's leader. And Thaddeus would follow his friends to the ends of the world. They did not need the pronouncements of the prophecy to tell anyone that.

But when Thaddeus was ready to ascend to the throne of the Griffin Isles, that situation could never be allowed to continue. The King of Griffin must be his own master, make his own decisions alone, to lead his people into the future.

Lodovico wondered if Thaddeus would realize the full ramifications of his new position in society. The Portolan looked at Augusta through eyes that felt as if they had sunk to the back of his head, an ache developing deep in his head. He intuitively suspected another of her worries—she was afraid of losing Aidan's affections. She was his first love, he hers, not many such adolescent relationships survived the transition into adulthood. The Portolan's sympathies lay with her – neither of them wanted their loved ones to grow up so quickly – they could very well drift away as their views on life matured.

'Aidan intends seeking his staff, he believes he'll need it to aid us in our fight against the One,' Augusta continued quietly. 'But firstly he will search for Tragen within the Darkness. And, of course, we'll not allow him to travel there alone; he'll never succeed on his own. We will protect him. He's agreed to us accompanying him…not that he had any choice in the matter.'

Hugo looked askance. 'Highness, I would be failing in my duty to your father if I allowed you to put yourself, again, in such grave danger. You have just survived immense peril by the skin of your teeth and …'

'Captain,' she said haughtily, her back ramrod stiff, her head just reaching his broad shoulders, no-one could mistake her royal upbringing, her glare brooked no nonsense. 'The decision is not yours to make, you cannot stop me or my friends. We will go with him—we will not be parted,' and then she relaxed slightly, her severe mien lifted. 'But rest easy for now; we have to find a place of safety before we go. We shall wait until we reach Prince Griffin's home.'

Hugo stared at her unwilling to end the argument. 'I'm sorry, Highness, Lord Aidan must be dissuaded...'

'Enough, Captain,' she ordered brusquely. 'We will not leave Tragen in the Darkness if there is any possibility of rescuing him. We've made our decision and there is no going back on it!'

'Highness, Prince Griffin as heir to the Griffin Isles, also has responsibilities that must be considered before I risk him entering that foul place again,' said Lodovico Portolan as anxious as the Mantovarian captain.

'Ah, Lodovico, I so agree with you,' said Bazyli Montetor, interrupting. 'Nonetheless, we cannot forget the prophecy for even one moment.' He stared at his new compatriot with compassion. 'We have both found a treasure beyond imagining, in Thaddeus. Having an honourable heir for my clan has lifted an enormous weight from my shoulders. But the boy, or young man as he is now, has a greater mission than just caring for our people. It would be selfish in the extreme to hold him back for our sakes...even if we could. He has to fight the Darkness along with his friends in order to save us all.'

Lodovico, his face troubled, stared at Bazyli Montetor and then at Marcus Janne, he turned to the others huddled near.

'I'm sorry, my friends, it's just the terrible risk. I...I will not be able to bear the loss of Thaddeus. If he is overcome...' his voice faltered. 'I have had his awareness, his life, returned for such a very short time,' his voice nearly broke altogether as his awful memories returned. 'I have watched over him for so long...fifteen years and not a murmur from him, and now...dear God, I see the sense in what you say, Bazyli, but I do not like it. Our heir, it seems, has grown to adulthood before he has lived a childhood.'

Lodovico strode to the side of the Grim under their watchful silence, their sympathy almost tangible. He stared out over the ocean continuing to think of all the terrible years he and Thaddeus had suffered since the boy had been thrust into Limbo—the years when Thaddeus had been unable to communicate with anyone living. The long years when Thaddeus' only experience of the life that should have been his, was gained by staring heartbreakingly through the wall of colours, yearning desperately for the life that had been denied him by demons.

A smudge low on the horizon to the north caught his attention. It was the uninhabited island of Moth, one of the numerous islands of the archipelago, aptly named for its mammoth population of the nocturnal flying insects. And Lodovico uttered similar words of despair to those spoken by Augusta in the dungeons.

'Why are we mixed up in this? We are small people, insignificant in the vast stream of life.'

'Aye, Lodovico, that we are,' said Marcus Janne sharing his friend's fears. 'But we are about to make one hell of a difference to some God's plans,' deliberately repeating the words previously uttered by Bazyli Montetor.

Silence returned as they dwelled on the marshal's words wondering now as they did then. What did they mean? Were they prophetic? Would any of them survive? How could they possibly fight a God? And which of the mad ones was it? So many questions…so much they didn't know.

'And talking of plans I suggest we start calling in at these islands as we pass and tell the people to come to Griffin,' said Leonid, looking aft over the poop deck at the blackness staining the sky behind and then indicating the island to the north.

'We don't have to worry about that island, Leonid. It is too far north. The wind never blows from the south in this region…the Darkness will pass well clear of Moth,' said Marcus.

'Moth? That is its name?' Leonid asked, puzzled.

'Aye…why have you heard of it?' Marcus asked.

'Moth? Yes, I…I'm not sure,' and Leonid frowning, stared hard at the smudge wondering if it was the same place the salamanders went to rest.

'It will be far better to wait until we reach Griffin and send out messengers from there. That way we'll reach more islands far quicker,' Bazyli said very pensive.

'Whatever, before the Darkness arrives, all those who cannot escape across the seas must be made safe in Bylani,' Leonid finished.

'Can Bylani give safe haven to thousands? There must be over two thousand in Griffin town alone,' asked the Portolan anxiously.

'We need not take everyone, Excellency. Those who have boats, and I imagine as it is an island, most people have some sort of boat in which they can survive on the ocean. Those can flee east to Drakka or north to Mantovar or better still go deep into the south maybe to Brakwanna. But whichever direction they take, they must warn people wherever they make landfall, that no-one can survive the Darkness. If they see the foul mist approaching, the people must be persuaded to flee immediately. No, I was thinking of those who will not be able to find safe passage. Those left behind can be taken into Bylani, my town and my people will welcome them for they have been preparing for such as this for a thousand years. Once everyone is inside the mountain a way must be discovered to seal off our refuge from the Darkness. I do not think my Elders envisaged a threat in this form.'

'Bylani is really large enough?' asked Bazyli.

'Bylani is vast…a country beneath a country,' he smiled. 'Well, at least an island beneath an island. The Green People have worked hard for this moment; it has been the prime mover in our life. We have huge resources, including ready built houses for the homeless. But Bylani is not limitless. Although we continue to expand into other, remoter caves, we cannot give home to everyone.'

'I think we must dissuade our people from sailing to Mantovar, from what the herdsman mentioned, the storm is still active between us and your country, Captain,' said Janne.

'He said that? By the Gods, and we dare not escape north to the frozen desert, even if we could get past the brigands of the Onyx Isles,' he sighed and tugged at his beard again. 'Tragen warned us to stay well away from the Ringwold.' Hugo felt as if he was losing his mind, wherever he looked there were horrendous problems to be faced, all of them with lethal consequences if he made a wrong decision.

'The Ringwold? What is that place?' Leonid asked.

'Supposedly the home of demons dwelling in Life,' answered Hugo. 'It is a long story, but apparently all of us on earth are protected from them only by the occupants of the frozen shores—the Giants. They are a people settled in place by wizards thousands of years ago, their express purpose to ensure our safety by keeping the demons isolated. Nothing or no-one is allowed to pass through their lands—in any direction!'

'Now that is a tale you will have to relate when we have more time, Hugo. I have heard tales of the Giants of the north, but I've always thought of them as just another race, although a solitary, violent people. I never realized their presence in that region was planned by mystics,' said Bazyli Montetor.

'How long do you think we have before the Darkness reaches Griffin?' Portolan asked, foremost in his mind the fact that as leader of his clan he had enormous responsibilities incumbent on him.

'That is an impossible question to answer, I'm afraid,' said Hugo. 'I tried to estimate its speed last night. At the rate it was flowing then, I think it would take weeks to reach Griffin. But I've a feeling that the aperture through which it is escaping is going to grow, allowing for a faster dispersion…and if the wind should pick up! At the moment it's anyone's guess.'

'Then I repeat we must send messengers urgently to the outer islands when we get back, Lodovico. We need to return as rapidly as possible to expedite matters, to begin the horrendous task of evacuating the town. And we cannot forget those in the hinterland either, we have to convince them to leave their homes and belongings. It's going to be a monster of a job,' said Bazyli.

'I agree. But have you any thoughts of how we overcome the tremendous difficulties in getting our two clans to co-operate?'

'Not yet, my friend, other than to deal with those problems as they arise,' answered Bazyli, a wry smile playing on his face.

'Can we sail any faster, Captain?' asked Leonid.

'Yes, of course. Hopper, set as much sail as you can,' ordered Locklear. 'Damn those masts, I wish we had had time to get replacements on Sanctity.'

'Can't the wizards repair them?' Janne asked.

'From what Aidan tells me, Marcus, the energy we'd expend would put us all out of action for days, especially as none of us know how a mast is made. It would likely be a very slow process, we'd need guidance each step of the way, even though we'd have the assistance of the best sailors in the world,' answered Augusta smiling at Locklear, paying him and his crew a well-earned compliment. 'But if needs be, and as a last resort, we'll attempt it.'

'There is no need, you may take your replacements from the forests of Bylani, Captain,' Leonid said astounding the veteran seaman. 'You are quite welcome to all the teak and oak you require,' and the Green Man laughed out loud at the confounded look on Hugo's face.

'Then obtaining them is also going to receive priority. We may need upwards of nine or ten good trunks of teak. Hopper that will be your job…choose the best!' Locklear smiled for the first time in days. 'Hopper will take a work party and accompany you to your forests immediately you disembark, Leonid. It shouldn't take more than a week to bring them to the quayside.'

Hopper smiled, at last work to distract his mind. And to be the first ever Mantovarian into Bylani, except for the wizards, was going to be a remarkable adventure in itself. He shouted down into the well deck to Trumper to get men aloft to increase sail.

Augusta taking one more look at the bustle on deck turned to go below to join her friends.

'Highness,' called Locklear. 'I beseech you to have a care. You are going into dangers that would make armies of grown warriors tremble with fright. You have to enter the Darkness; I understand that though I like it not. But if you succeed and there discover my friend and are able to communicate with him, tell him…tell Tragen I value his memory,' his voice nearly broke again as he turned away impatiently. He couldn't understand why he, a military man all his life, was unable to control his emotions as he always had.

Augusta brooded, her thoughts full of trepidation as she negotiated the dim passageway below the captain's cabin, a corridor still obstructed by the many bales and barrels transferred from the hold by Leash.

Recalling Locklear's words of caution and his obvious affection for the premier wizard of Mantovar, Augusta suddenly thought of her parents. In moments of real fear, when she thought that she'd never handle the panic gripping her, she wished that things were back as they used to be. That she was at home in Mantovar in the huge old castle built on the north bank of the River Mantovar. A few leagues across the river and towards the east, her father's hawking lodge lay, a restful place away from the hubbub and bustle of court life. She and Beatrix had formed the habit of going there on most weekends before leaving to attend at the emperor's court in Abferkarn. The chief hawker, who had also taught her father years before he had met her mother, had delighted in training both girls to handle the large birds of prey. And they had become expert in the sport, enough so to have competed favourably in a couple of contests against fully experienced contenders.

Augusta brushed away a tear impatiently, she missed her home and her parents terribly and she wondered now whether she'd ever see them again. But then she smiled nervously for her circumstances had changed out of all recognition. She was no longer the spoilt, selfish little girl always dressed immaculately, lording it over all others. She had grown these last weeks into a caring, very powerful young lady living with an unbearable fear that she might hurt her friends.

What would her parents think of Aidan and her relationship with him? For undoubtedly, since the kiss in the dungeon and again in the cabin earlier, there was now something tangible between them. Whether anything came of it, whether it would blossom into a full scale romance, was yet too early to say. And then she recalled the words her old nanny used to utter as she stared at the young courtiers in the castle, "young love is a wonderful thing…pity it never lasts". Was the "young love" mentioned the same as that she and Aidan shared? Was the outcome likely to be the same?

But she could foresee further insurmountable problems in her relationship with her father. He would never be able to come to terms with the fact that she had magical ability. He would never understand how powerful a wizard she was. As far as she knew no member of the royal family of Mantovar, or for that matter of Drakka, had ever shown the talent previously, certainly no ruler had ever been a wizard. Was she going to be the first in history? After all, wizards were anathema to most people.

Would Mantovar allow her to succeed her father?

And then her thoughts returned to the immediate future and she began to tremble with fear.

Passage between the Afterlife and Life had always been inconceivable, so ridiculous a concept that no-one had even considered it. Therefore the abilities the four of them now shared would be utterly disbelieved in the world—may even be thought of as blasphemous. The ability would have to be kept from all those who did not at present have the knowledge. Their friends had to understand that they must keep the secret, for the divulgence of such a power might have appalling consequences.

Most religions held the afterlife sacrosanct; the exceptions did not bear thinking about. She'd even heard of one particular people that refused to die—how they managed that she had no idea. But whichever religion, they all had one thing in common—their claim to be able to pass through holy provinces would be deemed evil, a profanity in the face of their individual Gods. Faith, in a poor man's world, was quite often the only hope that kept people alive. Ignoring the beliefs of the people she was destined to govern, would ensure she never gained their favour. And it would guarantee her failure to attain the throne—the duty instilled in her by her father.

There had only ever been one crown prince who had denied the throne, walked away from it for his own selfish reasons. And he had been disparaged for centuries, his offspring ostracized. And then Augusta shuddered, she recalled the reason he had made that choice—the prince had fallen in love with a witch and chose her over his own people! Fleetingly she wondered what had ever come of them; it had happened so long ago they had stepped out of memory. Was it on purpose?

The Prince of Mantovar was a very loving father, an excellent ruler of his people, and it had been made abundantly clear to her over the years that her primary duty was the health, safety and welfare of Mantovar. Surely, she could make him understand that the greatest and most important task she could perform for her country would be to help the others defeat the One behind the Darkness? And to aid her in that she'd need to use magic. But she doubted her ability to persuade him of that. What would she do if he ordered her to forget magic? Did she have the courage to disobey him? Would she be able to forgo the strange new skills she had acquired? Was she likely to be the second heir in history to be spurned by Mantovar? But maybe it wouldn't come to that if she could get her mother on her side, and Lady Cornelia would be an ally in that.

Thinking on her more immediate problem, Augusta was not worrying about the actual transition from life into death. No, she was just desperately anxious about their actions once there. She did not doubt their abilities, had no second thoughts about being able to return from the afterlife providing they were allowed to, providing nothing in the Darkness tried to stop them. No, she only wanted everything to go according to plan. But they didn't have a plan. They were going to enter the Darkness and hope for the best.

She was scared. She recalled the sight of the dread mist when she was in Limbo rescuing Aidan and Thaddeus. She recalled the revulsion she had felt at its nearness both in the afterlife and in the cavern on Sanctity, and she shivered uncontrollably. It was not just the sight and feel of it, though, but the stench as well. It was overpowering, it had assailed her nostrils to the exclusion of all else, even lucid thought disappeared overwhelmed by the gagging, acrid smell of rotting carcasses.

But that had been the effect of her feelings on the outside of the Darkness, at its edge. The thought of actually entering the clammy, black mists brought on the quakes.

Thaddeus' and Aidan's account of the evil within truly unnerved her. She didn't know if she had the necessary courage to accompany the boys. But she had no doubt that she would—there'd be no stopping her. Her emotional bond with her friends, especially Aidan – the one who made her tremble every time she was alone with him – that bond commanded her to follow him anywhere. She would never allow him to search the vileness for Tragen without her support. None of them would. But then she calmed down a little, smiling tentatively, she would also be sustained by the comfort of Thaddeus, Beatrix and Anders. Wouldn't she?

And then her feelings plummeted again. There was the loss of Tragen to come to terms with—her heart bled. Before she'd left for Abferkarn to attend the emperor's court she'd never really taken much notice of him. But this voyage had thrown her into close contact with the old wizard, an experience she'd found fascinating. She had developed an enormous respect for the man of magic, the man who had always been near, supporting her family in times of crisis. If she was finding the wizard's disappearance, or possibly his death, hard to deal with, how was Aidan coping? She had some inkling now why Tragen had been her father's best friend all these years and why he had always been someone they could rely on. He'd always been the stalwart figure, always been the one successful in any adverse encounter affecting the throne. And now, she realized close to weeping again, Tragen, despite her ignoring of him, had always been her mentor as well. But now his enormous presence was no longer near, his advice and support no longer on call. God she missed him!

An orphan of ten years, saved from the gutters by the old man, Aidan had earned the wizard's love, a love reciprocated tenfold. The young man's need to know the wizard was safe was now the driving force behind his present recovery. But love is a fickle emotion; it can make you think treasonable thoughts and commit terrible acts. For wasn't it Aidan's love for Tragen that had been the principal factor in him preparing, and even wanting, to commit suicide? He had needed to accompany Tragen into death; his love called for him never to leave his master's side.

But love had caused Aidan to put aside his own beliefs. Love had made him forget that those who committed the ultimate act of self-murder did not enter death, did not enter Limbo and pass on to the Light. Instead they were re-born again immediately in another body, born to re-learn the self-same lessons of the life they had just cut short—and to re-live the same agonies, undergo the same trials, though in a different setting and form.

Augusta bit her lower lip as she tried to make sense of Aidan's loss of faith. He had always said that harming your soul or anyone else's was wrong. But surely many people killed to protect others, her father had done so. And look at the battle in the cavern…they had slain others to escape the horror of torture. Was that wrong? And though it may have been a stroke of the purest luck, Leash killing Zorzecai had ultimately saved Aidan's life. So, was killing wrong in those circumstances? Nonetheless, Aidan had admitted not having all the answers. What would have happened to them if they hadn't fought Zorzecai? Giving in would have been tantamount to suicide. For dead they would have been, and in the cruellest manner.

But what had Aidan been about to say before he fell asleep earlier? Was he possibly going to deny that principle now, give voice to the loss of his fundamental beliefs and throw away his old tenets as if they no longer mattered? But if he did that, what would be the consequences be to him? How would it change him, for changed he would be.

She reached Aidan's cabin, the door standing ajar to allow a cooling breeze to blow through from the open porthole…the heat below decks was overpowering. The princess stared in at her companions and a lump rose in her throat, her emotions running very close to the surface these days. She loved her friends very much; she did not want to be parted from these three—ever.

Beatrix looked up from where she was sitting in the chair watching Aidan asleep. 'Augusta, at last, I thought you were never coming back, what do they intend doing?'

Aidan stirred on his bottom bunk and with a snort turned over and faced inwards, on the verge of waking.

Thaddeus lying down on the top bunk, worn out but afraid to sleep because he'd have nightmares, stared at the girl standing in the doorway, a very puzzled expression clouded his face. 'Hey, what the hell have you been doing, Augusta? Did you fall in a water barrel or something?'

'What!'

'Look at you, you're soaking wet,' he said.

Augusta looked down at herself, at the boys' shirt and tunic she had become accustomed to wearing, at the britches now filthy dirty, almost as black as her feet. There were big damp blotches in her armpits and around her neck.

Unnoticed by the others Aidan, hearing the peculiar question, opened his eyes and also stared at his princess who, before the storm had always been immaculately attired…even when she had run around the castle as a little girl.

'That is sweat, Thaddeus, my boy.'

'Sweat! Horses sweat, ladies do not…they perspire,' Beatrix said indignantly.

'Are you ladies, then?' the young man whose experience of life could be counted in days, asked still puzzled.

'Oi!' Augusta said, 'Do you want a smack on the nose?'

'And you stink,' Thaddeus continued, her retort not registering as in any way confrontational, not realizing what the blazing look in her eyes meant. His mother had taught Thaddeus an inordinate amount, but unfortunately had been unable to impart tact.

'Wha-at?' at a loss for words, Augusta and Beatrix stared thunderstruck at Thaddeus, the Prince Griffin.

Thaddeus innocently looked from one to the other. 'Now what have I said?'

And then they heard it. It was soft at first, but soon developed into a loud, deep belly laugh. Aidan curled up on the bed holding his stomach, tears, this time of joy, streaming from his eyes. And before they knew it, they had all joined in, the relief raising their spirits when they realized they had the old Aidan back—at least for a little while.

Leonid, who had come to the door at the very moment they all burst into laughter, silently wondered if these four youngsters were showing signs of hysteria.

'Excuse me, my friends, but the captain is seeking the advice of a wizard. It seems that some of the rats that live in the bilges are committing suicide.'

Nine

The warmth of the morning abated only a little in the cooling breezes of the early evening, a long low swell on the ocean. There was hardly a sound other than the wash of the waves against the hull as the Grim gently ploughed the seas. An undisturbed dusk eventually fell on the world and a lazy moon lifted above the horizon accompanied by a myriad stars glistening in the clear night sky.

Earlier that afternoon, as the four young wizards reached the quarterdeck, Thaddeus accidentally tripped over the storm-sill, falling forward he nudged Leonid in the back. The Green Man winced, for some reason his leg was paining him even more, although not enough to trouble the haggard young healer. He kept his silence.

'Sorry, the sun was in my eyes, I couldn't see where I was going,' Thaddeus said looking down swiftly at the offending board. He automatically lifted his foot and rubbed the pain away in his stubbed, dirty toes.

'Are you all right,' Leonid asked putting out a hand to aid his balance, his brow furrowing with concern.

'Aye, the bloody thing!'

'Thaddeus! Don't you dare pick up Aidan's bad habits,' Beatrix remonstrated.

'What do you mean…my bad habits?' Aidan asked rather put out by her tone.

'You know exactly what I mean. He swore the same as you always do…and in front of ladies. Thaddeus, we have enough of that with him,' she said. 'No more…'

'What's that noise?' interrupted Augusta referring to the shouting and something she hadn't heard in a long time, children's laughter.

'Oi! It's all right for you to swear then, is it?' Aidan persisted, taking umbrage.

'Me! I don't swear, thank you very much,' Beatrix said scandalized.

'Oh, aye, and how about what you said to that woman up at the manorhouse, you know…the one you called an old cow,' Aidan retorted.

'That was your fault.'

'Mine…how the hell was it my fault?'

'Shut it, you two,' Augusta ordered, 'let's see what all that noise is,' and the three of them followed Thaddeus over to the forward rail of the quarterdeck.

'That is something I believe you could all do with,' Locklear sniffed loudly and then smiled, seeing the four of them safe on his quarterdeck filled him with relief. 'They are bathing.'

In the waist of the ship below, screens had been erected and perforated barrels suspended above them. Men and women were now savouring the first showers they had had for years. Sailors were passing buckets of warm sea water and replenishing the barrels as fast as they were being emptied. It was the first shower the few children born in captivity had ever had. There were tears in many an adult eye as the little ones shrieked with laughter as they were scrubbed clean of the filth of years.

It wasn't long before Augusta and Beatrix joined them, dragging Aidan and Thaddeus with them despite the boys' remonstrations that they didn't need a bath. On pulling his shirt over his head, Thaddeus' ring caught in the sleeve. Panicking at the thought of losing it, he gave the Griffin ring to Beatrix for safe-keeping. But as he removed the ring from the middle finger of his left hand he was suddenly overcome with nausea. He felt distinctly uncomfortable and anxious, but just then Aidan threw a bucket of water over his head and they both engaged the children of Brakwanna in the only water fight the children had ever had.

At dusk the four young wizards were sitting on the poop deck relaxing, desolation and despair having disappeared among the crew and lifting momentarily in its passengers. The children, fed by Dolly and clothed in clean britches and shirts donated by the crew, were now listening avidly to lullabies sung by the ship's minstrel, Jason. And sitting on the foc's'le, Bartholomew was teaching a couple of boys to play the reed pipe.

But the water fight had brought back memories to Aidan of the time he had soaked Tragen and the rest of the crew, when they had been conjuring fresh drinking water from the air. There had been laughter that day as well. Aidan lowered his head, stricken again with the loss of his master.

Beatrix, ever the one to perceive a change in a person's emotions studied him sitting beside her, her face full of concern.

'What is it, Aidan. What's wrong?' She leant closer and whispered in his ear, offering comfort.

He breathed deeply and blinked, staring into her caring eyes, he smiled quickly.

'Oh, I'm thinking too much I guess,' he said taking her arm and putting it through his, holding her hand tight. He tried not to think of Tragen.

Although their purpose in coming on deck was to investigate the strange behaviour of the Grim's resident rats, their thoughts turned inwards as the alien events of the last few days intruded. Occasionally their morbidity was distracted by the very unusual sight of a large rat appearing on deck and making a sudden race for the scuppers. The rat would spend some time frantically swinging its backside from side to side, its long tail drooping until its body finally disappeared through the drainage hole, from whence it eventually dropped into the ocean. It did not swim for long before disappearing beneath the surface.

'Don't rats leave a sinking ship?' asked Augusta seriously.

'Everybody leaves a sinking ship, Augusta,' Beatrix said giggling. She couldn't help it, having her arm through Aidan's seemed so right.

'Aye, and talking about leaving ship, one of the sailors has disappeared,' said Thaddeus, 'the bo'sun's been searching everywhere.'

'Oh! You mean he's been lost overboard?' asked Augusta.

'Looks like it…they can't find him.'

'It couldn't be for the same reason these rats are jumping ship, can it?' asked Aidan.

Thaddeus shrugged. 'Hardly seems likely.' But however hard he concentrated Thaddeus couldn't understand the bizarre vibrations he was receiving from the rodents.

'The rat is not a very discerning animal; I can't connect with its emotions as I can with a larger, more intelligent animal such as a horse. Mind you, the rat isn't stupid, it does have primeval instincts, a certain amount of cunning and self-preservation; otherwise it would never survive, find food or raise its young.'

He stared at a particularly large specimen that had just appeared and been apprehended by Gregory, a very thin sailor with a very thin face and a long pointed nose. Some said Gregory looked like the rodents that fascinated him. He had even been known to eat them…hopefully cooked, Nkosi was heard to say, though he didn't sound too sure. Gregory had the animal cradled in his hands and was holding it up to the waning light and peering into its eyes when he suddenly shouted and dropped the animal onto the deck, cursing, he shook his fingers.

'What is it?' Aidan laughed, not in the least perturbed that the man had been bitten.

'Shush, Aidan,' admonished Beatrix, 'he may be hurt.'

'Who, the rat or Gregory?' asked Thaddeus smiling

'Shut it, you two,' glared Augusta.

'Any idea why it bit you, Gregory, they don't usually do they?' asked Aidan.

'No, Milord, that's the first time I've ever been bitten. It's strange, all the rats on this ship are brown but that one was black it must have come aboard from Griffin or the monk's island.'

Augusta tensed at the formal mode of address. Aidan, his head bowed stared at his hands thinking abruptly on his new status. It was expected, for his apprenticeship was now at an end. But he knew the reason the sailor had used the title was not because of that—he'd used it because he thought Aidan had inherited it on his master's death.

Augusta moved closer and seeing Beatrix's arm in his she put her own arm through his other and both girls clutched him tight. Thaddeus held his breath, not knowing what Aidan's reaction would be.

Anders stopped whittling when he unexpectedly found his eyes blurring. He was sitting cross-legged on the velvet grass and he stuck the misericorde into the ground between his knees. This time he was careful to ensure the hilt did not enter the wall—he wasn't too sure what would happen if the dagger disappeared into the colours. It never occurred to him to wonder how he still had the knife, the small dagger used for slitting throats that Dolly had secreted in his shroud the night before his burial.

Rubbing his eyes he recalled his childhood days living in the huge Castle Mantovar where his father bred the prince's horses and managed his stables. Anders had known Lord Tragen longer than Aidan had, although not as well. Anders' father had been friends with the wizard since before the cabin boy had been born. Anders sighed; his father would be devastated at news of the wizard's death. He suddenly swallowed deeply; his father would also be overcome by his youngest son's death.

Anders dried his eyes on his sleeve, he was perplexed, he should have left that life far behind by now. All he should have remaining were memories of lessons learned. He should be in the Light, in Paradise, resting and preparing for his next reincarnation when all the details of this life would be hidden deep in his subconscious. But he still remembered the love his parents and six older brothers had given him—and the love and companionship of his four friends. He picked up the dagger and the stick again and resumed whittling he knew not what, except that it appeared to be the same thing over and over—a bell with two handles. He again sighed, waiting for his friends to join him in Limbo, dreading it, for they would all enter the Darkness then in search of Tragen.

Aidan raised his head, his expression giving nothing away and he gazed at Augusta's face not a handbreadth from his. He paused a moment, licking his lips – he did like her mouth – dare he, he wondered? It would certainly shock her if he kissed her now. He turned and looked at Beatrix, at her mouth, her white teeth, wondering how she would react if he did the same with her.

'Aidan…Aidan, you all right?' Augusta asked, her heart breaking for him, not understanding the hungry look in his eyes.

Her voice brought him back to his senses, if she hadn't spoken then! He smiled; these girls were twisting his insides. He gazed over the starboard rail at the undulating sweep of the blue ocean. He smiled ruefully, he could still see the girls' faces…he liked swimming in their eyes.

He gently squeezed Augusta's hand. 'I've definitely got to find my staff,' he breathed deeply. 'But first I find Tragen…we find Tragen. He must not be trapped for much longer in the Darkness, the longer he's there the weaker he'll get, and then we'll find it harder to bring him out.'

'We'll find him, all of us, don't worry about that…we'll rescue him,' said Beatrix, nearly in tears herself.

Aidan smiled warmly. 'I'm glad I have you for a friend, Lady Beatrix,' he impulsively stroked the side of her face, a loving gesture that surprised him and nearly overcame her.

'Oh, Aidan,' and she instinctively threw her arms around his neck and hugged him. Relinquishing her hold, she dried her eyes with her small kerchief hidden in her tunic. 'But you can stop making fun of me…Lady…indeed.'

'But you are entitled to the honorific, Beatrix,' Augusta said, peering at her across the front of Aidan.

'Oh, come off it! I won't attain that until I reach the age of majority next year.'

'But you bear it in your own right, now. Beatrix, you're a wizard,' Augusta persisted.

'Oh, I know wizards have that title but I'm nowhere near qualified to earn it yet,' she answered, drying her eyes, 'so leave it, please.'

'Don't be silly,' Aidan interrupted. 'How many wizards do you know that are powerful enough to pass back and forth between Life and Death?'

'Well...I don't know of any, I suppose, except us but that doesn't mean I...'

'And how many do you know that can create a light bright enough to dazzle the sun and yet still be able to see through it when a normal person's eyes would be burned from their head!' said Thaddeus, smiling all over his face.

'Don't you remember Cornelia implying that you wouldn't be a lady's companion for much longer? She was right, although I suspect she didn't quite expect this to be the reason, you really are a lady...Lady Beatrix!'

'Oh...oh,' she uttered completely lost for words and the others burst out laughing.

'That thing was scared!' Thaddeus whispered, changing the topic, he had a knotted feeling in his stomach as if some part of himself was missing. And then he realized he was staring at Augusta again and he turned away wondering why he was doing it. He was getting very confused—he seemed to spend a lot of time looking at her while his stomach lurched. He tore his gaze away and instead studied the site of the disappearing rat.

'What do you mean? How can a rat be scared? They seem to spend all their time frightening me,' said Beatrix.

'I don't know why, but it was petrified...as if it was trying to get away from something. And don't ask me what. However, what I can't understand is why I found it easier to meld with the rats on Sanctity. I even directed their thoughts, their actions during the battle. Here I seem to be wading through mud with them. We'll wait until morning; perhaps something will become clear then.'

'Gregory, has it drawn blood? Do you need my help?' Aidan called to the sailor who was bent over the gunnel staring after his attacker and sucking his finger.

'Only a spot, there's no need for any healing, but I'm obliged to you, Milord,' and he touched his forelock, the chunky ring on his little finger glinting in the moonlight.

'Beatrix, I'll take my ring back now if you don't mind,' Thaddeus, seeing the twinkling and suddenly remembering, held out his hand as she rummaged in her pocket.

He replaced the Griffin ring on his middle finger and once more it glowed faintly as it settled in place. And Thaddeus had the absurd feeling that the ring was once again at home. He unconsciously stroked the raised figure of the mythical creature – a griffin – carved on its surface as his stomach settled and his anxiety eased.

'Well, we may as well retire now and try and get a good night's sleep, I could certainly do with one,' said Augusta rising from the deck. 'We'll arrive at Griffin late afternoon tomorrow, so the captain tells me. We can be at the manorhouse before the evening. I hope Cornelia and Mistress Barbat watch over us without being too frightened. They were scared silly last time,' she added pensively.

Thaddeus, Augusta and Beatrix walked away none realizing that Aidan was not with them until they reached the quarterdeck.

'Hey, aren't you coming?' Augusta asked him.

Aidan joined them reluctantly and as he reached the companionway abruptly changed his mind. 'You go on,' he said, 'it's a bit early for me yet, I'm going to sit on the foc's'le for a bit.'

'Are you all right,' Augusta asked her stomach churning, afraid to leave him on his own. 'I'll stay with you if you want.'

'No…don't worry…' and he smiled, 'I'm just not tired yet. I've slept most of the day haven't I?'

And Beatrix, her intuition working overtime, knowing that his real reason was that he needed time on his own to think of Tragen, grabbed her friend.

'Come on, Augusta, he'll be fine.'

Half an hour later Aidan, his head in his hands, was sitting miserably on the foc's'le with his back against the rail when Chief Mazumbai climbed the steps.

'May I join you, my friend?' he asked quietly. And when Aidan nodded he sat alongside him and stared up at the moon pensively.

'What a beautiful sight…I thought I'd never see it again. In the dungeon I thought my life had ended and I'd never see anything of the world again.' He paused and looked at the young man with so much power it shone from the very pores of his skin—and so much misery it turned his face dark, his eyes sunken deep.

Mazumbai looked up again at the stars and closing his eyes he breathed deeply of the salt air and listened to the gentle sounds of the sea.

'May I tell you of the man who counts grains of sand?'

'What?' Aidan asked, startled, his despondency laid to one side for a moment he looked at the small black man sitting beside him so full of concern.

'He is a man of my tribe. A good man who married a wonderful wife, their happiness fulfilled when they were blessed with a child late in life. Ndebesi, though, was a strange boy, even at his birth he never cried and in his short life, he lived until he was fourteen years of age, he was incapable of making friends. But the boy never seemed concerned, for his parents worshipped him and gave him everything willingly. They taught him what they knew of the sanctity of life and yet…and yet Ndebesi could never understand love.'

Mazumbai glanced quickly at the young wizard, and satisfied that he had Aidan's attention he continued.

'The boy could read and write and do his sums, he worked hard in his father's field and obeyed his mother. All as a matter of rote…there was no emotion in his life. Only great curiosity and a lack of patience! The boy wanted to know and do everything immediately, not unusual in a young boy you might think. But he had a particular trait, a characteristic that the rest of the tribe found disturbing. He was cruel! He managed to hide it successfully from his parents…or perhaps they were blinkered and chose not to acknowledge that side of his nature.'

The chief of the Brakwanna sighed and rested his head back against the rail, he was greatly troubled.

'What form did his cruelty take?' Aidan asked staring up at the dark sky, listening intently waiting for the point of the story, knowing there was bound to be one for Mazumbai never wasted words.

'He tortured…insects at first; you know pulling wings off butterflies, burning ants' nests just to watch them flee. But gradually it manifested itself in hurting his peers. He was a bully; he took great delight in creating misery and scaring the life out of other children. But one day…'

Mazumbai paused, sweat on his face, the memory of what he was about to relate still causing terror.

'One day Ndebesi took it on himself to investigate death…death in a human being. He could not take a victim from amongst the other children in the tribe for we watched him closely. So he killed the one person no-one dreamt needed our care—his mother!'

Aidan stopped breathing, the horror of the tale bringing back his time in the dungeon watching Zorzecai torture his victims.

'How?' he asked knowing the answer.

'He disembowelled her…and his father came upon him doing it.'

'Dear God! What…what happened?'

'Akumamba killed his son and then tried to kill himself. I heard the screams and found my dearest friend cutting his wrists. I stopped him.' Mazumbai's voice trailed away, the sight of that terrible tragedy rending him speechless for long moments.

'Akumamba, the man you named the bravest person you'd ever met?'

'Yes, for he is. He now has to live with the death of the two people he loved most in the world, knowing that one killed the other and he killed the survivor. But not only that he also lives with the shame of attempting to take his own life…life that he always held sacred.'

'How does he cope?' Aidan asked just above a whisper, his hands trembling.

'By counting grains of sand…the building blocks of nature. Whenever his memories get too much for him, he takes up a handful of sand and allows it to trickle between his fingers, one grain at a time. And he marvels that such matter can give birth to an oak tree.'

And Aidan laid his head on Mazumbai's shoulder and with the chief of the Brakwannans silently bearing him up, he wept as he'd never wept before. When he finished he rose and walked down into the waist of the ship. Alone, he felt better than he had for days knowing that eventually he'd learn to live with his shame.

'Goodnight to you, Gregory,' Aidan said as he passed the sailor leaning against the gunnel.

'Goodnight, Milord. I'll keep watch on the rats through the night, perhaps I can figure out what's wrong.'

None knew, of course, that it was to be Gregory's last night.

Ten

Elstan stared dumbfounded at the empty bench opposite him that had moments before been completely filled by the corpulent body of the librarian. He recognized the terror in the oriental sorcerer's voice, but he couldn't quite believe that he was listening to instructions from an invisible man. Elstan broke into a sweat—nothing like this had ever happened to him before. He was at a complete loss at what to do next, people simply did not do this sort of thing. People vanished, yes, but only after walking away and disappearing around a corner. He had never heard of a wizard powerful enough to make himself vanish. He sat afraid, not moving until he was thumped on the shoulder. Feeling Chong-An's breath on his neck and his hand on his upper arm, he jumped as the man again whispered in his ear.

'Quickly, move, he may detect the spell, don't forget my staff!' Elstan nearly leapt out of his skin. Looking hurriedly around the room for the owner of the finger boring holes in his back, his astonished eyes fell on the sorcerer who had just entered the room.

Tall and wearing a green robe, bald as most of them were, Elstan immediately recognized Brother Drudwynn, the magus' deputy. Drudwynn spent a moment glancing perfunctorily around the room, his eyes settling on the tavern owner he beckoned to him demanding instant attention. As the owner hurried across wiping his hands on his apron, Chong-An tugged at Elstan's arm and the man from Miskim automatically rose to his feet. He hesitated before picking up the sorcerer's staff along with his own sword, the misericorde he replaced quickly beneath his arm. Retrieving Chong's bag from the floor along with his own, in a daze, he prepared to follow the invisible oriental.

Immediately Chong-An, his hand gripping Elstan's arm, made a hurried exit through the kitchen door. Brushing past the cook and a couple of scullery maids they made their way out of the rear door into the yard and ran towards the stables at the back.

Chong-An, despite his large belly and bad feet, was a swift mover when he needed to be. Elstan was completely mystified, not only by this sorcerer, but at himself for obeying the man's instructions without argument. They continued on down the central aisle of the horse stalls until they came to the big double doors overlooking the front of the tavern. Here Chong-An abruptly reappeared. Peeking through the gap between the open door and the jamb, both men saw, drawn up in the roadway outside, an enclosed coach, its six black horses standing sweating in the traces, nostrils flaring as they dragged in air. The innkeeper, his hands clasped and bowing continually, was receiving instructions from the passenger within the coach.

'Why are we hiding from your colleague? And why am I carrying your bag and…and this, I thought no-one else could touch a sorcerer's staff without being hurt?' Elstan, staring wide-eyed at the staff in his hand, dropped Chong's bag on the floor along with his own. 'And how the hell can you make yourself invisible?' he shouted.

'Quiet man, have patience. As for the staff…it is not a sorcerer's it is a wizard's and I told it to allow your touch, I could hardly carry that and my bag through the inn. I think it might have startled a few of the customers seeing a bag and a staff floating through the air, don't you?'

'And your invisibility, how did you manage that?' Elstan asked frustrated ignoring the seeming difference between sorcerer and wizard.

'You can put the staff down now, give it here,' he placed it against the wall at his shoulder,' Chong paused, breathing heavily, the exertion of the last minutes telling on his unfit frame. 'Let me correct you. In the eyes of the world I am no sorcerer… I am an adept. But we "strong" adepts, those who lack one or two of the skills of magic, regard ourselves as wizards. Notice I said wizard—I do not follow the black arts as sorcerers do. My staff is special for no-one in the wizarding world believes an adept can create a staff—they are fools. I did not make myself invisible…that particular spell has been lost for many centuries. No, it was a spell of illusion I created, one of my many talents that the Brethren have no knowledge of and thus wasted by not making me a full member of the Order. I have been proficient with that exacting conjuration for many years; it comes in handy on occasion.' Chong-An turned from observing the coach. 'You know who walked through the door?'

'Aye, your leader's right-hand man, Drudwynn, his deputy isn't he?'

'That he is. He belongs, body and soul, to the magus…the only man I know of who wants to be as cruel as his mad master!' Chong-An glanced quickly at Elstan, 'which doesn't necessarily mean that Brenin is my leader just because he heads the Order.'

'You are a member of the Guild of Brethren, aren't you?'

87

Chong-An licked his lips wondering if he should lie. But reasoning he was hoping to spend a long time in the company of this man he thought it unwise to begin with an untruth. 'I have never been a full brother as I cannot mindmeld, and as of today I am not even that.'

'What do you mean?' Elstan asked his puzzlement increasing as he stared at the obviously terrified "wizard".

'By taking it into my head to follow you this morning, I have disobeyed Drudwynn's express orders not to leave the Tower. For that act he will kill me and also slay anyone with me...if he can apprehend us.'

Elstan frowned; this wizard was an enigma and no mistake. 'Is Brenin getting out of that coach?' he asked abruptly, hearing louder voices from outside.

'He is preparing to, I believe,' Chong said, scrutinizing the scene at the front door of the tavern.

'If you knew you'd be killed for leaving, why on earth have you followed me?'

'Well, I was going to be killed anyway—by Brenin. He does not trust me. And I have a feeling you and I are pivotal to each other's needs.'

'What...what do you mean?' Elstan was now suffering stabbing pains behind his eyes. 'Why doesn't Brenin trust you, and how the hell do I need you?'

'Later, I will tell you all, later. Get back, Brenin is alighting,' Chong said, leaping back from the door his vast bulk pressing Elstan against the board wall.

'Ouch! Have a care, you're squashing me,' Elstan pushed Chong away. 'Make yourself invisible again and you can watch him openly.'

'I dare not. Brenin has not attained the status and qualities of magus for nothing. He is only the second wizard in history to do so which makes him the most powerful sorcerer in the world. He can detect magic being used at great distances if he's a mind to it. And, anyway, a spell of illusion of that magnitude takes a lot of energy to create...and I am not a young man anymore.'

Chong paused, chewing his bottom lip he glanced through the jamb again. 'But why is he in such obvious haste? Those horses are nearly beat. Come, we cannot let either of them discover us here together. They'll need to change that team with another from in here.

We must leave,' and Chong-An moved back into the darkness of the stables. 'We can escape through the fields at the back and up into the Wolfshead.'

'Wait, you forget something. Why have I to escape? He doesn't know me, only you.'

Chong-An stared long and hard at Elstan. 'For years I have studied age-old texts, a lot of them concerning the Scissor Mountains and its inhabitants...human and others. Miskim, or a village with a very similar name, spelling evolves over time after all, crops up many times in tracts from all over the world. But however the name appears in the documents, the area is always indicated as being close to the frozen wastes, west of the Scissor Mountains.'

'The frozen wastes are nowhere near Miskim.'

'Thousands of years ago they were. The tundra has receded northwards as the world has warmed.'

'What is that to you? And what the hell do you mean by "inhabitants, human and other"?' Elstan asked beginning to lose his temper. Why was his birthplace in old texts? Why was this wizard so interested in his hometown? And why on earth did they need each other?

'Come, again we will speak of it later, we must go before we are discovered,' said Chong-An desperately, hurrying to the rear of the stalls.

'No! We will talk now or I will not go another step with you.' Chong-An sighed, holding Elstan's arm, he pulled him into an empty stall out of the direct line of sight of anyone walking past or through the stable doors.

'Can't you wait? I have already told you if Drudwynn finds me out of the Tower he will kill me! It is a long story!'

'So you say, so what! He will kill you not me, I have no worries on that score he knows nothing of me if I walk away. Now tell me why you are so interested in Miskim and why we need each other.'

'I have no time to speak of this now...we must leave immediately!'

'I will not move another step until you tell me more...Brother,' Elstan threatened.

'All right!' Chong-An stared at him through frightened eyes, deciding to give in but only a little. There was no way he was going to divulge the whole story, not here and now, there was no time and he couldn't trust this man yet.

'I overheard Brenin and Drudwynn discussing an enemy of theirs. They do not know I heard them but they were already suspicious of me because of something else. It is only because they need my abilities, for a reason of which I know nothing, that they have withheld my murder. I was ordered to remain in the Tower, denied permission to travel on the pain of death.'

'You keep telling me the same things, wizard. Tell me something I don't know.'

'Very well,' Chong sighed. 'Brenin wishes to question me. And those he interrogates never hold anything back...they never survive. My researches lead me to believe there is a crisis brewing between Man and the Gods. Brenin must never discover what I know!' Elstan was again astonished. 'I'll accept that no-one survives Brenin's questioning, I've heard that before. And I have just discovered there is something going on with the Gods,' he ran his fingers through his hair nervously, 'but what of Miskim, what of that place, and what of us?' Elstan asked, despite not trusting the wizard, Chong's words had the ring of truth.

'What do you know of the Gods? Tell me...it may be very important.'

'I'm not quite sure, but it's to do with something Brenin called the Darkness. Some sort of weapon of the Gods. Does that mean anything to you?'

'The Darkness?' and Chong-An lost all colour in his face. 'By the Gods, is that what the shadow is?' he spoke as if he was alone. 'Can you tell me more?'

'Later, Librarian, later...now what of Miskim?'

Chong-An's jowls wobbled, his hands trembled. 'How do I know of Miskim? Because I believe that town is the home of the artefact I have sought for years. It is a relic that needs explanation because it is unbelievably important for mankind.

'I have spent most of my life searching the mountains deep into the south and far into the east. I have looked all over the Dark Continent for news of the relic. These last years I have searched southern Drakka. Everywhere I have been I have discovered ancient treatises, scrolls, even minstrels' songs that mention an obscure village in the Columba, which I now believe is the hiding place of the ancient artefact. Why should a native chant in the backwaters of Brakwanna mention such a place? Miskim is a very strange place, it has an odd reputation. It is the largest town in the foothills of the Columba

Region…expected as the village I seek must have grown over the years. I do know that all mystics are drawn to the place at some time during their life. The town attracts magic – and its practitioners – like a lodestone and no-one understands why. These last twenty years it has drawn me, but circumstances and lack of knowledge have delayed me! Do you have anything to do with people that fly…I mean people with the codenames of creatures that fly?'

'What!' Elstan was shaken; this wizard was jumping from one end of a conversation to the other without speaking of what was in the middle. Elstan's mind was awash with dread and terror. This wizard obviously knew more than he was letting on. His words were already leading to a conclusion that Elstan wanted nothing at all to do with. But the last question rocked him—a query that was too damned near the truth for comfort! Elstan was being led deeper into a labyrinth, confused and fearful he did not have the courage or the inclination to flee the oriental wizard. He had to know what the librarian knew.

'Do you? Does any sort of insect or bird have any special meaning for you?' asked Chong-An becoming frantic, peering over Elstan's shoulder, continually watching for the magus or his henchman. Chong was convinced this man was the Fly, but needed him to admit it. If he didn't volunteer the information about himself, no way would he confirm the existence of his brothers or name them.

'Why? And don't fob me off with another question or I walk now and you can stay here on your own. I have had enough of your riddles and your very strange behaviour.'

Elstan shrugged his pack on his shoulder and strapped his sword to his belt. He hitched up his britches and turned from the oriental wizard, preparing to walk away, knowing though that he wouldn't dare until he knew the wizard's purpose. But he was positive he didn't want to hear the answer to his question. This wizard had strange knowledge and was sending shivers up his back…tremors of lightning.

Chong-An mesmerized the northern man. He was dishing out tit-bits like the cocoa-man in the marketplace—tasters to make Elstan's mouth water and his brain seethe with dread. Elstan had now become the wizard's follower; their roles reversed yet neither knew it. Elstan was in a fever. He needed answers or he'd be forever wondering about the purpose behind the librarian's questions.

But he was deathly afraid, he not only knew the nature of the artefact, but he had first-hand experience of it – it scared him witless – there was no way he was going anywhere near it again.

Chong-An made up his mind, he could have kept Elstan close by using magic, but that would have been enforced restraint and no matter how fearless a man is, being held captive was unlikely to lead to willing co-operation. In his heart he knew he needed Elstan's wholehearted willing compliance; he wouldn't succeed in the quest that he could foresee if he had to fight the man all the way.

'I specialize in reading the future, Elstan,' and he sighed, he had to meet the man part way, satisfy some of his questions or he was not going anywhere. 'Let us make ourselves comfortable for a moment; my feet are playing hell with me.'

With that the wizard slid to the ground and put his bleeding feet up on a broken rail and settled his back against the wall.

Elstan gazed down at him. Foretelling his future did not appeal to him in the slightest—no seer had anything good to say. Nevertheless, he knew this was going to interfere dramatically with his mission, he couldn't allow that. He had to get to Mantovar as early as possible with his news, with the information he had overheard. But first he had to get to Abferkarn, ascertain the name of the magus' spy if possible. But Elstan was not his own man at the moment – he was hooked – he had to hear what this librarian had to say and so he continued to stare into the yellow man's eyes.

'To understand my predictions is often times very difficult as there are many interpretations of what I see. Even then those interpretations can lead to a multitude of possibilities, the future is never certain, so many insignificant incidents can cause a change in the path.' He paused and moaned slightly as his feet gave him a twinge of pain. He bent forward and squeezed them attempting to force relief into his toes.

Elstan looked at the man's feet, distracted by Chong-An's pain for a moment. 'Can't you do something about them; you say you are a wizard?'

'I am no healer, but you are right, I will have to do something before we move on. I must find decent footwear. Meantime I must persevere with what I have. Can you pass my slippers, please?'

'Where are they?' Elstan asked picking up Chong's bag.

'What do you mean? Didn't you pick them up? You haven't gone and left the slippers under the table have you?' Chong said despairing.

'I didn't know they were there, they never crossed my mind. Don't blame me if you forgot to tell me to pick them up!'

'Have I got to tell you everything? I could hardly carry them, could I? We'd have had people thinking there was someone walking on air! There's nothing for it you'll have to go back for them, Drudwynn won't recognize you.'

Elstan bit off the retort that came to mind. 'What's the point in bothering; they're useless for the road.'

'What's the point? The point is, young man, they cost me an absolute fortune!'

'Then I'll return and barter them for suitable boots or you won't be going anywhere on foot.'

'Well make sure you get the very best quality or you'll be responsible for slowing us up.'

Elstan was so amazed at the injustice of the wizard's conclusion that he was struck speechless...but his voice returned rapidly.

'I have not decided yet to accompany you. You still speak in riddles. What have I to do with your forecasts?'

'Ah! Elstan,' Chong clasped his hands over his portly belly and lay back comfortably against the wall of the stall. 'I follow a fine art, a talent that is inexplicable to all but a very few—that is why the magus and his dog, his deputy, need me. To study the future I have also to study those predictions made in the past...the ones that have already come into being. To know what has gone before and how those events were interpreted at the time of their prediction, and what actually occurs later, help me to forecast the likely conduct of my auguries. Because of this need, as I've already told you, I study arcane histories.

'In several of the ancient scrolls I came across many predictions for this era, two or three spring to mind, two in particular spoke of catastrophe. One was particularly short and to the point, very unusual for any prophecy. The other was a lot longer and referred to the actions of others, although both concern a war with those who wish oblivion for mankind. I will not mention the longer of the two as its ramifications can have no bearing on us two—yet! But the second, the shorter, I believe concerns us now. Although it is very confusing and there is a lot in it that I do not yet understand. Listen and tell me what you think,' and Chong-An closed his eyes and clasped his hands over his ample belly.

'Five and three that is four and two and one come together.
To banish a shadow, young mystics awake.
Aid will be sought of three winged siblings that are four.
Green on white and a red legend will rediscover its fate.
And he who sees forward and looks backward knows.
A bane will be revenged at a second solitary sound.
But beware he whose hands have no limit,
For his wish will ensure mankind's bereavement.'

'My friend I see understanding in your eyes. Why is that?' asked Chong-An not daring to breathe.

'Perhaps I will tell you later,' Elstan spoke softly, the unusual numbers etched on his mind, unable to keep the creeping despair from his voice. Elstan hung his head. He had known that he did not want to know the librarian's story.

For better or worse now Elstan could never allow Chong-An out of his sight. His youngest brother's life depended on it. The Fly stared silently at the short, overweight oriental adept-come-wizard, the cause of his blinding headache.

Chong-An returned his steady gaze waiting for Elstan to voice the decision that in his head he'd already made. He was satisfied almost. Part of the riddle he'd solved years ago, "he who sees forward and looks backward" could only apply to himself. The shadow must be the Darkness. Undoubtedly this man was the Fly, but how could "three winged siblings be four".

Elstan sighed and walked to the front doors of the stable and again peered through the jamb. The activity around the coach suggested that Brenin and Drudwynn were about to end their list of demands on the innkeeper and enter the Vixen's Haven. If that was the case then it wouldn't be long before the team of horses was unhitched and brought into the stables to be fed and watered. But they might still have a little time yet, for the ostler would surely need to walk the sweating horses a while to cool them down to avoid fresh feed and water giving them colic.

He walked back up the central aisle between the stalls and examined the wizard's sore feet resting on the timber rail—they really were in a shocking state. He lifted up his canvas bag and rummaged around. Bringing forth a jar he handed it to Chong.

'This is a salve for your feet; use it liberally while I return to the bar and barter your slippers for some decent boots. Don't worry,' he said, holding up his hand as Chong was about to remonstrate, 'I'll make sure they're expensive boots in return for your expensive slippers. Shall I trade them with Drudwynn and Brenin, for only they'll be able to afford the damn things?'

Receiving a sickly grin, Elstan nearly smiled. 'Stay hidden!' He walked out of the rear of the stables and retraced his steps into the Vixen.

Elstan of Miskim threaded his way through the hustle and bustle of the very busy kitchen, this time taking care not to jostle the sweating staff, and peeped around the open door into the bar. He espied Chong-An's slippers in the hands of the man at the next table to theirs. He was grinning – drooling over the fine bonus that had fallen into his lap – but he didn't smile for long when Elstan sat on the bench across from him and did as before. Removing the dagger from his armpit he stabbed the blade into the table at his right hand and called for ale. The traveller recognized him and the dagger immediately. 'I thank you, friend, for taking care of my companion's footwear,' he said icily. 'You like them?'

'I thought you'd forgotten them, I...I didn't see you leave,' he stammered, fear on his fleshy round face as he pushed the expensive footwear across to Elstan. 'I was about to come looking for you to return them.'

'I believe you, friend. You do not have the look of a thief. But if you were so inclined then I'd have no qualms in cutting off your hand...or even killing you,' and Elstan smiled as he lifted the fresh foaming tankard of ale just delivered by a buxom barmaid. Elstan might not like the tavern's class of customer, that is those that preferred to reside and partake of refreshments on the second floor, but he was quite partial to the inn's beer.

The man quailed. 'Please, sir, take them. I do not wish to deprive your friend of their obvious comfort.

Elstan smiled again, after the initial terror; he now wished to instil a little ease. 'It is obvious to me, as it must be to you that they are far from comfortable for the Great North Road. It is also evident to me that you are an honest man with a good understanding of footwear. Now, my friend is not so knowledgeable on what is suitable to wear on his journey and wishes that he had remembered to bring his boots. Would you like to trade for them?'

'Trade? I don't understand, sir, I could never afford these,' he babbled, not fooled for a moment by the change in tactics, recognizing the opening gambits of a deal. He hoped he was not mistaken. 'I am but a poor salt merchant.'

'Who happens to be wearing a tidy pair of boots.'

'I beg your pardon!'

'My friend would like to trade his slippers for your boots…your feet seem to be of a similar size.'

The merchant licked his lips, he couldn't believe his ears. These slippers cost a fortune whereas his boots…well, were just ordinary boots and he had others in his luggage. He held his breath; his trip to Jasper was about to realize a worthy profit before he even entered the town.

'But I would then suffer the same problem as your friend, sir. My feet would hurt abominably before I entered Jasper.'

'True! I had not realized that you also had bad feet. Never mind, mayhap I'll find someone else here who is willing to exchange.'

The salt merchant broke into a cold sweat…a straight swop! Dear God what a deal! 'Um, all right, there's no need to look further, sir,' and he stooped and removed his boots.

'And your stockings, if you wouldn't mind?'

The salt merchant did not mind in the least. Handing the articles over, his eyes gleamed, he still couldn't believe his luck, and as Elstan left with boots and stockings in hand, the merchant placed the slippers on the table in front of him. He gloated as he examined them. They were worth the profit of half a year's trading and that is what he hoped to make when he sold them on his return to Abferkarn. No-one in Jasper could ever afford them.

Eleven

Marcus Janne had owned his fishing boat *Alessa* for years. He and the love of his life Thaddeus' diminutive nurse, Alessa Barbat, were at their happiest sailing the long, low swells on the seas around the island. Both were fanatical sea-anglers, partaking in sea-fishing competitions at the drop of a hat. They could be found on most weekends plying the currents outside the reef in search of tuna always accompanied by the then uncommunicative Thaddeus Portolan.

But the voyage this day of "Alessa" and its present occupant was very different.

Leash stirred painfully in the bottom of the boat and stretched his aching back. Groaning quietly he sat up and stared over the gunnels, looking round he searched the ocean for any signs of land. Thirst was playing havoc with him, dehydration was setting in with a vengeance and he was already suffering, along with blinding headaches, mild hallucinations. But what he saw on the horizon was no mirage.

The Grim, unmistakeable because of its size and its broken masts, sailed eastwards. Though it was too far away for anyone onboard the barque to see him, Leash nevertheless shrank back against the bottom boards. He hoped that if anyone saw his boat they'd take it for what it was…a fishing boat on the ocean, and they'd dismiss it and not come looking.

But he could not hide from the blindingly hot sun. There was no shelter on the small boat, its sail he had lost overboard when he had attempted to hoist it during the night. In the midst of a particularly lurid phantasm, he had fumbled with the spread of canvas when he'd seen the herdsman's face spread on its broadcloth. His demon had panicked and forced Leash to throw the canvas overboard. When Leash had come to his senses later he'd raged at his demon's catastrophic behaviour.

Leash had never been so thirsty. Satisfying the Wanting always left him with a raging need to drink—blood was salty as well as sweet. And this sating had been very exceptional; the copious amount of blood and the speed at which he had gulped it had surprised even him. He discovered no fresh water in the boat despite throwing nearly everything overboard in his search, for in the midst of his terror he had never thought to slake his thirst before fleeing Sanctity. Now he was forced to await the departure of the Grim before directing the boat to the nearest island, Moth, a smudge on the horizon to the northeast.

He settled himself as comfortably as he could and placed his head back on an old bit of canvas he was using as a pillow. He had, the previous day, placed this same piece of sailcloth over his face to protect him from the sun, but had nearly suffocated when he'd passed out momentarily because of the added heat. He'd given up that idea and now spent the time either with the back of his head to the sun – which gave his neck and scalp torturous sunburn – or with his arms over his face which, because he had no sleeves, resulted in gigantic blisters growing along his arms.

Suffering dreadfully, his lips cracking and blisters forming on the parts of his face he could not protect…or forgot to protect, his mind wandered. And Leash's thoughts turned to his incarceration in the dungeon across the dark and stinking passage from his second greatest enemy…Tragen. Grimacing, he thought of his first, his demon, the one he'd fought even longer than Tragen—the one he could do nothing about as yet.

Leash remembered screaming at Aidan in the dungeons, calling the boy a liar. Hearing Aidan speak memories of his mother had brought out the worst in Leash for he had reacted viciously, not wanting to believe the boy's story. Surely he'd have known if the woman had borne a son, she would have told him. Wouldn't she? Or had she? He lamented, he was losing his memories at a greater rate now, getting confused easier—it had been so long since the onset of his infestation.

Leash rolled his head on the makeshift pillow, his eyes closed against the harsh glare of the midday sun. He moaned, both at the memories he still had and his all-consuming thirst.

But he couldn't understand the overwhelming compulsion he'd had to attack Zorzecai. It wasn't just the need for blood to satisfy the demon's Wanting. No, he'd had the certainty of knowing that it was the only correct course of action. He'd had to save the boy's life even at the risk of losing his own. And his demon had been happy with the outcome, although for a different reason from just satisfying the Wanting. But Leash didn't know this.

He squirmed lower down between the thwarts into the bottom of the boat and placed his burnt arms across his eyes. He made an effort to forget his thirst, his mouth as dry as a desert. If he didn't find freshwater soon he'd be forced to drink seawater and, in a moment of rare lucidity, he knew that seawater killed a normal man. But would it kill him?

Adrift on the open ocean the current gradually drew him north-eastwards away from the Grim and away from Moth. Leaving the Griffin Islands behind him his mind roamed and he took refuge in his safe dream when he fell asleep again. He smiled, she was happy with Leash—the boy was safe. In his dream he wept as he looked upon her face while his body grew ever weaker.

But he also knew the lady in his dreams was no hallucination.

Twelve

The morning's weather followed the same pattern as the day previous. Warm and peaceful, the calm before the storm Beatrix thought, enjoy it while we may. Anxious for them all she couldn't seem to shake off her trepidation, the forthcoming night's activities terrifying her.

It was no light undertaking to travel into the afterlife. Like Augusta she had no qualms about her ability to do so, the reality, though, was that she to all intents and purposes, was going to die and then come back to life. An actuality that a couple of weeks before she would have thought impossible.

But not only was she passing over into death, there she would meet the boy with whom she had fallen in love, her first and only love. But thinking on her short-lived romance she was confused—her feelings for Anders were changing. She would definitely deny it to anyone who asked, but her love for him was undergoing a fundamental adjustment. It was as if they were…not drifting apart as such, her love could go no further and her mind and body was learning to accept it. Her love for Anders was now a cherished memory, she smiled, one she'd never forget.

But she couldn't understand her feelings for Aidan. Surely she couldn't be in love with him? Augusta loved him. And she loved Augusta, she was her friend she could never do anything to hurt her— Aidan was Augusta's and that was the end of it. But why did she need Aidan to hold her, comfort her and keep her safe?

Beatrix felt very lonely on times.

Augusta joined her on the quarterdeck; coming up alongside her she pushed her arm through Beatrix's, a welcome gesture but it made Beatrix feel even guiltier.

'Hey, you two,' called Thaddeus from the foc's'le, having to mindmeld for his voice would never have travelled over the sounds of the rigging stretching and creaking in the wind. *'Come up here.'*

Joining Thaddeus, they found Aidan kneeling down, his eyes closed and his arms stretched out in front of him pointing over the bowsprit, his posture similar to that of Tragen when he'd created the shield against the storm. Beatrix shivered, recalling that horrendous tempest she wondered if her feelings for Tragen would alter as they had for Anders. But she knew that she could never accept Tragen as a cherished memory until they discovered what had happened to him.

'He's teaching me how to cast my mind, let's see if you two can do it,' said the heir to the Griffin Isles, excited.

They spent the rest of the morning receiving lessons from Aidan in the use of basic magic—the first training that Beatrix and Thaddeus had ever received. Their own high magic they had no need of instruction in, they'd have to learn about that as they went along. Aidan could not help them, he had no idea how they created it. But when Augusta had been taught to look over the horizon a couple of weeks previously she had discovered the Griffin Isles. Time passed quickly and mostly with pleasure, laughing and joking, they were learning how to concentrate their minds…very difficult as thoughts of Tragen in the Darkness kept intruding.

Just as they were breaking up for lunch, Beatrix, who had been gazing northwards exclaimed, overawed at the range of her powers.

'Hey, you lot, I can see a boat out there and what's more I think it's Marcus' fishing boat.'

The last time she had seen the militia commander's vessel was when they had disembarked in the small cove not far from the sewer outfall on Sanctity.

'Where?' asked Augusta. 'I can't see a thing.'

'Over there,' said Beattie, pointing in the general direction of Moth.

'How do you expect me to see anything there, the sun's shining on the sea? You may be able to see through the glare, I can't,' said Augusta.

'What would it be doing out here anyway, we left it secured on that beach and we've had no storm to snap its mooring,' said Thaddeus. They searched for a while longer but in vain.

'How about you, Anders, can you see it?' asked Beatrix.

'I'm sorry, no. But don't let that surprise you, this wall of colours goes up and down and from side to side every time I look at the sea…it's a blur, and it's making me seasick,' he replied.

'How can it make you seasick you're a ghost…you don't eat, do you?' Augusta asked, puzzled.

'Shut it,' Anders ordered.

Early in the afternoon Griffin Island loomed on the horizon. The sparsely wooded, craggy slopes of the taller of the two peaks dominated the skyline. Mount Trespass, the towering roof of Bylani, Leonid's home, stretched skywards its catacombs not so intimidating now that the wizards knew they were the entrance to a haven deep within its bowels.

Between Mount Trespass and its sister, the smaller Mount Peaceful, smoke drifted in the air above the vale nestling at the feet of the peaks. Hidden beneath the smog was the curiously named town of Meltwater, its iron mines digging deep into the treeless, lesser mountain. The home of the ironmaster, Bazyli Montetor, was a hive of activity at all hours.

It was the following morning before they eventually came up on the island. The Brakwannans lined the rails, quietly watching the bustle, as the Grim sailed through the gap and into the lagoon sheltered behind the almost semi-circular reef around the deep-water harbour of Griffin Town.

Beatrix, leaning with her back against the starboard rail on the quarterdeck, studied the southern tribes-people rescued from slavery. She wondered what the small number of survivors must be feeling. She felt so very sorry for them, her eyes never far from tears each time she looked at their hunger ravaged countenances. They had suffered for so long it was even possible their miraculous survival still hadn't registered in their traumatized minds. Peering into their eyes Beatrix saw the full gamut of human emotions, bewilderment, confusion, sadness – anger and aggression in a few – peace, harmony and relief in others.

Mazumbai, standing amongst his people, a justifiably proud man, a leader of a very brave people, must have felt the maid's eyes on him for he turned, looking up he caught her gaze. Studying her very grave expression, he matched it for a moment and then smiled as he mindmelded.

'You see my people, young Wizard of the Light; we will soon be sailing to a home that we had all given up hope of ever seeing again.'

He paused and his face grew even more serious. *'We fought well together, you and I...your friends and my people, all of us. But I have a feeling that our fight is not over yet, we will need each other again and when we do, your Light is what will guide us. But until that time arrives we shall all need to come to terms with our survival—and our guilt at losing so many of our loved ones. But Brakwanna wishes you well and pledges you our support for as long as you require it.'*

Mazumbai resumed his thoughts; turning away he stared unseeing at the shore.

Towards noon the Grim tied up alongside the wharf of Griffin town. With the huge hawsers holding the ship tethered fore and aft, the bo'sun and his men lowered the brow to the quay. All other work ceased as the dockworkers ran to assist; surprise on most faces at seeing so many black people standing at the rails.

Hopper, barely able to control his impatience at wanting to be away, waited with a team of ten brawny sailors at the head of the brow, all preparing to accompany Leonid down the gangway. Marcus, standing at the starboard rail in the waist, called down to his militiamen on the quay to bring mounts and to escort the party through the town to its outer limits.

Leonid, quickly followed by the others, was the first to disembark; the superstitious dockworkers retreating hurriedly from the Green Man. Leonid glanced back up at the young wizards watching on the quarterdeck. Smiling his farewell, he turned his thoughts to his mission and the answers to the many questions he was to ask.

After preparing the Elders for the immediate influx of all those islanders who could not escape Griffin, he was to inform his people of the nature of the Darkness, so that means could be sought to seal off all the entrances and airways into the mountain. But before his departure, Aidan had also asked the green man to ascertain if anything had been discovered in the archives concerning the whereabouts of the elves.

But Leonid also had a private request. He sought the Elders' permission to accompany the wizards on their journey in search of the dragons. And he hoped the Elders would be able to enlighten him as to the reason for Zorzecai's statement that the Green People always disrupted the plans of those they came in contact with. Would his presence be detrimental to those plans of his friends?

Hopper could hardly contain his excitement. A veteran of many a voyage to strange lands, the trip to Bylani promised to be unique. And he now had work to occupy his mind, distract his morbidity. Obtaining masts from such an unusual source brought a smile to his face. The logistics of choosing, cutting and collecting ten of the best trees in Bylani's forest – and then transporting them to the surface and to the ship – was going to be exhausting work. He'd have no thoughts for anything else. But a mature forest growing beneath an island beggared belief; it was going to be a sight he and his men would talk of for years.

The dockworkers watched Leonid warily, but on Marcus Janne's shouted command horses were mounted and they wasted no time in leaving the docks.

No-one took much notice of the bandage around the Green Man's ankle.

Bazyli Montetor walked down the brow at a more sedate pace but equally as anxious as Leonid. Stepping on to the quay he met his deputy and henchman, Razor. To say that the Montetors were stunned by the change in their leader's appearance, at the vanished disfigurement, was an understatement. Bazyli explained quickly and delighted faces were turned in Aidan's direction.

But there were others, the Portolans, who were not so happy. These stared with mixed feelings but remained watchfully silent as they always did when the Montetor was on the waterfront. But Bazyli's next words were not so welcome with anyone when, with a few quietly spoken commands, he instructed his clansmen to await instruction from Lodovico.

'Do you mean we are to take orders from them Portolans, chief?' asked Cyryl Lewyn, a small, wizened, bald Montetor, disbelief making his high voice even shriller. His tone causing distress to his pet, the scraggy, tortoise shell cat snuggled closer into his neck, the animal's habitual place when not foraging. Not that his affection for the animal endeared him to many for he had the disgusting habit of feeding it mice on his shoulder. And as Lewyn didn't bathe very often, the smell of cat and carrion was overpowering about him.

Bazyli stopped in his tracks before striding off hotfoot into the town to the Montetor's headquarters in the "The Basking Shark" on Main Street.

'That is what I said, Lewyn, or have you lost your hearing as well as your hair!'

But this time the ribald remark did not draw the usual laughter. The strange order for all to obey the seneschal didn't sit well with either clan. None of them knew what it meant, but some realized they were not going to like it.

Before dusk had fallen arrangements for the evacuation by sea of the Montetor clan were well in hand, even though chaos was the chief impression. A messenger was prepared to leave in the morning to apprise those residing in Meltwater. Living closer to Bylani those townsfolk would probably opt for the underground haven for many were not owners of boats. But they too were superstitious people and would need reassurance. The only one who could supply that would be Bazyli himself. At the first opportunity he intended travelling to his home to lead his people into the mountain.

But it was also in the Basking Shark, before the first hour was over, that the Montetor informed his clan of their eventual merger with the Portolans under Prince Griffin.

Following discussions earlier that morning, Lodovico and Bazyli agreed that the status of Prince Griffin should be promulgated to each clan by its own leader at the earliest possible moment. Their hope was that it would gain more time to ease both peoples into the very unusual habit of co-operating with each other—essential for the success of the evacuation.

But the news that Griffin had a future king devastated Razor who had for years expected to be the next leader of the Montetors. Long before he went to bed that night resentment set in deep with the Montetor deputy and his cohorts. And it was Razor who sent the messenger on his way to Meltwater—but not with the instructions imparted by Bazyli.

Returning to the ship after watching Leonid, Hopper and his men ride off safely into the interior, Marcus Janne made his report and then remounted his horse and rode off again into the town. This time his errand was to roust out the mayor and to muster his militia to oversee the Portolans' reception of the elevation of Prince Griffin. The Portolans were going to be just as doubtful as the Montetors at news of a king to eventually lead both clans. And having to suddenly work with men they had been fighting for twenty years was going to foment trouble—difficulties that had to be settled quickly.

Lodovico Portolan studied his people as he walked down the brow. Awaiting his disembarkation was a crowd of intermingled Portolans and Montetors, many standing sullenly on either side of the gangway, others sitting on crates, bales and barrels. They numbered about forty or so dockworkers and possibly half that number again of inquisitive men and women straight out of the taverns, most with ale tankards in their hands.

Lodovico, seeking the foreman of the quay, espied the middle-aged, swarthy man wearing a red and white striped kerchief on his head. Beckoning him over, they met at the foot of the brow.

'Mr Lorrenzer, I need to talk urgently with you. We will use your office,' he turned and stared at the crowd silently watching.

'You men will remain here. When I return I will have tidings of supreme importance and instructions that you will need to act upon immediately.'

Lodovico Portolan paused, and gazing across the quay he caught the eye of his cousin, Dante Ernold, a tall man sucking nonchalantly on his pipe. Ernold removed the pipe from his lips and staring momentarily into the bowl he looked up and touched his forelock to Lodovico. His demeanour belied the fact that he was the Portolan's leader on the docks, the organizer of many a confrontation with the Montetors.

Lodovico and Bazyli had spent part of their discussions identifying those men they'd need to get on their side as quickly as possible if they were to have any sort of success in merging the clans. One of them was this man, Dante Ernold; the other his Montetor counterpart, Alexi Dambray. Standing either side of Ernold, Lodovico gazed at Dante's cronies, Caj Donnet and Sesto Corney both very hard men and long-time dockworkers—neither were ever very far away from their leader.

'Come, Mr Lorrenzer…your office, if you please,' Lodovico ordered.

A little while later a coach and four drew up on the jetty to take the young wizards to the manorhouse. Having taken an emotional leave of Mazumbai and the Brakwannans they disembarked and walked across the quay to the steps of the coach. Preparing to take their seats, their every move watched by the still ominously silent crowd that had now grown nearly double in size, they were distracted by a sudden disturbance on the deck of the Grim. The noise attracted the attention of everyone in earshot.

Aidan, Thaddeus and Beatrix turned as one and Augusta, standing on the steps of the coach her head bent to pass through the door, returned at once to the quayside.

They and the clans-people watched in amazement as the rat-faced Gregory balancing precariously on the gunnel, unexpectedly jumped off the rail. Mistiming his leap he fell between the ship and the jetty. He screamed as he was crushed between the two.

Stunned by the unexpected spectacle Aidan and Thaddeus, recovering quickly, ran to the aid of the Grim's crew. They raised Gregory above the surface of the water and then dragged his lifeless body along the wharf clear of the ship and hauled him from the harbour, laying him gently on the boards near the brow. The dead man's body was in a terrible state, one side of his face a bloody mess, chest crushed and his legs broken.

'What did he do that for, Mr Trumper?' Thaddeus shouted up to the bo'sun who was standing equally shocked at the head of the brow.

Normally unflappable, the red-faced man scratched his bald pate. 'I don't know, Highness, he raced past me raving, shouting something like "leave me be" and made straight for the side. Why he didn't use the brow I'll never know…he could have easily. I…I don't understand.'

'Oi!' Ivan Blouet, a tall, strapping Montetor dockworker, sporting a pigtail at the nape of his shaved head, shouted up at the bo'sun. 'Oi, Mister, why'd you call him "Highness" he's only the seneschal's idiot son, isn't he?'

Augusta swung round, instantly outraged her face purpled. 'Don't you dare…don't you dare call him "idiot", you…you cretin,' and she strode purposefully over to the man and despite only being tall enough to reach his shoulders, she smacked him across his face.

Dumbfounded, the crowd all stared at the fuming girl standing on tip-toe, her face thrust up under the chin of the huge dockworker.

Totally surprised, Thaddeus gazed at her open-mouthed. 'Augusta, please…um,' he mumbled lost for words.

Aidan and Beatrix left Gregory and rushed over. Moving into position either side of Thaddeus standing just behind the princess, their stance a warning they were a team ready to protect each other. They were already veterans of a vicious and bloody battle although no-one on the wharf knew it.

Staring at Augusta out of the corner of his eye, Aidan had mixed feelings, pride that her initial reaction was to defend Thaddeus, and annoyance at her aggression. A couple of days before he had stopped her killing Leash in a fit of rage. He sighed. He was going to have to tell her to control her anger, not an easy task…they'd probably end up quarrelling over it. Nevertheless, her quick temper could cause problems if she succumbed to fury within the Darkness. But he kept quiet; this was neither the time nor the place for a lecture. He watched for the big man's reaction—ready to use his magic to protect her.

Augusta, ignoring the response of her friends, continued her tirade her anger fully roused.

'If you but knew it this man is not only the Portolan's son he is also a very, very powerful wizard. He is Prince Griffin, your next king. You owe him fealty,' snapped Augusta as she stepped back and put her arm through Thaddeus' and held him close. 'Be warned…no-one is to show him disrespect, especially when I am around—no-one! You hear me, sailor!' She screamed at the unfortunate dockworker who, through his ignorance and asking of a perfectly understandable question, had earned her ire.

Ivan Blouet returned her glare, being hit on the face by a woman usually resulted in a beating for that woman, but her words gave him pause. A wizard! He licked his suddenly dry lips and fell back into the crowd, disconcerted by the iron in the eyes of her friends. Were they also wizards? Refusing to rub his face where her finger marks showed plainly, he disappeared at the back of the Montetors to stand alongside a very quiet man, Alexi Dambray, ex-priest of Tarria. He was Razor's rival within the clan and the leader of the Montetor dockworkers. Razor hated him but was always very wary of the battle-hardened, learned man.

'My dear, Princess, I thought I was supposed to announce my son's new status, not you,' Lodovico Portolan smiled wryly.

He'd rushed from the foreman's office when he heard Gregory's scream. Witnessing Augusta's outburst with shock, quickly turning to amusement, his chest filled with pride at the earnest display of deep friendship and affection for his son. He watched with eyes glistening as he saw her grab Thaddeus and pull him even nearer.

'Is it true, Seneschal, what she says? We owe him allegiance?' asked Lorrenzer standing close by.

'Aye,' and he raised his voice so all could hear. 'Bazyli Montetor and I have named my son as our joint heir. He will become the first king of our country when I, and Bazyli, step down as clan leaders.'

'But you are not our clan leader, Paul your brother, is our chief. Are you usurping his authority?' shouted Sesto Corney, alongside a silent Ernold, seemingly engrossed in drawing quietly on his pipe, but not missing one iota of the proceedings.

'Aye, that he is! He's a Portolan isn't he? You can't trust a Portolan…and what's more Bazyli will never allow a Portolan to rule us,' shouted Cyryl Lewyn pushing himself towards the front of the crowd standing near the brow, but also making sure he never left the safety of other Montetors nearby.

'How come you haven't brought your brother and his wife home with you? Didn't you want to?'

The implication in Lewyn's tone was unmistakeable and a hostile murmur grew in the crowd.

Lodovico almost smashed the man in the face, but he held back. Violence now would lead to more violence later, and only the Gods knew how that would end.

'Listen to me, all of you. It is a part of the dire tidings that I wished to inform you of later, but I will tell you now of what you need to know.'

He strode purposefully over to the brow, the onlookers moving out of his way, and walked part way up the gangplank so that he could see and be seen by everyone on the docks.

'Thaddeus is not only a Portolan he is also a Montetor, being the nephew of your chief's twin sister—no-one can deny that. As for usurping my brother's authority, let me explain, though it grieves me mightily to say this now, it is information that should be given in a calmer atmosphere.'

Lodovico stared at the puzzled men crowding around him growing silent and perplexed. They were surprised at the tears running unknowingly down the seneschal's face.

'Those of you that know me well are aware that I would never seize Paul's authority—if he was still alive.'

He stared across at Dante Ernold suddenly sitting very still on the barrel of nails, his pipe resting forgotten in his hand. A pin could be heard dropping to the wooden boards of the jetty in the silence that followed those words.

Lodovico paused a moment, his voice choking. 'Dante, Alexi…Paul and Ariana are dead!'

There was a collective drawing in of breath, the mutual shock rendering them all mute. Portolan and Montetor alike had lived with the knowledge for years that the very popular Paul Portolan and his equally beloved wife, Ariana Montetor, were held for ransom by the mad Abbot of Sanctity. And it had become a habitual premise that whatever the trouble between the clans, unrest and violence ceased when the ransom had to be produced. It was always paid in full and on time. But the reason for the ransom had created animosity between both clans for half a generation. It coloured their attitude to normal trade, to a peaceful relationship, breeding discontent and distrust.

The Montetors blamed the Portolans, specifically Lodovico for allowing the hostage taking, for he was the one who had agreed to Paul and Ariana remaining on Sanctity until the clan leader was healed of his otherwise terminal illness. The Abbot had refused their return and demanded twelve lives a year to safeguard their persons. The Portolans had reacted violently to the unjust accusation of collusion in this betrayal. And hatred had become the norm between the clans.

And now to find that the ransom had been in vain left them feeling destitute. Moments later there rose an unearthly wailing in the crowd, no-one knew whence it started but it soon overwhelmed the Griffin islanders.

'How?' shouted Alexi Dambray, menacingly, bringing the wharf to silence once more.

Lodovico stared at the man for a moment. 'Alexi…my friends…the Abbot of Sanctity murdered them the first night of their incarceration.'

'Then we will kill him!' Dante Ernold said, his quiet, vengeful voice cutting the atmosphere like a machete through a slab of butter.

Thrusting his pipe into his pocket he stood and gazed across at Alexi, his erstwhile opponent on the docks, the look that passed between them showing they were in agreement for once. The plea of death was taken up by others—men raged in both clans.

'Yes!' agreed Kuba Garin, a Montetor who had once been in love with Ariana. 'Let's go now, let us sail there this minute and kill the bastard!'

Lodovico raised his hand for silence, and eventually the crowd quietened.

'My friends, the deed has already been carried out. Do you honestly believe that Bazyli and I would have returned leaving their murderers alive? The abbot is already dead…and so is his master, a demon we had no knowledge of.

'But I'm afraid the manner of their deaths makes a long story, one for another day. I promise you this…I will relate every sordid detail of our encounter on Sanctity; you have a right to know. But there are pressing matters this night that we have to deal with, so I beg your patience. We must spare a little time to allow his captain to investigate this poor man's sudden death,' and Lodovico turned to those standing around Gregory, silent witnesses to Lodovico's words.

'Two things need explaining, Lodovico, before we do. Firstly your son, my cousin Thaddeus…it is definitely agreed between you and the Montetor that he will eventually be king over us all?' asked Dante Ernold frowning.

'There is no doubt?' added Alexi Dambray.

'There is no doubt whatsoever—his inheritance is assured and cannot be withdrawn. And in accordance with the custom of our friends, the Brakwannans,' and he smiled up at the black men and women lining the rails of the Grim, catching Mazumbai's sombre eyes. 'When a new successor to the chieftainship of his people is determined then that heir is also given a new name. Thaddeus will be known as Prince Griffin from this day; he wears the Griffin ring of the Montetors bestowed on him by Bazyli and he carries the name of both our clans. And heed me well all of you. Every time I look at my son my heart fills with pride. He is no idiot as his friend, Princess Augusta, just warned you. Her words are the truth. My son's soul, absent for so many years has now claimed its body, and in the battle we fought with the demon on Sanctity he has proved himself worthy of all Griffin.'

And as he said this he held out his arms for Thaddeus, and Prince Griffin left Augusta's side and hugged his father before them all.

'You have now answered the second, cousin, but how did he recover?' asked Ernold.

'All in good time…that again is a long story which will also require a suspension of ages old belief! But I will tell you this, it was his friends that rescued him.' Lodovico answered, leaving more puzzled expressions in his wake as he turned to the dead Gregory.

'But if the boy is a wizard…how can he become king?' Dyta Peche, a woman of dubious morality voiced quietly to those standing near.

'Let's have a look at Gregory,' said Aidan. 'I can't understand why he jumped from the rail.'

The sailors, who had pulled the dead man from the water, stepped well back and made room for the young healer. Opening the shirt to examine the body, Aidan recoiled instantly, finding signs of something that he did not want to acknowledge.

'Oh, my God, the poor man!' said Augusta, coming up behind him, 'what are those?'

'How the hell can this be?' Aidan's voice shook. 'These boils…where's he been to be infected with these?'

Huge black swellings had erupted below Gregory's chin, in his armpits and behind his ears. Not quite overcoming his revulsion he prodded them and found them hard. The rest of the sailor's vest was removed and, as the girls turned away decidedly queasy, Aidan discovered further boils in Gregory's groin.

'By the Gods, I've seen those before,' Trumper having come ashore, bent over conspiratorially and whispered in Aidan's ear.

Thaddeus breathed the terrible diagnosis softly as he stared horrified at the dead sailor at his feet. 'I've seen them before as well—in the Darkness, those lumps are buboes.' He gazed at his friends and they paled at his words. 'We have…we have plague on the Grim!'

Thirteen

The shape-shifter had enjoyed Gregory. It had played with him much as a cat did with a mouse.

Gregory had kept his promise to Aidan and had spent the night in the bilges studying the rats in their nests. The rats didn't mind this particular human, they had a strange affinity with him, as he did with them. Gregory looked for unusual behaviour, signs that might lead him to ascertain the reason for their abnormal behaviour. He lay on the wet boards for hours watching the rodents that fascinated him and eventually he realized they seemed to scratch almost non-stop. This puzzled him.

But as the human studied the rats, so the shape-shifter examined the man. It was the first opportunity the demon of the Darkness had to really observe a live human. It smiled. It had tasted a man now it wanted to know more. It crept closer for this human did not smell of danger, he was no threat. In fact, to the demon, the man's vibrations were very strange—it was almost as if the human loved the rodents. The shape-shifter couldn't see the point of love.

Gregory sat up and the demon watched as the man held a rat in his hands, stroking its back and whispering inanities. Obviously the man did not know what the rat carried.

The shape-shifter scurried forward and nudged the man's thigh with his cold, wet nose. Gregory looked down and frowned. Replacing the rat on the boards he picked up the shape-shifter and held him in front of his eyes.

'Hello, what have we here? A black rat with a white stripe on its back…where have you come from then,' he ran his hand along the blemish. 'You are very pretty you know.'

The shape-shifter looked up at Gregory and ensnared him with his eyes. It didn't take him long to read everything in the man's mind…it could do this as long as it maintained eye contact. It could also implant visions in its prey's consciousness. And this it did. The images of his mother maimed in the Darkness, tormented by its demons and lost souls, drove Gregory insane. The fleas on its back gave him the plague.

It was very clever. It waited until the disease was well established in the man before allowing Gregory to make for the upper

113

deck with it hidden in his pocket. And as Gregory fell between the ship and the jetty, the shape-shifter jumped nimbly into the jumble of pillars beneath the wharf and quickly found a hiding place deep within. But it didn't stay there long before it found another ride.

Fourteen

Ryn, hovering above the crest of the cliffs that hid the liosalfars' listening station, had a bellyache. Something was worrying Shadra and that concern was infectious. Ryn had a hollow sensation in the pit of his stomach, a feeling he only got when there were sharks in the vicinity of where he was resting, bobbing on the swell of the ocean.

The sky was clear, the thermals this high in the Scissor Mountains were scarce, but the currents still held him aloft and he soared ever higher heading east. The feeling that Shadra and Anselm were not safe would not go away though, and he thought of his options if Shadra proved correct.

But his choices were dismally few. Follow them into the cave he could not; he'd already looked into the hole in the cliff and found it too small to accommodate even his collar bone. He could wait for them at the entrance, but if they'd been taken prisoner he could be there until the end of the world. He could never initiate a rescue attempt from the rift. The only real alternative he had was to explore the mountain and hopefully find another way into Alfhime.

He scanned the vast panorama of hills and vales below, spectacular slopes of windswept snow broken only by high rock outcrops and small copses of larch and pine. His irrepressible good nature, though, soon reasserted itself. Unable to remain depressed at being a part of such a scene, he again contorted his beak into a smile…it was getting easier to make the unusual expression. What an adventure this was turning out to be. Since he'd been gifted with his voice his solitary life over water had been transformed into one of companionship over land, even if he did tend to lose his friends on times.

He flew on between sharp, rocky, snow-covered pinnacles and over deep snow-laden valleys and broad plateaux. He crossed the peak – the bowels of which held the cave Shadra and Anselm had entered – and flew into the valley on the other side. Long and broad it revealed an unusual feature, low cloud-cover dense, fluffy and inviting…and probably very deep. He drifted towards the grey, frothy mass, the colour indicating an immense volume of snow suspended within its midst.

Ryn loved flying through clouds. If it was rain the water poured from his body in a cascade, snow he glided through as if he was sliding down a slope, hail he didn't like…it was lumpy and it stung. He loved slipping through the gloom of dark clouds, the woolliness always tickling his wings somehow soothing him. He wanted to feel the ease of happy days again, not the nagging of doubt, and he wanted to shout his head off—to tell the clouds that his dream of having a voice had come true.

He spiralled downwards excitedly towards the fluffiness below him preparing his senses for the loss of vision and sound. Animated, he shouted to the wind "I'm here, I'm here".

And he nearly broke both his legs as he came crashing to a stop.

Stunned, he stumbled, nearly falling forward on to his beak. He sat down hurriedly on his backside, his tail feathers quivering with the shock. Panting, he stared at the mass of clouds surrounding him and pulled in his wings so that he could massage his stinging feet with his newly re-grown fingers. He blinked his black eyes, wondering if his fantasies had become too much for him. He nipped his tongue to see if he was dreaming and minutely examined the billowing fluffiness beneath his webbed feet.

'What the hell!' He looked around mesmerized and not a little scared. 'I'm supposed to pass through clouds not sit on them!'

He stood up and took a few steps still expecting to fall through to the air below. Finding his footing still as firm as if he was walking on land, he tip-toed carefully across the valley. His anxiety increased the more he meandered up and down the length of the vale. It took him over an hour to realize that there was no passage to the ground. There was no way through the mass of frozen vapour covering the valley beneath.

He lifted off and flew to the edge of the cloudbank where it abutted the slopes of the high mountain. Here large rocks broke through and Ryn investigated the solidity of the mass adjacent to the land. Poking his fingers into the cracks between the clouds and the rock, he found it just as impenetrable. There was no gap deeper than his first knuckle whatsoever, no way down into the vale. It was an immense impenetrable lid concealing whatever was below.

He sat on the soft cushion in the centre of the abnormal bulging mass and studied the strange phenomenon. He'd experienced all types of cloud all over the world, but even in the frozen wastes he'd never come across anything like this. Feeling the texture of the clouds with his fingers, the tips sank up to the second knuckle and abruptly stopped. Immediately beneath the surface it was spongy, giving only slightly with the pressure of his hand. But the harder he pressed the more unyielding the snowflakes became. Exerting all the pressure in his large body only resulted in the surface becoming further impacted, the flakes changing to ice. If he continued in that manner the valley would be covered in one large, flat glacier.

Soaring above the mountainside and flapping his wings once he hopped over the peak, returning to the rift in the cliff face through which his friends had disappeared.

Settling on the crest above he decided to wait. And he waited the rest of the day and all the next.

Shadra and Anselm did not return. No-one appeared until dusk on the second evening. It was then, as the liosalfar named Xelnor walked out of the rift and made gestures to shoo him away, that Ryn's suspicions were confirmed—Shadra and Anselm had been captured again. The forest elf's initial fears had proved positive. They were again in danger.

Ryn knew, without a shadow of a doubt, that Shadra and Anselm were being kept prisoner in the valley below the impassable cloud. And he knew of no way to rescue them this time.

The Cragga watched Ryn and smiled. Use could be made of this bird!

Fifteen

'I think we'd better get him and us aboard right now, Milord,' said Trumper, cringing as he looked over Aidan's shoulders at the badly disfigured Gregory. He didn't much fancy touching the dead sailor

'No, we can't, you can take him but we have to get to the manorhouse as soon as possible,' whispered Aidan anxiously, afraid to raise his voice. If the crowd heard the word plague there'd be a riot. 'We have urgent business there.'

'Well, we'd still better get Gregory aboard fast, Milord, before others see the buboes. It'll be quicker with your help. You can always return ashore as soon as we have him settled,' said Trumper, and seeing Aidan hesitate he added. 'We have no choice, Milord, if we are to avoid trouble he has to be placed out of sight.'

Reluctantly, and using small magic, under the watchful eyes of the amazed islanders, Thaddeus and Aidan levitated Gregory's body and floated him up the brow, laying him gently on the deck in the waist.

Lodovico Portolan, following, called up to Hugo Locklear standing on his quarterdeck keeping a watchful eye on the restless crowd barely hiding its hostility.

'Captain, we have a problem, we need to speak.'

Safely on board the Grim, Trumper set a couple of men to the immediate task of wrapping Gregory in a tarpaulin. Locklear climbed down wearily into the waist and approached the body, the Brakwannans making way for the big man.

'Have you discovered the reason for his death, Milord?' Locklear asked, ignoring Lodovico Portolan for a moment. Hugo was Mantovarian and his allegiance was first of all to those caring for the Mantovarian princess of which Aidan, for all his youth, was now his chief advisor. Hugo's word was law at sea and on the Grim, but for all else Hugo was now honour bound to obey Lord Aidan.

But it was Lodovico who answered, loudly clearing his throat, his anxiety having suddenly dried his mouth. He scanned the inquisitive black faces and the smattering of sailors standing amongst them.

'Plague, Captain…you have the plague on your ship!'

'Dear God!' Hugo stared, shock and horror of the fell disease rendering him momentarily unable to think.

The symptoms of the actual disease – heavy, dreadful breathing, shivering, red spots on the skin turning black and swelling, the vomiting of blood and acute pain – always accompanied the rotting of the flesh whilst the victim still lived. Coupled with the physical ailments, dreadful hallucinations wracked the mind, ceasing only when the victim fell into a blessed coma. Dying occurred sometimes on the first day if the victim was lucky, but more often the end was delayed, sometimes for as much as a week.

But there was also the spread of infection to deal with and no-one was sure how it was transmitted.

The only solution for the dread disease throughout the last centuries was that born of desperation. Isolate the victims and abandon them to their own devices. In towns and villages alike victims were denied sustenance, boarded up in their homes they starved to death. To stem the spread amongst the populace quarantine was always imposed. No movements at all were allowed between an infected area and a clean one. And fire—always there was fire. Every corpse, every house, every street, whole villages where plague appeared, were all burned to the ground.

Parents looked on helplessly as sons and daughters died. Husbands and wives watched their spouses. And if they did not contract the plague themselves, it was not unknown for folk overcome with grief to jump into the flames of the funeral pyres, to die clutching their loved ones.

Fear ruled all—as it was wont to do, now, on the Grim.

'Dear God, Captain, how do we deal with this?' Trumper asked appalled, his ruddy face drained of all colour.

'We set sail, anchor outside the reef until the plague plays itself out.' He stared at Lodovico Portolan hard-faced, knowing what the ultimate price was. 'No-one…I repeat no-one at all is going to burn my ship!'

'Then we are like-minded,' said the Portolan grim-faced. 'No-one can disembark. I cannot allow the risk of infection to pass to my people. This ship has to be placed under quarantine until a month after the last reported case of disease. That is how it has always been.'

'No! No, don't you understand? We can't possibly wait that long. I have to find my master,' said Aidan, frantically looking around for a means of escape.

'And we have to get the people on the Grim, and those ashore, well away from Griffin Town and safe in Bylani. The Darkness will be upon us well before even this month is out, Excellency, and you are contemplating waiting weeks longer,' Augusta said extremely agitated. 'No, Excellency, I agree with Aidan, we cannot wait. If we do as custom demands we will be condemning everyone to die in that evil,' and she pointed westwards at a barely perceived blackness low down on the horizon.

'The plague or the Darkness…God, what a choice!' said Thaddeus helplessly.

Beatrix broke the heavy silence that followed. 'It's a bit late for quarantine anyway, isn't it?' she stated quietly, fear etched deeply in her face. 'You seem to have forgotten that there are members of our company already ashore and you, Excellency, may have already passed on the disease in your time on the wharf.'

Lodovico paled at the thought. Plague amongst his people, the nightmare infection starting with him. His clan were his family. If he was responsible for their deaths he'd never forgive himself.

'Dada,' seeing the rising guilt in his father's eyes, Thaddeus went to him and put a hand on his father's arm, 'you can't blame yourself for something you knew nothing about.'

Lodovico pulled himself together. 'You are right, Thaddeus, as you are also, Milady,' he replied sorrowfully to Beatrix's words. 'It is too late to recall Leonid; he'll be well on his way to Bylani now with Hopper and the others. And Bazyli and Marcus will have been in contact with countless numbers in the town. By the Gods, we are too late!' He despaired as he stared at his son—again Thaddeus' life was at risk.

'Well, we now have two threats of annihilation to deal with and we can simply do what we can, Dada. There is only one thing to do, that we know of, to beat the Darkness and that is to flee, find safety abroad or in Bylani until the day comes when we can find a means to rid us of it. The other, the plague, is less dangerous yet more urgent. We have to keep in mind the plague will kill many, maybe hundreds. The Darkness will kill everyone.'

Mazumbai had been very astute in naming him the Wizard of Understanding. His logical thinking, his perception of a situation was becoming more apparent as time went on.

'Does anyone know how the disease is passed from one to another?' he asked returning his father's heartbreaking gaze.

'No, my son, we do not know for sure…there are assumptions…'

'We have a theory in Brakwanna,' Mazumbai interrupted as Lodovico's voice trailed away, 'we believe it to be spread by rodents.'

'Yes, that is one of the stories,' Lodovico replied, staring at the small, black chieftain. 'I've also heard that at one time there was a cure.'

'Yes, but that was aeons ago and the remedy has long been lost…lost because the disease had been eradicated in the Griffin Isles for centuries,' added Bazyli.

'Do you know of one, Aidan?' asked Locklear.

'Not one that can protect everyone, no,' he answered. 'What do you say, Thaddeus?' Aidan asked hopefully, acknowledging that where animals were concerned, Prince Griffin was the obvious expert. 'It may explain the rats' unusual behaviour these last few days.'

'You may be right, but there's only one way to find out for certain,' said Thaddeus immediately animated. 'I'll need to get hold of a rat to confirm it…a black one that's come aboard from Sanctity would be best, I think.'

'But how is being aware of the disease's source going to help us?' asked Lodovico. 'We will still have people falling victim to the pestilence.'

'Yes, but knowing where it comes from, knowing what causes the plague may give us an indication of how to deal with it,' answered Thaddeus.

'Those onboard the Grim I can heal, Excellency,' Aidan said, Thaddeus infecting him with an equal excitement.

'Thank the Gods for that. But that doesn't solve the bigger problem—that of those who succumb ashore,' said Locklear.

'But surely that will depend on how many victims there are. Lord Aidan may be able to heal them all,' Trumper said.

'Even if he healed all those who fall ill here, the disease will still spread inland. Griffin is a large island with an immensely long coastline…the plague could come ashore at any time, at any of the thousands of small coves where out-islanders land. No, Bo'sun, you're clutching at straws,' said Locklear. 'Every outbreak of plague I've ever heard of has resulted in hundreds dead. Lord Aidan could never heal them all. And we still have to evacuate the people off this island or into Bylani. And there we'll have another problem…we may very well be exporting the disease elsewhere.'

'Oh, my God!' said Beatrix, her hand to her mouth. 'Leonid was bitten. The bite caused a swelling on his ankle…I know, I bandaged it for him when Aidan was asleep. Oh, Aidan, it looked so innocuous we never thought to have you look at it. Leonid's taking the plague into Bylani!'

'Then first things first, I need a rat—now. We can search while Aidan begins treating everyone,' ordered Prince Griffin, turning away he made for the bilges.

The next few hours were frenzied to say the least. But in order to keep the outbreak secret from those on shore, Aidan examined everyone in the captain's cabin. Crew and passengers alike queued to be checked over thoroughly. And it was the mark of the esteem in which Aidan was held that there was calm amongst those waiting. Many remembered his healing of the cabin boy, although Anders' life had been taken by natural means shortly after.

A few were found to have the plague in its early stages and Aidan initiated the healing, calming the victims with a confident smile. But each treatment exacted a toll on the young man's stamina. The Wizard of Life and Death was exhausted at the end of examining over four hundred people. And again he slept the sleep of the dead safely ensconced on his bunk in his cabin, someone watching over him all the time.

Nkosi, the sailor trained to replace Leash as the second helmsman, caught a rat easily in the nooks and crannies of the main hold; he was the fleetest in pursuit of the desperate rodents.

Thaddeus held the black rat in his hands as he stood in the main hold. Raising it in his left hand up to the light streaming through the hatch he was distracted, for a moment he could have sworn his ring glowed. Lowering his hand he examined the ring but the figure of the Griffin, raised in relief on its surface appeared in its usual form. He dismissed the flush as a figment of his imagination.

Resuming the study of the rodent, his sensations easily merged this time with that of the small animal and he found it suffering only discomfort caused by the tiny fleas feasting on its blood. Puzzled, he grimaced and then focused on the actual jumping insects and here discovered the real hosts of the disease. They had come aboard on the bodies of the black rats, the land dwellers of Sanctity, and these insects jumped from rodent to rodent and from rodent to human and then from human to human—biting as they went. There was also something else that he discovered.

'Dada,' he spoke his fears, his words overheard by those standing near. 'Dada…I believe the fleas were originally infected by the Darkness.'

'Good God! You mean that is how the Darkness is going to kill us?'

'The Darkness doesn't kill; it is a cover, a protection if you like for those demons roaming within it. It is the demons that slaughter. The plague is just one of the many means of murder devised by the One behind the Darkness,' Thaddeus said handing the rat back to Nkosi.

'Dear God, then Lady Beatrix is correct in her summation, it really is pointless us staying onboard. We cannot halt the Darkness and we cannot stop the spread of the plague. We must go ashore as soon as possible and get our people to safety,' Lodovico stated, his face ashen.

'But we still have infected rats aboard,' said Augusta,' surely we should destroy them before they can get ashore? After all it may be weeks before the Darkness reaches here, and until it does, it would be wrong of us to allow the plague to be carried into the town by these things,' and she sneered distastefully at the rat in Nkosi's hand, 'if we have the means to stop it.'

'There are other paths along which it will be brought to Griffin, my friends,' said Locklear. 'We must not forget the other refugees. Not all those on Sanctity were mindless monks and we cannot forget those islands that will be overtaken by the Darkness on its way here. As Lodovico said earlier, those people could land anywhere on these shores, as could the rats. They will bring the plague with them.'

'Aye, it seems that whatever action we take will ultimately have no effect on the result, the disease is going to end up on Griffin. We cannot quarantine the whole damn island. But Princess Augusta is correct…we have a duty to delay the infection for as long as possible. We must rid ourselves of the rats onboard. But there must be hundreds on this ship. Can it be done, Captain? Can we kill them all?' Lodovico asked doubtfully.

'I have never heard of any ship being cleared of the vermin entirely. It would be a tremendous task to root them all out of every hole in any ship, and this is the largest afloat…it's staggering what you're suggesting. But there are a great many of us. If we can find them and stop them fleeing ashore, we should be able to destroy them all.'

'With my help it should be easier,' Thaddeus said quietly, 'although I'll hate doing it.'

'Why, what are you going to do?' Beatrix asked.

'All those that are in my hearing I can call to me,' he stared at her miserably. 'I can then betray them. You can kill them as they appear.'

'Oh, Thaddeus, it has to be done to save our lives.'

'I know…I know, Beattie!'

'I can search for those that are too far away to hear you and chase them towards you,' Beatrix said, mentally shuddering at the job she'd set herself, but more concerned at the effect the action would have on Thaddeus.

'How are you going to do that?' asked Augusta, frowning, not yet realizing why Thaddeus was getting upset.

'They don't like a very bright light do they? If you come with me down into the bilges to ward my back and dig out those too stubborn to shift, I'll create my light. That should drive on deck those Thaddeus can't reach with his voice.'

'Oh, my God, it's filthy down there! Do you realize that?' shuddering, she grabbed Beatrix's hand and they both turned to go below.

'Never mind, Augusta, just think of that giant bath we saw up at the manorhouse,' Beatrix said and her friend's eyes gleamed.

'Wait, ladies, please. You just can't drive these vermin up here without us being prepared. Captain Locklear, may I suggest you order your crew to line the decks cudgels in hand? Mazumbai can you do the same with your people?' and at their nods Lodovico glanced over the rail at those on the quay.

'Damn! We'll not be able to conceal the activity from those ashore. Seeing us lining the deck wielding belaying pins is going to come as an unpleasant surprise. They're already restless and seeing us arming ourselves will, without a doubt, be misconstrued. We'll have a riot on our hands.' The crowd had grown even more as the evening had progressed.

'Perhaps you should tell them of what we face, Dada,' said Thaddeus glumly.

'Yes…no, my son. I think it's time for Prince Griffin to introduce himself and do just that. Now is the time for both clans to begin to work together. And telling them of the Darkness should be a job for someone who has first-hand knowledge of it. I could never convince them of its terror, I don't completely understand it myself.' He put his arm around Thaddeus' shoulder and gazed at the boy he'd loved and known and yet not known for fifteen years. 'They are your people, Thaddeus—you will have to convince them.'

Thaddeus glanced between those ashore and those on the ship; he licked his suddenly very dry lips. 'But, I could never…Dada, they only know me as the idiot. They probably won't even listen to me.'

'Then it's about time they did, Prince Griffin, your Highness,' said Augusta, very experienced at making public speeches, taking his hand she squeezed it tight. 'Come, Beatrix and I will stand with you, lend you our support while you speak,' and she led him to the rail where Beatrix joined them, the girls standing either side of him their faces grim.

Thaddeus had spent years watching people through the wall of colours in Limbo, his mother identifying those she knew. But nothing she had said had prepared him for this—he was absolutely petrified. Peering down at the immense crowd on the quayside did not unnerve him at first; it seemed very familiar gazing from above at something happening below. It was the realization that they were returning his gaze that nearly unmanned him. The sight of so many people looking up at him, awaiting his words, was a new and terrifying experience. He was afraid to speak.

'Go on,' urged Augusta and she smiled up at him, 'go on…once you've started the easier it'll get. Begin with "my friends",' and she released his hand to stand behind his shoulder, Beatrix doing the same.

'No, Augusta, stay,' and he grabbed her hand again and gripped it tightly, it was his turn to draw her near. He held out his other hand for Beatrix. And drawing comfort and confidence from both his friends, and with his father heeding his every word from behind, he made his first public speech.

Nonetheless, having no experience of oration he unconsciously spoke as if he was in each individual's home sitting across the table from those living there. Clearing his throat noisily, he went on to speak quietly, though his voice carried to everyone standing or sitting before him. And they listened to his words, firstly with scepticism and then with trepidation and finally with horror. But even at the end of his speech, when they were all in various forms of terror or disbelief, most heeded his instructions because of his beguiling voice, the earnestness of his tidings and above all his open honesty.

'Dante Ernold,' Prince Griffin, his voice trembling slightly, stared across at the big Portolan puffing on his pipe. 'Cousin Dante…and you, Cousin Alexi,' the ex-priest Montetor, frowned at being addressed as such, but then smiled wryly as he realized the boy was correct in his assumption of their distant relationship. 'First, please let me explain my recovery from being an "idiot". No, Augusta,' he said as she went to remonstrate with him, 'that man was right, to all intents and purposes I was an idiot. I couldn't speak, smile, cry or do anything for myself.' He searched the crowd until he found the man with the pigtail. 'You, sailor, what is your name?'

'Ivan Blouet…uh…Highness, at your service,' and he touched his forelock, puzzled.

'Well, Ivan, I have a story to tell, it is long and involved but I will relate as much of it as I can and hopefully most of you will believe the unbelievable reason for my condition.'

He searched the crowd again and found Dyta Peche sitting on her man's lap on a bale of cotton. 'Lady, I believe I heard someone call you Dyta, am I right?' and when she nodded and hurriedly stood up, he continued.

'Dyta, you must have heard that my birth was not a normal one. As a woman you are accustomed to knowing the dreadful complications that can arise in birthing a child. Well, Dyta,' and he smiled forlornly, 'I don't expect you'll have heard of the particular trauma that assailed my mother at my birth.' He paused and looked around knowing his next words would be scoffed at. 'At her most vulnerable time my mother was beset by a demon. And this demon wished to kill me…why me I don't know, all I know is it wanted me dead, wanted my soul.'

He paused and licked his lips; the memory of his mother's telling of her recollections making his mouth again dry. 'In her efforts to protect my life, my soul was denied my body and my mother and I both ended up in the afterlife. My mother dead and, I know this is going to be hard to believe, but my soul was still alive as was my body here. My soul became a separate entity remote from my body, although still joined to it by my lifeline. And I became the idiot you all saw before you. But the not so simple cause of it was that my soul was unable to bond with my body here in this world.'

126

At those words Lewyn burst out laughing, his mirth soon affecting others around him. 'You expect us to believe you were in two bits? No wonder we all thought you an idiot. Perhaps you still are,' Lewyn looked around for support and again sniggered contemptuously.

Others in the crowd, equally incredulous, taunted Thaddeus and this urged Lewyn to even greater insolence, which was when he made his mistake.

'This demon, wanting to kill you, was he a Portolan supporter of Paul keeping your father in line?'

But this was too much for those on the dock willing to hear their prince. They turned on Lewyn and the Montetor suddenly looked around afraid of the threats being voiced near him. He slunk away to disappear for the moment amongst the mob.

It was then Thaddeus saw his opportunity to regain his audience. He raised his voice and was again heard over their muttering. And the more he spoke, the more time went on, so his voice grew stronger, more confident. And his gaze, instead of remaining fixed on one point or on one person, roved the crowd making eye contact with many of the Montetors and Portolans alike—unconsciously establishing a rapport with many in both clans.

'For fifteen years I was adrift in Limbo, that place we must all go when we die. My mother…my beautiful, wonderful mother cared for me, denying her own rest, her place in Paradise. She, refusing to allow the demons to finish what they'd intended at my birth—to take my soul. And there were demons, my friends, thousands of them, but not in Limbo itself…no…at its edges. There on the border was the Darkness, a place of fog, of foul smell, of terror and torment, and of unspeakable death. It was and is a place of iniquity, home to demons of many kinds. It is a prison for the lost tormented souls ensnared by the foul beasts,' he paused to allow his extraordinary words to sink into the minds of those listening. 'And some of those souls may very well be the relatives of yours that have died in the last fifteen years,' he paused to allow time for the dread fact of that to sink in.

'The greatest of the demons are the Herdsmen, the Collectors of souls for the One behind the Darkness…the One who tortures all souls from his lair in Purgatory.

'I wandered lost for years in the Darkness along with my mother. Our life there was one of abject despair and horror. The only relief we got was when I visited the wall of colours to watch my father, for I would return and tell my mother of her beloved husband.' Thaddeus glanced at his father, his love showing in that short look.

'We were privy to sights that would make you go insane at the mere thought of them. We constantly lived with having to flee and hide from the demons. Otherwise our capture would have meant banishment to Purgatory…to an even worse existence if that was possible. For our pain and our terror was needed to sustain the God.

'But I and my mother were rescued by my friends here, Princess Augusta and Lady Beatrix of Mantovar, by the wizard healer, Lord Aidan and by Anders.'

At mention of his nephew's name, Hugo despaired and breathed deeply to regain control of his emotions.

Thaddeus hesitated, and then made up his mind not to tell them any more of Anders' existence. By their faces they were having enough trouble accepting the very strange facts of their prince's survival.

'My soul was returned to my body as you see. But unfortunately my troubles did not end there,' he smiled ironically.

'I awoke to discover that I was a wizard, powers given to the three of us standing here before you, passed to us by Lord Aidan.

'When the Abbot of Sanctity arrived early on Griffin, it was not to collect his Quota. He was here to capture the magical staff of Lord Tragen, and in that he eventually succeeded. But to lure us to Sanctity to carry out the deed he told us he was here to ask the Grim's captain to carry a cargo to Mantovar and while he was here he might as well take his Quota. At this, my uncle, Bazyli Montetor, finally had enough and demanded the release of Paul and Ariana. The abbot agreed as part of his ploy to get us to his home. But Bazyli did not have his quota in place, so he set Razor to capture us…his purpose being to add us to his share of the ransom.' Staring at Alexi he smiled at the surprise on his cousin's face. 'Naturally, the four of us fled and we escaped into the catacombs beneath Mount Trespass.'

'You, what!' said Dante Ernold startled. 'Only fools enter the Devil's Keep…and none have ever escaped from there.'

'Nevertheless, that was where we went and that was where we discovered the Green People—the original inhabitants of these islands.'

'So that is where he's from…that Leonid, he's one of the devils,' shouted Cyryl Lewyn panicking.

'Quiet, Lewyn,' ordered Alexi, 'if he was a devil you'd be dead and we'd all have peace and quiet.' Some in the crowd sniggered at this. 'Shut up, all of you this cousin of mine intrigues me…go on, Highness.'

Augusta squeezed Thaddeus' hand tightly, getting the big Montetor's support boded well for the rest of the tale.

'The Green People have spent the last thousand years living underground, preparing a haven for all those who cannot flee Griffin. It was a task handed them as a result of a prophecy,' said Thaddeus pausing to await the expected reaction. It wasn't long in coming.

Through the shouts and dismay it was Dante Ernold's turn to call for order. 'Why a haven? And why have we to flee our homes, cousin?'

'When the Grim departed Griffin for Sanctity with my father and my uncle, and the wizard Lord Tragen, their intent was to bring home Paul Portolan and Ariana Montetor, and to pay the last of the ransom. We followed…that is, we three along with Lord Aidan, Leonid the Green Man and Marcus Janne. But we were all captured by the abbot and his master and imprisoned in the dungeons beneath the volcano. There we discovered the true horror of the monastery and the horrendous manner in which Paul and Ariana died.

Thaddeus paused and studied the faces below him; all were hanging on his words. 'They were the victims of torture by ritual disembowelling!'

And at the collective intake of unbelief and horror, he continued. 'Imprisoned with us were the Brakwannans, for years enslaved and used as sacrifices in the same manner.'

The crowd could not hold their silence any longer and moaning erupted.

Thaddeus spoke above the growing anger. 'The master's name was Zorzecai. He was a herdsman, a master demon from the Darkness working in this life to further his God's evil aims.'

'And what are those aims?' interrupted Alexi grim-faced, fear and loathing in his eyes.

'Zorzecai's purpose was to open a gateway in the divide between Life and Death. So that the Darkness, the black, choking, evil mist, can enter this life and bring with it its demons to kill every one of us…so that his God can rule in this world as well as in the afterlife.'

'Hey, watch out,' shouted Cyryl Lewyn jumping up from his seat on a bollard at the edge of the jetty.

'Lewyn…quiet!' ordered Ernold.

'Didn't you see it?'

'What?'

'That rat, it was huge…and very odd.'

'Odd? How?' asked Ernold his anger rising he was, nevertheless, puzzled and couldn't help the question.

'It was black with a helluva long white stripe down its back…I've never seen one so marked. And then he panicked again. 'Even the rats have the mark of the devil!' he shouted, not realizing how close to the truth he was.

'Lewyn for the last time…shut it!' Ernold said threateningly.

And a new voice was heard from the Grim. 'With the passing of Lord Tragen, my master and my father, the Collector of Purgatory has succeeded—he has opened the door between Life and Death.'
Unbeknownst to those on deck Aidan had awoken and heard Thaddeus when he came up to investigate the noise.

'You still haven't explained why we have to leave Griffin, Highness,' said Dante Ernold, the words finally acknowledging Thaddeus as his liege lord.

'The Darkness is on its way here…bringing its demons and its diseases and its everlasting torment.'

There was uproar in the crowd until Alexi Dambray shouted. 'Quiet! No more…listen,' he said, his eyes narrowing. 'You are saying that we have to flee or die?'

'Yes, cousin!'

'How long do we have before it reaches here?'

'It may be a week or a month away, we are not sure it depends on the wind. But unfortunately it is preceded by a dread disease…a disease that we need your help to eliminate on this ship, so that we may slow the rate of infection into Griffin. This will give us the time to save the lives of more of our families before the Darkness reaches here,' said Thaddeus.

'What disease is that, cousin, what is it you want us to do?' asked Alexi, his face expressionless, his manner and his body rigid in its expectation of the worst.

'We must exterminate the rats on the Grim…let none escape. That should suffice for now,' said Thaddeus.

'Dear God…it's the plague!' exclaimed Cyril Lewyn. 'My granda told me years ago that the rats brought the plague. 'Do you hear me?' he screamed. 'They have the plague…burn them, burn the ship!'

As one the crowd took a step back from the Grim, utterly appalled. Thaddeus spoke quickly before the panic took irrevocable hold.

'Wait,' he shouted, releasing the girls' hands he raised his arms for silence. 'Alexi, Dante listen to me. If you panic, you will all die—if you heed me, most of you, and most of your families, will survive!'
The strength of their prince's conviction quieted some but not all. Those that were not prepared to listen, led by Cyryl Lewyn and his cat, fled the quayside carrying the dread news with them.

'What do you want us to do?' asked Alexi Dambray moving over to stand with Dante Ernold—an action that calmed the crowd that had turned, for a moment, into a panicked mob.

Lodovico Portolan studied those people remaining on the dockside. At present Montetor and Portolan were one clan. Thaddeus had succeeded in an almost impossible task, his honesty, had worked a miracle—at least on the quay, for the moment.

Sixteen

It was on the following morning after being welcomed into the listening station, that Anselm and Shadra awoke and realized at once that the liosalfar had betrayed them. It appeared that the dread tidings in the conversation Ryn had overheard between Roidan and Qillan might very well be carried out in the not too distant future. For Shadra and Anselm discovered they were prisoners.

Shadra's cranium was splitting, his headache the worst he'd ever suffered. He lay with his head on the hard pillow, afraid to move in case his head fell off his shoulders. Keeping his eyes closed he tried to recall what had come of them after they'd entered the cave. The last he remembered was sitting down and drinking Zilbor's wine and eating the wonderful meat broth. But he knew that a headache such as this could only have been caused by drugs…what drugs, of course, was pure speculation.

He waited for the buzzing in his ears to ease and then listened intently. Muffled sounds came from somewhere, many voices, some raised in anger, others placating. Nearer to hand he heard laboured breathing and he opened his eyes. Squinting against the dim light and turning his head very gently, he espied Anselm sitting up on another bed against the wall on the other side of the room. He was holding his head in his hands and taking deep breaths.

'Does it help, Anselm?' he asked softly.

'What?' he asked lowering his hands and raising pain-filled eyes slowly to meet those of the small, green, forest elf.

'The deep breathing…does it help the pain?'

'Somewhat…the hardest thing is actually sitting up to breathe. God help you when you try! I'd advise you to keep your eyes closed when you do it, or you'll see stars that hurt even worse. What on earth did they give us?'

'What's more to the point is why they felt the need to give it,' Shadra answered. He raised his hands from the bed to rub his temples but found they were bound tightly with a strong white twine that almost cut into his wrists. Moving his feet he discovered they were also tied together, the twine the same, the binding again far too tight, restricting the flow of blood to his toes.

Breathing deeply and slowly so as not to make any sudden movements and exacerbate the pain behind his eyes, he turned his head and looked around.

The room itself was small and contained the bare minimum of furniture; the two beds, both had feather mattresses Shadra noticed, a luxury in the forest. There was a table and two chairs, a side-table with a tall blue ceramic water jug standing in a blue ceramic bowl, a plain framed mirror on the wall above it completed the furnishings. In the wall opposite the foot of the beds was a solid hardwood door, to its right in the adjacent wall, a smaller door, probably the privy. There was no window to the outside world.

Through the closed door they heard the sounds of loud angry voices, the words of an obvious argument, indistinguishable. Occasionally there were footsteps as someone walked up to their door, stopped for a moment as if listening, and then retreated.

'What's going on, Shadra? How the hell did we get here? I thought your cousins were going to help us.'

'So did I,' he closed his eyes his memories returning. 'The last I remember is sitting down in the cave having food. God…' and he gazed at his fellow captive, 'there is something I haven't told you, I was waiting until we were alone but never had the chance. Wait a minute…let me sit up first, perhaps I'll be able to think better.'

The elf closed his eyes and, taking his time and heeding his friend's advice he slowly pushed his legs to the side of the bed and then sat up, holding his face in his hands as he did so.

'Are you all right?' Anselm asked a little later when Shadra eventually lowered his arms.

'No…but I'll survive,' he opened his eyes and smiled tentatively.

'What was it you haven't told me?'

'Ryn, he overheard Roidan speaking to that other one who was waiting for us. They were discussing how long to keep us alive.'

'Wha-at!'

'It's all right, Roidan said that he wasn't going to be the one to kill us and he wouldn't be party to any of the others killing us. But…' and Shadra grimaced.

'But?'

'Well, because of some prophecy it seems that schrats are very dangerous to the liosalfar and are not allowed in Alfhime on pain of death—the orders of their leader,' he rubbed both his knees absentmindedly. 'I'm sorry, Anselm, I have absolutely no idea what they're talking about.'

'Well, I expect they'll let us know before murdering us,' he smiled sarcastically as he felt beneath his left armpit for the dagger he always carried there, and found it missing…the liosalfar were not so dumb. 'They've taken our weapons and your bag,' Anselm said, struggling to stand up, he managed it by holding on to the headboard with his tethered hands. Putting his feet on the floor he moaned in agony as the blood constricted at his ankles numbing his feet.

'Did they have to tie so tight? God, I can't feel my toes!' and he sat back down on the edge of the bed.

'Sh! Let's see if we can make out what they're arguing about.'

Shadra and Anselm concentrated all their attention on the door, silent for all of two minutes.

'It's no good, that door's too damned thick, let me try something else,' Shadra said and he brought his hands up in front of him and wiggled his fingers. 'What the hell,' he dropped his hands and stared at them in his lap.

'What's wrong? 'Anselm asked, alarmed at the panic on Shadra's face.

'Sh!'

Shadra brought up his hands again and seemed to concentrate even harder, his brow furrowing deeply as his eyes nearly popped from his head. He ignored the increasing pain in his ears. Blinking slowly, his face pale, he stared at Anselm.

'They've taken my magic. I can't do a thing…whatever they drugged us with has robbed me of any ability.'

Stunned, the human looked at his small friend. 'By the Gods, what do we do now? Is it permanent?'

'I don't know. I don't believe so, I've never heard of anyone losing their magic forever. But that's not to say it can't happen, of course. It…it should surface sooner or later,' his voice didn't sound too hopeful.

'How long is "sooner or later"?'

Shadra gulped, visibly shaken. 'I have absolutely no bloody idea,' he breathed deeply. 'We'll just have to wait and see. But why…why have my cousins denied me magic? What is their purpose?'

'Obviously, so you'd be no threat to them…or their leader. I told you the Garda were dangerous.'

'Then why did your chancellor send you to find them?'

But before he could answer they heard a key being turned in the lock and the door opened to admit Crystal. She was wearing a loose fitting blue shirt and skin tight red leggings. She smiled hesitantly at them both.

'I'm sorry, Shadra, Anselm, but we had to restrain you for your own safety. Here, let me release your bindings.'

Shadra and Anselm stared silently as she untied their hands and feet. Anselm studied her, she was very upset, her eyes red as if she'd been crying. He couldn't hold back a groan as the blood once more discovered unrestricted access to his fingers and toes.

She jumped, startled. 'I'm sorry. Qillan should not have been so exacting in his efforts to keep you from harm.'

Shadra stared at her as she worked the twine. Waking and finding himself a captive of those he thought were family made him angry—very angry and very apprehensive. Despite the conversation Ryn had overheard, he instinctively felt a liking for Roidan, had believed him when he said that he'd be no party to treachery. He remained silent, giving nothing away not even groaning when the excruciating pain of normality returned to his limbs.

'What do you mean for our own safety, Crystal? How were we in danger?' Anselm asked, flexing his fingers, 'and why has Shadra…'

'Ouch!' The little elf shouted, interrupting, more to halt the next question than because he was hurt, he didn't want the liosalfar to know yet that he had realized he had lost his magic. 'Why did you drug us?'

She stood up from crouching at Shadra's feet and strode to the mirror on the wall. She hesitated, attempting to hide her vacillation by making an unneeded straightening of the frame, not meeting their eyes.

'To reach Alfhime necessitates a transition from one world into another, yours of the outside, into ours here in the valley. It is a very painful passage for outsiders, sometimes bringing on a fit of violent behaviour—hence the bindings. We did not want you harming us or causing harm to yourselves.'

'Couldn't you have asked us before drugging us?' Anselm said. He went along with keeping secret Shadra's loss of magic—in his profession he'd learned never to speak of matters that were not immediately relevant. Perhaps she might not even know.

'Would you have allowed us to give you the narcotic?'

For the first time she stood and made eye contact with Anselm, he flushed. Her eyes were large and seductively green…and full of misery. This particular liosalfar was unnerving him; she made him appear a little boy, gauche and tongue-tied. The last time he'd felt like this was the day he'd met his wife. He'd been young then, living in Miskim with his brothers. But then, his memories of that time horrifying him, he focused again on Crystal, she really was a lovely girl. Why was she lying through her teeth?

'Refreshment will be brought to you shortly. In the meantime I will leave the door unlocked but please do not leave this room. Reasons will be given you later.' She departed and two very worried people gazed at each other.

'Did you notice that she never looked at you, Shadra, only at me? And before you say it, I don't think it's my good looks that kept her eyes on me. Whatever's in that prophecy frightens the life out of her.'

All that first day and far into the second they remained incarcerated in the bedchamber virtually isolated. Their only contact was a young liosalfar girl who, remaining silent, brought in their food and drink.

It was dusk on the second evening of their capture, as Ryn was waiting at the entrance to the rift in the cliff that Shadra and Anselm were taken from their prison.

Escorted by Crystal and Roidan, the forest elf and the human walked through a long corridor, past several other chambers similar to that they had just left, and into a long, wide and bright room holding two huge tables running along the length of the walls. The room was clearly a refectory, a communal dining room. There were several liosalfar, some dressed in coloured clothing but most in white, partaking of their evening meal, the smells of the roast lamb and hot bread tantalizing.

Anselm studied the occupants as he walked through, worry on his face; he knew a barracks when he saw one. Not one of the warriors raised his or her head, even though each stopped eating while the prisoners passed. They exited through the door at the end onto a stone flagged courtyard large enough to hold a regiment of soldiers. Crossing this quickly, they joined a flagstone pathway leading onto a wide cobbled road that eventually joined the main street through the town.

The barracks had been built high on the slopes at one end of the valley and gave a panoramic view over the extensive, fairy-like town of Alfhime spread along the valley. The two captives were astonished, not by the town as such even though its beauty tugged at their senses; it was the climate that fazed them. The cloud cover was complete, its greyness heralding a blizzard. But there was no sign of snow anywhere and the valley was wallowing in the heat of high summer.

Anselm's anxiety increased, this weather was not normal. Glancing at Shadra, both looked behind them searching for the way they must have been brought. The barracks was a long, low, one storey building large enough to house a great number of liosalfar and it had been built below the entrance to a large cave. And at that moment, a small troop of six or seven mountain elves entered the valley, removing their white furs and talking animatedly as they did.

Flanked by Qillan and Zilbor, and followed by two others, Crystal and Roidan led Shadra and Anselm along the tree-lined road towards a tall stone building in the central square of the sprawling township.

In total contrast to the whiteness of the outside world, here there was colour everywhere. Greens, browns and yellows, the earth colours predominated in the walls of the myriad buildings, no two the same. There were single-floored homes with huge gardens front and rear, two- and three-storey buildings, one or two adjoining its neighbour, most detached and standing alone amongst trees or in open fields.

Orchards of apples and pears, groves of oranges and limes sprung up behind and amongst buildings of all shapes and sizes...tall and narrow, spire-like, staring haughtily down on others that sat almost frumpishly squat and wide.

They glimpsed farm houses on the outskirts of the town. On the slopes of the valley surrounding them were cornfields near ready for harvesting and livestock in enclosed fields. Small, brightly painted workshops sat on the banks of the slow-moving river meandering through the bottom of the valley. Many high and lofty bridges crossed the waterway at intervals along its length, these having a profusion of gaily coloured flowers growing on trellis work along guardrails. But even these blooms seemed oddly out of place, for the plants of this region should be short-lived, rapidly flowering alpines, such as rock-cress and milk-vetch, not these. These were flowers usually grown in sheltered valleys in the lowlands, roses and mallows did not survive above the snowline.

The liosalfar themselves, appeared to prefer all shades of the primary colours of reds and blues and yellows in their clothes. Their light attire of tight leggings and loose tunics and shirts were eminently apposite for high summer. Anselm smiled sardonically; it seemed that white was anathema in Alfhime.

Anselm continued to find the climate unsettling as they walked along the main highway. Sunlight streaming through dark clouds was not normal and it had an unnatural, clammy feel to it, as if it was being forced to fight off winter, and didn't want to, the overcast elicited misery. Looking across at Shadra, the human could see the same feelings engendered in the forest elf; Shadra's face was a pale, sickly green. Whatever was wrong with the clouds stopped natural sunlight breaking through to relieve the dark malaise of Alfhime.

Anselm came to the conclusion that the bright colours of the town were an attempt to fight off a desperate depression. There was a false cheeriness permeating the town and its people and however the liosalfar were occupied, none of them could hide their trepidation for long.

As Anselm walked through the town, taking in the wondrously multi-coloured sights, he shivered, something else was wrong—and it wasn't just the lack of birdsong, there were no birds. And then he realized what it was as they both encountered other liosalfar working in the fields and gardens or hurrying past them on unknown errands.

All activity ceased and the liosalfar stared wide-eyed, panic-stricken—Shadra the focus of their attention.

There was no acknowledgement of his nod; no cheerful greeting of a cousin came their way. Crystal, Roidan, Qillan and Zilbor stared ahead, their faces blank, their thoughts hidden.

Shadra and Anselm examined the town, its layout and its people, searching for a means of escape. The mood of the people frightening, they grew more sombre as the large building before them grew nearer.

It was four storeys high, green-speckled marble steps led up to a very tall, very wide double door, painted a brilliant green. Tall arched windows flanked the door and continued on to both ends of the flower-decked veranda running along the broad frontage of the stone Hall.

Alfhime, the ancient home of the elven races, emanated forced light, an artificial gaiety—and rank fear.

The colourful dwellings, the beautiful walkways and parks, the brightly hued clothes, instead of conveying happiness and life, only served to enhance the sense of despondency they desperately tried to hide. Silent and troubled, their shoulders slumped, the Liosalfar were not the jovial people of age-old fable.

Roidan, Crystal, Qillan and Zilbor escorted Shadra and Anselm through the immense doors and into their Moot Hall, to ascertain the fate of their prisoners at the hands of their leader—the Magician.

Ryn was tired, depressed and very hungry. His stomach rumbled reminding him that he hadn't eaten since the liosalfar had rescued them all with their potion back in the cave. He was very worried now; he'd wracked his mind searching for all sorts of reasons for his friends' tardy return. But none of them seemed to fit with the conversation he'd overheard. He contemplated the fate that might have befallen his friends. Surely they wouldn't have been killed? The Gods couldn't do that to him, couldn't deny him his friends, surely they weren't that capricious!

Waiting in vain for Shadra's and Anselm's reappearance he studied the terrain around the cliff for sign of life. There was none, even the liosalfar's footprints had disappeared in a fresh flurry of snow. It was deathly quiet apart from the soft moaning of the light wind blowing through the peaks and across the lonely, uninhabited plateaux. He sniffed, hoping to catch the smell of any life form, cocked his head and listened for the same. Nothing! For a brief moment he felt homesick, he missed the sound of the ocean, the waves lapping, the porpoises calling to each other. In the Scissor Mountains it was as if even nature held its breath waiting for his friends to return.

He lifted his feet, his talons tending to adhere to the ice of the rocks beneath. He'd have to be careful he couldn't stay in one place for too long. He'd freeze to the stone if he didn't move. He lifted his head high and sniffed the air again…nothing except snow and smoke.

He knew in his bones after waiting nearly two days that there was no chance of them coming out of the rift below him. He'd searched high and low for another entrance and discovered nothing. He had come to the conclusion that there was no alternative but to go in after them—only he was too big for the gap in the cliff. He thought of using magic to make himself small, but he had not the experience to know how long the spell would last or even if it was the correct spell. It might result in him remaining small, he didn't want that. On the

139

other hand the spell might last only until he'd entered the passage and then he'd suddenly shoot back up to his normal size. He was claustrophobic, being squashed in such a small tunnel didn't bare thinking about and he shuddered. He didn't want to die yet either.

He stamped his feet and flexed his fingers before his eyes, admiring them he was determined not to lose them again to frostbite. There was still no movement, no sign of the liosalfar. It was as if he was the only one left alive in the universe. Even the wind was dying down. He looked below him at the cliff of impenetrable black rock; impatiently he kicked at it and yelped when he stubbed his toes. In frustration he pecked at the cliff, a small bit of ice fell from the wall. He stared at it, a glimmer coming into his eyes. Could he make the entrance bigger?

Ryn hopped down the cliff and stood before the narrow gap of the listening post. He poked his head into the rift and followed it with his neck, thrusting in as far as he could, which was no great distance his vast body soon blocked it.

He strained to hear, meeting only silence. It was pitch black in the tunnel and the only thing he could smell was dampness, the only thing he could feel was a moss on the walls. He instinctively licked at the fungi and immediately spat it out.

'Nothing like your cooking, Shadra,' he whispered.

He withdrew his head and futilely looked around for sign of another path leading to another entrance. He flexed his fingers again, they were getting very cold. Examining the rock wall he thought on how he could enlarge it. Pecking at the black granite he yelped again when he nearly broke his beak. He raised his head sucking his tongue…daft bird, he thought. He spread his wings and stared at his fingers, curling them he looked at them closely. His nails seemed overlong, puzzled he instinctively rubbed them against the rock and saw the excess bits of nail fall away. He spread his fingers to the sky and studied them poking out from his feathers and thought of the miracle of magic.

Perhaps there was another way to use his gift other than making himself small, maybe he could locate his friends with its aid.

For the third time he stuck his head into the rift and, breathing shallowly, he closed his eyes. His concentration intense he pushed his mind forward along the tunnel in the same way that some wizards could overlook an adversary in a different room although, of course, Ryn didn't realize he was doing this. But in his head he saw the cavern in which the liosalfar had greeted his friends. The rock used for cooking and heating, long gone cold, there was no sign of life. He pushed forward more forcefully to reach the other end of the cave and suddenly screeched in pain. He fell from the entrance of the tunnel, banging his head on the rock wall as he did. Stunned, he massaged the rapidly forming lump above his eyes.

'Bloody hell, Ryn, what were you thinking of…that hurt…whatever it was.'

He thought back on the experience trying to identify the reason for the pain. He'd appeared to come up against a wall—a blockage at the far end of the cavern where no obstruction was visible. He recalled the tunnel dipping lower into the mountain and when he'd attempted to push his mind into it he'd felt lightning in his head. The blockage had tugged at his brain dragging all sensation from his mind and body. And it had burned him, made his mind thrum with the terrible loss. He knew that whatever it was he'd never get past it—he'd only just managed to escape its draw on his senses. He shuddered, the barrier wanted his magic and there was no way past it. And if that was the case, was it possible that Shadra had lost his magic to it, for that was the only other way out of the cave.

Depressed he flew back up onto the cliff top to recover. Waiting for his headache to disappear, all of a sudden elation filled his chest. He'd remembered his magic and, although the purpose had been foiled, he'd summoned it at will and been able to use it. He sniffed with delight and almost choked when he again smelled smoke.

'Hello, where's that coming from then? There was no fire in the cave.' Ryn often spoke to himself when alone as did the wizard who gave him his voice. It seemed that Aidan had passed on his habit along with the magic. But it was too dark now to go searching—the liosalfar would certainly hide the fire at night.

He tucked his head beneath his wing and settling down he dreamt of the wind-swept ocean.

Seventeen

Leash was delirious, lying face up in the bottom of the boat his legs bent over a thwart, his arms fallen to his side. His black hair, missing in places where his scalp had burned, strayed across his blistered features in the slight breeze playing across the gunnels. Occasionally the carefree gust dipped to sweep gently across Leash's face and cherry-red skinned arms. It brought no relief only more pain. Where he wasn't agonizingly crimson his skin had blistered to form huge bubbles, some of these pustules had ruptured, the skin beneath peeling to leave bare flesh to burn again. His lips were flaking and shrunken, pulled back to display strangely yellow teeth, his mouth produced no saliva, his throat had the consistency of sawdust. He was unable to swallow and his head pounded whenever he was lucid enough to realize that the excruciating pain was his.

He was dreadfully dehydrated, his hallucinations graphic.

And the demon had had enough of Leash's pain. If he did nothing he was going to lose his host and the consequences of that didn't bare thinking about. He should have transformed earlier when Leash had the strength, now he couldn't his host would never survive the shock.

The vampyrus shook Leash, both in his body and in his mind. The demon was desperate; if the man died then he would be forced to return to Purgatory. This time there would be no escape, his eternal existence forever tormented by his enemy, the rest of his unending life would become intolerable. In desperation the vampyrus examined every facet of his host. To revive this body he had to bring it to full awareness to ensure survival for them both and so he shook Leash again and again.

Leash's head lolled from side to side on the thwart, giving rise to a greater agony as his scalp tore beneath his few remaining long, black locks. But perhaps this is what saved him. He opened his eyes at the new pain and peered through narrow slits, the sun almost blinding him. He poked his puffed up tongue through his cracked lips, his first thoughts of water, and he struggled to pull himself up to the gunnel.

He knew that drinking sea-water would only cause deterioration in his condition, but the sea was liquid—and his condition couldn't get any worse. His body needed fluid, his flesh was drying out, eventually his skin would rupture and the flesh would fall from his bones.

But the vampyrus knew he had to be careful. What he was about to do could severely shock Leash's heart. So the demon dwelled in the aorta preparing to steady the beat of his host's heart if it should falter. And then, without a second thought, the demon gripped Leash, raised him from the bottom boards and he heaved himself over the side of the fishing boat and fell into the ocean.

Dipping below the surface he screamed underwater as the salt burnt his raw wounds. Almost drowning, he instinctively drove for the surface, the demon moving his arms and kicking his legs. He grabbed the side of the boat and clung there for hours, screaming all the while—until he had no more strength to cry out and he fell silent.

His body soaked up the water…and the salt. But he knew he had to stay in the water to have any hope of life. The ocean was the only shield his body had from the dread rays of the sun. He lapped water into his mouth, receiving only temporary respite from thirst—temporary because he knew that his thirst would grow rapidly now that he had succumbed to temptation.

But it also brought him and his demon a time of clarity, a moment when he could reflect on measures to gain safety. He dragged himself around the hull until he reached the tiller. It was swinging free in the current ensuring the boat went nowhere. He stretched his arm over the stern and, grabbing the short rope designed for the purpose, he secured the tiller amidships. The strain nearly loosed his hold, but at least the boat would now go in a straight line northwards with the current. He rested, constantly dipping his head beneath the water to wash off the salt drying on the skinned flesh of his face.

He waited until nightfall before climbing back into the boat and falling asleep. He dreamt his safe dream, but only for a short period.

The vampyrus was strong now and found it easier to banish her.

Eighteen

Gazing down from the quarterdeck Hugo Locklear bleakly studied the carnage, dead rats everywhere he set his eyes along the upper deck. He felt disgusted. Abhorrence at children handling the corpses, fear for those same little ones having to dart amongst the deadly cudgels wielded in hands that were becoming more tired by the minute, repugnance at the thought of the infected fleas jumping all over their assailants. But, above all, he seethed with hatred, an acute revulsion at the aim of the Darkness to kill humanity indiscriminately, for an end that could only be surmised. What was the point of the One crossing into Life if all he found was death?

The annihilation of the vermin appeared to go as planned. On the Grim passengers and crew lined the rails, all with a variety of clubs in hand and with the scuppers blocked off to prevent escape. On the quayside, dockworkers were similarly armed and standing along the wharf, avidly watching the side of the ship for any rats that managed to reach shore by scrambling over the rails or shimmying down the hawsers.

Men, women and children moved like lightning when Thaddeus' high-pitched keening brought the rats. Black and brown rodents of all sizes rapidly boiled up from below, climbing and leaping up the stairways and over each other to reach the feet of Prince Griffin. But they didn't stay with him long; the instinct for self-preservation superseded the attraction of his call.

But as they arrived so the butchery began and they were pounded to death, most dying instantly. Later, as arms grew weary, the deaths were not quite as clean and swift and many a rat was thrown overboard with its back broken but still breathing, to drown in the murky waters of the harbour.

Thaddeus felt like a traitor. Surely his gift was not to be used in this way, for the purpose of killing animals that came to him because they trusted his call. He felt ashamed and that sentiment made him irritable and unforgiving. The others learned early on to leave him alone.

The battle went on for hours above them as Beatrix and Augusta crawled amid the stench and stagnant water in the bilges. Beattie's light caused panic amongst the rat population too distant to hear Thaddeus. Deep in the bowels of the ship they stirred and fled her brilliance in search of safety, only to find death.

But the girls were not without mishap. Unused to worming their way on all fours between decks less than half their height they inevitably suffered injury. One terrified rodent, driven from its safe haven beneath straw in the forward hold, ran over Beatrix's legs. Augusta jumped up from its path hurriedly as Beatrix screamed, leaping to her feet at the same time. Both girls cracked their heads together and for the rest of the night they nursed thumping headaches.

'Aye, well, at least your heads are still aching…those rats are dead because of the headaches they're getting,' Thaddeus said unfeelingly.

It was a good hour or so after the last rat had appeared on deck before the assailants took their rest. Some fell to the deck where they were, others managed to get to bed before falling asleep, weary to their bones and stinking of blood—that of the rats and of their own. Those on the quayside were equally weary, mostly though from pent up tension, not wanting to miss any escaping rodents. They took it in turns to remain on watch while most slept on the dock, none went home. A hard cadre led by Alexi Dambray and Dante Ernold never took their eyes from the Grim.

But it didn't stop the infection from breaking out on the wharf. People panicked when they woke and discovered several sick and dead lying amongst them.

'Oh, my God, what are we going to do?' asked Dyta weeping, cradling the head of her partner, a man who had delighted in ribald singing and bawdy humour as he clubbed the occasional rat. He had mercifully died in his sleep, the buboes huge beneath his chin.

Looking down at her tears falling on the black pustules, she cried. 'He's been in my arms all night, I never felt him going…my lovely Jem,' she said, rocking back and forth, smoothing his hair from his forehead.

'What's the betting I've got it now?' She looked up at the Grim moaning, the thought of others getting it made her heartsick. 'We can't let any of them come ashore! We're not going to stop the plague like this,' and in her despair she exclaimed. 'The ship needs burning!'

And the cry was taken up by others.

Locklear, standing on his quarterdeck, paled; though he sympathized with the plea his duty came first.

'No-one burns my ship,' he shouted, his face purpling. 'Trumper, arm the men. I want every man jack on deck now, archers and crossbows aloft.'

And the Grim's crew came racing on deck some climbing the sheets and shrouds to the spars, others spacing themselves along the rail, all facing down on the crowd of stricken Griffin islanders.

The sudden appearance of armed men on the deck of the Grim forced those on the jetty into a reciprocal show of armed aggression. One or two individuals wanting to open fire immediately were only stopped by Alexi Dambray and Dante Ernold. Others, taking cover behind crates and bales, prepared to return fire if the Grim's crew shot first. But some stayed in the open, braced ready to accept death, determined to allow no-one on the ship freedom to set foot on the wharf—prepared to kill the foreigners before breathing their last.

Thaddeus was in a quandary—these were his people on the quay, his countrymen and his responsibility to protect. And yet, here on the ship were his friends, his father—his loved ones, also now in grave danger. He stared at the frightened people on both sides, knowing their terrible fears were justified. He couldn't allow violence to erupt, yet felt powerless to stop it.

The islanders, single-minded in their purpose that the plague should not come ashore, and those on the ship equally determined that no harm should come to the ship or its crew and passengers, stared across at each other stalemated, waiting for the first bolt to be fired, the first arrow to find its mark. The crisis point was reached when Cyryl Lewyn and three of his cronies appeared from around a warehouse brandishing burning torches in their hands.

Alexi Dambray and Dante Ernold, like their prince, seemed at a loss as to what to do next. Dante knew Dyta, had lived and worked with her for years as had Alexi. Their habitual reaction in normal times would have been to support her in her demands without any hesitation, but these were not ordinary times. If blood was shed now by either side, and their prince's warnings ignored, whatever plans were in place for fighting the greater terror, the Darkness, would be gone out the window. They'd all die.

'Lewyn! Put them down, man, there's no need for them yet,' ordered Alexi, glancing at Dante who was equally adamant that no fires be set.

'Says who? They are not going to kill us. You should have listened to me yesterday and burned the ship then. If you had, my friend Jem and the others would still be alive.'

He walked forward with the others; all four had found their courage in drink otherwise they'd never have answered the Montetor leader in such a flippant manner. But opposition to Lewyn came from an unexpected quarter.

'Your friend Jem! Who are you flummoxing, you great turd...my Jem detested the sight of you,' Dyta Peche screamed, tears flowing freely down her face. 'And what's more, if he was alive now he'd never have anything to do with you. He'd throw you in the harbour and spit on you as you drowned. Don't you dare use his name for your crazy actions! Piss off, Lewyn!'

'You're deranged, woman, you don't know what you're talking about,' Lewyn said, but he hesitated afraid to come any closer to the aggressive, grieving woman. 'The plague killed him...and that's where the plague came from,' he brandished the torch at the Grim. 'I say burn it...burn it now!'

'Wait,' shouted Lodovico from on deck, distracting the quarrelling pair. 'I am the Portolan...you will listen to me. All of you,' and he stared up at Locklear including him in whatever he said next.

Thaddeus strode over, knowing his place was at his father's side; standing alongside the big man, no-one was in any doubt that Prince Griffin was supporting his father.

'Shut it, all of you, let's hear him out,' shouted Ernold over the raised voices on shore.

'Aye,' Alexi added, 'we don't want needless bloodshed.'

'Thank you, Dante, Alexi,' and the Portolan and his son walked to the head of the brow to stand deliberately between the men on the quay and those on the ship.

'If any one lets fly from here on the ship or on the wharf,' he glanced behind and up into the rigging, 'they will answer to me for disobeying my orders. I repeat...I am the Portolan and I will be obeyed. Captain Locklear you are in my port, under my jurisdiction...that is the law of the sea. You agree?'

'Aye, Excellency, but this ship and its safety is my responsibility and that is also the law of the sea.'

'Aye, Captain. Alexi, Dante, as harbourmaster I will be obeyed on the wharf, that is the law of Griffin, is that not so?'

'Aye, but not the town,' said Alexi. 'We both have jurisdiction there.'

'And I am your prince, heir to the throne of Griffin, and I hold jurisdiction over all,' Thaddeus shouted, not knowing where his courage or the proper words came from. 'You agreed to my succession only yesterday, did you not?'

Lewyn shouted. 'Not all of us agreed. It was never stated explicit! Not all of us Montetors want to be one with the Portolans, do we lads?'

'And not all of us want to be associated with you, rat-face,' a voice shouted from the back of the crowd.

'Shut it all of you! Lewyn I've had enough of you,' snarled Alexi. 'You do not speak for me…but I do speak for you. Not another word do I want to hear from you…not another word. Do you understand, shit brain?'

Everyone standing between them broke apart leaving an open space between the Montetor leader of the dockworkers and the Montetor troublemaker. Alexi was livid, the veins standing out on his neck. Only once before had anyone seen Dambray lose his temper and three men lay dead not long after.

'Drop those torches…now!'

And with no second thoughts Lewyn and his cronies complied and four flaming torches were doused with water.

Alexi turned back to speak to his prince, but as he did so Dante Ernold strode over and stood silently not two feet from him, studying closely his adversary of twenty years. Everyone waited with bated breath not knowing what this heralded.

And suddenly Ernold grinned and held out his hand to be gripped in turn by an equally grinning Dambray. They both looked up at Thaddeus.

'Aye, Highness,' Dante said, 'we all agree that you will become our first King of Griffin and that the clans are to become one. We salute you.'

And Alexi, grinning wide, called to the man behind him. 'Is that explicit enough for you, Lewyn, you dog breath?'

Cyryl Lewyn looked around at those near him and finding no tangible support walked away, seething and vowing vengeance. Mumbling very quietly to his three cohorts he, his tortoiseshell cat back on his shoulders – now there was no naked flame near – disappeared the way they had come.

The shape-shifter, hiding in the shadows of a warehouse not far from Lewyn, watched the cat clinging to Lewyn's shirt. It had heard every word spoken on the wharf but had not understood half of what was meant. But it did comprehend emotion. And the raw fear expressed amongst the humans pleased it. Still in its rat structure it was desperately looking for a new shape, this one no longer tenable, but it needed to touch a figure to copy it. It instinctively shied away from the humans; in its present form any human would kill it as soon as it was sighted.

But it fancied the cat—and its ride.

Thaddeus swallowed, for one moment he thought nervousness was going to make him sick, but then he grinned down at the two leaders on the wharf and instinctively bowed from the waist.

'And I am proud and honoured to be your prince…cousins.' He smiled even wider, his grin infectious as the mood of the crowd shifted from one of pure desperation to one of hope. 'Please…all of you, heed the Portolan…I am also very proud and honoured to be his son.'

And Lodovico Portolan, overcome with love and pride, couldn't halt the tears flowing…and the people understood. And perhaps it was his tears, and the respect shown to the dockworkers by the prince, that averted tragedy.

Behind Thaddeus, Augusta stared wide-eyed at his back. His regal manner and his intuitive obeisance to the dockworkers' leaders had astonished her. His behaviour was demonstrably unforced and she wondered what this heralded in their future relationship—both heirs to thrones. Thaddeus may not have experienced much of life, she thought, but his natural instincts for reading people had not failed him. She was very proud of her friend. Turning to Beatrix she found her friend weeping tears of pleasure, her hands to her mouth.

'Clan Portolan, Clan Montetor…Griffins…listen to me, there is no plague on the Grim. We have all worked hard to rid the ship of the disease, burning it now, or preventing anyone disembarking, will not make a blind bit of difference to those on shore,' Lodovico said.

'No, but we need to be sure, Excellency,' a rough voice interrupted.

'Jonas, I recognize your voice, come here.'

A bulky man, a belaying pin at his side, came forward and stood resolutely in front of the crowd of dockworkers staring up at his liege lord.

Portolan examined the man's face. 'Jonas, you know me. Do you trust me?'

'Aye, Excellency, you've no need to ask that,' he answered, affronted by the question.

'You think we should burn this ship and everyone on it to stop the plague spreading?'

'Well, everyone knows that fire kills the disease.'

'So it does. Are you going to burn me?' Portolan stared unblinking into the man's eyes.

'What! I can't do that,' Jonas said shocked to the core.

'Why not?'

'You are my chief, the Portolan!' Jonas said, spluttering with anxiety. 'Please, Excellency, be serious.'

'I am, Jonas, I am very serious,' and he turned to the crowd. 'Are any of you, Portolan or Montetor, going to kill me? Are any of you going to burn my son, your prince?' Portolan stepped to the side and stared into the crowd. 'Are you, Dado Cambar?' He called to the middle-aged dockworker standing in the second row. When Cambar shook his head and looked away guiltily, Portolan walked along the rail in front of them all, catching the occasional eye and asking the same question. He returned to stand at the head of the brow.

'Well, if none of you are going to kill me, or Thaddeus, and you believe the plague is still onboard, what is stopping us carrying the disease when we come ashore for you to burn the ship?' Consternation spread swiftly among those listening and no-one missed the Portolan's words.

Thaddeus interrupted. 'Cousins, friends, please heed me when I say that all those who caught the plague on the Grim were healed by Lord Aidan. No-one here is sick or carries the foul disease and you've seen for yourself there are no more rats aboard this ship.'

Lodovico put his hand on his son's shoulder. 'There is more that you all seem to have forgotten. The Montetor, Marshal Janne and Leonid of the Green People have sailed on this ship and all have been ashore since we docked yesterday, as have the First Mate and a squad of sailors. It is unfortunate, but we did not know of the plague before they disembarked and they may very well be carriers. There is nothing we can do for them at present, but as soon as we catch up with them Lord Aidan will administer healing and we will search out all with whom they have come in contact.' He turned quickly and glanced at

Aidan, feeling guilty at putting the young wizard under so much pressure.

Aidan shrugged. 'That goes without saying, Excellency. But there is something I can do immediately…I can check these good people on the quay. With their permission I will go ashore.'

'But how about those who may have caught it in the Town, Lord Aidan, can you heal them?' Dyta Peche shouted over the audible sigh of relief at his words.

'What say you, my Lord Aidan? Can you heal the townspeople of the plague?' Portolan stared at the young wizard who had rescued Thaddeus. He greatly wished that he didn't have to ask him; Aidan was desperately in need of rest himself, he looked as white as death. Was he expecting too much of the boy? But, of course, Aidan was no longer a boy.

Aidan studied the faces staring up at him, these frightened people, scared witless for their families and themselves. Aidan sighed, thinking of Gregory—it seemed that this disease sent men mad before killing them. If the plague spread too far, healing them all would be an impossible job, a mammoth task. It would require reserves of energy far greater than he had and take up time that he could not spare.

Even now Tragen was trapped, probably in utter degradation and despair, lost, unable to find escape—waiting for Aidan to find him. For Tragen knew that his boy would never stop searching for him. Tragen was Aidan's priority, not these people. Yet he could not abandon them to this most horrible of deaths. Perhaps discarding the islanders, leaving them to their misery, was part of what the Darkness wished.

Aidan moved to the rail. 'You realize, don't you, the plague will be brought ashore elsewhere by others fleeing the Darkness?'
Alexi nodded, along with others. 'We know, Milord, we can only ask you to do as much as you can.'

'Good, because healing takes a lot of stamina, energy that I can ill afford to lose,' he stared at them through sunken, dark eyes. 'But I will heal as many as I can today, for this night I must rest. I have something of the utmost urgency to do tomorrow morning. Those of you that are not ill should flee the island, get well away from here, those who can't will find shelter in Bylani below the catacombs,' again there was consternation and he was interrupted.

'We must pass through the Devil's Keep, Milord, we'll never return,' shouted Ivan Blouet from the back of the crowd.

'The Devils Keep is just a name fostered to keep people away, keep Bylani secret while the Green People constructed the haven. There is no devil…there never has been,' said Prince Griffin.

'What happened to the ones who disappeared then?' asked Dyta.

'They were given a safe life in Bylani, but couldn't be allowed to return for fear of divulging its existence,' Augusta replied.

'And the Green People have built a truly wonderful place in which to live,' Beatrix smiled widely, her eyes glinting. 'It is beautiful and magical, there are homes and work for everyone and safe places for your children to play. There are forests and orchards, a river for swimming and fishing, farms… everything you will need to survive. You will never believe you are deep underground, it is vast. There is no need to fear.'

'But it is not large enough to take everyone on the islands. Most of you must sail away and return when we have banished the Darkness,' Thaddeus added, eager that his last words give encouragement to the doubters, hoping that they wouldn't detect his ignorance of how he was to stop the devastating weapon of a God.

And Dyta, premonition playing hell with her, asked another question that sent shivers up the back of everyone listening. 'Highness, is there something else that we should know about, I mean, this God has given us the plague, is there anything else the damned Darkness might have sent?'

'Dear God, Dyta, that doesn't bear thinking about,' Thaddeus said, losing colour.

Aidan broke the appalling silence 'I will need you to search the town and bring to the quay all those you believe are ill and I will heal them here. But go quickly; if there are too many, then I am not going to be able to help the last who arrive.'

'Aye, Milord,' said Dante turning to the crowd. 'You heard him, leave once Lord Aidan has checked you and fetch the sick here.'

'And as you go around,' Alexi added, 'tell the people they must evacuate Griffin Island immediately. Tell them they must sail far away to protect their families. They are to take what they can carry in their boats and give aid to neighbours who have no means to sail away. Don't forget what I said…I mean anyone, we are one people now. They are to return only when the Darkness has left these shores.'

'Move away, you men, let the healer at the sick,' ordered Dante waving his arms at those around Dyta and the bodies on the wharf, two of which were already dead, four others quite likely to succumb.

It followed Lewyn until he entered a tavern in the street behind the dock. As soon as he was settled at a table with his mates, drinking rot-gut ale and scheming, the shape-shifter called the cat. The animal hearing the voice in its head perked up its ears and jumped down from its master's shoulders. It walked out the door, looking around it perceived what it thought to be an ordinary rat at the corner almost hidden in the shade, and it salivated. The shape-shifter, despite its danger of being seen by the humans, played with the tortoiseshell for long minutes before it allowed the cat to catch it.

Later, Dyta having laid her man wrapped in canvas on the boards, walked over to a nearby tavern to fetch a jug of ale. On her way she stumbled over Cyryl Lewyn's cat lying dead in the road and fell against Augusta standing close by, nearly knocking her over. Dyta kicked the scruffy animal into the gutter.

'Sorry Highness! Bloody thing, I could have sworn that cat was around Cyryl's shoulders when he ran off. Did you see it?'

'No, I'm sorry, all I saw was that man's shifty eyes and the way he sneered at everyone,' Augusta shuddered. 'Horrible looking thing isn't it?

'Like its master,' Dyta laughed.

Augusta giggled. She'd had a tortoiseshell once, they seemed very unlucky cats. Hers had chased a mouse right over the battlements of the castle and forgot to stop until it hit the ground. Her father wouldn't let her see it to bury it.

Aidan was again sleeping, this time on the coach seat facing Beatrix and Thaddeus, lying down his head in Augusta's lap. Augusta had her arm across his chest doing her best to stop him sliding to the floor. It was dusk and they were finally on their way to the manorhouse, hopefully to have a few hours rest before setting off after Tragen.

Augusta studied Aidan anxiously. It seemed that these days all he did was heal and sleep…and worry himself sick over Tragen. He had healed the four sick dockworkers right away and had discovered another two, all within minutes of disembarking the Grim. Examining close on a hundred more on the wharf he had found three others

153

infected. But the sick had trickled down on to the quay all day from the town, some brought on stretchers, others walking. But not all were suffering the plague. Aidan found himself healing all kinds of maladies from colds to chicken pox, broken arms, cuts and bruises. And it was not in him to turn anyone away—he'd done enough of that on Sanctity.

In the end it was Alexi and Dante – seeing the deterioration in Aidan's condition – that separated out the not so serious cases. But Aidan was still totally exhausted when they eventually departed the quay.

Augusta wondered how he could sleep on the bouncing seat. The coach rattled its way over the cobbles of the winding roads through Griffin Town heading for the high promontory and Thaddeus' home. She tenderly brushed the hair out of his eyes and worried. Aidan was not just white, he was ashen…pale beyond belief. He'd been that exhausted Alexi had had to lift him into the coach; Aidan hadn't the strength to stand or lift his arms.

Anders, watching Aidan accept people's gratitude, breathed a sigh of relief. At one time Aidan could not cope with people thanking him…their appreciation always made him feel guilty. He had the absurd notion that sick people made him happy because of the pleasure he received from healing. Anders smiled…finally an end to silly tantrums. And he sat at the Wall watching and eternally whittling sticks that bore a vague resemblance to bells.

'How are we going to enter Limbo tonight with him in this state?' Augusta asked of no-one in particular.

'Is there any way we know of to keep him sleeping?' asked Thaddeus.

'Good God, Thaddeus, we dare not! Even if we knew of a spell we could use, he'd never forgive us. Can you imagine what he'd be like if we kept him from Tragen tonight and then tomorrow night we discovered that for want of an hour we could have saved Tragen's life? No, no we cannot, not without asking him first,' Beatrix sighed.

It was at that moment the coach was rattled by something thrown at it. The next minute a stone came hurtling through the open window in the coach door. It landed with an audible thump against Thaddeus' leg.

'Ow! What the hell,' Thaddeus shouted, bending down instinctively to rub at his shin.

Shouting erupted in the roadway right outside and the coach abruptly came to a halt when the coachman cried out and fell from his seat. Peering out the windows in both doors they found they were in the middle of a riot.

Augusta bent forward to look closely at a face she glimpsed in a shop doorway and she recognized Cyryl Lewyn. He was standing behind a crowd of townsfolk urging them on to hurl abuse and missiles at the coach.

'Don't Augusta, for Gods' sake stay back, any of those stones can kill us,' said Beatrix frightened out of her wits. She'd never been the brunt of anyone's aggression before, not counting the terror of Sanctity, of course, but that had been something entirely different to this.

Thaddeus pulled up the shutter closing his window whilst Augusta did the other. Shutting out the sight of the rioters didn't stop the attack and suddenly the carriage was shaking from side to side, nearly toppling over as the driverless horses panicked and screamed in terror in the narrow road.

Lewyn had ambushed them very efficiently. Seeing no guard accompanying the coach – it not entering anyone's head that they were in danger from the residents of Griffin Town – Lewyn and his cronies had run ahead of it and had quickly organised a rabble to attack in one of the darkest lanes in the town. Lewyn smirked and watched his handiwork. These youngsters had humiliated him and they weren't going to get away with it. To gain his revenge he'd travelled the taverns recruiting, with his lies, the dissatisfied, depressed and drunken lowlife inhabiting such places.

Aidan, still sleeping, cracked his head against the wall of the lurching carriage. Augusta, unable to hold his weight, watched as he slid to the floor unconscious.

'Aidan…Aidan, you all right? Answer me,' shouted Augusta, frantically. She dropped to the floor and sat beside him cradling his head in her arms.

'Leave him Augusta, I think he's only been knocked out. It doesn't look serious, he's safer lying on the floor,' said Thaddeus. 'Come on, we've got to stop these people.'

'I'll stop them,' Augusta said menacingly, 'the fools, idiots— don't they realize who they're up against. Thaddeus open that window,' she ordered as she opened hers. 'Beatrix your light…dazzle them!'

And that's what she did. Her light poured from the coach as Thaddeus and Augusta then flung open the doors. The stone throwing ceased as suddenly as it had begun, so did the shouting. The drunken rioters stood in amazement in a road that was now bathed in a light brighter than the sun at noon. The last thing they expected to see was a blindingly bright radiance pouring out at them and they immediately shielded their eyes from the glare. Augusta, smiling grimly, lifted the cobbles in the road and the rioters fell to the ground as the stones were pulled from beneath their feet. She raised the differently sized rocks above the heads of the aggressors and then dropped them. Men, and the occasional woman, were knocked senseless where they sat.

Cyryl Lewyn, sheltering in his doorway, took the hint…and the easy way out. He ran through the shop and out the back. He disappeared deeper into the town chased by his irate accomplices, none of whom had realized they were attacking wizards. Lewyn, his cat draped around his neck sneezing uncontrollably – the shape-shifter hated the cat's long hair – never looked back.

But the dazzling light, the cobblestones dropping from mid-air and the frantic yells of the rioters terrified the horses even more and they stampeded. Trampling all in their way, the coach nearly overturned again as its wheels bounded from the road surface.

'Thaddeus, stop them!' Beatrix screamed.

'I will, I will, don't worry, let's just get far enough from here first,' he said, laughter bubbling from him.

'What are you laughing at you…you, stop this coach now we'll be killed!' Augusta shouted frightened out of her wits, the horses running in the narrow streets scared her more than the rioters had. And Thaddeus calming down, complied a moment later as the coach turned a second corner. He was finding it easy now to connect with and control any animals, and the horses halted their flight of terror, and stood panting and sweating in the road.

'Dear God, those fools still blame us for the plague,' Augusta moaned as she again dropped to the floor to cradle Aidan's head.

'I don't know…they looked drunk to me, perhaps that Cyryl never told them the truth,' Beatrix said.

'Aye, you may be right, but I think our major problem has been solved…at least for tonight,' Thaddeus said looking down at Aidan.

'What's that?' asked Beatrix.

'I think that knock on the head is going to keep him out for a while, and when he does come round even he'll see he's in no fit state to be entering Limbo tonight,' he couldn't keep the relief from his voice.

'What in hell's going on here?' a gruff voice shouted from outside.

'That's Bazyli,' said Thaddeus. And the Montetor arrived at the open door, peering in he repeated his question.

'Well, my friends,' he stared in at the suddenly silent foursome, 'is anyone going to tell me,' and then noticing Aidan lying on the floor of the coach, a lump the size of an egg forming on his forehead, he paled. 'Dear God, what happened?'

So they told him.

Nineteen

It was the dead of night, that hour when man is at his lowest ebb, if awake he desperately needs to sleep, if asleep he fights off awareness in his dreams.

Leash lay once more on the bottom boards of the fishing boat attempting and failing to find ease for his hurts. He was one massive pain. He couldn't think clearly around the blinding agony. Even his soul hurt. All his skin burned, whether it was exposed to the sun or not, the blisters crept beneath the frayed cuffs of his britches, the torn sleeves of his shirt. There was no original skin growth left on his chest, that and the curly blond hair had burnt away. New blisters, large and small had formed, the pustules rupturing raggedly with jagged bits of skin hanging loose to irritate him even more. In his delirium he had picked at the fronds and the flesh beneath had burnt again.

The only relief from the excruciating pain of sunburn was to suffer even more pain immersed in the ocean. Unconsciously he had formed a routine, fifteen minutes in the boat and an hour in the sea clinging to the gunnels of Marcus' fishing boat, changing hands constantly so that each hand burned at an equal rate.

It was his demon that fought to keep him alive, to give him time to find fresh water when dehydration forced him to drink the sea. His kidneys found it increasingly difficult to expel the salt from his body—he had to urinate more fluid than he drank, causing greater dehydration.

But all the time the boat drifted northwards and this is what saved him in the end. For eventually it encountered the edge of Zorzecai's storm and was blown at a faster pace along its western edge. And the violence of the stormy waters brought a blessed relief as it was also pouring with rain. The freshwater deluge soothed his body's burns, slaking his thirst and salvaging his sanity.

He slept fitfully and dreamt—or thought he dreamt.

But it was not his safe dream that consumed his mind, for she had disappeared into the far, deep reaches of his utter confusion, his pain. The demon blocked her out. But he was a hairsbreadth away from death and perhaps that is why the vampyrus felt so close to Leash.

'Who is she, Leash?' the demon asked.

The vampyrus instinctively knew she was an enemy in the other world, the afterlife. He grimaced, well used to having enemies, for every living being in this world was a foe—in the Afterlife, the dead were. He was puzzled; the woman was not a demon out of Purgatory. No, but anomalies of this magnitude seriously worried him. In all the hosts he had infested over his millennia-long existence, not once had he ever encountered anything like this, and he didn't like it, not one little bit. Ignorance had unknown consequences for his survival.

She had not always been with him in Leash, just the last decade and a half. For the first five years Leash's lover had helped fight off his influence. He pursed Leash's lips as he wondered why this one bothered with the man. Was she the same woman? What was she looking for? He had never been able to discover her identity in all these last years. But he had hopes now he was stronger, far too strong for her.

But Leash was weak, dangerously fragile, nigh to dying. The vampyrus needed to exercise extreme caution or it was the end of them both. He didn't like to think what would happen then. Surely she wouldn't follow Leash into Purgatory? All the same, her feeble attempts to keep in contact with Leash only fuelled the demon's contempt. He laughed at her, but he could not see her or speak with her—and that's what also made him fear her. She wouldn't allow either.

'Who is she, Leash?' he repeated, his innate curiosity getting the better of him.

'Who?'

'That woman…the one you speak to.'

Leash licked his healing lips, feeling the cracks closing. 'If I tell you then you will share her with me. I will not share her with anyone…except…' and he closed off his thoughts.

'Except?'

'Keep out of it, demon!'

'She's dead, yet not a demon or one of your Gods. How come she still talks to you?'

Leash ignored him.

'Why does she want to protect you?'

The question puzzled Leash. 'Does she?' he asked, the question surprising him meant that he could no longer shut out his demon's voice.

'You know she does, she fights me. Was she your lover?' he asked curiously.

'What do you know of love?' Leash asked contemptuously. 'You are an evil, unlovable creature.'

'You'd be surprised, I have experienced it. Even the Gods love, you know.' He'd only ever had one lover, but that had been so long ago he'd forgotten what she looked and sounded like, but he did remember her touch. And he still lived with the consequences of that love. 'And who do you think you are calling evil? I am not!'

'Don't be an idiot, of course you are.'

'You love name-calling don't you? I'm an idiot as well, am I? Well who's the one keeping you alive, hey? This idiot is who. Now tell me who she is.'

'Never…I told you, keep out of it. You may have corrupted me, you will not corrupt her.'

'Ah, well, it matters not. You are mine and whoever she is, she cannot help you now.' The vampyrus laughed easily and, with only a little trepidation, put her to the back of his mind.

He contemplated the results of his efforts to keep his host alive. His worries fading now, Leash's death would have meant a forced re-acquaintanceship with Purgatory. But that potentially dreadful fate had now receded well into the future, and would stay there as long as Leash survived. Throughout most of the long years of his existence the demon had managed to stay out of the reach of the God who ruled that fell place. With all the loathing his demented soul possessed he hated that God. But he worried, even demons could be subjected to torture and torment and oblivion. And the God wanted to make him suffer for eternity—would never let him attain oblivion; never allow him to escape again. The God wanted vengeance and would never forgive him for what he had done.

The vampyrus trembled. He had to cling to this body for Leash was his last chance to remain free. The indisputable laws of existence dictated that he was only allowed so many different hosts before he was compelled to pay homage to his God. To exist in Life the demon needed his deity to renew his ability to seek hosts—and his God hated him.

And because of the accident which forced the early transfer from his previous host into Leash's body, the vampyrus had no option but to keep the helmsman alive. Leash, being the last host, increased the almost insurmountable pressure on the demon to ensure the man's survival.

Leash interrupted the demon's morose thoughts. 'Who are you?'

'I am your demon…you know that.'

'Yes…but what is your name? If I am to share my body I'd like to know who with.'

The vampyrus laughed. 'What do you mean "if"? You have no choice! I am with you until you die or until I decide to leave.'

'Then tell me your name. Or are you afraid?'

'Afraid…of you? Never…you may name me Saviour, after all I just saved your life.'

'Saviour? No, you have condemned me to a living hell. I want your real name, or are you so insignificant in the scheme of life that you deserve no name?'

The demon bristled. 'Insignificant…you dare to call me such.'

'Then give me your name.'

'If I tell you, you must never speak it aloud.'

'Come off it, why ask? You can stop me speaking before I form the words. Why can't I say it aloud anyway?'

'Never you mind—just don't! You agree?'

'Yes…yes, just tell me.'

'All right. It's Balar! Happy now?'

'Happy? Don't be absurd. What does your name mean?'

'Persistence…what does your name mean?' he asked, again curiosity getting the better of him.

'Leash? Ah, Balar, a leash is a tether, a means of holding an animal prisoner unable to escape…the one tethered unable to attain freedom. Apt, don't you think?'

'Fool…you don't hold me prisoner; I can leave at any time I wish.'

'Then leave me now, if you can.'

'I've got used to you, I'm happy here, besides I require another host before I leave you…and as we are alone where am I going to find one,' Balar said feeling uncomfortable at the direction of the conversation.

'What if I commit suicide…kill myself? What happens to you then?'

'I won't allow you to.'

'No? Then satisfy my curiosity. There can be no harm in that for you, can there? What happens to you if I die before you find another host?'

'I would return to Purgatory.' He nearly told him that he'd never be allowed another host.

'Your home, hey. Wouldn't you like that, I mean, go home for a rest?'

'Believe me, it would be no rest.'

'Why?'

'The God and I do not see eye to eye.'

'The God? Who is he?'

'Never mind, he is someone no-one should ever meet…not ever. Leave me be.' Balar closed his mind, talk of the God always scared him, for his name must also never be spoken aloud—his God would hear. He'd fantasized on many occasions about reaping revenge, a useless pastime as most fantasies were. Besides he didn't like the analogy of a leash and him.

'Ah, my turn to nag, Balar…upset him, have you?'

'Who?'

Leash laughed for the first time in years. 'You know who…your God. Did that other demon know him?'

'What other demon?'

'The one I killed on Sanctity, notice I said me not you—the one you hid from.'

'Who said I was hiding from anyone?' Balar licked his surreal lips, his mouth suddenly dry.

'Come off it, you were so deep in my bowels I could have shit you!'

'No need to be crude, go to sleep.'

'Tell me first, did he know your God? Who…wait a minute,' Leash smiled, 'He knew you, didn't he? That's it…Zorzecai knew you, that's the reason you hid. What have you done, Balar, what have you done?'

'Go to sleep Leash…now!'

And Leash did.

It was later in the afternoon that Leash woke and managed to regain Balar's attention. Not that it wasn't too difficult, Balar hated being alone. Leash turned over in the boat for the rain to fall on his back to cleanse any residue of salt clinging to his bare skin. The freshwater brought immense ease, but it still left him with a pounding headache.

'Balar, how long did you infest your previous host?'

'I don't measure time as you humans do, but I suppose in your reckoning it would be about three or four years.'

'You've possessed me for twenty years...that's not fair! Why did you leave him after such a short time, was he dead?'

'He was in the very best of health when I transferred to you.'

'Then why did you come to me?'

'I don't know, as it happens,' Balar paused, not liking the question.

It was true he had no idea at all why he'd left his previous host and thinking back on it made him anxious. He hadn't done anything out of the ordinary but couldn't remember what it was that he had done. He'd always been the one to make the conscious choice of a new host and always the previous host had died.

So why hadn't either happened this time?

'And I don't suppose you're going to tell me why you were so scared of that herdsman, either.'

'Go to sleep, Leash!' Balar roared.

Twenty

Elstan, threading his way between the tables with boots and stockings tucked under his arm, left the bar of the Vixen's Haven with mixed feelings. Elated to have succeeded in so short a time in obtaining adequate footwear for Chong-An, it was tinged with the distinct feeling he had made a serious error in judgement. He should have bargained harder for appearances sake, got more from the merchant although no more was needed. He'd left the man crowing over those slippers and like all merchants he was garrulous, unable to keep a good deal secret once completed. Transactions were a merchant's lifeblood and the salt merchant had just made the deal of his life. He'd be telling everyone now of the stupid man travelling in the company of an oriental fat man, trading jewelled slippers worth half a year's income for a pair of old boots and stockings. They must have been desperate, he'd be saying.

And it would be the desperation that would register with Brenin and his deputy, Drudwynn, not the bragging of the salt merchant.

Elstan hurried across the yard, impatient with himself because he had allowed the oriental's words to rattle him, for if he hadn't have been then he'd never have made the mistake. He entered the rear of the stables. Full dark was nearly upon them, but locating the sorcerer was no problem…he followed the smell. Chong-An had plastered his feet in Elstan's sweetly scented unguent and the aroma wafted across the central aisle, overpowering the stench of horse sweat and dung in the other stalls.

'Dear God, how much of that have you used? The Guild will be able to track us from leagues behind just by sniffing,' Elstan said irritably.

'My dear man, my feet are in desperate need of a healer, as there is no chance of finding one in the Wolfshead tonight, I thought I'd administer a double measure immediately, to save us having to halt in the woods before daylight. I take it we do intend travelling through the night?'

'Aye, we'll have to. I don't like being this close to Brenin. Here, I managed to get stockings as well. Hurry up.'

'Ah!' Chong groaned moments later, 'my feet feel better already,' he wiggled his toes in the silk. 'I feel almost human again.'

'Well you'll be a dead human before long if we don't move. Drudwynn was coming down the stairs into the bar as I left. Your magus has taken a room for the night, which gives us time to get well away from here. But,' and he paused, tugging at his nose, 'there's something up with the deputy now, and I might be the cause.'

'Tell me.'

'Well, he seemed all right coming down the stairs, but I took a quick look at him as I came out the door and his face was manic when he got to the bottom.'

'Why would you be the cause of that?'

'Well,' and he cleared his throat guiltily, 'coming down those stairs he had line of sight with the merchant I left your slippers with. He could well have seen them.'

'Elstan,' Chong-An said turning puce at the thought of what Drudwynn would do to him, 'Elstan, please, do not refer to Brenin as "my magus". He is not mine. I have now severed all links with that organisation. Must I remind you that I will be killed by anyone in that order? Moreover, the sorcerer who takes my life will be rewarded handsomely.'

'Then bloody well stand up and get out of that stall, we're wasting time babbling!'

The Chancellor of Mantovar's agent, accompanied by the ex-librarian of the Guild of the Brethren of Wisdom rapidly departed the stables. Creeping around the back of the building, bypassing a large tump of horse manure, they came up against the boundary fence. They followed the pinewood rails until they reached the lower slopes of the Wolfshead. At first the going underfoot was easy; the landlord of the Vixen's Haven had cleared the ground to use as grazing for horses, cattle and sheep belonging to his customers. But as they left the paddocks and entered the woods, so the terrain changed from fairly flat field to that of hidden rocks, and tussocks grown by a mischievous sprite of nature to purposely twist ankles.

Elstan led the way, slowing his pace to allow for the overweight wizard to keep up. Chong was taking care; his feet were hurting, but not nearly as much as they had been. But he knew that eventually the pain would return and the chances were, trudging over this ground, it would be sooner rather than later. The aching would become unbearable forcing him to rest when he should be moving. He coped by remembering who was behind him, for it wouldn't take long for Brenin to organize a hunting party.

Elstan reached a small rise, the grass underfoot partially hidden by a screening of pine needles, a relatively springy surface for Chong's feet. He stared down the hillside at the rear of the Vixen's Haven; lamplight showing brightly in several of the upper rooms and from the open kitchen door. When Chong reached him he cautioned the wizard to remain silent and he cocked his head listening for signs of pursuit.

But all he heard was the harsh crying of the nutcracker searching for berries before night fell completely, larks singing unconcernedly and owls hooting in their nocturnal quest for small rodents. Relieved, he looked up at the night sky and watched as bats flew across the moon.

And he winced. Bats recalled harsh memories of a tragedy that need never have happened. If only he and his brothers had listened and obeyed the Elders.

In the undergrowth, a little way ahead, he heard the high-pitched howling of a lynx and the mad scrambling of mountain hares escaping. As they ascended higher into the mountains they'd quite likely come across brown bears and packs of wolves hunting anything that moved. They'd need to be on their guard. But fleeing hastily from the Vixen's Haven meant that Elstan's hunting skills would be called on sooner rather than later. They had nowhere near sufficient provisions for a journey into the Drikander, let alone enough to get to Abferkarn.

Again Elstan listened intently his head to one side, the night sounds were all they should be. Unless the Guild had followers that could float over the ground and pass silently through trees, they were safe until the morning. But he had the distinct feeling he was being watched and kept glancing around nervously. The hairs on the nape of his neck were standing on end, a sure sign he was in someone's line of sight. He halted, and for many minutes while Chong-An waited and watched him, he studied the rear windows of the inn. Finding no sign of anyone looking his way, he turned and resumed his climb into the Wolfshead.

The magus did not need a window to look through in order to see the fugitives. He sat in the only chair in his room, facing the window but back from it and he had his eyes closed. Barely holding his temper he cast around for the oriental.

166

Brother Drudwynn stood to one side, perspiration dripping from his face, and not because he was hot. He had returned from the bar carrying Chong's slippers. Glancing down into the bar from the stairs he had espied that which he should not have. Elstan had been correct in his surmising. His face purpling with rage, he had rushed across the crowded room up to the foolish man gloating and caressing the footwear on the table top in front of him.

Lost in rapture the merchant had suddenly become aware that someone was standing over him. Looking up, he'd recognized Brenin's deputy staring wide-eyed at the slippers. Drudwynn, his face fit to bursting a blood vessel, confiscated them leaving the merchant in absolute terror after being questioned harshly.

Drudwynn, quaking with fear, returned to his master. He stood behind him afraid to breathe awaiting his fate, bemoaning the fact he hadn't killed the librarian when he'd had the chance. As for the slippers he'd had no choice, he daren't hide them, daren't conceal the fact that the oriental was loose and making his way north. He contemplated keeping the knowledge from Brenin, but only for the barest of moments, fear made him disclose the information immediately. The consequences of his master discovering his complicity in the escape of the librarian, for his silence would be construed as such, did not bear thinking about. He had no option and stood waiting now, desperately hoping Brenin would not decide on the ultimate penalty for maybe placing his plans in jeopardy.

Brenin cast his mind wide as he gripped the oriental's slippers tightly in his hands. It was always easier to locate a quarry if you held an item belonging to that person. It wasn't long before he found Chong-An and his companion trudging up the hillside through the trees.

Brenin seethed, his manner distant he dripped ice into the room, enveloping his deputy in quaking terror. As he watched the two fugitives climbing into the Wolfshead his thoughts turned on Drudwynn. Like all common men, the man had succumbed to stupidity, lack of foresight. He now had to pay for the consequences of his failure to act—he had become dispensable. Chong-An should be dead, should have been killed days ago. Brenin had warned Drudwynn of the penalty.

But circumstances had forced a change. Chong-An now had to be taken alive and interrogated rigorously, for the oriental would not have disobeyed his curfew without good reason. And that motive had to be ascertained. If Chong had information concerning Brenin's plans then the magus needed to know exactly what it was and if he'd passed it on to anyone…maybe to the man leading him up the mountain.

'Who is the man with Chong?' Brenin asked menacingly as he watched the overweight adept struggling up the mountainside. He could not keep the venom from his voice; Drudwynn had placed Brenin at risk and that could never be allowed to happen again.

'I'm sorry, Master, the merchant did not know him, had never seen him before, but he does believe the man to be extremely violent…as most are these days. The merchant described a profusion of weapons about him, more than was needed by an ordinary hunter. He could possibly be a mercenary,' Drudwynn swallowed hard. 'There was one other thing he mentioned,' and he paused, his throat choking on the words, instinctively knowing that it was going to be received badly.

'Well, have I to guess?' Brenin sneered.

'Sorry, Master…the man had a northern accent.'

Brenin sat up straight and turning to his aide he opened his eyes, suddenly anxious. 'How far north?'

'He seemed to recognize the accent of Mantovar.'

'For your sake, he'd better not be from there,' Brenin snarled and then he tensed. If the man was a Mantovarian he could only be…

'You are a fool, Drudwynn, an utter idiot, a cretin. You have failed me and botched your task of securing my back,' he rasped hoarsely.

'Master! I don't understand, why should a man of Mantovar give you concern. We get a few of them here every year and…oh, my God,' his voice trailed away, all at once he found he could not swallow, paling he stared petrified at the leader of the Order.

'Ah! You realize now the identity of the man?'

'The Fly! Dear God, Master, I had no idea…'

'What I didn't want was a meeting between these two but it has now come to pass, cretin, the oriental and Sevenoaks' agent have joined forces. There is only one summation that I can reach…both men know of my plans,' he raged. 'You are a bumbling idiot, Drudwynn, you had better rectify matters immediately or I will delight in putting out your eyes with a spoon and making you eat them.'

Brenin sat back in the chair and, closing his eyes, he again resumed his scrutiny of the two men wending their way up through the woods. He concentrated on the Fly, the stranger leading the slow

168

walking librarian. Brenin could make out nothing of the man except that he was not tall, his hood was raised over his head and he was dressed all in black.

'You will follow them, Drudwynn, they are heading into the Wolfshead but I've a feeling they are making for Abferkarn through the Drikander. Their destination could not possibly be elsewhere. You are fortunate Chong-An is walking slowly, he must be having trouble with his feet again,' he sneered. 'Send a messenger now to the Tower for guards to accompany you, and for Brother Edmund to aid me.'

Drudwynn's stomach turned over, if he needed confirmation that he had made a mistake, the name of his rival within the Guild was it. He'd be lucky to hang on to his life let alone to his ranking within the Guild.

'Yes, Master, you can depend on me,' he said, nearly urinating in fright. 'I will kill them both.'

'No, you fool,' Brenin screamed, 'I need information,' and Drudwynn fell back, his terror nearly making him wet himself. Brenin breathed heavily, taking a moment to regain his composure. 'The men you send for should all be here by dawn. Take a sufficient number with you and follow Chong and the Fly into the mountains. When you come up with them, bring both to me and they had both better be able to speak when they are before me. I don't care what physical shape they're in, you can do what you like to them. But I must be able to interrogate both. Edmund and I will travel by road to meet those I must on the way. Bring them to me in Mulkie's Cross…or else! Go!'

Chong-An trudged along, glancing up from searching the ground for an easy pathway, to stare at his companion's back. Though he was of slight build Elstan's physique had been well nurtured over the years, there was not an ounce of fat on him. His way of life demanded it.

The oriental chewed his bottom lip and watched the Mantovarian striding powerfully along. He was very well armed—a crossbow slung over his shoulder, his sword in its scuffed scabbard hanging from his black baldric, a small axe in the belt at his waist and various knives in another belt across his chest. The whole served to instil a wary confidence in Chong-An. Confidence because this man, his hands never very far from a weapon, was obviously capable of handling himself well in any conflict. Wary because the man did not trust easily and he was yet to accept Chong as his ally though he was prepared to accompany him north to Abferkarn. But Chong needed him to travel even farther north.

The oriental was anxious. After countless years of study, leagues upon leagues of travelling interviewing numberless scholars and indigents, he now believed he was on the verge of discovering the meaning of his long life. This man of action, man of Mantovar on a perilous mission of his own, was going to lead him to it. The prophecies implied as much, if he hadn't misread the portents. Now all he needed to do was work out what the rest of the cryptic statements meant. Why were all prophecies written in a manner that could be so easily misconstrued? What was this Darkness that Cumbria had mentioned? Was it the shadow mentioned in two of the prophecies? He was convinced now that he and Elstan figured largely in both of them and, if it was true, then why not in the other divinations he had discovered.

The problem was he needed someone with intimate knowledge of the ancient Green People, and their language, to help him decipher the contents of their documents. At present he was making informed guesses—but conjecture could lead them all astray.

Nevertheless, he was adamant that a lot of the answers to the many enigmas were to be found in the Drikander, in the Green People's library. He recalled the day he'd stumbled over the ornate fountain completely overgrown by the forest – again it was his sore feet that had led him to it. After weeks of searching, following obscure hints he'd discovered in the Guild's library referring to a cache of arcane documents, he'd sat on a stone to massage his heels and, losing his balance, he'd fallen backwards only to look up into the face of a green woman. She was holding out her arms as if to lift the beautifully carved green child nestling in his armpit, her smiling stone gaze falling on the oriental.

He'd nearly screamed with joy when he recognized an ancient spell of illusion breaking down, but had realized that the Grekkos accompanying him would come and investigate if they heard him call. He'd found the entrance to the library. Ecstatic, he recalled the entry spell he'd known of long before he knew what the door actually looked like. His first exploratory journey through the ancient halls beneath the forest had confirmed that the library was immense and he'd spent hours in the darkened labyrinth but not as long as he would have liked. The Grekkos were already suspicious of his forays through their territory and they'd have come looking for him if he'd lingered too long.

So he'd departed and created his own spell of illusion to hide the entrance. He'd laughed; the spell would even keep out the Green People, if there were any left. He'd revisited the library many times since, but had never been able to stay long enough to glean all the information he needed. Nevertheless, his searches had whetted his appetite and he was impatient to learn more. He smiled, now with Elstan's help, perhaps …

He couldn't allow the Guild to stop him. Nonetheless, it was going to take all his skill to evade the evil magus and his equally evil, but far less powerful, deputy. Brenin and Drudwynn were both intensely ambitious for power. How were they going to attain it, though, he had no idea, but then he paused, perhaps he did. The Darkness was evidently a tool of the Gods. And then there was the mysterious agent on the emperor's council. Who was the traitor? It was going to take a lot of luck to discover what the Guild's intentions were. But in that, his and Elstan's aims seemed to be very similar. He sighed and massaged his brow too exhausted to think straight. He put his speculating out of his mind…but not for long.

He stumbled on a tussock; the hill was getting steeper, the trees growing closer together, a blessing and a curse. The gradient was killing his feet, but the increasing density of the forest was concealing them from ordinary prying eyes.

'Elstan,' Chong panted, 'do you think anyone saw us leaving?'

Elstan halted, turned and looked down on the inn, the Vixen's Haven looked remarkably attractive from up here, he thought, almost like a child's playhouse lit up for a festival. Even from this distance he could see the lamps flickering in the many windows and in the stable yard. He studied the scene silently for a moment and then shivered; the breeze was becoming a cold wind the higher they climbed into the mountains.

'I'm not sure. I saw no-one in the yard or at the sides of the inn when we left, no-one stood at the windows and we were alone in the stables. And yet…I have this feeling of being watched all the time.'

Chong-An swallowed, nervously scratching his bald head he looked around. He trusted this man's instincts even though he hadn't known him long. And knowing intimately their enemy's abilities he understood the man's anxiety.

'Brenin does not need his eyes to see you.'

'What do you mean?'

'He can cast his mind to search us out.'

Elstan stared at him, his face giving nothing away of his inner turmoil. 'Yes, a hedge-witch friend of mine told me she could see inside a loved one's head. I didn't want to believe her, but she proved it to me.'

'Well, I've never heard of a hedge-witch with the skill. She must have been an extraordinarily powerful woman. Are you sure she wasn't a wizard for she should have been. Where is she living, perhaps I could meet her sometime?'

'She is dead…and yes, she was extraordinary, a wizard though, I don't think so. She was the prettiest and the kindest-hearted, the most adoring …' his voice trailed away, his thoughts momentarily far from the Wolfshead.

'You loved her?'

'Yes, but not in the way you mean. She was another's…and I loved him very much. I have never met another woman like her, not even my wife. By the Gods, you wizards,' and he paused, his words revealing his helplessness and disgust in the face of the outlandish abilities of sorcery. 'Able to see as well as talk with your mind, no wonder no-one trusts any of you. But, I suppose, if Brenin and Drudwynn can see us from down there then there is no point in seeking to conceal ourselves.'

'I'm sorry, my friend, I must disagree with you, there is every need to hide. Although the skills of the mind are far-reaching and sometimes not what you may wish, they do have limitations. But you will admit that the ability to throw your mind has its uses.'

'I suppose…but what are these limits?'

'Brenin cannot see us if we are over the horizon or at a great distance, so we should be relatively safe on the other side of this mountain.'

'Until he comes after us,' Elstan rubbed his nose. 'And mindmelding, what of that?'

'Well, again distance reduces the ability to read someone's mind. You cannot mindmeld very far, a few leagues maybe. The degrees of restriction of both are much the same, but not being able to speak silently myself, I am not too sure.'

'You cannot mindmeld?' Elstan asked, raising an eyebrow. 'Are you implying then that you can cast your mind?' he asked, staring intently at the oriental's pudgy face. He noticed sweat dappling

Chong's face and he wondered if it was stress or fear or, feeling magnanimous recalling the state of the man's feet, perhaps it was pain.

'Yes, I can see at a distance with my mind,' he smiled tentatively. 'That is how I first saw you climbing to the roof of the Tower and then later, when you were in your room at that hotel. Seeing you settling down for the night I took the opportunity to return to the Tower and gather my few belongings to follow you.'

Elstan sighed. 'Few being the operative word…you didn't bring a lot,' he said looking at the canvas bag slung over Chong's shoulder.

'No, I have not. I do not require much, mostly herbs for pain relief and unguents for my feet.'

'So, you didn't need my salve?'

'Oh yes I did. I never turn down the opportunity to try anyone's remedy. Who knows I may find a permanent cure one day. What I do bring with us, though, are my skills. The Guild may not recognize me as a full wizard, but I am far more than they realize.'

'What do you mean?'

'You will see, my friend,' he paused. 'Now, as we have reached the summit of the Wolfshead will you answer my question?'

Elstan stared at his companion and dropping his hood he combed his fingers through his black hair. 'What question? You have so many.'

'All right…tell me first why your chancellor is so interested in the Guild?'

'I've told you, Brenin's accomplice the Abbot of Sentinel grabbed power in Mantovar and it was with the help of the Guild. But Brenin wants more, as does the abbot—and we want to know what and how he's going about it. Come on, let's rest among those trees over there,' and he nodded towards a small copse of pine trees, 'the ground is covered in needles so it should be soft for your feet.'

They both walked across and Chong-An settled his bulk on a fallen log and bent over to remove his boots.

'No, leave them,' ordered Elstan, 'your feet have swollen you'll never get them back on,' and the chancellor's agent sat down next to him with his back against the log and rummaged through his bag for something to eat. He passed a portion of dried hare up to the sorcerer and shared a skin of wine.

'Ah, that's better, Elstan, I didn't realize I was so famished.'

'I suspect you are hungry every time you do not have food in your hands,' Elstan said wryly.

Chong-An laughed. 'You may very well be correct there. Now the answer to my next question, you promised to answer when we reached this place.'

'What question?' Elstan asked, sighing, he knew full well what the wizard was getting at but tried to gain more time. He hadn't yet made up his mind whether to tell him the truth.

'I seek three people with the codenames of something that flies. I believe you are one, the Fly. I desperately need to know of the others.'

'Why?' Elstan tensed.

'For two reasons. Firstly, Brenin is very concerned about someone he names the Fly and, secondly, because the Fly and two others form a major part of the prophecy that seemed to frighten you. Although there is another part to that I can't figure out at all—how can three be four?' Chong-An gazed at the small dark man chewing his lip. This was one time he desperately wished he had acquired the gift of mindmelding. 'Why did the prophecy scare you so?'

Elstan's thoughts went into overdrive, perhaps there was a way that he could combine the two answers in such a way that the oriental would never suspect the full truth. He could never tell him why three make four.

'Well maybe they're both the same question,' he paused. 'I can trust you, ex-librarian…ex-Guild brother?'

Chong-An smiled ruefully, hearing out loud those words he now realized fully the outcome of his disobedience of Drudwynn's orders. They confirmed his complete severance from his erstwhile colleagues and the sentence of death that will have been passed on him.

'Do I need to answer that?'

Elstan sighed. 'My purpose in being on the Tower was to gain as much knowledge as I could of the Guild's plans. To be specific, I need to ascertain the identity of the magus' spy on the emperor's council. I failed to discover the name, but I believe Brenin is on his way to Abferkarn to meet with him…or her.'

'What makes you think that?'

'I overheard him speaking with someone, although he was alone. He must have been using the scry. I heard them talking of a darkness that was on its way to Drakka. A fog that is drifting through a rift,' he paused, puzzlement creasing his brow.

'What rift?'

'I'm not sure, but he did mention the Afterlife.'

Chong-An braced himself. 'What did he say exactly?'

'Well, he asked this other person, it was the Abbot of Sentinel by the way…he asked him how it would kill. Cumbria said differently to that in the Afterlife. What that meant I have no idea. But the news was received with excitement and resulted in Brenin leaving the Tower straight away, heading for Abferkarn to meet his agent and put his plans in motion.'

Chong rubbed the calf of his left leg, equally puzzled he also wondered about the mysterious darkness and what it held for them. And then it hit him—a way to ensure Elstan went with him deep into the Drikander, to the Green People's library.

'Are you sure he's meeting his agent in the city? Did he actually say his rendezvous was in Abferkarn?'

'Well that's where he said he was going, but that was after he'd been to the Drikander.'

'Then couldn't he be meeting his agent somewhere along his route…perhaps in the Drikander?'

Elstan carried on chewing the hare, mulling over the oriental's words. 'That never occurred to me,' he sighed. 'I must be getting old. By the Gods, I have no option but to follow him. As you say they could very well be meeting in the forest, or maybe even before then…in Mulkie's Cross.'

'Tell me,' Chong was careful not to smile, to show his elation too early could alienate the man who was now unknowingly his ally. 'How did you manage to climb the Tower?'

'I have specially adapted gloves and slippers…another hedge-witch made them for me, she specializes in "eccentric" footwear. I can climb anything anywhere using them.' He looked at Chong's feet. 'Maybe she can even make slippers comfortable enough for you,' he smiled.

'God, please let it be so!' Chong answered feelingly.

'Aye, Chong-An, perhaps I'll introduce you, we may meet her on this journey of ours. But I digress. I have been well trained in all the necessary techniques of surveillance but no-one else has these tools of mine. And this may satisfy the rest of your curiosity. I am one of a small company of men…all loyal to the Prince of Mantovar and all schooled by experts in espionage employed by Chancellor Sevenoaks. All of us have codenames…I am known as the Fly. And I think we'd better rest now.'

Chong-An's sharp intake of breath was loud in the stillness of the Wolfshead as another piece of the puzzle fell into place.

'The Locust…you know of him?'

'Aye, he's my brother; he's working in the north. What do you know of him?'

Chong ignored the question. 'Is there another? I mean one with another codename of a bird or an insect that flies?' He held his breath, desperate to know for these could be the three of the prophecy.

'There are many others, my brother and me are not alone in fighting Cumbria. Why?'

'I don't know…perhaps I clutch at straws, but it is so vitally important. There must be three…must be!' Chong studied his feet, the throbbing had resumed with a vengeance. Then something occurred to him.

'The three I seek are siblings, Elstan. Have you another brother?'

'I will never say anything of him,' and the look on Elstan's face was enough to send a chill up the spine of even Chong-An.

Twenty-one

Ryn woke with the dawn, yawning, he stretched his wings savouring the fresh breeze ruffling through his feathers and tugged his toes from the cold rock. He licked his beak he was hungry again, sniffing in search of free-running water; snow was not enough to satisfy his thirst and he needed a river to fish.

The air was crisp and cold, the wind picking up in the early hours of the new day. He was used to waking alone on the vast reaches of the ocean but peering around him this morning his senses told him different. He knew what it was, he was lonely. Missing his friends, he lifted off and soared above the peaks, coasting to the other side of the mountain he landed on the cloud cover of Alfhime. Again he pecked and prodded at the mass searching for a way through and failing. Dejected, he flew into the air again and turned northwards searching for another entrance. For in his restlessness overnight he'd deduced that if ever Alfhime was under siege then surely the liosalfar would not hide in a valley that had no escape route.

Coming to rest on another cliff in the next valley he suddenly recalled that he had smelled smoke the night before. Raising his beak he sniffed again wondering if his needs, and his loneliness, had misled him. It took him a while and several stops in a few valleys before he detected it again. He flew towards it and discovered a cottage clinging to the hillside, the smoke drifting upwards from a small chimney. He hovered above it, not understanding how it came to be here, wondering who could possibly live in it, for it would not be Roidan's kin they were safe in their own valley.

Alert for trouble, he circled the grey stone cottage spiralling downwards as he did. He was puzzled, the cottage was too small to house a troll and anyway trolls would never live in a habitat that was patently a human's home. Warily he landed on the slope across the hillside a little way from it and watched the closed door, the light of a lamp emanated from a chink in the drapes of a small window alongside it.

He sat motionless waiting for any sign of its occupant, ready to flee at a moment's notice. He sat patiently for most of the morning, just staring and listening, minutes before noon he heard her. His sharp hearing picked up the sound of slow, shuffling footsteps coming up the mountain track at his left. He twisted his neck and pointed his beak lower down the slope and a short while later around the hill and into sight walked a small, extremely old woman a brown cloak wrapped warmly around her, its cowl raised obscuring her features.

He waited until she reached the top of the sloping track where it levelled off in front of her cottage before clearing his throat. She halted; puzzled she lowered her hood down around her shoulders revealing a grizzled face and long wispy grey hair blowing in the wind. She stooped, her back bent, and in one gnarled hand she held a thumbstick and in the other, two dead trout hanging from a string. The albatross drooled.

She didn't see Ryn at first; her eyes were not too good she told him later, a white bird against a background of snow was almost invisible to her. Shaking her head and with small careful steps she ambled over to her cottage, mumbling to herself. It was his shadow falling across her path that made her look up again and she halted in her tracks utterly bewildered. Ryn and the old woman stared at each other, both speechless for moments.

Trembling noticeably, her skinny body shivering, either because of the cold which she was well wrapped up against or because of the very dramatic sight of a gigantic bird gazing at her, prompted her to speak. She smiled, the beam transforming her old depressed expression to one of delighted surprise.

'Well, well, well! Are my eyes deceiving me? I don't believe it! My, you really are a big bird aren't you...a big, very handsome bird. I wonder where you've come from. Lost I expect, there are no other birds like you in these mountains.' She seemed to be having a conversation with herself.

'But it's very strange, Helydd, almost as if time is turning the clock back, now that I see him up close,' she paused, 'the last time I saw a bird as big as this was...never mind, old woman you're rambling.'

She breathed deeply for moments, it had been a long climb up the track, and then she smiled again at seeing Ryn's mystified expression. He crumpled his beak into a most odd shape, contemplating her words he wondered, surely there never had been another bird as large as he? And how could time possibly go backwards?

'I wonder if you're hungry. I expect so, birds are always hungry,' and she looked down at the fish she held in one hand. 'I'll cut up one of these and share it with you. I'll break up some bread as well…I should have a little spare.'

Ryn waited saying nothing; he was perplexed. This mountain range was very hostile, no place for a strong, hardy human to live in let alone an old woman who talked to herself non-stop. He watched as she entered the cottage and set about stoking up the fire. She hummed a tune as she cooked the fish in a black pan almost too heavy for her to steady on the great iron hob alongside the fire. Ryn salivated at the smell of freshly cooking trout wafting out towards him. A while later the old woman came out of the cottage with a plate of trout and bread and placed it on the ground in front of him. He stared from her to the food waiting for her to step back.

'Ah, silly me! I've cooked the fish! You silly old woman, birds eat fish raw. I'd better take it away and fetch the other one.'

'No,' Ryn shouted, the thought of the delicious food disappearing brought on a panic attack. 'Please, I like cooked food, especially fried trout.'

She was astounded, staring up at him wide-eyed, mouth agape she brought her hands to her face. 'Am I going mad? I'm sure I heard him speak. You've been up here too long, Helydd…no bird can speak!' and she turned away leaving the plate on the floor.

Ryn lunged for it, gobbling it down; he rattled the tin plate making a noise that reverberated around the valley.

She stopped in her doorway and looked at him again. 'Oh, you certainly enjoyed that; you must have been very hungry to eat cooked fish. I'll fetch you some more,' and she re-entered her cottage.

This time as the fish cooked and Ryn licked the juices around his beak, the old woman placed a rocking chair outside her cottage door. Removing her cloak, she sat clothed in a long, heavy wool dress and thick cardigan. The only jewellery she wore was a necklace of tiny, variegated blue, red and yellow oval-shaped beads, each encased in its own glass shell, the rope hanging to her waist. She twirled it in her fingers. Resting her eyes, she rocked back and forth in her chair. Ryn waited patiently, the aroma of the cooking fish flooding his senses and numbing his mind to all else. He momentarily forgot his anxieties, Shadra's and Anselm's plight relegated to the back of his mind.

When Ryn smelled the fish on the verge of burning, he looked to see if the old woman had noticed. But there was no sign of her waking. Ryn was desperate; he had to rouse her while there was a chance of salvaging the fish. He walked towards her and prodded her with his beak.

She jerked awake and stared at Ryn in her face. 'Oh dear, what is it now? Have I frightened you, my dear? I didn't mean to drop off like that it's just I had a terrible long walk down to the river to get the fish. The fish!' and she screamed. 'Quick out of my way, it's burning,' and she pushed at Ryn's neck to make way to her kitchen.

She hurried back and put the plate on her lap. 'There, I just managed to save it. If you hadn't woken me it would have been lost. Come, share it with me,' and she threw a portion of the trout on to the ground between them.

Ryn, forgetting himself picked it up with his fingers and placed it in his beak and swallowed. The old woman shrieked. 'Helydd, I can see fingers…on a bird! First I imagine it has a voice and now I'm seeing things as well. Those liosalfar have a lot to answer for, the cruel harlots. They've driven me mad.'

'No, lady, I can speak and these are real fingers…honest. A wizard gave them to me,' and he waved his fingers in the air. 'Pretty aren't they? Thank you for the fish, another friend taught me how to enjoy cooked food.'

Ryn stared at her and wondered if he should have remained silent. By the look on her startled face and the way she clutched her chest, he might inadvertently be the cause of a heart attack.

'No, Helydd your ears are playing tricks on you, girl. A bird…talking, a bird with fingers. Are my eyes going as well? It must be all this snow; you were warned it'd send you doolally. She rose from her chair and walked towards the door of her cottage.

'No, please, Helydd is it? Is that your name? You are not mad, really, and I am desperate for your help.'

She stared at him, her eyes glistening. 'I don't believe I'm going to talk with a bird.' She held her face in her hands and stared amazed into his small black eyes. 'I have prayed for company for so long now…and it comes in this form.' She returned to her chair. 'Yes, my name is Helydd, do you have a name?'

'Yes, I am Ryn. I am a Wandering Albatross of the Giant Albatross family. I was hatched in the Deep, the vast ocean way to the west of here.'

'Well, you have wandered a fair distance from your home, Ryn, and no mistake. How come you to be in these mountains?' she asked, again curling her necklace in her fingers.

'A wizard wanted me to deliver a message to a princess' father. But I was attacked and wounded in the prince's castle and had to flee into the forest. I was rescued by an elf and a human.'

'An elf,' she hissed, venomously, sitting up straight she glared at Ryn. 'You are friends with the liosalfar?'

'No! I most certainly am not, Helydd. Shadra is a small forest elf, cousin to the liosalfar and my friend. But he and my human friend, Anselm, have been imprisoned by them and I don't know why.'

'I know why,' the menace back in her voice, 'they are an evil race...they hold my daughter prisoner, a child who made a silly, juvenile mistake years ago,' her eyes brimmed. 'However many times I ask them, they will not return her. But I will not give up...I will have her released to me some day.'

'Then, maybe, we can help each other,' Ryn said quietly. Moved by her tears and her desperation, he warmed to her. 'How about we talk over a cup of tea, eh?'

She dried her eyes on her sleeve and smiled. 'Now, I haven't had a chinwag over a cup of tea with a friend for as long as I can remember.'

Twenty-two

The coach, escorted by a six-man squad of the Portolan's militia, rolled through the iron-gates of the home estate and along the smooth, packed earth of the circular driveway leading up to the tall mahogany doors of Thaddeus' home. The manorhouse was large, three-storeys, built of grey stone blocks, windows running the breadth of the house on all three floors.

Standing in the portico to welcome them were two ladies. The first was Lodovico Portolan's love, the Lady Cornelia, overweight, middle aged companion and lady-in-waiting to Princess Augusta. The other was short and slim, also of middle age, Alessa Barbat, Thaddeus' nurse of fifteen years, betrothed to Marcus Janne. Both women, tears in their eyes, curtsied as Prince Griffin stepped down from the coach.

'What on earth are you doing?' Thaddeus asked, appalled.

'Welcoming you home, Highness,' said Alessa smiling proudly.

'For God's sake, don't you dare curtsey to me again…you've cared for me and loved me too long for that. I mean it…don't you dare!' He grabbed her and pulled her into his arms, kissing her as a boy kisses his mother.

But there was immediate consternation and concern when Aidan was carried from the coach in the arms of the coach driver, another militiaman delegated to the task after the riot. Aidan was still unconscious from the knock on his head and following the instructions of the nurse, was put straight to bed.

The following morning Aidan woke feeling fuzzy and light-headed. A little disoriented he pulled himself upright on the truckle bed in the dark bedroom he and the others had shared on their last visit to the afterlife. He held his head in his hands – the lump still sore on his forehead – unaware, at first, of who was in the room.. Alessa Barbat held a steaming mug of herb tea in her hands as she knelt beside the low bed.

'Come, Aidan, drink this it will ease your headache,' she ordered, her brusque manner contradicting the concern she felt for the young man who had brought "her" Thaddeus home from the Afterlife. 'The others have told me you will not allow anyone to use magic to

182

heal you. This is not magic. This, young man, is a good old-fashioned remedy for a knock on the head…pure and natural.

Aidan raised his head and took the cup in both of his hands, warming them. Alessa believed in fresh air for all cures and had the window wide open, "to blow away the cobwebs" she said. But the resultant cold breeze down off Mount Trespass made him shiver and his hands shake.

He sipped the hot brew cautiously, the menthol vapours clearing his head. 'What's in this?'

'A bit of lavender, some ginger, vinegar, honey to taste and a couple of other bits and pieces of my own mixing. There are about fifteen different ingredients,' she smiled. 'The Green People have a variation of it but I think mine works faster.'

'The Green People? You've met them?'

'Yes! When you departed with Leonid and Marcus a Green Woman turned up here with her children. I've never been more surprised in my whole life…were we not, Cornelia?' The nurse turned to the lady-in-waiting, another woman who loved Aidan dearly.

The young wizard returned her affection, though Cornelia had the power to scare the life out of him when she shouted. He had once healed her of a broken ankle and at the same time of the "old bones" disease and for that had earned her undying gratitude. To her, Aidan could do no wrong, but she never took any messing about from him, and he'd never dream of upsetting her.

'It was the morning after you'd sailed away,' Cornelia hugged Augusta standing alongside her, She couldn't seem to stop she was that relieved to see all of them back safe. Nevertheless, she grieved heavily for her friend Tragen and took to wearing black in his memory.

'She knocked on the door as brazen as brass, frightening the life out of Mistress Lacey. In fact the cook swooned at sight of Jasmina on the porch with her three children.'

'Leonid's family are here? Why?' Aidan held the mug in his lap, resting a moment, colour returning to his cheeks.

'Apparently she disobeyed the Elders and refused to stay behind. She wouldn't give us the reason,' said Thaddeus. Walking into the bedroom he carried a tray spread with a bowl of soup and fresh bread, the aroma overwhelming the potion in the patient's hands. He was followed by Beatrix holding the hand of a very young Green child.

'How are you feeling, Aidan?' Beatrix asked, sitting down at his head, the girl promptly sitting in Beatrix's lap.

'I've been worse,' he smiled at the little girl.

'You remember Kataya?'

'Of course...but I thought her name was Bella?'

'It was. But the Green People allow their children to add another name to the first on their fifth birthday, if they wish.'

'Yes, and I'm called by that until my tenth birthday when I can add another name. I have to keep all three, then,' the little girl interrupted.

'Oh,' and he grinned again, 'how are you, Kataya?'

'I'm fine,' and she held out her hand for Aidan to shake and as they shook she continued. 'I wish my brother was...are you going to help him?' she asked rubbing her suddenly watery eyes.

'Here, eat this food, we'll tell you everything while you get it down you,' said Thaddeus, pushing his way through the crowd around the invalid.

'I think we'll leave them alone for a while, Alessa,' said Cornelia, 'it's getting a might too full in here.'

'I agree. I have to supervise that dreadful woman's cooking of lunch anyway. You know I'm sure she's getting more sullen by the day.'

'Yes, and I'll return to Jasmina, try and persuade her to rest, the poor woman's had no sleep since Leonid left. Not that I expect she'll listen to me, understandably I suppose.' Cornelia's voice faded away as she went through the door. 'The best thing I can do for her is tell her Aidan's awake at last.'

'You eat all of that, young man,' the nurse ordered, departing the room, she turned to go below to the kitchen.

'Close that bloody window, will you,' asked Aidan of no-one in particular.

'Ooh, you naughty boy!' said Kataya looking up at Beatrix. 'The naughty boy swore, Beattie, did you hear him,' she asked, scandalized.

'Oh no, not another one,' moaned Aidan, rolling his eyes feigning disgust. 'It's enough having her shout at me, Kataya,' he laughed, his eyes twinkling. He tucked into the soup finding he was ravenous; he couldn't remember the last time he'd eaten, the evening before last he thought.

'Anyway you ought to hear what Beattie says sometimes,' said Thaddeus implying that the maid did not always have good manners.

'What! Beatrix would never say naughty words…don't you fib,' she retorted, curling up closer on Beatrix's lap, her thumb in her mouth.

'All right, now tell me which brother is ill and what's wrong with him?' asked Aidan staring up from the bowl of hot vegetable broth on the tray in his lap, his initial hunger pangs sated.

'It's Prile. I'm afraid he has the plague, Aidan,' said Augusta mournfully. 'Alessa and Jasmina have been treating him with some foul-smelling concoction, but whatever's in it doesn't seem to be working. He's deteriorating,' she said shaking her head, her expression telling him there was little hope.

'Bloody hell! Why didn't you wake me? Help me up I'd better get to him, now!' Aidan shouting, nearly tipped the tray passing it to Thaddeus and he rose from the bed far too quickly; Augusta grabbed him and held him, dizziness making him lose his balance. He was still dressed in his clothes from the day before; Alessa had thought it better not to disturb him by changing him into night attire, saying the most important thing was rest for his head wound.

The young wizard-healer hurried after his bigger friend, Thaddeus, along the corridor to Jasmina's room, Augusta, Beatrix and Kataya scurrying behind. They found Prile tossing and turning in his bed, his mother constantly bathing the infant's head, the tell-tale black buboes plastered with a sweet-smelling cream. Jasmina, her eyes red and swollen with grief and weariness, was sitting at his head, her sleeves rolled to her elbows, her long black hair hanging loose from its tie at the nape of her neck. She was desperately offering comfort to her delirious youngest child, a lad of two years.

She looked up through dark, sunken eyes, her anxiety making her tremble as the wizards walked through the door. 'Oh, Aidan, thank God, you are all right now?' At his nod, she stretched out her arm to him. 'Can you help my Prile, my baby, please?' She begged bursting into tears and pulling him towards her son.

'Excuse me, out of the way, I have to get to the bed,' ordered Dom, eleven years of age and the oldest of Jasmina's children. They made way for him and he pushed his way through carrying another bowl of cold, scented water. 'Here you are, Mum, the nurse said there won't be any need for more.'

'Oh, no! She thinks he's going to die?'

185

'No, Jasmina, she means there'll be no need because Aidan is here,' said Cornelia. Aidan glanced at her standing at the foot of the bed. 'The others told me that you healed those on the Grim who had the plague, Aidan. Can you do the same for dear little Prile?'

He went straight to the bed of the youngest son of the man who had found, and ultimately saved them. They had been lost in the catacombs beneath Mount Trespass, fleeing Razor Montetor and his cutthroats. Ignoring Jasmina he placed his hand on Prile's head and closed his eyes. They all watched in silence as Aidan entered the mind of the little boy. They held their breath, the only sound that of Prile's laboured breathing.

Aidan shuddered, grimacing he opened his eyes and stared down at his friend's very ill son. 'This is a disgusting disease, Jasmina. I don't know what you've given him but it slowed the infection, although it hasn't cured him. But if you hadn't administered that salve he would have died hours ago,' he turned on the others and suddenly shouted.

'Why didn't you wake me? You nearly left it too late for me to save him.' He glared at them, each in turn before continuing his tirade. 'By the Gods what do you do when I finally wake? You give me food which delayed me even more! He could have died. Where was your sense? How the hell am I supposed to trust you in the Darkness if you don't think!'

Turning his back to them he put his friends out of his mind and knelt alongside the bed placing his hands on the boy again.

The others stood by, stunned. His outburst coming as a complete surprise, none of them had ever seen him in such a temper before, not even Anders. Shock stilled any retort from Augusta. Beatrix, though, burst into tears and releasing Kataya's hand, she ran from the room, Kataya shouting and running after her. And Thaddeus raged, for Aidan's words held the ring of truth even though unjustified…for they had tried to rouse him.

There was no need to speak to them like that, they did try to wake you' said Anders on sentry duty in Limbo.

'They didn't try hard enough.'

'They were only thinking of you.'

'Yes, when they should have been thinking of Prile. Now leave me alone…all of you, while I see to him.'

His words, spoken aloud, confused Jasmina but she bit her tongue. Wanting to defend the others she couldn't deny her maternal instincts, Prile came first. And she watched Aidan working on her son, she clenched her hands together, her knuckles white.

And as they watched and bristled with mixed indignation and guilt, the buboes on Prile's skin paled and began to reduce in size; in the next few hours they would disappear entirely leaving the boy's green skin unblemished. The stench of rotting flesh waned as the boy opened his eyes and stared around him, confused. In moments Prile was in his mother's arms, she hugging him nearly to death her tears falling on his face.

'Thank you, Lord Aidan,' said Dom through his own tears. 'If there's anything I can do for you…you just tell me.'

Aidan rose from the bed, ruffling Dom's hair he spoke sharply. 'It'll be a while yet before he's fully healed so be careful of him. How did he catch the plague, Jasmina? It shouldn't have reached here yet. We're the first to get here from the harbour aren't we?'

Cornelia startled, stared wide-eyed. 'Leonid! Leonid and Hopper were here yesterday, they stopped off on their way to Bylani. Leonid…he spent an hour with his family before departing.'

'Hell…Hopper and his men, where did they spend their time?'

'The stables, I think…yes, the stables to see to their mounts,' Cornelia answered.

Staring at Aidan, she was seeing a different boy to the one that had left for Sanctity. This was a young man, fully grown, authority and desolation written all over his face. He was no longer a naughty boy to be corrected; he was now a man to be obeyed. His manner frightened her.

'Leonid, do you think he carried it here?' Thaddeus asked.

But before he could answer Jasmina looked up from Prile, appalling shock on her face. 'My Leonid! Do you think he has the plague? If he has, he's taken it into Bylani.'

'Oh, please, Aidan, go after him. You must heal him. He…he cannot die he is my husband. Please!' and she stretched out her hand again to hold his arm. 'We Green People, once we pledge ourselves to another we…we cannot bear being apart from them for any length of time. That is why I left Bylani. I had to be with him…me and our children. We cannot live alone once we are trothed. If Leonid has the disease and…and dies without the proper ritual only I as his wife can perform, then I will die also and my children will be left orphaned. I cannot allow Leonid to enter the Afterlife without me being present at his end. Please, Aidan, I beg you.'

'I'm sorry,' he said, unable to meet her eyes, 'I can't go yet, Jasmina. I'm sorry…I can't. I have to find my master first,' and he gently shrugged off her hand and striding past the others, ignoring them all, he stormed out of the room and downstairs.

'He's a very nasty boy to make you cry,' said Kataya, again sitting on Beatrix's lap, this time in the summerhouse that had been built by Thaddeus' mother just before she died. 'Is he always horrible? If he is, I won't like him.'

Beatrix dried her eyes and tried to smile. 'That's just it, Kataya, he's not usually…not nasty and horrible, I mean. I've never seen him like that before. He loves people, cares for them. You saw him healing little Prile, Aidan is very kind.'

'Then why did he shout at you?'

'He's very worried, I suppose. He loves his master very much, like you love your Dada. His master's in grave danger, we have to go and look for him. And, well he was right; it was thoughtless of us to give him food when Prile was lying in bed very ill.'

'But he said you should have woken him. You tried…I saw you, you couldn't.'

'No, but he doesn't know that. He has no idea that we stayed with him all night watching over him,' she sniffed loudly. 'We were very anxious for him, weren't we?' she shuddered. 'There was a time we thought he'd never come round.'

'Is that why you were crying? You were squeezing his hand very tight, you know.'

'Yes, I suppose I was. We all love Aidan very much and we…I…I don't know what I'd do if I lost him,' and her voice shook, close to tears again.

Beatrix suddenly looked up at the rose strewn doorway when she heard a footstep and saw Aidan watching her silently. She looked back down at Kataya who had suddenly tensed in her lap.

'I'm sorry, Aidan,' she mumbled. 'We just didn't think.'

'No, Beattie, I'm the one who should apologise. I shouldn't have lost my temper. You're right…I can't get Tragen out of my head. He's being tormented in that terrible place, I know it. I have to get to him as soon as I can…I have to rescue him from that horror.' He stared over her head at the roses growing on the trellis, distracted for moments at the beauty of this world in contrast to that of the Darkness. 'He's been like a father to me. But every time I think we're ready to set out, to cross over and search for him, something else crops up to delay me…delay us. I'm desperate, Beattie, at the end of my tether.'

Aidan sniffed and looked at his feet. 'I don't know if I can explain it, but…'

'There's no need, Aidan, I know how you feel about him.'

'But I must tell you. If I can make you understand why I shouted perhaps I can get my feelings under control again…for they aren't, Beattie. I feel as if I'm going nuts.'

'Come and sit down, then. You haven't really spoken about him since that terrible night. Maybe you'll feel better talking it out.'

Aidan sighed, sitting on the wicker chair opposite her he paused, waiting in vain for his trembling to cease. 'Tragen has always been there for me. When he took me in first, I was wild…a thief and a liar.'

He looked up at her and grasped her proffered hand and held it tightly. 'I'd use my magic at the slightest provocation, any insult justified or not, or at any thoughtless response from those around me. I'd hurt people just to get away. But whatever I did to him, or however disobedient or nasty I was, he never lost his temper with me. He'd just sit there and stare at me until I calmed and then he'd smile and hug me. He was the one who taught me not to use the magic maliciously…for I did lots of times in my first years with him.'

Beatrix bit her lip, she recalled memories of stories she'd heard back home in the castle when she'd been a lot younger. There had been tales of an angry boy creating havoc and the wizard having to control him. She and Augusta had been warned by Princess Maria to stay clear of him, but the restriction had been lifted when the boy began to behave himself.

Aidan paused, his memories coming thick and fast. 'And sometimes there were times I'd burst into tears,' he bent his head not wanting her to see his shame, but now that he'd started his story he didn't want to stop. It was important to him to make Beatrix understand his feelings…and what Tragen truly meant to him.

'I'd be sitting at the table having dinner or whatever, talking to him or playing with the dog he got for me, and all of a sudden I'd start crying. And he'd hold me…hug me until they stopped. He'd drop everything and run to me. He used to tell me that nothing was more important to him than my happiness and my safety.'

'Oh, Aidan,' she said, almost crying herself. 'I never realized...it must have been terrible for you. I never knew your childhood was so unhappy.'

'But that's just it, when Tragen was around, I wasn't unhappy. And when I did feel the miseries coming on I'd go looking for him and...and everything seemed all right again.'

'Have you any idea why you'd suddenly cry?'

'Yes...it's almost unbelievable, but not to Tragen, he always believed me.' He wrapped his arms across his chest as if he needed to hold himself together and he stared into space for a moment.

'This strange feeling used to come over me. One minute I'd be totally engrossed in making potions or reading a particularly hard script, or whatever, and I'd suddenly look up and I'd see a woman smiling at me from across the table or from across the room. She was sitting at an open window at one time, her long black hair blowing in the breeze, her mouth was moving but I couldn't make out what she was saying. And I knew without a shadow of a doubt that she was my mother. She smelled lovely,' and he smiled, his memories very vivid. 'She always smelled of lavender, you know.'

'Yes, I remember you saying. You still miss her terribly then even though you were very young when she was killed?'

'Always...I see her face in the most unlikely places as well. I once saw her staring up at me from a hayrick in the stables at home. I don't think she was too happy with me at that moment...I think it had something to do with the girl I was being friendly with,' he blushed and looked up at Beatrix.

'I don't cry so much for her now, unless I'm alone. Don't laugh, will you, but that's one of the reasons why I hate being on my own.'

'Oh, Aidan, I'd never laugh at you, I...' And she stopped, afraid to continue not quite knowing what she'd say, her instincts telling her to hide her feelings for him, that there were consequences brewing here that neither was quite prepared for yet.

'Do you still see her?'

'Not as much as I did, but...'

'What?'

'Sometimes I see a man standing behind her, his arms wrapped tightly around her. His head is bent down in her neck and she's got one arm lifted stroking the side of his face. I can never see what he looks like though, his hair is dazzling me, blond like bright sunshine and her hand is in the way. But I know she loves him.'

'Is he your father?'

'I don't know, he may be,' he sighed. 'I've never told anyone any of this before, not even Tragen,' gazing at Beatrix his voice unexpectedly trembled. 'I don't know what I'd do if I lost you, either. I'm sorry.'

He stood and put out his arms, tears rolling down his cheeks. Putting Kataya down, she rose into his embrace taking comfort from the warmth and love of his nearness.

It was at that very moment Augusta and Thaddeus came upon them. Augusta's stomach lurched when she saw Beatrix in his arms. She glared, not saying a word as she halted abruptly in her tracks.

But when they arrived in the doorway of the summerhouse, Kataya squealed with delight. 'It's all right now; they've made up, the nasty boy said sorry for being horrible to everyone.'

Thaddeus pushed past Augusta. 'Has he, indeed. We've been looking everywhere for you,' and when Aidan turned, Thaddeus saw the tears in both Aidan's and Beatrix's eyes. 'Hey, what's up with you two?'

'I'm sorry for losing my temper, Thad…I shouldn't have. I'm sorry,' and he held out his hand to Augusta.

Augusta, in her confusion, hesitated before taking it, her mind in turmoil wondering if she had reason to be jealous, though in her heart she knew that Beatrix would never do anything to hurt her. Aidan mistaking her reluctance released Beatrix and pulled Augusta to him.

'Please, Augusta, I couldn't stand it if you didn't forgive me.'

'Oh, Aidan, what are we going to do with you?' she said returning his hug, at the same time promising herself that she'd be keeping an eye on him and Beatrix from then on.

Later that afternoon, they were all sitting around the table drinking freshly made lemonade, discussing their future plans when Aidan made up his mind.

'We'll go tonight, when I've fully recovered. Okay?' he said. 'Will you be ready for us, Anders?'

'Aye,' Anders answered from his place at the wall of colours. *'Are you all coming?'*

'Of course we are,' said Augusta tersely, 'we'd hardly let him walk into the Darkness on his own.'

'Well, we won't have far to walk, now. It's a lot closer than when you saw it last time,' Anders said, his arms clasped across his chest, his back resting against the oak tree.

'Can you see any sign of Lord Tragen?' asked Beatrix, the thought of entering that dreadful place scaring her silly.

'I can see a pinpoint of light in the distance, I don't know if that's him. If it is then we aren't going to like it, it seems to be right in the middle of a moving mass of activity. The Darkness seems to be a lot denser there and the mist is pulsating very fast. That must be where it's forcing its way through the hole into the cavern on Sanctity.'

'You don't have to come with me…any of you. I won't hold you to your promise, it's going to be very dangerous searching in that lot,' said Aidan staring anxiously at the table beneath his hands. He clenched his fists to prevent them shaking, betraying his fear, Tragen's face in his mind's eye. The more he thought of his mentor the more desperate he was getting. He wondered how the wizard was coping. He was bound to be confused and scared, for if no-one could see into the blinding light of the magic within the cage, then he could very well be unable to see out.

'Don't be silly, of course we'll be with you,' said Augusta putting her hand over his on the table.

'I'll get us some more lemonade,' said Beatrix rising from her chair, Kataya clinging to her like a limpet.

'Where are you going tonight? Can I come with you?' Kataya asked, her big eyes glinting in the sunlight.

'Is she stuck to you?' asked Thaddeus amused.

Kataya poked her tongue out at him as she trotted off with Beatrix.

It wasn't long before Beatrix, her face ashen, was back without the lemonade and Kataya.

'Aidan, I'm sorry, Leonid's been taken gravely ill, they think he's dying. They need your help desperately.'

'What?' he asked suddenly full of foreboding.

'Jasmina is packing, getting ready to leave immediately with the children. When I walked into the kitchen they told me there was a messenger from Bylani at the house. I ran upstairs and Cornelia told me. Leonid has the plague, Aidan,' she stated desperately, her hands to her terrified face. 'He's going to die!'

'No…no, please, I have to find Tragen. I can't put it off any longer,' Aidan, all colour draining from his face, had expected the plea as soon as he'd seen the distraught look on her face.

'Oh God, please don't do this to me.' He groaned, his anxiety rending him bereft, he held his head in his hands.

Twenty-three

'Can you cast your mind now, search out Brenin and see what he's up to?' Elstan asked, sitting on the ground in a small grove of loblolly trees, his back resting against the half-buried log that Chong-An was sitting on. He tugged gently at a bed of trailing azalea, its pink flowers growing on short stems, its soft fragrance calming.

It was dawn, the sun hidden above a cloud-filled sky, a slight drizzle falling promising a storm later in the morning. The fresh smells of wet undergrowth, the trilling of the wood warbler in a nearby oak tree and the sad song of the chiffchaff had woken both men early despite them only resting for a few short hours. They were now well up into the mountains above the Wolfshead, the white peaks of the Scissor Mountains looming ever vaster and loftier above their campsite.

The Vixen's Haven was still visible as a pin point winking in the floor of the valley below, but there was no possibility of detecting any movement of individuals at this height and distance. Nevertheless, as the tavern was still in line of sight, Chong-An knew he'd be able to overlook the magus, as long as he did it very cautiously. Brenin was powerful enough to detect his searcher's probing, the tendrils of Chong's mind and his emotions, if the oriental was the slightest bit careless.

Chong-An sighing, peered through the woods and down the hillside, looking everywhere in fact except at the inn. He loved the forest, always had, he was at peace amongst the trees and the undergrowth. He was very fond of most of its inhabitants, the forest elves especially; he'd spent many a month as their guest in the Great Forest north of the Drikander. He forced himself to gaze on the Vixen's Haven again, tensing visibly. He didn't want to do this, he loved life too much, lived it to the full. Now he was risking death. For Brenin could kill him simply by following the mind link back to its origin and snipping the lifeline in Chong's brain.

'I will try Elstan, but you must ward me. Promise me that if you see me trembling or disturbed at all you will awaken me in any way you are able.'

'Why would you react like that?' asked Elstan suddenly anxious for the wizard who was almost a friend, a man whose courage he was fast learning to respect.

'Because, Elstan, it will mean that Brenin has discovered me watching him, and he will be endeavouring to ensnare my mind. And it is quite possible he will succeed. If he does, then he will delight in terrorizing me, forcing me to do things I would not normally. Promise me you will wake me at the first sign.'

'Aye, all right, but what kind of thing is he likely to make you do?'

'Well…kill you, for one. For once he sets the compulsion on me I'd never be able to break it.'

Elstan licked his suddenly dry lips. 'I'd appreciate it if you weren't caught.'

'Then let us get farther into the forest, find a relatively safe place to hide before I attempt it. It will be advisable for him not to see us in the open. We don't want to make it any easier for his underlings to locate us, for the chase will undoubtedly begin this morning.'

Elstan, helped his friend to his feet and moved off when Chong-An was ready. It was becoming increasingly painful for Chong to walk, his feet had swollen grotesquely and the flesh of his lower legs was hanging over the tops of his boots. To take Chong's mind from his hurts as they trudged higher into the forested slopes, Elstan tried to get him talking.

'While we walk,' he asked, 'tell me of yourself, I'd like to know more about the man who has the courage to disobey the magus.'

'Oh, my dear Elstan, you do not realize what you ask, I am my favourite topic of conversation,' Chong chuckled, 'you may be sorry, I could talk forever of myself and bore you silly, I'm sure. But I will tell you a little of my early life, how I came to study magic,' he stared up at Elstan walking ahead of him, and then he remembered something else. 'You know that Brenin has been expecting you in this region?'

'I'd guessed as much. Do you think he's identified me?'

'He's no fool. Drudwynn will have told him of the man from Mantovar trading my slippers. He'll put two and two together.'

'How do you know he knows of me?'

'I was hidden in a cupboard, in Drudwynn's rooms and overheard Brenin speak of you.'

'What did he say?'

'Oh, nothing much except that he could sense you near the Tower, and that he wanted to question you. He knows you work for the chancellor. He set guards on the Tower to apprehend you...obviously they failed.'

'Aye, they weren't very good,' he smiled grimly. 'I left a number bound and gagged. So, you think he may have realized that the Fly accompanies you?'

'It is probable.'

'Then we had better be extra careful, I'd hate for him to get into my mind, it'd put a lot more than just we two in jeopardy.' He peered amongst the trees on both sides of their path as if expecting Brenin's minions to appear at any moment. And then his brow furrowed, looking puzzled he turned to his companion. 'What were you doing in a cupboard?'

'On one of my journeys of exploration around this country of ours, I discovered the original plans to the building of the Tower and they included the secret ways hidden in the walls. I was proving their authenticity when I stumbled into a cupboard in Drudwynn's apartments. Unfortunately it was just then that Drudwynn arrived in the company of Brenin and they sat on the other side of the door to where I was secreted. I had no choice but to remain where I was in case they heard me leaving.'

'Oh, it wouldn't have anything to do with you wanting to eavesdrop, of course?' and Elstan smiled when Chong-An had the grace to blush. 'Where did you find those plans?'

'In a place of no importance,' Chong said suddenly wary.

'Of no importance? I seriously doubt that, my friend. I cannot imagine you discovering such documents without a great deal of time and effort on your part. And if that's the case their location would be of the utmost relevance,' Elstan stared at him through narrowed eyes. 'And where there is one document of such significance there may be others. Where did you find it?' Elstan demanded, his tone broking no nonsense.

Chong stared silently for moments. 'Oh, very well, I will not dissemble, my friend. I discovered them in a long-lost library of the Green People hidden in the Drikander.'

'The Green People? I thought they were a fable. Is that the reason you have cajoled me into accompanying you into the Drikander? You mean to return to the library?'

'Hardly cajole, my dear Elstan.'

196

'That is exactly the word. You have been directing me there since I met you. Now, do you intend visiting it on this journey?'

'I'm sorry, Elstan, but I really need to. It holds countless documents of unimaginable importance on the shelves there. But I have not prevaricated, not cajoled; I honestly believe that Brenin may also meet his agent in the villages of the forest.'

Elstan gazed at Chong, his eyes stony. 'I believe you believe that, wizard, but I warn you…keep nothing from me again, if you have aims that involve my cooperation, ask first,' and he turned and resumed his relentless climb up the hill. 'Now, let us get back to the story of your life.'

Chong-An breathed a sigh of relief, obtaining the prophecies with just this man's aid should be a lot easier, now. 'Have you ever travelled in the Orient?'

'No, but I came quite close to it once. I accompanied my brother through the Scissor Mountains into the Great Desert on the other side. We were on a mission to the sand nomads for the chancellor,' he shuddered. 'I don't like deserts…too much sand…and other things. The Orient is at its far side, I believe. Am I correct?'

'You are. But it would take many months of walking through the desert to find my home. Which brother was it?'

'What?'

'Which brother did you accompany?'

'Oh, the Locust…Anselm.'

'Do you all follow your Chancellor?'

'What do you mean?'

'Is it just the two of you, you and Anselm? How about your other brother, doesn't he follow as you do?' and Chong waited with bated breath.

'I will never divulge anything of him. Don't ever ask again.' Elstan's tone, though soft and low, bore a menace that sent a cold shiver down Chong's back. 'Now, we were talking of you, Chong. Don't change the subject.'

And Chong-An thought he had his answer. It couldn't possibly be any other, could it? Elstan and his two brothers had to be the three winged siblings, although he had no idea how the third fitted in yet…or how three could be four, or why Elstan would not speak of him. The oriental wizard kept his silence, the same implacable look of violence had returned to Elstan's face.

Chong-An stopped to catch his breath, they'd just pushed their way through dense bearberry and patches of yellow broom. The woods were rapidly transforming into the dense forest visible from the road, the trees here mainly larches and pine with the occasional redwood towering over its neighbours. The sporadic small clearings – the ground covered in fallen leaves and pine needles soft underfoot – were now becoming more infrequent. Chong breathed deeply, he adored the smell of pine it reminded him of home. He closed his eyes for a moment and listened to the sound of crickets clicking their wings nearby. Glancing down at his feet, whilst trying to flex his toes, he noticed the eggs of the pine-cone bug adhering to the pine needles and he gently moved away, not to disturb them.

The ground between the trees was getting harder to traverse, the undergrowth thicker. He was going to have to rest before long and, despite his good intentions, he was going to have to apply more salve to his feet, how though, he had no idea. He believed Elstan when he'd said that if he removed his boots he'd never get them back on. But he desperately needed to treat his feet with something if they were to maintain the present pace, which even he realized was not excessive.

But, of course, what he really required urgently was the services of a healer of the First Order. And for the first time since their flight began, Chong doubted his ability to reach the other side of the Wolfshead, let alone get to the Drikander. For it was not only his feet that was troubling him but his knees and his lower spine…his arthritis had flared up beyond anything he'd ever known before.

He struggled on, the need to gain more distance, more height before he probed for Brenin, imperative. The more secluded a site he could find, the more difficult it would be for the magus to follow the link back to Chong's psyche for if the environment hid him, Brenin's line of sight would cease. Chong-An examined the sky, the drizzle had all but stopped, the increasing wind dispersing rapidly the dark clouds overhead. There were now breaks in the overall greyness and the sun was shining through, its rays lifting his spirits a little. There'd be no storm this day.

Elstan was an expert at hiding his tracks and Chong could hide his own to a certain degree without using magic. They'd need to, Brenin's guards were violent, ignorant brutes and there were expert trackers among them. And, of course, there was always the possibility that Brenin might even employ the services of a wizard tracker. But they were very few and far between and if memory served him there had not been one present in the Tower when he'd left. Chong-An looked farther ahead up the wooded slope around the slight build of Elstan following a trail only he perceived. He stared up at the summit of what Elstan liked to call a hill, but to Chong was a very steep mountain. He inhaled sharply, his lumbar going into spasm. And then he smiled wryly, Brother Drudwynn had called him a pain only recently.

'Well, I'm waiting, Chong,' said Elstan.

'I'm sorry, Elstan, I was far away,' he paused. 'Let me see. I was born in Cuomo, a territory renowned more for its rice than its people. It's in the south of my country, Cuo-Absoma, not far from the coast on the edge of the Yellow Ocean. The people are very quiet, nondescript you may say. We've never had an uprising in Cuomo like they've had in other parts of the country. We are a very boring, peace-loving people who are only interested in our family and our close neighbours and friends.' He laughed, his jowls wobbling beneath eyes that were twinkling. 'We do have the occasional spat, mind you, usually on a Friday night after work has finished for the week. The men would all congregate in the local wine shop and sometimes the rice wine would be overly imbibed and fisticuffs would ensue over a comely wench…but not often. The men usually ended up singing loudly and causing a ruckus into the early hours. We have always maintained that the primary purpose of a Saturday morning is to recover from the night before…and to wonder why our wives' voices always take on a strident note on that particular morning.

'But I have strayed. I knew nothing of rice wine at the time of which I speak. I was only seven years old and the apple of my mother's eye…and my father's, though he was too much of a man to tell me to my face. But I did overhear him once talking to a friend…' Chong halted again, pain darting through his head rendering him speechless for a moment, but the ache had nothing to do with his arthritis.

'Don't worry, my friend, we're nearly at the top, you can rest there.'

'Thank you, Elstan, I'd appreciate a respite. Where was I? Oh, yes. The Cuomoans rise early with the sun and are usually tending the crops within the hour. The women bring food out to the fields and paddies at midday and we return home when the sun drops below the horizon. There is a river running through my village, the Salaka, wide and very deep in places; it flows from the Indikara Mountains, way to the north. Many a villager's life has been saved during a famine by the trout and carp we tickled in the Salaka.' Chong-An smiled at his memories, even after all these years he missed his home.

He'd returned a few years back for a visit but it had been a dreadful mistake. All those people he'd known, been brought up with, had long gone, not even their great, great, great, ten times over great grandchildren were alive. Sometimes longevity was a curse he thought. He stumbled for the umpteenth time.

'I'm sorry, Elstan, I must rest a moment. You go ahead, I'll catch up.'

Elstan stared anxiously. 'I tell you what, I'll go on and set up camp, get a small fire going, they won't see it from down there, and get dinner started. You take your time.'

Chong-An smiled his thanks and sat down gratefully, wheezing his way through his pain, willing it almost with the strength of his inner being, to disappear. And while he waited, he gazed down the mountainside trying to glimpse the valley bottom through the trees. He failed for they were now blessedly deep into the woods.

When the pain subsided he rose to his feet and plodded slowly up the remainder of the hill and sat on a convenient tree stump in front of the cheerful campfire that Elstan had set. Chong scolded himself; he'd been far longer than he intended, climbing the last part of the slope. Elstan had used the intervening time to catch a couple of conies. He was roasting the two rabbits on spits and he had broken bread ready on platters. Pouring wine from a skin into a mug, Elstan handed it to the distressed wizard.

Elstan tried very hard to hide his anxiety. If they were pursued, and he didn't doubt they would be, then there was no way they'd escape if their pursuers were fleet of foot. Chong-An needed a healer yesterday. It was not only the pain that the man suffered that concerned Elstan…it was the man's weight. Many a man in his condition had succumbed to a heart attack. And Elstan had come to like this oriental, gentle, man.

Speaking through a mouthful of hot rabbit, Chong continued his story. 'It was the river that brought me to the attention of the Hangwue Monastery. I woke one morning extremely tired. It was as if I'd never been asleep and had spent all night bent over in the paddy fields planting rice. My back ached, I could hardly move my arms and legs and my eyes seemed puffed up, the lids almost stuck together.

'My mother was very worried and sent for the physician. He could not give a diagnosis despite almost frightening me to death as he manipulated the acupuncture needles. So he called me lazy and told me to get out of bed.' Chong chewed more hot meat from the remains of the rabbit's carcase and sighed.

'I was shamed before the whole village. No-one would believe me when I informed them I'd been up all night fishing. My mother listened to me, of course, and I acquainted her with my night's activities. I told her of the fish I'd caught in the shallows, the backbreaking weight of the many baskets I'd pulled up the river's bank and left outside our house. She was puzzled; the river was very deep for leagues in both directions, so she asked me where the shallows were.

'And I laughed at her and said they were right in the middle of the village because of the drought. What drought she asked me, and I looked at her silly. I said the river had been dropping for weeks because of it. The paddy fields were drying up, the rice plants dead, the wheat withering in the fields and we were all starving because there was no fish in the river either. But the many baskets of fish I had caught last night by the light of the full moon were enough to save our lives and those of our neighbours.

'Everyone thought I was mad. But a few weeks later the river did drop, the rice and wheat withered and the fish disappeared. And I seriously irritated very anxious people when I told them not to worry, that when the river dropped to almost nothing at a full moon, then we'd have a harvest of fish to see us through the drought.

'And that's what happened, two moons later. Why the river filled with fish at that point we do not know. But I ran around waking everybody that night and we waded into the middle and just scooped them up with the baskets. The following morning the fish disappeared again.

'The monks of Hangwue heard of my presage, for that it was, and took me at seven years of age into the monastery to learn more of augury,' Chong smiled ruefully. 'I never saw my family again.'

Elstan stared at him, the tragedy of the portent's outcome utterly appalling. 'My friend, talking of rivers, there is one on the other side of this hill. A week's walking north should bring us to Mulkie's Cross.'

'You may have to leave me, Elstan. I don't think I'll manage to get there if we are pursued quickly. But if we can reach that town I know of someone there who can help us find a healer.'

'You'll get there, my friend, even if I have to carry you. But as for us being hunted perhaps you'd better try and find out.'

Twenty-four

R yn hunched down on his belly in the snow, the oils in his white plumage keeping him dry and insulating him from the cold. His small black eyes studied Helydd sitting on her chair in the doorway of her cottage, cup in hand. She had wrapped a blanket around her legs and slung a heavy, bright red scarf around her neck…to ward off the chills, she told him. Her eyes twinkled, radiating warmth and bemused affection as she returned his look.

She reminded Ryn of his mother, at least his mother's manner during the first few weeks after his hatching. She had cared for him then, fed him and taught him how to fly. But the affection had ended abruptly when he'd been kicked out of the nest to fend for himself, as soon as he'd accomplished his first flight.

'You are truly an amazing bird, you know, Ryn. Being able to speak the human tongue and eat using fingers, it's…' and she giggled like a young girl, shaking so much she nearly tipped her tea, 'it's unbelievable!'

Her pleasure made him smile. 'Thank you, Helydd. You have a pretty name what does it mean?'

A momentary darkness clouded her eyes, although Ryn never noticed. 'Ah! My people are very loving creatures and very wise despite what others believe. My name means "battle",' she smiled fleetingly. 'I always found it strange that they'd name me such. But I now believe they must have been prescient, you know. They must have had inkling as to my future, for it is very apt. I feel as if I am fighting a war. I was an only child, Ryn, very unusual, my people normally had three or four young ones,' she sighed. Her guilt at deceiving him making her feel uncomfortable although not all she uttered was a falsehood. 'Do you know your name means "leader"?'

'Yes, the princess who named me told me so.'

'A princess! You must tell me your story. It sounds highly intriguing. Please…go on, I'm all agog.'

'Why have the liosalfar taken your daughter prisoner?'

'That is a long story. Perhaps I will relate it after you tell me yours. How come a princess gives you a voice and fingers, and how are you here deep within the Scissor Mountains leagues upon leagues from the ocean?'

'All right, I'll tell you,' slurping the remainder of his tea he laid the empty cup on the ground between them. 'I do get very thirsty the longer I speak, though.'

'Ha! I can take a hint, here, pass it to me.'

He supped at his replenished cup and clicked his beak in satisfaction. 'Wonderful.'

'You have enough sugar or would you like more?'

'This is fine, thank you. You are very kind, sharing this with a perfect stranger.'

'Oh, I don't look on you as a stranger, Ryn. Strange, yes, after all you are a bird with very odd abilities. But no, I feel comfortable with you…you are no stranger. Here, have one of my biscuits.'

His mouth watered with the smell of freshly baked sugar and fruit and he gulped the crumbling, sweet confectionery, noisily. He munched happily as he told her his story.

'My family live in the far reaches of the Great Deep…a long way west of here, it is a vast ocean. Have you seen it?'

'Once or twice…long ago. Go on.'

'We are a solitary people and we do not mix generally with others not of our kind. I spend most of my time on my own, flying here, there and everywhere. I love exploring and gladly spend my life doing just that. But one day I was called by a wizard. Ooh, this is a lovely biscuit,' he said meaningfully, grinning as she gave him another.

'I'm confused, you said a princess not a wizard.'

'There are both in my tale. Well, I was merrily resting on the ocean…when I've just eaten I am particularly fond of floating up and down on the wave tops bathing my toes. Well, as long as there are no sharks about, of course. Anyway, there I was, dozing after a wonderful meal of fresh sprats and wondering whether to fly north or south, or perhaps even east or west, when I heard someone calling to me. I opened my eyes and looked around and couldn't see a soul. But as the voice kept on shouting I followed it and ended up perched on the biggest ship I've ever seen in my life…it was huge. Five masts, although two were broken, I don't know how but…'

'Never mind that bit. Tell me about the voice,' she said frowning a little.

'I discovered the owner of the voice was a young wizard and he'd called to ask me if I would deliver a message to the Prince of Mantovar on behalf of his friend, an older wizard. And when I say old

I do mean "old"…he was ancient. Aidan, that was the young wizard's name, gave me a voice in return for doing the favour. He also gave me magic…accidentally a friend of mine thinks, because I didn't ask for that. Well, I'm not a carrier pigeon and told him so, but the old wizard asked me very nicely so I agreed.

'A friend said you have magic? Which one, the forest elf or the human?'

'Shadra, the elf,' Ryn said. 'Anyway, as I told you before, I was attacked and wounded in the Castle of Mantovar without seeing the prince, and I escaped into the Great Forest. There I met Shadra…Shadramintamablinski, what a mouthful, hey,' and he smiled. 'Shadra is the forest elf who healed me. He was on a journey here to the mountains and I decided to accompany him. And on the way we met my other friend, Anselm, a human also fleeing the castle. We all escaped some nasty monks chasing us through the forest, but trolls captured Shadra and Anselm and I had to rescue them. We nearly died from the cold later but the liosalfar found us just in time and saved us.'

'What a strange friendship…a bird, an elf and a human.' She gazed at him full of wonder and then her eyes clouded. 'I've heard of a bird and an elf before, but where? Oh, my memory's going at my age, never mind,' she smiled ruefully. 'Your friendship is a thing of tales, minstrels will sing of you in years to come. But tell me, what of the accursed liosalfar, why did they capture your friends?'

'Well, the liosalfar had saved us from imminent death, so when Shadra said they were his cousins we trusted them when they said they'd take us to safety in Alfhime. It was a serious mistake, for they took Shadra and Anselm into the cliffs through a gap that was too small for me…that was two days ago. I haven't seen them since.'

'They are an evil people, Ryn, they betray their history. If your friends are in Alfhime then you have cause to worry. Let me relate a little of my story, perhaps then you will understand a bit more,' and she settled back in her chair and wound her necklace around her hands. 'Years ago my daughter, Manon, and I came into these cold mountains looking for a new home and we encountered the liosalfar. They were kind at first, helped us build this cottage and so we settled. It was hard here, but we survived by picking berries and bartering hares and such like for other provender in the village a few valleys over,' again she didn't look into his eyes.

'But they were treacherous. My daughter wasn't feeling well this one day, but I had to go into the village as we were short of provisions. The liosalfar offered to look after her and medicine her while I went down to ply my wares in the market. I went off happy knowing that Manon was safe, but on my return they told me that she had harmed something belonging to them. I asked them what she had done and they wouldn't tell me…they said it was secret and that I didn't need to know. But they told me she needed punishing and because of the seriousness of her actions, they were going to imprison her for life. I'd never see her again.' Helydd burst into tears and spoke through her hands covering her face. 'Despite my entreaties they still hold her.'

Ryn was appalled. 'Will they ever release her?'

'I don't think so. But I will not leave here until she is free even though it may well be my death I await.'

Ryn became very agitated. Was this the fate awaiting Shadra and Anselm? And then he remembered. 'What of the Cragga?'

'The Cragga…what is that?' Helydd asked quietly, staring intently in his face she wondered how much he knew.

'You've never heard of it?' Ryn replied.

She shook her head, looking puzzled. 'Should I have?'

'The liosalfar were fleeing it. They seemed very scared of whatever it was.'

'I'm sorry Ryn, I have no idea. But I do know of another way into Alfhime. It will take a long time and will need a lot of strength. But I believe you may succeed with my help.'

Twenty-five

The shape-shifter sat on Lewyn's shoulder eating yet another interminable mouse. It wondered if the cat ever ate anything else. The slimy taste and cold feel of the little carcase slipping down its unaccustomed small throat, although inviting at first, was now getting a little monotonous. It wanted something larger and warmer…the cat might be small but the shape-shifter in its normal state was not. It licked its lips and rubbed its furry cheek against the rough stubble on its ride's neck. It wondered what reaction it would get if it just raked its claws across the protuberance humans called "adam's apple". It smiled and began washing its face with its paws. One thing was certain, Lewyn would not be happy if his neck suddenly burst open and blood gushed forth from his mouth instead of the usual rubbish he spoke.

It remained alert as Lewyn walked across the tavern floor carrying a jug of ale and, pulling out a stool, sat across the table from his leader, Razor Montetor.

'Here, Razor, me old mate, you look as if you need cheering up have a refill on me.'

Razor looked at him through eyes narrowed to fine slits. 'Since when have I been your mate? I've things on my mind, go away.'

'Aw, come on, no need to be like that 'cos the boss has dumped yer for that idiot kid. You ain't the only one that doesn't want him as king, yer know.'

'Yeah, well, perhaps yer right,' and that was the nearest Razor had ever come to apologising or agreeing with the cat lover. 'We got to do something about him…get rid of him somehow.'

'Which one, Bazyli or the kid?'

'The kid o' course! We can't get shot of Bazyli until he names me his successor.'

'Well, he ain't gonna do that while our so-called prince is alive.'

'Lewyn, you love stating the obvious don't you.'

'You gotta get rid of both of them.'

'Again, the obvious, you're getting on my nerves, and keep your bloody voice down.'

'Sorry,' and he leaned forward over the table.

Razor drew back instinctively, the smell on Lewyn was overpowering. The cat, though, was staring him in the eye, and this made Razor very nervous. It was licking its lips the way it did just before killing its prey. If Razor didn't know better, it looked as if its fangs were longer.

'Perhaps we won't have to worry if the kid goes off in that ship with his friends, like we overheard,' Cyryl Lewyn sniggered, a sound that made the shape-shifter feel right at home. 'He could be gone years, we won't get him interfering.'

Lewyn supped his ale and, dipping his finger into the mug, he offered the wet digit to his cat. The shape-shifter sniffed and then run its rough tongue over the wetness and, liking the taste, it purred its pleasure. Lewyn tipped his mug and allowed the cat to drink from it, smiling he took another sup himself and turned his gaze once more on his disgruntled leader.

Razor turned up his mouth in disgust. 'One day that cat's going to poison you,' and he resumed staring sullenly into his own mug. 'The kid going off in the ship won't help me at all; in fact it could be the worst thing. He'll still be Prince Griffin and too far away for me to do anything about it.'

'Yeah, pity that. I'd much rather have you as the Montetor. That ship'll have its new masts any day now.'

'That bitch princess said they were all off somewhere and no-one was going to stop them,' Razor said before taking a large swig of the sour ale.

'Where they goin', then?' Lewyn scratched a fleabite on his neck disturbing the cat.

'I don't know. But I do know they need that ship wherever it is they are heading. Now if we can stop it, hey, ratface!'

'Stop the ship? How you gonna do that?'

'Well, first of all, perhaps we could delay it until that fog drifts in, it wouldn't get out of the harbour with that down on us. Then maybe we find a way to scupper it for a few weeks. Nobody will ever see us under that; we could get very close to the hull, do some damage. If I thought they wouldn't see it I could maybe set fire to a boat and hitch it to the hull. If the fog's thick enough they'd never see it until it was too late. Risky though.' Razor, emptying his mug, slammed it back on the table and sneered. 'Maybe the kid will accidentally trip in the dark and fall in the harbour between the ship and the wharf, like that other one did.' Razor's eyes gleamed and he called across to the bar for brandy.

'We can't wait for that fog, though, can we? What about them demons?' Lewyn's face ticked below his left eye, a habit he had when he was scared.

'What demons?'

'You know, the ones they said was in that Darkness.'

'You didn't believe that load o' shite, did you? That's a story they've put around to make things easier to get the kid crowned. Distract the people with a story of terror, keep them running in circles, and then make him king when everybody's looking elsewhere for demons. After they've done it, hoodwinked everybody into having him, they'll come out with another story and say the demons have all run away because we have a king...or something!'

'I never thought o' that. Are you sure there's no demons, Razor?'

'Of course I am, you think I'm stupid. When was the last time you saw a demon, hey? Now shut it while I think of a way to hold that ship at the dock until the bad weather comes in.'

'All right, while you're thinking I'll get us another refill. Tybalt's just come in, he owes me a round or two for a bit o' work I done him.'

'You, do some work, that'll be the day!' Razor looked over at the squat, thick-shouldered man standing at the bar talking to the innkeeper. 'Hey, isn't Tybalt the haulier the Portolan hired to bring them replacement masts down from the mountain?'

'Aye, he must be making a packet out o' them two wagons.'

'Only two?'

'Aye, they are the only ones long enough on Griffin to carry them trees.' Lewyn, somewhat worse for wear for the ale, lurched up from his stool and started for the bar and the man who was going to buy the next round.

'Wait,' called Razor, 'get back here.'

'What?' Turning quickly the shape-shifter nearly lost its hold and dug in its claws, pain spasmed in Lewyn's face. 'Careful, Hyacinth girl,' and he stroked her back.

'Find out all you can about them wagons, when they're due back and how many journeys they're likely to make. And find out how many men will be with the wagons on each trip.'

'What you thinking of, then?'

209

'Never you mind, turd, just do as yer told. And be careful…I don't want him knowing I'm asking.'

Half an hour later, Lewyn stumbled back to an increasingly bad-tempered Razor sitting morosely at his table, rotgut brandy in hand and a lot more in his belly. There was no sign of the cat, judging by the smell on its owner, with good reason, the stench poured from him along with the sweat.

'Dear God, man, don't you ever wash?' Razor asked.

'What's the matter?' and Lewyn raised his arm and sniffed. 'That's them bloody horses you can smell, Tybalt stinks of them.' He dropped his arm and took another swig of his ale.

'Well, what did you find out? Razor asked, leaning back against the wall to get as far from his underling as possible.

'There's one due back this afternoon, Tybalt's meeting it outside of town to redirect it. There's been a flood, fountain bust or something on Bramble Hill, the wagon can't get through there,' Lewyn sniggered. 'They were gonna use Bramble as the easiest way down to the docks, Bazyli and the seneschal have spent all morning keeping that route clear. Portolan's gotta think of another way to bring it now and its giving him and Bazyli a right headache. He's been asking after you, wants you.'

'Who wants me?'

'Bazyli.'

'He can want…I'll see him later. What's the new route?'

'What? Oh…that's why Tybalt's in here now, he's waiting for his new instructions.'

Razor's mind went into overdrive. 'It hasn't taken them long to get the first trees cut and loaded, has it? I wouldn't have expected the first lot here until tomorrow.'

'Tybalt said that an' all. But it seems these green people have magic and can bring the trees to the surface in double quick time. He doesn't know how.'

'Where are Striker and Snake?' Razor asked abruptly, wondering where the two most productive of Griffin's pickpockets were working.

'Those two could be anywhere, there's ripe picking in these crowds. No looting though, Janne's watching for that, the militia's out in force. There's panic everywhere and people ain't being careful. I'm surprised this place is still open.'

'You know Fendrel, anything for easy coin; he'll be the last to close. Go and find Striker and Snake, bring them to the Bottle's Neck. You do know where that is?'

'Aye, top o' Bramble.'

'Bring them by noon. I've a few things to organize before I meet you, so wait if I'm late.'

'Aw, come off it, it's bedlam out there I'll never find them!'

'You will! If I have to come looking for you you'll wish you hadn't been born…you and that damned cat. Go, look for the biggest crowds that's where they'll be.'

'There's no need to take it out on Hyacinth, Razor, she's done nothing to you.'

'Except reek and I don't like the way she's giving me the eye lately…she looks as if she's plotting something, gives me the creeps.' The deputy rose from the table, swallowed the last of his brandy, and walked out.

Cyryl Lewyn followed cursing under his breath, he didn't like anyone maligning Hyacinth, although he admitted, she was not her usual self lately…must have been something she ate.

Razor was correct; Striker and his partner, Snake, were working Laudanum Square behind the docks. Here the crowds were massed, baggage in hand, making their way down to the Portolan's naval ships, all of which were taking on refugees and sailing for Drakka. Other boats of all shapes and sizes, from freighters to trawlers, and of all nationalities berthed in the harbour, had also all been commandeered to carry the people of Griffin. Bazyli smiled his satisfaction, he and Janne's organization was working well, most of the townspeople would have vacated their homes and be away to safety by the end of the following day.

Lodovico Portolan watched as his pride and joy, the Porpoise, sailed through the reef carrying the Brakwannans home. He had given her over to Mazumbai for as long as she was needed by him, for he and the chief realized that their homecoming might not be an easy one. Power loaned to another had the habit of corrupting as Lodovico knew well.

'What's he want us for?' asked Striker disgruntled, Lewyn had just jogged his arm in the act of purloining a purse.

'Don't know, but you'd better not hang about he's not in a very good mood,' answered Lewyn.

'Sulking is he?' sniggered Snake.

'Shut it, fool,' Striker said clipping Snake around the head, 'if you slip up and say anything like that where he can hear you, you'll be dead before you can fart.'

'All right, keep your hands off,' Snake said rubbing his head. 'But don't he realize the rich pickings here?'

'Aye, he'll know. So it must be important for him to call us away, his share's gonna be down as well,' and then he smiled. 'Maybe he's found richer pickings.'

'Watch out, there's a militiaman over there walking this way.' Lewyn nodded his head towards the other side of the square.

It didn't take them long to remove themselves from the vicinity. Hurrying up Sweet Lane, a narrow passageway that did not live up to its name behind the Golden Turtle, the three were soon on their way to meet Razor in the Bottle's Neck, another less than salubrious tavern about a half hour's walk away.

Razor examined the large fountain, its size indicating that it was not just used for recreation but also by the local residents for the collection of fresh drinking water. The wall holding its reservoir of water had been ruptured, probably by a collision with a wagon driven too hastily for the narrow street. It was a stupid place to have the ornate structure, at the top of a hill overlooking a road just wide enough for a decent size coach to traverse.

The Montetor's deputy sat on the wall along from the break watching the water pouring through and down the road. The flow was washing away the surface cobbles and leaving a deep channel in place. He swept his eyes over the area close by, at all the houses now vacated because of the barmy demon story. Razor was disgusted at people's naiveté. To give up all you own, to run away on the say so of two traitors. Bazyli and Lodovico, so obviously in collusion to install the usurper prince, how anybody could fall for the story was beyond belief. Razor picked up a cobble and dropped it in the water its loud splash jarring him. He again examined the surroundings. No-one was walking in the road in either direction. If it hadn't been for the noise floating on the air from streets over the way, and the absence of kids playing, you'd have thought it a pleasant day in the sun. It was unnerving. Bramble Hill, being a main thoroughfare, was very rarely empty.

Razor put out his hand and felt the stones at the edge of the break; they were loose and wouldn't take much effort to remove. He prised one away, the torrent increased slightly and more stones shifted. He could see why Bazyli wouldn't allow the wagon to attempt this road. It was lethal.

Razor grimaced, he would teach Bazyli not to do him out of his rightful inheritance…the Montetors would rule the Portolans, not the other way around. He walked off to the Bottle's Neck smiling; the fool hadn't even put a militiaman at the bottom of the hill to warn travellers.

Selkirk, holding the reins of the six-horse team, hummed quietly as he drove the wagon south along the road to Griffin Town. His companion, Rowan, a sailor off the Grim was sitting alongside him lolling on the seat, feet hard against the buckboard his eyes closed, relaxing under the sun. They had talked for a while on setting out with the first two trees on the bed of the stretched-bed wagon but their conversation had soon stilled in the warm breeze. Both men were comfortable, happy in the knowledge that the journey was going well. Selkirk glanced behind at his cargo, shorn clean of all branches and knobbly bits by the use of magic, the trees were now bare poles you could barely put your arms around and forty foot long.

Earlier, Rowan had tried describing Bylani to him, but the stories all seemed so far-fetched Selkirk had tended to switch off. Even though the evidence was on the wagon, who had ever heard of a forty foot teak tree growing in a cave? But he'd find out for himself soon, his family already on their way underground…the price extracted by Tybalt as his fee for delaying his own departure. Nevertheless he worried. He was not usually a superstitious man but he'd grown up with stories of green devils taking you into the catacombs and never giving you up. Despite what the prince and his friends had told him there was still that nagging little doubt that wouldn't go away. And then again there was the future to come to terms with. What on earth was he going to do down there, did they need hauliers? If not, though, he could always work on a farm—but a farm underground? The concept beggared the imagination. And how were they going to cope with the knowledge that there was a host of demons above them digging their way down to annihilate them. For whatever was in the Darkness would undoubtedly try and gain entrance to Bylani. Was hiding in the green people's haven a premature burial? He sighed deeply, it was no good worrying about tomorrow, just let's get today over and done with first.

He resumed his humming as he came into sight of the town and prepared to negotiate the narrow streets. It was not usually too difficult getting these wagons around corners, but their normal freight was iron ore, piled high, these trees, although not as heavy perhaps, jutted out of the wagon a good ten feet or more. It was going to be dicey in several places, especially at that damned fountain on the top of Bramble. Still, he'd been told that the rest of the route would be clear, all the way to the ship.

Razor watched the wagon rolling cumbersomely towards him, its front end riding lighter than the rear due to the overhanging poles. A team of six, a lot of horseflesh to have milling about frightened, he'd have to be careful, keep well out of the way. He'd send Snake in to finish off the driver and the passenger.

Snake liked killing as long as there was no prospect of his quarry fighting back. He'd just proved it by sneaking up behind an unsuspecting Tybalt listening to Lewyn talk nineteen to the dozen. He'd hit him too hard of course, the crack of the haulier's skull was heard a hundred yards away. Razor had nearly lost his temper with him, not expecting the noise. But he had already decided how to hide the body from the questing eyes of Janne who would, of course, investigate the tragedy.

Another one with uses was Lewyn, as long as it involved his tongue. Standing in the front bedroom window of an empty house overlooking the bottom of the hill and Hawthorn, the road running across the bottom of Bramble, Razor smirked. Lewyn was about to employ his gift of the gab in giving the driver a message purporting to come from Tybalt. As the wagon drew into the end of the bottom road the deputy signalled to Lewyn, and Cyryl stepped out, frightening the life out of Selkirk who had to haul on the reins sharply to halt the wagon.

'You stupid bastard, Lewyn! If you wanted me to stop why didn't you call from over there?'

Rowan roused quickly when he nearly slid off the seat. 'What the hell, crazy sod.'

'What you want?' Selkirk asked, he knew the cat-carrying man of old, had done a little business with him, mainly contraband brandy. But he also knew that Tybalt employed him on minor tasks running errands.

'Tybalt sent me to warn you, the fountain's been breached at the top o' the hill. He said you've no need to worry, they've begun repairing the wall but the road is a bit slippery.'

'No need to worry? Does he realize what a sod this is to drive?'

'Course he does, that's why he sent me. You're to pick up speed, do it at a run from here, get the horses trotting before you come to the bend at the bottom and you'll get up there. Don't slow down whatever you do or you'll never get up. He said it looks worse than it is.'

'Bloody hell, I love going round corners at speed, plays hell with my heart,' Selkirk grumbled. 'Well, you heard the man, sailor. Hold on tight!'

It was a good team. Selkirk, a very experienced driver, had driven a six-in-hand many times but he was tired. It had taken him a good day and a half to drive up to the catacombs and he'd expected to rest until the following day. But by nightfall he'd turned around and was half way back to the forest—haste imperative. If he hadn't been exhausted he might have got down first and had a look up the hill, but he took Lewyn at his word.

He cracked the whip and the horses moved off at a goodly pace; speeding up as they got to the bend. Selkirk wasn't worried about the wagon overturning; the weight of the trees would keep its wheels on the ground. But his tongue clove to the roof of his mouth when he saw the veritable river running across the road. It was too late to stop the wagon it would have slewed and upended, probably killing the horses in the process. He did the only thing he could, he speeded up even more. But he hadn't seen the channel cut across his path. He did see the men at the top repairing the fountain's wall suddenly turn and throw stones at the horses at the very moment the horses found the deep rut in the road. Selkirk lost control.

The wagon juddered throwing Rowan into the feet of the panicked rear horses; he was kicked unconscious before the weight of the toppling wagon crushed him. He drowned beneath the fast-running water. Selkirk managed to jump clear but he stumbled and went to his knees. It took but moments for the waiting Snake to bash him over the head. Striker dragged Tybalt's body from where they'd hidden it behind a hedge and he and Snake slung both bodies amongst the screaming horses.

'Get out of here,' shouted Razor highly delighted at the sight of the two poles breaking loose and sliding back down the hill.

They disappeared into the surrounding buildings leaving six stricken horses screaming in terror and three dead men—and the first delivery of replacement masts a shambles. It would take at least a day to salvage the poles, the wagon wrecked beyond repair. With only one wagon remaining to bring down the other eight, it would take nearly two weeks to get them all to the Grim, weeks more to step them—plenty of time for the fog to drift over Griffin.

But what was more important, the Prince Griffin would be marooned on the island. He wouldn't be going anywhere with his friends. Razor almost laughed aloud as he went to the docks to report the accident, and to put the next part of his plan into operation.

Twenty-six

Locklear, standing on his quarterdeck at noon the following day, watched as the two bare poles were laid on the quay alongside the Grim. Hopper had chosen well, he'd never seen trees so well prepared for making a mast.

'What a tragedy, three men dead to bring us two trees, I wonder if it's worth it,' he said aloud.

'It is, my friend, but I agree, I never expected to pay such a price and all but one of the horses killed,' Lodovico shook his head. 'Why on earth did he attempt that hill? The haulier was told to bring them through Cobb's Road, I just don't understand it.' He turned his back on the wharf and stared out to sea at the approaching fogbank, easily seen now it was that close. 'How are...' and then he was interrupted by the sound of horses neighing loudly and crowds scattering on the quay.

Forced to a walking pace, the two riders made their way through the mob to the side of the Grim the first, on reaching the ship, shouted up. 'Captain Locklear, may we come aboard, we have tidings?' And two green men lowered their hoods startling those near them.

Moments later both men were on the quarterdeck refreshing themselves with the best Enzorean wine in Locklear's larder, and staring around the ship, their large eyes even larger in their wonderment.

'Gentlemen, you have news?' asked Locklear pulling at his beard.

He didn't care for more trouble at this time and these two had definitely caused a stir on the waterfront. Even though a great number of the islanders had now heard of the green people's reappearance and would soon be sharing their hospitality, only relatively few had actually glimpsed Leonid. It came as a momentous shock to actually see a green man in the flesh...and here were two arriving in one hell of a hurry.

'I'm sorry, Captain, but being in the outside world is mesmerizing, your ship and the sea equally so,' and he smiled. 'Allow me to introduce myself, I am Lowis and my friend here is Revvie, we are tree sculptors. It was thought best that two be sent here to aid you in making your masts, but also in case one of us became a victim of another so-called accident.'

'So-called? What do you mean?' asked Lodovico, his insides starting a bellyache. But then he felt sure he could feel a rumble beneath his feet, he looked down disconcerted.

'Don't worry about that tremor, Excellency, we'll explain in a moment. But as for the loss of your wagon, it was no accident,' answered Revvie.

'How do you know? The Montetor and Marshal Janne are even now at the site and they've reported no foul play, and…' Lodovico again halted in mid-sentence as the rumbling increased, noticed now by others on the quay all looking around for its source, consternation on many faces. 'What is that?'

'Please, patience and all will be explained, there is no danger,' said Revvie. 'As for knowing it was murder, we have means that you will not understand yet. Later, when we have time, you will learn more of us…as we will, you. No, the wagon driver and his passenger were definitely killed by others. Although we did not see the third man slain we assume he was, as his body was found with the other two and his death was not by natural means.'

Locklear and Lodovico stared at each other, both lost for words. Then all four men suddenly made a grab for the rail, the tremors now becoming seriously violent and the sea just inside the enclosed harbour beginning to boil at the foot of the beacon's cliff. Everyone stared east.

The green men laughed aloud and Lowis shouted so that everyone could hear. 'Do not be afraid. What you are about to see will be amazing and believe me when I say it is no demon that you will see….' The rest of his words were drowned out by an almighty crash as the side of the cliff suddenly blew out, rocks flying everywhere followed by a great torrent of water bursting forth. With it, as if shot by the most colossal bow in the world came a krynx, forty foot long and huge of wrinkled girth. The krynx shot two hundred feet into the air before falling gracefully into the lagoon. Riding atop it was a green figure, lying prone, gripping on for dear life. Behind it falling like a salvo of arrows, were tree trunks all shorn as those on the quayside.

In the tremendous silence that followed, the freed river pouring through its natural outlet for the first time in centuries, Locklear asked the question that all wanted answered.

'Dear God, what was that?'

'That, Captain, is the rest of your masts being delivered,' said Lowis, grinning from ear to ear.

'Mattie will bring them into the harbour and then we'll levitate them to the quay. Simple, hey?' and Revvie laughed until his sides ached.

It was later, when matters had calmed and they were watching Mattie riding her krynx around and around the logs pushing them towards the ship, that an explanation was given.

'You see, Captain, when the vibes told us the accident was a deliberate action we decided that another means had to be employed to get your masts to you. And we suggested the river, we and Mattie,' said Revvie.

'We will still have to replace the cliff before the Darkness arrives otherwise it will be another entrance into the heart of Bylani. Besides, you have no water in Griffin Town at the moment, the level of the river has dropped, no longer constricted at its mouth,' Lowis added.

'How long will that take you?' asked Lodovico.

'A couple of days, I fear,' answered Lowis.

'Then we will not have the time to step new masts before the fog is upon us,' said Locklear. 'So, once you have raised the poles from the water, instead of placing them on the quay can you put them straight aboard the Grim? I believe there is a safe anchorage at Moth, we will sail there to complete repairs.'

'Revvie, Lowis,' Mattie now alongside the ship called up to her fellow countrymen, 'Revvie, do not go near the humans!'

'What…' answered Lowis, 'what do you mean?'

'It's Leonid, he has the plague. You may be carriers,' thankfully no-one ashore heard.

'Then we will send for the healer,' said Lodovico, 'he's up at the manorhouse. It won't take him long to get here.'

'No, he's not there. A messenger has already been sent from Bylani overland. The healer is on his way to Leonid,' Mattie said.

Twenty-seven

Aidan, at the end of his tether, felt he was losing his mind. Once again something had cropped up to thwart his attempts to get to the Darkness and to Tragen. He even wondered if the Gods were conspiring to keep him from his mentor.

He'd had no option other than to see what he could do for Leonid. But acceding to his friends' sympathetic pleadings meant putting off his rescue attempt for at least another three days, an appalling delay that was breaking his heart. It would take a day to get to the catacombs, possibly a day to get down to Bylani, heal Leonid and return to the surface and another day to get back to the manorhouse. And they'd all agreed, it had to be the manorhouse where they left their bodies—they couldn't trust anyone else but Cornelia and Alessa to watch over them. He was devastated; anything could happen to Tragen in that time, it didn't bear thinking about.

But what else could he do? Besides being a friend, he owed Leonid. The Green Man had rescued the four of them when they'd fled from Razor into the catacombs. They'd been utterly lost wandering the black tunnels with only Beattie's light to guide them. Not even Anders, from his place at the wall, had been able to identify the route back to the surface. It was at the height of their despair that they had stumbled into the cave where Leonid had been waiting for them.

Aidan reined in his horse a little, his impatience and concern dictating he speed up. But he was tending to outpace the coach carrying the womenfolk and children.

Thaddeus, though, did not seem to be having any problems, despite the fact this was only the third time he'd been on a horse. His ability to align his psyche with the emotions of animals had grown into something phenomenal. It had started with him playing with insects on his hands, enjoying their antics. But that had been fairly small magic. Then his ability had leapt in unparalleled bounds to controlling rodents in battle, something that was unheard of in the wizarding world. And what he had done on the Grim in calling the rats to their death had also been incredible, though Thaddeus would have called it unforgiveable. No other wizard could control the animal kingdom as Thaddeus did. His personal magic was becoming more powerful by the day—it was frightening him. He didn't want to control any animal, his empathy with all fauna was deep, and he felt it in his soul. All animals should be free to lead their own lives. He vowed again never to deliberately call an animal to its death—he'd never handle the guilt.

And Aidan had no idea why. Magic was not supposed to grow in this manner. Was someone or something helping him? There was so much he didn't know, so much that he wanted Tragen's advice on, he felt overwhelmed, grossly inadequate. He was feeling guilty at wanting to put the search for his master before that of healing Leonid. This culpability, added to that he was already suffering over Tragen's passing, was almost too much for him to bear. His desolate mood deepened, his isolation from his friends desperately offering comfort, became greater.

Nonetheless, he couldn't seem to get Beatrix out of his head. Her face and Augusta's were getting mixed up in his mind and he didn't know what the hell that meant, so he tried to lock them both out of his head. But doing that only increased his loneliness, his misery, he needed them both.

His silence was grim and forbidding as he rode towards Mount Trespass, past the relatively new trees planted to revive the old forest after the depredations of the iron mines and charcoal burners in years gone past. Their destination, the catacombs beneath the taller of the two peaks, Mount Trespass, the tombs known locally as the Devil's Keep, were still out of reach until the morrow.

The Devil's Keep, so named because all those who had entered in search of treasure had never returned. Superstition, nurtured by the Green People, had flourished among the Griffin islanders. Bright, winking lights were often seen at rifts in the mountainside. They were thought, by the islanders, to be demons on watch for intruders, but were in fact salamanders standing guard to frighten away inquisitive people. Nevertheless, the salamanders and the intruders were only a part of the actual story.

A thousand years previously the original inhabitants of Griffin Island, the Green People, had made the decision to reside below ground to answer the requirements of the Prophecy—the dying Elder Findar's Prophecy, delivered to Elder Zoran, the present day leader of his people.

'The shadow's bane is nigh when young sorcerers defy the design of the Dark One, to search all under the sun.

A haven must be found for all those who are bound to flee the vile shadow, and ensure life will follow.

One sorcerer to heal the bane, a second to reassure its pain, a third to show it the light, a fourth to aid its flight. And one all-seeing, to guide, but not in this world does he bide. When five strive together succeed the Dark One will never.

When thunder rolls and that which cannot toll, tolls in the hands of Edele's enchanted, salvation will be established.'

The Green People had dedicated themselves to creating the haven in an infinite assortment of huge caverns in a subterranean world beneath Griffin Island. It would be a place of safety for those fleeing the shadow at a time when five wizards would come together to seek the bane.

And now the wizards had emerged in the world, Aidan to heal, Thaddeus with his strange magic, was to reassure. The young women, Beatrix to show the bane the light, and Augusta, the warrior wizard to aid in its flight, the latter perplexing them all for none knew quite what that meant. The fifth wizard, the most amazing of the five, was Anders, dead for weeks and watching over them at the vastly complex wall of colours in Limbo—spending his time deciphering a panoramic wall of perpetually changing shapes and colours while he whittled away at carving bells.

Aidan, deep in his memories on the journey to Bylani, wondered on the identity of the bane. The shadow was easy enough to understand, that was the Darkness now flowing free in the world and bringing untold terror along with its demons.

But the identity of the bane? They had struggled with unravelling that mystery in their discussions with Elder Zoran and had come to the conclusion that it could only be a dragon—an animal that had not been seen for thousands of years. But where on earth could they search for such a beast? One of the few facts known about dragons was that the elves used to ride them. Elves and dragons lived in close harmony together and both races dropped from knowledge at roughly the same time.

So someone suggested asking the elves for information. But which elves? There were the small forest elves supposedly still inhabiting the Great Forest in Drakka and Mantovar. There were other, taller elves long exiled from the known world, no-one knew where they were. And there were other darker elves that legend implied lived to nurture violence—no-one wanted to know of them. So they'd made the decision to search for the small forest elves and if there was no luck with them, if they had no knowledge of the whereabouts of the dragons, then hopefully they'd be directed to the taller elves.

For the shadow's bane was intrinsic to the requirements for defeating the One behind the Darkness.

'Aidan, you're going too fast,' called Thaddeus from his horse behind, 'slow down the coach can't keep up.'

Aidan eased his pace even more, not bothering to look behind him at those following; he studied the terrain, river to his right and the forest on his left. Aidan sniffed the air; he preferred the countryside to that of the towns…cleaner, fresher, the pace of life slower, and a lot less hassle. In the past he and Tragen had often gone hunting, not just for food but also for the different plants and herbs the old wizard needed for his potions—and Aidan required for his healing salves.

The young boy's gift had flourished in those years, grown with his learning of the different ingredients needed to support his healing. His healing magic was only used as a last resort, for employing the gift usually exhausted him, the depth of his fatigue depending on the seriousness of the ailment. So whenever it was possible he refrained from using magic and employed instead the natural remedies to be found growing in sometimes the most unlikely of places. He and Tragen laughed and grew closer as they collected peppermint to relieve pain, lavender to aid sleeping disorders, green tea to reduce the risk of some cancers, and even encouraging the eating of mustard to those who had lost their appetite. Aidan smiled; he had not believed a number of Tragen's remedies and had told him so on many occasions, only for Tragen to laugh, his great belly laugh, and prove him wrong.

Thinking of Tragen brought despair to Aidan's eyes. 'I won't be long, Master, honest…honest. I'll get you out of there, the Darkness is not going to keep you, I promise.'

He kept his head turned away from Thaddeus now riding at his flank. Drying his eyes surreptitiously on his sleeve he accidentally rubbed against a fungus growing on the bark of a birch tree. He had wandered closer to the trees in his musings. Rubbing the squashed, yellow brain fungus from his arm he dismounted for a moment and picked at the brown, fairy ring mushrooms growing at the foot of the tree. He stared into the woods enjoying the peace and quiet of the forest, the normal teezing sounds of the tree pipit, and the soft rattle of the redstart. He looked at the ground and smelled the aroma of the violet coloured tufted vetch and fodder vetch. He sighed and remounted, twirling a mushroom in his fingers as he rode along, throwing it away when the coach came up with him.

'Hey, what's that on your arm? I'll have that,' Dom, his head hanging out the window, pulled free a lump of the brain fungus that Aidan had missed and promptly ate it. 'Smashing,' he said, licking his lips, 'cauliflower mushroom…very sweet. My Mum gave me plenty of that when I was ill last year.'

'What was the matter with you,' Aidan asked, curious.

'My skin was itching something awful and Mum used to cook them with some other funny things.'

'What funny things, Jasmina,' Beatrix asked sitting opposite her and cradling Kataya, fast asleep, on her lap despite the bouncing of the coach on the rough track.

'Oh, there were many things, among them nettles and burdock, and a little alfalfa. A spoonful three times a day did the trick.'

A little later Prile stirred on his mother's lap and, opening his eyes, he studied the slow flowing river. 'Mum, there are trout in there can we stop and tickle a few?'

'Not now, we haven't time.' She did not stress her anxiety, not wanting to frighten her children, but it was very evident in her manner and appearance that she was worried sick. She was extremely agitated, unable to remain still on her seat. 'When we get back you can run next door, I'm sure Primrosa will have some for you.'

'Oh, Mum, I like tickling them, please.'

'No, Prile, not now, we can't stop we have to get home. Dom can take you to the river tomorrow.'

They travelled on through the night, afraid to tarry in case Leonid succumbed to the disease before they reached him. Aidan wouldn't have stopped anyway; his concerns more for Tragen, though he never mentioned it.

When dawn broke over Mount Trespass, the party arrived at the catacombs utterly exhausted, Prile and Kataya very fractious. Dom, the only one of the children to have an understanding of the urgency of their journey, held his mother's hand attempting to bring comfort to her despairing mind.

224

Augusta and Beatrix climbed down – aching and weary from the coach – helped by Thaddeus and the coachman. Stumbling after came Jasmina and her children. Hurriedly pushing past Nkosi and two others – securing on a flatbed wagon the last of the tree trunks to be brought to the surface before the novel way of the river was used – the green woman and her children made for the entrance to the catacombs and quickly disappeared inside.

'Good morning to you, Milord, Highness,' Nkosi said touching his forelock to the wizards.

Aidan stopped a moment and examined the tree trunks. 'How goes it, Nkosi, you have enough?'

The black helmsman laughed cheerfully. 'Oh, aye, Milord, the green people found another way to get the trees to the Grim, these are extras. As we're going back by horse we might as well take them with us.'

'How much longer before you go?' Thaddeus asked.

'Tomorrow I expect, Highness, as soon as the first mate comes up.'

'Where is Hopper?' Aidan asked.

'In Griffin Town.'

'What, he never passed us,' said Aidan taken aback. 'What is he doing back there?'

'Sorry, Milord, it isn't our Griffin Town, it's the Green People's Griffin Town. They name their caves with the location of the place on the surface directly above it. There's Elk, that's over on the west of the island, they breed cattle there. Then there's Timber in the north and Moth and…'

'Okay, I get the message. If I miss him, tell Hopper that I'll need to check you for disease before I leave tomorrow.'

Aidan, Thaddeus and Beatrix strode towards the entrance, leaving the horses in the care of the coachman. Augusta lagging behind glanced quickly down the mountainside towards Griffin Town sparkling in the early morning light. She stared out over the town and into the harbour beyond and could just make out the Grim tied up to the jetty. She wondered when they'd ever see it again—it already seemed like weeks since they'd disembarked.

Lifting her eyes to the horizon she drew breath sharply. 'Aidan,' she called. 'Aidan, Beattie, Thaddeus come and have a look…now,' she ordered.

When they came up to her she stretched out her arm and pointed west at a dark smudge on the horizon. 'Is that what I think it is?'

'Dear God, it's moving faster than we thought,' answered Beatrix as the boys stared silently. 'Anders, is it the Darkness?'

'It is, the opening into the sewer has been widened and it's now drifting a hell of a lot quicker!'

'Any idea how the hole got bigger?' Aidan asked.

It was Thaddeus who answered his voice full of dread. 'Demons…demons have been used to break out of the cavern. They are here.'

'Come on you lot, there's a krynx here to give us a lift,' shouted Dom from the cave.

'Coming, Dom,' Augusta said as they gazed at each other, the dread and menace of the Darkness filling them.

At that moment a horse galloped into the rock-strewn forecourt of the catacombs and its rider fell from its back in his haste. 'Highness…Highness, please I have a message!'

Again Aidan, Thaddeus, Augusta and Beatrix emerged from the cave. 'What is it?' Thaddeus asked the man almost collapsing with fatigue.

'I'm sorry, Highness,' he gasped. 'I've ridden here at speed from Meltwater. The Montetor needs your help. There is rioting and he needs you to help him persuade the people to leave—they don't believe what he's telling them.'

Aidan's face fell but Thaddeus was the first to speak. 'Aidan, we have two days before we leave for Tragen…two days. You don't need me in Bylani, I have to go. When I've finished I can meet you back at home, I'll go straight there. Please understand, this is my duty now.'

'Aye, Thaddeus. But you understand me, whatever the outcome I leave in search of Tragen in two days with or without your help—I wait no longer.'

Thaddeus nodded and turned for his own horse. 'Thank you, I…' he hugged Aidan quickly.

'Wait, there's no need for you to go alone, I'll come with you,' said Augusta, unexpectedly afraid for him. 'It sounds dangerous, you'll need someone to watch your back,' she smiled tentatively and, her jealousy forgotten for the moment, she whispered in Beatrix's ear.

'Take care of Aidan; you know what he's like when things aren't going his way.'

Aidan and Beatrix re-entered the catacombs and climbed on to the krynx's back for their bumpy journey down to Bylani. All four, though, had misgivings at the splitting up of the party. Uppermost in Aidan's mind was the delay in getting to Tragen. Beatrix worried about her awakening feelings for the young healer. Thaddeus couldn't hide his anxiety for the troubles in Meltwater and Augusta couldn't understand why she'd suddenly felt an overwhelming need to be in the iron town—or was it because she wanted to be with Thaddeus.

Twenty-eight

Chong-An opened his eyes and stared at Elstan, an amused expression flickered across his face. 'Oh, dear me!'

Elstan sat up quickly from where he'd been resting against the fallen branch of the loblolly, keeping an anxious watch on the oriental wizard sitting with his eyes closed, casting his mind for Brenin. There had been no sign of any unusual distress in his friend but, of course, casting one's mind was not exactly a normal everyday thing to do. So Elstan hadn't been too sure what he was supposed to look for. What was unusual in the unusual, he thought, very confused.

The afternoon was peaceful; insects buzzing in the nearby bushes, a cloud of midges drifting up from one of the many tributaries of the River Wry hovering nearby, not yet a nuisance. Elstan's fingers sank into the deep bed of pine needles he'd been hoping to sleep on this coming night, the taste of freshly cooked conies lingering on his tongue.

'What is it?' Elstan asked worriedly, puzzled by Chong's smile.

'I'm afraid Brother Drudwynn seems to have seriously upset his master. I found Brenin; he was sitting on a chair alongside his bed in the Vixen. Fortunately his mind was on other matters, he had no idea I was looking in on him.' And then his eyes lit up. 'But, of course, he doesn't know I can cast my mind, only those who mindmeld are able to do it. It's very strange that, you know. Why I can't cast my thoughts as well, I should be able to. It seems I have some sort of blockage in my head—it's never occurred to me before. You are having an untold influence on me, man of Mantovar! But, never mind, it's a relief to be back'

'What do you mean? Elstan looked askance. The only influence he wanted on this man was to change his mind about going to Miskim. 'You mean you can half mindmeld? Seems a bit odd to me, as well. Well, go on, what did you see?'

'Brenin has a new companion, Guild Brother Edmund,' Chong grinned widely, for once his mind off his feet. 'He happens to be Drudwynn's arch enemy, his rival for the job of deputy to the magus,' Chong giggled. 'It may be that Drudwynn will be somewhat distracted in his search for us…they absolutely hate each other.'

'Do they now?' Elstan thought of the trouble that could be engendered within the Guild with that priceless piece of knowledge. Sevenoaks would make some use of it, no doubt.

'Drudwynn is hunting us?' he asked abruptly.

'He is preparing to,' Chong said all of a sudden depressed. 'I found him in the stables, him and a few others. I couldn't make out how many there was a lot of milling about, guards by the look of them though, not wizards thank the Gods. They were loading a mule with supplies. The Guild is not known for their hunting abilities…well, the hunting of animals for food anyway, humans are a different matter. So whenever they set out on any sort of expedition that is likely to take them into out of the way places they have to carry their food with them. And they are idle…they use animals or porters whenever they can.'

'How long before they set out, do you think?'

'An hour or two perhaps, then a day to reach here, the mule is bound to slow them up, not long enough for us to reach safety, though.' Chong said bleakly.

'Don't give up yet, my friend. I know these mountains Drudwynn doesn't. I'll get you to Mulkie's Cross if it kills me…or them. First thing you do is hand me your bag, I'll carry both. Second thing, we'll cut you a crutch from this,' and he tapped the birch branch behind him. 'This and your staff should aid you walk,' Elstan fell silent and looking thoughtful asked the question that had been at the back of his mind since they'd fled the Vixen. 'Tell me, can't your staff aid you more, you know conjure a spell to make you walk easier?'

'I am not a healer, neither is my staff. Even if it could, Brenin would detect the use of magic at this distance. He doesn't think this is a wizard's staff. To him I am merely an adept and adepts don't have staffs. Probably thinks this is just a walking aid. But he doesn't know I have the power to hide our path from his detection…well, to a great extent anyway,' and he laughed.

'Well, why haven't you?'

'At the moment it is obvious we are traversing the Wolfshead and it is only the Drikander we can possibly be heading for. Using my skills to hide behind would be a mistake. I do not want him to know how potent I am yet. We may need to surprise him later.'

Elstan frowned. 'All right, my friend, I see the sense in that. But you may be forced to use it before long or they'll catch us on the mountain. But if they do come up on us and you are forced to use your magic, I want you to promise me you'll use it to enable us to flee…not to fight them.'

'Oh, you do not mind appearing a coward?' Chong smiled.

'No, of course not, misplaced bravery has got many a man killed needlessly. Alive, we can fight again, my friend. Come, at least Mulkie's Cross is downhill from here, but I will concede a small change of plan,' and he rose from the ground and retrieved his small axe hidden beneath his pack.

Measuring a suitable length for Chong's height he lopped off a fairly straight section of the birch branch keeping the remains of a v-junction at its end.

'Pass it here, I'll finish it off,' said Chong and promptly stroked the stirrup that was to play host to his armpit. 'It's all right; this is small magic, too small for Brenin to feel.'

His actions smoothed the knobbly bits on the wood making it a more comfortable fit. He then fished from his own pack a length of leather strapping and cutting it to size he wrapped it around the top of the crutch to allay any friction burn against his soft skin.

Elstan looked at him, amazed. 'I almost forgot you were a wizard for a moment,' he said admiring the finished article.

'Not one of the First Order according to the Guild, I'm afraid, but I suffice. What is this change of plan?'

'We'll make for the Great North Road. It should only take us a couple of days down the mountain to reach it and then we'll mingle with the other travellers. We should blend in,' he laughed abruptly, 'we'll be looking pretty haggard by then.'

'Drudwynn will have caught up with us well before we reach the road,' Chong said despondently. 'It's your turn to promise something now. I want your oath that you'll leave me when he catches up with us. Drudwynn is an evil man and delights in torturing his captives. Among his favourite methods of torment is making a victim watch a loved one, or a friend, being mutilated. I don't think I could bear that.'

'He has to catch us first…I am a woodsman don't forget, he's only a wizard,' Elstan grimaced. 'He will not find it easy to take us, especially if the guards are as inept as the ones I put out of action at the Tower.'

Magus Brenin sat in his chair staring balefully at his erstwhile deputy, although Drudwynn was totally unaware that in Brenin's mind he'd already been deposed. But Brenin was cunning, he wanted to keep Drudwynn on edge, keep him hopeful and he'd strive harder to succeed in the task given him. Drudwynn was taking his leave, reporting all in readiness for the chase into the Wolfshead. The ex-deputy resisted the urge to shuffle his feet as Brenin scrutinized him. Though he was full of trepidation he didn't want to give Edmund, standing at the window smirking, the satisfaction of knowing that he was afraid.

'I have located them at the summit of the Wolfshead,' said Brenin, menacingly. 'Do not fail me!'

'Do not fear, Master, I will have them in my clutches and in Mulkie's Cross before the week is out,' Drudwynn promised, bowing his head.

'You had better or you will wish you were dead,' Brenin suddenly shouted, making both his companions jump. Startled, Edmund stared at the back of the magus' head for a moment and then, raising his eyes, he again smirked at Drudwynn staring down at his feet, too terrified to catch Brenin's eye.

'I want them both alive and in front of me. I must know what Chong-An and the Fly are up to. And Drudwynn,' his voice dripping venom, 'you will feed on your entrails if they know too much.'

Drudwynn paled—he was no match for Brenin and knew it. But he also knew he was vastly more powerful than the oriental adept and he took hope from that. If he could apprehend both fugitives and ascertain their knowledge, then present it to his master quickly, he'd be reinstated in Brenin's favour. And Edmund would be sent packing. Drudwynn would no longer be under threat of death—or worse.

'This man, the Fly, I could not see his face despite remaining in the cast longer than was wise. Are you sure you don't know him?'

'I'm sorry, Master; I have never seen him.'

'You have any idea what his connection is with Chong?' Drudwynn shook his head at the question. 'Well, we know he's one of Sevenoaks' band of renegades, therefore by consorting with him Chong is also a danger to us. For all we know they may have been conspiring for years. Go, Drudwynn, and if you fail pray that I give you a quick death.'

Chong had not been wrong in his estimate; Drudwynn reached the summit of the Wolfshead in the middle of the following morning. Elstan and Chong stared back up the mountainside behind them and

231

counted the number of men carelessly outlined against the skyline about half a day's distance behind.

'Ten plus Drudwynn. Do you reckon that's enough to send back to Brenin with their tails between their legs?' Elstan asked grinning all the while.

Chong-An quickly smiled, he was getting used to Elstan's sense of humour even if it was inappropriate. 'The only way you'll return any of those to Brenin is in a box. They'll never give up until they're dead, they're too afraid to quit…any of them. Brenin wants us and he won't care what condition we're in, as long as we're alive and able to answer questions. He needs to find out what we know, and we'll never hide anything from him, my friend, have no doubt of that. And then he'll slay us…slowly.'

'Don't be so cheerful, Chong, you'll split my sides,' and he gazed back up the hillside. 'That mule won't like coming down these slopes, he favours his feet, and won't want to slide,' said Elstan smiling broadly. 'We're now out of Brenin's sight, any chance of causing a little accident with that staff of yours?'

Chong-An looked at him, wondering if he was being serious. The gleam on Elstan's face was all the confirmation he needed that his friend meant what he said. He looked up at the ridge and watched as his long-time, hateful adversary gave his orders and thought why not. Give it a go, show Drudwynn that he was in for a fight, even though the odds were stacked heavily in favour of the hunters.

'I thought you wanted to run not fight?'

'Ah, look at them. It seems too good an opportunity to let go by.'

Chong leant against a nearby aspen, and taking a minute to settle safely, he rested the crutch in his left armpit. He studied the men above him and then cast his eyes over the terrain between him and them, and grinned.

'I'll have to be careful, Brenin may not be able to see us but Drudwynn can. All right, let's see if I can use a little magic, just enough we don't want him detecting it right away.'

He raised his staff in both hands, studying the runes etched in its surface. He smoothed a finger over a particular one that had the appearance of a dragon coiled around a nest of eggs.

'You know, Elstan,' he said, not taking his eyes from an icon displaying a picture of a star, 'many of these runes have several uses.

This one can give light as well as…watch!' he said grinning all over his chubby face.

He held the base of the staff in his right hand and pointed the knuckle up the slope directly at the mule taking its first steps down off the ridge.

Elstan stared avidly, not taking his eyes from the party above. He had no idea what to expect and didn't want to miss a thing. He listened to Chong chanting an unintelligible string of words and nearly jumped out of his skin when Chong finished with a tremendous shout that sounded like a clap of thunder.

The mule reared on its hind legs as if it had stepped on a rattlesnake. Braying loudly and frantically it landed with its forefeet on the shoulders of its driver. The man was dead as soon as he hit the ground, his chest crushed, his neck broken. The mule, with bales shaken loose, made a run for it back over the ridge followed by the other guards. And with Drudwynn screaming his rage at their provisions disappearing down the Wolfshead back towards the Vixen's Haven.

Elstan, startled, gazed at his friend. 'That was unbelievable, what happened to it?'

'It doesn't like shooting stars—especially in daylight,' and he grinned mischievously. 'One down, ten to go.'

'Oh, boy, are they in for a surprise. I feel better already, my magical friend,' and he laughed himself silly.

'Let's move, Elstan, while I can.'

The two wended their way slowly down the mountainside following a narrow game trail to a stream they could hear and smell just ahead. Chong had one arm around Elstan's shoulders; his other hand gripping his staff, while Elstan carried the crutch and his companion's bag. Chong sweated with the strain of keeping his full weight off his heels and trying not to jar his knees at the same time.

Elstan, his own bag on his back, found the crutch cumbersome; it was catching every few steps in the undergrowth, his stamina was fast leaving him, fatigue and muscle strain exhausting him. Chong's weight was too much. Elstan looked around for a place to hole up as they arrived at a gently flowing stream running down from the north.

'Chong, go and sit on the bank, put your feet in the stream, let the water run over your boots, its cold enough to reduce the swelling. I'm going to search for a place for us to hide a while. I'm afraid we're going to have to let them pass us—you need rest desperately.'

'But they're following our tracks. If they no longer see our trail they'll cast around here until they locate us.'

'Ah, my friend, I told you I'm a woodsman. I'll be away for a couple of hours setting a false trail, get some rest. Don't get found,' Elstan ordered, helping Chong to sit.

'You've no need to worry on that score, my friend. No-one will see me unless I want them to,' and he winked.

Twenty-nine

Leash raised his head from the hard, unforgiving thwart. It had ceased raining the afternoon before and it was again getting hot—but this time he was prepared for it. He now spent most of the daylight hours out of the boat and in the ocean. And whilst hanging on to the gunnels he managed to catch food, mainly sardines and pilchards which he ate raw, sometimes not even bothering to kill the wriggling fish first. He kept to a routine, enforced by Balar, of immersing his whole body in the sea to evade the ravages of the sun on his skin. Although the fresh water of the storm had not actually healed the burns on his body, it had gone a long way to relieving the pain. But it had had no effect on his mental health.

He tossed and turned at night unable to dream his safe dream. She had disappeared behind Balar. Totally obscured by his demon, he was forgetting her existence. There was the occasional disturbance as she shouted to gain his attention, but Balar had found a means to counter those attempts. He sang. And his terrible lack of tone gave Leash a thumping headache—which was Balar's mistake. Leash knew why the vampyrus sang and that kept her alive.

Leash awoke in the morning with another interminable ache behind his eyes when his fishing boat was bumped heavily and almost overturned.

'What…' he groaned as someone jumped into the boat behind him.

'Is he alive?' a guttural voice asked.

'Aye, just about,' was the answer in a tone just as hoarse as the first.

'Bring him aboard, if he survives he'll do, set the boat adrift we don't need it,' a third voice ordered.

And that was the last he was cognizant of as he was knocked unconscious and manhandled into a ship that was infamous in the north. He woke a few hours later incarcerated in the brig, a small cell deep in the bowels of the bows. His only view, between the bars of the door, was that of the feet and shins of the two hundred or so oarsmen sitting at their rowing stations.

The *Alessa,* in the following week, eventually drifted into a current flowing south.

'What the hell!' He looked around bewildered, his head splitting; he felt a lump rising on the back of his skull. Lifting his hand to touch it he abruptly screamed when he was prodded in the stomach none too gently with the end of a whiplash handle.

'About time, you lazy bastard raghead. What are you doing out here in the middle of the ocean on your own, hey? You'll tell me before this voyage ends or I'll skin some more off your back.'

The owner of the harsh voice squatted down above him on the walkway of boards forming an aisle between the two sets of rowers. The man was stripped to the waist, barefoot and covered in tattoos all over except for an area on his neck where there was a strange scar—it looked like teeth marks. The man was sweating profusely beneath the black tarred topknot bouncing on the top of his head as he stared at his prisoner.

Leash groaned and put his head between his knees. He knew where he was; in fact he recognized the oars-master. His name was Gunter and he worked hand in glove for the most notorious brigand of the Onyx Isles, Captain Jos Osvaldo. He was on the Lobos.

'You know this bag of shite?' Balar asked.

'Aye, demon…of old. And I hope he doesn't recognize me or you'll be looking for a new host earlier than you expected. But there again, perhaps I should tell him who I am. At least I'll be rid of you.'

'So you would, at least in this life. But I'll ensure you come straight to Purgatory with me—for eternity,' he warned, *'and you won't like that place either.'*

Leash shuddered…for once he and his demon were in agreement.

'Tell me about these people. Why are they chained in this hellhole and how do you know our genial captor?'

'Gunter is an old acquaintance of ours,' Leash sniggered. *'Don't you remember meeting him? It must have been at least fifteen years ago. He was one of the few who ever got away from you after we'd sunk in my teeth.'*

'Fifteen years ago I was not as strong as I am now' Balar replied, his pride wounded. *'And you released quite a few before I managed to control you. But rule you I did in the end,'* he swaggered. *'He was one of those you felt sorry for…this thing of shite?'*

'Well, I didn't know he was a slaves' overseer now did I? I thought he was just another nutter off the docks. He was still a human being, though, not a foul, disgusting demon owned by the devils, like

236

you,' Leash sneered, his memory of fighting the vampyrus returning briefly.

He'd managed the escape of more than a few victims of Balar in the early years, before the demon had taken full command of his host's urge for clemency. Gunter, although a despicable excuse for a human being, did not deserve to die at the hands of a vampyrus and so Leash had overcome Balar's insatiable lust for blood. It was Balar that forced Leash's teeth into Gunter's neck and commenced his disgusting sucking. But it was Leash that had forced Balar to relinquish his hold. Balar had been seriously upset more than a few times during those first years. Leash smiled, it had almost been a game between them then— see how many he could liberate before Balar killed them.

But looking around the darkened, slaves' hold where the light creeping in through the oar ports gently bathed the sweating bodies of two hundred men sitting in two tiers – the lower having two men to an oar the upper having three, forty oars on each side – lassitude set in again. He was finding it increasingly difficult to remain mindful of his surroundings, and the effort of talking, even be it in his own psyche, was exhausting him. He'd been ill near to death for days and, despite the efficacious treatment of the rain, he was still very unwell. His head swooned; his consciousness ebbed and flowed like the tide on some hellish black beach. Pain, weariness and absolute hopelessness were dragging him down to a depth of desolation that was past the need for death. For he knew that demise would not be a release, it would be an endless continuation of the same torment.

Leash's state of mind began to worry Balar for he knew that hosts sometimes succumbed to great depression, with the result that their brain atrophied and eventually died.

'I am not owned by any devil, Leash. Get used to it. I am my own boss…I do as I wish.'

'Aye, until your God grabs hold of you.'

Balar trembled. He did not want to think of his deity at this time—or at any time. *'And I am not a foul, disgusting demon…I have my standards.'*

'Standards! You live on other people's blood, you…you suck them dry, kill them in your greed!'

'I'm not a glutton. I only feed when the Wanting is on me. What's wrong with that? You eat meat…now that is really disgusting!' Leash was almost lost for words. *'Of course I eat meat…and you do, you even complain if it's not prepared properly.'*

237

'Can you honestly say you prefer raw fish to cooked fish? No...I know you don't, you were sick too many times for it to be agreeable.'

And Leash recalled the acid taste of the still living fish he'd caught, but he'd been desperate enough over the last week to have eaten the boat if there had been any possibility of digesting it.

'I need meat to stay alive.'

'And I need blood to stay alive. This argument is pointless. Now tell me, who is this Gunter?'

Leash gave in; he could never understand his demon's reasoning. 'He is a pirate...a brigand. He sails the open seas in charge of the slave oarsmen for Osvaldo. And you do not want to meet Jos Osvaldo. He is the worst of them all.'

'Well, there's no fear of this Gunter recognizing you, not even your mother would know you now.'

'Why not? His memory can't be that bad, he's bound to remember the man who bit his neck and left that terrible scar. Look at it you can see the marks of my teeth plain.'

'Why do you think he called you raghead?' Balar asked exasperated.

'I don't know. It's just another insult, isn't it?'

'He called you that because you lost most of your hair when the sun burned your scalp. All you've got left are little tufts here and there. Haven't you noticed? You look ridiculous really; you ought to shave your head it'll grow back normal then.'

Startled, Leash took moments to reply as he raised his hand and rubbed it over his head, pulling away more black hair as he did. 'Of course I haven't noticed, I've been a little unwell lately...or haven't you noticed?'

'Who in hell's been healing you, Leash? Don't be ungrateful.'

'Ungrateful! You...dear God what have you done to me? To think I had lovely hair once. At least she always said I did,' he added quietly.

But not softly enough for Balar heard him. 'Who said?'

'Never mind! And how the hell am I supposed to shave my head? Have you a razor handy? If you have you can cut my throat as well, I think I've had just about enough, now.'

'Stop whining,' and then Balar fell silent as they were rudely interrupted again.

'Wake up, raghead! Don't dawdle,' Gunter said. He opened the door and indicated for Leash to leave the cell. As soon as he did, Gunter laid about him with his whip. 'Move to that station there,' and he pointed at a vacant seat at an oar on the lower tier. 'Row, you bastard or I'll throw you over the side for the sharks!'

Leash screamed again as the leather strap cut into the newly exposed skin of his back. He felt the blood flowing warmly, dripping to his waist.

'I think you'd better remain quiet for the moment,' advised Balar sinking into the recesses of Leash's mind. *'You can tell me more when you're resting.'*

It was hours later when a halt was called and Gunter allowed the slaves to drop their aching arms and hang their heads over their oars. His surroundings penetrated slowly into the mind of Leash. The silent oarsmen sat too worn out to talk. They could not stand at their post even if they hadn't been chained. The deckhead – the roof over the slaves – was just three feet above the heads of the upper tier of slaves, at the same height as Gunter's chest. Built beneath the deckhead were shelves, these used as storage space for a multitude of items, all stolen from other ships waylaid by Osvaldo. The hold stank as nothing in the world had ever stunk before. There were no latrines, men were periodically unchained and allowed to use an open shutter in the bows but in bad weather they often missed. Between times they emptied their bladder, or evacuated their bowels where they sat. In storms they vomited over each other unable to avoid the man sitting on the bench in front or below, and they were never allowed to bathe while at sea in case they attempted to drown themselves in the ocean.

Their breaks, taken at regular intervals unless they were in pursuit of prey, or when the Lobos fought an oncoming wind, were never for very long. The slaves prayed for a following blow for then they could rest as the ship's sails billowed full. The poor wretches sat for hour after hour hunched over, sweating between hot decks. And that was the time their minds succumbed to despair and loneliness. For each man was in his own little world, uncaring and not sharing of any other's plight. An hour for a late afternoon meal, a thin gruel and a jug of water, then they took up their oars again. By night time, Leash was nearly comatose with exhaustion and pain, his hands were torn and his back bled. He almost wished that he was back in his fishing boat getting burnt. The routine never ceased, it went on for days. Sleep for two hours, row for four, rest for one, row another four, sleep again for two hours, and then it would start all over again.

It was Balar and his own instincts that ensured Leash's survival. Balar would not allow him to drift, lose himself in desolation—in his own way the vampyrus had become very fond of his host. He didn't know why. In all the thousands of years of his existence this was something else that had never happened before. It had always been a case of infest, feed, use, ignore the host, kill and invade a new one. But ever since he'd been forced into Leash's body – and because of the great length of his infestation – Balar's demeanour had changed. He'd got to know Leash, become comfortable in his body.

Besides, keeping Leash alive meant life for Balar, for if he failed in his endeavours and Leash died, then it was a case of "hello God!" and "ah, the pain!"

The enmity had begun aeons ago when Balar had inadvertently taken as host another human who had been a disciple of the same God. It was not the done thing to infest a body of a fellow devotee—he should have possessed the body of another God's adherent. When the rogue infestation had been discovered, by the God himself – who had wanted the human for his own reasons – Balar had ignored the deity, a very foolish thing to do. And he'd got away with it the first time because the God had not realized the consequences of not taking action. The vampyrus, although a very active demon, was not overly intelligent, but it was very powerful and cunning. And he did have the benefit of longevity as long as he wasn't careless. But Balar transgressed again…and again. His God had ended up incandescent with rage, the vampyrus more than an immense irritant. It seemed that everywhere he turned, Balar was somewhere about causing mayhem, a huge thorn in his God's side.

But then Balar did something that was truly unforgiveable—the God could no longer allow him to remain free.

So the God set out to apprehend him, extract what he needed from the vampyrus and then get rid of him, destroy him. But however hard the God searched he could never locate the vampyrus. He sent out other demons to apprehend Balar and they always returned empty-handed, or died never to be seen again. In time, capturing the vampyrus had become a dire necessity—and the longer Balar remained at large so the deity's hatred grew. And so the God relentlessly set in motion a chain of events that had astonishing repercussions for everyone.

Balar was forced to hide for even lengthier periods in the disciples of other Gods…Leash was a follower of Tarria, the Goddess of Healing and Mercy. But Balar was stubborn, and courageous, some might have said foolhardy. When he'd said that he was his own boss he'd meant it. He kowtowed to no-one, least of all his God. And now Balar wanted revenge—being the hunted had gone on far too long. He wasn't going to let anyone kill him or deprive him of his freedom— even if it was justified in their eyes.

The God could be defeated. He just didn't know how—yet.

Leash was another who wanted revenge. He wanted Balar's head on a block if that was possible. The never ending battle to retain his sanity was wearing him down. But, unfortunately, a side effect of a vampyrus infestation caused the host memory loss and this hurt Leash more than anything. But the loss of a host's memories usually happened within the first few months—yet not with Leash. For some reason amnesia had taken years to reach the stage where his recollections of his previous life had all but disappeared. Nonetheless, Leash still clung to his most earnest memories, those feelings that were very deep seated in his core being, the essential Leash—if that was his true name.

And Balar was very disappointed in his host. He hated Leash remembering and that woman intruding when he wasn't looking!

Leash felt on times that there were three people occupying his body. There was a war going on between Balar and the lady—the prize being Leash's sanity. When she got the upper hand, Leash was almost happy even though Balar was there always in the background. But when Balar got the upper hand, as he had now, then Leash despaired for the vampyrus was strong and getting stronger each year—and the lady was getting weaker. He very rarely heard her these days and he knew that this pleased Balar, for with her aid Leash had often denied him his feasting.

But Leash also knew that it was Balar safeguarding his life now. He sighed. Did he want to carry on this despicable existence? Did he want to remain alive at all costs? Did he have any choice?

Thirty

An hour after leaving Chong easing his feet in the stream, Elstan had retraced his steps up the hill and was now peering from behind the trunk of an immense redwood. He was watching Drudwynn, his nine remaining men and the mule. All were treading anxiously along the narrow, hummocky trail which eventually would lead them to Chong-An.

All ten men were in a foul mood. The guards' worn leather armour was clanking noisily, the occasional strap catching in the undergrowth whenever they passed too near the edge of the track, tugging them to a stop, jarring their joints. None of these men, including Drudwynn, were used to chasing fugitives through forested mountain terrain, and whenever they reached an obstacle they profaned the air in their efforts to get past it. Their morale was low – these guards hadn't volunteered for this mission – for when called on by their masters they could see no safe way to refuse. None of them wanted to be at the receiving end of Brenin's wrath. They glared at Drudwynn behind his back, cursing him silently for not using his magic to ensnare the fugitives. They envisaged a long chase before them, with great danger a constant companion.

What the guards did not know was that Drudwynn had one important failing that he hid well, even from Brenin. He could not control his magic wherever there were oak trees, for they partially absorbed his conjurations.

Drudwynn scowled, he was in no mood to tolerate slackness, his thunderous face enough to urge the men on faster. But although the guards wanted to travel at a quicker pace, the mule was resolutely slow. And no amount of coaxing made the slightest difference to its temperament; the mule was impervious to all entreaties. The constant battle to get it around, through and over fallen trees and dense bushes caused tempers to fray, men to fall suffering painful grazes. Their failed attempts to cajole the fractious beast into hurrying had the effect of merely lowering morale even further.

But Drudwynn's irascibility was not just a result of the mule running off for no apparent reason, killing a guard in the process. Drudwynn suspected magic…in fact it stank of it. He could always smell conjurations in an area that he traversed, and he confirmed its use when he reached the site of Chong's spell creation. He halted and sniffed the air as he looked around studying the woods and the trail leading down the north side of the Wolfshead. He could feel the residue of the stale magic in the air he breathed, its taste and smell he identified as that of the eastern adept.

'Sergeant,' he called.

'Brother,' answered a tall, heavyset man rushing to the sorcerer's side and saluting by touching his forelock.

'Warn the men, sorcery has been used here—they are to remain alert at all times. I will not tolerate another death unless it is at my hand. You understand?'

'Yes, Brother,' and he turned away, a cold sweat running down his spine. Sergeant Brom had been a mercenary all his life, paid by petty potentates in all corners of the empire. It was a hard existence, but he'd almost accrued enough coin to retire. It was not the time of his life to be working for sorcerers but the superb remuneration, and the high status, was too much of a temptation to refuse. All he wanted now was a quiet life and, normally, the fear in which the Guild guards were held ensured that. But not on jobs like this. He'd never expected to do any actual fighting for the sorcerers. Who in their right minds would ever confront Brenin? The very few who were stupid enough to complain about the Guild, or the Guild's guards, soon learned their mistake. Nevertheless, he'd always avoided any battles in which sorcerers were involved. Brom licked his lips and snarled at his men, he didn't want to begin now, besides being too old for it, it was far too dangerous.

'Right, you scum,' he ordered the white-faced men after he'd informed them of Drudwynn's words. 'You'll be all right as long as you keep your eyes open; your ears cocked and shut your mouths. How the hell do you expect to come up with the bastards if they can hear you on the other side of the mountain?'

'But magic, Sarge, I didn't bargain for that.' Rorkes, a tall thin man from the depths of the plains to the west of the Drikander, drawled apprehensively.

'So what are you going to do about it—run?' whispered Gil, another of the guards. 'What do you expect when you work for sorcerers?'

Elstan, listening from behind the tree, sympathized greatly and smiled, this was going to be too easy he thought. But he was wrong, for at that moment Drudwynn detected his presence and also let slip that he knew who he was hunting. And he made an almost catastrophic error of judgement.

Drudwynn turned and appeared to stare right at him. With his eyes closed the sorcerer could see Elstan in his mind's eye and he gloated. 'Well, well…welcome to my web, little fly.'

The guards stopped in their tracks not understanding their leader's words or his manner. And then Drudwynn raised his right arm and pointed his staff, knuckle foremost, at the group of trees concealing Elstan. A red light shot from the gnarl and ignited a small group of pine trees shielding the base of the giant redwood. The trees immediately erupted in flames, a conflagration that would have annihilated Elstan if he'd been the actual target. But Drudwynn only intended to clear a pathway for the guards to apprehend him.

'Get him,' Drudwynn screamed when Elstan emerged from behind the huge tree, fleeing eastward away from the flames. 'Bring him to me…alive!'

But as the guards, led by the sergeant ran forward, the wind shifted and the flames ignited other trees and a burning branch fell on one guard, mercifully braining him before burning him to death. The guards came to a panicked halt, unable to see through the smoke or negotiate a safe route around the fire. And then the wind shifted again and blew down off the ridge.

And the fire made a beeline for Drudwynn and his guards.

It took all of the sorcerer's stamina, and the rest of the day and following night, to quell the fire before the whole forest went up in flames, which would have killed their quarry and themselves.

Elstan escaped, delighted with the death of another of his pursuers, and a lot wiser. For the first time he realized he was fighting no ordinary man. Elstan grimaced; his initial impressions of the guard were as he thought…not very bright. But the state of their scuffed and tattered armour indicated that they were experienced fighters, albeit of the tavern brawling type, but fighters nevertheless. He wasn't going to underestimate these men—Brenin's guards would fight like cornered wolves when caught. He recalled their weapons as he strolled quickly and quietly back towards Chong-An sheltering at the stream. They wore their swords and crossbows with an ease of constant use with swords in baldrics and knives in belts, all very close to hand.

And there was Drudwynn. The man might be a fool divulging he knew the identity of his quarry. But he was still a very powerful sorcerer to have conjured a fire that immense without a warning of any kind. But Drudwynn had also disclosed a trait that would be useful to Elstan—the man was very short-tempered. Nevertheless, Chong was going to have his work cut out fighting him, it was certain Elstan could not. He sucked in breath through closed teeth. Being present at open combat between a sorcerer and a wizard was not conducive to long life. And he wasn't sure who would win that conflict. But he knew one thing for sure. Now was the time to resume the attack, while their pursuers were all fully occupied extricating themselves from Drudwynn's foolish conflagration.

Elstan turned about and circled northwards up the hill ensuring he halted below the ridge so that he wasn't outlined against the sky. From here he looked down the slope at the fire, the wind blowing from behind him. Two hours later he found a safe niche within a long bowshot of the guards and studied the insane melee in front of him. The guards and Drudwynn were using anything and everything from thickly leaved branches to their own bedding to beat out the flames. Drudwynn was conjuring spell after spell in his efforts to douse the flames, the overall intention of extinguishing the blaze failing badly. For as soon as he extinguished the fire on one tree so other flames jumped across and re-ignited it.

They all fought the fire frantically except for the mule's driver; his exertions were fully occupied keeping the terrified beast calm. Elstan, never one to miss an opportunity, took advantage of the driver's preoccupation, aimed and loosed a bolt at him, hitting the guard squarely in the chest. The mule, startled by the sound of the bolt skewering flesh, caused more pandemonium when unexpectedly finding itself at liberty. It decided to flee through the flames. Finding it could not, it attempted to trample the other guards before being brought under control.

Elstan walked away, highly pleased with the night's work. Another two down and the hunters delayed even longer.

Chong could hear Drudwynn and his men shouting and screaming at each other – and the mule frantically braying in the distance – when Elstan reappeared. In all that time Chong had sat on the bank of the stream allowing the cold water to wash over his boots and his ankles. He couldn't see if the swellings had reduced in size within his boots but the pain in his feet had abated…they were numb because of the cold. Chong felt Elstan approaching through the forest long before he came into sight. The oriental was attuned to the gentle breeze blowing near him and he felt the air being displaced by the wiry man's body. And then, of course, Chong could smell Elstan's body odour. A fact that worried him, for if he could smell his friend, so could their hunters.

'This way, Chong, I've found the bole of a tree we can hide beneath, maybe sleep for a few hours. They're fully occupied at the moment and will be for the rest of the night, hopefully. I've laid a track over that spur, they'll follow it for quite a while tomorrow,' he pointed to the northeast at a tree-covered low hill a few leagues distant.

'What's all that noise? Surely they don't expect to come upon us when they're making all that racket?'

Elstan laughed. 'At the moment they're fighting a fire that your ex-colleague inadvertently started and at the same trying to quieten a mule going berserk.' He patted his crossbow still in his hand. 'Another two down, Chong, although only one by my hand,' he smiled, 'eight to go!' And when he looked at the oriental's astonished face, he added. 'Well, it was my turn—you've had one, Drudwynn had the next and I had the last!'

'Tell me or I'll never rest.'

Later, as Chong lay sleeping with his feet up on a large root, Elstan listened through the man's snores to the dying fight on the slope above. Drudwynn and his seven remaining men and the mule finally quieted. And Elstan slept the sleep of the innocent knowing that it would be the afternoon at the earliest before the chase would resume.

Drudwynn's loud cursing woke Chong the following noon and he sat up quietly, the long rest working wonders on his aches and pains, but unfortunately not rendering a cure.

'God, that mule would come in handy, my friend,' Chong said wistfully, kneading his ankles and his knees and arching his back. He spent a few minutes watching their stalkers take the trail over the spur. 'How far will that take them?'

'It'll be full night before they realize it's a false trail.'

'Good, Drudwynn though is probably casting for us every so often; he'll get suspicious way before then.'

'The man's an idiot. He'll get suspicious, yes, but he'll see our spoor and doubt himself. I know, I've done the same with sorcerers for years.'

'Elstan, you amaze me.' Chong groaned and stretched before settling back against a fallen branch. And then he took notice of

246

Elstan's sudden concern. 'Don't worry too much, my friend, when you get to my age your body begins to fall apart,'

'And what age would that be?'

'Umm…four hundred and three…I think.'

Elstan's mouth dropped. 'You're that old!' Chong nodded. 'Well if that's the case, your body has every right to complain. And what's more I agree with you, that mule would come in very handy. Do you reckon it's strong enough to carry you?'

'What do you mean? Of course it is I'm not that heavy.'

'Aren't you,' Elstan said, pointedly looking at the oriental's portly belly. 'Stay here, and don't you worry. I may be gone past nightfall,' and he left their haven.

Chong shouted after him. 'Where are you going?'

'To get you a ride…and, with a bit of luck, a little extra food to fill that belly of yours.'

Elstan waited until the early hours before taking action. It hadn't taken him long to come up behind their hunters. Drudwynn was walking in the middle of the column, two guards ahead of him heads down studying the false tracks, four guards behind him and the mule and its driver bringing up the rear.

The track meandered through dense woodland for leagues. Elstan circled ahead of them and awaited their appearance at a narrowing of the trail. He hid behind the large trunk of an aspen tree. Sitting on the crushed leaves of lemon-scented fern, with his legs bent, his chin resting on his knees, he watched the sorcerer and his guards striding past him, the mule and its driver plodding way behind. But this time Elstan remained alert, watchful for any undue or unnatural movements from the sorcerer.

Elstan studied the newly assigned driver, another thick-set man with dirty shoulder-length hair, black eyes, and a knife scar running from one ear across to end just alongside his nose. He appeared to be a man well used to taverns, his paunch indicating a liking for the heady ales brewed in Jasper. But he was distinctly nervous and kept peering into the undergrowth on each side of him as he passed. He was obviously experienced in fighting with a sword or a dagger; his hands were never very far from either weapon. The guard was evidently alert, not wanting to end up like the previous two mule drivers, dead and abandoned to the wolves.

Stealing the mule quietly was also going to be extremely difficult, but Elstan knew of a way. He had the solution in his pocket. Earlier in the day he'd noticed a patch of blue dream-sorghum not far off his track and he'd filled his pockets knowing that it would come in handy, although he wasn't expecting to use it this early and for this purpose. The small blue leaves, when crushed and rubbed in the nostrils of a human, resulted in the onset of immediate torpor, the mule being a lot larger he'd just need to use more that's all…he hoped.

It was a couple of hours later that the pursuers halted and made camp for the night. 'Move it, Sergeant, I want a fire lit and supper within the hour,' Drudwynn ordered.

'Rorkes, Artus, Gil break out the makings and get a fire going, Jake don't let that animal out of your sight, unload him and tether him back up the track he shouldn't stink us out from there. Joss, Owain stand watch, and keep your eyes open. I don't suppose they'll attack us here, but who knows? I can't see that little fella wanting to backtrack here with the lead they'll have. Can you see a broken-down, fat, old man and a little squirt daring to attack us again?' the sergeant grimaced not expecting an answer. 'But if they do, I don't want to have to let your cronies back in Jasper know that you were beaten by those two. Telling them you lost wouldn't do a lot for your credibility—your little line in extortion wouldn't last very long.'

'If you fail, you will have nothing to worry about—your lives will be forfeit,' rasped Drudwynn.

Elstan smiled. If things went to plan tonight then the "squirt" would be leaving the deputy and his guards with more than egg on their faces. He settled in the undergrowth overlooking the campsite from where he could see all three sentries. Judging by their body language, Drudwynn's cohorts were fed up, tired of trudging through the woods at the edge of the Great Forest, and absolutely terrified of their leader. But it had been interesting to learn of the Tower guards' involvement with the criminal fraternity of Jasper. The emperor would be very grateful for that information. It may even be enough of a reason to curb the machinations of the Guild, if that could be managed. But niggling at the back of his mind was Drudwynn's referral to the spider and the fly, for it was confirmation of what Chong-An had mentioned earlier. Brenin knew who he was chasing—and that put an entirely different complexion on the need to escape.

However, Drudwynn's malice was not just directed at Chong-An and his companion, he was also venting his spleen on the Guild's guards. Drudwynn was not happy; he didn't like this trek through the woods chasing a man he should have killed days ago. And he was worried, almost panicking at the thought of failure and what his rival, Edmund, was up to behind his back. If he returned without Chong and the Fly it would be the end of him.

He had seen the magus find and kill a man at a distance of some leagues, just by using the powers of his mind. No, Drudwynn was living on the edge of reason, of his own sanity, for he had to succeed to save his own life. Scuppering Edmund's scheming came a very poor second to that. He reasoned that he had two, at the most three days, to apprehend the fugitives. He peered around in the dark, using his eyes this time and not his mind. He was too exhausted to cast. Extinguishing the forest fire had taken it out of him; it would be days before he fully recovered. And if he lost any more men it was going to become even more difficult to capture the yellow man and his little insect.

Jake, the mule driver, slept at some distance from the others around the campfire, for the man now smelled of the beast and the others would not have him near. The three sentries had been relieved at midnight and it was now Rorkes and Artus on watch. Both men were tired, and agreeing with their sergeant's initial words, neither saw the need for this duty and it wasn't long before they dozed. Gil, the lucky one left to sleep all night, had been delegated to have breakfast ready for the others when they woke; he also had the unpleasant task of rousing Drudwynn. Joss and Owain slept either side of the sorcerer, close to the fire to keep warm in the chill night air, and the other three were dead to the world when Elstan struck.

Thirty-one

The vestibule of the Moot Hall was large and airy. Portraits lined the walls alternating with niches holding branched, silver candelabra. Tall doors led off at the rear into the interior of the ground floor, and staircases, one either side of the Hall, led to a landing that stretched the whole breadth of the building. It was gloomy, the high, narrow windows at the front of the building allowed in sufficient light during the day, but now it was close to dusk and the candelabra would need lighting before long.

Anselm studied his surroundings, looking for a means of escape if they should need it. Roidan ascended the staircase to their right, Shadra and Anselm following slowly. They had to, the risers were constructed for tall people not short elves and Anselm repeatedly dragged Shadra up the steps. Crystal, bringing up the rear, couldn't help but smile affectionately…children had the same problem. Reaching the landing, Roidan walked past two stout rosewood doors before halting at a pair of heavy teak doors with ornate gold fitments.

The four waited silently, staring at the intricately carved panelling, each panel portraying a different scene of liosalfar life, each scene separated from its neighbour by a depiction of immense branches of a stylized oak tree. Shadra, fidgeting as he waited, looked behind and saw the rail of the long landing was also carved, each post and rail entirely covered in flowers of all shapes and sizes and colours. Without a warning or indication of any kind, the doors suddenly opened and Roidan walked through. Shadra and Anselm glanced at each other before shrugging and entering behind him.

The room was huge, running deep into the building to five tall windows in the rear wall. Each side wall was again intricately carved depicting a verdant forest, the trees intertwining and seemingly blowing in the breeze. Running the full length of the room and all facing forwards were rows of elaborately decorated benches, an aisle running down the centre and a further two aisles, running down on either side of the auditorium.

Roidan led them down the centre aisle to the raised dais at its far end. And as they reached it the candles in the wall sconces suddenly ignited. They illuminated the meeting room and bathed it in a light that left in darkness, the features of the tall, dark figure standing before a high chair placed in the front of the middle window.

Roidan and Crystal separated and moved to either side of Shadra and Anselm and at the same time bowed low to the darkly cloaked man, his face obscured by his raised cowl.

Standing in a line in front of the silent figure, breathlessness overwhelmed Shadra and he started sweating. Something was wrong he could literally feel malice in the air. All of it emanating from the man on the dais.

Anselm frowned, his spine chilling, as he tried to discern the man's features beneath the hood.

'A schrat and a human…' the figure's voice hissed, 'a strange pair of companions. I thought schrats avoided the race that forced them off their ancient lands.' As Shadra went to answer the figure raised his hand to stop him talking. 'You speak when invited. I have not asked you yet.'

The figure turned his attention to Anselm and Shadra bit off the retort that was on his lips. This offensive welcome was not the one he expected.

'A human…we have seen none of your kind here for a generation and we hoped to see none ever again.' He paused, moving back he sat in the high chair as if it was a throne.

'What is it you want here, human?'

Anselm continued to stare at the intimidating figure. 'Civility and hospitality are renowned attributes of the legendary liosalfar. Have we believed a lie all these years?'

Roidan and Crystal shuffled their feet, with trepidation or embarrassment the captives weren't sure, but the figure again raised his hand for silence.

'I ask again and for the last time. What is it you want here, human?'

Anselm licked his lips, he didn't at all like the way things were panning out. 'Your friend, Chancellor Sevenoaks of Mantovar, sent me here to seek your aid in opposing the monks of Sentinel and its evil abbot,' Anselm said, once more failing dismally to make out the man's face.

'Your chancellor is no friend of mine,' the dark figure answered bluntly. Turning his head he focused for a second time on Shadra. 'The appearance of a schrat in Alfhime portends grave danger to the liosalfar. Why are you here?'

'Grave danger…from me! Why do you say that?' Shadra asked astounded, he could hardly believe his ears.

'For the last time, I ask the questions. Why are you here…schrat?' The menace in his voice was growing and Crystal gasped at the implied contempt for the race of forest elves.

Shadra glanced at the tense woman and from her to Roidan staring ahead of him his face totally blank of any expression. 'I was drawn here,' he said softly, his answer directed at Crystal.

'Drawn here? By whom and for what purpose,' the figure sneered.

'Who are you?' Anselm interrupted. 'I was led to believe that the liosalfar were allies of my chancellor and that you guarded something that was of great benefit to mankind.'

'I am the Magician—and I am elf-kind not mankind. I repeat, I am no friend of your chancellor's, human. Remain silent until I wish otherwise. Now what drew you here…' and he paused significantly, 'schrat?'

'I do not know,' and Shadra seemed to hesitate, he'd never expected a conversation such as this, 'but I feel it,' and drawing in a great breath he decided it was pointless hiding the fact of his loss of magic, they already knew. 'Where is my magic?'

The magician sniggered. 'Your magic is where it is meant to be. Where all magic is meant to be—in my hands—for me to use for the protection of Alfhime and the liosalfar.'

He turned to Roidan and waved his hand dismissively. 'Take these to the cells; they are to remain secured until I decide what to do with them. The schrat's captivity is your responsibility since you disobeyed my orders by bringing him here. You will suffer greatly if he, or his companion, escape.' And with that the hooded figure of the menacing magician stood and deliberately, contemptuously, turned his back on them.

Leaving the Hall and re-entering the vestibule, the guards waiting there immediately secured the hands of the prisoners, and with a rope, tethered them in line one behind the other. Crystal and Roidan remained silent until they were far from the Moot Hall and heading up a path leading to a cave entrance in the mountainside across from where they'd entered the valley.

'I'm sorry, Shadra, for the magician's attitude, but he does have our best interests at heart. We live under continual threat of annihilation and…'

252

'Enough, Crystal! It is not our duty to apologise for the magician. He knows of matters that we do not. His attitude could well be justified and if so your apology is tantamount to treason.'

'Roidan, please, I meant no disrespect.' White-faced she remained silent as they were led into the cave and down the steps inside.

The steps were old and led deep into the mountain. The lower they progressed so the air got cooler and dampness pervaded their clothing. Their breath clouded before their mouths and they trod through the occasional puddle of icy water.

And as the lighting dimmed in the tunnel, Shadra spoke through chattering teeth. 'So, you rescued us from dying of exposure in one cave only to allow us to die of exposure in another. Am I right, Roidan?'

Roidan glanced across at Crystal uncomfortably, not knowing whether he believed his own answer. 'No-one said that you were going to die. Your cell is heated and as hospitable as we can make it. You will be treated honourably.'

'Honourably! You amaze me if you expect us to believe that,' retorted Anselm.

'He went out of his way to insult us—especially me,' said Shadra.

'Who is "the Magician"? My chancellor always spoke of him cordially…they were friends. What's happened to change that?'

'Perhaps this magician is not the magician your chancellor speaks of,' said Crystal, thoughtfully.

'What do you mean?' Shadra asked blowing on his bound hands.

'How long is it since your chancellor met with our leader?' Roidan asked frowning.

'I don't know,' answered Anselm, 'maybe twenty, thirty years ago.'

'Then that explains it. They are different people…your chancellor's friend must have been Gabriel. He died because of an accident twenty years ago and Jehan was then elected our protector. You must have patience now. I know that matters appear very bleak for you but there are some here that read the complex prophecies differently,' said Roidan.

'And now that we actually have a schrat in Alfhime, they may prevail. Before Jehan's time, all strangers were made welcome,' added Crystal, her eyes filling up again.

'Crystal—enough,' warned Roidan.

They arrived at a solid oak door, a barred window cut at head height and a huge iron bolt securing it closed. Opening it, Roidan led them into a warm room.

'There are your warming crystals,' and Roidan pointed at a sack of the same pellets they had seen in the listening station, evidently it was these that had heated the stone for cooking. 'If it gets cold place a handful of the crystals on that iron dish on that pedestal and add a little water. But take care, the heat given out can be immense if you use too many.'

But as he turned to leave after freeing them from their bonds, Anselm asked the first of the two questions that had been troubling him.

'Why are you all so frightened of Shadra?'

Roidan sighed as he locked the cell door, glancing at Crystal and avoiding Shadra's eyes, he answered quietly. 'The prophecy the magician brought with him states that a schrat will be responsible for the death of all that the liosalfar protect. And if that is the case then our purpose for life will end—and we also will die.'

'Wait!' And Roidan turned once more to the cell door and peered at Anselm, his face outlined in the barred window. And he asked the second question. 'Wait a moment—have you all lost your magic?'

'We have.'

'Why?'

'We surrendered it to the magician. He holds it all and wields it for our benefit and protection,' answered Crystal, staring at Roidan daring him to issue another reprimand.

'Ah! So that is why Alfhime is so deathly afraid. It's not because of the Cragga, is it…or Shadra. You all fear the magician,' Anselm shouted at their departing backs.

Thirty-two

Tragen, his eyes closed to shield his retinas from the intensity of the light emitted by the magic in his staff, was barely conscious. It made little difference though as the brilliance passed through his eyelids, but it did ease the pain in his head a little. He had tried for a time to exist with his eyes open but all his senses could perceive was the vividly bright, white light. Nothing took form within it, and he knew if he persisted in straining to look through it he'd burn out his eyes.

Closing his eyes also gave his other senses ease to examine his body. He could feel the vibrant staff clutched in his hand, the mind-carved runes enhancing the staff's power cutting into his palm. The tips of the fingers on his left hand, along with his eyelids, were the only parts of his body that he could move at first. He had laboured long and hard to unclench his fist from the staff and had failed miserably. The staff seemed to have a will of its own and would not allow him to release his grasp. Tragen, exhausted, eventually desisted and debated the reason for his failure and gradually the cause surfaced from the depths of his anguish. The staff—his sentient self—was keeping him alive. If he relinquished his hold he'd die. How he knew he was not sure.

He had no concept of what was happening around him, he felt nothing except the inflexible confines of the cage, heard nothing and tasted nothing. But there was an offensive smell—of what he had no notion, only a suspicion that he did not want to voice. And that was another part of his body he was in control of, almost—his throat. He swallowed convulsively, panic almost choking him.

He did not know where he was, except that he was still imprisoned in the cage. He was aware of the mesh holding him rigidly in its embrace, constricting his chest, making breathing difficult and painful. But he didn't know where the cage was.

He licked his lips, the magic and the fear drying his mouth. And then he grimaced, he'd moved another part of his body. He wondered if the demons knew that his mobility was increasing, albeit slowly. For he knew there were demons around him, what, how, where, he was not yet cognizant of, but given time—and his survival, awareness would return in his body. And then it wouldn't be long before he discovered the full facts of his predicament and maybe ascertain a means of escape.

He was going to have to think of something to halt the magic both in his body and his staff. Too much use of the power would eventually drain his stamina to the point where his heart would implode—and he was nearing that now.

But the staff sensed his weakness and its probable consequences. It directed part of its energy into sustaining the wizard's physique, nurturing his heart muscle, feeding Tragen with additional magic only when and where necessary. But the larger component of its magic went elsewhere, where that was Tragen wasn't sure. But the staff was a prisoner the same as he. And if that was so then the magic's source would remain in the cage unable to escape. He fervently hoped that was case for that meant it was close to hand—available if only he could determine a means to use it.

But then he recalled what Zorzecai had said that the magic could not pass through the cage until his God needed it. Is that what was happening now? Was the God – whoever it was – utilizing the staff's magic, bleeding it from the cage without his knowledge? Surely he'd be able to feel it if it was so.

Tragen's mind drifted free. He tried to remember what had gone before, but most of the events were blurred—by the light and by the terror. The horror of his imprisonment and of what he'd seen whilst suspended above the basin of fog had been too much for his brain. His ability to reason had shut down in an effort to protect his intellect, shield his sanity. But it had succeeded only marginally.

Uppermost in his mind was the memory of Zorzecai maiming those members of the quota sacrificed on the altar to the demon's God. He recalled their sweat-sheened desperate bodies stretched out on the slab, held motionless by the black magic of the herdsman. The inhuman method of their death, the torture, the ritual disembowelling that resulted in a demise that did not end their suffering. For their souls now joined all the other ensnared victims, to be tormented for eternity within the Darkness. But the demon's name, Zorzecai, tugged at the very depths of his intellect, his memory. He knew the name and knew it was vital that he remember.

Tragen struggled to survive the madness of his memories for he knew that regaining his full understanding was essential for his complete recovery. His revival crucial to aid his escape, for he felt his part in forthcoming events was not yet ended, despite Aidan seeing his death.

And then, thinking of Aidan, he recalled all that had transpired before and after their incarceration in the dungeons. Tragen recollected the purpose behind being coerced into setting in motion the magic in his staff—the magic that was now feeding on itself, building towards an unknown, irrevocable climax.

Aidan, a healer for all of his short life, a young man who hated the very idea of pain and suffering, had yielded to his inner feelings and used his curative powers to block the pain of those under torture. But Zorzecai had inevitably become conscious of the fact that his victims were no longer suffering physical pain.

Tragen had created his own magic in a forlorn attempt to hide that being used by Aidan.

And, discerning the reason, Zorzecai had delighted in discovering another wizard. Intimidating Aidan into killing himself had been an added torture for Tragen. The deed was designed to inflict more pain and anguish, all to succour the One behind the Darkness.

But in bringing forth the magic of the staff Tragen had assured Zorzecai's success.

For the magic in Tragen and in his staff combined to emit a power immensely more potent than ever seen before. But it was confined within the God-created mesh unable to roam free and disperse in a safe manner. The result was an unstoppable chain reaction. The magic within the cage rebounded off the mesh and fed itself—it grew out of all proportion to that it was meant to be. And it was that which the God used to open a doorway between Life and Death.

Had he saved Aidan's life? Tragen didn't know, but there had been an occasion once before when he'd wondered whether Aidan had died and knew then that somehow he'd have felt the passing of his boy. Again, this time he had not felt any such thing—he had to assume his boy was still alive.

Tragen sighed. The last thing he remembered actually seeing, although it had been a blur through the intensity of his magic's brilliance, was Leash beheading Zorzecai. Aidan had definitely been alive at that point and the wizard knew in his bones that Aidan's friends would have moved heaven and hell to stop the foul deed of suicide.

And if that was the case, if his boy had survived, then Aidan was going to come after him, follow him to wherever he was now. And the only place the cage could possibly be was in the Darkness. Trapped within his magic within the cage, Tragen was helpless…except to pray.

He pleaded vehemently that Aidan would find him quickly for the boy would remain in the black mists until his search succeeded. And all the time Aidan was hunting for his master he would be at grave risk. He would need to use magic to locate the cage and the demons would detect him, find him out. And wherever Tragen was imprisoned, that was where the greatest number of demons would be.

Tragen agonized, Aidan did not have the power to beat these demons without a staff—and he had not yet made his.

Then, despite his terror, his abject pessimism, Tragen suddenly smiled. He recalled the startling conversation he'd had a few weeks previously, when he and Aidan had spoken of the apprentice's first visit to Limbo. If Aidan had been right in his assumption that he'd discovered the Tree of Paradise and that it had called him, then the implication was that Aidan was quite likely the most potent wizard ever known. The tree could provide his boy with a staff of such power, it would be unassailable.

And because it was such an unknown quantity – the tree a legend amongst legends – the normal rules for manufacturing a wizard's staff might not apply. It may not take Aidan weeks or months to create it!

Tragen rested, closing his mind to everything, the only way to resist the overpowering desolation of his situation. The only thing he could do now to assist Aidan was to ensure the boy's search was not in vain. To conserve his strength Tragen blanked out everything and went to sleep.

He was determined not to die—quite yet.

PART TWO

DISASTER

And his God spoke:

'You have done well Zorzecai.
You are the first to open a gate.
Another will open one more.
Prepare to lead the horde.
The key must be found!
The boy must be killed!
I return you to Life to find the key.
You must kill the boy!'

Thirty-three

Leon tossed and turned in his bed, throwing off his blankets only for them to be replaced immediately by his nurse, their neighbour, his wife's sister, Primrosa. The disease had taken full hold, the black buboes in plain view in his armpits and under his chin, the rotting flesh giving off a putrid, overpowering odour of decay. Groaning weakly, the sweat pouring from him, he fitted, the convulsion thrusting him upright on the bed. The spasm weakening him even more he fell back on his pillows exhausted, deep in delirium. Staring wide-eyed from a face that had lost its flesh, his green skin pale and stretched taut over his cheekbones, his black hair long and lank, he recognized no-one.

Jasmina ran frantically to his side and, uttering a mournful cry, she hugged him to her chest turning her weeping eyes on Aidan.

'He's nearly gone,' she cried hoarsely.

'Let me get to him, Jasmina,' Aidan said and added cryptically. 'I cannot see that his life is at an end yet.'

'What do you mean?'

'His aura doesn't show his imminent death…there is time yet.'

The young wizard of life and death shook his hair out of his eyes and took her place at the bedside. Laying Leon back gently against the pillows he commenced stroking the green man's head and chanting the song of relaxation. Leon quietened almost instantly, his moaning ceasing altogether, his eyes closing in a natural sleep.

'Beatrix, you'd better leave us, take the children with you. Jasmina, I'll need your help to undress him.'

Beatrix, gripping Kataya's and Prile's hands gently in her own, led them from the room. Dom departing reluctantly, not taking his scared eyes from his father until Beatrix closed the bedroom door after them.

'Come, Dom, let's make tea,' she smiled reassuringly and put her arm comfortingly around the young boy's shoulders. 'If anyone can heal your father it will be Aidan, and what's more, I'm positive they'll all need a hot drink when they finish their ministrations. Come, show me where everything is and you can help me,' she smiled to hide her worry. She'd never seen anyone look as ill as Leon – almost cadaver-like she thought – but that could have been because of the green pigmentation of his skin.

She glanced out the kitchen window into the broad vegetable garden stretching down to a road that wound away around a bend in the distance. She stood quietly for a moment, shutting out the terrible sight of Leon. Regaining her composure she found herself marvelling at the abundance of fresh beans and peas ready for picking. The neatness of the weed-free rows exhibiting a love of growing nature's harvest that was unknown amongst most humans. The Green People were guardians of Mother Nature and this subterranean world of Bylani was its ultimate proof, there was no doubt.

The township was built on a circular basis, dictated by the shape of its immense cavern. Rows upon rows of brightly painted cottages and shops – which must have taken countless numbers of years to build – had been constructed around the high Moot Hall where the four young wizards had met with the Green People's Elders on their first visit. It was at that meeting the wizards first heard Findar's Prophecy and, as a result, a lot of previously unexplained happenings had taken on new meaning.

In front of the Hall was a large central square, home to a magnificent fountain depicting a family of Green People playing beneath the strangest tree imaginable. Arranged around the fountain were wooden benches festooned with intricately carved depictions of flowers from all over the world. The river itself – flowing gently across broad shallows and through the town – appeared from nowhere at the farther end of the cavern and it disappeared into the tunnel from which they'd entered. It eventually flowed beneath Meltwater and the town of Griffin, supplying both with fresh drinking water. And intermingling haphazardly with the homes and shops, warehouses and small workshops, were small parklands. Beatrix, distracted by the noise of a crowd, turned her head and glimpsed in the distance a small throng of people playing some kind of ball game. She dropped her eyes momentarily and swallowed. Life was proceeding normally in Bylani despite the near death in the next room.

Looking up again she studied the overabundance of empty dwellings interspersed with occupied homes throughout the town. There were four or five houses that had yet to be lived in for every single one that held a green family. When they'd entered the town on their first visit, she had been puzzled at seeing these and had enquired the reason of the Elders. They'd been informed that these were the homes awaiting the influx of the refugees from the surface world of Griffin Island.

With a sudden premonition of hard times ahead, Beatrix wondered if both races could live alongside each other for any length of time. Two such dissimilar cultures forced together in a time of crisis – even if that coming together was planned – was bound to create problems. Initially the frightened and traumatized refugees would be grateful that they were safe and, although the haven would be very strange, most people would settle fairly quickly. But as time went on, the complete change to their environment and their mode of living would cause a reaction and give rise to bewilderment and loss of hope. Some would deem the future bleak, would see their long-term plans for their families' future brought to an early end. Psychological problems would cause friction between the races—the hostility ending only when people returned to the surface and their homes.

Opening the front door Beatrix peered out and found Hopper striding aimlessly back and forth in front of the white picket fence bordering the front of Jasmina's flower garden. He seemed to be at sixes and sevens, an expression of permanent astonishment lighting his face.

'Master Hopper, what on earth are you doing out there?' Beatrix shouted from the door, and not waiting for an answer she continued. 'I'm making tea, will you join us?'

Hopper opened the white picket gate and strode up the garden path saluting as he came. 'Thank you, Milady, very kind of you, I will, but if you don't mind I'll sit on this chair out here. Bylani astounds me, I just can't get enough of looking at it—it really is amazing. Besides, I don't want to drag dirt into the house.'

'That's very thoughtful of you, thank you. But I agree with you, the first time I came here I couldn't keep my eyes still. I wanted to see everything at once,' she grinned and stood away from the chair for him to sit on the porch. 'I won't be a moment. Dom another mug if you please, we have a guest.'

Within minutes Hopper was ensconced on the wicker chair a mug of hot tea in one hand and puffing on his pipe. 'How is Leon, Milady?'

'Aidan and Jasmina are with him now,' she shuddered, 'he looks very ill.'

'Aye, that he does. I've been helping Primrosa look after him, he's a heavy man. But don't worry yourself; I've seen Lord Aidan heal ailments worse than this. Leon will be fine and up and running this time tomorrow, you mark my words!'

Beatrix sat on the step alongside him; sipping her tea she smiled weakly, despite his words she couldn't keep the anxiety from showing. 'But Aidan looks so very ill as well. He's exhausted—he hasn't recovered yet from what happened to him on Sanctity. And he's worrying himself silly about Lord Tragen, as we all are, but…I don't know. We are so new to magic—none of us even know if we are healers. But there again, even if we were, Aidan wouldn't let us use magic on him to heal him. Mr Hopper, what are we to do, I'm so very frightened for him?'

'That young man is a lot stronger than he seems, you heed me, a few days rest and he'll be as right as rain.'

'But we haven't got time to rest. You know what we intend doing in a couple of days—what we would have been doing before this if the plague hadn't come to Griffin,' she said almost crying. 'I don't know if he'll have the strength to survive the Darkness. It's highly likely we'll have to battle our way through to seek Tragen. I don't think he'll have the strength to fight, but he will—and he'll be killed—we'll all be killed.'

'Lord Aidan has friends—good friends, Lady Beatrix, the best a man could ever need, and you are wonderful people, brave and true and immensely capable,' he gazed down at her full of compassion. 'Have faith in yourselves and you'll bring him through. You'll all survive—I've every confidence in you.'

'Thank you, Master Hopper, I do so hope you're right,' she smiled tentatively, and then she found the need to change the subject. 'Are you free of the disease? Your men, are they ill, do you think any of you have caught the plague?'

'None of us show signs, yet. But we are expecting to, me especially, we've been in Leon's company for too long not to escape it. But Lord Aidan will see us right and then we'll return to the Grim. That's why we're still here; we need him to check we'll not be carrying the disease with us.'

And from the doorway behind them, where none had heard his approach, Aidan spoke wearily. 'I agree, Master Hopper, you'd better bring the others here right away. I don't have much time to hang about.'

'Aye, Milord, I've already sent for them. I'm afraid we learned of Leon's illness too late to keep ourselves in quarantine until your arrival. We had to choose the right trees for the mast and then ship them out. When we found out that Leon had gone down with it we kept ourselves isolated as much as possible in one of the houses in the forest.'

Beatrix smiled up at Aidan hiding her worry but still shocked at his haggard appearance; he'd been in with Leon a full hour and looked as if he didn't have the strength to stand. She grimaced—Aidan had been right when he said that using magic took it out of you.

'Okay, you lot,' Aidan gazed at Dom standing at the window and at Kataya sitting alongside Beatrix sucking her thumb; Prile was stretched out on the hearth behind playing with a kitten. 'You can go in now, but not for long. Your father needs sleep to get well, so go and say goodnight.'

'He's going to be all right?' Dom asked his face alight with hope.

'Aye, but it'll take time.'

'Thank you, Aidan,' Dom said as he was almost bowled over by Kataya and Prile running from the room, 'thank you, so much,' he burst into tears and followed his sister at a rush.

'You also need sleep, Aidan, you look terrible but have some tea first,' she said smiling.

'Aye, I could murder one. How long will it take to step the new masts?' Aidan asked, straightening up from where he'd been leaning against the doorjamb.'

'Two masts to step? At least a week, probably more. But there again, there are tree sculptors amongst the Green People,' he grinned, 'I don't quite know what they are capable of but they seem confident.'

'Well, let's hope they're good. I've a feeling the Darkness will be upon us within the week. Have you any idea what Captain Locklear will do if it is?'

'He's already made plans for that eventuality. He'll up anchor and move around to the north of the island and wait for you there. And if all of Griffin Island is overwhelmed before you reach him, he will wait at Moth. Forever if needs be. He'll not leave any of you behind; nonetheless, he hopes you won't be too long before you return.'

Aidan nodded as Beatrix handed him his tea and both looked up as a stranger opened the gate and walked up to them through the front garden.

'Excuse me, my friends,' said a tall, green man bearing a remarkable resemblance to Leon. 'Please allow me to introduce myself. My name is Adler, I am Leon's older brother, my wife Primrosa tells me you are here to heal him.' Primrosa had disappeared not long after their arrival saying that she was going to fetch her husband. 'I'm afraid that I was far from here in a new cavern we are excavating beneath Meltwater. I've been investigating a grave problem that we have discovered there.' He wiped his brow with a kerchief pulled from the pocket of his britches and joined Aidan and Beatrix as they moved into the kitchen and sat at the table, leaving Hopper to enjoy Bylani in peace. 'Thank you for hastening here, we are in desperate straits,' he said slumping in the fireside chair.

'Where is Aunty Primrosa?' Prile hearing the new voice rushed from his father's room, his young voice excited. 'Mummy said she'd have trout and I'm starving,' he licked his lips expectantly.

'Oh, she's gone to lie down, Prile; she's very tired. It's taken it out of her nursing your father for the last couple of days. Wait till she wakes, my lad, and you'll have all the trout you can eat,' he smiled wearily. 'How is my brother?' he asked, turning to the wizards.

'He'll be fine, Aidan has set the healing in place,' answered Beatrix squeezing Aidan's hand affectionately.

Aidan stared at the haggard man saying nothing until Beatrix poured Adler's tea; he passed it over to the troubled man. 'There's no need to worry about Leon, he'll be up and about in days,' said Aidan, his words only bringing a momentary relief.

'Thank the Gods,' and he sighed, 'that's one less problem to concern us at least.'

'What do you mean?' Beatrix asked, frowning.

Adler rubbed his eyes and drank noisily from his mug. 'Vugocite!'

'Pardon?' Beatrix said, taken aback, Adler's reply didn't sound at all proper.

Adler looked at her and then at Aidan. 'Vugocite…it's a black rock, very porous and very anti-magic. We've discovered a huge amount of it in the new cavern. I don't know what we can do about it,' he shrugged helplessly. 'We'll never be able to seal it off—the seam is just too vast. We can block off the cavern, of course, but that'll take months and waste years of work. Then again we can use salamanders for a while; perhaps they can keep its influence at bay. God, I wish Leon had come home earlier, we've been battling this for the last couple of weeks, and he's the expert,' his ramblings ceased as he emptied the mug.

'I'm sorry…you've lost us. What exactly is wrong with vugocite and why does it need to be sealed off?' Aidan asked perplexed.

'Oh, I'm sorry! Here I am prattling on and you have no idea what I'm talking about,' Adler pursed his lips.

'Very well, vugocite is a very strange rock and not very common…well, up until now that is. For upwards of a hundred years we've been expanding a natural cave beneath the town of Meltwater to make way for the building of new homes. In fact we've already landscaped a fair stretch of it and houses are already under construction. Everything was going so well, access tunnels had been drilled, the ceiling reinforced as well as the walls, drainage, sewers and the main roadways laid down. And then two weeks ago there was a cave-in at the northern wall. Small at first but as we cleared away the debris to ascertain the reason, for it is very unusual for a cave wall to collapse once reinforced with natural magic, we found the black rock. And then, as we're standing there debating our next move, more of the limestone covering the face of the vugocite fell, and more—and even more.' He shook his head in despair and banged his fists on the table. 'It is huge; it spreads everywhere—all over the north wall. An impossible hazard, it…' he ceased speaking and bowed his head.

'You still haven't told us what vugocite is exactly, Adler,' said Beatrix.

'Vugocite is a very porous, extremely hard rock whose nature cannot be changed by the natural magic of the earth that we control. In fact it negates any of our magic used in its vicinity. Being porous it will allow the passage of water. You might not think that is much, but we are deep underground and we battle water seepage continually. It has to be controlled you see or we'll have a flood in the cavern and that can have disastrous consequences. But there is just too much of the vugocite to allow us to use magic to manufacture the drains to funnel the precipitation away, especially when it rains in the outside world. It means years and years of work gone to waste, just when we need the new cave to supply employment and homes for all those who will take refuge here.

'And there is another reason why the vugocite is so perilous at this time, although we knew it not until Leon came home,' he swallowed convulsively as he caught Aidan's eyes.

'Go on…what is it?' asked Aidan

'When there is no water to block the pores it allows the passage of air—we cannot stop it.'

'Dear God!' Aidan said, his face draining of all colour.

'What? What does that mean? We need air to breathe down here, don't we?' Beatrix asked anxiously, the look on Aidan's face frightening her.

Aidan stared at her. 'We have to seal it, block it off before it's too late. Beattie, where air can percolate so will the Darkness. This…this vugocite is a gateway for our deaths.'

Thirty-four

Creeping up on Jake, asleep not far from the mule quietly munching on a cone bush and a nearby patch of common box, Elstan drew his misericorde from beneath his armpit. Putting his hand over the driver's mouth to stifle any shout and then slitting his throat, didn't take long. There was surprisingly little sound, a slight gurgle and a hiss as the blood spurted from the man's jugular and that was the end of Jake. Elstan had no pangs of conscience in murdering the man; he knew Jake's type, had met many men like him and had fought them on numerous occasions. But he did show mercy, of a sort, by ensuring the man died quickly.

The mule raised its head and ceased chewing, disturbed by the unexpected smell of blood. It shuffled its feet, moving to the side to get as far from the odour as its tether would allow. Elstan moved quietly and quickly to the mule so as not to startle it more. He held a handful of berries out to the animal and as the mule ate them held a bunch of the crushed dream-sorghum to the animal's nose. The mule inhaled and its mouth fell slack, ceasing to masticate, the uneaten berries fell from its open jaws. The mule's normally wild eyes clouded over as it was led away silently on the pine-needles covering the track. Elstan walked the beast away for half an hour before re-tracing his steps to the campsite. Judging it too dangerous to proceed with stealing any of Drudwynn's supplies – for it was nearly dawn – he concealed his and the mule's tracks on his way back to the dazed animal.

The sun was well above the horizon when Elstan and the mule arrived back at the stream to find Chong-An fretting at his companion's long absence. But the oriental sorcerer soon forgave him at the wondrous sight of a ride to ease his feet. That night, they reached the promontory overlooking the Great North Road, Chong-An, astride the mule, with Elstan humming a happy tune. Looking down over the long slope Elstan estimated that in another two days they'd be at the road.

Drudwynn, meanwhile, having woken and discovered the driver dead and his mule gone, went utterly berserk and beat his men with the only thing close to hand, his wizard's staff made from hefty lengths of ebony, mulberry and larch. He only stopped his ranting, and his assault, when he realized that he needed the guards to carry the

271

provisions. Weighted down and grumbling quietly to each other in case the sorcerer heard, they came to the end of Elstan's false trail and madness truly took hold of the desperate sorcerer. And again he took out his wrath on the guards. Drudwynn raised both his arms before him, and with magic crackling in the air, he struck out at the foremost mercenary for leading him on a wild goose chase, killing him instantly. Rorkes quite literally exploded in his boots, the only bits left of him strewn far and wide over the trees and undergrowth, up and down the trail…each little piece of flesh emitting a tendril of foul-smelling smoke.

'We'll make straight for the road, that's where they'll have gone. Move it, you cretins, move it.' Drudwynn was beside himself, a rage he'd never felt before was on him. He was determined to make Chong and the Fly suffer the pains of purgatory when he caught them. Hell bent on having his satisfaction before handing them over to Brenin, this time he took the lead. They turned southwest making for the Great North Road below Mulkie's Cross. And next morning Drudwynn's all night haste bore fruit for in the early light they cut across their quarry's tracks again—and this time they were fairly new, no more than hours old. The fugitives were making for the river and Drudwynn smiled. There was no way they were going to make the crossing before he caught up with them.

'Now, you morons, move! We've got them…and remember this,' he said hissing through his teeth, 'I want them alive. I want my way with them before Brenin gets to interrogate them. And afterwards…' he dribbled in his excitement, 'I get to kill them—very, very slowly.'

The unidentified rustling behind them came ever closer but it couldn't mask the noise of the hunters farther away. Both sounds were coming ever nearer, the tension in the fugitives rising as a consequence.

Chong's feet hurt abominably hanging down either side of the mule, the arthritis in the joints of his insteps aching for support, though the respite from pressure on his heels was a blessed relief. Elstan, walking behind, studied his friend his concern growing. The oriental no longer had healthy yellow skin it had faded to a sickly pallor, his face deeply lined with pain.

'What is that animal following us?' Chong asked, his reverie interrupted by a violent scrabbling in the undergrowth.

'You're the one who can cast his mind…can't you see?'

'I have tried, the woods are dense over there and very dark, but I get the impression it is a fairly large predator.'

'How large?'

'Well, smaller than this mule. It surprises me that this beast cannot smell the other and start acting up.'

'The breeze is in the wrong direction, I expect whatever it is can smell the mule…and us,' Elstan sighed, abruptly realizing what the animal was. 'Ah, dear God, that's all we need—it sounds like a boar tracking us! Can you make that mule go faster?'

'I'm trying,' Chong said kicking his sore heels at the mule's flanks, the action having no affect whatsoever, Chong found it impossible to land hard blows on the beast, his feet hurt too much. The mule plodded along the wildlife trail – halfway down the north side of the Wolfshead – at its usual unhurried pace and Elstan understood now why its previous drivers had lagged so far behind Drudwynn.

'We'll have to find another place to hide,' Chong stated the obvious.

'We can conceal ourselves from humans but not from a boar,' and Elstan withdrew his sword from its scabbard. 'We'll have to leave the track, go deeper into the undergrowth. The trouble is we'll have to abandon the mule; he'll leave a trail a league wide even a blind man could follow. And maybe that's best, the boar will follow the mule it has the stronger scent. Furthermore Drudwynn will follow the boar; it'll be making the most noise. We can flee in the opposite direction.'

'Then, perhaps now is the time to leave me, my friend, for I cannot abandon this mule. If I dismount I will collapse…my feet will not carry me another step.'

'Ah, Chong…Chong, I'm not deserting you, my friend,' and he patted the fat man's thigh, 'forget I mentioned it. But I wonder if our pursuers realize there is a boar between us and them. Maybe they think it's us. Drudwynn will wet himself if he comes upon it unexpectedly. Not that that is likely with the racket its making.'

'Well, let's see if I can reduce the noise of the boar somewhat, just enough to really make them think it's us. Whatever, it might delay them while we get off this trail and find somewhere to hide,' said Chong, grimacing at a twinge from his feet.

'He'll detect your magic,' said Elstan.

'But only when it's too late. You can attempt to hide our tracks when we move into the undergrowth.'

'But that's just it…I can't, the mule is too big,' Elstan said frustrated.

'I said attempt, not succeed. I have a plan that involves them following us deeper into these woods, but you must keep up the pretence for a couple of hours at least.'

'You want them to follow us?'

'Those who are left after the boar has finished with them…yes.'

'What is this plan?'

'Wait, my friend, have patience!'

'Chong!' Elstan warned a scowl on his face.

'All right, but you won't believe me. It is dangerous for it will mean you having to watch over me for perhaps a day and a night after we escape.'

'Go on,' Elstan urged as the oriental sat on the mule saying nothing.

'Well, it'll mean me using an inordinate amount of magic. I'll be drained of all energy and I'll need that long to recover. But it will be worth it, we'll keep the mule and we'll be safe from Drudwynn for a while—and my feet will be rested.'

'Do you want me to guess or do you intend telling me when we've been caught?' The Fly's extreme anxiety was resulting in sarcasm that he used only when he was in the most parlous situation. 'We haven't much time, Chong, will you get on with it!'

Chong told him and the oriental was correct—for Elstan didn't believe a word of it.

'They've gone quiet, Brother,' said Brom, unnecessarily.

'No! I thought I'd gone deaf,' said Drudwynn derisively. 'They are not far ahead even though I can't see them in this gloom. I can smell the animal, Chong can't hide that.'

Drudwynn walked in front of his men, leading them down the trail that Chong and Elstan had just left. He was a lot happier than he'd been the day before; he could almost feel the oriental's neck in his bare hands, see Chong's eyes bulging in his face. He strode the trail, not allowing the pace to slow, excitement brimming he felt the animal plodding along just over the crest less than a half hour in front.

Sergeant Brom and his subordinate, Gil, walked a couple of yards behind the feverish deputy, the others straggling farther back up the track studying the undergrowth, nervously expecting an ambush.

274

Gil whispered. 'He's mad you know, sarge, he'll get us all killed.'

'Not if I can help it.'

'He's a sorcerer, man, he'll protect himself and throw us in at the deep end—you know that.'

'Quiet, that man's got phenomenal hearing. There's nothing we can do for now.'

Drudwynn suddenly halted, beckoning to Brom he pointed into the undergrowth to his right. 'Would you say they left the path here?'

Brom examined the ground and the bushes, evidence of their passing could barely be seen but Elstan had done as Chong suggested and had not completely covered the mule's tracks.

'Aye, Brother, they went this way,' he smiled, 'the mule is too big to hide in this brush.'

'Then why do I still smell the animal farther on down the track?' Drudwynn sneered. 'They've set this deliberately to throw us off their trail. That Fly must think I'm stupid!'

'Fly, Brother? I don't understand,' Brom asked bewildered.

'You aren't meant to. No, we keep to this track. Have your men get ready and remember…I want them alive. It doesn't worry me how much alive as long as they can answer Brenin's questions later. I will create a spell to conceal your noise and,' he wrinkled his nose in disgust, 'your smell, you will keep as quiet as possible. I want to come upon them unawares.'

It was night before Drudwynn raised his hand below the brow of a steep hill, barely discernible he again called Brom forward. 'I cannot cast my mind over this hill but I can hear the animal grunting, Chong and the Fly must be sleeping. We will all run from here, we should be on them before they stir. Do not stop for any reason, any man who hangs back I will kill,' he snarled. 'I want their necks in my hands before the morning.'

'It's dark, Brother, how will we see them?' asked Brom.

'I will float a ball of light above our heads when we are over the crest—you will see everything there is to see. Wait for my signal.'

Brom fell back and stood alongside Gil, the others closed up behind them, all anxious. The thought of a sorcerer running with them prepared to kill them if they stopped, and a sorcerer in front of them wanting to kill them if they didn't, put them all in a bad mood.

'Let's make the best of it, lads. Go hell for leather and get it over with,' said Brom.

'Sarge,' whispered Gil.

'What?'

'Mules don't grunt!'

The boar was in a foul temper having lost its prey and it was in no mood to tolerate being attacked by one sorcerer and a bunch of soldiers.

Running over the crest, Drudwynn creating his spell was looking up in the air to float the ball of light at tree height, glancing down he nearly tripped over the grey, whiskered boar rooting for grubs on the far side. The deputy's instincts more than anything saved his life for he flung himself into the undergrowth at the edge of the trail. Brom, immediately behind him, fell the other way. It was Gil who tripped arse over tit across the wild boar's bristly back landing further down the path, breaking his arm. Rorkes and the others managed to pull up a few yards from the incensed animal before racing for the trees in terror.

The wild boar made for Drudwynn rolling over in a bramble bush, all cuts and bruises. He incinerated the animal as it was about to close its jaws on his outstretched hand spouting blue flame…this time, a relatively small flame that did not ignite any vegetation in its vicinity.

Drudwynn screamed his frustration. And without being told they all turned and made their way back to where Chong and the Fly had veered from the path. Brom strapped Gil's arm to his chest as they walked silently side by side. Gil had been positive about the grunting.

'All right, climb on behind me,' ordered Chong.

'What? The mule can't carry both of us…besides, the tracks it'll leave even Drudwynn will fall into.'

'No he won't because we won't leave any. Come on, my friend, trust me.'

Elstan shrugged his pack into a more comfortable position on his back. With Chong's bag and makeshift crutch in one hand he climbed up behind his friend and clutched the oriental's waist.

'Hang on tight, if you get nervous,' said Chong.

'I'm hardly going to hurt myself falling off a mule…what the hell?' Elstan shouted as he felt the mule lift off the ground.

'Quiet, we don't want them looking up, now which way do we go?'

'This thing is flying—I don't believe it!'

'I did tell you. Now have faith in me, I am levitating the mule Elstan…it cannot fly. But I don't want to take it too high in case we break cover or the mule panics. We'll drift along just below the tops of the trees but well above the undergrowth so no trail will be left, apart from that of magic. And Drudwynn will only detect that if he suspects that I am more powerful than he thinks. But remember what I said, the longer we're up here the more tired I'm going to get, so…which way is the river?'

'There,' and Elstan pointed down the hill. 'But wait a minute; if our tracks disappear at this point he'll know magic's been used.'

'Yes, but he won't be sure which direction we've taken.'

'He's not a total idiot he knows we're making for the road.'

'Elstan,' Chong spoke patiently, 'of course he knows, that is why we'll not go down there yet. We'll go back up the hill away from them, circle round behind and with a bit of luck reach the road further north than they. And if we're really lucky Drudwynn will join the road a lot farther south and he'll wait there hoping we'll catch up with him.' Chong smirked. 'We might even get to Mulkie's Cross while he's still waiting. But don't bank on it. This spell will leave me incapacitated for at least twenty-four hours. He may take it into his head to make straight for the town…or wait in the woods above the road.'

'All right, let's fly, Chong,' Elstan said behind the sorcerer, 'but please be careful or I'll get vertigo.'

'Vertigo! But I've seen you on a Tower vastly higher than we will go.'

'Yes, but my feet were on something solid…not fresh air!'

For nearly an hour they drifted between the trees, the oriental adept-come-wizard and the chancellor's agent, both sitting astride a strangely docile mule, its eyes closed. The beast only murmured once and that was when a call of nature caused it to defecate, the resultant deposit falling to splatter on the branch of a larch growing tall amongst a profusion of rose coloured petals of moss campion.

Once Elstan had got used to the slow, if gently sickening, motion he studied the terrain, calculating how long it would take them to reach the river. At this rate, if they could levitate like this all the way, they'd cross the river at noon the following day. But, bearing in mind Chong's warning, close to the end of the hour he was searching for a place to hide for he could feel the weariness in his friend. It was going to take at least another day after his recovery before they'd reach the road. The Fly smiled, no-one would believe this journey—travelling through the air on a silent mule. Would Drudwynn comprehend this sort of action?

'Okay, Chong, down and to your right, I see a cave big enough for us all.'

Thirty-five

Aidan and Beatrix weren't long arriving at the new excavation. They'd hitched a ride on Adler's krynx, Everard being a male, was a lot longer and broader in girth than Clarinda. Everard, ensorcelled by the Green People's magic, travelled at an enormous rate and it powered its way through the city of Bylani travelling eastwards. An hour later Aidan realized that they were traversing a high tunnel beneath Mount Peaceful and the ironworkers' town of Meltwater. On the way they had passed through several vast caverns, their roofs so high that Aidan wondered how they didn't collapse under the weight of the island above. The internal walls of these artificial caves were sometimes leagues apart. Bylani truly was a world beneath a world. Nevertheless, its survival relied on the natural magic of the Green People. And that magic could be destroyed by vugocite—and the people by the Darkness.

They arrived at the new cavern as a horde of Green People emerged from its high and wide, rocky entrance.

'What's up, Brickel?' Adler shouted to a short, stocky man standing to one side seemingly counting the others as they exited.

'Oh hello, Adler, another fall, I'm afraid. Its extended the previous collapse by a factor of ten and I think it's running now beneath the floor of a mineshaft, too close for comfort.'

'Can we shore it up?'

'No, the vugocite is too close; our magic can't find a permanent hold. It is as we feared, Adler, I can see no alternative but to abandon the work here altogether—a hundred years wasted, it's heartbreaking.'

'After all this toil there must be something else we can do,' Adler fretted. 'I've brought the human wizards to see if they can do anything. I'm sorry, Milord, Milady, I am ignorant and don't mean to be, allow me to introduce Brickel, he's in charge of the excavation. Brickel this is the Lady Beatrix and Lord Aidan. Will you allow us passage?'

'Welcome Milady, Milord,' and he bowed. 'I have heard great tidings, news travels fast in the tunnels,' he smiled. 'I thank you for healing my good friend, Leon, we all would have grieved terribly at his passing,' he shook Aidan's hand, the pleasure on his face short-lived. 'It's very dangerous,' Brickel said looking anxious. 'You must have a care and not remain long.' He stood away from the entrance and the dwindling flow of miners to make room for Everard.

'Oh, Adler,' he shouted after them as they entered the dingy cave, 'we seem to have mislaid a salamander, keep an eye out for it will you…it may be injured.'

'Right you are,' Adler said and then turned to the two wizards. 'There won't be much light in here, we haven't created all the banding yet, so watch your step.'

'Banding?' Beatrix asked.

'Yes, the quartz lighting that runs in lines throughout the rock walls and ceiling. We have it in every cave and even in the tunnel through which the river runs to the sea. It takes years to gain the optimum luminosity. Until then we often use salamanders to supply a mobile light.'

Beatrix's eyes wandered everywhere. Peering through the gloom she found the sight of the unfinished workings very depressing, hope in the future wasted. Everard undulated over a well-trodden road, the verges of which clearly required a lot more work, partially dug drainage ran intermittently, pipes standing on end here and there. Half-built homes of all sizes littered pre-planned housing estates, piles of bricks and stacks of cut timber standing in amongst excavated foundations. Everard pulsed his way past vast open spaces, already cordoned off and obviously delegated as planting areas, agricultural or recreational she had no idea. All signs of activity throughout the huge cavern had ceased but up ahead, a good league away, Beatrix detected the presence of a large cloud of dust.

They came to the bottom of a scree slope that stretched endlessly from side to side. Dismounting, Aidan, Beatrix and Adler examined the uneven fall of rock before them, predominantly limestone with various other minerals mixed in.

Aidan picked up a black, shiny rock and studied it. 'Is this vugocite?' he asked Adler.

'No, my friend, it is an extremely hard coal used by the ironworkers to manufacture coke for their kilns. Vugocite does not break into little pieces. In fact I have never heard that it breaks at all.'

'What do you mean?' asked Beatrix.

'What I said. It doesn't crumble when exposed to weather, does not crack. It is unbreakable by any means known to us. When we come across it, which isn't very often, we turn away from it, shun it altogether. It is one of the natural creations of nature that we, nature's guardians, avoid like the plague.' Adler trembled and continued in a whisper. 'There is something of the devil about it—it is evil.'

Aidan glanced at Beatrix warily. 'I think you'd better stay here while I climb up and have a look at it.'

'Oh, don't be silly,' she retorted and began scrambling her way up the hill of loose rocks. Stumbling at one point, she nearly fell as a stretch of rusty red nodules gave way below her feet...they had reached an enormous area of the tumbled rock.

'What is this stuff?' she asked Adler.

'That is the blood ore that the miners of Griffin delve for,' he paused. 'It may be that one of the mineshafts has already collapsed,' he paused, his eyes expressing an even deeper anxiety. 'And if that is the case it will not only be extremely perilous for the miners of Meltwater, but there will also be greater access into Bylani for the Darkness.'

'You mean that you've excavated that close to the surface?' Aidan asked, aghast at the safety implications of digging the ground away from beneath a tunnel in which men worked.

'No, my friend, we have never made a habit of putting you humans at risk. It's just that when we discovered this cave it was more or less columnar...a deep shaft running vertically through the mountain. We surveyed every surface and found that there was one very deep mineshaft running across the top of the column. The men in that mine were lucky—as were we, for we might have been discovered. The floor on which the miners walked was about to collapse into this cave. But with our magic we managed to reinforce it, in effect shoring it up safer than if they were walking on the surface. But now that floor is again in jeopardy, no-one can walk it in safety anymore. Somehow they must be warned.'

'Then why has your magic failed? Aidan asked perplexed as they reached the summit of the scree slope.

'Because of this!' and Adler, disgusted, smacked the surface of the vugocite. 'This rock stretches all the way up to the mine—we can do nothing in its vicinity, nothing! We...we are helpless,' he moaned, his voice desolate.

Aidan stared upwards attempting to see the top edge of the black rock, it was concealed in darkness. He stroked the surface of the vugocite feeling a sense of unease that was somehow familiar but one he couldn't place. Examining the surface even closer he found it had the consistency of small round balls, each ball squashed slightly against its neighbour leaving tiny gaps between the individual nodules. 'I can just get the tip of my finger in between each of these lumps. Beatrix, make a light let's have a closer look,' Aidan asked without thinking.

Beatrix glowed a little, enough to see the surface clearly, roughly a yard around them.

'How can you use magic, it should be impossible this near the wall?' Amazed, Adler stared open-mouthed at the girl when she bent closer to peer at the wall.

'Oh, I never thought,' and she shrugged. 'Um…I don't know, do you, Aidan?'

The young wizard scratched his head and stared at her for long moments. 'I suppose it's because the magic you're using is unique. No-one else can create light quite like you.'

'Ugh, it smells,' she said taking a quick sniff of the wall.

'It does?' asked Aidan puzzled. 'I can't smell anything.'

'Neither can I,' said Adler sniffing. 'I've never known of anyone complaining of any sort of odour before. But there again we've never made a habit of staying in its environs for long.'

Beatrix looked at them as if they were mad. 'Of course it smells…it's…it's disgusting, it reminds me of…' and then she grasped Aidan's arm. Peering closely at the black rock she suddenly paled, her face shocked she could hardly stand.

'What is it, Beattie, what's wrong?' Aidan asked.

'It smells like the Darkness, Aidan,' and she stared at him full of fear, 'and I know why.'

'What do you mean?' Aidan cast his senses into the rock frantically searching for any indication of the enemy and found none. 'I can't feel it here, Beattie,' and as she looked at him still afraid, he reassured her. 'Honest, I can't, and anyway it won't have got here yet,' he pulled the frightened girl into his arms, worried because she was trembling.

'The rock, Aidan—it's the same,' and she gasped, squeezing him tight, so hard it hurt. 'Don't you understand?'

'No, what are you on about?'

'The fog in the basin…the fog that held the Darkness on Sanctity, I saw the rock beneath it. Aidan, I saw exactly what it was like because of the light from Tragen's cage—somehow the sacrifices changed the hard rock into the fog. It's the same rock!'

'Dear God! Are you sure?' her face told him the answer.

'What has happened to the rock, there,' Adler, not understanding their conversation, interrupted and pointed all of a sudden fearful, at a small section of the wall as big as his fist.

They both studied the spot he'd indicated, it taking many minutes for what they were seeing to sink in. The horror of that place beneath the volcano on Sanctity unexpectedly appearing here in Bylani rendered them incapable of grasping anything.

'It doesn't seem as dark as the rest, does it?' Beatrix asked, finding her voice first.

Aidan nervously stretched out his hand and stroked the area. 'It feels different as well, not so knobbly,' he withdrew his hand quickly. 'Why has it altered, Adler?'

'I don't know it's never changed its appearance before—ever.'

'It's because her light touched it, young wizard.'

Aidan abruptly pulled apart from Beatrix at the sound of the small voice and searched around for its owner.

'Who is that? Where are you?' Aidan shouted, startled.

'What's the matter?' asked Beatrix.

'I'm down here at your feet, wizard.'

Aidan looked down at the ground and discovered a dark-red lizard about two feet long. It was sitting back on its haunches and looked to have one of its front legs broken; it was hanging limply against its side.

'Good God, who are you?' Aidan asked totally dumbfounded.

'Are you all right, Aidan,' Beatrix asked perplexed.

'Yes, Beatrix, it's talking to me, can't you hear it?'

'No!' And she stared at the small animal its head moving back and forth gazing up at them, abruptly she grinned. 'Like Ryn spoke to you?'

'Aye,' and he laughed.

'Is it a salamander?'

'It is, Milady,' replied Adler puzzled. 'What do you mean, Milord? Salamanders cannot talk. And who is Ryn, you've lost me?'

'I am not an "it"! I have a name in your tongue…Hector. And I can speak with the wizard of life and death.'

'What's it saying?' asked Beatrix.

'I'm not an "it",' shouted Hector, his temper rising. *'Tell them!'*

283

'I think I've had this conversation before,' Aidan said, dropping to his haunches in front of Hector. He grinned recalling Ryn and his unusual demand. 'Don't tell me—I suppose you want a voice as well, do you?'

Thirty-six

Thaddeus and Augusta travelled a long and twisting road, sometimes over a good hard level surface, at other times the way was rocky and pitted with irregular craters where rainwater had washed down the mountainside and across their path. It was a highway that traversed the whole island from west to east. The western end was used primarily by fishermen bringing their catches of herring, haddock and the huge tuna to Meltwater and Mount Peaceful. The hinterland stretch across the moors and through the forests was used by hunters of bear and otter, deer and the sneezing black grouse.

But it was the stretch east of Mount Trespass that was the busiest. Here many villages had been established, arising because of the eternal search for the bloodstone. Alongside the numerous open mineshafts, the entrances of which were dark and a little menacing, heaps of red rocks were piled to await collection by the wagon transports of the Montetor clan. However, the people and the buildings of the sometimes large, more often small neighbourhoods, all shared a common trait. All were covered in the fine red dust of the iron ore dug from deep within the bowels of Griffin Island.

Peppering the slopes of Mount Peaceful, stretching high above the island, were numerous adits. Abandoned by the mining families, they were strangely peaceful now. Augusta and Thaddeus were a little surprised, though, as no-one had passed them making for the catacombs. The guide informed them the miners and their families were gathering in Meltwater where the Montetor was ordering them to evacuate into the catacombs.

In the valley between the two peaks, the foundries had been sited amongst a profusion of hills of coke imported from other islands. And it was here that the large town of Meltwater had grown over the centuries into the hub of the ironworkers' lives.

After a day of hard riding Thaddeus and Augusta arrived at a junction where the road up from the south met the road running east and west. A small stream gurgled over rocks as it fell down the mountain. Here their guide, Artur, called a halt for the night and dismounting he began setting up camp. It was a site clearly used many times by travellers as a permanent fireplace in a stone circle had been built. Alongside it was a stack of tinder and Artur commenced laying a fire, he handed a pot to Thaddeus and asked him to fill it at the nearby stream.

'How long before we get to Meltwater?' Thaddeus asked on returning.

'We'll get there at noon tomorrow, Highness,' answered Artur, not looking at them he hung the pot from an iron tripod over the fire. He retrieved boiled bacon, cheeses and bread from his saddlebags.

'It's not going to be very comfortable sleeping here,' Augusta muttered. 'Why don't we see if there's a spare bed in that house over there?' She nodded at a small stone building about half a league away on the road to Griffin.

'People round here don't like strangers poking about their homes when they're not there, Milady,' Artur said, spreading out his blanket near the fire. The only one with any sort of bedding, he did not offer it to Augusta.

'But I think there is someone there, I saw a light.'

'Can't have, Milady, everyone's in Meltwater,' their guide turned over onto his side and drew the blanket over his head. Moments later he was snoring.

An hour later Augusta stood up from where she had been trying to sleep on the grass verge and stretched her aching back. Staring across at the stone cottage she kicked Thaddeus.

He awoke startled. 'What?' he said not opening his eyes but rubbing his thigh where her foot had connected.

'I can't sleep,' she said.

'I can,' and he turned over.

'Come on, get up, we're going over there,' she ordered.

'What?' opening his eyes he sat up. 'We can't go over there, you heard what he said. Whoever's house that is, is not going to like us wandering about their property.'

'Thaddeus,' she said impatiently, 'think on it. No-one is going back to that cottage for the God knows how long when the Darkness gets here. And who knows what those demons will do to it when they do get here. Anyway I did see a light there, I'm convinced of it. So move, I am not sleeping on stones any longer.'

Grumbling he stood up, glancing at their guide fast asleep in his blanket, Thaddeus decided not to rouse him to tell him where they were going. He rushed off after Augusta striding purposefully down the road. A full moon shone its light on them in the warm night, an owl hooted in the distance, and walking with Augusta, Thaddeus discovered he was happy. He stared at her from the corner of his eye and had the overwhelming urge to grasp her hand. What would she do, he wondered? Probably think he was crazy and hit him around the head, he thought. But as his hand twitched and his fingers uncurled to slide over her hand, they reached the small gate in the white picket fence facing the red stone built cottage.

And Thaddeus also saw the light winking in the gap between the curtains of the only window alongside the open door. And he did grasp her hand, pulling her to a stop.

'What's the matter?' she asked, surprising Thaddeus by gripping his hand tighter.

'Why's the door open?'

'I don't know—it is hot tonight,' she added staring into his concerned eyes.

'Yes, but it's late. There must be bandits on this road.'

'Don't worry, dearies, they're all in Meltwater,' came a pleasant voice from the cottage. Moments later a middle-aged woman, with a yellow shawl around her head and shoulders and a long red dress, stood in the doorway blocking the light. 'You're quite safe here and welcome. I noticed there were travellers up at the crossroads and I thought you'd come and avail yourself of my hospitality—poor as it is. Come, come on in, I have water on the boil, I'm sure you'd like some tea.' She turned and walked back into the room behind.

Augusta glanced up at Thaddeus, shrugged and releasing his hand, she followed the woman into the cottage. Thaddeus licked his lips, held up his empty hand where he could still feel her fingers, and sighing he walked after her.

The room stretched the whole length of the cottage and held a fair-sized table, half a dozen straight-backed chairs around it, and two comfortable, heavily cushioned chairs either side of the fireplace. A door in the corner led into what must have been a bedroom and both side walls were covered from ground to ceiling in shelves holding a vast array of items. Augusta was fascinated, it almost looked like a shop, yet the cottage was not.

Noticing Augusta's gaze, the woman smiled, her teeth white and even. Removing her shawl and letting her long black hair settle down her back she lifted the kettle from the hob and poured water into a teapot. 'Please, my friends, sit at the table and drink this. Luckily I've just made some biscuits you can share them with me.'

The smell of the hot sugar bringing a flush of saliva to his mouth, Thaddeus wasn't long tucking in. Augusta was a little slower as her eyes were constantly examining the shelves. Bright yellow and red striped ribbons, the royal colours of Mantovar, streamed from hooks screwed into the wood haphazardly. Behind these was an abundance of attractive and fascinating objects. And abruptly she was lost all at once in a woman's world of cross-stitch, embroidery hoops, pouches of sweet smelling herbs and odd knick-knacks of jewellery and figurines. She was utterly enthralled. Augusta couldn't resist her sudden urge to explore and leaving her tea she walked over to the nearest wall.

'Augusta what are you doing?' Thaddeus asked, her manner in ignoring their hostess surprising him.

Augusta turned and realized her bad manners. 'Oh, I'm sorry, I didn't mean to be rude, it's just that everything is so fascinating.'

'Don't worry, my dear. You go ahead, pick up anything you like, have a look. I'm so glad someone likes them, I've spent years collecting them.'

Augusta, smiling tentatively, gently touched each object as she walked along the shelves. Afraid to pick them up she thought some of them very delicate and didn't want to trust her fingers, for some reason her hands were trembling. She stooped and examined the various odd little figurines that caught her eye, the captivating jewellery ranging from etched rings of gold and silver to ornaments of jade and other colourful, unknown stones. But one piece sitting at the back in the shadows of a bottom shelf caught her attention immediately. Drawn inexorably towards the article she picked it up. Studying the object closely she found it consisted of a circular disk of red stone suspended amongst a series of short irregular bands of red leather. Without thinking she slipped the fingers of her left hand through the bands.

'Oh!' she exclaimed, staring at the object.

'What's the matter?' Thaddeus asked, not overly concerned as she was smiling.

'Its soft,' she said prodding the stone with her finger. 'When I picked it up off the shelf the disc was hard, but it's suddenly gone soft. Look, it seems to have moulded itself to the curves of my palm, I can hardly feel it there,' and she held up her hand for Thaddeus to get a closer look.

'You have a very discerning eye, my lady,' said their hostess. She left the table and strolled over to Augusta. Holding Augusta's hand in hers, the woman stroked the stone in her palm.

'What is it?' Augusta asked staring at the circle of red – embossed with a depiction of a stylized castle and a river that she hadn't noticed before – nestling comfortably in the palm of her hand.

'It is the rarest of bloodstone, mined here on Griffin, it is indestructible. Yet very attractive is it not, unique jewellery for the palm of a unique hand. But, of course, you know that. You are the first to ever wear it correctly.'

'I am?' Augusta asked not taking her eyes from the disk, its etching reminding her of home.

'Yes, everyone else places the disk on the back of the hand, a very uncomfortable mode, if I may say so. I had given up hope of ever parting with the glove until I saw the way you handled it. It rests easily in your palm, does it not?'

Augusta nodded. 'It almost feels as if it belongs with me. A glove, you say? It's a very strange one but it fits me perfectly,' and she smiled from the bottom of her heart – she could not describe the fulfilling sensation in words but her expression said it all – the glove was a part of her. 'It seemed to call me and now it feels as if it's at home,' she suddenly looked embarrassed. 'I know it sounds daft, but... you want to part with it? I don't understand...it is beautiful.'

'So it is, but it is not for me, never has been.' The woman, beaming, returned to the table and picked up her cup of tea. Augusta sat alongside her unable to take her eyes from the glove. 'Take it as a gift, a present for a warrior,' she stretched across and patted Augusta's arm leaving a faint trace of lavender.'

'A warrior?'

'Oh, yes—it is a gauntlet of war,' and the woman smiled again. 'Please, take it as a gift.'

'Then let me pay you for it,' said Thaddeus.

'Oh no, you must not. It will not work for her if you pay coin and the both of you will offend me if you persist. Now you must rest, you face great danger. In the morning you must take her from here.'

With those words their heads dropped to the table and they slept where they were. But Thaddeus could have sworn her last words were in his head.

'Heed me well, young Prince. Care for her all your life, for she will surprise you mightily.'

They woke at the same moment, the following morning, refreshed as if they'd lain in a bed all night not bent over in a chair their heads on their arms. They sat up and looked around at an abandoned cottage. Nothing was the same except for the fireplace, even the table was smaller. There were no shelves crammed with the trinkets of the night before. The room was cold, the fire in the grate having died days before. Bewildered they stared at each other.

'Was it a dream, Thaddeus?'

'If it was, it was a very realistic dream. Look at your hand,' he said.

Augusta raised her left hand and stared at the gauntlet, the red disc moulded softly to the palm, the webbing comfortably in place across her hand and wrist.

'I don't understand. Who was she?'

But before he could answer there was a shout from outside. 'Bazyli will be waiting, Highness,' Artur said anxiously, 'we must go.'

Thaddeus and Augusta left the cottage and remounted their horses that Artur was leading.

'How did you know we were in there?' asked Thaddeus.

'Your tracks, Highness,' and he turned his horse to the road. 'Come, we must not waste any more time.'

'Do you know who lived here, Artur?' asked Augusta.

'Aye...old Mel. Some say she was a hedge-witch—she could heal the small things, warts and what-not. But she died weeks ago.' With that he put his heels to his horse's flank and rode off.

It wasn't until much later that they gave up wondering at the woman knowing who they were and her strange words. Augusta never even thought of removing the gauntlet, the disc had become her.

They reached the outskirts of Meltwater at noon as Artur promised—and found the town fortified. There was a barricade across the road with an opening just wide enough for them to go through in single-file. The town was crowded, the people from the outlying villages camped on every spare piece of ground and in the alleyways. Armed militia manned the barricade and perimeter of the town.

A semblance of normality was being attempted in the life of Meltwater. Behind the hostile stares of the townsfolk directed at them – as they rode past on their way to the Town Hall – were the everyday shouts of shopkeepers and wagon drivers. What was missing was the merry banter of hardworking neighbours, happy voices coming from the rear of houses where later that evening most of the miners, having finished work for the day, would be bathing in tubs of tepid water, their offspring laughing and playing or occasionally arguing nineteen to the dozen.

There were still the faraway sounds of heavy hammers banging metal and the dull background roar of blast furnaces. The mining families were going about their business on every street. Women were walking with baskets on their arms or men with canvas bags on their shoulders. The occasional drunk was weaving along the road a jug in hand, or else lying comatose in small alleyways, the common eyesore of many a town.

But there were also bands of men standing on street corners armed to the hilt with pikestaffs, crossbows, swords and cudgels. There were others walking around with daggers stuck in belts and staffs in hand. This was not the customary behaviour of any peaceful town untroubled by events in the greater world. Swathed in gusts of black smoke, the heavy-laden ore wagons trundled along lazily over cobbled streets amidst hawkers continually plying their wares among the predominantly wooden buildings. But neither was it the normal behaviour of a people preparing to evacuate to a safer haven beneath the catacombs.

Nevertheless, there were no riots.

'What's going on, Artur? Everything seems quiet…there's no riot. But why does everyone look as if they're prepared for a war. They can't fight what's coming with these weapons,' Thaddeus asked puzzled.

'And why is everyone glaring at us as if we're the enemy?' asked Augusta.

'Bazyli must have finally put a stop to the riots,' he said, glancing quickly at his prince but again not meeting his eyes. 'He said to meet him in the Town Hall, shall we go?' He dug in his heels and his horse moved off at a trot, uncaring that the street was crowded and people had to move frantically out of the way to avoid being trampled.

Augusta hung back a moment with Thaddeus and grabbed his arm. 'I don't like this, something smells,' she said.

Thaddeus grinned worriedly. 'Aye, that'll be the furnaces, won't it Anders,' he asked their friend watching from his place at the wall of colours.

'Well, ignoring the armed men, I can't see anything wrong, everyone's going about their business as people always do, but…'

'But what?' asked Thaddeus.

'Shouldn't they be getting ready to leave?' asked Augusta, interrupting. She was scared. Earlier, as they reached the outskirts of the town she had peered south at Griffin Town. She could just see the ocean reflecting the last of the sun's light. She shuddered; she had also glimpsed the Darkness looming on the horizon. 'How far off is it now, Anders?'

'At its present speed, it'll be with you in a day or two.'

'Can you warn Aidan?' Thaddeus had asked anxiously.

'He's very deep underground now, I can barely hear him. I think he's on that animal, that worm, and its body rubbing along the floor is drowning out his thoughts.'

It was Razor who met them on the front steps of the imposing red bricked, two-storey building at the north end of Bloodstone Square, Cyryl Lewyn, his cat on his shoulders, stood behind him a small cigar hanging from his lips.

'What's going on here, Razor,' Thaddeus said as he and Augusta stepped down from their mounts. 'Why aren't people moving out?'

'Bazyli is inside, he'll tell you.'

Lewyn's cat dropped from her master's shoulders as they walked through the double doors into the vestibule and she rubbed her body against their legs nearly tripping them. Unfortunately, though, she was moulting and several cat hairs clung to their clothing. The cat's welcome distracted them for vital moments.

Thaddeus and Augusta were clubbed senseless, from behind, as they entered the main meeting hall.

Thirty-seven

'Aidan...Beattie! Can you hear me?' Anders screamed. 'Answer me, for God's sake, *Aidan...*'

'*All right, all right, we can hear you, what's the panic?*' Aidan asked.

He, Beattie and Adler were returning to the town of Bylani on the back of Everard. Hector, cradled in Aidan's arms, was sleeping; resting after displaying one of its many unusual attributes—salamanders could re-grow their limbs once lost, and they had all watched as he did just that. Before their amazed eyes he shed his broken front leg and another grew in its place. But it was something else that made Aidan smile, his grin permanently stuck on his face. The thought of having given a voice to two previously dumb creatures utterly astounded him. He wondered briefly what had become of Ryn, if he'd managed to deliver Tragen's message. But thinking of Tragen wiped the grin from his face, depression again deepening his loss. It was Anders' voice that brought him out of it.

'*I don't know what's going on, but Thaddeus and Augusta have been knocked unconscious and captured by that man who was chasing you...Razor I think his name is.*'

'*Where are they?*' Beattie asked, startled.

'*In Meltwater...in the Town Hall. They walked through a door and men jumped them from behind. They had no warning.*'

'*What's happening to them now?*' asked Aidan, his body tensing, his spirit plummeting once more. Was this going to be another incident to delay his search for Tragen? So many problems all at once and all he wanted to do was rescue his master. He was becoming convinced there was a conspiracy to keep him from the afterlife.

'*They've been imprisoned somewhere beneath the Town Hall, at least that's where I think they are. They were taken that way anyway. Nobody seems to be bothering with them at the moment, though, except for that cat.*'

'*What cat?*'

'*That man Lewyn's cat. It's crawling all over them rubbing its body against them...it's very strange. I've never seen a cat as affectionate as that before, or one that looks so odd.*'

'*What do you mean?*' asked Beattie.

'Well it's a tortoiseshell with a perfectly white hind paw...very distinctive, very unusual.'

'All right, damn the cat...keep an eye on them for now. Let us know when they wake or if they're moved. We have something else to do first before we can do anything about them,' said Aidan, sighing.

Whatever course of action he decided on to rescue his friends in Meltwater, it seemed that the task set them by Hector had to take priority, simply for the fact that they were so close to its fruition. It was potentially the most important factor for the survival of Griffin. Again he'd have to forget about going after Tragen, but not for much longer he promised himself—and his mentor.

'What's that?'

'We found a salamander in a cave down here and he's told us how to render vugocite harmless,' Aidan said aloud, forgetting that Adler knew nothing about their ability to talk with the dead.

'I beg your pardon, Milord, what was that?' Adler asked.

'I'm sorry, Adler, we've been talking to Anders, a friend of ours,' said Beattie, and then, of course, she had to explain, which left Adler speechless, a condition he was rapidly getting used to after hearing Hector speak.

'What is vugocite?' Anders asked having waited impatiently for Beattie to cease speaking.

'It's a black, unbreakable, porous rock that is impervious to natural magic. The Green People have discovered a vast seam of the stone in the cavern they're excavating beneath Meltwater. It's frightening, Anders, for Beattie believes it to be the same rock that the fog was formed from on Sanctity.'

'God! Can anything be done about it?' asked Anders.

'Aye, for it seems that Beattie's magic has an effect on it, her...'

'And yours, Aidan, don't forget you were almost touching the rock yet you still managed to use your magic to give Hector his voice,' she interrupted.

'Bloody hell, I hadn't realized that. Wait, though, my magic didn't make the slightest difference to it, only yours did. Well, let's hope Hector is right then, telling us to get hold of wandwood.'

'Who is Hector?' Anders mind was in a spin, struggling to take in the consequences of vugocite being present in Bylani; he was becoming more and more confused by their strange conversation.

'Oh, he's this salamander we rescued. I've given him a voice and in return he's told us that Beattie's light, channelled through wandwood, would be enough to seal the vugocite, render it safe,' Aidan said matter-of-factly.

'And Adler is taking us to the only known source of wandwood,' said Beattie excited. 'It seems that I am to have a wand, not a staff!'

It was later that afternoon when Aidan, Beattie and Adler stood before the fountain in front of the Moot Hall of Bylani. It was quiet in the square, the occasional green man or woman making their way home, the aroma of orange blossom wafting on the soft breeze.

The three of them, and Hector, studied the strange looking tree which formed the centrepiece of the fountain. They ignored the family of Green People depicted playing beneath it.

It wasn't long before they were joined by two of the five ancient leaders of the Green People, Elder Zoran and his wife Elder Varna. Both of them were unbelievably old. Elder Zoran had been the first to receive Elder Findar's prophecy which ultimately condemned the Green People to live below ground for a thousand years…their purpose to build the safe haven.

'Are you sure this is wandwood, Adler?' asked Aidan scratching his head. 'It looks very odd to be wood let alone a tree.'

'It is the only one of its kind, Lord Aidan,' Zoran answered as he and Varna walked over to stand at the side of the two wizards.

'And this is what we need, Hector?' Aidan asked the salamander, still cradled in his arms. 'You are sure?'

'Of course I'm sure, think I'm daft do you?'

'No…no…I'm sorry,' he answered hurriedly, stroking the salamander's back, placating him.

Beatrix glanced quickly at Hector and sighed…it seemed that another animal was beginning to sound like Aidan.

'It is true,' said Varna clasping her husband's arm and staring at the lizard, 'we have a talking salamander in Bylani.' Smiling at the animal snuggling close to Aidan's chest she stretched out her ancient arm and stroked Hector's head. 'Welcome to my home, Hector, I am very pleased to meet you.'

'And I you, but forgive me if I correct a misunderstanding—it is our home as well, not just yours.'

295

There was an awkward silence, the Elders taken aback, very rare were they ever corrected.

Beatrix cleared her throat tactfully. 'And how am I supposed to get a wand Hector. It is a very beautiful tree; it would be criminal to just break a piece off.'

The tree was a profusion of colours, different shades of each forming lines and patches which pulsed and gelled haphazardly to form new lines and shapes and even different colours. But it was the tree's shape that was the most striking. Its branches grew uniformly straight and horizontally from its thin trunk in a series of concentric rings climbing the bole, long branches of uniform length at the bottom gradually reducing in size to very short branches at the top—and not a leaf in sight. Water spouted upwards from the apex of the trunk and cascaded down over the stone family gambolling beneath, the flow clean and fresh to drink.

'Perhaps you should ask it,' Hector suggested.

'What do you mean?' Beattie looked at him nervously. 'I just can't talk to a tree.'

'Why not,' Aidan interrupted. 'When I find the tree to make my staff I'll sing to it.'

Beattie glanced at him and then said excitedly. 'Do you suppose this is the Tree of Paradise, you did say there was only one?'

'No, that tree is in Limbo.'

'What is the Tree of Paradise?' Zoran asked, frowning. 'I've never heard of it and that is very unusual as we are the guardians of nature.'

'It is a legend, the only tree of its kind. It is said that the Tree of Paradise will give me the most powerful staff in creation. I hope it's right, we'll need all the help we can get to defeat the One behind the Darkness.'

'But why is that staff to be yours, Lord Aidan, forgive me you are very young for such a responsibility. Surely it should go to another older wizard?' asked Elder Varna.

'Does the prophecy state the wizards' ages, Elder?'

'No, Aidan, you are right of course,' said Zoran bemused, this was the second time an Elder had been corrected in as many minutes.

'The Tree of Paradise calls only to me, therefore it is mine,' Aidan said, no sign of arrogance in his voice, just complete acceptance of the fact.

'Then it seems there are two trees in this world that are unique,' said Zoran.

'No, my husband,' Varna answered, 'you miss the point. Aidan's Tree of Paradise is not of this world, this…' and she indicated the tree of wandwood in the fountain, 'this is just one of many unique trees in our world, this, the only wandwood that we know of. But I'm afraid, Beatrix, that we know of no means to obtain a wand from it— we thought it only a quaint name attributed to it over the years. We never believed that it could actually supply a wand.'

They studied the young girl gazing glumly up at the wandwood tree towering above her. She was at a complete loss. But the more she stared, the more its colours reflected off her pretty face and deep in her ever-changing eyes. The constantly fluctuating hues and tints of the tree mesmerizing her until she gradually perceived a pattern that her mind somehow attuned to.

'Yes,' she said gazing rapt at the wandwood. 'I have to breathe in tune with you, don't I?' she said speaking to the tree, ignoring those watching her. She waited a while. Her emotions were the first to synchronize to the gentle pulsing of the tree, her blood the next—her heart beat in time with the regular pattern that only she could see. She stepped resolutely into the pool and walked beneath the fall of the water and, stretching out her hand, she stroked the lowest array of branches—and the next one above.

And then she levitated slowly up the tree, touching each array lovingly as she came to it, until she reached the topmost. At this point her feet were twice Aidan's height above his head and she discovered that the exit point for the water was in itself a branch of the tree—a single long hollow twig pointing skywards. This she grasped in both hands and it came away from the tree without the need for her to break it free. Holding the branch aloft her heart soared—the wand was hers and rightfully so. She understood that the wand had been waiting for this moment—waiting for her.

And she kissed it.

She stared down at the water, now flowing from the stunted trunk of the tree and, as she watched, so a new budding emerged; a new branch grew to replace the old. But she knew in her heart that this was the only wand it would ever relinquish gladly.

Beatrix came back to earth slowly, her heartbeat returning to normal but not her emotions. She walked from beneath the water, she and her clothes perfectly dry. She and Aidan gazed full of awe at the wand in her hand—the colours still pulsing, the lines and shapes almost mimicking that of the wall of colours in Limbo. But these colours beat in time with Beattie's life force.

'Bloody hell, Beattie…that was impressive!' Aidan exclaimed.

'Stop swearing, Aidan, we have guests,' and suddenly she screamed in ecstasy and flung her arms around him, hugging him tight. Returning her embrace he was utterly bewildered for he knew she loved him—and tears started in his eyes.

A couple of hours later Beattie felt as if her arm was falling off. The strain of holding the wand up, though it was not heavy, made her arm ache for it was taking forever to render safe the vast expanse of vugocite.

The first time she used the wand surprised everyone, its effect had been truly astonishing. She stood before the wall and placed the tip of the wand nervously against the rock not knowing what to expect. But this time when she created her light it did not flow from every pore in her body, the wand concentrated her power and the magic streamed through it into the vugocite and spread throughout a large area. The rock altered its composition—turning white and fusing the nodules into one completely impervious mass even more rigid than it was previously. But the seam of vugocite was massive, so very much of it that Aidan worried about her waning strength. Beattie was deep into her reserves when transmuting the last of it.

It was as she finished that a messenger arrived and spoke urgently to Adler standing at the foot of the seam with Hector at his side. Both man and lizard were enthralled, watching the young woman levitate across the wall leaving a stretch of harmless white rock where there had only been black threat.

'Aidan, I have to go I've just had terrible news,' he said turning quickly to career down the loose scree to mount Everard. 'We have another case of plague. It's Primrosa, my wife, she…she must have caught it off Leon,' he shouted over his shoulder. Distraught, the Green Man nearly fell from Everard as he turned her in his panic.

'Wait, Adler, wait for us…a few more moments won't harm. Beattie's nearly finished now and I can't leave her here alone, she's about to drop with exhaustion. She'll need your krynx to return to Bylani. Don't worry; I'll heal your wife.'

'Thank you, Aidan, but there's more. The plague is about to spread throughout Bylani—my wife went to market earlier, and it was very busy there. She must have come in contact with hundreds.'

'Aidan, can you hear me,' Anders shouted.

'Aye, Anders, what is it?'

'Augusta and Thaddeus have come around but I can't speak with them, and from their frantic actions they seem...'

'What do you mean...frantic? Anders I can't handle any more problems, I have to get to Tragen,' he replied, despairing, knowing that Anders' hesitation would inevitably mean another delay.

'They've lost their magic!'

Thirty-eight

Helydd sat on the mountain slope alongside the cloud-cover denying Alfhime normal sunlight and a natural climate, her back resting against a cold rock. She was wrapped closely in her heavy blue cloak, her hood raised against the sharp wind, watching Ryn hard at work.

She was morose, full of guilt and ashamed at deceiving the bird, but she was afraid to confide in him. She so desperately needed his help to break into Alfhime and rescue Manon that she'd go to almost any lengths to achieve her aim. She could not go anywhere near the magic of the shield, for if even one tiny wisp of cloud touched her, an alarm would sound in the liosalfar town. The thought of the elves becoming aware of her forcing entry, frightened her silly. Although they couldn't kill her or her daughter, they could still keep Manon from her mother, hide her deeper within their mountains where Helydd would never find her. But if she told Ryn the truth, let him in on her secret, he'd probably recoil in fear as everyone did and, ceasing her bidding, he'd fly away. Her heart bled.

Nonetheless, in the last twenty years this was the closest she had ever come to succeeding. She recalled the last attempt when she had unwittingly allowed an enemy – of both her and the liosalfar – to gain entrance. The demon had thwarted her attempts to follow him through the gateway. She was determined that wasn't going to happen again. And it shouldn't this time, she'd been more careful in her assessment of Ryn. The albatross was not an enemy and moreover he had the same aims, his worries for loved ones the same as hers—his desperation to rescue them just as ardent. And Ryn, a Wandering Albatross of the Giant Albatross family, had totally captivated her.

But ever since the enemy had entered the valley of Alfhime, the liosalfar had increased their efforts to keep her at bay. They had begun by fortifying this cloud-cover with an incredible potency and raising other defences as well that she could not breach. She could no longer enter the listening post through the rift in the cliff; the enemy's magic now sealed the way. All to deny her daughter's rescue. At least that was the purpose of the liosalfar—the demon had another. She stared at Ryn still ploughing away at the clouds, and she raged impotently—the unfairness of the elves' decision rendered her bereft.

The tall, white-skinned elves were zealots. Manon had been very young when she had caused the accident in all innocence. But the mountain elves were blinded by their purpose, blinkered by their guardianship. Any threat to the legend, however accidental, was punished inordinately. And Helydd was dreadfully aggrieved at the monumental sentence imposed on her daughter—life imprisonment for a being that could not die!

But she couldn't deny a twinge of conscience every time she thought of the last time she'd tried to penetrate the shield. The rescue attempt had been going so well until she had been betrayed at the last step, deceived so unexpectedly. She hadn't realized the nature of the enemy, or its intention, until he'd entered Alfhime. By then it was too late. But there again, she thought, perhaps the liosalfar deserved a share of her torment for what they had done.

She twirled her necklace in her fingers. At least the enemy wouldn't gain possession of the legend if that was truly his aim. But then again he'd been in Alfhime for twenty years—why hadn't he yet realized his mistake? She wondered, maybe the demon wasn't as clever as he thought he was.

Ryn paused in his task of pulling away little pieces of cloud from the vast mass of feathery vapour on which he was standing. It was a laborious undertaking he'd been set. Helydd had told him what to do but that's as far as it went, she made no move to help. He put it down to her age…she was an old woman, with all an old woman's aches and pains he assumed. But at least she'd promised to feed him. He was thankful for that…she was an excellent cook, nearly as good as Shadra. And thinking of his friend he twisted his beak in misery and plucked at the cloud with more vigour. But this job was going to take forever, he sighed.

She'd told him there was no way he could force his way through the clouds, pushing against its bulk only made it sit firmer—but pulling at it was a different kettle of fish. He hadn't quite understood the allusion to his favourite food, but he did see that tugging at the cloud broke pieces away, although they were mighty small bits. And she'd warned him not to break through the bottom most layer until they were both ready to enter Alfhime and that couldn't be until after nightfall. But before that he had to ensure that the space he cleared would be large enough to allow them entrance. However, at this rate it was going to take him at least a week just to make a dent big enough for him to stand in.

She added, with a note of caution, once normal sunlight burst through into Alfhime then the magic of the cloud-cover would disperse. Moonlight though was something else, it had a different effect. The dispersal and eradication of the magic would be slower and would not at first be seen. If they were lucky it might even go entirely unnoticed until the dawn. Perhaps, by then, they'd have found Manon and the others and be far away, for she knew where the cells of Alfhime were located.

She didn't tell Ryn that there were two enemies of vastly differing capabilities in the valley below. The liosalfar, for all their blind stupidity, were decent people at heart and very courageous. Their guardianship proved this—they had surrendered their lives to one purpose, to protect the legend for eternity if necessary. The legend might be needed again. So their paranoia at the accident caused by Manon was, to a certain extent, understandable, but no less hurtful.

But the demon, the second enemy, was by far the more dangerous of the two. He was not a normal foe and would react cataclysmically to the disappearance of the clouds. Helydd could feel the increased malice within the conjuration of the vapour, evidence that his presence was even more evil. She'd have to be very careful to safeguard Ryn, and whether she liked it or not, shield the liosalfar themselves, from the evil one's lunatic intentions.

How the liosalfar would react after all these years to the sudden acquisition of normal sunlight and a natural world was anyone's guess. But Helydd, despite her loathing of them pitied them, for the monster within their midst would show no mercy if crossed. She had never had the opportunity to inform the mountain elves of their danger—but they probably wouldn't have believed her if she had.

'I'm feeling a little peckish, Helydd, any chance of lunch?'

She smiled at him. She did like him. He had the childlike, honest quality of the new-born about him that was endearing. Manon would dearly love him, she thought. 'Yes, my good friend,' and she dragged from behind her a basket of goodies, hot baked trout swimming in garlic butter, and for dessert a large pink blancmange…he loved blancmange. And she was going to surprise him by presenting him with his own knife, fork and spoon. She grinned and wondered if there'd be enough room in the pouch that he wore around his neck. She'd asked him once what it contained, but he'd become very reticent and had tucked it back within his chest feathers. She'd let the matter rest for it could not possibly hold any threat for her, he had no idea who she was—but its contents had seemed very important to him.

Shadra paced the floor of his dungeon while Anselm stretched out on his back on his bed, his hands behind his head, staring up at the grey, knobbly, rock ceiling.

'How much longer do you think before he decides our fate?' asked Shadra.

'We've only been here a couple of days. I can't see the Magician making up his mind quickly, can you? I get the impression that the longer he keeps us locked up the less danger we are to him. Even if he let us walk around Alfhime, I can't see us winning any sort of popularity contest and persuading the liosalfar to help us escape. I think they're more afraid of the Magician than we are. And as for fighting a battle—you have no magic and I have no weapons.'

The little green, forest elf shrugged his small shoulders. 'There's definitely something about that Magician that doesn't ring true you know. He didn't smell like a true elf.'

'What do you mean? I haven't noticed that you smell much, but there again you've an absolute mania for washing.'

Shadra looked askance. 'Perhaps you could do with a little more bathing, it wouldn't come amiss.'

'Oh, yes! And where do I bathe? That fountain in the corner,' and he pointed at a small spout of water coming out of the wall in the rear of the cell, 'is both very cold and hardly sufficient. I need a bowl to catch enough to dunk my head…and there's no soap.'

'Why didn't you say you needed soap I could have given you some, here,' and he pulled his bag from beneath his bed on the other side of the cell to Anselm's. 'I should have plenty in this,' and he rummaged around the interior of the canvas sack. 'Damn,' he said after a while withdrawing empty hands, 'the magic has gone from my bag as well. I wondered why they'd returned it.'

Anselm sat up and swung his long legs to the floor. 'Never mind, the longer we're here the more chance of your magic returning before they do something really bad to us. You did say that it won't have disappeared for good, didn't you?'

'I know but I've never had it taken from me before. I don't know if the Magician has some means of retaining it permanently— he's taken the liosalfars' from them hasn't he, and the way he talked he seems to have had theirs for years. I think that's why he hasn't killed me. If I die my magic dies with me, perhaps he needs all the power he can get. I don't know Anselm, being without my magic is so terribly difficult. I feel as if part of me, the biggest part, is dead. I feel empty. If it wasn't for the fact that you're here, I think I'd have gone mad by now.' He hung his head and all of a sudden clenched his fist and hammered the wall alongside him.

'Whoa, Shadra, take care, we'll get out of this somehow. Is your hand all right?'

The elf kneaded his bruised knuckles. 'All this waiting, hanging around when we should be out there searching for the reason for me being called here. If we don't get out of here before long, I am going to go crazy.'

'Haven't you any idea why you came here?'

'No, Anselm. I woke one morning years ago with the compulsion to explore this part of the Scissor Mountains. I'd had a strange dream about becoming friends with a white bird and…I don't know, there were lots of other things as well, but everything got so muddled.' He stopped pacing and sat on his bed. 'I had that same dream many times over the years before I went and sought advice from the shaman.'

'The shaman…he's a soothsayer isn't he?' asked Anselm his full attention caught by the story.

'The shaman is many things—soothsayer, healer, advisor to my king. But Namamonatama went all quiet on me when I asked what the dreams meant. He said I'd know when the time was right. So I asked him when that would be and he told me "when I was needed". He kept replying in the same mode never giving me a straight answer. But he did tell me that I had to complete my duties before leaving on my search. And my King wouldn't give me leave until this year.'

'Your duties…what were they?'

'   I was, and still am, the King's Ranger—the Soldier Guardian, Commander of the army of the forest elves and Chief Deceiver. There aren't many rangers, but enough to protect the hunters and farmers and of course our families. It is my duty to train my people and lead them in time of conflict.'

Anselm was startled; taking a deep breath he remained silent, digesting the new revelations. His small friend was not just any old forest elf. He was a warrior—and a great warrior amongst his people, if his title was anything to go by.

'You are someone of importance among your people, then?'

'Everyone is someone of importance among our people, Anselm. Do not make more of it than it is. But the compulsion to come here would not leave me and finally the King relented and gave me one year to satisfy my urge. I think the shaman persuaded him in the end.'

'And does your compulsion still tell you that you are in the right place?'

'Aye, it does Anselm. That is what's so odd—I know this is definitely the place. And the right time,' he smiled. 'And haven't I become friends with a white bird?'

Anselm laughed. 'That part is undeniably correct. Ryn must be getting seriously worried by now.' Anselm ceased speaking and stared into space thinking of their mutual friend. 'I bet he's spending his time trying to find a way to rescue us, and what's more if anyone can save us I think he will. I've a lot of faith in that bird. Wait a minute you said you were the Chief Deceiver, what exactly does that mean?'

'Before me, have you ever seen another forest elf?'

'It's strange; I've always thought you were a myth.' He didn't look at Shadra, the elf not noticing that he had ignored his question.

'Well, that is because of the work of the deceivers. We hide our people from humans in every way that we can—by setting spells of concealment, sometimes hexes such as that of distraction. But we also use normal means—many times I have led humans along false trails. We forest elves live throughout the Great Forest and there are lots of us. Yet only a very few humans know of our existence and that is only because we have allowed them to meet us. We are deceivers…we deceive your sight and your hearing, your nose, touch and even your sense of taste.'

'You amaze me, Shadra, you really do.' And he smiled with more respect for his small friend than he'd ever shown before. 'But I also have a purpose here. I should be out there trying to enlist the aid of the liosalfar in my fight against the Abbot of Sentinel.'

'Isn't it about time you told me of your mission?' Shadra asked. 'Why does your chancellor need their help?' He sat up on the edge of his bed, swinging his legs he waited expectantly.

Thirty-nine

Anselm sighed and, pulling a toothpick from his belt, began cleaning his teeth. He lounged back comfortably on his bed, stretched out his legs and stared up at the ceiling again. Distracted a moment he gazed at a globule of moisture clinging to a small nick in the roof. The rest of the ceiling was bone dry and he wondered where the dewdrop, for such it looked, had come from. Grunting, he gathered his thoughts, putting them in logical order deciding to hold nothing back. He trusted Shadra; they'd been through too much together in the short time they'd known each other, for the elf to be playing fast and loose with him. Learning the elf's true status among his people only confirmed his integrity. Shadra could never be in league with Mantovar's enemies. Returning the toothpick to his belt he took out his tobacco pipe from his bag that he'd been allowed to keep. Puffing manfully on the liosalfar's mild tobacco, he exhaled a long stream of smoke and related his tale.

'I suppose the real trouble started about twenty years ago, about the time Cumbria was elected, or rather usurped the title of Abbot of Sentinel. The previous incumbent, a man by the name of Lawren, had died in a hunting accident…we now believe arranged by Cumbria.' He squirmed deeper into the mattress, relaxing his body though not his mind, and continued.

'That Cumbria, now…he's a devious, dangerous bastard and no mistake. But he's also extremely charming; butter wouldn't melt in his mouth type…when he wants to be. His chance came when the Prince was up north checking his borders; there'd been reports of skirmishes with unfamiliar insurgents out of the frozen wastes. Well, he started in on Princess Maria first, befriending and advising her on matters personal as befits his ecclesiastical responsibilities…although no-one is quite sure which God he worships. Are you keeping up with me, my friend?' he asked, stopping to relight his pipe. The tobacco seemed somewhat damp again, which was peculiar as it had been perfectly dry when he'd accepted the gift. But there was unexplained moisture in the air on occasion; he glanced up again at the ceiling and, yes, the globule of water was still there. But the mountain elves had been true to their word, the cell was warm and comfortable. He wondered if they knew of the strange humidity, maybe he'd ask if he remembered.

'Get on with it, Ansclm, you've aroused my curiosity, stop dithering.'

'Well, the trouble escalated a few months ago. We know that Cumbria engineered the illness that brought down Countess Dotrice, Beatrix's mother, and…'

'Hang on, who is Beatrix? You've never mentioned her before.'

'No, there'll be a couple of strange names for you in this tale, Shadra. Well, Beatrix is the friend and companion of the heir to the principality, Princess Augusta. Countess Dotrice is one of only two close confidantes of the Princess Maria of Mantovar. The other is Lady Cornelia…she also is companion and lady-in-waiting to the Princess Augusta. Augusta is in Drakka finishing off her schooling at the court of the emperor. Apparently she has been earmarked to marry Crown Prince Gerhard, the emperor's son and heir…but that's bye the bye. Are you following all this? It does get a bit complicated.'

'I am…just. Go on,' Shadra said, shuffling to the top of his bed and resting his back against the wall.

'So we now have the princess' two greatest friends out of action as it were, one very ill and the other a few hundred leagues away. Well, neither was able to advise her. And Cumbria seized the opportunity and went at the Princess like a bear at the honey pot—he became her only advisor. And as Prince Cedric is besotted with his wife, Cumbria eventually became his advisor in the absence of Lord Tragen, Cedric's best friend. He's been sent south on the Grim to bring Augusta home.'

'The Grim, what is that?' Shadra interrupted, saying the first thing that came into his head for it was the name of the wizard that disturbed him.

'The largest warship in the world, captained by Hugo Locklear another great and very dear friend of the prince's which, of course, also had the consequence of depriving Cedric of the advice of his trusted chief naval officer. And also out went Chancellor Sevenoaks…only just holding on to life.

'But it seems that Prince Cedric suddenly had a change of heart about deposing Sevenoaks and installing Cumbria, for he set me to warning the chancellor. The prince ordered me to get Sevenoaks out of Mantovar because he thought Cumbria wanted the chancellor dead. So

I did, well as far as the town anyway, Sevenoaks wouldn't flee any farther. But he is safe, hidden with friends...or he was. Knowing him, though, he's already started the fight-back without me, without waiting for the liosalfar to aid him.'

'Does the prince know you're here?'

'I doubt it, because from the day Cumbria was appointed chancellor, the prince and princess have not been seen. There'll be quite a little war breaking out when Lord Tragen returns home...he's a very powerful wizard, you know, and...'

'Yes, I've heard of him,' said Shadra fully alert. Events that had encroached on his people over the last year were rapidly being explained.

'You have? How is that?'

'I told you, we reveal ourselves to those we know and trust. Lord Tragen had a mentor, Lord Herman; he was one of those we befriended.'

'And Lord Tragen, of course, he knows of you as well doesn't he? But it's strange I've never heard him speak of you.'

'Because he does not, we forbade Lord Herman to ever tell him.'

'Why on earth? He's one of the most honest and loyal, good people I have ever met!' exclaimed Elstan.

'It is a long story, but I'll tell you this. We have always known that Lord Tragen would make an unforgiveable error of judgement. That mistake will deprive three people of love and a normal life— three innocent people condemned to unutterable torment because of his ill-thought out actions. It is known that as a consequence, those three lives have been put in jeopardy. And they are of vital significance in the future of this world. They, along with others, will face monstrous malevolence and, if not successful in beating it, possible obliteration of all life on earth will result.'

'But...I don't understand. Lord Tragen is hundreds of years old, have you hidden yourselves from him all that time for an "error in judgment"? Who are these other people you speak of? You talk as if those three can halt the end of the world,' he laughed nervously, 'surely you don't put any credit in that.'

'We do. As for naming the others and the role they will play... I'm sorry. I cannot divulge any more details. Only my shaman can authorize their disclosure.'

'But Tragen is a decent man; he even took under his wing my...' here Anselm paused for no discernible reason, his hands trembling slightly. 'He adopted an orphan boy for God's sake.'

'We know of the boy Aidan, know who he is. We watch over him, and care for him, more closely than he knows.'

'Then you realize you aren't the only ones doing that.' Anselm lay back on his bed. He and Elstan were aware that the townsfolk of Miskim had nurtured Aidan during his early childhood until ceding responsibility to the wizard. But why are the elves tending Aidan? What could Tragen's lack of judgement possibly be to justify the forest elves not making themselves known to him? There was no more honourable and admirable man in the empire. If Anselm and Elstan had not known Tragen's reputation, the boy would never have been allowed to stay with him.

'Aidan is a very great healer and all the townsfolk cared for him. He is a remarkable lad, a lovely boy,' again his voice trailed away. 'My brother watched him heal a shire horse once, and to hear him tell of it...' Anselm smiled as the memory evoked good times. 'But why do you tend him?'

'He is the subject of prophecies. He is mentioned in the same prophecy as that to do with Lord Tragen's great error. In another he is in company with other wizards. And there are more again—he is highly crucial, that one.' Shadra brought up his knees and rested his arms on them. 'Now, let's get back to what we were talking about, go on with your tale,' the forest elf ordered. And Shadra wondered why he thought this wasn't the time to tell Anselm that both Tragen and Aidan also figured in the dream he'd had for years—along with Ryn.

'Well, okay. Anyway Tragen, being the wizard he is, will ransack Mantovar until he finds Cedric. But I'm afraid he won't succeed on his own. So my dear Shadra that is our aim—to help Chancellor Sevenoaks and Lord Tragen rescue them from the clutches of the abbot. And we also intend putting a stop to the machinations of the Guild of the Brethren of Wisdom.'

'The who?' Shadra asked sitting up straight, startled, he suddenly felt squeamish.

'Magus Brenin's bunch of power hungry black sorcerers—they are somehow involved. My brother, the Fly, is in southern Drakka hopefully ascertaining his secrets.

'The Fly?'

'Aye, like me, all agents of Chancellor Sevenoaks have codenames…it hinders Brenin's spies. His real name is Elstan.'

Shadra looked frightened. 'Why the "Fly", why name him that?'

'Because he can crawl along a ceiling without being seen…and besides,' and Anselm laughed, 'he wants to shit disease all over Brenin and watch him die slow!'

'And you…what is your codename?' Shadra asked, his face a sickly green.

'Why are you so interested in codenames?'

'Please, Anselm, it is important. What is your codename?'

'I am the Locust,' and Elstan grinned widely. 'I just want to starve Brenin to death.'

'Is there another one, another one of you I mean,' Shadra asked even quieter, his hands beginning to shake, 'another brother?'

Anselm suddenly glared at his friend, all humour gone. 'If there is, we never speak of him,' he answered cryptically. 'Why?'

'I'm sorry, Anselm, if I've upset you. It's just…I don't know, something I read at home…a prophecy. The shaman, no…it doesn't matter,' and Shadra closed his eyes and rubbed his face in an attempt to relieve his panic. *"Aid will be sought of three winged siblings"* ran through his head and, like Chong-An whom he'd never met, he wondered if Anselm and Elstan were two of the three. And if they were—why wouldn't Anselm speak of the third? The other bit of the puzzle—three that is four—what on earth did that mean? Could Anselm have the answer and not know it?

'By the Gods, Anselm, we are in deep trouble. We must get out of here as soon as possible. I need to return to my people and warn them. I must prepare them for the coming conflict. I have no doubt now that war is coming. For long have we watched Brenin,' he stared fearfully at his friend.

'War? Aye, you may be right for the abbot and the magus plan together and whatever those two plot cannot be for the good of the rest of us.' He stared glumly into the bowl of his pipe; the tobacco had once again gone out. 'God, now I'm really depressed. And talking about depression, have you heard the mournful sound that fountain makes when you wash your hands?'

'What the hell are you talking about?'

Shadra, mystified, went over to the corner and cocked his head to the quiet flow, hearing nothing untoward he stuck his hands in the water as Anselm came up behind him. They both bent their heads and listened again to the water gurgling quietly as it dropped into the shallow depression below and disappeared through a drain in the cell floor. But when Anselm put his hands in the water with Shadra, they did hear something—it was indeed making a sound, almost as if someone was singing a dirge.

'Ah, we must be imagining things,' said Shadra shaking his head and walking back to his bed.

'Aye, maybe, but remind me all the same to ask for a wash bowl when they come with our food. I can't wash my head under this drip.'

Forty

Far away in the west, across the vast feral snows, ravines and peaks of the Scissor Mountains, across the breadth of Mantovar and the Deep beyond, another pair of prisoners were wide awake in another cell.

The small room was situated deep below ground, accessed from a door hidden behind ancient, dusty ale barrels in the cellars beneath the Town Hall of Meltwater. The thickly timbered, black door led into an old mineshaft, long disused for its primary purpose. Its existence had been forgotten over the years until Razor had stumbled upon it one night seeking a place to secrete the spoils of an attack on a Portolan wagon. Not even Bazyli Montetor knew of it – the door or the loot – for he would never have condoned the murder of innocent Portolans.

Augusta and Thaddeus were a lot less comfortable than Shadra and Anselm. On the island of Griffin, Augusta and Thaddeus stared at each other in the gloom, both desperately afraid and utterly shocked.

'What's happened, where's it gone do you think?' Thaddeus asked, scared witless.

He didn't remember being incarcerated but he knew how—his head ached and he could feel a lump the size of a duck's egg beneath his long blond hair. Touching it gingerly he pondered on whether the unnecessarily hard knock had fractured his skull. It certainly felt like it.

Seeing his fingers probing beneath his hair, Augusta sat up quickly and knocked his hand aside. 'Here, let me see,' she said and she gently spread his locks until she could examine the violent, blue and red striped swelling. 'Ugh, leave it alone, they must have hit you harder than me, my head is not near as bad. I wish I had some water to bathe it.' She dropped her hands and Thaddeus abruptly grabbed them. There were far more pressing worries than his head—the reason for their profound shock being paramount.

'Do you think it's gone for good,' he asked.

'I don't know. Aidan said our magic was with us forever. If he's correct then this loss can only be temporary,' she said white-faced. 'God, I hope he was right. Oh, Thaddeus, I'm frightened, I hate being without my magic,' she flung her arms around him and hugged him tight.

He looked over her head, squinting to somehow see more of their surroundings. The room was not that small, not large either. It was made of rough timber planks. No windows, just one door in the wall opposite the hard, wooden bench they were sitting on. The floor was uneven hard-packed earth and rock. The only other furnishings, if you could call it so, were a number of broken wooden crates against the wall, a three-legged stool in front of them and a bucket in the corner. Thaddeus didn't even want to think what that was for. It was the coarse planks of his seat that had probably contributed to his headache, for he'd woken stretched out on it with the back of his head overhanging the end. As he'd sat up he had disturbed Augusta, also prone alongside him and she'd risen on her arms full of concern hearing his groan. And as their eyes met so they had discovered their loss. Their magic had disappeared.

'Anders will be watching out for us, don't worry,' he whispered, stroking her hair all other thinking suspended, he looked down at her—despite their predicament, cuddling up to her he was in seventh heaven. He plucked a cat hair from the top of her head.

A day and a half's riding west of Meltwater lay the catacombs, the gateway to the town of Bylani deep beneath the surface of the island of Griffin. And it was there, in the town of Bylani, where Aidan was closely following the actions of a salamander. He watched diligently as Hector displayed another of the several unusual abilities of its species.

The salamanders were primarily employed in creating a ghoulish light at the many airways into the labyrinth below Mount Trespass. The purpose being to deter unwanted visitors so that Bylani would remain a secret until it was needed. But another of their attributes was that of being able to destroy disease. But it was not without risk.

Salamanders were able to generate warmth that could be felt several feet away, in fact unwary observers standing too close had often been set alight by these creatures. The body of a salamander glowed red when called upon to create heat, the higher the temperature the lighter the colour red until a salamander turned a brilliant white— no-one stayed anywhere near a salamander displaying white heat.

But a salamander could also use heat in another surprising way. It could send warmth into a body, whether human or animal it did not matter, and use the heat to gently wash a disease out of it and burn it to destruction.

But in Primrosa's case the plague was very deep-seated. The buboes grew in the midst of her flesh and delved deep down to her bones and, at the surface of her skin they erupted into hard black mounds of rotting flesh. At Hector's suggestion Aidan waited and watched as the salamander walked very gently all over her as she lay comatose on her bed. Hector wanted to ascertain the minimum amount of heat to sluice the plague from her system and then destroy the fell disease without burning any tissue of the woman. Aidan was standing by just in case things went wrong. He watched closely while the salamander emitted a deep red heat, flashing a shade lighter every time it came in contact with a particle of the disease. Hector was succeeding in drawing out the infection and destroying it but it was slow, very, very slow.

Nevertheless, a lot depended on Hector's total success, for if the plague spread throughout Bylani then salamanders would be used to heal any future victims until the forgotten remedy was rediscovered. Aidan, perforce, would be elsewhere and because of this the cure was being pursued with a vengeance in the Green People's archives. For however successful the salamanders were in their healing, it would not be sufficient to cater to the devastating needs of a plague at loose in Bylani.

But there were only so many salamanders and they would also be required to stand sentry at the entrances into the catacombs to burn away the Darkness, if it was possible to do such a thing. Nobody was looking forward to the first attempt for if it didn't work then the mountain would have to be sealed from the upper atmosphere. A nightmare scenario for the Green People could only produce a limited amount of breathable air and they were expecting to harbour a colossal number of refugees, far more than they'd ever envisaged. There were other locations around the island through which fresh air was provided, but these were already being sealed. The island of Moth would end up being the only supply point, and it being at such a distance from Bylani, its air always tasted stale.

While Primrosa was being healed, Beatrix was sleeping in Leon's home next door being watched over by Jasmina and Kataya. She had completed the extraordinary task of sealing the vugocite and as far as anyone could see had succeeded beyond their wildest dreams. For not only had the composition of the vugocite changed, the Green People could now create magic within its vicinity, something they deemed miraculous.

Aidan, waiting for Beatrix to waken, continued to watch Hector closely. His anxiety was making him very irritable and he fought desperately to control it. He'd promised himself he would enter Limbo after two days and the time was nearly up. But once again something else had cropped up to delay him—he had to rescue Thaddeus and Augusta before he could go. He agonized, finding it increasingly difficult to manage his emotions.

'Dear God, Master,' he said quietly, 'dear God, Master, hang on...I won't be much longer, I promise!'

Chong-An and Elstan came down out of the dense forest to ground that had levelled off for quite some distance. The forest this near the road had thinned out, the trees growing farther apart, the undergrowth higher yet sparser.

The two had left their refuge in the early hours of that morning having rested for most of the day and half the night. Chong had been utterly exhausted, unable to keep his eyes open and greatly disorientated when they'd alighted in front of the gaping hole in the mountainside. The cave itself had only been visible from the air, on the ground it was all but obscured by dense foliage. Their strange flight on the back of a mesmerized mule had indeed been fortunate.

Elstan had all but fallen carrying the nearly comatose wizard into the deepest recesses of the head-high cave. The mule, still ensorcelled, had dropped to the ground just inside the mouth and had remained quiet for most of the evening, only stirring as night had descended. It didn't forage for long before it slept in its usual stance, standing up and legs locked.

Elstan, seeing that his friend and the mule were safe, had gone searching for sign of their pursuers. Concealed behind rocks on a high hill amidst the woods, he'd located them a long way south and still travelling east. He'd watched them for a while nearing the clearing in which they'd soared aloft and he'd smiled at the sudden flare of incandescent light as Drudwynn again lost his temper. Elstan had then returned to the cave in the mountainside to wait for Chong to awake.

The River Wry was between them and the Great North Road and both ran parallel to each other, two hundred paces apart, for about three or four leagues at this spot. The ground on both banks of the river was a land of low scrub and gorse leaving very little cover in which to hide, except for the occasional clump of bramble and small grove of stunted olive trees. To the north, Elstan espied the only ford for leagues and he massaged his face, disappointed—they'd never reach it before Drudwynn was upon them.

On the road, coming up from the south, was a long line of gaily painted wagons, brightly dressed people and strangely exotic animals. Behind the carnival were other travellers some on horseback, most walking, all going north to Mulkie's Cross. There weren't quite so many people travelling south.

Elstan glanced back up the track they'd just used to come down the Wolfshead. Although their hunters were not in sight at the moment, both fugitives could hear them running fairly close behind. The sojourn in the cave had done wonders for Chong's feet, the rest momentarily easing the pain but, unfortunately, the inordinate amount of time the wizard had needed to recover had given Drudwynn and his guards enough time to catch up with them.

'It's my turn now, Elstan.'

'What do you mean?'

'Like we said before…you are the woodsman, I am the wizard. Get to that spread of gorse with the bramble at its other end. Go on,' Chong urged when Elstan hesitated.

As they reached the blackberry bearing bushes the mule suddenly raised its head, its ears lying flat on its head, its nostrils abruptly flaring at the presence of the brown bear that neither of them had seen feeding on the berries.

'Bloody hell!' Elstan cursed as he grabbed the animal's head to stop it fleeing in terror and bucking off its rider. 'Hold the bloody mule, Chong, will you,' he reached over his shoulder for his crossbow. 'Don't just sit there!' he shouted.

'Wait, don't panic,' and Chong-An raised his right hand and gesticulated in the bear's direction. The bear immediately reared up on its hind legs and peered around bemused, its huge black nose sniffing the air. 'Quick…help me down.'

'Don't be daft stay on there the mule is faster than your feet, turn back to the woods.'

'Oh, yes, back…into Drudwynn's arms. Listen to me, help me down while the madman's still in those trees,' Chong glanced quickly at the copse of larch about a league behind and then hurriedly dismounted. Elstan taking the full weight of his friend nearly went to his knees.

Elstan kept his feet, his eyes on the bear still standing upright on its back paws, towering over them twisting its head from side to side totally confused, a bunch of blackberries hanging from one front paw.

'Get the mule to lie down,' said Chong urgently.

'How the hell am I to do that, there's a bloody great bear over there that wants to eat it…and us!'

'Don't be silly, it can't see us or the bramble bushes now, that's why it's so puzzled, hang on.' Chong waved his hands about, this time in the mule's frantic face, and it quieted. 'There, now the mule can't see the bear or smell it either. Now lean on it heavy, we need it lying on the floor it'll be easier to hide.'

Elstan stared appalled, firstly at the mule then the bear and finally in the direction of their pursuers. And at Chong's insistent demand he did as ordered, pushing and pulling the dumb beast, he finally got the mule stretched out on the ground on its side He slumped down alongside it worn out with the struggle.

'Hey, did you notice back there, they seem to have lost another guard?' asked Elstan breathing heavily.

'No, I haven't been counting; now hold that animal still.'

'Drudwynn is either getting desperate or very careless, my friend,' Elstan said drying the sweat on his face with his sleeve. 'But whatever the reason, his behaviour suggests utter madness.'

Chong-An stared in the direction of their pursuers for long moments and then indicated for Elstan to lay down alongside the mule. The oriental wizard stood for a moment longer and waved both his arms over them, chanting a short litany. The bear suddenly dropped to all fours and raced off into the trees to the north leaving the berries on the bramble, in moments it had disappeared.

Chong, grinning widely, sat down alongside Elstan and patted him gently on the arm. 'Now we wait.'

'Wait?' Elstan asked staring wide-eyed at his friend. 'Are you mad as well?'

Chong laughed. 'I am a wizard…the master of illusion. All Drudwynn will see here is an expanse of bramble and gorse. My conjuration will hide us and your friend the mule. Now sit quiet and wait.'

'My friend…the mule? Ah, well,' and he looked pointedly at Chong. 'I suppose my friend is a donkey,' and he sniggered when Chong's expression abruptly dropped when he comprehended the jibe. 'Well, I only hope our hunters are not hungry.' Elstan's fear reappeared and he brooded not daring to believe in his friend's spell. 'Hey, wait a minute you said Drudwynn can detect magic. Won't he discover this?'

'No, for two reasons—firstly he is in a blind rage and can't think straight, anyone can see that, secondly he won't come anywhere near us. He now follows the bear.'

'What!'

'Watch and smile.'

Drudwynn, the sergeant and his four remaining guards came into sight walking fast. Using magic, Drudwynn had increased their walking pace to well past that of normal. Chong smiled, they couldn't keep up that pace for much longer. The men looked terrible, the haggard look on their faces telling of abnormal strain. If Drudwynn kept them at it much longer eventually their hearts would explode and they'd drop where they were.

Elstan tensed, his sword in one hand a short dagger in the other, not quite believing his eyes, he watched amazed as Drudwynn hurried on past and on into the trees after the bear.

Ten minutes later, Chong stood and motioned Elstan to his feet. 'All right, the mule can get up now as well, I'd appreciate the ride, my feet won't be good for long,' and he grinned.

'Okay, I can understand that if you blinded the bear and the mule to each other, then you also blinded Drudwynn and his crowd to us. But surely they are not going to follow those tracks, I know they're stupid but not even they are dumb enough to mistake the bear's spoor for ours.'

'What bear…what spoor?'

Elstan exasperated turned and looked up the trail that Drudwynn had just followed. 'Uh! What…' he was suddenly lost for words. There were no paw marks of any bear.

'A little trick I learned some while back. At the moment the bear is running and leaving behind it what looks like our footprints and it will do so for quite a while. But I suggest we get away from here pretty sharpish, in a few hours or so Drudwynn and his friends are going to catch up with it. I calculate we should be on the road by then, and with a bit of luck lost among the carnival performers,' and he grinned again into Elstan's startled face.

Forty-one

Leash lowered his head as Captain Jos Osvaldo, a tall, lean man immaculately dressed in a knee-length blue frock coat and epaulettes embellished with silver embroidery. His long, red hair flowing in the breeze, he hurried past towards the prow of the Lobos. It was an automatic reaction, not wanting the brigand to catch his eye. For despite Balar stating that no-one could possibly recognize him he didn't want to take the chance, even though he couldn't remember if he'd ever met the pirate before.

'Cowper,' Osvaldo shouted for the first mate of the pirate ship and, as the big heavy-set man arrived at the run, everyone looked up knowing by the captain's tone that something was amiss. 'What do you make of that?' and he pointed somewhere ahead.

'I'll go aloft,' and Cowper scrambled up the foremast shrouds, and shielding his eyes he studied the ship hull down on the horizon ahead of them. 'I think it's the Hound.'

'You thinking is no good to me.'

'Sorry, Captain, yes it is definitely the Hound,' he answered, once more on the deck at his side.

'So, Connors is searching for the Lobos' treasure again, is he? But where Connors is so is Bartram. Did you see him?'

'No, there's no sign of him, he must be over the horizon probably ahead of Connors.'

'Yes, but if he's not, where will he be…east or west? Gunter, get these slaves breaking their backs I want to catch up before the Hound reaches shore.' With that parting remark Osvaldo returned along the slave-master's walkway to resume his place aft, pacing his quarterdeck.

'What's wrong, Balar, why are you trembling?' asked Leash mystified.

'I'm not…you are.'

'You are scared. Why? You don't know Osvaldo…or do you know Connors?'

'Never heard of him now leave it.'

Gunter, at his station aft of the slaves, abruptly turned from staring over the side at the faraway ship and striding forward, he laid his whip across Leash's back.

320

Leash gasped, the pain agonising in his already lacerated thorax. Even so, the ex-helmsman realized that Balar had somehow influenced Gunter to lash out at him at that precise moment. Leash was shocked; his demon had never before set anyone else to actually cause him hurt. What had Osvaldo said to elicit such fear in the vampyrus?

It took all day to come within hailing distance of the smaller Hound, a modified galley with an after-castle, forecastle and two masts, but only one row of thirty oars on either side. It had been taken in a fierce fight from a Drakkan merchant's mercenary escort some years earlier.

Captain Marcus Connors, a fat, gaudily dressed man, was the arch rival of Osvaldo on the islands' ruling council. However, both men were subservient to the admiral of the Onyx Isles, Alberto Lonsdale.

Open enmity had never actually broken out between the Lobos and the Hound though all Onyx knew that Connors craved Osvaldo's status as first minister. It was tradition amongst the brigands that the first minister, in this case Jos Osvaldo, always replaced the admiral at the end of his tenure or, of course, at his death. But to gain the ascendency Connors would need to kill the Lobos' master—a very difficult task. Nevertheless, if he could do that there'd be a bonus. Impounding Osvaldo's treasure trove by killing the crew of the Lobos would be relatively easy.

Connors also had a following. Chief among his supporters was Alex Bartram, master of the North Star, a very fast sloop traded from Osvaldo after a particularly successful season the year before. And where the Hound went, the North Star was never very far away.

Osvaldo planned to purge himself of Connors at the earliest opportunity and then exact the same justice. He'd seize the Hound's treasure and recruit the crew or slay them. It made no difference to Osvaldo whatever the outcome as long as he succeeded. But he'd never completely eradicate the threat of assassination. There were others who fancied themselves as admiral. Osvaldo, of course, had his own cronies on the ruling council and more importantly, within the community. He needed them to watch his back and he paid them well to do so. There was no shortage of killers in the Onyx Isles, especially for the tremendous fee Osvaldo's head commanded. And all wanted a share of the Lobos' reputedly enormous booty. This was the primary cause of Osvaldo's problems—he was too successful.

Jos Osvaldo trusted no-one except his first mate, Cowper, and his ally ashore. His greatest supporter had come to him twenty years before and his faith in her was boundless. None knew of Karnica, Osvaldo's secretive advisor, except for Cowper who hated the black witch. She was usually enough to protect him on shore, but even she couldn't forewarn him of everything. How she knew the things she did Osvaldo could never ascertain but he followed her advice without question.

That was what Cowper loathed, his master and friend in the clutches of a Hag living deep within the bowels of the island beneath Osvaldo's home. And she would be consulted immediately they reached shore, she always was.

But Cowper was well aware that civil war would erupt if Osvaldo and Connors miscalculated and moved against each other too soon.

Meanwhile, Leash had again worked himself into a stupor. The repetitive motion of pulling on the oars was causing numbness in his arms, his feet straining against the deck making his legs tremble. On top of that the lashes across his shoulders when he flagged, the heat and the smell of the rowing station, all served to cause his senses to shut down. He took refuge in his memories, the few he had left. Relying constantly on his instincts, he futilely studied his reasons for saving the life of Aidan.

But Balar, from deep within his host's psyche, listened to all around him for what he had heard mentioned by the pirate captain unnerved him completely. He debated discussing it with Leash, but decided against it. It would be giving away too much information, all of it centuries old, and he wasn't quite sure how Leash would react to it even if he could understand.

'Cowper, I want every man armed, the first watch crouched down against the larboard bulwark we'll come alongside him on that side. Let no man show his head above the rail. All that can be spared of the second watch are to stand against the rail. I want them hiding the first from the watchers on the Hound; have their weapons at their feet.'

'Back the oars,' ordered Osvaldo and the helmsman directed the Lobos to come alongside the Hound and stand off from it two oars' length. 'Oars inboard,' commanded Osvaldo and he stared across the intervening water at his rival's ship.

Connors waddled to the starboard side of his after-castle, smiling, his eyes missed nothing, including the probable concealment of men below the Lobos' rail. He had men similarly concealed along his deck, although his bulwark was not as high. It had become a habit when these two ships met at sea, just in case one or the other made a mistake, so that battle could be engaged immediately with success assured.

'To what do I owe this dubious pleasure, Connors?' asked Osvaldo, no smile creased his face; he had no need to ingratiate himself.

'My dear, Jos, you always greet me in this manner. Why? There is no need, you know, I come in friendship.'

'What do you want?'

'Jos, Jos, please…do we conduct business with all listening? Join me aboard for supper. I have a stimulating claret, newly won from a skirmish a couple of days ago.'

'Don't fall for that, Captain, you can't trust the man,' whispered Cowper in the refined speech of an aristocrat.

'You do not need to state the obvious, but it's the only way we'll find out what he's up to—and maybe where that damned Bartram is.' Osvaldo, ignoring both Connors and Cowper, looked around at all points of the compass and perceived an empty ocean.

'Where is the North Star, Connors?' he asked.

'Ah, my friend has sprung a leak I'm afraid. He is still in harbour in Armadillo.'

'A leak,' Osvaldo frowned. 'Then he needs the dry-dock?'

'Yes…but there is a problem. Lonsdale will not allow him to leave the quay without paying upfront for the dry-dock's use. And, of course, your Serpent of the Seas still occupies it, Connors smirked. 'I also have a message from Admiral Lonsdale, he demands your fee now or he'll stop the work on the Serpent and eject her.'

'He…what! There's at least another week's work needed to get her ready for sea. I'll crucify him, what gives him the right to demand anything of me?'

'Ah, I'm afraid there has been a slight change of priorities in Armadillo since you've been away. Lonsdale has usurped unilateral authority and the council now follow only his orders—to the letter.'

'What has happened?'

'It seems Lonsdale has unusual supporters—backers that no-one wishes to disobey. Who they are or where they're from no-one exactly knows. Speculation is rife. But Lonsdale is now the proud owner of a weapon that can blow holes in a ship—from afar. And he is not afraid to use it on people either. If you are unwilling to come aboard here, may I join you ashore to discuss matters? It will be of mutual benefit.'   'Blow holes in a ship…are you serious?'

'I'd hardly lie about a matter like that, Jos. It would be too easy for you to discover the truth of the matter. We both need to discuss this, unlikely as it may seem, we might even join forces.'

'You intrigue me, Connors,' a feeling grew in his gut giving him bellyache, 'but there will be no tricks from you or your men hiding below your bulwarks.'

'Very well…of course the same goes for you?'

'Before we proceed, why doesn't Bartram pay up?' Osvaldo asked, more puzzled by the minute.

'It seems that Alex needs to set to sea to obtain the fee,' Connors sniggered, 'he is broke. You know him…he loves to gamble with other people's coin, but a couple of nights ago he got seriously drunk, played with his own money and lost the North Star to old Barnacle Billy. Of course, when the lucky man came to claim his prize Alex killed him, but in the process the Star was holed. And now,' Connors shrugged, 'no-one will lend him any coin because he reneged on his bet.'

'He's your partner, why don't you lend him the necessary?'

'Oh, come Jos, Alex may be a long-term friend but I wouldn't trust him with my money as far as I could throw him,' and he laughed.

'A falling out, Cowper, do you believe that?' Osvaldo whispered.

'I don't know, it seems unlikely and yet they did come to blows a couple of months ago and that was over money.'

'What can this weapon of Lonsdale's be, have you heard anything?'

'No, I'd have told you.'

Osvaldo tugged at his chin and turned to Connors again. 'I must land my cargo first before I sail for Armadillo. Our discussions can await our arrival there. You may return to Bartram and tell him I will be along shortly.'

'Ah! An addition to the famed Osvaldo treasure trove, hey? One of these days, Jos, you really are going to have to spend some of it otherwise Onyx will sink beneath its weight.' Connors laughed loudly and stared from his after-castle down at his crew making sure his men were ready for any eventuality, not yet prepared to disperse them. 'I tell you, my friend, I don't think our discussions can wait that long. What say you I bring this claret ashore and share your hospitality?'

Osvaldo tapped the upper edge of his quarterdeck rail, taking his time mulling over the decision, worrying not a jot that everybody on both ships were waiting on his words. He stared hard at his long-time first officer, Cowper, not even giving that man any inkling of his thoughts.

Cowper stood as he always did when not in action...patiently. Having full confidence in his captain, knowing that whatever Osvaldo's decision may be, as the nearest either of them would have to a friend, he'd go along with it and ensure the man's orders were fulfilled. The first mate was a hard man; he needed to be within the hierarchy of brigands, all of whom were violent men existing outside of any country's laws. The only rules they obeyed were those of the Council of Onyx and that only when they felt like it.

Cowper was the younger son of a Drakkan noble denied any inheritance through the accident of being conceived later than his brother. The only opening to assuage his jealousy and feed his tremendous ambition was to go to sea. Appointed a midshipman in his father's grain ships, he served for years waiting for promotion, which was granted only when a senior officer died or failed in his duty.

Sailing the northern waters off Mantovar his ship had been attacked by Jos Osvaldo. After a fierce battle, fought to a stalemate by the bravery and leadership of Cowper, the Drakkan noble had astounded the brigands by surrendering his ship to Osvaldo. But only on the condition that he became the pirate chieftain's second in command. Jos Osvaldo, a keen judge of men, did not hesitate and had never regretted his choice of aide.

'What do you think? Shall we invite him to dinner ashore?' Osvaldo asked.

'I'd like to know more of this weapon before we enter Armadillo.'

Osvaldo again tapped the rail unable to make up his mind. 'Is Bartram incapacitated? I wish I knew for certain.'

' How long to unload...two hours perhaps? As long as we hide our path from his prying eyes, direct his gaze away from the Needle when we transport the cargo to the caves in the morning, we should be ready by noon,' said Cowper. 'But I agree. Not knowing the whereabouts of the North Star makes me nervous. We'll need to set a careful watch on the Hound and its crew.'

'That's if all his crew are aboard.'

'They must be we followed him here, he hasn't had the opportunity to land any men.'

Osvaldo suddenly straightened, his back ramrod stiff, his face darkening. 'He might not have, but what if the Star isn't in Armadillo, what if it's around the next promontory, east or west doesn't matter. Bartram may already be ashore waiting and watching.'

'Then we leave the unloading until we know for sure. But…I don't know…he may be lying about Bartram but I can't see him lying about Lonsdale's weapon,' Cowper smiled grimly. 'We have got to learn more of that.'

'We will, if anyone knows, Karnica will.' Ignoring his first officer's look of utter loathing he turned towards the Hound. 'Connors,' Osvaldo shouted across, his face giving nothing away, 'I will be only too happy to extend the hospitality of my home to you. Just keep your crew aboard your ship when you tie up at my jetty. I will send for you when I am settled at home.'

Before dusk had fallen, both ships had berthed in Comfort Bay, the Lobos' base in Onyx, a town entirely owned, built and fortified by Jos Osvaldo.

Leash stumbled up the three steps placed inboard of the bulwark; his feet numb as he crossed over and stood on the brow. He lifted his head and squinted at the long low house up on the hillside, painted a brilliant white it sparkled in the late afternoon sunlight.

The captain of the Lobos was not one to hide his success, unlike his treasure. His home shouted his wealth, his love of opulence perhaps his one weakness although his vanity screamed in everyone's face.

Leash nearly fell again as he was tugged down the brow to set foot on the jetty. Earlier he had been forced to wait along with the other slaves, until the officers and crew had landed. Nevertheless, all the slaves were glad to be on deck savouring fresh air instead of sweltering below decks in hot and rank rowing stations. Chained together with heavy links at their ankles, they shuffled one behind the other along the jetty and on to the wharf. They squatted at the bows of the ship, after being herded into place by Gunter swinging his whip menacingly in front of downcast eyes well used to physical abuse.

Leash, despite his injuries, watched the Hound come alongside and tie up abaft the Lobos as Osvaldo and Cowper hurried up the slope to Jos' home.

Moments later Cowper stood behind his captain as Osvaldo unlocked the door into the windowless dressing room next to his bedroom at the back of the house. The pirate captain stepped back to allow his aide to enter first. Following behind, Osvaldo moved to the side of the room and indicated for his first mate to pull aside the heavy carpet on the floor to disclose a trapdoor. Osvaldo handed him a key to the heavy padlock and Cowper pulled on the heavy brass ring and the trapdoor opened upwards to expose a stairway descending into darkness. Osvaldo grasped the lantern always kept on a hook at the head of the stairs, lighting it, he led the way below.

Surprisingly, the air smelled clean and fresh, the underground passageway was ventilated by shafts leading to the surface, their upper ends well camouflaged from prying eyes. The steps were dry and dusty. It took almost half an hour to reach the bottom before entering a long tunnel that eventually debouched into a large cavern, a slow-flowing stream running through the centre of its rock-strewn floor.

A small bridge crossed the stream and on its farther side, ignoring them, was the Hag.

Both men halted at the entrance, unable to move forward because of a shimmering in the air, the Hag's protection against unwelcome intruders. Stretched across from wall to wall just within the tunnel, the shield could barely be seen and did in no way obscure the many runes, sigils and pictures painted or carved on every available space on the walls and rocks of Karnica's home. Some of the designs were huge straight line patterns; others were patches of dark colours that seemed to merge when glimpsed from the corner of your eye. But then there were a number, darkly sinister, of intricately drawn depictions of life forms that were definitely not of this world.

Cowper shivered, he hated this place and its inhabitant and he knew that Karnica reciprocated his loathing. He only accompanied Osvaldo at his friend's order despite voicing his detestation. Jos invariably derided his fear and his hatred.

'She requires your presence, why I do not know. But it is enough for me, so you will stand beside me and keep silent—whatever she says.'

'But she despises me, hates me. I do not trust her, Jos.'

'Your trust is not required…mine is…and she is my Hag.'

The finality in Osvaldo's voice silenced Cowper even though he was convinced that the old woman belonged to no mortal. He looked across the stream and watched her as she stroked the back of her familiar, a sleek, black, weasel-like creature, a devilish rodent unlike any he had ever seen before. The animal's mouth stretched from beneath one ear across to beneath the other and it held two rows of long spiked teeth. Growing upwards between its ears stood a horn almost the same shape as a wild boar's tusk; its eyes pierced his very soul whenever it looked Cowper's way.

'Karnica,' Osvaldo called loudly, 'open up.'

'Ah, a stranger and the despicable one return,' she replied, looking up.

Cowper saw blood dripping from her mouth and in her hand she held a half-eaten rat. She gave it to the weasel they seemed to have been sharing it.

'I am no stranger.' Osvaldo glanced quickly at his companion, he did not understand the Hag's disdain of his friend, but shrugged it away.

'No, indeed you are not.' She waved her hand, the shimmering disappeared and the gateway opened.

Osvaldo strode down the stone pathway winding its way to the bridge, Cowper following in his wake, his skin crawling the nearer he got to the weasel. It was cold, bitingly cold at this depth, how she survived in these temperatures was a mystery to him. Osvaldo didn't seem to notice his breath fogging the gloomy atmosphere. His lantern he put down to one side, it was not needed the other side of the bridge for the Hag had her own lighting. The runes and sigils glowed with a green fluorescence casting a sickly glow over her unkempt appearance. The Hag had long, straggly, grey hair knotted and bunched on top of her head, sticking out all shapes above her ears. She was old, ancient, her face deeply lined her jowls drooped, the skin on her neck flapping as she spoke. She wore a plain black dress enveloping her from neck to toe; her feet were hidden beneath the heavy hem. Cowper thought he had glimpsed her feet once, but the sight of them had caught his breath. His imagination getting the better of him—he could have sworn they were cloven.

But it was her eyes that seriously frightened him. Only once had he looked and he'd almost frozen when her pupil-less white eyes stared into his. Now, he never raised his eyes above her flat chest. He couldn't understand how Osvaldo could speak to her as he spoke to normal people. He was not fazed at all by her. Whether it was courage or some other emotion that blinded him to her unnatural attributes, Cowper was still trying to figure out.

'You have news, old woman?'

'Perhaps,' she replied, her voice strident.

'What is this new weapon of Lonsdale's?'

'Why have you brought a demon to Comfort Bay?' she asked querulously.

'A demon? What on earth are you talking about?'

'Comfort Bay smells of a demon.'

'The only one I've brought is Connors. He's no demon, just a fool who thinks he can take my treasure.'

'Our treasure,' she said. Pushing the unnatural animal from her lap she wound her fingers in the only bit of jewellery she wore, a small pendant hanging from a gold chain.

Cowper started at her words; surely Osvaldo didn't mean to share their booty with the old Hag. He stared at his friend her words going over his head. Cowper began to sweat, there was more to this relationship than met the eye.

'Tell me of this weapon.'

'It is only fire and noise—it can be overcome. I will tell you how.'

It was as they were leaving the cavern an hour later, this time Cowper leading, that she spoke a warning.

'Beware the demon, Osvaldo; it can harm you far more than the southerner's weapon. And be cautious of betrayal…there is one amongst you who detests insects.'

Her last comment did not mean much to Osvaldo, but Cowper's face lost all colour.

Forty-two

Captain Connors wore his usual long brightly coloured frock coat with a wide-brimmed hat sporting an ostrich feather, on his flowing auburn locks. Along with his first officer, Meecham, more soberly dressed in a short black jacket and dark blue pantaloons, he took his time walking down the brow of the Hound. He glanced quickly at his men lining the deck overlooking the wharf. Each man was armed to the hilt with an assortment of weapons, cutlasses being favoured by most. Both men came ashore and strolled slowly up the slope to the white house, followed by the captain's servant carrying the crate of claret.

Connors cast his eyes to left and right noting the headland with its watch-post to the west, the small town of Hampton a little farther on. Connors smiled, before his and Osvaldo's open escalation of rivalry, Connors had spent many a night in the Oyster Tavern in Hampton's High Street. The buxom madam, Sophie Tucker, was still the proud owner and, from what he'd heard, had also kept her good looks. He'd like to meet her again and he would if only Osvaldo wasn't so intransigent.

To the east, at a distance of perhaps three hundred paces – so that its foul odour could not encroach on the tranquillity of the residence – the slaves' barracoon was sited. A large complex of buildings and open yards, it housed accommodation for upwards of five hundred slaves, the largest number held by any of the Onyx brigands.

Pausing halfway up the hill Connors, ostensibly out of breath, peered out to sea and chewed at a bit of dry skin on his lip, the ocean was deserted, the lowering sun glinting off a calm surface. Resuming his short walk, he passed through the gateway in the waist-high boundary wall and walked up the cobbled path edged on both sides with whitewashed rocks. The pathway led to a long veranda stretching the whole breadth of the front of the one-storey house, its doors and windows open wide to allow free passage of the cooling night breezes off the ocean. He glanced quickly at his short, dark servant carrying the case of claret and wished that he could have drugged the drink. Matters would have been so much simpler. But he knew that Osvaldo would never fall for such a trick, he'd ensure his guest drank first from a bottle of his choosing. And then he sighed again. He needed Osvaldo's aid against this new weapon—neither of them would survive if it was left in Lonsdale's hands.

An hour earlier, Cowper had walked down to the Hound and invited Connors and Meecham to the house to partake of dinner. The captain of the Hound had been taken aback at the ashen face on the Lobos' first mate, he'd looked positively ill. But Cowper had left him smartly enough and continued on. Striding across the wharf he spoke to Gunter sitting in a chair overseeing the resting and very quiet slaves at the bow of the his ship.

'Right, get them up and moving to the barracoon. The captain has decided not to unload the cargo tonight.'

Gunter stood immediately, throwing a cheroot into the harbour's waters. He screamed his orders and accompanied them with switches of his whip across the nearest backs. It wasn't long before the slaves were shuffling into their home. Mercifully the trek was short and Leash, gasping with relief, bent down to massage his ankles when his shackles were removed. Straightening, he turned away in hopes of finding a place to rest but, as he did so, he was jostled violently from behind and fell to his knees.

'Out of my way, scum,' roared a deep, menacing voice.

Leash looked up, instantly wary, to stare into eyes devoid of life, a look that he knew well. His assailant was huge and had an arrogance and manner born of drugs and desolation. As Leash struggled to stand up, the man-mountain walked off and a short, stocky, weather-beaten sailor – another slave – helped him to his feet.

'You're the new one, aren't you? Don't worry about him; he's the same with everyone. He's nuts, just stay out of his way and maybe you'll survive.'

Leash took a moment to catch his breath before speaking. 'Thank you, who is he?'

'His name is Vlad; he used to have his own ship until Osvaldo took it. Now all he has is naxix leaf and goorani.'

'Naxix I've heard of…but goorani?'

'Take my advice; never drink it unless you want to forget who you are and where you are. Believe me it's guaranteed to take your memory quicker than the naxix.'

'I don't have that worry,' Leash answered under his breath.

'What?'

331

'Doesn't matter,' and he looked his advisor in the face for the first time, seeing a man of middle age and stubble prematurely grey. 'What's your name?'

'Nicholas…and yours?'

'Leash,' he stared around his new home. 'By the Gods, I've heard of these places but never expected to see the inside of one.'

The barracoon was a long low building; the brown boards bleached a dirty, harsh grey by the tropical sun. It was used for shelter from the violent storms that hammered the islands during the rainy season. But, Nicholas told him later, most slaves avoided it, preferring to remain in the open under the torrential rain than suffer the abominable stench of the shed's interior. The open compound was encircled by a head-high wooden board fence, also bleached of any colour and gaping in places affording a restricted view of the outside world. Latrines had been dug at the northern boundary behind the building, but the south side was where everyone sat on the ground to eat. There were discarded bones lying here, there and everywhere among the four hundred or so slaves presently sitting silently, recovering their strength awaiting their supper.

'Don't worry, you'll get used to it if you live long enough, just remember to stay clear of Vlad,' Nicholas said.

'He doesn't worry me,' said Balar.

'He does me,' Leash said, his weariness bringing on forgetfulness and he spoke aloud.

'What was that?' Nicholas asked, puzzled.

'Sorry, ignore me I've not been well, I'm rambling,' Leash answered, his headache returning with a vengeance he rubbed his scalp causing more hair to fall out. 'I need to rest and I need to eat something decent…what are the chances of either?'

'Ah, you'll have food shortly, good food, better than onboard; Osvaldo needs us fit and well. We'll be carrying his ill-gotten gains to the caves in the morning and they're a fair way from here. As for resting, come, we can sit over there,' and he indicated a stretch of wall on the south side. 'One or two of the boards are missing we'll get a fresh breeze to take this stink away and we can look out to sea… a far pleasanter sight than staring inwards at the others.

Leash sank wearily to the ground and sat immobile, staring through the gap at the long white sands and the sweeping surf rolling in from the south. The sight of the blue water and white foam calmed his shattered nerves. Gradually peace stole up on him, the first for weeks, and he found himself drawn to the past unable to think yet of his future.

The past, for over half his life, involved Balar and his unnatural existence. Before the infestation he'd been a young teenager full of life and passionately in love. But then there was the stupid escapade planned by him and the others to cock a hoot at the Elders. And then the totally unexpected consequences brought about by that irresponsible attitude. How old had he been…fifteen…twenty years ago. He held his tears in check. No-one was to blame for what had happened—they'd only been passing it back and forth between them, a totally innocuous object. And then there had been the interruption—the flash, the jolt and the scream. The gradual realization over those first half dozen years that he'd become a host for a vampyrus, utterly devastating him.

The vampyrus, Balar, was a demon who lived on draining a human of blood. In his haste and greed he had the habit of tearing the head from the body in the process. A violent and sickening way for anyone to die—and Balar didn't care who he killed when the Wanting was upon him. And yet, now, the vampyrus was scared. Leash could feel Balar's fear.

But why had Balar fought so hard to save Leash's life since his escape from Sanctity? Was it truly because this was the last infestation he could initiate without receiving the renewal rite—the ritual that could only be granted by his God? Leash's thoughts tumbled together. Balar had stated that time had not the same impact on a demon's life as it did on a human's, long or short had no meaning in his life. Yet Balar worried about Leash dying and it wasn't because he was the last. Leash almost felt it was because they had become friends. He caught his breath and his eyes widened at the absurd notion of friendship. And yet? So why did the demon struggle to remain in Leash's body for a matter of a few years, a negligible time in the never-ending life of a vampyrus. Why didn't he relinquish the mammoth effort of infesting Leash and allow him to die? True, he'd have to return to his God and take his punishment for whatever he had done. But, having served his penance, he could then resume his life of infestation free of limitation for another eternity. Even if his God did keep him in Purgatory for a millennium or two, it would soon pass for Balar.

But Balar was truly terrified of his God. What had he done to incur the wrath of that sentient being? All Gods had disciples who obeyed their deity without question, so why had Balar disobeyed his?'

'Balar,' Leash called, 'Balar, who is your God?'

'Uh?' Balar answered startled. 'Never you mind...you've no need to know. Too much knowledge is a dangerous thing, or have you forgotten that.'

'Don't be silly. What can I possibly do to endanger you by knowing his identity?'

'There is no need for you to know,' Balar reiterated. 'Listen to me; I will not say it again. His name will not pass my lips. Now leave it be or I shall be forced to hurt you.'

'That's another thing. I've never known you solicit someone's aid to harm me before. Why did you make Gunter beat me?'

'Did I?'

'Yes! I know you have the power to influence the action of others. I've seen you do it many times over the years. You do it to trap your victims. So...why did you make Gunter beat me?'

'Because you wouldn't shut up!'

Leash sighed and took the hint. But he wouldn't forget it for he knew that Balar had hurt him out of pure desperation. Now, if he could discover the reason for the vampyrus' fear? His stomach turned over. Could there possibly be a chance to end his intolerable existence?

He turned and sat with his back against the stockade wall and studied the compound and its habitants. There were slaves of all ages and colours, some sat in groups or pairs as he did with Nicholas, others including Vlad, sat alone. Pirates stood at the gate, both inside and out, talking to each other and smoking the interminable foul-smelling cheroots. Armed with pikestaffs, as well as the ubiquitous cutlass, their purpose was to ensure discipline was maintained. Any infringement would be put down immediately. But he noticed that everyone stayed well away from Vlad, including the guards. It seemed that the huge man could do as he wished—except leave.

Leash wondered if there was any way he could relieve the sentries of a weapon. With Balar's aid he was extremely strong and fast so he shouldn't have much of a problem overcoming even the biggest pirate or perhaps even two of them. But Leash knew he'd have to regain his strength first. Balar had saved his life by healing him of the worst of his injuries. All he needed now was health-giving rest.

But if Vlad took it into his head to persecute him, would he be able to end that as well? However, he was a lot shorter and far weaker than Vlad. If he used the strength of his demon in front of witnesses it would appear out of all proportion to the size and state of his body. It would cause consternation and he'd become the focus of everyone's attention, maybe even Osvaldo. He'd be watched continually. No, to deal with Vlad he'd have to be cunning, do it in such a way as to appear normal, if violence was normal. But to escape he needed to keep his head down, blend in, become inconspicuous. Killing Vlad would have to be a last resort. Besides, he needed a weapon to defend himself and to aid his escape. He sighed; the question of obtaining a weapon would have to wait until nearer the time to flee. If it was found on him before he made his escape then the consequences didn't bear thinking about. He stared through the gap in the wall again, continuing to watch and study the short stretch of beach visible to him. As for escaping—he had no clear idea yet on a destination after he fled the compound. He needed to know more of the islands—and his captors.

For escape he had to. Slaves had no future. Just a few years extremely hard, dangerous labour and then, if they were lucky, an easy death. That was not the future he envisioned for himself. He might be blighted with Balar, but he was determined to search for a means of attaining freedom, not only from this prison, but also from his demon.

Dropping his head he almost gave in to despair. Had his flight from the ceremonial chamber on Sanctity been a pure waste of time? He'd suffered terribly on the fishing boat drifting north. But then he smiled—so had Balar. He'd nearly frightened the life out of the vampyrus by dying on him. And then something else occurred to him.

'Balar,' he called.

'What now,' the demon yawned.

'Are you tired?' Leash asked surprised, he hadn't realized his demon slept.

'Yes… why?'

'Never mind, just tell me this. You told me all your previous hosts died when you left their bodies except for my predecessor, is that right?'

'Yes, now leave me alone I want to go back to sleep.'

'How can you sleep when I'm wide awake?'

'Easy…I'm not you. So what do you want and make it quick.'

'I'm just beginning to realize that there's a lot about you I don't know, isn't there?'

'Yes…hurry up.'

'Why did you fight so hard to keep me alive?'

'You're my last host, I told you.'

'I'm not, though, am I?'

'Of course you are…we've gone over this before. Why do you keep on?' Balar asked impatiently.

'You told me that each of your hosts die when you finish with them, that's why you move on. It is their soul that is counted for your God. I mean…one life dead, one soul tallied against the total you can have before returning home. But there's one you didn't finish with of your own accord, isn't there? My predecessor is still alive—his soul doesn't count in your tally. In other words you still have a soul to spare. I am not the last. You don't have to go back to your God when you leave me…when I die.'

Balar was afraid to breathe, that fact hadn't occurred to him. Would it be enough, he'd have to find that man again, re-infest him when Leash died. But there again he was happy in Leash, although the man did seem to end up fighting for his life more often than not. There was no getting away from it, Leash was a survivor. He couldn't resist a secret admiration for his present host.

'You may have a point, Leash. If I can go to the Drikander and find that man again…'

Leash's heart turned over. *'I didn't mean that!'*

'What did you mean?'

'I'm not sure—I don't want you re-infecting the man when I die, that wouldn't be fair on him.'

'You don't have to die when I leave you. It just so happens that the others did because they were weak. You're hardly weak, Leash.'

Leash didn't know what to make of that admission. Was it true?

Balar continued musing. *'If I infest a body for a period of time and leave him alive when I desire another? As long as I don't collect his soul—does that mean I can go on indefinitely; I won't have to return to Purgatory?'*

'Nicholas,' Leash turned to his new acquaintance, more black hair had come away in his hand as he massaged away his enormous headache. 'I don't suppose you have anything resembling a razor, do you?'

Forty-three

Drudwynn lost another man when they came up with the bear. By that time Chong's soporific spell had worn off leaving the large, black ursine beast with terrible toothache. It was in no mood to tolerate humans attacking it. It killed one guard with a mighty sweep of its paw and in the same action nearly decapitated Drudwynn. Its long claws grazed Drudwynn's face, he promptly panicked and fell and broke his arm. In his rage, the ex-deputy again pointed his finger and this time the bear exploded, splattering everyone with gore.

The guards, understandably becoming used to the situation, did not need telling to retrace their steps. Although completely exhausted, all but one made it to the ford by daybreak the following day. The one who did not, suffered a brain seizure as a result of the abnormally fast pace Drudwynn's magic insisted on. Later that night he constituted supper for a series of nocturnal hunters.

They relocated the fugitives' tracks at the bramble at which the bear had been eating the black fruit. Drudwynn, his sergeant and the two guardsmen remaining to him, followed the mule's hoofprints down to the ford across the river Wry. Crossing wearily hours later, Drudwynn commandeered the campfire and dinner of the poor unfortunate tinker family they discovered on the opposite bank.

Having eaten and calmed a little, Drudwynn braced himself and mindmelded with Brenin requesting horses be brought up to meet them. He had the presence of mind to ask for eleven, not wanting the magus conscious of his losses. But he did make him aware that he'd herded the fugitives onto the Great North Road and he expected to come up with them very soon. Brenin replied with another warning concerning failure, one that Drudwynn, seriously worried at his catastrophic failure so far, did not need. He and his three remaining guards rested at the roadside awaiting their mounts, if they but knew it only a few leagues south of Chong and Elstan.

Up ahead on the Great North Road, Elstan led the mule, with Chong-An still atop. They were gradually creeping up on the train of the carnival. The Fly took his eyes only momentarily from his objective as he walked, though his hearing was continually attuned to everything about. It seemed there were people of all nationalities treading the road. He walked amongst people speaking the lilting tongue of Qula in the south, and the guttural sounds of the tribesmen of Talka, the desert region on the other side of the Scissor Mountains. But mostly it was the slow drawl of the plains people of western Drakka, mixed in with a smattering of accents of those from north of the Drikander, that he heard.

He glanced up at Chong every now and then, his concern for the oriental begging haste; the ex-librarian's stamina had ebbed to a dangerously low level. Elstan had no idea how the man had survived the last hours frantically fleeing across the Wry. He must have been calling on reserves of strength desperately enhanced by magic.

It hadn't taken the fugitives long to reach the river after Drudwynn and his few remaining men disappeared over the promontory north, heading deep into the forest following the bear. They had left the safety of Chong's illusion and walked briskly to the river and followed it north to the crossing point. The stubborn mule had eventually been coaxed into the ford but the water reaching its knees seriously upset the beast. The animal's psyche was in turmoil, troubled by confusion after its period of flying through thin air and lying on its side amongst the bramble. It was also still suffering the lingering after-effects of the dream-sorghum administered only a couple of days before. The water swirling about its trembling knees seemed to be the last straw. It snorted and bucked, its hind legs leaving the water throwing Chong heavily onto the rock-strewn bed of the river.

The oriental wrenched his back and badly sprained his left ankle, with the result that his arthritis immediately flared up again worse than ever. The relief he had gained from his rest of a day and a half, forgotten now in the midst of renewed agony. Elstan had struggled to help him regain his feet and his seat on the mule, but the oriental's health deteriorated rapidly shortly afterwards.

'Don't worry, my friend,' Chong smiled bleakly, 'we'll make it yet.'

'Aye, we will that,' and he patted Chong's thigh encouragingly, careful not to touch the man's aching knees. 'Damn!'

'What?'

'You see that caravan way up ahead behind the leading one, the one with the red, green and white stars painted all over it? I painted those; I've spent many a night sleeping under it. We may have a problem,' he said, dejected.

'Elstan, you're making me anxious, what sort of problem?'

'I've worked this carnival many times over the years,' he sighed again, 'but maybe old Lembek will still take us on as acrobats, if...'

'Acrobats! If...if what?' Chong suddenly straightened and stared at his companion askance. 'Are you serious? I can't even walk let alone tumble...mind you I could fall easily enough. What's this "if"?'

Elstan smiled ruefully. 'I'm sorry; I didn't mean you for the acrobatics. I've used my skills at climbing walls and jumping from roof to roof to masquerade as an acrobat in this circus. I have a tightrope act that'll make you cringe,' he suddenly laughed. 'It'll make a change to fly in full view again...not hidden in the dark. It's a wonderful feeling soaring through the air...I wish I could explain it properly. If we can get over my little problem it'll be a perfect cover if Drudwynn ever catches up with us. He won't expect me to perform openly in front of crowds and we'll ensure you'll be safe hiding among the carnies.'

'You have a lot of ifs. As for our safety, I wouldn't be too sure if I was you. The man has tipped over the edge of insanity. He will probably see flies everywhere, as well as little yellow men. Or not so little I suppose,' he added tapping his belly, knowing that Elstan would not enlighten him yet as to the "if". 'That reminds me, I am a little hungry.'

'You're always hungry. Still I agree with you, I'm feeling peckish myself and I do know of a rather beautiful lady in this circus who cooks extremely well. Trouble is we daren't meet her.'

'Elstan, do you intend telling me, or are you going to wait until I say or do something which will drop us in it inadvertently?'

'I will, I will, my friend, but for now I think we'd better hurry, I don't believe it'll be much longer before we see our pursuers again. And I'd much rather they didn't see us.'

Despite the urgency they took their time coming up to the star-painted caravan, Elstan averted his eyes as they did so. But both realized haste on this road would have drawn curious glances and the unusual was always a topic of conversation over a campfire. Drudwynn would soon understand that his quarry had been sighted and, the mood he was in, he'd rip the carnival apart in his search for them.

In the late afternoon, the carnival halted for the night and made camp just off the side of the road at a place that must have been used many times before for the same purpose. There were remains of numerous campfires, the grass flattened over a wide area bordering large woods which were obviously used to supply kindling.

The two walked on past the carnies, the children already running to the river with buckets in hand to fetch water. The older carnies were stepping down from their caravans and carts, stretching stiffening limbs before moving off to set up camp and prepare supper. Elstan continued to lead the mule hoping to locate Lembek, the circus master, in amongst the vast crowd before he was recognized by old acquaintances. Staring at the myriad faces of all colours and ages he found himself smiling at his memories of good times as he glimpsed familiar faces. He reluctantly turned his face from them. It was a carnival acrobat that had completed his training, teaching him the tricks of his now clandestine trade.

But all of a sudden Elstan dropped his head and hunched his shoulders. Up ahead a huge, giant of a man had just walked out from between the two leading caravans, the star-painted vehicle and the larger one obviously the ringmaster's. Elstan slowed until he fell back alongside the mule.

'What's wrong?' Chong asked looking down on his guilt-ridden companion. Who is that man?'

'That is Otto, Lembek's son, he's the strong man of the circus and I honestly don't want him to see me.'

'You are afraid of him?' Chong asked incredulously.

'I have seen that man lift a board with ten men sitting on it and run with it two hundred yards and not even break into a sweat. He can bend iron bars as thick as his arm and then straighten them again. I'd be a fool not to be wary of him.'

'How have you upset him?'

'That's a long story; I'll tell you when we're settled for the night. Now come on, let's find the ringmaster.'

Aerial acrobats, those that performed aloft on the trapeze or the tightrope, were always in demand. The profession called for people with nerves of steel and an expertise second to none. Many tried it – the pay was well above average – but the foolhardy amateurs literally fell to the wayside. Consequently there was always a shortage of men and women prepared to work at the dizzy heights. But it wasn't until the fugitives neared the head of the caravan that Elstan's fears found fruition. His enquiries elicited the knowledge that Lembek had died and his son, Otto, had inherited the circus.

'Never mind, my friend, whatever you've done Otto will surely know of your skills. If you are as good as you imply then he'll jump at taking you on,' Chong said cheerfully, even though Elstan's face was a mild shade of sick.

'Aye, that's what I'm afraid of.'

'What?'

'Him jumping at taking me on…I wouldn't last a minute! Damn that Juliana!'

'I beg your pardon.'

'Otto's wife, Juliana. Well, I didn't know it was her at the time, I thought she was her sister, Messalina.' He looked up at Chong, a sheepish grin now suffusing his face. 'They were twins, identical twins. I didn't know they both fancied me, did I?'

'Oh, my God! Are you a fool, couldn't you control yourself? We need to hide among this carnival if we're to evade Drudwynn!'

'Chong, don't shout at me, I didn't know anything about this then, did I? This was six years ago. But it's not only him I have to hide from—Messalina will probably join Otto in trying to kill me. God, if they recognize me…we've got to think of something else.'

Chong stared at him utterly perplexed. 'Dear God, the things I've had to do since meeting you. Well, I suppose we'd better make sure they don't recognize you, hadn't we.'

'Ah, Chong, your skills may hide my face but he'll still know my act.'

'Then change your act.'

'How the hell am I going to do that? It takes years to get a competent performance together, especially on the high ropes.'

'Elstan, we haven't come all this way, gone through all we have on that damned mountain, to come a cropper now. I suppose you'll have to audition, show him what you can do?'

'Of course, he's not going to take me on without seeing me perform. He'll know me straight away.'

'Am I right in thinking the next actual performance before a paying crowd will be in Mulkie's Cross?'

'Of course, that's where the circus is headed. It always performs at Kaneshi's Festival. Why?'

'Then we only have to satisfy him of your skills at your audition. If we can do that, we have shelter to reach our destination and you won't have to stay with the circus once we're in Mulkie's

Cross. I am a wizard, aren't I? Just do as I say and don't look surprised at what you can do.'

'Whoa, now, what are you going to have me doing?'

'You said you fly…so I'll make you soar. We'll work out an act that will be the best in the world. He won't be able to say no. But first I'll modify your good looks in such a way that no Juliana or Messalina will want you near them. Let's find somewhere nice and quiet and very private.'

Later, after much cajoling from Chong, and an assurance that the modification was not permanent, Elstan, his nose now altered to twice as long as normal with a large wart growing on its tip, approached the circus master.

Otto was huge. Sitting on the mule, Chong still had to look up at him. He was bald with a bushy red moustache that drooped majestically either side of his mouth, the jewel braided ends hanging below his chin. He seemed fascinated by the wart and couldn't seem to look past it to even see the colour of Elstan's eyes.

'What can you do?'

'I'm a flyer.'

'I have fliers aplenty. I've just engaged the services of the Soaring Myners from Qula.'

Elstan paused; he'd heard of them, they were a very famous troupe of aerialists. None could eclipse their act in all of Drakka.

'I'm better,' he said, keeping his fingers crossed behind his back, hoping that Chong's illusions would be more than adequate.

'Better! Get away, man, there is no-one better,' he roared and called up to a very beautiful woman who at that moment poked her head out of the caravan having heard Elstan's boast. 'Juliana, find Billy Myner. Tell him there's a fish here with a shrimp on his nose who says he can fly better than him. Ask him if he'll set up a line in the morning, and then we can all watch the fun.'

Elstan, bristling at the insult to his face, raised his hand to his nose. He hoped to God it wasn't permanent, but despite the disfigurement he was nervous at allowing Juliana to see his face. Her smile as she flounced past him, her red dress full with a low bodice showing more chest than he'd seen in a long while, stirred him, the feelings totally inappropriate when he was talking to her husband. But his gut lurched at Otto's next words.

'Messalina,' he shouted his voice enough to drown out thunder.

A woman, the spit of Juliana walked around the end of the star caravan, her hair just as black, just as long as her sister's with eyes as black as night, she turned her gaze on Elstan.

And his heart stopped.

'What now, I'm busy,' and with that a girl of about five or six brushed past her from behind and seeing Chong-An sitting on the mule squealed with delight.

'Mama, he's beautiful, can I have him?' She skipped over to the mule and run her hand down its face gently stroking his cool muzzle. Laying her face on the beast's cheek, her long black, curly hair bouncing with her quick motions, she kissed the mule and then looked up at its rider. 'Please, Master, can I have him, Uncle Otto will give you a horse for him if you want?'

'I'll what! You want me to give him an expensive mount for a load of shite like this?'

'Stop swearing, Uncle,' and she looked up at Chong again. 'Don't worry, Master, he's an old softy at heart. We'll talk him around later,' and as she turned away fear appeared in her eyes. 'You don't want him, do you...the mule, I mean. It's just my Megan died a couple of weeks ago, she was a lovely mule, I'd had her from the day I was born. I really do need another one, honest.'

'Trinity, come here darling, don't bother the travellers. What do you want Otto?'

An observant man might have noticed wetness in the huge man's eyes as he looked down with affection on his niece and stroked her small head with a hand the size of a bucket. 'Trinnie, I want you and your mother to make supper for these two, they are my guests until after the little one's audition.'

He picked up a rope hanging from the back of his caravan. 'And what is it that you do oriental? By the looks of you on that thing you could make an excellent jester, though I can't see you tumbling.'

'God forbid, Ringmaster. I'm just a fellow traveller, a friend met on the road. He's been kind enough to aid me; I have problems with my feet.'

'Very well, but I can't afford to feed hangers-on for long,' and then he warned. 'Stay close to my wife's sister and her daughter, strangers, I am not fond of those I don't know roaming loose among my people.'

Chong-An belched his pleasure. Leaning back in a chair, his aching feet resting on a padded stool belonging to Trinity, he contemplated the scene being enacted between his three companions, Elstan, Messalina and Trinity. Rubbing his belly, full for the first time in weeks it felt, he watched as Elstan sat cross-legged on the ground playing pat-a-cake with the little girl who had enchanted them both. And as Elstan taught her the game of synchronisation where they patted each other's' hands and knees alternately, speeding up as the game progressed, he wondered what had become of his friend.

Elstan hardly spoke, never looked directly at the slim, black-haired Messalina, although Chong was convinced he was looking at her from the corners of his eyes. And he took no notice of Juliana when she visited to tell them that the Soaring Myners would assist Otto in judging Elstan's performance in the morning. It would be the last full day of travelling before reaching Mulkie's Cross. Otto wanted to enter the town with the carnival in full cavalcade at noon, the busiest hour the day after.

But Chong noticed a bemused look on Messalina's face. She seemed fascinated by the short, weathered man and it was not his wart. Chong wondered how long it would take her to realize that the man, introduced as Cenward, was the lover who jilted her.

Nevertheless, Chong was also puzzled by the antics of the usually bad-tempered mule. He'd discovered it, just before supper, standing at the back of the caravan having broken free of the communal livestock compound. It had been resting its head on the shoulder of the little girl as if on guard. She in turn was speaking to it as if it understood her, and for all the oriental knew, it possibly did. Now the mule was grazing unfettered between the caravan and the woods, refusing to be returned to the compound.

The child's laughter broke into his reverie as both she and Elstan collapsed in hysterics.

'Why have you got such a funny nose?' Trinity asked innocently.

'Trinity, that's rude, you should not ask people about their looks,' Messalina scolded.

'It's all right, I don't mind, she can ask me anything she wishes,' Elstan said quietly as he held both her hands in his, smiling up at her as she'd bounded to her feet before him. 'I don't think this young lady has a shred of malice in any of her bones.'

'I'll agree there,' said Chong, 'even that stubborn mule loves her already.'

'Aw, he's not stubborn, he's lovely, just needs a cuddle that's all,' Trinity said.

'Well, talking about cuddles it's time for your bed. Come, Trinity, say goodnight.' Messalina stood with her hand out ready to take her daughter inside. But a ring on the little finger of the woman's hand caught the attention of Chong.

'That is unusual, Messalina, may I see?' Chong asked.

Holding her hand he examined the ring with Elstan looking on, it had a little blue stone set in a clamp of gold.

'That's my Dada's ring,' Trinity stated proudly, 'he left it to her before he went away. That's why I was named Trinity—Mama, Dada and me, three of us together. We will be one day.'

Elstan hissed sharply, shock striking him dumb. Messalina and Chong glanced at him quickly, his reaction totally unexpected. Trinity didn't seem to notice the effect of her words she grabbed hold of her mother's hand and pulled her.

'I must say goodnight to Giddy before I go to sleep, Mama,' and she went over to the mule and pulled its ears until it stopped feeding so she could kiss his face.

'What's wrong, Elstan, even under that illusion I can see you're pale? Are you sickening?' Chong asked as mother and daughter disappeared through the gaily coloured door at the back of the caravan.

'I'm fine…I'm going for a walk.' he said abruptly and stormed off leaving Chong biting his lip wondering if his suspicions were correct.

The following morning it seemed that half the carnival performers were standing in a ring awaiting Elstan's audition. He had been the object of many a ribald comment over supper the previous evening. It hadn't taken long for his boast to get around the camp. The Soaring Myners had set up a high rope between two very tall oak trees and secured rope ladders at each end. Billy Myner and his brother, Roderick, were smirking when Elstan walked into the centre of the ring accompanied by Otto.

Chong sat in a chair at the edge of the crowd not wanting to be in full view. He was about to perform serious magic and didn't want anyone noticing. But staring at Elstan he was seriously worried. His friend was unnaturally silent and distracted, an unfortunate manner when he was about to climb a hundred feet into the air and perform on a tightrope. The ex-librarian looked about studying the crowd, the merriment increasing as time progressed towards the comeuppance of this stranger from the north. But Chong was confident that he could make Elstan appear more daring than the Myners, even if he wasn't too sure how clever the brothers were.

The act he and Elstan had planned overnight was spectacular, but Elstan would have been happier if he could have rehearsed it first. Elstan had tried to inform Chong of the more dangerous tricks and flips, but the more he elaborated the more the oriental became confused. So they settled on a trick that seemed simple to look at but everyone in the circus knew was extremely difficult. And what's more the lead up to the flip was to be exceedingly fast—a speed that was mind-blowing. The climax of the act was to entail Elstan standing in the middle of the rope perfectly still, a feat in itself. He was then to make a back-flip and catch the rope in his hands. From this position of hanging below the rope he was to commence swinging until he swung over the rope. The swing was to take up momentum and when the crowd was utterly enthralled with the speed, Chong would halt the swing with Elstan doing a handstand on the rope. Elstan would then walk on his hands to the end of the rope. Chong assured Elstan that nothing could go wrong, he would be completely in the magician's care from the moment he began the swing. It would be easy to hold him in the handstand and on the walk.

The crowd quieted when Elstan walked across the clearing to the rope ladder and commenced his climb. As a safeguard Billy Myner was already at the line, for despite competition between aerialists, they all stood by ready to help each other in case of accidents. Billy, at one end of the rope, stared at Elstan flexing his arms and legs, preparing to step out.

Moments later Elstan was performing the simple tricks and flips that all aerialists did to limber up for the big one. And as he did, so his concentration returned to the matter at hand. No more did he think of Messalina and Trinity and the totally unexpected situation in which he'd found himself. No more did he think of Drudwynn some way down the road hastening to his capture. And neither did he think of Chong, his friend the wizard. The tightrope took him to realms of peace that he'd almost forgotten. His love of the high line and the tricks and flips returned so easily, he felt as if he was flying like the birds and he gave himself over to his skill.

Below, Chong did as everyone else did. He sat quietly not taking his eyes from his friend. He marvelled at the ease displayed as Elstan walked along the rope on his feet and then turned and ran the other way. His jumps and flips and falls to catch the rope were as good as the Soaring Myners any day. The performance mesmerized all, everyone applauding a superb act. Elstan was good, his acrobatics perfect, but all knew that this was just the intro and the crowd wondered. Was he going to prove his mastery over the Soaring Myners?

Elstan halted at the end of the cable and wiped his brow first in one sleeve then the other. This was the signal that Chong awaited. He looked about to see if anyone was watching him and paused when he again saw a puzzled look on Messalina's upturned face. Turning from her, putting her out of his mind, he dropped his arms to his side and flexed the fingers on both hands. Any moment now he'd place his hands, palm upwards on his knees, and commence his gesticulations under the cover of a blanket he was using ostensibly to keep a draught off his old legs.

Elstan walked across the tightrope, back-flipped to exclamations of surprise and caught the line in both hands. And Chong took over, his fingers on his right hand moved and his friend swung around the cable, he moved the fingers on his left hand and Elstan swung even faster. Chong raised the fingers on both hands ready to halt the swing and Trinity jumped on his lap, squashing his fingers, completely disrupting the spell.

'This is boring, Master Chong, come let's play pat-a-cake it's more fun,' and she grabbed hold of Chong's hands and held them in the air. There was absolutely nothing Chong could do without revealing he was a wizard. He glanced quickly up at his friend, the swing going on far longer than it should. He couldn't push her away or tell her to keep quiet because that would have upset her and attracted unwelcome attention. He couldn't make the required gestures because Trinity was holding his hands. And he couldn't disentangle them from hers without hurting her. When Messalina came to stand alongside them he despaired. He could do nothing but watch and pray.

Up above the Fly began to panic waiting for Chong to halt his progress. He swung forever before he realized that something was wrong. His hands started to sweat and slip on the rope, he could feel the skin on his palms burn and the blisters burst. He desperately closed his eyes against the pain and clamped his mouth shut as he felt a groan in his throat. He frantically unclamped his left hand to ease the pain and the crowd gasped as he continued to swing one-handed around the rope. The noise brought him back from the brink and he clasped both hands to the rope again, but couldn't hold it and he eased his right hand from the rope.

Billy Myner, clinging to the tree couldn't believe his eyes; no-one had ever flipped so fast or with just one hand. Roderick Myner shinned up the ladder to get a closer look, and his eyes nearly popped from his head when Elstan changed hands yet again.

It was the crowd that persuaded Elstan that he had to stop the swing himself. With thoughts of strangling Chong when he reached the ground, Elstan's skill saved him. He slowed the swing and halted with his legs in the air—a perfect handstand from a speeding flip, but his hands hurt too much for him to do the planned walk. Mumbling imprecations against Chong he brought his feet down either side of his hands and stood up straight. To the ecstatic applause of the crowd and the admiration of the Myners, all thinking the abortive trick was part of the act, Elstan walked to the end of the rope and made his way to the ground.

Messalina was the only one who was puzzled. As she administered salve to his hands, she wondered where she'd seen him before.

Forty-four

'Fire, iron and a dreadful noise…that is his weapon,' said Connors sitting back in his chair, replete after a sumptuous dinner of roast rack of lamb and sweet potatoes eaten off solid silver plates. Osvaldo's hospitality was renowned throughout the islands and Connors sipped his coffee sweetened with honey. 'Thank you,' he took the cigar proffered by his host, lit it from the candelabra in the middle of the table, and taking a long puff he spoke through the exhaled smoke. 'The result is devastation the likes of which I have never seen before.'

'What do you mean, fire is fire is it not, and iron is iron? And I've never heard of anyone dying because of a noise,' said Cowper lighting a cigarillo, he preferred the smaller packaged tobacco.

'Oh, yes...fire that can fling a ball of iron hundreds of yards through the air?' Meecham said, raising his eyebrows and noting Osvaldo's puzzled expression, he continued. 'Let me describe the weapon for you, he calls it a cannon by the way. It consists of a long iron pipe which is partly filled with a black grain – Lonsdale calls it gunpowder – and then he drops an iron ball in on top of it. He does something or other with a lit taper and there is an enormous bang and the iron ball is propelled from the pipe's mouth. Depending where he points the thing it demolishes everything in its path, whether it is property or men.

Connors took over and went on for more than an hour describing the carnage already perpetrated on the populace of Armadillo.

The devastation was almost incredible and Cowper wondered if the remedy that the hag had come up with was truly enough. He smiled. The fat pirate sitting opposite Osvaldo had no idea how to battle the fearsome weapon and he had no intention of telling him of the simple solution. But he had no idea yet how they were to get close enough to the cannon to destroy it.

'Alex Bartram and the North Star, how do they figure in all this,' asked Osvaldo. 'If the Star is as badly damaged as you say he's not going to be of any help to us in gaining the upper hand. Are there others who will come onboard with us?

'There are, but we have to lead and be seen to have a chance of success,' he sniggered derisively. 'You know the calibre of our compatriots. Most are cowards and will come aboard only on the winning side. But I thought to utilize Bartram's men if we can get the North Star into position in the dry-dock. The weapon is sited across the wharf from there,' he grinned, 'at the moment it's trained on the Serpent.'

Osvaldo sucked air through his teeth at that. 'If Bartram's men are that near then they are at grave risk if we attack.'

'True, Alex's men may come to grief but he won't mind that as long as you promise to have the North Star repaired,' he chuckled. 'Without a ship he is dead meat,' said Connors manfully removing from his mouth the residue of his meal using his toothpick. 'He will also require paying.'

'At the moment Lonsdale has that cannon trained on our ship? Can he really destroy the Serpent?' asked Cowper incensed.

'He can blow it out of the water or, in this case, out of the dock,' Connors answered.

'Bartram is willing to trust me?' interrupted Osvaldo.

'Of course, Jos. As long as the Serpent is taken from the dock and the Star is already in place when the fun starts. If his ship is too badly damaged he can always take Lonsdale's Shark in its place. It takes a long time to reload the weapon from what I've seen. So if we allow him to fire it, then while he's doing whatever he has to do to shoot the damned thing again, we distract him. Maybe we can get him to swing the thing around and point it somewhere else. If he does, then Bartram's men can attack him from the dock.'

'And how do we distract him, Captain,' asked Cowper.

'Well, this is where your men can play their part. It's no good putting them on the Serpent while that's in dry-dock, Lonsdale would notice and take action before you've completed the move. But if you attack him from the beacon on Marlin Point to the east of the harbour, I can support you with my men if the Hound is alongside the quay. There is sufficient cover amongst the warehouses and cargo stacked there. With both of us attacking Lonsdale on the wharf we can give Bartram enough time to race ashore and overwhelm the weapon. Once it's in our hands we can turn it on Lonsdale and watch the man crawl on his hands and knees to kiss our feet.'

'If we know how to use it,' added Osvaldo thoughtfully.

'The black southerner, master of the weapon, and his aide are always at its side—if we can take them alive we have the means to fire it,' Meecham added.

'Tell me more of those two, they intrigue me. You say they are southerners but from which nation on the Dark Continent?' Osvaldo asked.

'I didn't say he was from the Dark Continent. I said they were southerners and black. But he looks strange or should I say they look strange.' Connors frowned. 'They have pointy ears.'

Cowper straightened suddenly, gripping his fork with which he was about to spear a portion of melon he stared wide-eyed at the fat man. 'Black…how black?' he asked quietly.

'As the night, why? Have you heard of them?' Connors asked, himself startled at the mate's reaction.

'There is a legend back home in Drakka of black elves, Svartalfar they're named. But it can't be they, surely. The stories say they died out with the other elves millennia ago, though…' Cowper peered into space his brow creased.

'Though? Come, man, what have you heard?' asked Osvaldo irritated.

'Well, they were supposed to be masters at the art of creating weapons. It was they who supposedly supplied all the weapons to both sides in the wars of the sorcerers, thousands of years ago.'

'What wars?' asked Connors.

'It doesn't matter…stories told children to frighten them into going asleep,' Cowper said shrugging his shoulders, though the puzzled look remained on his face.

'There are no such people as black elves, Marcus, just tales,' said Jos Osvaldo raising his eyebrows.

'Now, this is where I must divulge a little knowledge that quite honestly will astound you,' with that he glanced at his companion, Meecham, and licked his lips. 'Our dear Admiral Lonsdale knows of the Needle.'

The only thing to be heard in the silence that followed was a cockatoo calling in the distance, not even a breath registered on their senses. Tension was thick in the air as Cowper reached for the dagger in the baldric across his chest, the belt that usually held his sword at its lower end. Osvaldo put his hand over his mate's and spoke just the one word.

'How?'

'You have a man by the name of Smudge, or rather you did. Lonsdale took him and eventually killed him. Did you know the man hated slugs? He was quite paranoid about them in fact. Our admiral discovered this and waylaid your Smudge coming out of the Mermaid. How he discovered that Smudge was alone must have been pure luck. It is well known that none of your men are allowed in Armadillo unaccompanied as all of them know the location of your hoard. But when Lonsdale placed him in a hole in the ground with hundreds of the fat, slimy creatures for company, I'm afraid we were all enlightened.'

Cowper stared at the fat captain, startled. So Karnica had been right, a man afraid of insects would betray them. He shuddered; he was himself terrified of moths, so it wasn't to him she had been referring.

'All?' Osvaldo asked softly, the menace in his voice holding his facial muscles rigid.

'I'm afraid so, Jos. I think Lonsdale wanted to show us his new power. And what better way than to discover the closest kept secret in the islands. Needless to say you won't have your treasure beyond the end of this week, for in five days' time he will have taken it all.'

'Not if I'm here to stop him.'

'Ah, my dear Jos, but you won't be. He is at this moment planning to trundle another of these weapons to the Needle. He has two of them…didn't I tell you? He also has around half a thousand men accompanying it. It's surprising how men will shift their loyalties when promised a share of your fortune. Not even you can survive those odds. No, as I see it, you have three options. One, allow Lonsdale free reign to take your treasure and escape with your life. Two,' and Connors held up a second finger, 'fight him at the Needle and get annihilated or three—join battle with him before he leaves Armadillo.'

'Or four, shift my treasure before he gets here—and then kill him,' said Osvaldo pulling at his beard.

'And how long will that take, my friend?' asked Connors.

'Too long,' broke in Cowper.

'Too long before we can get it to safety, yes, but we can load it tomorrow on both ships. Sail with it into Armadillo, slaughter Lonsdale and then find another secure site where this time no-one can get at it.' Osvaldo stood and walked slowly over to the large picture window looking over Comfort Bay.

'Both ships, Jos? You wish to put your treasure on the Hound?' asked Connors, not believing his ears.

'You and I, Marcus, have something in common,' and he turned from the window and stared at the fat man at the table. 'We keep our word! You swear to me that you will not run off with my booty and I will give you a substantial share of it. You attempt to run off with it and I promise you I will follow you to the ends of the earth. And you will die a very slow death at my hands. There, I have made you two promises, what say you?'

Connors stood up from the table, laying his napkin to one side he looked his rival in the eye. 'I swear by all that's holy to me that I accept your conditions, provided...' and here he paused for a moment before his voice hardened. 'You will also swear never to do me out of my share and in future we will be partners and rule this island together.'

Meecham held his breath as did Cowper. Both aides looked at their masters knowing that at the outcome of their swearing they would both sink or swim together.

'Done!' and both captains shook hands.

Leash could hardly walk, or see to walk, his back hurt, a gash above his left eye bled down his face, his eyes had puffed up and his nose was broken. Unable to call upon the supernatural strength of the demon, he'd been beaten savagely by Vlad.

The big man existed on the locally grown naxix leaf and the powerful narcotic had rotted his mind, just as lypyn weed did for the indigents of Drakka and the mainland countries. But there was a substantial difference between lypyn and naxix—the former made you love everyone, the latter made you hate them but also strangely compliant to orders. For this reason the chewing of naxix leaf was encouraged and freely supplied by the slave-masters. Coupled with it was the consumption of the almost neat alcoholic drink, goorani. Both were used as the favourite methods of keeping the slaves under control.

'You should have let him take the chicken; it was only a measly little leg, not even cooked properly.' Balar said not in the least bit perturbed, Leash had been far nearer death than this.

'It was mine!'

'So?'

'He has too much already,' Leash cradled his head in his hands. Feeling the swellings on his cheekbones, he spat out the remains of a broken tooth, one of several smashed by Vlad's huge fist. He suddenly grasped his nose and groaning loudly he jerked the broken appendage back into place.

'Strange, I never noticed he had more food than you,' said Balar wincing at the unexpected pain.

'There's more to wealth than enough food. Look at him, Balar, he's rich.'

The vampyrus was mystified. 'He can't be, he only has the same as you…dirty britches and an even uglier smile. Mind you, at the moment you run him a close second,' Balar sniggered.

'Ugly? Now that's a comment I've never heard before…I used to be told that the sun shines out of my face when I smile.'

'Uh! Who on earth told you that?'

'As you said to me earlier…never you mind, it's none of your business. Why didn't you help me?' he asked.

'Oh, yes, and have everyone notice that you were abnormally strong. How long would it have taken them to discover me? There are enough of them to kill us, you know. Besides I'm healing you aren't I,' he added, aggrieved at Leash's lack of gratitude. 'Now going back to my question, who on earth told you that you were handsome?'

'How do you know the one who told me is of this world?'

'Oh, it's her again, is it? Isn't it about time you forgot her?'

'Whatever you do to me, and howsoever long you subject me to your loathsome presence, something of her will always get through to me. I'll never relinquish her…get used to it.'

'You're a fool—forget her, you'd be a lot happier with just me,' receiving no answer he returned to his original query. 'So, tell me how this animal is richer than us.'

'I didn't say us…I said me. He has something I don't have…his freedom. A man is wealthy beyond his wildest dreams if he is free.'

'He's a slave! He's imprisoned the same as you…he has no freedom. You're not going insane on me now are you? I wouldn't want you going mad…it'll get very uncomfortable for me.'

'You are a fool, Balar, why I bother with you I don't know.'

'You bother with me because you have no choice…and there's no need to be insulting. You still haven't explained how that mindless hulk is free.'

'He is alone in his body, isn't he? He has no demon but that of his own making in his head. He can make his own decisions, he...' and Leash broke down, sobbing he bowed his head and held it in his hands.

'Oh, dear me, it's back to the tears. I thought you were a grown man, Leash, not a baby.'

'Hey, man, you'll survive,' said Nicholas returning to his side with a wet cloth. 'At least he didn't kill you, come on hold this to your face,' and he sat down alongside Leash.

Moments later Leash raised his head and looked across the compound at Vlad sitting alone chewing his naxix, a vacant expression on his face. Leash sighed and ignored both Balar and Nicholas. Vlad couldn't help what he was; despair had turned the man to the drug, the combination of that and the goorani made him violent. Nevertheless, Leash knew he would have to do something about him, the next beating he received at his hands could very well mean his death.

And despite Balar, Leash did not want to die, whatever he might say in the depths of his desolation.

'You okay now, man?' Nicholas asked offering him a cup. 'Drink this, but rinse your mouth out first you won't want to swallow a tooth.'

Leash took the proffered drink, washing the beer around his mouth. He winced as the cold fluid entered the newly created cavities and spat it out. He drank the rest quickly through the pain of toothache.

'Thank you, God my face hurts,' he said holding his head in his hands.

'Well, perhaps you'll listen next time. When Vlad comes up to you, as he will, he loves dishing out a beating, just sit still and give him whatever he wants. If he gives you a kicking—take it, he'll get fed up in time and leave you alone.'

Leash smiled his thanks for the advice he knew he could not afford to take. He picked up the leftover chicken thigh from alongside his leg that Vlad had thrown down after wrenching it out of Leash's hands. He turned it idly in his fingers staring at it as a means of distracting his thoughts away from Balar and the well-meaning Nicholas. It was a fairly thick bone for a chicken, fairly straight and as long as the palm of his hand—and it gave Balar an idea. Leash rose from the ground and shuffled over to shelter in the lee of the big barn-like structure most never sheltered in. Nicholas watched him scrabbling about in the sand until he picked up a small, sharp-edged, rough rock. Leash commenced cleaning and sharpening the bone.

'What are you doing?' Nicholas asked.

'A good question, Balar, what are we doing?' asked Leash.

'Preparing,' answered Balar.

'For what?'

'You'll see.'

Leash smiled grimly and studied the bone for moments before realizing what his demon was making him shape. *'I am not going to kill him. I have spent twenty years trying to stop you killing people...I am not going to give up now.'*

Balar ignored him. Having full control of Leash's muscles he continued to sharpen the bone.

The next day was hot and dry; they'd had thin gruel and watered-down rancid wine to break their fast, a standard of food that Leash had got accustomed to onboard, but it was not what he'd received the night before.

'Why are we back to eating this disgusting stuff, Nicholas?' Leash asked gently rubbing his hurt nose to see if it had displaced whilst he'd been sleeping.

'I don't know, it's hard work off-loading booty from the Lobos, we are usually well fed. But something is going on, I've never seen the crew up this early before, unless we're sailing.'

Balar was equally upset and continually grumbled as Leash ate. Leash ignored him and smiled—the more he was disregarded the more Balar became distressed. And he loved having the demon discomposed.

Not long after, Gunter walked into the compound lash in hand accompanied by a band of half a dozen pirates. He quickly trod the dirty sand prodding slaves with the handle of his coiled whip. The slave-master was just about to walk past Leash when he noticed the appalling state of his face.

'Bloody hell, what happened to you,' he said bending over and peering closely into his face. 'Another fight like that and you ain't gonna last, boy. You'd better come with me now, I'll need to get some work out of you before you depart this world,' he laughed and laid the lash across Leash's back.

Leash was tethered in a line of twenty men, five behind Vlad at the head of the rope, Nicholas behind. He waited as other slaves were similarly formed up making ten lines in all before they moved off. Gunter, striding along a little way ahead, led the lines out of the compound and headed along the coast, his lash resting on his shoulder and swigging goorani from a pewter jug.

'I told you something was up,' Nicholas whispered, 'I've never seen this number mobilized before. We should be going to the ship first to tote booty to the Needle but the crews are stripping both ships for some reason, look.'

Glancing back along the quay, Leash noticed the frenetic activity amongst the crews, they were off-loading all extraneous equipment including sails and bedding.

'Where are we going?' Balar asked.

Leash's eyes, squinting through the harsh swellings, constantly roved the terrain hoping to find a means of escape. *'How the hell should I know? Wait and see I expect we'll find out before long.'*

Balar grumbled and did as he was told, not liking it one bit. He watched everything through Leash's eyes, faintly disgusted at the obvious health of the verdant forest on the one side of the track they followed, and the lively strength of the ocean rolling on to the broad sandy beaches on the other. They climbed a steep path to the top of the cliffs and shuffled along for maybe an hour before descending into a small cove its western promontory jutting well out to sea. They halted at the foot of the escarpment and here the slaves were told to sit and wait. Gunter continued on towards the rock wall and it was only then Leash realized there was an open fissure, a natural cave situated behind a column of freestanding rock, a needle towering above their heads.

Gunter shouted in at the entrance and Captain Osvaldo appeared wearing a short blue naval jacket with gold epaulettes and braiding, tight, white trousers and a cutlass at his belt. The vain, broad-shouldered man sporting a freshly shaved face stroked his thin ginger moustache, the same colour as his immaculately brushed shoulder-length, curly hair, and studied the slaves.

He placed a long black cigar in his mouth, dragged on it and blew the smoke into Gunter's face making the slave-master cough. 'You're late.'

'Sorry, Captain, the men were slow gathering the slaves. I have the first couple of hundred as you ordered.'

'Good. Well you'd better release them they can't carry anything tied to that rope. Move it, I haven't all day,' and he turned and walked back inside the cave.

Leash walked into a fortune house, all the stories he'd ever been told of pirates' treasure suddenly before his eyes. There were chests upon chests of gold bullion, silver coins, gems and precious stones. In amongst the chests were sacks full of precious ornaments, candelabra, picture frames and mirrors. Bails of silk and other exotically coloured fabrics lay to one side of the cave—everything looted from ships at sea over many years. Leash and Balar stared mouth agape.

'Move it,' Gunter ordered, 'grab a chest each, pick it up and carry it outside, use the stretchers if needs be. Come on, you can gloat as much as you want when everything has been taken away. You are to tote it all to the Lobos and the Hound, hurry,' and he swung his lash at a poor unfortunate standing nearby. 'Captain Osvaldo wants everything shifted and stowed by nightfall.'

It was well after dusk when Leash finally collapsed, exhausted, back in the compound. All day they had trudged with the heavy chests on shoulders or carried between them on makeshift stretchers, passing others along the way with great difficulty on the narrow cliff-top path. And now the treasure was stowed above the oarsmen's pits and on the decks of both ships, under guard of pirates bemused at the sight of so much loot and equally amazed at co-operating with a crew treated previously with great suspicion…if not enmity.

And again Vlad came for Leash, a smirk on his face, evil in his eyes.

But this time Balar was ready and as Vlad bent down to grab the chicken leg from Leash's plate resting in his lap, the demon thrust the sharpened thigh-bone into the big man's eye and using the heel of Leash's hand he hammered it on through into his brain. Vlad screamed and clapped his hands to his face—and everyone watched as the huge man, blood dripping down his face, reeled around the compound in agony until he dropped dead. The silence was heavy and all stared at Leash, not one caring to make a move to help the dying man.

'You bastard, Balar,' Leash said, tears in his eyes.

'You and your merciful ways, Leash, will be the death of both of us.'

358

It was the following morning before Vlad's body was taken away and Leash found himself again on a bench an oar in his hand.

The Lobos was again following the Hound, both ships heavily laden with Osvaldo's treasure, were low in the water. They headed west hugging the coast to Armadillo on a bright morning, riding the swell, pushed along briskly by an easterly wind. Slaves rested at their oars, raising their eyes every now and then to stare at the gold and silks arrayed above their heads, the crates and bales barely allowing room to sit upright.

Nicholas, sitting with Leash at the same rowing station, remained silent. Gunter did not allow talking. He was a firm believer that camaraderie amongst his charges bred rebellion and he walked from stern to prow and back again, continually studying the slaves for any breach of his regulations.

It was mid-afternoon, the eastern promontory of Armadillo bay, its huge beacon built on its highest point to warn the town of danger from other countries' navies, in sight on the horizon. The Lobos slowed to allow the Hound to enter the harbour. Connors was to hand over the required fee to Lonsdale and sealed orders from Osvaldo to the captain of the Serpent. That evening the Serpent was to vacate the dry-dock to be replaced by Bartram's North Star. The Serpent was to stand off at the harbour mouth until morning to hide the Lobos' approach.

'Take in the sails, Mr Cowper, we don't want Lonsdale to see the moonlight reflecting off them,' ordered Osvaldo, 'and tell them to do it quietly, I don't want any sound travelling to shore.'

The Lobos watched the Hound round the headland and enter harbour. Osvaldo wondered fleetingly if Lonsdale would notice how deeply she was riding. But it was too late now to retreat. Jos Osvaldo seethed. All these years he'd put up with the strutting of the island's admiral, principally because Lonsdale was useful, he could keep order amongst the undisciplined inhabitants. His overbearing manner, though, grated on Osvaldo, he should have got rid of him long before now. Well, the man had now asked for it, and the consequences were going to be lethal for him.

But what of this weapon, what had Karnica and Lonsdale called it…a cannon, yes, that was it. He'd never heard of grains that could propel a missile, and he'd never heard of pointy-eared, black men, what had Cowper called them…svartalfar! Who were they? Where had they come from? He'd been tempted to go and ask the Hag before he left home, but knew she'd be incensed at the removal of their treasure. And to actually trust his rival with it—she'd be livid. He had not been in the mood to put up with her tantrums.

He paced the deck for another hour before turning to his mate. 'Cowper, take over, I'm going below to rest. Keep her here; hold this side of the headland. Wake me at dawn with the shore party ready to land.'

The slaves slept. The crew did not, too pent up with the prospect of violence in the morning. They spent their time honing cutlasses as well as the many daggers and pikestaffs. Leather was unwrapped from the handles of cudgels, cleaned and then rebound to ensure a tight grip. And, unlike the crew of the Hound who drank themselves into a frenzy to acquire courage before a fight, the men of the Lobos did not. They were contemptible of those who needed false courage to enter battle. And this was the secret of Osvaldo's success. His men fought stone-cold sober and made every thrust of their blades count. Drunken men just lashed out, most of their strokes wasted their losses greater—and they usually lost the battle.

At dawn all seemed ready. The Serpent, just glimpsed inside the entrance of the harbour, should have been out more towards the sea but the current at that spot was racing. Perhaps her captain was not happy with the uncompleted repairs to allow his ship into faster waters. The North Star should now be in the dry-dock and the Hound alongside the quay. Osvaldo, on the Lobos anchored off the headland, prepared to disembark with his men. It wouldn't take long to cross over the intervening hill. He waited for the signal.

Forty-five

'What happened up there?' Messalina asked, her eyes narrowing, she applied the greasy, green salve to the rope burns on his right hand. Her heart was in her mouth, she knew this man, at least the feel of him though not his features. She knew the sound of his voice though he spoke little in her presence.

'What is that?' he asked staring at the gel she was applying, desperately seeking time to come up with a plausible answer.

'It's the sap of the crocodile tongue plant…very good for burns and other things.'

Elstan did not meet her eyes as he savoured the relief, the burning almost but not quite, disappearing. How could he answer the question truthfully? She'd always been able to catch him out when he lied. There might have been a parting of nearly six years but who was to say her instincts had changed. There seemed to be secrets on both sides in this dormant relationship. Why hadn't she told him, been in contact with him? She could have found him easily, he wasn't always hidden. Carnival people had an intelligence network second to none; Chancellor Sevenoaks used it on many occasions.

He'd used the excuse of pressing work to leave her – she knew a little of his secret work for the chancellor – but he'd been lying and she must have known that. He'd really left because he was ashamed, full of remorse, still was. But looking back on that night he felt stirrings that made him feel even guiltier. Juliana had been a devil that night. Before he'd been with her ten minutes he'd suspected something different, Messalina had never done the things her sister did then. No…it hadn't taken him long to realize who he was with but by then it had been too late. He couldn't stop and neither could she. And in the morning, being the coward he was, he couldn't face the woman he really loved. He made his excuses and run. But would he have, if he'd known what he was leaving?

He'd still had his other work, though, he could not leave that unfinished too many people depended on him. Besides, there was the search. He'd promised himself that he'd go back to her once both were completed. He'd beg her forgiveness for he'd have to tell her. Better it came from him than Juliana.

'Well, are you going to tell me?' she interrupted his thoughts.

'I've lost my gloves, thought I'd manage without them,' not exactly a lie, he had gloves but not ones she'd recognize. Still, he'd been a fool damaging his hands, the tools of his trade.

'Did you mean to flip that fast?'

'I don't know what came over me; once I started I couldn't stop.' He hadn't lied then, that was definitely the truth. He was going to play havoc with Chong's neck once they were alone. 'It was exhilarating, though,' he smiled bleakly.

'Exhilarating! I thought you were trying to fly through the air and when you took one hand off the rope, my heart stopped. I thought you were going to fall. We all did.' Messalina wiped her hands on a towel and replaced the lid on the pot, putting it away in a cupboard she looked at him again.

'For one second, at the beginning, I thought I almost recognized the act, but the man I knew could never have flipped at that speed, even the Myners were amazed.' She sat on the bed alongside him, pursing her lips. 'Where did you learn it and why haven't we ever heard of you? I mean, we carnies are a close-knit community, even though we seldom meet up we do talk of what we've seen when we do.'

Before he could answer and come up with a lie she'd see through, Trinity flew through the door nearly tripping over Elstan's feet.

'Master Chong said I could keep Giddy when we reach Mulkie's Cross, Mama,' her excited voice shrill, her eyes wide. 'Oh, sorry, Master Cenward,' she wrinkled her little nose at the green mess on his hands.

'Trinity, will you be careful, how many times have I told you not to run through the door? What does Master Chong want for the mule, we haven't a lot of coin you know?' she asked suspiciously.

'Nothing…he said its payment for his food and he won't need Giddy when we get to Mulkie's,' she answered rummaging in a box of biscuits on a cupboard.

'Oh,' and she turned to "Cenward" narrowing her eyes, 'is he leaving you when we get there.'

'I don't know what his plans are, like we told Otto, we only met on the road,' he couldn't take his eyes from the little girl, she fascinated him.

'Can I keep him, Mama, please?' she jumped up onto Messalina's lap and hugged her.

'Did he mean it,' she asked, returning her daughter's embrace, 'or did he say it just to shut you up?'

And distracted by Trinity's artfulness in persuading her mother, he looked up quickly and caught Messalina's eye. 'If Chong said it, he meant it,' he answered, hurriedly glancing away.

But it was too late she screwed up her eyes, startled. 'Do I know you?'

'Oh, Mama, don't be silly, we've never seen that nose before,' and she giggled. 'Master Chong said he's loaded all the pots and pans and we're ready to go and Uncle Otto said to move it he's not waiting any longer for you!'

Uncharacteristically silent, Messalina stood up and left the caravan with Trinity following closely. 'Master Chong said I could ride on Giddy with him, Mama, so he could get to know me. He's silly, Giddy already knows me.'

Her voice faded away as Elstan remained sitting on the bedside. He was in trouble, Messalina had always told him he had eyes that she could swim in. His identity would soon come to her. Hopefully it would be after they'd reached the town, for then it wouldn't matter, he and Chong would have left the carnival. But he was deceiving himself again. Of course it would matter—it would matter more than his life. He didn't want to leave her again—or Trinity.

Later that afternoon Chong was lying flat on his back on a mattress in the back of one of Otto's flatbed wagons, his feet raised and resting on a bale of straw. He was fast asleep and snoring loudly. Elstan was sitting on the duckboard, reins in one hand driving the single horse. Smoking his pipe, he kept a wary eye out for pursuers, but his mind dwelt on Messalina and a situation totally unexpected. He was at a loss; he just didn't know what to do. Stay or go, only two options to consider. But was staying an option? He had a mission to complete—and a crazed sorcerer on his tail. He had to go, desert Messalina again…and Trinity. But could he go without telling them? He wanted to return when his job was done—to care for the woman he loved and his daughter.

Although she had not made mention of her suspicions again, he had caught Messalina looking at him on numerous occasions over the last hours. He'd wanted to return her gaze directly but the risk was too great. Despite his abnormally long nose and the disfiguring wart at its end, if she looked for any length of time into his eyes, she'd know him.

Otto strode past the slow moving wagon towards his own caravan leading the procession. He smiled at the pensive man, unable to catch his eye, he wondered if the adulation earned by his extraordinary acrobatics was in some way troubling him. Elstan did not look at all happy.

'You all right, man?' Otto shouted his voice deep and loud.

Elstan looked up. 'Tired that's all and mad at myself for not asking the Myners if I could borrow their gloves.'

Otto laughed and hurried ahead. 'Don't worry about that, as long as your hands are all right tomorrow.' He'd spent all morning enthusing on the new act, promising Elstan all sorts of coin as long as he performed similarly at the festival. Elstan heard him muttering as he climbed up alongside Juliana driving their caravan.

Towards early evening Otto halted the caravan and the circus folk set up camp for the night in open ground off the road nearer the river. Smoke from the houses in Mulkie's Cross was visible in the distance, three or four hours driving. Sitting at Messalina's fire, arranged like her neighbour's on the inner perimeter of the circle of wagons and caravans, Chong heaved one of many sighs of relief as he ate the lamb stew cooked with the exotic spices purchased in Jasper. He relished the respite from the bouncing wagon exacerbating the hurts in his spine. He dreaded the continuation of the journey in the morning, knowing that the wagon was the only viable alternative to his feet aching as they swung either side of the mule. He'd relinquished the mule earlier that day into the safekeeping of Trinity and would probably do so again on the morrow, having been forced to ride in the wagon again.

Putting his empty bowl down on the ground alongside his stool, he heaved himself to his feet with the aid of his staff and shuffled off slowly between the wagons to relieve himself behind bushes at the river. Returning, he heard a disturbance from down the road. Peering from behind tall reeds he heard the harsh rasping of their enemy. Drudwynn was berating his men. And despite the pain, the sudden rush of adrenalin enabled Chong to reach Elstan swiftly. The chancellor's agent was sitting with his back against the wagon, brooding. Chong dragged the silent man to his feet and between the caravans.

'What the hell, Chong, what's up now?' he asked bleary eyed, for the first time all day he'd nearly managed to get Messalina out of his head.

'Listen...do you hear that?' Chong asked, cocking his head towards the southern end of the road.

At that moment there was a shrill scream and loud shouting, and Drudwynn rode through and into the centre of the circle of wagons. With him came his three remaining guards, Sergeant Brom dragging a little girl, forcing her to run to keep up with him, her little hands clasped around the big hand entwined in her hair.

'Dear God, that's Trinity! What's the mad bastard doing now?' Elstan shouted frantically.

'I'm afraid the man is beyond madness, my friend. He has no intention of searching the circus for us, he's going to demand our surrender or he'll kill her. And there's not a blind thing we can do but comply, unless...'

'Unless what?' Elstan stared at him wild-eyed.

'We make a break for it—let Drudwynn see us fleeing; he might let her go then.'

'I wouldn't bank on it.' Elstan quieted. 'Chong, grab our bags and hide in the river, in the water upstream. I'll find you later.'

'What are you going to do?'

'I can't risk him killing her. Look...' and he stared at his friend all hope gone from his face, 'there's no need for both of us to surrender. I'll go out there, walk up to him, you never know I might get lucky, get a chance to stick him with this,' and he tapped the misericorde in his left armpit.

'You're fantasizing. You'll never get near him, what do think those guards are for. Besides he's a sorcerer, all he's got to do is lift his hand and you won't be able to move a step. Anyway, he wants me as well...probably more so.'

'God, I can't even get at my crossbow in the wagon. I can't reach it to shoot him without those guards seeing me.' He dragged his hand across his eyes, sweat dripping from his brow. 'She's my daughter, Chong, my daughter!'

'I'd guessed as much, she looks a lot like you and it explains your silences. Right,' and Chong rubbed his hands together, 'now you wait a minute, my friend, this calls for subtlety. You grab our bags I haven't the strength to run with them,' and he raised his staff. 'Go, man, you cannot aid me in this.'

'You don't honestly think I'm going to leave her, do you? I tell you what, you kill the mad bastard…the guards are mine. Quickly, while we're arguing they're hurting her.'

Chong moved to the inner end of Messalina's caravan and peered around the tailgate, he took the situation in at a glance. Drudwynn was astride his horse in the centre of the camp, his broken arm strapped to his chest. Standing at the stallion's head was Brom, his hand still gripping the long hair of Trinity as the girl knelt at his feet sobbing. Gil, also with his arm strapped to his chest, stood the other side of the horse, sword in hand. The third guard stood behind the horse, sword unsheathed, watching their rear.

But the noise had roused Messalina resting in her caravan. She opened the door at the rear and climbing down she came up unnoticed behind Elstan and Chong. Looking over their shoulders she couldn't believe her eyes; she screamed and tried to push past Elstan.

He wheeled around and immediately grabbed her around the waist from behind. 'Wait,' and as she struggled to break free he shouted in her ear, unthinkingly using his pet name for her. 'Wait, Sal, we have it in hand, Chong is a wizard, he's going to use his magic.'

'She spun in his arms jolted out of her fear at the name he'd used. 'What did you call me?'

'Sh!' Chong ordered sharply. 'We waste time, watch and run for her when I give the word.' He raised his staff and commenced the incantation just as the giant ringmaster stepped in front of him obstructing Chong's line of sight.

Chong halted the spell when Otto spoke, the tension among the carnies eliciting a silence promising violence at the slightest provocation, a violence that would result in their deaths. For no way could they battle a sorcerer and win.

'What do you want, Brother? We have done nothing to harm the Guild.'

'No? Then why do you harbour the Guild's enemies?' Drudwynn smiled maniacally, the graze on his face pulling down his right eyelid making him appear even more evil. He glanced down at his captive. 'Hand them over immediately or she dies.'

'Who, Brother? We are carnival people, gathered together from all over the known world to perform at Kaneshi's Festival in Mulkie's Cross. If your enemy is among us, then search for him, it's no good asking us, most of us don't even know each other.'

'You have a mule in your string I recognize, this child was on its back. I am its owner. The thieves are my enemies.'

Otto sucked in his breath knowing immediately who Drudwynn meant. He looked around quickly, not seeing either Elstan or Chong; he licked his lips and shuffled forward hoping to get close enough to grab Trinity. He walked towards Sergeant Brom, his arms out to his side.

'Please, Brother, this girl is my niece, it's not her fault she has taken a liking to a strange mule. I now know your enemies, release her and we'll all help you apprehend them.' With that he turned sideways to again look into the crowd hoping to see the fugitives, not wanting to give them up, but having no option.

But his movement opened a line of sight for Chong. Before Otto could turn and once again look at Drudwynn, people screamed. A horde of rattlesnakes appeared from beneath the surface of the ground and slithered towards the captors. Otto instinctively retreated, revealing a full view of the man on the horse. The horse reared; terrified it bucked Drudwynn from its back. He was knocked unconscious when he landed on his head. The horse bringing its forelegs to earth again abruptly kicked out with its hind legs and the guard standing too close behind, caught both hoofs in his thorax. He landed some feet away dead before he hit the ground, his ribcage caved in.

Brom and Gil stared goggle-eyed at the reptiles making for them and, releasing Trinity, the sergeant drew his sword and both men attacked the snakes, slicing them in bits. But Chong hadn't finished for as each reptile was cut so each severed piece swam together. The snake reformed and continued its attack.

At Chong's nod, Messalina ran through the mass of wriggling reptiles and, picking up Trinity in shaking arms, she fled into the crowd.

Chong and Elstan fled into the river, the two fugitives wading north. It wasn't long before they stole a boat, to the immense relief of the oriental, the cold water was purgatory.

During that night, just on a week's travelling from Jasper, the oriental wizard and his occidental friend reached the outskirts of Mulkie's Cross.

They delayed their arrival at Elstan's safe haven until the early hours of the morning. They left the boat moored in amongst other boats to conceal its whereabouts, just in case their pursuers discovered their means of escape. Elstan and Chong-An slinked along in the shadows of tall buildings and along dark alleyways towards the centre of the town. Those townsfolk they encountered, even that time of the morning, took little notice of more strangers. The town was inundated with country people in for the festival and with the normal travellers on the road. Reaching his destination, Elstan persuaded Chong to find concealment behind the very quiet tavern. He then went off to wake the innkeeper and search for Chong's contact.

Chong-An sat exhausted behind another spell of illusion, at the foot of the low wall at the rear of the Drovers Bar. He grimaced through his pain though he was feeling smugly proud of himself. He'd thought several times that he'd never make it to the town; the pain in his limbs had become almost unbearable. But he'd persevered and with the aid of his crutch and his staff, Elstan's strong back and the mule, he'd made it down off the mountain. And then the never-ending journey to Mulkie's Cross, pummelled by the motion of the wagon, had been completed by stealing the boat to travel upriver. He smiled. The last part had been the easiest. Elstan had done all the rowing while he'd slept.

Elstan brooded as he walked the town. What was Messalina thinking now? She'd known him at the end because of a slip of the tongue—Sal. Would she forgive him for deceiving her…once again? But he and Chong had rescued his daughter, his lovely Trinity. His heart bled. Would he ever see either of them again?

He halted at the corner of an alley where it joined a wide street and leant against the wall with his hands in his pockets. His options were now decidedly limited. He had to follow the magus into the Drikander for Chong might very well be correct in his assumption that the forest was, in all likelihood, the venue for Brenin's meeting with his agent on the Emperor's Council. He just hoped the meeting had not already taken place on the road up from the south. If it had, then there was nothing to be done about it now. But maybe he could determine the exact relationship between Brenin and Bartraz. Elstan had long suspected that an alliance existed between the Guild of the Brethren of Wisdom and the Drikander tribes led by Bartraz. If the rendezvous was not at Llyshame, the home village of Bartraz, then Elstan had to follow Brenin along the mystical paths through the forest to Abferkarn. For there, surely, the identity of the traitor would be discovered and the ultimate aims of the magus become known at last.

Back at the wall Chong was also examining his options. He also had his immediate future mapped out for him, a chart that showed no possibility of any diversion. He had not forgotten his need to get to Miskim in northern Mantovar. He was – as others in the past – being called to that town. But unlike those aimless wanderers of the past, Chong-An knew he was to search for an artefact. The prophecies intimated as much. And locating the relic was the most important task of his centuries-long life. How it was to benefit mankind and all the other races on this earth he did not know, that knowledge was yet to be ascertained. But to find the relic he needed Elstan, the Fly, agent of the Chancellor of Mantovar, for the man possibly knew its location. Elstan was a native of Miskim and, even if he didn't actually recognize what he knew as ancient magic, he knew of something unusual in the town, knew enough to be scared witless by it.

But first, Elstan had to help him get to the Green People's library in the Drikander. There he could obtain the rest of the prophecies and then move on to Abferkarn. But then it would be Chong's turn to help his friend discover the identity of the traitor advising the emperor. With the documents in Chong's hands, the spy known—both could proceed north.

'The fool has got himself into serious trouble,' said Elstan suddenly dropping alongside the wizard, it was now mid-morning the sun well up in the blue sky.

Chong jumped and an involuntary groan broke from his lips. 'Dear God, don't do that again! You frightened the life out of me…you nearly sat on me, be careful.' He stretched his hands out to his feet but didn't touch them, he was too afraid to.

'Sorry, I didn't see you until I was up close, that illusion's pretty good someday you are going to have to teach me how to do it. Anyway I thought you wizards had no problems detecting people.'

'Normally I wouldn't, but as you can see I'm not feeling too good. Tell me, how am I supposed to teach you how to conjure magic you aren't a wizard?'

'There's magic in my family,' he answered softly.

'Is there?' Chong's head came up sharply. Something else this man had surprised him with.

'Never mind, perhaps we'll talk of it later,' Elstan stretched his legs out in front of him and closed his eyes a moment. Another slip of the tongue, he thought, one of these days he was going to say too much.

Chong settled back against the wall. 'All right, what trouble is the "fool" in?'

'Oh, he's only being executed tomorrow for heresy.'

'Heresy?' Chong said, startled.

'Aye, he's been passing himself off as a pardoner for Kaneshi and approached the wrong people. I am told it was easy to trap him, the idiot. He's not a pardoner is he?' and Chong shook his head. 'Well, he only tried to sell one to a priest of Kaneshi. That priest has now arraigned him for blaspheming against the God of Disease and Despair.'

'Dear God, I've heard of him being mixed up in some wild schemes before, but that takes the biscuit. But first things first, we'll worry about him later, can you find a healer without Cledwyn's help?'

'Yes, my friend, I can and I have,' he stood and held out his hands to help Chong to his feet. 'We've been lucky; I bumped into the best healer in Drakka, an adept in the art of healing. He's down here on business. He also happens to be a supporter of Sevenoaks. I've used him many times in the past, he's very discreet. And he has another thing in his favour as well. He hates the Guild and all it stands for.'

'Why?' Chong interrupted.

'What?'

'Why does this healer hate the Guild?'

'Ah! The Guild has an abhorrence of lepers, does it not,' and at Chong's unspoken acknowledgement he went on. 'Well, this healer has spent his whole life in leprosaria doing his damndest to heal the victims of the foul disease and at the same time trying to stop the Guild from killing them. He is now waiting inside this tavern very impatiently. He's all dressed up to go to a meeting with the local bigwigs. So, my friend, while he's administering to you I'm going to relax and have a few ales,' and he asked again. 'Are you sure we really need this Cledwyn?'

'Yes, Elstan, for he knows the way to the library.'

'He does? How come you don't, you've been there many times, so you said.'

'Come off it, you know the Drikander–the Grekkos keep changing the direction of the pathways. Cledwyn has the knack of bypassing their magic, knowledge that I should have because he's always promising to teach me, but he always finds an excuse not to.

370

Sometimes I think he has his own magic. The ability to unravel magical illusions is, in itself, very powerful.'

'Bloody hell,' Elstan laughed derisively, 'he didn't know the difference between a priest of Kaneshi and an ordinary townsman. And yet he knows how to read Grekko magic. This man must really be something. Perhaps he knows how we can rescue him from a lynch mob of hundreds?' Elstan threw his arms in the air, exasperated. 'I've changed my mind I'm going to down a jar of brandy...I think better when I'm drunk.'

Chong-An lay on the bed in the dingy upstairs room of the rundown Drovers Bar studying the man preparing to use his skills on the swollen flesh of his feet. The healer flexing his fingers, though, was definitely not rundown. His raiment was that of a man of substance, a tall, middle-aged man of reckoning within the town. He was arrayed in a red silk waistcoat and a white ruffled silk shirt over blue cotton leggings and he had placed carefully over the back of the only chair in the room, a heavy dark-blue cloak trimmed with gold brocade.

'What have we here, Elstan, another of your miscreants?'

'He is a friend, Makepeace, a very good friend and I'd be obliged if you'd minister to his hurts good and quick, we have a long way to go.'

'Yes...and some not very nice people chasing you I hear.'

'News travels fast.' Elstan said preparing to help the physician remove Chong's boots.

'Like you, I have spies everywhere, not that I needed them in this case,' he laughed. 'You caused quite a stir at the circus camp yesterday. Brother Drudwynn has concussion and his arm is going to take weeks to mend. He's placed a rather large sum of money on your heads.'

'He came to you?'

'No...I went to him. Being the man he is, he had to have the best treatment did he not? Though it will be slow healing, he would not allow me entrance to his head. But the cretin hasn't paid me, mind,' he grimaced. 'And I'm unlikely to seek recompense. Come to think of it, he probably won't pay the reward either. Now, I'm afraid my man, we are going to have to cut these boots from your feet, your ankles have swelled over the top...very nasty...very painful. And I'm mortified to say it but you're in for a lot more pain when the support of the boot is removed. Hopefully it won't be for too long.'

'I can't allow you entrance into my mind either, I'm afraid,' Chong said.

'I've learnt over the years not to satisfy my curiosity where Elstan's cohorts are concerned. In fact I actively engage in ignoring your secrets, it's safer for me. But because of your stipulation you must follow my instructions to the letter or you'll never heal.'

'You can save my feet?' Chong asked.

'Well, I don't believe the green sickness is in them yet, I can't smell it. You're lucky. Did you get the brandy, Elstan?'

'Of course, I well know how you work.'

'Good, a large one for me please, and a smaller one for our friend here.'

'A small one, healer? I think I'm going to need a very large one,' Chong interrupted, a tremor in his voice as Makepeace's fingers dug into the flesh around his ankle.

'You may very well think that, and possibly a large one would work miracles for your constitution, but I don't want to risk you spewing over my new clothes. I have a reception to attend after I've seen to you. Allow me to introduce myself as our ignorant friend has neglected the niceties,' he said as he commenced delicately cutting the leather of the boots with an extremely sharp razor. 'My name is Athelstan Makepeace and I am an Adept, the premier healer for Mulkie's Cross. Please,' he held up his hand quickly to stop Chong speaking, 'I do not wish to know your name. I've a feeling our mutual adversary from the Tower may well ask me and if I don't know who I'm healing, he can't detect a lie.'

'I am a man of the East…you won't be able to hide that.'

'Then I must ensure I do nothing to alert his suspicions,' and he dropped the first boot to the floor, the clatter accompanied by Chong's agonized groan as the bones in his foot spread, no longer restricted by an over tight sheath of leather.

Chong and Elstan watched closely as the master healer of the First Order of Physicians went about his work, with just the occasional pitiful moan from the patient. Setting the healing in place took nearly two hours and by the time Makepeace had manipulated the slipped disk in his spine back into place Chong was worn out. And so was the healer.

'Am I correct in believing that Brenin is also on his way here?' Makepeace asked washing his hands in a bowl on the side-table. 'I have heard rumours of many meetings between him and others on the road.'

'Ah, I was wondering why he was such a long time getting here. I thought he'd have reached Mulkie's ahead of us,' Elstan frowned. Was one of the meetings with the traitor?

Forty-six

Thaddeus opened his eyes to a damp and dreary world. The room seemed to be a shed built to house tools though there were none anywhere in sight. It was dark, the only light leaking through chinks in the board walls, came from a lantern outside the door.

He heard a rat scuttling about in the corner and tried to communicate with it. Failing, it deepened his depression and he tried to cast around searching for other life forms but only glimpsed a spider up in a corner of the roof. He wondered if Augusta was afraid of the insects, like Beatrix.

Thinking of Beattie he wondered if Anders had been able to tell her and Aidan of their predicament. His mouth dried abruptly and he felt a flicker of fear run down his spine. What if Anders didn't know? But surely he must have been watching them. Aidan had told him to keep an eye on them. Then again Anders had problems seeing anything in a tunnel and all Thaddeus' instincts told him he was underground somewhere. Nonetheless, the only tunnels in Meltwater were mineshafts and by the look of this shed, it was a long abandoned mine.

He looked down at Augusta fast asleep in his arms and his heart filled with love and his head with misery. She was Aidan's. He was not going to steal his friend's girl; Aidan had more than saved his life. He had rescued him and his mother from the hell of the Darkness. And seeing his mother enter the Light after fifteen years, Thaddeus would be forever grateful.

He stroked Augusta's hair, taking it from her eyes where it had fallen. Having her nestling in his arms, her head on his chest, he wanted to hug her even tighter, but was afraid to disturb her in case she sat up. But stir her he had to, the bench was very hard and he ached in muscles he didn't know he had. Both had lain on the seat, it was just wide enough for both of them, huddling together all night for warmth and comfort. It was hours before they eventually fell asleep exhausted, mortally afraid of what the future might hold for them. And desperately attempting to become accustomed to living without their magic, both knowing they never could.

Augusta awoke, but didn't open her eyes as she lay at ease against Thaddeus. Thinking over the previous night's events she now knew what people meant when they said that you never missed what you never had. Up until a few weeks ago she had not had magic and therefore had not missed it. But now there was an empty feeling in her belly, an ache in her chest and bewilderment in her head. The ability had disappeared so unexpectedly for a moment she wondered if it had been her fault, if it was something she had done. The magic was there one minute and gone the next. But the more she thought, the more she became confused and her head ached even more.

She surreptitiously touched with her finger the red disk moulded to the contours of her left palm, receiving reassurance from it. It seemed that even losing her magic did not lessen the knowledge that the glove belonged with her. She had no idea of its purpose and was faintly perturbed that it was called a war gauntlet. She didn't want to kill, not after Aidan explaining the consequences to her soul if she did. Nevertheless, the only gauntlets she'd ever seen in her life were what her father and his army of knights wore…long mail gloves reaching well past their wrist. They bore no resemblance to this one moulded to her hand.

Not wanting Thaddeus to move she remained perfectly still, feigning sleep. She felt safe with his arms around her.

Nonetheless, her mind was in turmoil thinking back over the last day. She'd definitely had magic when she'd accepted the gauntlet—she'd felt the glove calling her. Or was she mistaken? But no, she remembered her hand automatically reaching for it as soon as she discovered it on the shelf. She remembered the heady feeling of completeness as she pulled it on her hand. So the loss was incurred after that. Nothing untoward had occurred when they rode through the town. She recalled the tension in the air, the black looks of some of the people, mostly armed men, they'd passed. But the townspeople hadn't done anything, she'd felt threatened but that was all. Then dismounting and walking through the door of the Town Hall—and oblivion. Was it the knock on her head or had Razor done something when they were unconscious? But how could he—he knew nothing of magic.

She lay in the circle of Thaddeus' arms, pressed up against his side she could feel his chest rising and falling, the rhythm and his warmth calming her fears. She didn't open her eyes when he stroked the hair from her face. She didn't want to destroy the moment, feeling his eyes on her she smiled and snuggled in closer. She forgot Aidan for a while.

Thaddeus tore his eyes from her face and examined the shed more minutely in the light leaking in between gaps in the boards. It was dreadfully cold and smelled abominably. There was some straw on the floor, not changed for months, but who would renew straw on a shed's floor. Large enough to hold at least four more prisoners, it had only the one bench and the bucket in the corner. It was foul-smelling now, they'd both been forced to use it the night before, each affording the other privacy by standing at the door and facing it, trying not to listen to nature's noises. No-one had disturbed them all night except for Lewyn's cat which kept appearing at odd moments to rub its coat against them, leaving even more hair clinging to their dirty clothes.

Thaddeus watched from the corner of his eye as the cat arrived again by pushing its way through the small hole down in the corner. He'd examined the aperture the night before by feeling with his hands and had managed to break off a little piece… and tore his finger in the process. He had hopes that he could enlarge it more but, at Augusta warning him that Razor would wonder why he was bleeding, decided to wait. Their captors would surely not starve them so they'd give it another go later.

The cat strutted over to them, its green eyes unblinking when it returned Thaddeus' stare. It unnerved him. For the first time since he'd returned to his body he didn't want to read the sensations of an animal. And as he looked at the tortoiseshell he shivered, there was something unearthly about it, something not quite right, but he couldn't put his finger on it. His eyes were drawn to its back legs, having one perfectly white paw on a variegated brown body looked very strange…and it seemed to lope not walk.

Augusta stirred eventually, aching, she couldn't stay still any longer and they both sat up when she felt the cat rub against her leg. 'That blasted thing! Look its moulting so much its leaving most of its coat on us,' and she stretched her cramped muscles and tried to brush the fur off her leggings. But most of it stayed, some clinging to the short golden hairs on her arms and catching in the straps of her gauntlet.

Staring at it Thaddeus noticed a bald spot on its side. 'It's too affectionate for my liking and it's not natural to lose that much fur in one place. It may be diseased.'

'It's creepy like its master,' and she pushed it away. 'You know, I can't get it out of my mind, but I was sure that cat was dead.' she said pushing it away again as it jumped up on the bench.

'What do you mean? It looks lively enough to me.'

'Yes, but…it was just after Aidan started healing those people on the dock. That woman you spoke to when you were making your speech, Dyta…well, we were fetching water and nearly fell over a dead tortoiseshell cat. It was lying not far from the water barrel so we kicked the body into the gutter. We both thought that was Lewyn's cat.'

'Well it wasn't, 'cos that there cat is mine,' laughed Cyryl Lewyn, his face pressed up against a gap in the shed door. He juggled the key in the lock and flung the door open wide. 'Don't make any false move or I'll skewer you,' he warned, brandishing a long, evil-looking dagger.

'Out of the way, Lewyn,' Razor said pushing him roughly to the inside wall alongside the door. 'Well, idiot, I'm glad to see you've had a good night,' he said staring right at Thaddeus.

'Don't you dare…' Augusta started to say.

'Shut up, girl, this is man's talk,' and he smirked, 'not for little girls.'

'Be courteous, Razor, or you'll be sorry,' Thaddeus stood, his hands forming fists at his side, ready to lunge at either of their two captors.

'You are the ones to be sorry, and if you want to get out of here alive you will do as I say.'

'You can't kill your prince, Razor, too many people know he's here,' said Augusta. 'When Bazyli arrives he'll put an end to you.'

'If he arrives, you mean. It's a long way here, a long and dangerous road in places. But you needn't worry. My men have already told me he's on his way, left Griffin Town sometime yesterday afternoon after he'd stirred up the Montetors on the coast. I've been told there's a very long line of refugees making for the catacombs, all those who haven't left by sea. Bazyli's a fool listening to you and your stories of gibberish.'

'They aren't gibberish, Razor, and if you had any sense you'd know what I said was the truth. I don't speak nonsense. The Darkness is on its way and the demons within it will kill everyone they catch. We saw the black fog as we rode into town and you'd see it too if you went and looked to the horizon beyond the harbour.' Thaddeus fell silent, keeping one eye on Lewyn's dagger, hoping for a chance to overthrow the little bald man. But in his head he knew that without his magic he didn't stand a hope in hell of beating Razor, the vastly experienced street brawler.

Razor laughed when he perceived his prince's blatant intention and he withdrew his misericorde from his belt. 'Don't even think about it, brat. You'd be dead before you took one step and your girlfriend wouldn't be long behind you. I didn't earn my name for nothing,' and he tapped the point of the very narrow blade at a spot just below his right eye. 'I've seen your so-called Darkness. I looked last night; the fog was almost at the harbour mouth. And that's just what it is—fog. By this time it'll be in the town, but there's nothing new in that, we've always had fog rolling in from the sea. This is an island, its normal weather. The only difference is this time it just seems a little thicker that's all, nothing to worry about.'

'But it's not fog,' shouted Augusta, her face ashen.

'Yes it is! And that's what the high and mighty prince here is going to tell the townsfolk of Meltwater tomorrow,' he grinned at Thaddeus. 'You will also have to inform them of Bazyli's untimely death—and that he wished me to succeed him as the new Montetor.'

'You are going to kill Bazyli? But you can't he's done nothing wrong. He has always put the clan first, you know that,' Augusta said frantically.

'He won't be very easy to murder,' said Thaddeus, his mouth dry. If Razor's insane ambitions succeeded, with Bazyli's death then there was no protection against the Darkness for the Montetors. Fear made him tremble; he knew that without his magic there was no way he could escape to save his uncle.

'Take my word for it, the matter is already in hand. You forget—Bazyli trusts me; he will not be expecting an assassin.' And then Razor lost his temper. 'Bazyli is a fool for listening to you. His time on Sanctity has more than addled his brain, you…you must have done something to him,' and for a moment he looked to have tears in his eyes. 'He's not fit to be clan leader any longer; he's betrayed us to those green devils.' He ceased his ranting and stared at the floor until his composure returned.

Meeting the mania in Razor's cold eyes, Thaddeus knew there was no way they were going to change this man's mind. The disappointment at his loss of the inheritance had tipped him over the edge. The man was no longer sane.

'It will be the easiest thing in the world to kill Bazyli, as it was to capture you two…and you are supposed to be wizards. Some wizards, hey,' he laughed contemptuously and glanced at Lewyn grinning foolishly in the corner. 'Why haven't you used your magic to escape?' he sniggered. 'Just goes to prove that you're both liars, if you can lie about being wizards you can lie about this Darkness.'

'We are wizards!' shouted Augusta.

'Prove it,' retorted Razor. 'Go on use your magic, try and silence me that should be easy enough. You can't can you,' he sneered when there was no reaction from his prisoners.

'I…something's happened to us, we seem to have lost our magic. But it won't be for long, Razor. No wizard loses his magic forever. And Lord Aidan will come after us, soon,' Augusta said finishing lamely, and then even more strongly she added. 'You cannot doubt that he is a wizard.'

At that moment the ground beneath their feet began to shake. Lewyn, scared, gripped the wall. Razor spread his legs and rode the tremor as if he was on the deck of a ship and Augusta grabbed hold of Thaddeus. The floor steadied with a last violent rumble.

'What was that,' Thaddeus asked.

'Don't worry it's only the river running below here. That's why this mine was abandoned in the first place—the floor ain't too safe,' and he laughed. 'The last miners sunk iron rods to test for the river's roof. They ran when one rod fell straight through the floor. You'd better hope you don't disappear the same way.'

'They might, Razor, an' all. That's the worst I've felt it,' said Lewyn rubbing his arms nervously.

'Ah, shut up. If they do go it'll save us the job of killing them.'

'Aidan will rescue us before you can do that,' Thaddeus warned.

'No chance, he doesn't even know where you are. Besides, if he really believes that fog is the Darkness then he'll be trapped underground with all those refugees blocking the entrance to the catacombs. And then he'll have all his time taken up with healing the victims of the plague. For as sure as your God made little apples, the plague is now rife amongst the people of Griffin. Because you…you brought it here. He'll never keep it out of Bylani. But, even if he does manage to get to the surface and you are correct, then he will also be trapped in your so-called Darkness. He won't get here before the fog reaches us and when it does—it will prove your lie.'

'We are not lying! Listen to us, the demons will kill everyone,' Thaddeus shouted, knowing it was futile to continue the argument. But he lost his temper and acted completely against his nature. He kicked the cat across the cell, its constant rubbing against his legs seriously annoying him.

'Oi! Leave my Hyacinth alone, she's not harming you,' said Lewyn picking up the uninjured cat and stroking it. It snarled at the prisoners, its eyes unblinking.

'You have the rest of today, Highness,' Razor mocked, 'to make up your mind. When you stand before the Montetors and tell them what I've said, you will make them believe it. You will do as I say or your girlfriend dies before your eyes,' and smiling maniacally he waved his misericorde in their faces before turning away.

'But they know Thaddeus is their prince and has been named as first King of Griffin, they'll never believe Bazyli changed his mind about that,' said Augusta.

'Some will, enough already waver in their beliefs especially when I told them that Prince Griffin is responsible for bringing the plague ashore,' he laughed. 'People weren't too happy about having a wizard for a king anyway, and now that the plague is ashore it was highly unlikely, anyway, that he'd ever be crowned.' Razor, chuckling loudly, turned and walked out the door, Lewyn and his cat followed, immediately locking the door behind them.

'What the hell!' startled, Thaddeus looked at Augusta.

'What is it?'

'Well…for one moment I thought that cat smiled at me. God, the ground shaking like that frightened the life out of me. I'm being stupid; this place is really getting to me.'

'No, it's they are the stupid ones,' said Augusta as they heard their captors walk away down the passage.

'Insane fools. God, I hope Anders heard every word of that and tells Aidan,' said Thaddeus slumping back down on the bench.

'He will have, the trouble is though Aidan is deep in Bylani. He'll never get to the surface in time to save Bazyli, even if we knew how Razor intends killing him.'

'Aye, and if the Darkness is in Griffin Town now, it'll be in Meltwater in two days. God, what's happened to our magic?' He put out his arm for Augusta and they both sat without saying another word, again taking comfort from each other. But this time a little guilt crept into the back of Thaddeus' mind as he held Augusta. Aidan would never understand or condone the pleasure that Thaddeus was feeling just holding the girl. 'Come on; let's see if we can work on that hole in the wall.'

Thaddeus knelt at the wall while Augusta sat on the floor with her back to it, her arms on her knees. He struggled to remove another small piece of the board but it was heavy going. The board had rotted near the floor but higher up it was still solid and he couldn't shift it. He gave up eventually and sat alongside Augusta staring silently at the bench opposite her.

'It's no good the timber's too thick to break.' Receiving no comment he glanced at her face. 'What are you looking at?' he asked breathing heavily.

'There's something glinting under the bench. Look, it's right at the back, poking out of the ground,' and she scrambled across to it and started tugging at it. 'Help me, it won't move.'

'What is it?'

'It feels like an iron bar or something. Perhaps it's one of them rods Razor was on about, that tremor must have moved it. Maybe we can use it to pry that board loose.'

'Strange place to test the ground, isn't it, under the bench?'

'Don't be silly this bench must have been put here afterwards.'

'Wait, I'll see if I can drag some earth from around it,' and he stretched out on the floor with his head beneath the bench. 'Keep jerking it, it's loosening the soil.'

Later that day three men stood in front of Razor. The traitor sat at Bazyli's desk in the Montetor's office on the second floor of the red, stone built Town Hall.

Cyryl Lewyn and his cat sat on a bench behind him, Lewyn still smarting over the treatment meted out to his cat. He'd had "Hyacinth", as he'd named her, ever since she was a kitten and they were inseparable. He smoothed her coat as she lay on his shoulder purring in his ear, allaying her master's fears. It was almost as if she could read Lewyn's mind for the man was puzzled. He couldn't remember her having a white paw or moulting as much as this, but her obvious happiness reassured him. He held up his hand and studied the tortoiseshell hairs in his fingers, frowning at the cat's bald patch. She must be coming down with something, he thought, and being kicked wouldn't help her. He raged—he wanted revenge on her attacker.

Razor played incessantly with his misericorde, tapping it below his eye, rubbing it against his nose and picking his teeth with it. He smiled inwardly, knowing that each of the calculated movements unnerved his cohorts even more than did his grey, dead eyes. Alvar and Godun shuffled their feet, nervously glancing away, cringing every now and then, their leader, Lyell, stared at Razor unflinching. Lyell was a hard man in his forties, a long-time opponent of Bazyli Montetor. He had his own reasons for wanting revenge on his leader. He was also the smartest of the three despite having a liking for naxix and "bludgeon" the rotgut brandy brewed illicitly on the island.

'You know the spot, it will be nearly full dark when he gets there,' and Razor threw a purse on the table, it jingled as it landed. 'The first half now the rest when you come back in the morning with his head. You don't see any problems with the job…do you? You will be able to do it?' he asked threateningly.

'No problem…it'll be a pleasure, I've wanted to do this ever since he flung me in the cells ten years ago,' answered Lyell.

'You were lucky; if he could have proved murder he'd have slung you in the Quota and we'd have been waving goodbye as you sailed for Sanctity. Go, all of you and don't fail me or you'll never see another daylight.'

When the three had departed through the door, Razor turned to Lewyn. 'Follow and let me know what happens,' he glared. 'I'll need time to make other arrangements if they fail. Be back here well before noon or else…understand?'

'Don't worry, Razor, depend on it. If they're not up to it Hyacinth and me'll finish him off,' he gloated. 'We'll have the gold then, won't we?'

Razor nodded and glanced askance at the animal. He always became uneasy when Lewyn mentioned his cat as if it was an ally he could rely on.

Anders, at the wall of colours, had heard every word in the shed. *'Aidan you have no choice, Bazyli is going to be killed tonight and tomorrow sometime Thaddeus and Augusta are going to be forced to deny the truth about the Darkness—and then they'll also be killed. Razor can't afford to let either of them live.'*

'I can't get to Bazyli in time you know that,' Aidan said desperately. 'It would take me at least a day to get to the surface, all right half a day on a krynx, yes, but it'll still take me a full day to intercept Bazyli.'

'But we can get to Thaddeus and Augusta before the morning, Aidan,' said Beattie equally despairing. 'We can't let Razor kill them, they're…they're our friends.'

'I'm not saying I'm going to let him, Beattie. I love them just like you but…but I love Tragen as well…oh God!' he held his head in his hands and wept. 'I'm never going to rescue him, am I?'

'Yes we will, I promise you. We've no need to go to the manorhouse to make the transition into Limbo. Hopper's told us that Cornelia and Alessa are at the entrance to the catacombs, they'll be here shortly. They can watch over us in Leon's home. And that gives us time to get to Meltwater tonight, rescue Thaddeus and Augusta and get back here by noon. We can go after Tragen tomorrow afternoon, Aidan, and nothing will stop us this time. I promise you.'

That's cutting it fine. It's not going to be that easy to get them out of that shed. I never saw the entrance to the mine but there's bound to be heavy locked doors between you and them. And what's to say that there's nothing in that mine that could take your magic? Something took theirs. But I promise you as well, Aidan. Tomorrow we search the Darkness, whatever happens,' said Anders, ceasing his whittling. He dreaded the task and for just a moment followed Razor's habit of tapping his misericorde against his face.

'Well, don't forget this…we're wizards. Thaddeus and Augusta were unconscious when they lost their magic, they had no warning. I don't believe we will lose our magic, Beattie, without us realizing it. So we'll go careful. Razor has no chance against us,' he squeezed her hand reassuringly. 'Adler can you get Everard to take us to the cavern below Meltwater?' Aidan asked sighing with relief that this was the last delay anyone was going to impose on him before he went for Tragen. 'We'll go through that mineshaft in the roof.' He still had misgivings but locked them away in the back of his mind. He denied the feeling that something else was bound to crop up, he shook it off—nothing was going to stop him this time. 'Whatever happens we go after Tragen tomorrow,' he warned Beattie and Anders.

Adler nodded, the one-sided conversation he was hearing was confusing but he got the gist. 'Yes, I can get you there within hours. But how are you going to access the mineshaft?'

'Use what I did when I got my wand—levitate of course,' said Beatrix, her relief at going to free Augusta and Thaddeus bringing a grin to her face. 'But we'll have another problem that only you and your people can deal with.'

'What's that?'

'Anders has told us that no move has been made to evacuate the people of Meltwater. They will not now have time to reach the catacombs before the Darkness engulfs the town. You will have to bring them here through the same mineshaft we'll be using to enter the town. And you'll have to bring them down into the cavern.'

'Can you do that?' asked Aidan.

'Yes, of course, I'll gather helpers, enough to levitate them to safety. We can use the platforms we work from when we're reinforcing the roofs of the caves. Oh, saying that we may have to make a few more, I'll run now and make arrangements while I get Everard. I won't be long,' and then he hesitated. 'Hector really has succeeded with Primrosa, hasn't he; I mean there's no fear of her succumbing to the plague again?' Aidan smiled his assurance. Adler's face flushed with unshed tears of relief as he took a hasty look at his sleeping wife, kissed her forehead and rushed from his home.

'Anders, try and locate Bazyli. I know there's nothing you can do, but let us know what's happening with him, will you?'

'Shite! I don't want to watch him being murdered. I like him, he's a decent man,' he hesitated. *'All right, I'll do as you say.'*

'Good, but let's hope it doesn't come to that. As you say, he's not going to be very easy to kill.' He turned to the salamander basking in the heat on the hearth in front of the fire. 'Hector, can you organize your friends to help those others struck down with the plague?'

'Of course, it's already in hand.'

'Thank you, I'm not sure what we'd have done without you,' said Beatrix kneeling down and stroking the salamander's head. 'And you, Anders, go and wash out your mouth!'

384

Forty-seven

Tragen opened his eyes and yawned. Such a natural reaction, in desperately unnatural surroundings, somehow focused his mind. He didn't know how long he'd been sleeping and dreaming.

The white glare was ever present, even more brilliant, but it did not hurt his eyes as before. And he wondered. Could he be getting used to the light. If so, what did it mean? Was it good or was it bad? If good, did it mean his sight would return? But he couldn't remember being struck blind. As far as he knew he still had normal sight. But he stared into the whiteness and saw nothing.

What if it's bad? How bad could the consequences be? The worst, of course, was the blindness—could he cope with being blind? What did he need sight for anyway? His brow furrowed what a silly question. He needed it to get about, move around the country unaided. Nonetheless, there was no chance of either, imprisoned in this place, so he didn't need it for here. What else was there? Oh, yes, reading. He'd always been an avid reader. He'd miss his tomes and parchments terribly if he couldn't see them as well as touch them. But there was no reading material here either, so again it was not needed at the moment. But if he was elsewhere, if he did escape without his sight, what then? There were friends who could read to him, of course, the solution wasn't in any way satisfactory but he'd learn to cope. However, there were the highly personal tasks of caring for his bodily ablutions. Well, that went without saying. He wanted no-one wiping his backside. Could he live with the lack of dignity if it ever came to that? Nevertheless, there was no need for concern on that score either. Until he escaped there wasn't any requirement to worry about personal hygiene, the magic in his staff took care of that.

No, the worst thing about being blind was he'd never see the faces of his loved ones again. And he so needed to look on Aidan.

He closed his eyes momentarily to hold back the tears. He wasn't going to give in and he used the moment to scan his other senses. The smell was still the same, putrefaction, he recognized it now. The sweet, cloying, dreadful smell of rotting corpses and it was stronger from what he recalled earlier. He remembered Aidan and Thaddeus telling him of the maimed bodies wandering lost within the Darkness and he knew it was those he smelled. Impotence at his own helplessness to aid them nearly overwhelmed him and he understood a little more of how Aidan must have felt. Why Aidan, who had lived for healing the sick, had gone temporarily insane at the sight of so many defenceless, lost souls.

Tragen licked his lips and discovered saliva, the taste of magic wasn't drying his mouth as much as before either. He was relieved. He'd always hated a dry mouth, and then he grinned in the whiteness…a mischievous, boyish grin. Quite often he'd used the excuse of a dry mouth in order to get a drink, usually the alcoholic sort. Aidan had been wise to him and had always taken full advantage of his master's goodwill. He'd often accompanied Tragen in finishing off a jug or two. And then he recalled relating the story of the wolf to Cornelia and the two young girls, Augusta and Beatrix. Would he ever see their beautiful faces again?

Tragen clutched his staff even tighter, again to control self-pity. And he thought of his sense of touch and worked his way through his muscles. It took him a long time but no-one bothered him, he wasn't disturbed. And hope returned, albeit very slowly. He wiggled his toes and felt the restrictions of the straps on his sandals loosen across his insteps. He flexed his kneecaps, the ligaments tensing at his call, and he became aware of the cage bars pressing against his buttocks. He cast his mind to examine the organs in his abdomen and found them to be in perfect order, despite his lack of movement, none were atrophying.

However, he was losing weight; the fat content of his belly was fast disappearing. He'd have to watch that, lose too much and he would die of malnutrition, but strangely he didn't feel hunger. Was his staff the culprit? He'd always been a little overweight, was the staff now controlling his nutrition, forcing him to diet…lose the flab? There was nothing he could do about his diet though, except depend on his staff to supply the necessary sustenance. Nonetheless, there was one benefit of his weight loss, he could now flex his arms and open his hands. And he determined at that point to exercise. True, he had minimal movement at the moment, but it was still more than it had been the last time he'd been awake. He could now turn his head slightly and the agony of renewing muscle movement was excruciatingly delightful.

And then some sound disturbed his enjoyment and he stopped moving altogether…to listen.

'Touch the cage, cretin,' Zorzecai ordered.

Tragen's mind recoiled in terror when he recognized the herdsman's voice. It still bore the sibilant hiss of a snake and the enjoyment of horror. The wizard recalled the last time he had heard that terrible voice. It had been ordering Aidan to hold the dagger aloft as the boy lay on the altar, awaiting the command to commit suicide. But Tragen was puzzled. Leash had killed the demon before Zorzecai had been able to give the order. It had been one of the last things the wizard had seen before the light grew too bright for him to see. Tragen had watched the vampyrus tear Zorzecai's head from his shoulders. Didn't that mean that the herdsman was now dead? If so, what was he doing outside Tragen's prison ordering someone to touch the cage? And then he realized. Of course, everyone was dead in the Darkness…except himself. Nonetheless, it could never be a coincidence that Zorzecai was still with the cage.

'Please, Master, I'll burn…have pity.'

'Now!' and Tragen felt a body rebound off his cage as it was flung heavily against it. And Tragen recognized the scream. The same scream as Brother Dyfrig, Abbot of Sanctity, had used when Zorzecai had thrown him into the dense cloud of freezing black fog.

'Please, Master, have mercy,' Dyfrig moaned, weeping copiously.

'Mercy? You are fortunate, cretin, despite your folly my God succeeded in his quest to open the door into Life. For that he rewarded me with a return of my body to continue with his search. And you are going to help me in that seeking. And this time you are not going to fail me. Embrace the cage!'

And Brother Dyfrig did, screaming not an inch from Tragen's ear the whole time. Standing against the mesh, Dyfrig wrapped his arms around the cage as if hugging his lover. And for moments Dyfrig disappeared from Zorzecai's sight within the intense brilliance. The magic bathed Dyfrig, for although it could not leave the confines of the cage, the magic filled the mesh. And Dyfrig grasped the web of iron to his body. He unexpectedly ceased his screaming when he realized he could actually feel the wizard's magic coursing through the bars—and through his fingers entwined in the open mesh. He was astonished. No dead soul could feel a living being and yet Tragen's magic was sentient.

Dyfrig stepped away from the cage, not taking his eyes from it. 'What, Master, I don't understand. Am I now alive?'

'For now,' and he again laughed, thoroughly enjoying himself. 'You can easily die again, and probably will many times in the foreseeable future.'

'What do you mean?' Dyfrig asked, his heart almost stopping, dreading the answer.

'I have a task for you…a relatively easy task. You are to protect the cage, ensure my demons do not accidentally open it,' and he sniggered. 'You are to die if needs be to ensure that never happens. But never mind…there is a compulsion on you that each time you die you will re-embrace the cage. You will constantly regain your life to resume your task. There is no means to break the spell.'

'I am to suffer the pain each time, Master? It will not ease?'

'On the contrary, cretin, the more you die the greater will be the pain each time you touch the cage. So be vigilant—do not allow the demons anywhere near it.'

'But why do I have to live to stop them, can't I stop them while I'm dead?' Dyfrig, in his abject terror of the pain, preferred death.

'No dead soul can touch a demon, Dyfrig. Demons have a corporeal body the dead do not.'

'Why can't the cage be opened?'

'You really are a fool, aren't you? This is the wizard's soul—his body is trapped within the cage in Life. If the cage is opened here then the cage will open within the rock below the black miasma. The wizard will be crushed. My God does not require his death until the search is successful!'

'The search…what search?'

'You have no need yet to know of that, cretin. I must leave now…do as I say.'

Within his prison Tragen no longer heard Zorzecai near him, only the weeping of Dyfrig. And he also wondered about the search.

And he prayed that when Aidan did find him—he wouldn't open the cage within the Darkness.

Forty-eight

Ryn continued his never ending task of ripping bits of white cloud from the measureless expanse on which he was standing. Under the watchful eye of Helydd he was very careful not to rupture the bottom-most level. She said he'd know when he was near it because it was not so dense, the light from the valley below him would shine through. Every now and then he rested and, stretching his neck, he studied the edges of the cloud base. He was hoping against hope that he could detect an area of a darker colour that might indicate the surface of the mountain was near and therefore the depth a lot shallower. But he was clutching at minnows and he knew it.

The area he had cleared varied in depth from just a few feet to places where it was deep enough for his grave, he shuddered at the horrible thought. But this was his second day of digging away at the mind-bendingly boring task and he sighed, fed up he wanted a break. 'How much more of this stuff do I have to get rid of, isn't it large enough for you yet, it is for me.'

Helydd stared at him. She so much wanted to tell him what the immediate future held but couldn't. She was terrified of losing his friendship. She did not have any friends, everyone was too afraid of her. She was a loner, forced into solitude by others' fears. Yet she liked and respected the large albatross and he liked her. Would he spurn her if he knew the truth? Yet, the albatross was not human and did not have the same outlook on life as they did. Nevertheless, he had a voice and spoke as a human; he had fingers and used them as a human, he ate human food. Did that mean he had the same fears of nature as humans did?

The only chance she had of entering Alfhime was in her present form. As a human she was small enough to get through the clouds without actually touching any of the vapour. But this form held inordinate danger, as it was it took a lot of her strength and power to remain in the shape of an old woman. But she needed every ounce of stamina and magical ability to hold forth against the demon. She dared not remain for any length of time in Alfhime, in her present form, while the demon was there. She would have to regain her true form. She had access to her full power only in the shape in which she was born. But maybe even that would not be enough to slay the enemy.

She thought of the liosalfar, their true plight unbeknown to them. She could have told them many times but their prejudices would have ensured disbelief. They were blinkered against her because of what her daughter had done. And, of course, the magician's purpose would not have allowed any credence of her tale to take root.

The liosalfar were blind fools, first in their zealousness in guarding a legend they no longer held, a fact of which they were ignorant. And secondly, for ceding all their magic to the magician, the one they had elected leader in their ignorance and fanaticism. They had no idea he was not of them.

No, she had to enter Alfhime as an old woman. Assume her true form at the earliest opportunity, to have any chance of rescuing her daughter and now Ryn's friends. But her true likeness was colossal.

'Oh, you have a ways to go yet, my friend. Don't forget there are three others to bring out of the cells and we might have the mountain elves chasing us. We can't afford any delay in escaping caused by a route that is constricted.' She also couldn't tell him that the magician, being a creature of the dark, would find it easier to stop them escaping at night. His powers would be enhanced to such an extent he could annihilate even her as long as it was dark. No, to avoid the possibility of being thwarted, the rescue had to be carried out in daylight when the demon magician's power was at its nadir.

Helydd went over her plan time and time again in her head while staring at Ryn, not seeing him. The timing had to be just right; the rupturing of the bottom-most layer had to be under cover of darkness. Their entrance into Alfhime and the location of the prisoners also had to be at night—but their escape had to be in daylight. She couldn't foresee any problems, but knew there would be.

Ryn considered her answer and found it logical, but he did wonder how large a hole she needed. Did she want one as large as the Tower he'd stood on in the castle of Mantovar? And he smiled at the thought, a hole that size in this cloud would surely be a magnificent sight, birds from leagues around would flock to play in it. It would certainly be plenty big enough to aid their escape. He carried on grubbing at clumps of clouds, throwing them into the air where they blew away.

But across the valley something stirred. It lived amongst the clouds, was one with it. It could feel the breeze gently tugging at each particle of vapour, each cloud caressing its neighbour. Luxuriate in the gentle warmth of the natural winter sunlight.

And it felt the sundering of the clouds as if someone or something was wrenching at the sinews of its heart.

It woke fitfully from its long sleep, its antennae probing the clouds searching out the reason for the disruption in its tranquillity, the unknown cause of its anxiety. Listening intently it heard the mutter of conversation, although it had no recollection of ever hearing speech before. The vibrations in the air told it that this was the source of its concern. It sniffed but detected nothing in the air, it was too far away. And although it had no sight, immersed as it was in the clouds, it could still perceive shapes within the limits of the valley using its two stalk-like antennae. And so it turned its head in the direction of Ryn and tasted the thinness of the clouds about the bird.

It knew birds of course, they often flew across the valley and through the upper-most level of the clouds and it had learned to ignore them. But they never, ever flew down through the mass into the free air below. They couldn't unless they knew the secret of the magic.

However, it understood what was happening, that somehow this bird was succeeding where no other bird ever had. Was it because it was the biggest avian creature it had ever encountered? Could its size have anything to do with discovering the only way through the enchantment? It didn't think so; the creature was phenomenally large itself. So it stirred. Howsoever the bird had found the secret, it could not be allowed to progress any further. It struggled out of its torpor and lashed its tail angrily. It popped its greyish-white antennae above the clouds and peered over the valley. Finding its quarry, it swiftly dropped below the surface again. Hidden, it swam towards the shattering of its home.

Its speed was not great, its vast bulk did not allow for rapid movement. But it was fast enough to reach Ryn before the albatross had advanced much farther in his task.

The cloud-serpent had been a creation of the liosalfar when they had set up the cloud cover at the time of dragons, tens of centuries before. Its purpose was to protect the liosalfar. From within the clouds, it kept them safe from predators and interlopers attempting entrance to Alfhime from above. In all its long existence it had only ever been called once previously to carry out its duties. That had been twenty years before, when a similar but smaller disturbance had occurred.

At that time the cloud-serpent had been drowsing for centuries. Not moving, it had become fat and slothful, its brain atrophying. The inevitable physical degeneration it suffered had not been accounted for by the liosalfar who had all but forgotten its existence above their homeland. It had been too slow or the interloper too fast—for whatever had gained entrance to the valley below had long since disappeared. And the guardian had no inkling of anything untoward happening as a consequence.

Helydd was the first to detect its presence. Her place on the hillside watching Ryn was hidden from the cloud-serpent whose full attention was on the bird breaking up its domicile.

Helydd, as if reading the monster's mind, was thinking of that first incidence. It had been at her instigation that the enemy had laboured such as Ryn was doing now. She thought the enemy was a man who had taken pity on her and wanted to aid her in her rescue bid. But she had been fooled so very easily and had confidently shown him the only possible way into Alfhime. But he had betrayed her and slipped through a rupture he had tunnelled beneath the cloud cover. No sunlight or moonlight had ever touched it. It remained open long enough for him to disappear. And the clouds had soon gathered back over the enemy's entrance.

She had raged and in her despair had fled to her cottage. She had not noticed the slight regular movements in the clouds, actions that were not normal to such a weather formation. So she had missed the cloud-serpent on that occasion—but not on this.

The first inkling she had of anything amiss was when she saw a gigantic head poking through the wall of the hole directly behind Ryn. The bird, unknowing of the lethal presence watching it, carried on tugging at the clouds oblivious to his danger and Helydd sat immobile—shocked rigid.

And, although the cloud-serpent was slow in its undulating mode of travel, it was not slow when its body was free of the restrictions of the thick clouds. It lunged across the intervening space at Ryn its mouth stretched wide open displaying two tremendous rows of razor-sharp teeth.

And Helydd, roused by its movement, reacted instinctively by raising her hands and a dense wall of ice formed in the air between the cloud-serpent and its prey. The huge serpent's lunge smashed its head into the thick wall and such was the great impact that the ice shattered in an explosion of sound. Shards erupted everywhere, falling on Ryn,

Helydd and mercifully one large shard severed the head of the cloud-serpent. It collapsed onto the floor of the hole where its life-blood formed a very large pool as it drained from the colossal body. Its lifeless eyes stared up at Helydd in reproach.

Helydd quickly stood and breathed heavily, immensely relieved when she saw that Ryn was safe, even though he was almost completely buried under the broken ice shards. 'Ryn,' she called, 'are you all right?'

He did not answer, afraid to move he just stared up at her.

'Ryn, my friend, what is it?' Helydd, panicking at the look in his eyes, rushed to the hole and her heart turned over when she saw the blood, for she knew it was not all from the serpent. 'Oh, my God, Ryn where are you hurt—don't move, I'll look. Please Ryn stay still, I did not mean for you to be hurt, it…it was going to kill you. I had to do something.'

She floated down into the hole; her feet landing on the ice she had created. Her powers, although diminished because she was not in her true form, were still vast. Careful not to touch the cloud, she peered through the ice at Ryn's body. She paled when she discovered the shard pinning his wing to his side and knew that if she removed it he would bleed to death in an instant.

'Oh, my Ryn,' and she burst into tears. 'Oh, my Ryn, I'm so sorry…I'm no healer, I cannot help you.' She wrung her hands helplessly and crouched down to stroke his feathers, not taking her eyes from his.

'It looks that bad, does it?' he croaked terrified.

'I'm sorry Ryn; it seems that every time I come close to rescuing Manon, something goes wrong. I never wanted you hurt…honestly!'

'You've tried before then, you must tell me later. I don't understand any of this. God, it's beginning to hurt now and I'm getting tired. That's not good is it?'

'No, dear Ryn, it isn't.'

'You have magic, Helydd, don't you, that's how you saved my life?'

'And killed you, Ryn.'

'I'm not dead yet, can you move the ice from me…slowly?'

'If I do that then the shard in your body will melt and fall out and that will finish you.'

'Helydd, my friend, the shard is melting already, it is buried in my hot body,' and he surprised her by smiling. 'Aidan, the young man who gave me my magic, must be the greatest wizard in the world,' he laughed quietly, 'and the most accident prone. Along with my voice, his magic and the power to mindmeld, I didn't realize until now that he has also passed on his ability to heal. He is going to be astounded when next we meet.' He smiled to reassure her, her sorrow draining her face of all colour. 'I have set the healing in place but I do not have enough strength to free myself from this ice. Can you do it? I suggest you hurry for the ice is forming a solid block around me and lowering my body temperature to a critical level.'

Helydd stared, astonished at his words, it took moments for her to realize what he was saying and when she finally complied the ice flew from the hole leaving Ryn liberated. But he was still disabled in the bottom of the hole, his feet wading in the blood of the serpent, and a little of his own.

'One more thing before you explain, Helydd. Can your magic lift me out of here? Healing doesn't half take my stamina,' he said wearily. 'I'm afraid our rescue attempt is going to have to wait awhile for me to recover.'

'My lovely friend,' she said weeping tears of happiness, 'my magic is enough to carry you down the mountain if you wish it. Shall I take you back to our cottage?'

'Aye, lovely Helydd,' he smiled, his beak all awry, 'I could murder a cup of tea, while I listen to you explain everything.'

Helydd again sat on her chair in the doorway of her cottage drinking tea. It still amused her to see this huge bird delicately holding a cup and munching one of her buttered scones. It was while she studied him that his long white feathers fluttering in the breeze jogged her memory. She'd seen it before, back in the past. What was it about a giant white bird? It was niggling at the back of her mind, something from way back. She sipped her tea…it would come to her if she left it alone. The more she probed the further it receded.

She sighed, where to begin her tale. She'd have to be careful how she explained matters; she didn't want to frighten him. She couldn't tell him everything he'd never understand. I'll feed him a bit at a time, let him get used to what I've told him, let him digest it before telling him more. She didn't want to lose him. She loved his friendship, his companionship—and she needed him yet, to rescue

Manon. He brushed his feathers on his chest and again she wondered. Ryn was important for other reasons—she didn't know how, yet.

Ryn interrupted her thoughts. 'If you can't find the words to tell me let me see your thoughts. It may make it easier for you.'

'See my thoughts? Mindmeld you mean? I have never allowed anyone into my mind except my Manon. You amaze me, Ryn. All this magic gifted to you by a human. I've never known of it before. This wizard of yours is truly exceptional, is he not?' and she smiled tentatively. 'We'll do a bit of both, I think. It's a long story, if you wish more cake, there's plenty, and tea, help yourself as I speak,' and she sat for long moments twirling her necklace through her fingers.

'Thank you, Helydd, my friend,' he broke the silence. 'Perhaps I can start you off by saying that I've guessed you are the Cragga. I'm right, aren't I, but you don't look dangerous to me,' and he waited patiently for her to speak.

'Friend?' and she smiled at the wonder of it. 'I've never had a friend before.'

'Until I met Shadra and Anselm I had never had a friend either. We have a lot in common, Helydd, but go on, please; I want to know more about you.'

'I am a shape-shifter, Ryn. This is not the manifestation in which I was born.' And now that she'd started it flowed from her, her thoughts, her knowledge and her fears. She'd never had anyone to talk to before, except for Manon, and it was because of that and Ryn's palpable innocence, she found her earlier misgivings taking flight. She held nothing back.

'I am a creature of water…in all its forms. I can shift my shape to take on the appearance of anything that contains water—rivers, snow, glaciers and even tsunamis,' she paused when Ryn was startled at the word. 'You know what a tsunami is? Of course you do, you are a creature of the ocean.'

'You can really become a tidal wave of such greatness?'

'Yes, my friend, but it's not quite as it seems. I am not explaining myself properly. I can form a tsunami and live in it. I am not actually the tidal wave. I am a living entity with no formal, identifiable shape. I can take on the outward appearance of a river and live in it. And this present shape—I can appear as an old woman and live like this for however long I like, for humans are mostly made of water.'

'So are birds—can you fly as a bird?'

'Well, birds are very small and you do not hold much water, not enough to hold me at any rate. I suppose Manon could, she is small. No, I take the form of a cloud sometimes but I'm afraid I am not a very good flyer, I am slow and need to rest often.'

'Then you must fly with me, I'll take care of you.'

And her heart broke for the honesty of a mortal bearing his friendship for her so openly, worrying for her safety. She—a being who could snuff out his life with an intake of breath.

'Many centuries ago, maybe thousands of years I'm not sure now my memory only goes back so far, I came to live in this valley as an old human woman. I can't remember my reasons except that it was after a period of great turmoil in the world. Don't ask me what it was for truly my memory lets me down about that period. I know that I was in great need of rest and these mountains suited me. I love snow,' she giggled. 'Manon and I delighted in sliding down the hillsides. We used to race often,' she stifled a cry, her memories painful.

'We'll find her, bring her away, Helydd, I promise on my life,' he said forcefully. Ryn gave her time to compose herself and when she looked up and dried her eyes in her shawl he asked the question that when answered was truly to astound him. 'How old are you?'

'I am as old as the hills, my friend.'

And the story she related took his breath. For as she spoke those lost memories of thousands of years earlier, returned. But she was still too terrified to divulge them all.

Forty-nine

It was long before dawn when Captain Jos Osvaldo resumed his pacing of the quarterdeck of the Lobos. It was a beautiful night in the tropics, if you didn't desire secrecy. A full moon and fading starlight glinted off the waters…and the Lobos, with its sea anchors strung out, at rest around the headland from Armadillo Harbour. A soft breeze, barely enough to fill the sails if they'd been hoisted, wafted gently off shore, bringing with it the smells of frangipani and orange blossom. But men were careful not to breathe too deeply for mingling in with the sweet fragrances was the acrid sting and spicy odour of an over-populated town with inadequate sewers. At this time of the morning there was hardly a sound, only the occasional creak of a board as the ship tugged against the anchor awaiting the signal from ashore.

On board the Lobos tension was a tangible emotion. The crew hunkered at the bulwarks their weapons close to hand, the moonlight glinting off the occasional naked blade. The only movement was that of Osvaldo quietly pacing the deck from side to side behind his first mate. Cowper was standing at the side of the helmsman, looking down into the rowing stations far below. There the slaves were also at rest, most asleep, taking advantage of the lull before the violent action to follow. They were all mindful that, in all likelihood, they would be caught up in the battle despite being helplessly tethered to the oars.

Leash groaned and stretched his aching back and looked up at the fading stars. Glimpsing those on the quarterdeck he ignored them and inhaled deeply, gagging only slightly at the taste of unwashed humanity confined in too small a place. He was getting accustomed to the odour of vomit, urine and sweat.

'Quiet, Leash, or our friend will be along with his whip,' warned Balar.

'Perhaps any noise I make will upset Osvaldo's plans, might even result in his death,' Leash replied.

'Or ours fool. Anyway, how will his death serve us? If he is attacked out here and in the furore he dies it will quite likely mean our deaths. The only way to kill him is to sink this ship and we are chained to it. Do you want to end up in a watery grave? He will not relinquish *the Lo…'* Balar swallowed convulsively. *'He will not cede the ship while he is alive.'*

'Maybe you're right,' Leash answered, despondency in his voice he didn't notice the hesitancy in Balar's. *'But we will still keep my eyes open, who knows we may see an opportunity to escape.'*

'Go to sleep Leash, keep dreaming. We'll be lucky to get out of this with your life.'

Osvaldo ceased his uneasy pacing and stared up at the huge beacon just visible as a darker patch on the headland a league away. 'Cowper,' he whispered, 'I don't like this, I have a bad feeling.'

Cowper didn't stir from his spot but, nevertheless, he straightened his shoulders even more. He glanced quickly at his captain, noting the wary look on Osvaldo's face. The man's uncanny instinct for trouble had served to forewarn them of danger many times in the past. Cowper looked up at the masts, inspecting the men standing on the footropes gripping the spars, ready to unfurl the sails when ordered, and waited for his master to continue.

'We are going ashore now, Cowper,' Osvaldo decided abruptly. 'I'm not waiting any longer. The Serpent should be into the entrance farther than it is and I want to know why it's not.'

'We could always send someone to investigate.'

'The harbour is in shadow, these hills will have blocked out the moonlight. Whoever we send will never see all, besides he'd never return before sunup. No…get the men into the boats.'

It didn't take long. The manoeuvre was a well-practised one—the Lobos had raided ashore many times. The men shinnied down the rope webbing hanging against the hull, dropping into the boats silently they took up their oars. They didn't have far to row over the low swell to the shore. As his boat touched the sandy beach below Marlin Point a lone, male, smooth-billed ani, guarding its nest and young, whined a warning to its mate searching for the night-time flower thrips feeding on the coffee plantation to the north of the town. Osvaldo leapt ashore; turning impatiently he watched the others as they arrived. Cowper strode across to him from the second to land, his men pulling the longboat up above the waterline to join Osvaldo's. Other boats were drawn up farther along the beach.

'Take your men up the hill from the west and move round so you come up inland of the beacon. Any men there will either be asleep or staring out to sea. They won't be expecting a raid from the harbour. Do your damndest to ensure the beacon is not lit—I don't want the

town warned. I'll bring the rest up this side. If we time it right we'll both attack the beacon at first light. From there we should be able to see what's going on in Armadillo.'

'Do you think Connors has betrayed us?' Cowper asked.

'No, I trust his word. But Connors may have been betrayed.' Osvaldo stared at his mate, his eyes glinting steely in the moonlight.

Cowper moved off, his men following silently, snaked up the hill and shortly disappeared west. Osvaldo waited on the beach his men crouched against the hillside. He gave Cowper half an hour to get into position before leading his men up the steep incline towards the unlit beacon.

Standing amongst clumps of citronella, smelling strongly of lemon, Osvaldo paused to get his bearings. He looked back at the Lobos at anchor, its outline just visible in the fading moonlight. He pursed his lips, ducking automatically as a bulldog bat, returning from fishing in the shallows, flew low overhead. The ship would be fully visible to those at the beacon in an hour. But Lonsdale will have known of its presence the previous night. The watchers would have informed him as soon as the Lobos appeared on the horizon. Would the admiral expect an attack? Unlikely, even though the ship waited outside…no ship entered the harbour at night unless it was up to no good. Lonsdale was no fool, though. But not even he'd suspect an alliance between the two arch rivals, Osvaldo and Connors.

'Tell them to be quiet, Sturges,' Cowper whispered to his second mate. 'Listen…' and he cupped his ear.

'I can't hear a thing,' the brawny man, festooned in knives and carrying a naked cutlass, whispered.

'How many times have you been up to this beacon and not heard a sound, hey. There's always been someone making a noise, either singing or messing about with the whores. It's never quiet this place—so why is it now?' Cowper crouched on the path leading up the gentle gradient from the town of Armadillo. The track was well-trodden, hard-packed earth used for bringing up supplies for the lookouts and timber for the beacon.

'They can't possibly know of us, can they?' Sturges mouthed in his superior's ear.

Cowper bit his lip; the unusual always made him suspicious. The lookouts, usually numbering two or three plus their women, habitually partied up here. It was a light duty sought after by many as a place to unwind, for no-one ever sighted an enemy out at sea and watching inland never occurred to anyone. No-one would ever dare attack Armadillo; the brigands of Onyx were just too many. Cowper smiled, the Lobos was about to put an end to that tradition. Could the watchers be sleeping off their carousing or did they believe that the Lobos actually meant to attack and were keeping a sharp lookout? The former was doubtful so it had to be the latter, unlikely as it seemed. But if they were prepared for an attack, there'd be a damned sight more than two or three men at the beacon.

'Spread out, we'll proceed in a line across the hill. Warn the men—I've a feeling we're going to have a hard fight on our hands. Tell them that once we're engaged they are to scream their heads off, keep the enemy's attention. I want them to believe we are the only attack.'

'Osvaldo doesn't want the town warned…if we scream the noise will travel there,' Sturges mouthed quietly.

'If there is fighting, the town will hear us anyway,' he grimaced. 'But if we can pull it off, the captain will give Lonsdale one hell of a surprise.'

Osvaldo and some hundred men worked their way silently up the hill from the beach, each man holding his cutlass in his hand in case it collided with a rock and made a noise. He was a hundred yards below the top when he first heard shouts and then the clash of arms as battle commenced.

Cowper, along with his twenty men, had surprised the fifty or so of Lonsdale's brigands standing guard. But only half the defending force turned inland to answer Cowper's initial charge, the others stayed resolutely facing the other way, waiting for an assault from the sea. The commander of the beacon forces, a large, ruddy-faced man sporting a livid scar around his neck – incurred when someone tried to hang him – espied Osvaldo and his crew racing towards him up the gradually easing slope above the beach. And, while Cowper was grappling with the men behind him, he gave the signal for the beacon to be lit. It roared into flames, illuminating everything and everyone on the hill. The defenders, outmanned and with their mission in warning the town completed, fled north to disperse amidst the coffee plantation, leaving three men down.

Osvaldo and his second in command met on the top of the hill, well away from the heat thrown out by the gigantic, burning bonfire.

Frustrated at the loss of surprise both men swore and waited the few moments longer it took for the sun to rise above the horizon. The town and harbour of Armadillo were spread out before them and Osvaldo cursed again at the sight that greeted him. He now understood why the Serpent was not within the entrance of the harbour. It had been tethered between two smaller ships and was being used as a barricade to stop the Lobos entering the anchorage.

Bartram's North Star had sunk at the quayside only the tops of its mainmast and foremast visible above the waterline. Connors' Hound was anchored in the middle of the harbour, intact but probably not for long. As the men at the beacon looked on there was a tremendous crash from the quay, a cloud of smoke, a strange whistling noise and then the mainmast and most of the rigging on the Hound collapsed. The roll of thunder continued for many moments and the watchers stared in amazement at the carnage. But they were not surprised when the cloud dissipated on the quay to reveal a throng of hundreds of men. They were clustered behind and to the sides of the cannon, its long muzzle, appearing small from the beacon, the last to give up its tell-tale trail of smoke.

Cowper, his gaze switching from the Hound to the quay, was the first to speak. 'How in hell do we fight that?'

'We have no choice; half my treasure is now on the Hound. I don't know how he got wind of our partnership...but he must have had spies at Comfort Bay. I want Lonsdale's head in my hands before this day is out,' snapped Osvaldo. 'A change of plan is called for, I think. Send for every slave on the Lobos, I want them here in one hour. Leave a skeleton crew and get everyone else with us. Karnica said to drown the cannon and that is what we'll do. When we succeed it'll shorten the odds to about two to one,' he removed his hat and ran his fingers through his hair. 'We have all been betrayed.'

Leash wasn't the only slave to be surprised at being landed ashore on the sandy beach. Roped together they were led up the hill to stand in front of Osvaldo in five ranks of twenty. Surrounded by the crew, Leash grimaced; there was no chance of escape. Leash and Balar looked down at the town of Armadillo and saw at once the problem. The Hound was helplessly at anchor in the middle of the harbour, though Connors was lowering boats to ferry his crew to the quay. It seemed that Connors was not giving up the fight and was sending his men into battle. But his hope of distracting Lonsdale from the men on the hill was forlorn and the second cannon had now been trundled on to the quay. The first was now being trained on the Hound's boats, the second along the quay, awaiting the attack from the Lobos.

'You slaves are about to be given the chance of freedom!' Osvaldo shouted over the heads of the surprised, shackled men in front of him.

Cowper – along with the rest of the astounded crew of the Lobos – stared at their captain. The order to bring everyone to the hilltop had puzzled the crew, though not the first mate. He thought it perfectly obvious what was intended. The slaves and the crew now totalled close on five hundred men. Against those in the town it was good odds, they'd fought harder numbers before. But the difference this time was that a hundred of the Lobos' men were slaves and Cowper couldn't see them ever fighting for Osvaldo. But four hundred crew fighting Lonsdale was still fair odds. He had every faith in the Lobos' crew. They'd slaughter Lonsdale and his cohorts—if the cannons were disabled. If they weren't, none of Osvaldo's men would escape death. Cowper, his hand on the hilt of his cutlass, the other holding a dagger, listened to his captain. And his grin grew wider the more he heard—but it was still going to be a desperate action calling for a lot of luck. But Osvaldo had the reputation of being lucky.

Before Osvaldo could continue there was another earth-shattering rumble. A cacophony that made everyone on the hill clap their hands to their ears and stare transfixed with horror at the cloud of smoke on the quay. Amid the strange whistling noise that followed, a wail of fear erupted as a ball of iron abruptly appeared from the cloud of smoke. They watched as the ball seemed to float through the air and slowly drop towards a boat full of the Hound's men. There was another enormous boom and the longboat exploded. The hilltop attackers watched in terror as men were flung into the air, the boat – splinters flying everywhere – sinking beneath them. The screams of the dying drifted over the water.

'Frigging hell, Captain! I thought Connors said it would take a long time to ready the weapon again after firing,' Cowper said appalled at the sight.

'How long do you estimate, ten minutes?' Osvaldo asked.

'Cowper turned his ashen face from the boat to the quay. 'Aye, about that, and they have two.'

'They must have been practising. Can you see the svartalfar?' Osvaldo asked taking his glass from his belt and peering through it. 'I see one at the farthest cannon but where's the other? Never mind, we'll deal with them when we've got them in our hands.'

'We'll be blown into the water if we charge them,' Cowper whispered.

Osvaldo laughed. 'What did Karnica say—water is the answer? We'll feed them to the fish.

'Slaves,' he shouted, 'you want your freedom? Then you must kill those weapons. You've heard them, seen them, felt the terror of them. Listen to me. They can be killed! If you're quick and nimble, stay away from the front of them, charge each from the side and push the buggers into the damned harbour, your freedom will be assured.' It hadn't occurred to him that if the slaves got that close to the weapons then there would be no need to push them into the water. The cannons would be in his hands to use as he wanted. But when Karnica ordered, he obeyed—to the letter.

He waited for the reaction of the terrified slaves knowing that each man was desperate to change his life, even at the possibility of losing it. He'd lost many a slave to suicide. Wasn't this just another method of self-murder, this one a lot swifter than most? And who knows they may succeed. But they would die trying anyway, he was determined on that. Nonetheless, he had to offer more or they'd never move.

'To each of you that survives, I will not only grant you your freedom I will pay you enough gold to live comfortably the rest of your lives, wherever you wish to go.' He wondered if they suspected he wouldn't keep his word. 'And to enable your success my crew will accompany you. My arbalests will shoot their bolts over your heads for they will be stationed on the roofs of the warehouses at this end of the quay. Swordsmen will be behind you and alongside you. Their task will be to kill Lonsdale's men. Your task will be to kill the cannons for that is what the smoking devils are called. But be warned, all those who fall back or do not attempt the kill will be slaughtered by my men. Understand! I will have no attempt at premature escape. If you jump into the harbour and swim for the entrance you will be slain by those men on the Hound. If you flee into the town, my arbalests will kill you. There are only two paths to freedom—to the left or the right of each cannon. Overwhelm each as you pass and push it into the water. Are you with me?'

'Well, Balar, what do you suggest?' Leash asked amid the clamour of acceptance.

'You don't honestly believe the man will give you your freedom, do you?'

'No, but what is the alternative?'

'You can swim, can't you?'

'I'll never get out of the harbour you heard him. But even if we did, we'd have the ocean ahead of us. I don't think even you'd have the strength to swim across that.'

'I don't mean to go that way.'

'Tell me quick then, I don't fancy running hell for leather along the quay either.'

'No, we'll swim beneath the quay. We emerge and mingle with Lonsdale's men, approach the cannons from behind and push them into the harbour.'

'Oh, aye, on our own?' he asked, sarcasm dripping venom.

'No, we take two men with us. They can grab the southerners and hold them whilst we throw the cannons into the water.'

Leash, quiet for moments, examined the plan and grimaced, it might work. Whatever, it was the only plan with any chance of success. 'We'd need our own weapons, knives at the very least, just in case. Did you notice that Osvaldo never mentioned arming us? And do you honestly think I am strong enough to push those things over?'

'Of course, with me you are,' said Balar.

'But you said yourself we couldn't trust him to free us.'

'He won't set free all the slaves; he needs them to man his ship. But two or three of us he might. But what's to stop us fleeing inland when we climb out of the harbour?'

'We couldn't do that either, from what Nicholas has told me this island's too small to hide us. Whoever wins will seek us out and either put us back on the oars or kill us.'

'Then we've no option but to ensure Osvaldo wins. Even if he doesn't free us we'll have gained more time to seek escape. Put the plan to Osvaldo, now, before he sends us to commit suicide,' Balar said.

'Captain, excuse me, can I say something? Can I put another plan to you, one I believe that will help you succeed?' Leash held up his hand to attract the man's attention.

Osvaldo stared at him. 'Aren't you the one we picked up adrift on the ocean a few weeks back?'

'Aye, Captain.'

'Well, you seemed resourceful then and what's more to the point…lucky.' He beckoned Leash over. 'Tell me quickly, don't waste my time.'

Leash didn't as he gave a brief outline. 'I'd need two other men; more would be noticed by those above us on the quay.'

'And armed, you say?' added Cowper. 'You really expect us to give you knives?'

'How do you propose to push the cannon into the harbour if your two accomplices are holding the svartalfar prisoner? On your own?' Osvaldo sneered.

'Tell him we'll go for Lonsdale as well…go on,' Balar said when Leash hesitated.

'The southerners are not together, Captain. There is one at each of the cannon. So we'll grab Lonsdale, force him at knifepoint to order his men to push them into the harbour.'

'They are not together? Where is the second one?' Osvaldo asked turning to peer into the town.

'Standing in the doorway of the warehouse alongside the nearer cannon, he is black and cannot be distinguished easily in the shadows,' said Leash.

Osvaldo stared through narrowed eyes until he saw the svartalfar come out of shelter and move to the rear of the weapon. 'You have good eyes, man. Your plan is audacious to say the least, but it has possibilities. Cowper, assign two men to go with him…and arm them. We've nothing to lose.'

Except my life, Leash mused. 'If I may, sir, I'd like to take Nicholas,' asked Leash.

'Whatever! Be quick about it, you can slip into the harbour under cover of my arbalests taking up position. Cowper, you'd better tell them what the bastard, Lonsdale, looks like.'

An hour later crossbowmen were in place on the roof of the nearest warehouse at the eastern end of the quay and the Lobos' crew and slaves were making their way down the hillside towards the town. As they deployed across the breadth of the quay, Leash and his companions slipped unnoticed into the water of the harbour. There was silence as both armed antagonists stared at each other along the length of the waterfront. Sizing each other up, cutlasses and daggers were loosened or held in hands ready for use and the arbalesters held loaded crossbows in nerveless fingers.

It was the muttering, the indrawn breath and a soft rustling getting louder as moments passed that made Cowper look round. At first the parting of their men to either side of the path puzzled him. But it wasn't long before he understood and he nudged Osvaldo still peering at Lonsdale's men.

'What is it, man? I'm thinking,' and then he looked and sucked in his breath. Shuffling along, between the men fearfully making a path for her, was a little old woman dressed all in black, her back bent and leaning on a stick. Across her shoulders lay the familiar form of the grossly ugly and deformed weasel, its two rows of white fangs glinting in the sun.

'Karnica, what are you doing here?' Osvaldo hissed, ignoring his men watching horrified as the Hag lifted her head and stared at their leader's livid face.

'You think you could run off with my treasure?'

'I was not running off. I am keeping it safe while I deal with this cretin aiming to steal it, you fool.'

'Fool? Me…the fool? You don't know what you've done. You don't believe that idiot Connors is going to give it back do you?'

'Connors may be many things but he has never gone back on his word, old woman. And when I have Lonsdale under my heel, he will return it.'

She looked past Osvaldo at the milling crowd clustered around the cannons preparing to attack. 'Then you will need my help or you will never destroy those weapons,' she said, stroking her familiar's head.

'You can help? How? You've already told us to throw them in the waterhj and that is well in hand,' asked Cowper swallowing convulsively. He hated this woman. She was pure evil—he could feel it emanating from her very pores.

'Me and my little friend here, coward, can ensure success, so keep your tongue still,' and she raised her hand and stroked the weasel's head again. The animal returned her affection by opening its jaws wide and licking her hand with a snake-like tongue.

Cowper shuddered, but he couldn't leave the jibe pass without refuting it, there were too many listening. 'I am no coward, Hag.'

And she laughed. 'You will be. Shut him up Jos, or I will,' she warned.

Osvaldo raised his arm. 'Enough of this bickering, how are you going to help?'

Fifty

Elstan sat in the chair in the corner keeping well out of the way, drinking his brandy fascinated by the proceedings. But his mind kept wandering from his friend's pain, the alcohol not having the usual effect. He brooded, it was either watered down or his problems drove the fumes away. He couldn't keep his earlier promise to Chong and get drunk.

He was in a great deal of trouble. He ignored his fascination with the healing of his friend's feet and analysed his problems again, hoping that the more he examined them the easier he'd find a solution. He had a mission which could only be completed by reporting to his chancellor in Mantovar. But it was no good appearing in front of Sevenoaks without either the identity of Brenin's spy or without ascertaining the aims of the Guild. Knowledge of both was intrinsic to the success of the chancellor's overall aims to rid Mantovar of the Abbot of Sentinel and the influence of the Guild of the Brethren of Wisdom—and to re-instate the rule of the Prince of Mantovar.

Elstan sighed; he had spent the last few years fruitlessly searching for the spy and for what the guild was up to. He'd followed each of the members of the emperor's council to no avail. The only ones to ever meet the magus that he knew of were the emperor, his son, the crown prince and Prince Leofric, the emperor's brother. He'd followed up every lead on the guild only to find himself drawn to a dead end. He knew Brenin's ultimate end must be to gain more power. The how of it, the when and the where, was what he needed to know.

It was unfortunate that the Guild had become aware of his presence. Inevitably it seriously undermined his prospects of success. He couldn't hide from them for any length of time without leaving the area. That he could not do. He had to keep close to Brenin to follow him now, and hopefully he'd observe his meeting with the traitor. But, the nearer Elstan got to him, the easier his discovery would become because of the magus' ability to cast his mind in search of him. Magic would be employed to catch him—and therefore only magic could deflect the Guild's search. And for that protective magic he needed Chong-An's aid—the desperately disabled oriental wizard lying on the bed hardly able to move a muscle at present, being administered to by one of the cleverest healers in the country. Elstan and Chong were very fortunate. Athelstan Makepeace had been brought up in Mantovar, his and Sevenoaks' families were very close, related in some way. He was an ardent supporter of his childhood friend, and very loyal to Prince Cedric.

Nevertheless, Elstan felt that he was at last on the brink of achieving his aims. And it was meeting Chong-An that had brought it about.

But even if Chong-An had been physically fit, young and full of energy, he and Elstan could not travel through the Drikander without the help of a guide. The state of affairs amongst the Grekko tribes was always annoyingly fluid. Alliances had the habit of changing overnight—as did the pathways. The Grekkos had a certain magic, the ability to change the direction of the tracks in their lands, much as Aidan suspected the Green People of being able to do. The tribesmen employed the magic to mesmerize and confuse travellers. That was the reason a toll was always easily extracted from those travelling the Great North Road through their territory. It was simple to get lost in the huge forest, even on the road, for the road seemed to have a mind of its own and it went where it wanted. If you weren't careful or you got overly tired then you'd find it was extremely difficult to escape. Pathways that once went north suddenly veered and went east, or west, or double-backed without anyone realizing it. Tracks that led to established villages would disappear in a thicket or took a traveller to an entirely different village to that sought.

He could attempt the journey. He'd been through the Drikander many times before, but he'd always been alone, travelling speedily and very, very quietly and staying well away from the trails. His luck had never abandoned him and he'd always got the better of the Grekkos. But for some reason, Elstan felt that his luck was about to change for the worse.

Nevertheless, going alone was out of the question anyway. He couldn't leave Chong behind, even though part of him wished to do just that. There was the urgent need for Chong to salvage the ancient prophecies in the Green People's library. Though, more importantly for Elstan, Chong had spoken of his intention to eventually visit Miskim, Elstan's hometown. Yet, taking the oriental wizard there frightened the life out of him.

Elstan sighed, knowing with his luck the library was probably at Llyshame, Bartraz's home village. And Bartraz, the supreme leader of the Grekko tribes, was in league with the Guild. He was almost certainly meeting the magus somewhere along Brenin's route to Abferkarn. Bartraz! Elstan hated the name. Bartraz was an extremely dangerous Grekko, a very powerful man holding a grievance against the Emperor of Drakka. He was a chief intensely ambitious for himself and his people, and he returned Elstan's hatred, they having crossed swords many times over the years. That was the other reason he needed a guide, for Bartraz would never allow the Fly passage through his lands. If he even had a whisper Elstan was in the vicinity – and, of course, he would know because Brenin would tell him – then he'd set the tribes hunting him.

So Elstan and Chong both needed Cledwyn, the guide who knew the location of the Green People's library. A native of the Drikander, Cledwyn knew the paths and the spells used to make them change direction. But more importantly, Cledwyn knew the counter-spells, the words and gestures to return the paths to their original purpose. Before he'd fallen asleep in the boat, Chong had told Elstan something of the history of the man they needed to find.

Cledwyn had been chased out of the forest by numerous tribal chiefs for one reason or another, usually for smuggling goods and denying the chiefs their fair share of the profits. But Cledwyn, though, had always maintained his contacts, they were legion amongst the honest and dishonest both in the forest, and in Mulkie's Cross.

But the finest of all Cledwyn's contacts was Bartraz's own personal hedge-witch in Llyshame, the majestic Mistie…thirty stone in weight with arms to fell a tree. She had the normal magical knowledge that all hedge-witches shared, coupled with herb lore and a certain amount of animal lore. But her true power lay in the fact that she was the proud owner of a jinka, aptly named Morbid, a catlike creature with an immensely long tail, deeply cloven at its end. This tail the jinka carried hovering over her back, the split end of the tail above her head. She used the two fingers of her tail to lift food into her mouth and to groom her short coat. But this was not the only odd thing about a jinka. She had large bulbous eyes and communicated with her mistress by using a series of hums and thuds that reminded people of a cat coughing as it purred. Mistie was the only one who could read the myriad sounds, for Morbid could read people's minds and she told her mistress all.

But the real reason Elstan wished Chong would go away, preferably far to the south of Drakka, was Chong requiring his aid in Miskim. And the Fly was going to do all in his power never to step within a hundred leagues of the border town. He knew what Chong was searching for, what the oriental maybe needed to confirm some of the findings in his ancient documents. And he was absolutely terrified of the strange relic.

But he couldn't allow Chong to find it and use it. For the artefact was the originator of his family's personal nightmare and if its power was called upon again it might very well kill his youngest brother. And whatever his youngest brother had done in the interim, he was not to blame, did not deserve an early death, or the opprobrium for crimes he couldn't help committing.

For all four of them had been at fault. And he and Anselm had been searching for twenty years to find the answer. To make recompense for their appalling transgression.

Elstan sweated for his youngest brother. Kenric was quite likely the third of the "three winged siblings"—and he had no idea what that meant for the future.

Elstan looked across at Chong through a haze of alcohol fumes. But if he and his brothers were the three mentioned in the prophecies, perhaps the solution they craved was in them as well.

Elstan needed Chong, Chong needed him—and to get where they wanted and achieve all their desires, they had to rescue a man being beheaded for heresy, in front of the whole town.

But then his reverie was broken. Someone was banging heavily on the door shouting for Makepeace and sending shooting pains through Elstan's head.

The innkeeper burst in. 'I'm sorry to disturb you, Master Makepeace, but you're needed downstairs urgently. The militia are here and want you to accompany them. The heretic tried to top himself and the mayor wants you to heal him enough to be executed. If you don't there'll be a riot to end all riots. A lot of people have spent good money to get decent seats.'

Travis, the tavern owner, a man of dubious repute who had been paid well for the room, didn't want any backlash from either Elstan, or the town militia. If the Fly and the oriental were apprehended on his premises then the innkeeper would stand alongside them all on the same scaffold. Ted Travis' Drovers Bar had been used often in the past as a safe haven and, if the truth be known, it was only Elstan's custom that kept the place open for business. Ted Travis was not known for keeping a decent ale or an orderly house. It was very bad news that the militia were downstairs for they would have been told to keep an eye out for an oriental and a short dark man.

Makepeace hurriedly glanced at Elstan. 'I'd better go. Finish removing this bandage; he'll never walk with it in place...and keep him warm. Make him drink this potion three times a day...it's a very efficient painkiller. If I can, I'll be back this afternoon to let you know what's going on. If not, meet me in Tomos' bakery on Frog Street this evening. You never know something may occur to us if we know the present situation with Cledwyn. But if I was you, I'd get your friend out of here before noon. Everyone knows Drudwynn is seeking a seriously injured man. There are too many curious faces in Mulkie's Cross today and they'll all want that reward.'

An hour later Chong was more alert than he'd been for days. 'You look worried, should we listen to the good physician and get out of here? I'm feeling a lot better now,' Chong asked quietly, watching his friend standing at the foot of the bed massaging his feet, the pressure both deliciously painful and relieving.

'I don't believe there's a need yet, the more rest you get the faster you'll be able to move when we've got to. We'll wait till this evening. It's rescuing Cledwyn that's worrying me. The bloody fool selling false Kaneshi pardons at Kaneshi's Festival!'

Chong breathed a sigh of relief, he knew his recovery would be seriously impaired if he got on his feet too soon, and was glad his friend acknowledged this. 'I know what you mean; he's worried me a few times over the years. He might as well have tried selling Lobos' pendants. At least he'd have been killed instantly for that.' Chong chuckled and sat up straighter, pulling himself to the head of the bed and resting his back against the boarded wall. 'Kaneshi's disciples would really have loved pulling him apart if he'd sold those unlucky charms.'

'What do you know of them? I've only ever heard the myths surrounding Lobos, it's not only pendants that he has, there's other jewellery as well, isn't there?' Elstan asked ceasing his manipulation of his friend's feet and sitting on the end of the bed. The tension wouldn't leave him; he hoped Chong's story would take his mind off his problems.

'Oh, yes, many types, there are bracelets, sword pommels, brooches...'

'And they all carry the same device?'

411

'Yes, depending on what it is they're either triangular or pyramidal in shape, some have three dots on each face, one in each angle. But, of course, they're all fake. I think Kaneshi would send a bolt of lightning to visit anyone who had a genuine Lobos jewel.'

'Aye, I believe you. Do you know the story behind it all? Is it true that Lobos tried to kill his father? I mean...I thought Gods couldn't die.'

'Ah, Elstan, of course Gods can die—it just takes a long time. But to murder one, as Lobos tried to murder Kaneshi, now, that is really something.'

'Then it's true?'

'Oh, yes! Lobos tried to kill him with magic trapped in a pendant. But it never worked.'

'Why not?'

'Well, Lobos made a fundamental error; he manufactured the pendant using vugocite.'

'What is vugocite?'

'It's a very hard, black rock...made of shiny lumps squashed together for want of a better description. Lobos tried to neutralize Kaneshi's magic with it but it only nullifies nature's magic not that of a God.'

'Then why did he use it?'

'Because he was advised to.'

'By whom?'

'Now that I do not know. The name was not in any of the documents I've read so far,' answered Chong. 'But whoever it was, Lobos will never have forgiven him. When the attempt to murder his father failed, Kaneshi imprisoned Lobos in Purgatory to suffer for all eternity. But, so the story goes, that same advisor also holds the key to free him from his imprisonment.'

'Do you know why Lobos wanted to kill his father?'

'Not really...but why do all the Gods fight each other? Power, jealousy...you name it.'

'How do you know all this, it's not common knowledge, is it?'

'I am possibly the world's greatest historian, Elstan. And I don't mean to sound arrogant. Nevertheless, I have been reading arcane documents for nearly four hundred years. Now, my friend, to change the subject I think we'd better find a way to save Cledwyn from the axe, don't you?' Chong couldn't help it; he suddenly had a vision of a head rolling about in the dust. He shuddered.

'How long have you known him?'

'Cledwyn? Since he was born…his mother was a very comely wench in her day.' Chong paused and took the opportunity to lower his feet to the floor. He very gently put a little weight on them, testing their vulnerability he found them still seriously weak. He raised them back on the bed and resumed his tale.

'He's always been a bit wayward but never evil, never a bad lad. I lost all track of him for a few years, he completely disappeared. Then, when he did turn up out of the blue, about twenty years ago, he was a changed man. Something very bad had happened to him in the interim, he'd lost weight and he was very furtive. He used to walk about looking over his shoulder continually and he'd jump out of his skin at the slightest noise. He hid in the forest for nigh on ten years…I think he felt safer there. But the chiefs didn't,' Chong laughed. 'Although they find him useful, they run him out of the Drikander every now and then to teach him a lesson. But I don't think there's any one of them who'd want to see him dead…not even Bartraz, and he's not known for having a forgiving nature. No, there's something about Cledwyn that's totally engaging. Perhaps it's his warped sense of honesty, he's very loyal to his men and they return it. He's just a lovable rogue.

'But he's also the best guide I know; his knowledge of the pathways in the hinterland is second to none. He knows when they're likely to change and their correct route. He's forever running back and forth doing business with the tribes, smuggling in booze and tobacco, herbs and spices, anything in fact that would usually call for Bartraz's tax…not that he pays Bartraz,' Chong grinned. 'But because of his illicit business he knows people that can get us past Bartraz's warriors. Cledwyn even consults Mistie on a regular basis, so I'm told, though I'm also told he's terrified of her. I'm not sure why. There are several weird and wonderful stories concerning him, most of them put about by Cledwyn himself. It helps build his reputation no end and the not so lawful follow him even more eagerly. He has quite a little army of felons in and out of the forest.'

'If that's the case, perhaps we can use his so called army to rescue him.'

'I don't know how to contact them and we haven't much time,' said Chong worriedly. 'But I have been thinking while I was being subjected to immense pain…God, Makepeace hurt. Perhaps I can utilize a spell of illusion…my repertoire is rather vast. If you can get me near Cledwyn, I may be able to cause some sort of distraction and you can spirit him away.'

'You make it sound easy.'

'The simplest plans are always the best—there's not so much can go wrong,' Chong laughed. 'Have you a safe house nearer the Town Hall? That is where he's being held, isn't it?'

'Yes, in the cells below the Hall. But we do have a haven nearby. Tomos' bakery on Frog Street is on the square opposite the Town Hall.' With that there came a discreet tap on the door, opening it Elstan admitted the innkeeper.

'Makepeace sent news. That fool Cledwyn took an overdose of lypyn weed and seems to have changed his mind at the last because he sent for a physician.' Ted scratched his thinning hair. 'I didn't know you could die of an overdose of lypyn unless you hadn't used it before, but saying that, I've never known Cledwyn to touch it at all. He's always had a mania for being in control of himself—he's terrified of having blackouts. He was in here once drinking himself sober and I heard him say that he's got to know what's happening to him at all times. And then he said something very strange. He said he was not going to lose himself again. Mistie wanted to hypnotize him once. He nearly wet himself,' and Travis laughed.

'Then if he's never taken lypyn weed before, the man is up to something, Elstan. I suggest we get to this bakery if not tonight before first light in the morning. Cledwyn may very well have thought of an escape plan already.'

'You may be right. Do you know how Makepeace was traced here, Ted?'

'Aye, the militia's out in force searching for you two. A patrol noticed him alighting from the coach outside and walking in here,' he rubbed his hands against his chest nervously. 'I'd appreciate it if you disappeared before long; somebody's going to wonder why the chief healer is in a backstreet tavern.'

'We'll go this evening, don't worry, no-one's going to come searching for us here before tomorrow. The town's going to erupt with excitement this afternoon when the circus arrives. The watchmen and the militia will have their hands full policing the crowds. The cutpurses are going to have a field day,' said Elstan.

'Elstan,' Chong interrupted, tapping his chin thoughtfully, 'today is the first of Kaneshi's Feast Days, is it not?' Chong asked.

'Aye, that's why the carnival arrives today. It always begins on the first day. It's the circus folks' way to perform for the lepers, to assure Kaneshi of their good will.'

'Yes, well Master Travis I'd be obliged if you could get us a few things before we leave. Two cloaks, black and as old as the hills, also a few bits of old calico as well, the dirtier the better.' and Chong beamed. 'Oh, yes, and two bells. Meet the two latest recruits to Kaneshi's pilgrims,' and he laughed at the astonishment on both faces. 'Don't look so surprised, Elstan. I told you I am the master of illusion. But I don't always need magic to hide behind.'

That evening, Elstan walked through the noisy suburbs, into the town square; a misnomer the northern side was longer than the other three. Roughly in the centre of that side were three stone buildings, the Town Hall dominating the one on either side, a lane separating each. Walking past reeking alleys and around rats rooting in piles of discarded rubbish; he stepped over pools of dubious, stinking fluid. Halting in a closed shop doorway, its shadows hiding him from all but the most curious eyes, he looked across at the Town Hall.

Studying the podium built in front of it, the staging for the execution on the morrow, his gaze was drawn to the wooden block, the last resting place for Cledwyn's neck. He shivered. If things went wrong tomorrow and they failed to rescue the heretic, Elstan hoped the executioner was experienced. If he wasn't it was highly likely that more than one blow with the axe would be needed to sever Cledwyn's head from his shoulders. A gruesome, terrifyingly painful way to die, he had witnessed a botched beheading once before…he didn't want to ever see another.

He crossed the square and walked to the rear of the staging. He shuffled past the end of the first lane running between the Hall and the three-storey, stone-built house belonging to a rich and powerful man…Elstan knew him. The magus, Brenin, used it occasionally on his trips to the Drikander and Abferkarn. In his absence it was always left empty, except for the servants employed by the Guild to keep it clean and inquisitive visitors away. He walked on past the Town Hall and into the other lane. The house here was similar to that of the magus' but a lot less plush. It was intentionally so, its occupant, Mayor Smallwood, did not want to give the Guild the impression he was competing with it. He wished the black sorcerers would forget he even existed.

Elstan turned in alongside the mayor's home, pressing up against the high stone wall, constantly peering over his shoulders into the gloom, he quickly passed through. Drudwynn had taken up residence in the mayor's huge house and it was extremely unlikely that he would be sleeping this early. In his madness, he would be casting his mind searching for his quarry. Elstan knew what would become of him if he was discovered right outside the mayor's front door.

Beyond the square, he strode warily into the busy industrial compound, home to warehouses and workshops. By the smells, the noise and decrepit buildings, it was also the seamier side of town with many a tavern home to a brothel. He wandered through the complex, ignoring the workmen carrying assorted bales and crates to and fro, and the rundown harlots leaning against wooden walls plying their trade.

He emerged within sight of the wide wooden bridge – now showing evidence of long neglect – straddling the river Wry. It led to Kaneshi's shrine at the edge of the forest about a league farther north. Elstan had often wondered why this bridge continued to exist for its purpose of carrying the road across the river was no longer necessary. In years past the river had worn away its banks southeast of the structure. With the silt build-up in the river bed the result had formed a large ford. Appearing, seemingly from nowhere, an easier crossing point for livestock and people had superseded the bridge.

Elstan stepped back into the shadows cast by the moon on a warehouse stacked with fleeces, the smell abominable, and studied the ground across the bridge. The carnival had pitched camp along the northern shore of the river, extending from one end of the bridge down to the ford. Its vividly coloured gigantic show tent was standing proud, erected along the path to the shrine. Staked out along the river bank were the caravans and wagons, the homes of the carnies, performers and labourers alike. Further north and to the east the livestock had been secured in a railed enclosure. Out to the west was an open area, cleared except for long trestle tables, this was where the lepers would be fed by the townspeople.

At this time of night the carnies were finishing off their evening meal, the smells of their exotic cooking lingering in the air. The bustle and noise muted as adults and children savoured the peace before retiring for the night.

The Fly looked over to the star-painted caravan about a hundred paces to the left of the big tent's entrance, Otto and Juliana's

416

caravan next to it. He watched Messalina sitting on a chair at the rear of her van with Trinity standing, facing him her back to her mother, having her long black hair brushed. The peaceful, unthreatening scene brought a lump to his throat, his memories and his guilt tears to his eyes. The woman he loved and his daughter, spending their evening as they'd probably done for the last five years, caring for each other, sharing their love. If he hadn't been such a fool…

Looking back on Trinity's rescue he recalled the moment of recognition in the large, dark eyes of Messalina. The shock, or was it disgust, knifed his heart. If he hadn't used his pet name for her he could have gone on believing that she still cared for him. But that look had put an end to his dreams. However, saying the name had been instinctual. With Messalina in his arms, the smell of her remembered perfume lingering and the feel of her flat belly beneath his hands, all served to drive away sensible thought. Would she ever forgive him…or would he lose her?

But if he and Chong were to rescue Cledwyn he needed her help. Her aid to gain the cooperation of Otto, the man he'd cuckolded. He walked slowly across the bridge his footsteps echoing hollowly on the boards in the almost quiet evening.

And it was as if Messalina sensed him. She stilled her brushing and, looking up, she caught his eye. For moments there was complete silence, just him and Messalina in the whole world, nothing intruded until he noticed the tears in her eyes. He continued to walk forward, his legs moving automatically, not daring to look down or break her gaze. He suddenly felt a stinging in his eyes. He blinked his eyes quickly to disperse his tears and, failing, he stepped from the bridge.

Trinity at last detected something different and she turned and glanced up at her mother. She followed her eyes to Elstan. But something told her to remain silent as Elstan raised his arms.

'Please,' he said, breaking the silence.

And it was as if the river had broken its banks when Messalina ran into his tight embrace.

'Mama, what's wrong, why are you crying?' Trinity implored, tugging at her mother's dress.

'Nothing's wrong, my darling,' she said breaking from his embrace retaining a hold of his hand. 'Everything is fine…at last,' she quickly kissed Elstan, 'except for his nose,' and they both burst out laughing and hugged again.

'Trinity, this is your Dada,' she said at last.

'Don't be silly, you always said my Dada was handsome. Elstan is nice but he's ugly.'

Elstan knelt before her, grinning. 'Watch, young lady, this nose is magic, an illusion created by my very good friend, Chong.' He lifted her small hand and placed it on the wart and commenced rubbing her hand against his nose.

Taking her hand away after moments, she saw the results of her ministrations. Gone was the elongation and the wart, in its place his normal nose. 'Did I do that?' she asked amazed.

'You removed the spell. Do I look better now?'

'Oh, yes,' and she whooped and flung her arms around his neck and kissed his cheek. 'Are you really my Dada?'

'I am, my darling Trinity,' he smiled and lifting her in his arms he regained his feet and turned to Messalina.

'I have a story to tell and forgiveness to beg, if you'll hear me out.'

She stared at him with her hands on her hips. 'I love you, Elstan of Miskim, always have and I always will. But I am no fool. I know what you and my sister got up to, and so does Otto. Before I allow you back into our lives you promise me the truth…that'll be a good place to start. Trinity can go and play while we talk and we'd better get inside before Otto starts in on you!'

Two hours later, Elstan was nursing a black eye like no-one had ever seen before. But it was worth it, he thought, for he had gained Otto's aid if not his heartfelt friendship. With a bit of luck, Chong's need of a distraction was in place.

'So, let me get this straight. You want me to send the horses into the square as soon as this Cledwyn appears,' Otto said. 'You realize the Elders of the town are not fools, they'll be expecting something to happen, they'll know it's a diversion.'

'Yes, but if you can get the Myners to sling a rope across the square and do a free performance, all as part of the proceedings, everyone will be distracted from your distraction. With a bit of luck and with what Chong has in mind, there'll be utter confusion.'

'Aye, and don't forget Otto,' added Messalina, 'Smallwood loves his property. If his shops and stalls are in danger of being demolished by the horses, he'll forget all about the execution,' she grinned. 'He'll probably have a heart attack.'

Elstan stayed with Messalina the rest of the night, only leaving her and Trinity in the very early hours after assuring them of his return when the rescue had been completed. But his heart was still heavy for he'd have to leave them both later, until his mission for the chancellor had been completed—and when his intention to keep Chong from Miskim had been fulfilled.

Fifty-one

Shadra paced rapidly, his nerves all on edge. A denizen of the forest used to open spaces he was suffering claustrophobia confined in this cave. His head was pounding, his stomach churning and his normally emerald skin was a pale shade of pea green. He was tense and irritable.

Anselm was getting increasingly anxious, ever since he'd woken that morning he'd borne the brunt of his friend's changed behaviour. He had never seen Shadra in this mood, as snappish and as restless as he was now. But the chancellor's agent well understood how his small friend felt; he also had spent most of his life in the open air, ranging far afield on his clandestine forays. Life in this cell was depressing them both; they were uncomfortable and both smelling abominably.

Shadra at least had struggled with the small flow of water in the corner and managed to bathe at the fountain. But what had come as a surprise was the refusal of the Liosalfar to provide a bathtub for them. They were supplied with a granite basin instead, totally inadequate for Anselm, barely sufficient for the forest elf.

Shadra, walking back and forth incessantly, hands in his pockets accidentally kicked the basin full of water across the floor from where he'd placed it at the head of Anselm's bed. 'Hell's bells, now what have I done?' he moaned looking down at the mess of soap suds spreading under Anselm's bed and across to the wall beneath the fountain.

'I was going to use that to dunk my head,' Anselm said abstractedly.

'Don't be disgusting, I've just washed in that,' Shadra wrinkled his nose. 'We'd better call for a mop or something to clean it up.'

'They won't come yet, not until they bring us food. We'll just have to be patient.'

'Patient! I've had enough, how you can lie back there contented I'll never know.'

'Who said I'm content?'

Shadra stopped his pacing and stared at the fountain. He hunched his shoulders. 'I'm sorry, Anselm. It's this place I can't cope much longer. I didn't expect to be imprisoned here at all and we've been here days.'

'Neither did I, still…never mind. If I put the bowl under the fountain you can keep filling it for me and I'll duck my head in it.'

'Oh, yes, well if you're going to stand in my dirty water, you might as well wash your feet the same time.'

'Are you saying I've got smelly feet?'

'Yes, can't you smell them?'

'All right, your soap suds are bound to be better than not washing them at all, I suppose.'

Ten minutes later, when the bowl finally filled with cold water, Anselm removed his boots and stockings and stood on the wet floor at the fountain. He poked his finger into the basin below the flow of water. 'God, that's icy,' he glanced at his friend. 'Do you think they'll give us hot water if we ask?'

'No, don't be a big baby; get your head in there.'

'Are all forest elves merciless bullies?' Anselm asked grimacing at the water. He was cold all over for some reason as if standing in a draught. He'd noticed it before but he and Shadra had searched the cell and failed to find any movement of air. They put the feeling down to the heightened humidity, the cell was usually warm but Anselm couldn't get rid of the sensation of frost on his skin.

'Be ready with that soap I'm not staying under for long.' He put both his hands either side of the bowl to hold it steady, rubbed his bare feet on the wet floor to gain a safe purchase and suddenly dunked his head in the bowl under the fountain. And before Shadra could even lift his hands to put soap on the human's head, Anselm shot up straight, a look of total bewilderment on his face. Water dripped down his face and onto his shoulders.

'Give me a chance, Anselm. You didn't give me time to do anything, bend down I can't reach.'

'I…I…' He suddenly spun around, his eyes wide he peered around the cell suspiciously, staring into each nook and cranny, although there weren't many places to hide. He turned back to the bowl and stared down into it intently.

'Oi! Stop that, you're soaking me. What's the matter with you?' Shadra asked.

'I think I'm going bonkers.'

'Wha-at?'

'When I stuck my head in the water, someone said "hello".'

'Uh!'

'I did…it sounded like a little girl's voice. I heard her distinctly.'

'What…when you stuck your head under the water?' Shadra laughed.

'Don't laugh—I did.'

'Don't be daft, you're hearing things.'

'I know—she said "hello".'

'Do it again.'

'What?'

'Go on…stick your head under the water, tell me if you hear it again.'

Anselm licked his lips, stared at the water momentarily and again stuck his head under the flow—and brought his head up just as quickly. 'Yes, I heard her again, plain as anything. Here, you do it,' and he moved away for Shadra to immerse his head.

'Come off it…I'm not falling for that,' Shadra said, very sceptical

'No, I'm not kidding, go on please, I mean it.' Anselm pleaded.

'This had better not be a joke.' Shadra plunged his face into the remaining water in the bottom of the bowl and under the slow pouring fountain. 'You're having me on. I never heard a thing.'

'You didn't?'

Shadra shook his head, perturbed, he could see by the look on Anselm's face that something strange was happening.

'All right, out of the way little elf, I'm going under for longer this time. I don't care how cold I get.'

Anselm refilled the bowl and fifteen minutes later with the water still pouring into the bowl, he took a deep breath and dunked his head. He stayed under for what seemed like two minutes before coming up for air. He shook the water from his head and stood with his hands under the flow of the fountain. He turned to Shadra and smiled broadly. 'Take your boots off,' he ordered the bemused elf.

'Oh, aye, you never give up do you,' and Shadra laughing, started to walk away. 'Give me a good reason why I should believe you.'

'Wait, Shadra. She said your feet must be wet, but there's no need for our heads to be wet, she can talk to us if we put our hands in the fountain.'

'Are you insane?'

'Please, Shadra, I think she's very lonely.'

'You are mad, and I must be for listening to you—this place must be really getting to me,' Shadra said taking off his boots and wiggling his toes on the cold, wet floor.

But the look on the forest elf's face was out of this world when he joined Anselm in placing his hands under the falling water of the fountain.

'Hello!' she said.

'Uh! Um…hello,' answered the forest elf automatically.

'Who are you?' asked Anselm, tickled pink he couldn't stop smiling.

'I am Manon, who are you?'

'I am Anselm and my friend is Shadra.'

'What are you?'

'What do you mean,' asked Shadra finding his tongue.

'What manner of creature are you?'

'Oh, I am an elf and Anselm is a human. What are you?'

'An elf? No, I will not talk to an elf you are despicable creatures, hateful beings, you are cruel,' she replied the fear in her shrill voice contagious.

'Why are elves cruel, Manon?' asked Anselm. 'Shadra is not, I don't think he could ever be.'

'The elves have kept me here for eternity. I must go.'

'No, wait Manon. Shadra's not liosalfar…he's a forest elf,' urged Anselm, realizing immediately who she was referring to. Afraid that she was about to keep her threat and leave he went on. 'We are prisoners of the mountain elves as well. Is that what you are, a prisoner?'

'I am a hostage of the liosalfar, yes. They are elves and your friend is an elf, he said so.'

'Manon, do you know what forest elves are? Have you ever met any?' Anselm asked holding a finger quickly to his lips to keep Shadra silent.

'No, I don't think so. I might have I suppose long ago. I don't remember and I don't remember my mother ever speaking to me of the creatures.'

With doubt creeping into her voice she spoke to Shadra. 'Aren't you the same as the white-skinned ones?'

'I am an elf, four feet tall, green skinned and live in the Great Forest. The liosalfar are six feet tall, have white skins as you say and live in the Scissor Mountains. We are cousins, distant cousins…very distant at the moment since they hold me against my will. This is the first time I have ever met them. They disappeared from history eons ago. But our stories have always said they were gentle, caring folk and if that's the case, something's happened to them. I think it may be something to do with the chief liosalfar, the Magician.'

'This Magician is not liosalfar; the others were—the one who imprisoned me initially, and those that came after. This Magician killed the last one.'

Shadra almost stopped breathing, his instincts had been correct. All along he knew the Magician was not quite as he seemed. 'The Magician killed the last one? Are you sure?' he asked.

'Of course I am.'

'But…why? Have you any idea?' Shadra's fear was growing.

'Yes, silly—he wanted their magic and now he's got it.'

'What manner of creature are you, Manon?' Anselm interrupted.

'I am a water-sprite.'

'Where are you, how come we can speak with you and yet not see you?' Anselm asked, mystified. He'd heard of them but only as creatures of myths and fables.

'You can see me—at least part of one of my forms. I am all through these caves, can't you feel me?' and there was a sweeping sensation of cold water on the human's face.

Anselm raised his hand to the sudden wetness, staring at the glistening droplets of dew on his fingers. 'This is you,' he asked his brow furrowing. 'I don't understand.'

And Manon giggled a sound so childlike and honest it tinkled in their ears. 'No, silly, that is how I travel and speak with you. I am water, so wherever there is water there I can be—in it!'

'So you are in this cell with us?' asked Shadra equally perplexed.

'Part of me is. The liosalfar deliberately keep the fountain in the corner of your cell very small to stop all of me travelling—and, of course, escaping. But a little of me can pass back and forth in the stream, if it was larger more of me would be able to enter your cell. That's the reason they wouldn't let you have a tub in here to bathe—in case the amount of water in it would be enough for me to get away.'

'Oh, I see,' said Shadra although he didn't, the whole concept confused him. 'And is that how you talk to us because we are standing in water with our hands in the trickle?'

'Yes, it was frustrating, though, waiting for one of you to get your head and feet wet at the same time. There is no need for you to do it anymore. Now that we have made contact you will be able to speak to me through the vapour in the air. But please do not allow them…' and she paused significantly, 'to become aware of us communicating. They will move you far away to a drier cell. That would be very cruel after all these years, now that I can speak with other creatures.'

'How long have you been imprisoned?' Anselm asked.

'I do not know. But there was only one dragon, the last one, in the world when my mother and I came here first.'

'A dragon! You have seen a dragon?' Shadra asked excited. 'They are the legend that the liosalfar protect, Anselm,' and then he stopped suddenly. 'But if that was the last one, God—that must have been thousands of years ago. That dragon is surely dead, now. But if that's the case, what are the liosalfar guarding today?'

'Eggs,' Manon answered.

'Eggs?' asked Anselm.

'Yes…dragons' eggs. They are in a cave below us, though they weren't always there.'

'What do you mean?' asked Shadra.

'That is the reason I was imprisoned so long ago. The eggs were kept in a shrine alongside the river that runs through the valley. It was a beautiful place, all colours of the rainbow…I like rainbows…I used to slide about in them,' she giggled.

'The eggs…Manon?' Shadra asked.

'Well, I was curious. I was very young then, although very old in your years I suppose. I didn't realize that I couldn't pick one up. I am made of spinning water and when I engulfed the egg it…it smashed,' all of a sudden she wept. 'I didn't mean for it to happen. But the liosalfar wouldn't believe me. They thought I'd return and break the others. They used their magic to lock me up and won't let me go back to my mother.'

'Dear God, no wonder you hate them,' said Anselm. 'I didn't know they could be so inhuman.'

'They are not human, my friend,' said Shadra. 'But I know now, that we must all escape at the first opportunity. If they can keep one creature imprisoned for over a thousand years, they'll keep us here until we die.'

'You will help me?' Manon's voice sounded a yearning that sent a shiver through both Anselm and Shadra. 'You will help me escape and find my mother?'

'Yes…where is she?' Shadra asked his heart going out to her.

'She is outside the valley of Alfhime, in the mountains waiting for me.'

'Who is your mother?' Anselm asked, although he thought he knew the answer.

'The Cragga.'

'Dear God,' Shadra said staring at his friend, 'what does your mother look like?'

'Oh, she is absolutely huge in her birth state,' Manon said breathlessly, her pride evident in her tone.

'What do you mean "birth state", Manon,' Anselm asked, a twinge of anxiety creeping in.

'We can change our shape and appear as anything that has water, you know like rivers and glaciers. My mother was born as a hurricane. But my favourite shape is that of a human child. My mother says I am a beautiful little girl—Mama likes to take on the shape of an old woman.'

'Oh, why that shape?'

'It's less destructive!'

Fifty-two

Anders stared into the wall of colours watching Bazyli Montetor riding his bay horse. The leader of the mining clan was alone on the north road, travelling towards the junction with the great east-west road leading eventually to Meltwater. Anders moved his eyes slightly to the left and upwards on the endless tapestry of Life. Here he watched Razor's assassins nearing a deep, narrow gorge a few leagues south of the junction. The murderers and their quarry were moving inexorably towards each other and he estimated they would meet sometime that evening.

Anders seethed. The spot chosen by Razor and the killers couldn't have been better suited for the act of betrayal. It was close enough to do the deed and be back in Meltwater by noon the following day. Perfect timing for Razor's announcement of the Montetor's unfortunate death and that Bazyli had named him his successor. Razor would then be able to instigate the penultimate part of his plan. He would force Thaddeus to admit his lies about the Darkness and his culpability in bringing the dread plague ashore on Griffin Island.

But some in Meltwater had heard Bazyli's instructions to flee urgently to the catacombs. And, on seeing the fog on the horizon approaching the harbour of Griffin Town, had begun preparations to heed their leader's words. But none had actually departed. Razor had spoken to each and convinced them it was a rumour spread by the Portolans to install the rule of Thaddeus as Prince Griffin.

The idea appalled them. The thought of having an idiot as king over both clans was beyond contemplation. Bazyli had omitted the fact of the boy's recovery. He fully intended explaining Thaddeus speaking before them as an act of magic, a spell created by the wizard Aidan, a friend of Lodovico Portolan. And this story would be believed because they distrusted wizards and from time immemorial the clans had avoided the catacombs. He had told them that it was the aim of their enemies to have clan Montetor disappear forever beneath the mountain. So no-one packed up, instead they armed themselves and built barricades and awaited the arrival of the Portolans.

Anders shifted his eyes to the catacombs and studied the first arrivals at the rift in the cliff wall above and behind the Portolans' hunting lodge. The long line of people up from Griffin Town and the surrounding countryside was led by Lady Cornelia and Mistress Alessa Barbat. Having met the Green People before, they were instrumental in calming the fears of the evacuees. But it was hours later before the two ladies eventually walked into the tunnels themselves. The Green People had made preparations for the initial welcome by installing what seemed to be pockets of quartz in the walls along the route to Bylani—a journey likely to take them a full two days of walking. A recovering Leonid had put a halt to using krynxes explaining that the surface people would be frightened enough without having to ride on a monster.

But now Anders frantically paced the green velvet grass in front of the wall of colours. He was no longer whittling strange bells from bits of wood that just appeared in his hands when he needed one. He frowned anxiously and spent the time tossing his misericorde from hand to hand, never failing to catch it even though he never once glanced at it. The more he deliberated on the situation the less he could accept that there wasn't a way he could rescue Bazyli. He had to find a solution—there had to be something he could do.

He glanced at the wall again and saw Aidan and Beattie racing to the new cavern on Everard, the krynx. Once there they'd levitate into the mineshaft above the rockfall and hopefully walk into Meltwater, arriving before Razor carried out his threats. But Aidan and Beatrix could do nothing for Bazyli Montetor.

Anders flung the dagger back and forth between his hands, the motion a blur. Bazyli's rescue was his responsibility. His head ached even more and his stomach lurched with fright, when he noticed that his fingers accidentally brushed the wall, his knuckles disappearing into the colours.

He spent the rest of the day, pacing faster and faster, tossing the misericorde even more rapidly from hand to hand, a continuous haze before the wall. His mind seething, his eyes never leaving the tableau in the colours as the unsuspecting leader of the Montetors rode blindly to his death.

Lyell favoured the assassin's weapon, the stiletto, and he held it in his hand as he positioned himself on one side of the road, looking down into the gorge that Bazyli had to ride through. Godun, short sword in hand, was in a similar position lying flat on his belly behind a rock on the other side. Alvar would be the one to actually halt Bazyli. He was sitting at the northern end of the gorge his back against a boulder, his drawn cutlass hidden behind him. He was pretending to be hurt and would seek his leader's aid. Bazyli would dismount and at that precise moment all three would attack him—Lyell and Godun from above and Alvar as soon as the Montetor turned his eyes upward. Anders could see Razor's simple plan falling neatly into place.

There would be no warning. Three strikes it would take and Razor would be the next Montetor, for without his magic, Thaddeus would capitulate in order to save Augusta's life.

But, of course, obeying Razor's orders would not save Augusta. Razor would kill them both once he was leader.

And while Aidan and Beattie raced to the mineshaft, and Bazyli rode to meet his assassins, Anders looked from his misericorde to the wall and back again frantically trying to remember something that was scrabbling at the back of his mind.

He waited, and prayed, and struggled with his memories for he knew that whatever niggled at him was of the utmost importance. He stared at the assassins hidden in the rocks, every ounce of his will obsessed with finding a solution.

The two young wizards arrived at the new cavern beneath Meltwater with Beatrix holding her stomach, sick after riding on Everard. The nausea almost took away her anxiety for Augusta and Thaddeus. Sitting directly behind Adler driving Everard, she felt Aidan's hands on her waist holding her steady from his saddle behind. His constant nearness reassuring, that comfort making her feel guilty.

Neither of the two wizards could figure out how the krynx was being controlled but both assumed Adler must have some sort of mind touch with it much as Thaddeus did in sensing the emotions of animals. Whatever it was, Everard seemed to know what his master wanted almost before he did and didn't falter once on the long journey taken at great speed.

The cavern was vastly busier than it had been on their first visit. Now that the vugocite had been rendered harmless by Beattie's use of her wand, the Green People had resumed work with an almost superhuman rapidity. Beattie heard the unmistakeable sounds of hard toil before they'd even slowed to cross the threshold of the congested entrance. The noise of construction work greeted them, hammers beating loudly, saws screeching madly, shouts of the many different artisans mouthing all sorts of instructions, and the braying of donkeys. Amongst it all were strange flashes of white light; Adler told them this was the visual evidence of certain earth magic being created. No longer were piles of timber left untouched or heaps of bricks ignored, carts of all shapes and sizes dragged supplies to all corners of the cave. Where bare foundations had once been, new walls grew upwards at an alarming rate. Once-vacant channels, excavated alongside the many highways, now held drainpipes of sometimes staggering dimensions, some lying parallel with the road, other smaller drains leading off into the grounds of diverse buildings. And then there were the myriad smells common to all building sites…wet and drying grey and black mortar, fires in iron braziers giving off a red heat, the tang in the air near these bitingly acrid.

Accompanying these manmade odours were those of nature. The sweet, cloying aroma of fresh and drying dung spread over large fields and small garden plots. Boxes and boxes of new plants and seedlings, piled haphazardly in every available space, all waiting to be planted.

Adler ignored all and raced Everard past the frenzied activity to the scree slope against the foot of the farthest wall. A wide and unbroken smooth expanse of white rock formed the wall stretching to the immensely high roof above. The rock was now no longer the ominous black of normal vugocite denying the Green People's magic.

But it was at the foot of this scree of fallen rock that they discovered the activity was at its greatest. A multitude of Green People were making large platforms that looked like rafts. Each one was able to accommodate fifty people seated, and around the edge of each raft the green People were erecting handrails, more it seemed to give the impression of security than for the actual fact.

'Bloody hell, Adler,' and then Aidan bit his tongue. 'All right Beattie I'm sorry, okay?' He smiled and held up his hands. The smile though was his tacit recognition that her standards were at last registering a little on his nature …even if it was only learning to moderate his language. 'You intend using those platforms to ferry people down from above?'

Beatrix was surprised at the uncalled for apology, the fact he'd cursed hadn't quite registered with her she'd been too intent on studying the work in front of her. She grabbed his hand, her hold enough of an answer. She found herself holding his hand more and more often now. She blushed and, at a twinge of anxiety, blocked out Augusta's face.

'Yes, Lord Aidan. We'll find it easier and a lot quicker to transport the large numbers of people living in Meltwater to safety here,' he glanced above at the roof, his anxiety palpable. 'It isn't feasible to bring them down individually.'

'How many have you made?' asked Beattie, unable to hide her admiration, she grinned at all those nearby.

'We hope to have ten of these platforms ready by the morning,' he answered, exhaustion in his voice. He seemed not to have slept for days, worrying over first Leonid and then his wife. 'That's right isn't it Brickel?' he asked the overseer who was busy inspecting the lashings on the rails of the nearest raft.

'Aye and we'll have ten men to levitate each platform…they're resting at the moment. It's going to be utterly nerve wracking keeping the people quiet and very exhaustive for nature's magic. But I've got plenty of volunteers standing by to take over,' he smiled quickly. 'It's a long way to bring inexperienced, frightened people through the air, so we thought we'd use some of our children to calm them. You know, sit a couple amongst them to show them there's nothing to be afraid of.'

'An excellent idea, Brickel, I salute you,' and Adler grasped the man's hand and shook it vigorously.

'I hear the salamander healed Primrosa,' Brickel suddenly asked very concerned.' She will be all right, won't she?'

'Yes, my friend, Hector worked a miracle. And he now intends going off to Moth for a well-earned break.'

'From what I've heard he is a miracle in his own right. A talking salamander, whatever next! So, we can rely on the salamanders to heal us of the dread plague?'

Adler grimaced. 'They are slow, very, very slow, and I'm fearful there won't be enough of the creatures available to us if the plague runs rampant. But there's nothing we can do about it, we'll just have to cope the best we can,' Adler shook his head dubiously.

'I'm sorry to interrupt, Adler, but we must get going,' said Aidan barely containing his impatience. 'Can we levitate to the mineshaft now?'

'Of course…of course, my apologies my young friend. Brickel,' he said, 'I shan't be long. I'll accompany these above and return shortly.'

'Wait, there's a problem in the mineshaft. It's blocked. The roof of the tunnel has collapsed just along from where the floor fell here. You won't be able to get through to Meltwater yet, Lord Aidan. But we were fortunate, Adler, your nephew Dom was here with the young krynx he's training. Being small it wasn't too heavy to levitate and they're both now in the shaft working to clear an access hole through the fall.'

'But isn't that dangerous? I mean, isn't it impossible to bore a hole through something that isn't solid. The fall is loose rubble, isn't it?' asked Aidan anxiously.

Beatrix squeezed his hand tighter. 'Dom's not in danger is he? I'd never forgive myself if anything happened to him.'

'He'll be fine, there are adults up there supervising,' said Brickel. 'We aren't too sure how deep the fall is but Dom is adamant that Halcwyn is quite capable of processing the rock. As long as his speed is checked he'll accomplish the task easily.'

'Halcwyn, that's Dom's krynx?' and at Brickel's nod Aidan asked. 'What do you mean "as long as his speed is checked"?'

It was Adler who answered. 'Like all young animals and Halcwyn is very young, two years old. He tends to be headstrong and will go like a bull at a gate at the rockfall. Speed, I'm afraid, could be fatal to all up there—that's why Dom has not been left on his own.'

'Oh, God, Aidan, let's get up there before something bad happens to him,' Beattie said her face draining.

'I'll come with you,' said Brickel, her anxiety infectious. 'I've told Dom to clear a hole just large enough for you and your young man to gain access into Meltwater. He is to clean the remainder of the fall when you are through so there is no obstruction for the people of the town. They are going to be nervous enough as it is without having to clamber through a roof fall. Don't worry, Milady, Dom is a good lad he knows what to do.'

A little later, Aidan still holding Beattie's hand, and accompanied by the two Green Men, levitated towards the roof. Beattie didn't take her eyes from Aidan's face as they rose through the air. She wondered if Aidan had noted Brickel's words earlier. Could Aidan possibly accept that he was "her young man" or was she pinning her hopes on a false dream? But she again thought of Augusta, her childhood friend, in love with Aidan. She would never condone Beattie's feelings when she didn't understand them herself. A cold shiver ran down her back. Was she betraying Augusta? But she wanted Aidan, and she wanted him to be more than just a friend.

It was a long lift to the roof and it gave Aidan pause for thought. Was this rockfall going to be the straw that broke his back? Was the delay going to kill Tragen? Beattie and Anders had said that whatever happens in between, they'd all go off tomorrow in search of the wizard and Aidan was going to hold them to it. Beattie had promised him. And then he recalled the very same words that Beattie was mulling over. Was he her young man? He liked the sound of it but at the moment he was Augusta's young man. He didn't know quite what to do but knew he'd have to face the problem at some time. Or everyone was going to get hurt. But for now he contented himself with squeezing Beattie's hand… he did like that.

All four rose through the rupture in the mineshaft's floor and entered a gloomy tunnel with just enough height to stand in. Light emanated from two salamanders emitting red heat. The resultant red light was somewhat unnerving if you weren't used to it and, of course, Aidan and Beattie were not. Still red was better than white in this confined space; white heat would have fried everyone within the mineshaft.

Brickel's colleagues were frantically digging at the rockfall that filled the whole tunnel at the Meltwater end. Glancing over his shoulder behind him at the tunnel disappearing into the distance Aidan saw little obstruction in that direction and wondered fleetingly if there was access to the town that way. He didn't think on it long as the floor at that end sloped ever downwards, deeper into the very heart of Mount Peaceful.

Beattie, fed up of squinting in the unnatural light, raised her own light illuminating the work at the fall. The Green People were assisting Dom and Halcwyn by shifting rock and dust that fell by the wayside. They were then hardening the walls of the aperture as the young krynx, a little way ahead of them, buried its head into the loose detritus in front of it, devouring what it could. The noise was almost intolerable, a perpetual sound of crunching stone in huge teeth, the gulping. The krynx, though small, burped loudly enough to be full grown and as Beattie walked closer there was a continual whooshing sound.

'Not too much light, Beattie, you may need all your strength when we get out of here,' Aidan warned speaking quietly.

Beattie couldn't hear him over the din of the krynx and she turned her head towards Aidan. 'What?'

'Don't stand there,' screamed Dom.

But it was too late. Beattie had inadvertently walked up directly behind Halcwyn merrily munching away at the rock. His digestive system was working overtime and nutrients were being added pell-mell to the minerals in its gut, with the inevitable result that the produce was defecated from the vent in its tail. Beattie received a full blast, spraying her from head to toe. She was dumbstruck, too surprised and disgusted to do or say anything when she was pulled clear by an amused Green Man.

'Ah-h,' she screamed when she eventually found her voice. 'What is this?' she asked holding up the new soil in her hands. 'It smells absolutely disgusting,' she said shaking her hands free of it, brushing down her shirt and running her fingers through her matted hair.

Aidan and Dom were laughing too much to answer.

'What are you laughing at, you pigs? Ugh, it smells like a sewer.'

'Well,' and he rubbed the tears from his eyes, doing his damndest to stifle his mirth. 'Well…it would.'

'What?' And then it dawned on her. 'Oh no! Leonid said krynx's…you know…' and she blushed beneath the grime, 'everything they eat immediately. Is this what's…what's all over me?' she stared down at her clothes, the horror on her face bringing on more smiles until she lost her temper and began throwing handfuls of shite at them.

The Green People standing back towards the hole in the floor to make way for the wizards, looked on bemused, their behaviour reminding Adler sharply that these were young people, not children maybe, but still very young. And he was saddened. The future was so very dire for them. Full grown, experienced warriors would balk at the fearsome task facing these two young wizards and their friends. The thought that they're young lives could very well be cut short—as would everyone's if they should fail, nearly broke his heart. 'I think, my friends, we had better check progress.'

And it was then there came a fresh fall of rock, the dust billowing out obscuring Halcwyn and Beattie's light. 'Dom,' she screamed and she grabbed him, Holding him close while Aidan wrapped them both in his arms and instinctively raised a shield waiting for the fall to settle.

Fifty-three

'Dear God, this robe stinks,' moaned Elstan, his bell tolling its warning "beware", at the top of his staff and shuffling along as befits a leper.

Chong, walking beside him also dragged his feet, it was easier…he didn't have to pick them up so high. Athelstan Makepeace had worked wonders, but not miracles and he'd implored Chong to take care or he'd undo all his good work. He ordered the oriental to be cautious, make no sudden movements, take things slow or he'd end up worse than he had after previous healings. Makepeace also told him bluntly that if he didn't follow his instructions then he'd never recover and this time it would quite likely be a permanent affliction—he'd never walk again. And that's what frightened Chong more than anything—not being able to walk around any library, no more exploring and searching for answers.

'Stop complaining, Elstan. We're out and about aren't we? No-one will recognize us in these clothes,' said Chong-An, puffing behind the horrible stench of the calico across his mouth. However much he blew the fabric from his mouth, it still made contact with his lips. It tasted abominable.

'You're not wrong there. Where'd Travis get these rags, the local midden?' Elstan asked, desperately trying to keep down the contents of his stomach. He struggled on; gagging at what he saw on his friend's robe, knowing the foulness was also on his. 'How are you managing?' he whispered, head bowed, no leper ever made eye contact with those not similarly afflicted. The ignorant thought that the maimed had the evil eye and would pass on the malady just by looking at them. Many lepers had lost their lives at imagined glances. Today, though, crowds parted as if by magic allowing free passage to the two heavily shrouded, very dirty, diseased disciples.

Elstan's long night with Messalina had worked wonders on his state of mind. Nonetheless, Messalina had not been at all happy at him leaving that morning, so he'd spent a bit longer going over everything with her again. But it was up to her if he left under a cloud…and that she would have none of, this time. Promising to wait for him she delayed his departure another half an hour before kissing him

435

goodbye. Lastly, he'd leant over Trinity's cot and kissed the sleeping girl's head, caressing her face as he left.

Returning to Chong he was walking on air. Explaining his absence, the oriental had smiled. Elstan no longer fidgeted, jumping at every unexpected noise, though he didn't seem to have had much rest. Elstan grinned behind the calico mask when his friend mentioned his exhaustion. Chong's face turned blood red after moments.

The townsfolk jostled each other in their haste to gain the best seats. Those who failed battled for at least a good place to stand so as to have an unobstructed view of the execution. All were surprised when they saw the Soaring Myners rigging a tightrope across the square in front of the podium.

Unlike at previous feasts, there were now three entertainments promised for today—the aerial acrobatics above the square, the execution of the heretic and in the evening the vastly popular circus making their second appearance. Included in tonight's show was the contest of carnival skills. It was always magnificent; carnies from all over the known world were there to perform their specialized feats of excellence. Reputations were made and lost at the Mulkie's spectacle, the successful artistes commanding large fees at castles and mansions all over the empire.

The Elders of Mulkie's Cross always played host to the circus on Kaneshi's Feast Days. The purpose was twofold. The first, in order to worship the God of Disease and Despair, and the second, because it drew people from all walks of life to experience the wonders of the big-top. The Elders milked the spectators of every coin they possessed. In Mulkie's Cross Kaneshi was worshipped, by the Elders at least, for also being the God of easy wealth, though no-one ever voiced this. They could have joined Cledwyn at the block for their heresy.

But as well as the trapeze artistes, bear wrestling and boxing booths, the people had the added attraction of the beheading of Cledwyn. There were never many official public executions in Drakka, though there were many unofficial…a solution to problems meted out quicker, whether it was justified or not. But this putting to death of the Grekko felon had all the hallmarks of a classic exhibition.

The spectators, stall-holders, richer merchants and travellers kept glancing at the low-standing wooden block Cledwyn would lay his neck upon, a wicker basket placed conspicuously on the boards in front of it. Chairs for the Elders and Kaneshi's many high priests had been placed around the two sides and across the rear of the high staging. In front of the podium, on the cobbles of the square, long rows of unstable benches had been placed. These were for spectators who had paid exorbitant fees for the privilege of witnessing the head fall into the basket. And the mayor, looking out of his office in the Town Hall behind the stage, gloated. He was in for a huge profit on the day.

Cledwyn had always been a source of intolerance and rage for Smallwood, his differing felonies usually resulting in a loss of revenue for the chief merchant. But now the mayor was going to have his revenge and at the same time reap a fortune in viewing fees. Smallwood grinned, the fool grekko was about to suffer a pain in the collar above all those pains in the neck he had always visited on him. He smiled; the idiot was about to meet the Grim Reaper …let him suffer the arsehole.

The crowd began gathering early in the morning, streets around the square a throng of moving citizens, the festive cheer bringing the best and the worst out in people. Scuffles broke out amongst those who had purchased prized seats, the losers turned out of the square by the local militia. Urchins of the town were already pushing their way in and out of the half-awake crowd with a cheery laugh and a handful of purses lifted from unwary pockets. Hot pie vendors did a roaring trade as did the jellied eel sellers and cocoa men with sweets on sticks—all of them paying a tax to the mayor.

But, whoever they were, high or low, fat or thin, pious or blasphemous all moved out of the way and made room for the lepers. There were a number of the sadly stricken people already congregating in front of the execution dais. They caused much annoyance to the paying customers whose view of the beheading was likely to be obstructed.

The militia had no alternative but to allow any of the equally bloodthirsty, although disfigured, individuals to take up a place standing at the podium. There was nothing anyone could really do to thwart the status of the lepers—it was a sin to harass them on these three days. Not even Smallwood's elite band of law-keepers was allowed to manhandle the victims of the dread disease. But the lepers did not take advantage, even when drunk, for their safety was only assured during the days of the festival. Aggrieved people with long memories came looking for the miscreants after the feast. And so the lepers disappeared into the forest within hours of partaking of the best meal in their sorry lives.

Kaneshi, Lord of Disease and Despair, required his feast once a year to remind people that if they did not worship him in the correct manner, then foul ailments and abject desolation would be their lot. And that's why lepers were the town's guests demanded by the priests of Kaneshi. The victims' sole purpose was to remind the unwary that Kaneshi's displeasure would result in everyone suffering the disfiguring skin lesions, thickening nodular skin, the loss of feeling and the amputations. And, of course, the priests of Kaneshi's shrine expected and got ample donations to tide them over the forthcoming year. So no-one ever chased the lepers out of town on these days. On the first two days the townsfolk celebrated with the carnival. On the third the lepers feasted before his shrine, their faces uncovered and served at table by those same townsfolk.

Although the execution was not scheduled until the late afternoon, by noon the powers that be were taking their places choosing the best seats on either side of the platform, their eyes resting every now and then on the low, hardwood block, covered in ugly brown stains. Smoking tobacco, drinking brandy and wine and generally comporting themselves in a dignified manner befitting their status, they did as they always did—they peered down their noses at the peasants. They sat, preening themselves like peacocks before peahens, and watched the crowd watching them.

'How are you feeling,' Elstan asked once again over the din of the spectators.

'A lot better than these poor beggars,' Chong said indicating the disabled walking before them.

'Aye, perhaps you're right. Well, this way,' and Elstan moved to the left making for the bakery on the corner of the square with Frog Street. The crowd melted from in front of them, people afraid to look the poor lepers in the eye, shuffling quickly away.

They approached the front of the only shop on the square with double doors. Made of old pine they were flung wide and the delicious aroma of fresh baked bread and savouries wafted across the heads of itinerants already in the shop purchasing the baker's wares. It also streamed over those making their way to the execution dais.

Chong grabbed Elstan's arm as he stepped up on the boards lining the road on that side of the square. 'Hang on, this may be Kaneshi's Feast days but I don't think it's seemly for two lepers to walk in at the front door. The customers would have a fit. There are people in this square looking for the unusual—we don't want to be

438

more conspicuous than we are. No leper would dare walk in any shop whatever day it was.'

Elstan paused, his foot already on the threshold, he glanced around quickly chewing his bottom lip behind the dirty calico strips wound around his face, leaving only his eyes free of obstruction.

'Aye, perhaps you're right.' He led Chong around the corner into Frog Street and to the alley at the side of the bakery where supplies were delivered. They both pushed their way around sacks of flour piled haphazardly at the doorway and walked past the huge red-brick ovens into a small office at the rear of the busy shop.

They pushed the door open and strode into the middle of one almighty shouting match. Athelstan Makepeace, red-faced, and a stocky, middle aged man wearing a bright yellow kerchief knotted tightly about his head were going at it like a hammer on an anvil. Standing between them with his arms outstretched, a big hand on each of their chests was the baker. Barnaby Routh, a sandy haired man with massive shoulders and a temper ready to burst, now had his hands full keeping the two protagonists from coming to blows. All three stopped in mid-flow at seeing two lepers walk in on them.

'What the hell…' Routh, his face already suffused with anger, stared at the interlopers. 'No lepers are allowed in my shop. Get out, now!'

'Tut…tut, Barnaby, where are your manners?' Elstan said, dropping his cowl around his shoulders, and pulling down the rags hiding his face.

'Elstan, by all that's holy…am I glad to see you. Hey, that's what I call a disguise man…you smell though,' he said wrinkling his nose in disgust. 'Stay well away from my produce I don't want you contaminating my bread,' and Routh laughed as he greeted his friend with a huge backbreaking hug. 'You're just in time to sort out these two idiots for me.'

'I beg your pardon; no-one calls me an idiot…you fool of a scullion maid.' Makepeace gripped the front of Routh's shirt, pulling it part way from the apron tied around the baker's waist. And despite Routh's weight, Makepeace lifted him bodily to one side so that he could get at his opponent.

Routh, too dumbfounded at the insult and too surprised at actually being lifted off his feet, stared mouth agape at the gentlemanly healer. None of them ever having seen Makepeace in such a temper

439

before, they were all astonished at the healer's display of almost superhuman strength.

'Do not speak to poor lepers in that fashion in front of me,' he stormed. 'No leper is at fault for having the disease and it is only your crass ignorance that makes you afraid of them. They are deserving of your sympathy, not your scorn. Fool!'

'Okay…okay, Athelstan, calm down, I didn't know they weren't real lepers now did I?' Routh held onto Makepeace's hands, desperately glad they weren't around his neck.

'That's not what I meant. Cretin!' he shouted, purple with rage. 'All right…all right,' the baker paused, his brow furrowed in puzzlement; Makepeace had lost him in his tirade.

'What did you mean then? I'm nobody's bloody fool…fool! I'm no ignorant peasant and you've no right to call me such…' Routh stopped in mid-sentence; Makepeace's face was all the colours of the rainbow now.

'By the Gods, I've said it enough times over the years, haven't you been listening. Lepers are not contagious when treated with the correct medication. Do you understand? You are not going to catch leprosy from a victim receiving the proper care. I ought to know, I've spent my life treating them.'

'Aye, man, and how the hell am I supposed to know whose receiving treatment? They all look the same wearing them masks, don't they?' asked Routh, his normally purple nose turning an even darker colour.

'Whoa, you two, leave it, we've more important matters to discuss,' said Elstan interrupting, hoping to calm things down.

But his words only served to antagonize the healer even more and Makepeace turned on Elstan, venting his spleen. 'Nothing…I repeat…nothing is more important to a leper than the disease!' he snarled.

'All right, I'm sorry, I should have said we have more urgent matters to discuss, okay?' and Makepeace, controlling himself with a tremendous effort, held his tongue as Elstan studied the object of Athelstan's initial fury.

'Who is this Barnaby?' he asked inclining his head at the third man now standing flat against the back wall, who was finding it expedient to remain silent.

'This is Beeton, an ally of Cledwyn's, trying to organize his escape. This is the oriental sorcerer we've all been hearing about, is

440

it?' The baker asked, his voice struggling to regain its normal composure as he watched Chong removing the dirty calico strips to reveal his face.

'Aye, gentlemen, meet Chong-An, ex-Guild and very good friend of mine who is also going to assist us in rescuing Cledwyn. By the way, he's a wizard not a sorcerer. He doesn't practise the black arts.'

'I'm glad to hear it,' said Routh.

'Chong-An you say?' Beeton asked frowning. 'I've heard Cledwyn speak of you, he's taken you into the Drikander many times hasn't he?'

'What else has he been saying about me?' Chong asked suddenly nervous, wondering if Cledwyn had broken his oath and mentioned the Green People's library.

'He said you were fat and a right pain in the arse when you got a notion in your head. He also said he trusted you with his life,' the thief smiled to take away any insult. 'And if Cledwyn trusts you, then so do I. Welcome to Mulkie's Cross,' and he held out his hand to be shaken by Chong.

'Cledwyn may be a rogue but he's the best guide I've ever met,' and it was Chong's turn to smile. 'I also trust him with my life. I'm not too sure whether I'd say the same about my purse…he does make a lot of money out of me. But Elstan and I need him desperately now to get us through the Drikander ahead of our pursuers.' Chong sat himself on the edge of the table used as a desk by the baker.

'Ah! You haven't many pursuers behind you now, my dear Chong,' said Makepeace smiling, 'the last count was three and that includes Drudwynn.'

Elstan smirked. 'I told you the man was careless, Chong. The two he has left must be getting very nervous by now.'

'What about the magus, any sign of him yet?' asked Chong.

'I overheard the mayor speak of him,' said Makepeace amused. 'It seems that Smallwood is rather perturbed at the magus' visit at this time—he's never been here at the time of Kaneshi before or at the same time as his deputy. Drudwynn has planted himself on Smallwood's hospitality, even demanding the best bed, which of course is Smallwood's. If Brenin arrives tonight or tomorrow, Mayor Smallwood and his family are going to move out. He doesn't want to be on the square at the same time as those two. But he's got a small problem, there's no room at the tavern he's picked, he has told the landlord to throw people out ready for him…and they're not having it.'

'Good,' said Beeton, 'Smallwood's always been a pain in the arse; it's about time he got some trouble back.'

'Brenin seems to be travelling very slowly on the road, he should have arrived here days ago,' said Chong puzzled.

'Yes, my oriental wizard,' answered the healer, 'it seems that Brenin has been holding meetings on the road with various strangers. They converse with him in extreme privacy and then ride away apace. And there have been many such clandestine meetings.'

'Putting his plans into operation…whatever they are,' mused Elstan.

'What plans?' asked Routh feeling out of his depth.

'Something I overheard, Barnaby, and I wish I knew what it meant. But whatever they are you can be sure they bear ill for us. So we have to initiate Cledwyn's rescue well before Brenin turns up.'

'Well, I'm sorry to have to bear bad tidings, my friends,' said Makepeace frowning, 'Drudwynn is taking pride of place at the execution. He wants to address, or should I say harangue the crowd, before the axe drops on Cledwyn's neck.'

Beeton quailed at the uncalled for vision of his friend's head in the wicker basket. 'Please, have you got to be so graphic?'

'That's going to complicate matters, Chong. Having Drudwynn actually on the stage when we are trying to get Cledwyn off it, is going to create one hell of a problem. Are you sure no-one else can take you to the…'

Chong interrupted Elstan quickly before he could divulge any mention of the library. 'Elstan, please, we've discussed this already. Cledwyn is the only one who can help us,' and he turned away. 'Can you tell us how he fares in prison, Master Makepeace?'

'Oh, Athelstan, please, Chong-An. You were correct in your assumption. The call was a ploy to contact me so that I could relay information to Beeton here. The fool was lucky mind. The lypyn overdose nearly fried his brain. I only just managed to pull him round.' Makepeace wiped clean a corner of the baker's desk alongside Chong-An and perched his backside on its edge, ensuring his clothes remained free of any flour. 'He wants Beeton to create a diversion with the rest of his cohorts and me to release him so that he can flee from the rear of the dais.'

'I gather you are to accompany the other dignitaries on the podium then, am I right?' asked Elstan.

'You are, and I am to choose a leper to stand with me.'

'A leper? Why on earth…what is the reason for that bizarre request?' asked Chong.

'It is Kaneshi's Feast and Mayor Smallwood wants to enhance his own profits. He's put it around that he's having a leper kiss Cledwyn before the axe falls. I'm sorry Beeton there's no other way to put it,' he said when the felon winced.

'The purpose being to pass on the disease, I take it,' said Elstan rubbing his neck. A tic beneath his left eye was troubling him the more he thought of the absurdity of this escapade.

'Yes, he's an idiot, another one who doesn't realize that leprosy can't be passed on when I am treating him. Besides, although Cledwyn is smart, I don't think even he will show signs of the disease in the little time between the kiss and his head falling off. Mind you,' and the healer smirked, 'I suppose it is the ultimate form of spewing your guts up.'

'Really, Athelstan, there's no call for that,' Chong-An remarked, desperately striving to hide a smile as he watched Beeton retch.

'Yes, well if we don't laugh over this situation we'll end up crying. But the mayor seems to think the crowd will believe it shows his sincerity where Kaneshi is concerned,' replied Makepeace brushing a speck of dust from his knees.

'So, you get the easy job of releasing Cledwyn,' said Elstan grimacing. 'Does he say how you are to cut him free of his bindings when the executioner, the mayor, the local hobnobs and Brother Drudwynn, are all on stage?'

'That's where Beeton comes in. The podium will be crowded with Drudwynn centre stage, hopefully standing in front of Cledwyn when he makes his speech. Beeton, here, will create a diversion while I carry out the deed.'

'You'll need one hell of a diversion, 'said Routh shaking his head.

'That's what Cledwyn wanted the healer to pass on to me. He's told me to use the horses that the carnival has housed in the stockade. We're going to loose them and stampede them through the crowd,' said Beeton triumphantly.

'And besides hurting and probably killing a lot of men, women and children in the square, it will also immediately alert everyone on the podium and they'll watch Cledwyn like a hawk—or kill him straight away. Will you convince him of that fact, Elstan? Makepeace asked. 'For that is what we were arguing about when you walked in the door.'

'As it happens we have that already organized,' said Elstan. 'Otto and I had the same idea in using the horses. He will drive them around the square, avoiding as many people as he can while the Soaring Myners perform above the podium as an added distraction.'

'Otto? Who is he?' asked Makepeace.

'The ringmaster…and friend,' answered Elstan keeping his fingers crossed, Otto had hardly shown friendship when he'd tried to dislocate his jaw. 'Otto is going to drive the horses into Smallwood's shops and stalls, which should suffice to give the mayor apoplexy and drive him, hopefully, from the podium. At least it will delay the execution.'

'Ah! I like it. Well, it puts an end to my arguing with this clown, anyway,' said Makepeace nodding at Beeton who decided to keep his mouth shut. 'If the mayor does run, so will others. I must have a chance to remain free, for if I'm caught helping Cledwyn then at the very least I will never be able to work in Mulkie's Cross, or anywhere in the south for that matter, ever again. My work with the lepers is very important to me as well as to them. I will not risk my treatment of these poor people for a stupid felon like Cledwyn. If I'm caught, Drudwynn is more likely to put my head on the block as well.'

'He is not a stupid felon, Makepeace; you don't appreciate him is all. He's done a lot of people a lot of good in his time, otherwise we wouldn't want to help him,' retorted Beeton.

'Then give me a chance of succeeding.' Makepeace shouted. 'You all might have worked out the diversions but everything depends on me being near enough to get him away.'

'Has Cledwyn made any suggestions as to how you are to actually free him?' asked Elstan, taking Routh's place and standing between the two protagonists squaring up to each other again.

'He wants the leper to cut his bonds when he is kissed. He trusts me to find a suitable candidate. You know one who isn't infectious and doesn't mind dying when he's discovered doing it,' Makepeace said unable to hide the sarcasm in his voice.

'Another easy job, my friend,' said Elstan grimly.

444

'Why let himself be kissed? It doesn't make sense, we don't want him with leprosy when he's free and as for the leper he's dying anyway,' asked Beeton.

And this time Makepeace did blow. He grabbed hold of Elstan and threw him out of the way. He lunged for Beeton who was very slow reacting and the healer swung a right-hander that would have floored a horse. It did floor Beeton and he ended up unconscious slumped against the rear wall with Makepeace panting above him.

'Very good, Athelstan, that solves a lot of problems, doesn't it. How can we formulate a plan with a comatose conspirator?' Elstan said impatiently.

'I don't care—a leper has the right to life.'

'Yes, Athelstan, I agree. But all the same, a leper's presence will be useful on the stage. Who gets to choose him, is it you?' asked Chong quietly, his voice and his words bringing order. Makepeace nodded.

'Very well...if you'll excuse me, my friend, we really do need him awake.' Chong-An walked across to the recumbent Beeton, placed his index finger to the man's forehead, mumbled and Beeton awoke with a start.

'Come, stand up Master Beeton and listen. There will be no more unthinking remarks from either of you,' he said glancing quickly at the healer astounded at the speed Beeton recovered.

'I thought you weren't a healer,' said Makepeace.

'I'm not, but I know how to wake a man.'

'What have you in mind,' asked Elstan, not in the least surprised. He was getting used to Chong's magic.

'How and when will you choose the leper?' Chong asked.

Makepeace was, for a moment, unable to find his voice. 'Um...I will take him from the crowd in front of the podium. He will accompany me onto the stage and we'll both stand either side of Cledwyn.

'Good. Make sure you pick Elstan.'

'Wha-at!' Elstan said suddenly losing colour.

'You will masquerade as the leper. Don't worry I'll create a spell to make it foolproof even when you lower your cowl to kiss him,' said Chong taking not a blind bit of notice at the panic on his friend's face. 'You will have all the appearance of a leper, the hard skin, puffed eyes...no nose.'

445

'No nose?' Elstan said in a voice that sounded as if he was being strangled.

'Yes, and you will have a knife hidden in your sleeves to cut his bonds. There'll be no need for you to worry,' Chong said, 'well, I don't think so.'

'You don't think so?' Elstan said his voice an almost silent croak.

'Where will you be, Chong,' asked Makepeace, smiling at Elstan's discomfiture.

'On this side of the square, so Drudwynn will see me. When Otto stampedes the horses around the square, I'll also cause another, hopefully more spectacular, diversion. With any luck those on the podium won't know what in hell is happening. And to cover your part in the escapade, Athelstan, for Elstan will be busy getting Cledwyn clear, you will be discovered later in the wreckage with your colleagues.'

'Wreckage?' asked Makepeace anxiously, his face also now draining of colour.

'I'll get my nose back, won't I, Chong?' asked Elstan plaintively.

'Of course, and I promise not to tell Messalina that you go around kissing men.'

Fifty-four

It was early evening when Bazyli entered the gorge half a night's riding still in front of him. He wasn't going to rest, his mission in Meltwater too urgent. He rubbed his eyes in the sudden gloom, weary to his bones he hadn't slept for two days and nights. He had spent the time cajoling, sometimes with anger, very often with the power in his arms, but mostly persuading with his smooth tongue and logic. The Montetors, the Portolans and the foreigners off the many ships found it hard to believe that demons were being brought to the island within the Darkness. Nevertheless, Griffin Town was evacuated and Bazyli raced past the people making for the catacombs on the old track past the forest the wizards had used on their first visit to Bylani. He bore right from the track and joined the north road to Meltwater, his duty dictating that he fetch the people there to safety. But he only had at the most one day to accomplish the task; the thought of failure was too horrendous even to contemplate.

He turned in the saddle and stared south at the horizon displaying the madness approaching with a rapidity that almost brought on panic. It did increase his impending sense of doom. The Darkness was devouring the town of Griffin, streets disappearing like magic, buildings once standing proudly under the sun, gone within moments. And he was petrified, for he fancied that even at this distance he could hear again the terrible moaning within the black fog.

He had this last day, if the mountain slowed the fog's advance, perhaps another half a day, to bring his people out of Meltwater and into Bylani. It was too late now to take them off the island. Every ship and small boat, including those of Lodovico's navy, were sailing east, west and south. All taken up with transporting Griffin's citizens to a safe haven some on the mainland of Drakka, others the Gods knew where. But if the wind continued to blow the fog east – and the wind stopping was against all the laws of nature – then Drakka would be threatened, overwhelmed in time. How far would people need to run to find safety? If the young wizards failed then nothing could stop the Darkness drifting over the whole world. No-one would escape the depredations of whatever demons travelled with the Darkness.

Bazyli was despondent. The only ship left anywhere in the islands was the Grim lying off Moth effecting repairs and awaiting the arrival of the wizards.

He sighed and again turned his horse's head to the north and walked his mare through the narrowing gorge. The Montetor was mortally afraid that he wouldn't have time enough to organize the evacuation. He mulled over the news he had received earlier by a messenger sent by Razor, the message forcing him to leave the evacuation of the remnant of his people to the Portolan.

Bazyli had had no option. He could understand why his orders to flee had been disobeyed by the townsfolk of Meltwater. They were abandoning their livelihood, businesses built up sometimes over centuries. No-one wanted to leave without protecting their families and their property. But Razor had failed to persuade them of the dire necessity, failed to convince them that their lives were more important than their shops and their mines.

His clan had always obeyed the Montetor in the past, always trusted his judgement. Why had they decided now to distrust him when, at this crucial time, every minute of every hour counted?

He brooded in the oppressive silence, only the clipping of his horse's hoofs, walking slowly, sounding in the gorge in the approaching dusk. He unconsciously eased his sword in its scabbard as he reached the narrowest place on the trail. It was a constriction of the road between high rock walls, excavated hundreds of years before to facilitate travel between the north and the south of the island. A location that had seen many a robbery before he'd managed to bring law to the road. For years people had now trod this highway in safety, but he was still wary and that was why he brought his head up abruptly when he heard an unwelcome voice calling out to him. He halted and peered ahead, his hackles rising.

'Excellency, thank God it's you. Can you help me, my horse threw me...I think I've broken my ankle.'

'Alvar, is that you?' Instinctively he tensed. Cautiously he looked around. Alvar was a Montetor clansman but not one of his trusted followers. Razor, though, did use him on occasion in troubles with the Portolans, but not with Bazyli's blessing. Alvar was a minor rogue and had been arraigned before the Montetor many times in the past, receiving trifling punishment, witnesses to his crimes very often failing to appear before his court. 'What are you doing out here?' he asked suspiciously.

'Razor sent me to warn you of the riots in Meltwater.'

'What riots…what are you talking about man? And why would he send you?' Approaching the stricken man he continued to study the road about him but, despite perceiving no threat, he nevertheless swung his right arm across his belly and grasped the hilt of his sword hanging at his left side.

Up above Lyell smiled. He waited a moment longer for his quarry to settle, he didn't want to fall on the man and find his sword point in his throat. Godun licked his lips, the excitement drying his mouth. He looked across the gorge at his leader, awaiting the signal to attack. It was going to be too easy, he thought, and almost laughed aloud. Alvar, though, was beginning to panic. He couldn't see his leader and wondered why Lyell was delaying the attack. Becoming increasingly anxious at the lack of action he prepared to run for it. There was no way he could keep up the pretence of an injury to his ankle if Bazyli examined it closely.

But Lyell was waiting for Bazyli to remove his hand from his sword and begin to dismount. He didn't have long to wait. As the Montetor took his foot from his right stirrup and leant forward to swing out of the saddle, Lyell and Godun fell on him from above. The combined weight of the two drove the rider heavily to the ground and the horse fled. At the same time Alvar jumped up from the side of the road and bashed Bazyli over the head with a rock. Bazyli, unconscious, his head bleeding, did not feel a thing as he was picked up and dragged over to a nearby oak tree. His arms were pulled back almost out of their sockets and roped tightly, his feet similarly secured, his head flopping on his chest. The three conspirators, breathing heavily, laughed nervously as the tension of the last hours wore off. They rested sitting on the roadway, their backs against rocks opposite the silent man, and gloated.

'Oh, boy, I'm glad that's over,' Alvar said wringing his hands to relieve the nerviness in his fingers.

'What do you mean…it was easy,' grunted Lyell revelling in the success of the plan. 'I think I must have crushed his ribs, did you hear them crack?' he smirked. 'Now we'll get to the really interesting bit. How long do you reckon before he comes around, Godun?'

'Shite knows! Alvar hit him a bit too hard for my liking. Perhaps that cracking you heard was his skull. You'd better have not done us out of our fun, Alvar boy, or we'll take it out on you instead,' he growled, meaning every word of the threat. He'd waited too long to have his revenge on the Montetor.

'Well, I had to knock him out didn't I? Nah, he's not dead…nowhere near dead yet. We'll still have our fun, you wait.'

'You'd better be right, pass the bludgeon this is thirsty work,' said Lyell unable to hide his elation.

Unseen in the trees a hundred yards or so up the road nearer Meltwater, Lewyn and his cat watched the attack and its aftermath. Cyryl was puzzled; they were supposed to kill the Montetor straight away not hang about. Razor would be on pins waiting news of his leader's death. He had urgent matters to prepare before he could announce his succession to clan leader of the Montetors. And then there was the execution of the prince and princess to be dealt with quietly. Lewyn grinned at the thought of the boy's comeuppance. There was no need for him to kick Hyacinth like he did. Lewyn stroked his cat's head and noticed the bald spot had grown, there was hardly any fur now on one side.

He watched the three assassins closely and, overhearing their talk of fun, he grinned again. This he wanted to watch—and so did his cat, it was purring. Bazyli had never had much time for Lewyn either, always poking fun at his bald head…him with his scar an' all! But o' course he didn't have a scar anymore. But the thought of witnessing his clan leader's torture was going to be a reward in itself. Nonetheless, Lewyn had never expected Lyell to delay carrying out Razor's orders, although, thinking it over it came as no surprise. Lyell hated Bazyli Montetor and everyone knew it. Everyone also knew of Lyell's liking for causing pain. Lewyn had been at the receiving end himself on more than one occasion when he'd upset the big man over something trivial. What was the last occasion? And then he remembered, Hyacinth had been thirsty and had lapped the big man's ale. Lewyn had been lucky to get away with just a gashed arm, the cat with its life.

Lewyn was worried, though. They didn't have much time to return to Meltwater with the news of Bazyli's demise. He was tempted to reveal his presence and tell them to hurry up, but he didn't want to bear again the brunt of Lyell's malice. He was quite likely to add another's torture to his night's entertainment. He waited, relieved at least that the Montetor had been taken and there was no escape for him. Lewyn smiled and stroked Hyacinth's head…the shape-shifter snarled, he hated that. Standing up quietly Lewyn turned away to relieve himself, the excitement playing hell with his bladder.

Anders sweated profusely, the perspiration stinging his eyes making him blink to clear his vision. He paced short, quick steps across the velvet grass beneath his feet, the verdant growth springing back up unharmed as he lifted his feet. There was no wind in Anders' Limbo, not even a slight breeze as he moved—but there were sounds. They were the everyday noises of Life leaping from the wall of colours, a constant murmur in the background intruding on his thoughts. He frantically puzzled a solution from his stagnant brain. His head was splitting, the ache unbearable as he raged impotently. His knife, Dolly's misericorde, was an unremitting blur leaping from one hand to the other in the stillness as he passed back and forth in front of the resplendent oak tree. He looked up at it, its knobbly bark catching his eye. He wondered if he banged his head against it would he perceive a glimmer of a plan to rescue the Montetor. Pummel a solution into his brain; come up with a way to stop the murder. He shook his head knowing the answer was not in the tree. He turned back to the wall, staring at it he prepared to watch the man's torture, knowing he was impotent to save him.

An hour or so later Bazyli regained consciousness, his groan unheard over the merrymaking of his captors. The drunken revelry bringing immediate remembrance of the attack, he remained motionless assessing the situation with his chin on his chest. He was aching all over. Their treatment of him had not been gentle when they dragged him to the tree and tied him to it. He hurt abominably. There was blood dripping slowly past his right ear, the gash throbbing in the cooling night air. His shoulders burned with the pain of overstretched sinews, his feet numb the ropes restricting the blood flow to his toes. Listening to the raucous noises of his attackers he eventually opened his eyes and squinted across the road.

Lyell was obviously in charge, his back against a large rock he was swigging from the jug of rotgut brandy, its heavy aroma drifting across the road and assailing Bazyli's senses. The man clicked his fingers and Alvar, sitting one side of him, passed him a lump of dried beef from the canvas bag at his feet. Godun lounging on the other side had his eyes closed, he'd always been a tired man, some said too tired to get out of his own way. But when there was illicit money to be made Godun could move just as quickly as any other. He had a very quick eye for a victim's lax security. None of them were taking much notice of their prisoner. They were enjoying themselves, the anticipation just as enjoyable as the actual torture was going to be. They were in no rush to get down to business.

Alvar commenced a very lewd song and picking his nose he studied avidly what he retrieved from his nostril and then flicked it away.

'Stop that, ya pig, I'm eating,' shouted Lyell cuffing Alvar on the side of his head.

'Ow, there's no need for that,' he said rubbing his head.

'Yes there is, if it wasn't for you we'd have had him dead and been long gone from here, by now.'

Godun opened one eye and glanced at the Montetor. 'Couldn't we throw a bucket of water over him…wake him up like?'

'And where are we going to get a bucket round here, let alone the water, dickhead?' Lyell growled.

Bazyli listened to their bickering. He seethed. He had no time to be waiting here he had to get to Meltwater as soon as possible. Each minute spent tied to this tree could mean countless numbers losing their lives in the Darkness, each hour meant sure entrapment maybe for hundreds. But then again, what the fools didn't realize was that the four of them here on this road would be the first to succumb to the evil.

He knew each of these men well, knew their reputation and they frightened him. Alvar was the least of the three, a minor felon. A fool who thought a lot of himself, he was an incompetent housebreaker who had been apprehended by the Watch when he fell off a roof and landed in the outside privy. Bazyli had put him in the stocks for a week and had ensured that there was plenty of rotting vegetables close at hand. The children of Meltwater had had a field day. Godun had been a different matter; he had been jailed for three years for assaulting Meltwater's only silversmith in a bungled robbery.

Neither man worried Bazyli too much, even trussed as he was, both Alvar and Godun were terrified of him and could possibly be coerced into freeing him. It was Lyell made Bazyli sweat. He had been in and out of prison for years, his crimes graduating in seriousness each time. The last time the Watch had arrested him, Lyell had been very lucky to escape the Quota. The only witness to the charge of murder had himself been unlawfully killed, the perpetrator never caught. But Bazyli was an honourable judge; he needed proof before he executed anyone. His mouth suddenly dry, he recalled the murder victim had been cut to ribbons before being killed.

He was in serious trouble; Lyell would delight in killing him, his eventual death long drawn out. Bazyli raged at their stupidity, he wouldn't be able to talk his way out of this. But he wasn't able to remain silent when the bot fly landed on his face looking for a host on which to lay its eggs. Bazyli instinctively shook his head dislodging the insect. His movement attracted the attention of Lyell.

'Well, my boys, fun time! Our lord and master is awake,' Lyell stood up hurriedly and strode over to stand insultingly close to his captive. He grinned when he caught Bazyli's eye and spat straight in his face. All three felons sniggered as they watched the spittle drip down the Montetor's nose.

Bazyli stared back at his tormentor, his face blank he fumed inside at the insult but would show no reaction to please Lyell. Impotence writhed in his belly; these dregs of humanity were going to be responsible for the clan Montetor suffering torment for eternity. No amount of pleading would persuade Lyell to release him, but maybe the others would.

'Nothing to say, Excellency?' asked Godun, slurring his words he'd never been able to hold his liquor.

'How much money do you want, Godun?' he asked looking over Lyell's shoulder.

And Alvar laughed as Lyell punched Bazyli in his stomach forcing an involuntary groan from him. 'We've got plenty of money from Razor…we don't need yours.'

Bazyli drew in his breath sharply; when the pain subsided he looked up again at Lyell. 'Razor put you up to this? I don't believe you, why would he do that?'

'He wants to be called Excellency, don't he?' Alvar shouted, walking over to stand alongside Godun, both men at the shoulders of Lyell.

'He wants my job? But I won't have it for much longer, he knows that Prince Griffin will become king.'

'Nah, he won't, cos Razor's got him as well,' Lyell laughed, 'he'll be dead in the morning an' all.'

Alvar sniggered and swung a fist punching Bazyli in the solar plexus. The Montetor gasped, temporary paralysis taking his breath, but he couldn't halt the moan of despair.

'Hang on, it's my turn,' and Godun punched Bazyli in the face breaking his nose, a fountain of blood spouted out and over Lyell.

'Careful…idiot,' growled Lyell. 'I don't want his blood all over me…all over the ground will do.' He grabbed Bazyli by the hair and pulled up his head. 'This is for sending me down for all those years, bastard,' and he kneed him in the groin.

Bazyli screamed. The three laughed uproariously when Bazyli doubled up, blood pouring from his nose and the gash on his head.

He don't look so pretty now does he…even without his scar,' Godun gloated.

'I thought he looked really ugly when he had that scar,' said Alvar.

'Well…why don't we give him it back, boys?' Lyell pulled up Bazyli's head again and pulled away the black eye patch. He laid his knife across the empty socket and down alongside the Montetor's nose. 'That wizard boy did me a favour getting rid of that scar for you—now I can enjoy giving it back.'

'No!' All pretence of bravery fled Bazyli, he never wanted the nightmare of that scar to return and for the first time in his life he begged.

'Please, Lyell, not that!'

And as Lyell and his cohorts laughed, the point of the knife dug into Bazyli's forehead drawing a small bead of blood.

But Lyell died before he could complete the action.

Anders had eventually found the answer. And as he raged at the wall of colours, he lashed out with the hand holding the misericorde. The next thing he knew was the knife entering the wall and passing through. It ended up where Anders directed it—skewering Lyell through the back of his neck.

Bazyli, standing in front of his torturer didn't see the dagger enter his assailant's neck but he did see the point of the narrow blade suddenly appear above the man's adam's apple.

In the stunned silence that followed, Godun stared at the knife appearing from nowhere. He whipped around searching for the man who had thrown the weapon. Seeing no-one he stared at Alvar gurgling in terror watching the dagger being withdrawn from Lyell's neck. It hovered in mid-air as the dead felon, eyes wide open in shock, fell to the ground without a murmur.

Bazyli and Alvar stared in disbelief as the knife moved through the air. It sliced the jugular of Godun standing dumbstruck, watching his death approach. Blood spurting from Godun's gashed neck covered Bazyli's chest, the oak tree he was tied to and the ground at his feet—surplus blood drenched Alvar's britches.

For horrified moments Bazyli and Alvar stared at the knife floating between them, neither understanding the disembodied hand grasping the hilt.

Abruptly Alvar screamed and turning rapidly he fled. But he didn't get very far—the knife followed and pierced him between the shoulder blades. Alvar fell, the force of the blow throwing his body along the ground until his head impacted against the rock alongside his canvas bag and the jug of bludgeon.

Bazyli watched as the hand withdrew the dagger from Alvar's body and rotated in the air to point at him. He thought he was going out of his mind when the blade cut through his bonds setting him free. Bazyli slid to the ground in a heap, his eyes wide, as the incorporeal hand of Anders waved the knife in salute and disappeared.

Anders held up the knife before his eyes, staring at it he grinned all over his face. 'Well, Beatrix, my old love, you can have your wand—I've got my misericorde!' His instincts had led him to the answer. He'd forgotten that he'd pushed his arms into the wall to pull his friends' souls through into the Afterlife. He smiled ruefully. He'd also forgotten that the hilt of his dagger had on one occasion disappeared into the wall as well.

Lewyn and Hyacinth had watched the unbelievable in stunned silence and Cyryl suddenly realized his life was now in jeopardy—but too late. The shape-shifter screamed in terror. It knew a good spirit when it saw one. It scratched Lewyn's neck to shreds – accidentally ripping open his jugular – as it jumped from its perch and fled through the trees north. Lewyn bled to death in moments.

Fifty-five

It seemed to take ages for the sounds of falling rock to subside. Aidan's shield spell protected them from inhaling the dust—the air filtered long before it reached their lungs. Aidan and Beattie stood for long moments in the black and eerie silence still grasping each other, with Dom squashed between them enveloped in their arms. It was Dom's muffled pleading for air that brought them to their senses and Beattie raised a cautious light. Visibility, though, was just about nil. There was a thick cloud of dust taking a long time to settle as loose rock continued to tumble.

'Are you all right, Beattie,' Aidan asked quickly, he knew that the young wizard of light hated the darkness.

'I...I think so. Dom, are you all right?' she asked. Looking down at the top of the young boy's head, she could only just make him out in the gloom.

'Has it stopped?' The boy asked, coughing, not opening his eyes and gripping her tightly around her waist. 'Is Halcwyn okay?'

'Raise your light a bit more, Beattie; let's have a look what's happened.'

She breathed deeply and her light increased to show a terrifying scene. The roof had collapsed all around them; how they hadn't been crushed she'd never understand. But, of course, it was Aidan's shield that had deflected any fall. They were completely cut off from the others in the tunnel. She thought she could vaguely hear Adler shouting in the distance but she wasn't too sure, it was probably hope more than fact. She examined her surroundings and became more afraid. The rockfall had created a cavern just large enough for them to stand in and walk perhaps ten paces in both directions before coming up against rocks, some nearly as big as themselves.

'There he is,' shouted Dom relieved, and covering his mouth, he rushed over to the Meltwater end of the mine. Kneeling down alongside a four foot length of Halcwyn's tail, the rest of him, another ten or so feet, was buried in the rubble; he heaved a sigh of relief.

'God, Aidan, it can't have survived that fall can it?' Beattie asked dreading confirmation and what it would mean for the green boy.

Dom heard her. 'Aye, course he has, he's alive, I can feel him breathing. It takes a lot to kill a krynx, his skin is very thick. But I think he's been knocked unconscious.' Dom, looking very anxious, started stroking the little bit of tail he could see. 'Hey, Halcwyn, you'll be fine in a minute, rest now and then you can dig your way out'.

Beattie went over to him and put her arm around his small shoulders. 'He can't hear you, Dom. Come and sit over here in case any more stones fall and hurt you. We can wait together,' and she pulled him to the centre of the mine floor.

Aidan scrutinized the rubble cutting them off from the Green People. With his eyes closed he attempted to penetrate the fall with his mind, to ascertain its depth. Opening his eyes he glanced worriedly at Beattie before doing the same at the other end. Minutes later he sat on the floor with his companions and rubbed his face, the look he turned on Beattie was full of fear.

'What is it?' she asked holding Dom close.

Aidan licked his lips. 'Unless Halcwyn wakes before long it will be too late. These falls are far too deep to breach. We haven't enough time.'

'What do you mean,' she asked his fear infectious.

'We will have used up all the air long before they can dig us out.'

'Oh, God!'

'It's all right Halcwyn will get us out of here. He won't sleep long now,' Dom said, the quiver in his voice showing that he wasn't too sure.

'Aidan?' Beattie didn't have to put in words what she feared.

'I honestly don't know. He could come around in the next few minutes or it may be hours, it depends on the knock he had. And judging by the size of some of these rocks…his recovery may well be too late.'

'Is there anything we can do, I mean…we just can't sit here and wait to…to… we're wizards for God's sake there must be something we can do!'

'Let me think a minute.' Aidan sat with his head cradled in his hands staring at the rubble strewn floor. His mouth was very dry now because of the dust, and anxiety had given him a headache. He thought back through all the years of his training for any comparable experience and he couldn't recall one that was remotely similar. He did recall his master's warnings against spell-casting in confined spaces. Nonetheless, for once he was going to have to create a spell in a very small space indeed, whatever his master advised. And then, of course, he remembered where Tragen was and this made him even more anxious.

'Aidan, Beattie,' Anders called out excited, *'Bazyli's all right, he's alive. I had to kill his three attackers but he's survived.'*

'What do you mean, you killed them? How?' Beattie asked so surprised she forgot where she was.

And Anders went on to tell them in great detail what he had done. *'You can keep your wand, Beattie, I have my misericorde.'*

'What! You think your dagger holds magic like my wand? Is that possible, Aidan?'

'I don't know, but there again it must have some sort of power to travel through the wall of colours into Life.' Aidan frowned, consternation creased his brow. Why on earth would two of his friends each have a magical artefact?

But thinking back on it all later, what really surprised Anders and Beattie was the fact that Aidan had not disputed the need for killing. It was almost as if he wasn't bothered. And neither of them was too sure if that was a good or a bad sign.

'It's a relief that Bazyli's safe, Anders, I only wish we could let Augusta and Thaddeus know. But we have another more urgent problem facing us at the moment,' said Aidan, and he went on to tell him of the rockfall.

'People don't breathe so deeply, use so much air, when they're sleeping. Can't you try that…if you can slow your respiration then you'll be giving your rescuers more time to break through to you?'

'What do you think, Beattie? I can't think of anything else.' Aidan stared at her frightened face wishing he could bring her comfort. 'If we use magic here and now to clear some of this rubble away, we'll use up the air even quicker.'

'Well, there's no way I'm going to sleep. Even the thought of closing my eyes in here terrifies me.'

'Why do you want to sleep? I thought wizards would be able to blast their way out of here,' said Dom his big eyes seeming even bigger in Beattie's light. Not hearing Anders he wondered at her words.

'To blast our way out of here would take immense power and skill, Dom. I don't have either.'

'But my Dada said he heard you were the most powerful wizard in the world, and I've heard of wizards using their staffs to do impossible things.' Dom looked at Aidan as if he was almost accusing him of abandoning them to die of suffocation.

'I haven't got a staff, Dom, I'm sorry.'

'Where is it then?'

'Somewhere in Paradise.'

'Well, can't you go and get it?' Beattie asked. 'I mean…you know you said once that you'd seen it. Perhaps it wouldn't take you long.'

'Get my staff? Bloody hell, Beattie, I only heard it once and that was when I was staring into an orchard.' He paused, biting his lips he mulled over her suggestion wondering if it was possible to get there and back in time. But was he looking for excuses? His stomach clenched at the thought of holding a staff. 'Even if I could find the orchard right away creating a staff sometimes takes weeks.'

'It takes that long when you need the wood of more than one tree. You said yourself that the Tree of Paradise called you. That is the only wood you'll need, isn't it?' Beattie grasped his hand tightly, ignoring his cursing she understood even if he didn't, that his retort was more because of fear of the staff, dread that he was not yet ready.

Aidan looked around their prison and without warning he felt a constriction in his chest and knew that it was because the quality of the air was already deteriorating. They really didn't have much time— minutes only. He turned back to Beattie and stared long into her eyes, she smiled, her faith in him showing no doubt.

'Hold on, you two! When Aidan heard the Tree of Paradise calling him, it was his first visit to Limbo—my Limbo. The tree he saw in that orchard then was one I created…you know…the way I thought the tree might look like. It wasn't the real Tree of Paradise.' Anders said very perturbed at the thought of his friend wasting time searching for a non-existent tree.

Beattie brought her head up sharply. 'Is he right?' she asked panicking.

Aidan winced. 'In a way I suppose, but looking at his version of the tree I felt the presence of the real Tree of Paradise. So…if I look at his tree once more maybe I'll feel the real one again…I don't know, maybe I'll be able to track it down quicker. But, whatever, it will take time…time we haven't got.'

'If you don't try, we'll die in here, anyway,' said Beattie chewing her lip and beginning to struggle for breath.

Aidan looked at her, hearing her laboured breathing, and Dom's silence. 'I have to try, don't I? Hang on, Beattie,' and he grasped her hand and bringing it to his mouth he kissed her fingers. 'Don't you dare die on me.' Eventually he tore his eyes from hers. 'Watch over my body I won't be long, I'll go and have a quick look.'

Aidan lay down, thought of Limbo—and completely disappeared.

Beattie screamed as Aidan appeared in the Afterlife and stood alongside Anders at the wall of colours. The ex-cabin boy was reclining against the oak tree still flinging his misericorde from hand to hand.

'What the hell?' Anders asked, startled, he ceased throwing his dagger about. Her scream nearly made him drop the knife, but it was the change in Aidan's appearance that truly astounded him.

'He's gone, Anders. He's not here…I mean his body's not here!' shouted Beattie.

'I know…he's here with me.'

'No, you don't understand. He's gone—all of him, his body as well!'

'Don't be daft, I've crossed over as we normally do,' Aidan said perplexed.

'Aidan? Thank God you're there, you frightened me,' and then realizing what he'd called her she immediately got her back up…she hated being called silly. 'Don't you dare call me daft! I know what I can't see and it is most definitely you.'

'She's right, Aidan. You look different, more…solid I suppose. Somehow you've brought your body with you.' Anders looked bemused.

'Bloody hell, am I dead?'

'No of course not, go back, let's see what happens,' Anders suggested.

And he did. And he did it a few times before it sunk in that he could cross between Life and Death without his soul leaving his body behind.

'What are you doing, Aidan,' Dom asked, 'I'm getting dizzy watching you appear then disappear. Can you do it, Beattie?'

And her senses were dumbfounded when she did it and returned safe.

'Dear God, what does this mean?' Aidan asked.

'I think it could be a way out of there for you...maybe you don't have to return to the same place. You could cross over to me at the wall and then return on the other side of that fall of rock.' Anders' suggestion was met with silence.

'And what about Dom?' Beattie asked.

'Try bringing him with you.'

'Oh, yes, and wouldn't that amount to killing him. We'd be bringing a live body into death!'

'You brought a dead soul out of the Darkness, didn't you?' Anders retorted.

'That was different...me and Thaddeus protected his mother with magic,' answered Aidan full of scepticism.

'Right! Protect him then...the same way,' Anders said, his patience running out. *'What have you got to lose? The air has nearly all gone in that pocket; he's going to die anyway, if you don't do something.'*

'Let's try it, Aidan. He's right we can hardly breathe now,' Beattie said her speech markedly slow, gulping for air.

'God almighty! All right, we'll have to be very careful and very quick, we daren't linger in Limbo, Beattie, you understand? I don't know how this will affect him.'

'Okay, but hurry up I've a feeling we've only moments left. Look at him he's as white as a sheet and he's gasping. He's going to die, Aidan,' and she grasped his hand again.

'Dom, stand up and close your eyes. I don't want you to open them until I tell you to, okay?'

'Why?' Dom asked, his voice quivering.

'We're getting out of here using very powerful magic,' Beattie said.

'What about Halcwyn I can't leave him,' the boy said his voice close to sobbing.

Aidan looked at Beattie and sighing he made up his mind. 'When you're safe I'll come back for him, I promise.'

Dom stood between Aidan and Beattie with tears rolling down his face. 'You really promise?'

It couldn't have taken moments. The two young wizards enveloped Dom in their arms as they had when the cave-in occurred. They crossed over into Limbo and stumbled against Anders. All four fell in a tangle.

Startled, Dom opened his eyes and stared around him, taking deep breaths and holding his arm where he'd banged it against the tree. 'Ow, that hurt. Hey, I can breathe better. Where are we?'

'Close your eyes, Dom, now,' Beattie screamed, 'don't look. Quick Aidan, get us out of here,' she ordered, all four scrambling to their feet.

Without stopping even to glance at Anders, they immediately crossed back into Life, this time nearly knocking over Adler digging frantically at the rubble.

'By Mother Nature, how are you here?' Adler asked shocked to his very core. He had never known of, or seen such a thing, as anyone appearing out of thin air.

'Halcwyn, Aidan, you promised,' Dom said looking up at him through tears that hid a strangeness in his eyes.

Beattie knelt down and held Dom's face in her hands. 'Are you all right, are you feeling all right?'

'I don't know, a bit wheezy I guess. Halcwyn, you promised.'

Beattie stood up, keeping hold of Dom's hand. 'How are we going to transport an animal as big as that?' Beattie asked, she had a bad feeling and glanced back at Dom. Something was wrong with the green boy.

'We?'

'You can't do it on your own.'

'Perhaps I can if I have my staff.'

'You haven't got your staff,' she said staring down at Dom, the feeling of dread persisting. 'Can we blast our way through to him, now? We have plenty of air this side.

It didn't take them long. Aidan, Beattie, Adler and the others directed three different kinds of magic at the fall. Coming up on the krynx's tail, the green people dragged him as Aidan and Beattie shored up the roof.

'There, Dom, we have him all safe and sound,' Beattie said as Halcwyn shook himself much like a dog.

But there was no answer. They looked around and discovered Dom slumped to the floor.

Fifty-six

'Hey, Sarge,' Gil ceased chewing a hot spiced sausage. 'I don't know 'bout you,' he wiped gravy from his mouth on his sleeve, 'I don't like this at all, honest, we start out with ten men and now there's only us two left.'

'What do you suggest we do…run? Shite, if we try it'll only be a waste of time the bastard will soon find us. With his powers he'll sense us leagues away.'

Sergeant Brom was worried; his normally rugged features showing more creases in his forehead, his face paler. The future was looking very bleak for the both of them. He'd been mulling over the same thoughts as Gil's for the last couple of days, going over and over their pitifully small options in his mind. But whatever idea he came up with always ended in the same conclusion. He couldn't see any way of escaping Drudwynn. He was on the verge of panicking, an emotion he hadn't felt since he was a rookie recruit setting out on his violent profession many years before.

'Come on, Sarge, there's bound to be something we can do. If the yellow man don't kill us Drudwynn's temper will…and if you ask me the man's nuts!'

'Aye, you may be right. What a mess to be in, working for a crazy, mad sorcerer,' he sighed. 'Go get us another of those, I can't think when I'm starving,' he said staring into the crowd. 'And this is another waste of time an' all. How the hell does he expect us to find anyone in this crowd? If they've any sense they'll be long gone.'

'Got any money, Sarge,' Gil asked holding out his hand. 'There ain't enough of us guards to get anything for free from this lot, especially when I've only got one arm,' he glanced down at the sling across his chest. The break had received healing but it was still going to take time before he could use it again.

'Frigging hell, Gil! You've never got any cash, what do you do with it all?'

'Oh, come off it, he ain't paid us for over a month and…what's up?' Gil suddenly stopped speaking as the sergeant's eyes opened wide.

Brom had unexpectedly stilled, his eyes looking over Gil's right shoulder, staring across the heads of those walking nearby.

'Sarge?' he said again. Getting no reply he turned around and gazed in the same direction, the remainder of the sausage almost forgotten in his hand.

'Shut it, a minute,' and Brom walked up onto the boards running alongside the eastern side of the square, Gil following. The sergeant suddenly smiled and nodded across the square at the opposite corner. 'You ever seen a fat leper, Gil?'

'A fat one? No, I don't think so. Why?'

'Well, there's one and he has the smell of the east about him.'

'Get out of it, you can't smell the east from here, this lot in front stink too much. Oh, yeah, I see what you mean. Over by that bakery?'

'Aye, and there's a little guy with him. Come on, they're looking into the back of that baker's shop, let's have a peep ourselves, see what they're up to.'

'Careful, Sarge, if that is the oriental don't forget he's also a very powerful sorcerer. Gawd…I should never have got mixed up with these sorcerers, me Ma always told me so. I should of stayed up north.' The sergeant, a lot taller than Gil, kept Chong and Elstan in sight as he moved through the people crowding the square. And, much like the lepers he was following, the crowd moved out of the way of the Guild's guards, everyone avoiding eye contact, not wishing to cause offence. The fear of the guards – reflected in the eyes of the crowd – differentiated from the dread of the lepers. The Guild's guards meted out a very quick death whereas death lingered with the touch of the lepers.

Brom and Gil were on the opposite side of Frog Street when Chong-An disappeared through the kitchen door into the bakery followed by Elstan, it never entering the minds of either of them to look behind for watchers.

'That confirms it, no self-respecting leper would enter any shop in this town,' said the sergeant relaxing a little.

'What now?' Gil asked.

'We wait,' Brom answered; standing in a doorway he dragged Gil in with him. 'Stay out of sight of the bakery, somebody could look out a window and see us.'

Gil peered up the road. 'Aye, and there's two men up there looking very suspicious, an' all.'

'Aye, I noticed them.' There were two men loitering along the square from the bakery, studiously avoiding looking in the direction of the shop. 'They could very well be lookouts for those inside.'

'If they are, they ain't doing a very good job—they haven't seen us yet,' said Gil smirking. 'Shouldn't we tell Drudwynn, Sarge? I mean, he'll go mad if he finds out we've found them and not told him.' 'Yeah I know, but think about it, what happens to us if we tell him? The mad bastard will send us in there after them and one and a half ain't enough for that job. Besides, I don't much fancy being caught between two sorcerers fighting it out, either. Do you?'

Gil gulped, his face losing all colour. 'I see what you mean, but we just can't stand here doing nowt.'

'We ain't. We're waiting for them to come back out and when they do, we go in. Maybe we'll see who they're meeting.' He massaged his bicep above his stripes where Drudwynn's horse had bruised him bucking off its rider. 'And if it's who I think it is, what say we have a chat with them, man to man like—see if we can come to some arrangement?'

'Who do you think it is then?'

'You are a dickhead sometimes, you know that. It has to be that Cledwyn's lot. Who else could get those two out of Mulkie's?'

'There's no need to be insulting, sarge. I can't help it if I'm not a great thinker like you. So…we going to betray Drudwynn, are we?'

'We'll play it by ear first,' he sighed. 'I feel the same as you, that mad sod's going to get us killed and I ain't ready for that just yet. So, for now we stay hidden here. I don't want anyone informing them in there that there's two of the Guild's guards watching the premises.'

Athelstan Makepeace looked up from rubbing flour off his new blue cloak, tutting all the while at the state of Routh's desk. 'I must go or Mayor Smallwood will be wondering why I'm late for Kaneshi's Day luncheon,' the healer grimaced. 'He deems it very important as most of his guests have paid exorbitantly to be present, though not me I hasten to add.'

'Oh, aye,' said Beeton, 'why not you?'

'Because, my dear felon, he doesn't wish to offend the healer of Kaneshi's disciples. But this is one lunch I am not looking forward to. Brother Drudwynn will be present.' Recalling the deputy's summons the day before, he unexpectedly smiled. 'The last I saw of him he was frothing at the mouth. He was jumping about like a fly on

465

shite to avoid being trampled by his own herd of horses…serves him right, all those horses for just the three of them. I was tempted to ask why he had so many, but his face was turning purple and I thought better of it.'

'Too many horses…what do you mean?' Chong asked his curiosity roused. 'How many were there? Did you count them?'

'Aye, I did as a matter of fact I was looking at them wondering which one would be unlucky enough to step on Drudwynn and disappear in flames…I saw him do that once with a cow. There were eleven. Is it significant?'

And Chong smiled. 'Oh yes! Elstan, my friend, Drudwynn has not informed Brenin of his losses in the Wolfshead.'

'So?'

'Well if we can somehow get that knowledge to the magus before he arrives in Mulkie's Cross, it will cause Drudwynn no end of trouble. Edmund will be unable to contain his scheming. He'll sow so much discord in Brenin's mind Drudwynn won't be able to breathe without asking permission first. And Drudwynn can't take much more pressure; he's losing his senses fast and his fear of the magus will ensure he makes even greater mistakes.'

'Losing his senses? My eastern friend, he has already lost them, the man is a gibbering maniac. He is no longer sane. And I mean that seriously.' added Makepeace leaving the office. 'Well, gentlemen, let us hope all goes well on the podium. If it doesn't…please do not acknowledge me in the mayhem. I would rather escape with my life. But, before I go, I wish to impress something on you all. These lepers are innocent victims of a vile disease; I do not want to see any of them hurt more. Elstan, there will be many lepers standing at that podium, please ensure you are at the foot of the steps. I won't have time to search for you. But as you'll all look very similar, take this,' and he handed the Fly a small yellow ribbon, 'tie this to your bell so that I can find you easier. And please…when I call you, do not hesitate or someone else may push their way in front of you. Now, goodbye gentlemen,' and he bowed as he moved to leave.

'Wait a moment. Will you be seeing Cledwyn before they take him to the block,' Chong asked ignoring the look of extreme distaste on Beeton's face.

'I don't know. Why?'

'You must tell him that when I commence my diversion, which will be after the horses arrive in the square, all three of you have to fall to the floor immediately. Drudwynn will be retaliating against my conjurations and his spells may hit you unintentionally, or on purpose depending on his frame of mind. But, whatever, it will be rather unfortunate if they do strike you,' he finished, grinning broadly.

'I don't like the sound of that,' Elstan said.

'Neither do I,' added Makepeace.

'Just do as I say. Make sure you are both standing either side of Cledwyn, drag him to the floor quickly and you should be all right.'

The two Guild soldiers shrank back into the doorway opposite the bakery when they saw the physician come through the front door followed immediately by Beeton. The two men standing sentry on the boardwalk walked up behind the physician and their temporary leader, all four disappearing into the crowd.

'Hey, Sarge, how are we going to know who the bastards are meeting if we wait for them to come out?' Gil asked, licking the cooling sausage fat off his fingers.

'Gil, can't you think further than the next minute! What do you think we should do? Do you suggest we break in on a wizard having a quiet meeting with what can only be a gang of the local criminals aiding his escape? I wonder if he'll wait to say hello before he blasts us to bits!'

'All right, all right, don't get ratty, point taken. But what if they decide to stay in there? Don't forget we've got to get back, Drudwynn wants us to escort that prisoner to his execution.'

'Aye and we haven't much time. Okay, maybe you're right for once. Come on we'll make out we want to buy something in the shop. Keep your eyes open.'

Brom and Gil stepped down from the boardwalk and pushed their way across the hard-packed earth and through the festive crowds until they reached the bakery. Climbing the wooden steps to the open front door they walked in bringing silence with them. All talking ceased and people moved swiftly out of their way, some escaping through the door into the square behind the two soldiers as they strode deeper into the shop. The place was a lot darker than the bright noon sun shining down on the square; it was also a lot hotter. The fresh baked bread and sweet cakes gave off the heat and heady aroma of just being drawn from the ovens at the rear.

When all noise ceased in the shop, Barnaby Routh looked through the door of his office. His heart almost stopped beating when he spotted the Guilds' soldiers. He turned back hurriedly closing the door as he did.

'Quick, out the back,' he ordered Elstan and Chong. 'We've got Drudwynn's soldiers in the shop acting very strange.'

'What do you mean…strange?' asked Chong hastily replacing the calico bandages across his face, Elstan doing the same.

'They're purchasing my produce, something no Guild's man ever does. If they want anything they always take it. Now go!'

'Wait, Elstan, unwrap your face again I have to get rid of your nose now. I may have no time later.'

'Do you really have to?' Elstan asked anxiously.

'Yes! Now stand still or I'll be removing your mouth as well.'

Elstan, quaking in his boots at the thought of losing half his face, squeezed his eyes tight shut and crossed his fingers. Chong placed his hands over his friend's face and, muttering quietly, slowly wiped his hands downwards. Dropping his hands to his sides he examined his handiwork and tutted with pride. Routh, on the other hand, seeing a black weeping hole where previously the Fly's nose had jutted, gagged and turned away.

Chong, startled, glanced at the baker quickly and then returned his attention to his friend. 'Put those rags back over your face quickly or you'll be causing a panic when we leave.'

'Have you got a mirror handy?' Elstan asked Routh's back.

'Don't bother…you really don't want to see what you look like,' Chong said dismissively.

'God, is it that bad?' Elstan, feeling queasy himself, lifted his hand to feel his nose but thought better of it at the look of horror on the baker's face. He replaced the bandages and picked up his staff jarring the bell as he did. Thankfully the ribbon he had secured to it had wound itself around the clapper so the peal was almost non-existent. Chong grabbed his staff and both men – again attired from head to foot as disciples – departed the bakery through the back door into the alley whence they had come.

'Gil, come here,' ordered Brom standing at the window overlooking the square moments later. 'I think our two lepers are leaving us,' he whispered as he watched Chong and Elstan walk from the alley and head towards the podium.

'Are you sure it's them? I don't remember one of them having a yellow rag on his bell before.' Gil frowned.

'Aye, it's them all right. Watch the fat one, his feet are hurting him…he's limping.'

'All lepers limp, Sarge.'

'He's the only one that's fat. Come on we'll follow them.' And it was as they stepped down into the square they received Drudwynn's summons.

The deputy's voice was hoarse with suppressed excitement in their heads. *'Come, cretins, it is time,'* he mindmelded.

Beeton and three of his confederates walked up to the railing enclosing the paddock holding the carnival's horses. There were close on a hundred of the beasts of all sizes and colours milling about cropping the short grass. The smell of dung wafting towards them was phenomenal although none of the four took any notice. It was fairly quiet here and about, the occasional townie walking hastily by on unknown business, from somewhere nearby a parrot cawed in the breeze.

'Miller,' Beeton whispered to a very thin, dark man alongside him, one of those who had been watching the shop earlier, 'walk all the way around and see if you can find the ringmaster. You can't miss him he's a giant. If you see him tell him we're here to help. Rowan,' the second of his cohorts, Miller's twin in appearance but who had a broken nose, turned from ogling the fourth member, 'go round the other way and do the same.'

Both men walked nonchalantly away leaving Ysmay, a very pretty sixteen year-old girl with long black curly hair, staring after them. 'Why can't I go? You're always sending them on lookout, Dada,' she pouted.

Beeton stared at her, he never put his daughter in danger if he could help it, which was not the only reason he kept her nearby. He didn't want to become a grandfather yet. 'Shut it, you'll get your chance.'

Twenty minutes later both men arrived back at the high double doors of the stables at one end of the paddock where Beeton and Ysmay were keeping out of sight.

'We found him and some others,' said Miller, 'they told us to bugger off they don't need our help with the horses.'

'I didn't like their attitude, boss, it was like they didn't trust us,' added Rowan peevishly.

'Aye,' continued Miller, 'but they do want us to take care of the mayor's watchman having a sly smoke in that alley over there. They think he'll sound the alarm when the gates are opened.'

'Any suggestions how we do that?' asked Beeton scratching his head. 'We leave this shelter, he'll be bound to see us and smell a rat wondering why we ain't out front.'

'The easiest way would be for you lot to stay hiding while I entice him over here,' Ysmay said.

Beeton studied his daughter. 'Don't you dare go overboard with him, nothing too sensuous, behave yourself I'll be watching you.'

'Dada, course I won't,' she grinned, her innocent look not deceiving her father.

'You'd better not,' he warned. 'Now just get him in here. I'll be behind the door ready to knock him on the head. Miller, you and Rowan stand on the other side in case he sees me. We'll tie him up and stick him behind them bales of straw,' he nodded behind him at a stack of fodder dumped at the rear of the stalls.

'What's all that noise?' Miller asked as a great shout came from the direction of the square.

'Hurry up Ysmay they must have brought Cledwyn up.'

In the square before the podium, the crowd were cheering. Up onto the rear of the stage walked the executioner with his black-handled, double-bladed axe over his shoulder and his head hooded, only his eyes showing. Flanked on either side by Brom and Gil came Cledwyn, hands tethered in front of him while behind them, an anxious look on his face, walked Athelstan Makepeace.

The Elders of the town, sitting on the seats behind and to the sides of the block joined in with the crowd, raising hearty shouts and glasses of brandy and wine. The executioner strode across the stage to stand on one side. Brom and Gil, gripping the heretic's upper arms, walked the silent Cledwyn, his eyes darting everywhere, towards the front to stand behind the block. Cledwyn, unable to hide the tremor running through his body his legs nearly giving way, looked down on the blood-stained depression in the top of the hard lump of teak.

Makepeace strode to the head of the steps on the side of the platform and looking down into the mass of upturned, bandaged faces he located the yellow ribbon on Elstan's bell and beckoned him up on the stage. Fortunately there were only two lepers between the agent and the steps and Elstan pushed his way through. Reaching Makepeace he confronted a very worried looking physician.

'You never mentioned the Guild's guards would be here,' Elstan whispered.

'I didn't know until they walked out of the cells with him. Apparently Brother Drudwynn insisted that he take over security until a certain oriental gentleman and his accomplice are apprehended.' Makepeace led him over to stand behind Brom, Cledwyn and Gil.

'This is no good…how are we to tell Cledwyn to get down?' the Fly whispered hoarsely. 'The moment the horses are driven into the square, those two are going to grab hold of him and hold him tight. We'll never get him out of their grasp.' Elstan searched the square in an attempt to ascertain the whereabouts of Chong. He was nowhere to be seen.

'Don't you think I know that…' Makepeace ceased speaking when the sergeant of the Guild glanced behind him and stared at Elstan.

Brom, smiling, turned back to Gil and winked. Gil, surprised, returned his look and was even more astonished when Brom mouthed silently. '*This is it, do as I say, when I say.*'

Just then Brother Drudwynn strode onto the stage accompanied by the Mayor of Mulkie's Cross looking as if the cat had got his tongue.

Elstan, staring at the sorcerer's back, wondered if he'd get the opportunity to instruct Cledwyn when he got to kiss him. He doubted he'd be able to say anything without the guards hearing. He stared round helplessly the crazy escape plan had just become impossible. He glanced above at the Soaring Myners performing on the tightrope, but even their purpose had failed dismally. No-one was now watching them, and they soon ceased their flips and tricks. All eyes were now on the crazy sorcerer.

Chong-An made his way through the crowds and around to the back of the imposing Town Hall. Finding no-one behind the high building, he levitated up on to the only flat part of the roof. This happened to be in between two huge chimney pots poking up at the inner ends of two long sloping tiled roofs. He was now on a level with the Myners and he nodded across to them to leave the rope. On hands and knees, he crawled painfully to the low, narrow balcony running along the front of the roof and peered through the short pillars down onto the podium. He'd just made himself comfortable when Drudwynn appeared below him. But he could not see Cledwyn; his view was obstructed by the Elders of the town now standing in fear. Chong, though, was not worried. He had enough faith in Elstan to know that his instructions to shield their guide would be followed to the letter. He settled to wait patiently for the arrival of the horses.

'People of Mulkie's Cross…beware.' Drudwynn threatened, his face purple with rage, the violence promised in his loud voice effectively putting a stop to any remnant of whispering amongst those at the back of the square. All conversation ceased abruptly.

People shuffled nervously in their seats glancing at each other, puzzlement on many faces. Those standing at the back of the square were in two minds to leave but innate curiosity dictated they remain and discover what it was they had to beware of. None welcomed the presence of the Guild at any function, especially this sorcerer, for he was known to be vicious and merciless. It had become common knowledge that he was being thwarted in his search for two fugitives and people looked at each other nervously. It would make him even more dangerous to any who got in his way.

'You are hiding two men that I want—and that I will not tolerate!' Drudwynn stared down at a field of upturned, frightened faces. He was now beside himself with rage and fear. His frustration that the long chase through the mountains and forest had only resulted in the deaths of nearly all his guards, had warped his judgement. His inability to locate the fugitives in the town and the resultant sniggering behind his back had served to increase his desperation. But above all his other worries, was his abject fear that Brenin would discover his incompetence. His sanity was long gone. His ability to think logically was lost in his mania. His obsession to capture Chong and the Fly dictated all his actions now. The only way he was going to get his hands on them before Brenin arrived was if he managed to scare these people into giving them up. In his panic it never entered his head that the vast majority would not know of their whereabouts. His madness dictated that everyone knew. He meant to frighten the townspeople out of their wits…for scared people divulged information they knew not they had.

He raised both arms, and chanting loudly, he pointed his fingers to the left of the podium; he swung his arms across his body slowly until his fingers pointed to his right having encompassed the entire boundary of the square. Lowering his arms, he again harangued the crowd, this time with a threat they could understand.

'Listen to me! None of you…not one solitary soul can depart this square until I say. A murmur arose as he called those at the back. 'You…' and he pointed at an old, stooped man in front of the bakery, 'you, walk into that shop. Now!'

Everyone strained their necks to watch the petrified old man singled out by the sorcerer, scared witless to disobey he reluctantly stepped up onto the boardwalk. Turning, he shuffled to the shop and put up his hand to open the door. But that was as far as he got, for as he touched the shield Drudwynn had placed around the square, he burst into flames and was dead before he could utter a sound.

'People, believe me when I say not one living soul will leave my presence while I am awake and standing before you.'

The crowd erupted in fear, wailing in anguish, some standing ready to flee at the slightest intimation of the relaxing of the spell. They all stared up at the sorcerer awaiting his next words, knowing that his demand for the surrender of the fugitives couldn't be met.

'I want the fat oriental and his partner from the north and I want them now. If no-one admits to knowing their whereabouts then you will all die—before this thing behind me,' screaming, he indicated Cledwyn. The heretic, his escape plan failing, was so frightened Brom on one side, and Gil on the other, had to hold him up.

Before he'd stepped from his cell Cledwyn had gone over in his mind each element of the escape plan. He knew it was risky but still had faith in his men. However, the moment he had come through the door into the darkened passageway below the Town Hall, things had started to go wrong. Instead of being accompanied by the physician, the Guild's guards had grabbed his upper arms, and their grip was harsh, even the one with the broken arm strapped to his chest had been strong. And now they were standing either side of him where it had been planned that Makepeace and the leper would be. There was no possibility that Makepeace could render the guards unconscious before his planned flight. Their close proximity would render impossible the leper's instructions to cut him free as he kissed him. Cledwyn sweated. Looking down at the wooden block he suddenly realized that he was about to rest his neck on it and say goodbye to his life. And then a sudden commotion invaded his thoughts and the guards immediately grasped him tighter and closed up to his sides.

Drudwynn paused in his tirade as he also became distracted by the disturbance to his left, though it was nothing to speak of at first. A gentle wave-like motion at the edge of the crowd suddenly erupted into loud shouting and everyone on that side of the square surged towards the stage. And amid screams of outrage and fear a line of horses appeared, firstly at a trot and then at full gallop as the rider on the lead gelding lay across its back and dug in his heels.

The rider led the stampede around the square as those on the podium stared in disbelief. But when the horses trampled the stalls, spilling goods all over the square, Mayor Smallwood gave a strangled cry and ran down the steps. Unfortunately, in his haste, he tripped over the hem of his robe and went flying, ending up somewhere amidst the crowd. His plaintive voice could barely be heard above the noise of the horses.

But Drudwynn knew the purpose of the stampede and he reacted immediately. He turned abruptly to his guards. 'Hold him, hold him tight, the fools are trying to rescue him,' he raged.

Moments later there came a crash from across the square and a haberdashery fell down amidst a cloud of dust, the rubble flowing across the boardwalk and into the crowd. After the initial shock pandemonium swept the already frightened throng. People fled from the demolition in the only direction they could—towards the Town Hall.

'Halt!' screamed Drudwynn afraid he was going to get overrun, and his voice amplified by his magic had the desired effect. People milled around in front of the stage pushed by those behind. But no-one came nearer the podium, too scared to infringe the lepers' space and too terrified of the expression on Drudwynn's face.

Drudwynn looked across at the fallen shop wondering if his shield spell had somehow caused its collapse. It was of necessity a very powerful conjuration; it had to be to enclose a very large area and an enormous number of people. Nevertheless, its fall surprised him.

'Listen to me…' but before he could continue another building fell. This time a confectioners on the side of the square and as Drudwynn looked at it so another collapsed on the other side. The clouds of dust billowing about and the noise of falling masonry caused even more panic and the spectators swayed to and fro, wailing, their fear infectious.

And the Deputy of the Guild of the Brethren of Wisdom smelled magic when another building fell—and it was not his own conjuration. He spun around looking everywhere in the square for Chong-An, for he recognized the spicy oriental aroma of the eastern enchantments.

'Chong-An!' he screamed. 'I know it's you…you are going to die!' He continued his diatribe as he searched the crowd and the buildings encircling the square. 'This is your last day on earth yellow man. I am going to enjoy killing you…so very slowly. Where are you? Show yourself or I will kill a few more of these cretins,' and he stuck his fingers out in a fan before the crowd. 'I warn you Chong, give yourself up now – you and the Fly – and I will release these people. Otherwise you can watch them burn!'

Chong-An, the master of Illusion, threw his image from the roof behind the podium and it appeared on the roof of the shop alongside the bakery.

'You are the fool, Drudwynn, you cannot reach me,' and he laughed derisively. 'Let me give you some news,' and he looked down at the horses now running panic-stricken from the square, the riders having dismounted were now mingling in the crowd unable to leave the square because of Drudwynn's spell. The shield had no effect on the animals.

'What news, cretin?'

'Edmund is laughing at you.'

Drudwynn convulsed, his face beyond purple, blood vessels broke in his nose. 'What do you mean?' he screamed. 'What do you know of him?'

'Oh, Drudwynn, you should have told Brenin you lost your men up in the Wolfshead. You should have informed him that we are still at large,' and Chong laughed again. 'You should have told him you failed. But don't worry…I've told him for you. He is not happy with you.'

Drudwynn went berserk, raising his arms he sent sparks of fire leaping at Chong-An. Everyone in the square and on the stage screamed and fell to the ground. Terrified they held their arms over their heads praying to their Gods to save them. Fires burst out in the buildings around Chong, the shops and houses engulfed soon succumbed and collapsed, the debris showering all those in their vicinity. It seemed to last for hours but in fact it was only minutes before Drudwynn calmed a little and peered through the dust and flames for his adversary.

The deputy had finally flipped, reached the end of his tether. Having Brenin know of his failure sent him over the edge into irretrievable madness. He had nothing to lose now by killing Chong and the Fly. Brenin would exact retribution as surely as the sun rose in

475

the mornings. He dropped his arms and peered wild eyed across the square. In the sudden silence many looked up at the stage, only to drop their gaze when they saw the manic glint in Drudwynn's eyes.

The silence lasted for eternity. 'YOU MISSED!' Chong shouted gleefully from the roof of the Town Hall.

Drudwynn turned slowly as everyone held their breath. Looking up, Drudwynn locked eyes with another image of Chong-An, he, himself, was now at street level hidden in a doorway alongside the stage.

Drudwynn raised his arms slowly and splayed his fingers at the image. 'You cannot escape me fool, you are too near.'

But Drudwynn had not been taken in this time and he had deliberately moved slowly so that he could read the apparition. He knew that any illusion always had an almost undetectable line to its creator. And Drudwynn found the line and spinning faster than light he followed the line to Chong in the doorway. He let fly with a bolt of lightning from his fingers straight at the oriental in the doorway. And suddenly Chong was no more as he went up in flames.

At the sound of Chong's voice Elstan, lying on the floor of the stage, peered up between his arms and his heart stopped as he witnessed the end of his friend.

Silence returned to the square, many of those who had fallen now stood up and peered at the spot where the oriental had died. Drudwynn straightened, smiling he searched the crowd. 'You cannot escape me Fly, I will have you next, do you hear. Your death will not be nearly as fast as this incompetent fool. I will have you and feed you piece by piece to the Magus. And I will be restored to his favour.'

'YOU MISSED!' Chong, proving once again that he was the master of illusion shouted up at Drudwynn from amongst the crowd. For, of course, he knew of the line and, unlike Drudwynn, had not underestimated his opponent. He had conjured an illusion from an illusion. Chong had remained in safety on the other side of the stage.

Drudwynn went mental. Utterly demented and screaming invectives, he flung thunderbolts randomly all over the square, some falling among the people and killing a few unfortunates. Other bolts demolished more buildings, but in his frenzy Drudwynn stumbled and one of his thunderbolts fell at his feet. The stage crumbled. Everyone on it fell amongst the rubble. And as Drudwynn went down so a large timber dropped on his head knocking him senseless—once more he was unconscious of his surroundings.

The magic ceased.

In the sudden hush everyone regained their feet although slowly and very warily. They looked around at the carnage, marvelling at their escape. Those on the stage when it collapsed now extricated themselves from the rubble. Standing up dazed they all in turn looked at the unconscious sorcerer half-buried beneath the timbers. But no-one made a move to go to his aid.

Chong helped Elstan to his feet. 'You bastard, Chong, you bastard! I thought you were dead you lovely, clever man. Don't you ever do that to me again.'

Chong smiled and hugged his friend. 'You all right?' and at his nod he glanced at Drudwynn out cold. 'Well, I think we'd better get Cledwyn and get out of here quick.'

'Aye, where is he?'

'What?' Chong asked suddenly wary.

They scrambled about amongst the wreckage and discovered Athelstan Makepeace brushing himself down at the side of the stage. 'Athelstan, didn't you two have hold of Cledwyn?' asked Chong.

'What, my oriental friend?' he asked, shaking a finger in his ear to dislodge dust, he'd gone temporarily deaf. 'Boy, that was some diversion,' he grinned and looked over at the people milling about in the debris. 'Well, I think my services are required in the square, if you'll excuse me.'

'Wait, have you seen him?' Chong asked again.

'Who?' Makepeace asked, holding his head in his hands a moment. 'God, my head aches.'

'Cledwyn…I can't see him,' answered Chong, exasperated.

'Well, he must be somewhere in this lot,' Makepeace answered looking down at the confusion he was standing amidst.

Beeton arrived with Ysmay and they spent the next few minutes searching diligently. All the while everyone kept at least one eye on Drudwynn in case he regained consciousness while their minds were elsewhere. There was no sign of Cledwyn, anywhere.

'He must have escaped,' said Chong. 'Why didn't you have him secure, like I said?'

'We couldn't, the guards were holding him,' answered Elstan.

'What guards?' asked Chong softly.

'The Guild's guards. Drudwynn had them holding him tight between them,' answered Elstan from behind his calico mask. 'We couldn't get near him. Bloody hell, I've got to get this thing off.' And before anyone could stop him Elstan pulled down the rags covering his face revealing the gaping, oozing hole where his nose should have been.

Beeton retched, emptying his stomach over his daughter who dropped in a dead faint.

'Dear God, Chong, did you have to be so explicit, not all lepers lose their noses you know,' said Makepeace grimacing.

Elstan put up his hand and rubbed his nose, for although no-one could see it behind the vile illusion, it was still in place. 'What's the matter with you all?'

'Cover yourself Elstan, I'll see to that later, for now we urgently need to ascertain the whereabouts of our heretic,' ordered Chong.

'Cledwyn wouldn't have run off unless he was forced to. He looked straight at me when he was standing up there behind that block. He wouldn't have gone anywhere without me,' said Beeton wiping vomit from his mouth.

'Any sign of the guards?' Chong asked.

'None and I think we'd better get out of here, Drudwynn is stirring,' warned Makepeace.

'Come with me,' ordered Beeton, I've a safe place for you on the other side of the river. Let's go, I'll send out a search party for Cledwyn later. He's got to be somewhere.'

'Hell,' Elstan said abruptly, 'you don't think the guards have run off with him, do you?'

'Why would they do that?' Chong and Athelstan asked in unison.

But Elstan never answered, they fled when Drudwynn groaned.

Fifty-seven

'I don't know if I appreciate this, Leash,' Nicholas said in the darkness, treading the water and cold slime beneath the quay. Spitting the evil tasting water from his mouth, Nicholas clung to a stanchion and looked back at where they'd entered the water. It didn't seem that far away though it felt as if they'd been in the water for ages. It was taking far longer than expected to negotiate a path through the wooden substructure underpinning the quay.

'Ah, shite!' exclaimed the third man, one of Nicholas' acquaintances a man by the name of Sawyer who had in fact been a carpenter on the Emperor's Purse, the ship renamed the Serpent of the Seas, when it had been taken by Osvaldo.

'Quiet man, what's wrong?' asked Nicholas.

'Like I said…shite! I think we're swimming through the sewer outfall.' He was a big man, shoulders big enough to carry a tree.

'It's still better than charging those bloody cannons…dear God!' said Nicholas wrapping his legs around an upright and clasping his hands to his head as another horrendous rumble sounded above. This time the second weapon had been fired and its effect was vibrating through the structure of the quay.

Screams erupted amongst the sounds of running feet and yelled orders. Osvaldo's men panicked and fled to the sides of the wharf. There they crouched in terror against the warehouses, others lying flat at the water's edge. Those who had been unlucky and caught the full blast dripped their life away into the boards beneath them, their blood flowing through gaps and falling on the swimmers below. No-one went to the aid of the injured.

Balar moaned but otherwise made no move to satisfy his awakening hunger as he had in the cavern beneath Sanctity.

Lonsdale's men crowded up on each side of the smoking weapon trained on Osvaldo, their presence obstructing passage of any counter-charge by the Lobos' crew. It also established them firmly facing the front of each column of cowering slaves. They moved forward slowly under the protection of archers and arbalesters standing on crates behind and looking over their heads. Those bowmen on the roofs above had their own separate battle with the Lobos' crossbows. The rooftop skirmish coming to a stalemate as each side could only let loose an arrow or a bolt by appearing in full view. Death was not long in arriving when they did so.

The two lines of slaves found themselves again forced forwards by Osvaldo's pirates, but unsurprisingly lack of space meant they re-united in a solid body in front of the cannon's smoking mouth.

Osvaldo called a halt and ordered the slaves to lie down on the boards giving his arbalesters, coming up behind, a clear line of sight to their enemy. A flurry of bolts and arrows cleared the site of the cannon, but only momentarily. Lonsdale ordered his own archers to let fly and another stalemate formed as both sides fell to the boards for cover.

'Lonsdale,' Osvaldo shouted, 'I want a word. We can settle this without further bloodshed.'

'Call your men off and I'll talk,' Lonsdale ordered through the smoke of the first cannon, it had just fired and sunk another of Connors' boats milling about frantically in the middle of the harbour. But one of the boats had pulled clear and was nearing the western end of the quay under the cover of the acrid black cloud.

'Withdraw,' Osvaldo shouted to his men, 'but wait at the end.' His face registered no emotion as the slaves and crew shuffled backwards, ignoring the pleas of the maimed.

Lonsdale laughed. 'Ready to admit defeat, Jos? There's no way you can beat me, even if you had a thousand men.'

'You know me, Lonsdale. I've never yet come second in a fight. I want to save your men's lives…and yours. We can come to an amicable arrangement and avoid all this.' Osvaldo stood legs astride, one hand on the hilt of his cutlass; with the other he pulled a cheroot from the top pocket of his frock coat and placed it between his lips.

'I'll settle for your treasure, Jos…all of it and let you sail away. How about that?' and he laughed again.

'Who are these svartalfar, where did they come from?' Osvaldo ignored the expected reply. He needed to know more of the weapons and that was the reason he'd called a halt to the bloodshed.

'I found them on a ship sailing to Mantovar. Unfortunately the captain had been too afraid to set up the cannon on his deck. He was afraid his ship would fall over.' With that sniggers arose amongst his men. 'You need not be afraid of that, Jos, the Lobos will sink under you. So, shall we continue or are you prepared to give in?'

'I will consult with my first mate.' Osvaldo turned his back contemptuously and strolled back to his men at the end of the wharf.

He attacked twice more before accepting the inevitable. He lost another fifty or so men in the abortive actions. He sighed, now was the time for Karnica's ruse. His losses were greater than Lonsdale's, over a hundred men and Lonsdale's hardly touched. He wondered if Leash was near his goal. That would surely surprise his enemy—and him, for he didn't have much hope in its success. He shrugged, he'd have to count them among his dead, not that they were important.

He was losing this battle and acid boiled in his belly at the thought of that unaccustomed outcome.

'Come on, we'd better move faster than this otherwise they'll all be dead before we get Lonsdale,' ordered Leash. Relinquishing his hold on the timber crosspiece before him, he struck out with long arms, his abnormal strength creating a violent wash behind him.

'Would it matter if they all died? Osvaldo couldn't hurt us anymore, then,' said Sawyer struggling to keep up with Leash.

'We'd never get off this island, Lonsdale would have us,' spluttered Nicholas, 'and he's just as bad, so I've heard.'

'Besides, there are a lot of men up there who don't deserve to die for the likes of either of them. I want them free,' added Leash.

'*Your virtue is making me sick,*' said Balar pretending to retch.

'*Shut it,*' ordered Leash and then ignored his demon's continued pretence at puking

It wasn't long before they reached their objective, a ladder leading up through the floor of the quay. Leash halted and clinging to the ladder he listened intently. 'I can't hear anyone directly above us, can you?' he asked.

'How the hell can you make anything out with all that shouting?' Sawyer asked incredulously.

'That doesn't mean no-one's up there, Leash. We don't want to come up in the middle of them,' Nicholas said giving a sickly grin.

Leash wiped the slimy water from his face and looked around. 'I'll climb up the outside and take a look. Wait for my signal and follow as quick as you can.'

Leash dragged himself from the stinking water of the harbour and climbed the timber supports of the quay. Moments later he poked his head above the boards and immediately ducked down again. Standing right at the edge of the quay was one of Lonsdale's men staring intently ahead at the melee along the wharf. Leash beckoned to

Nicholas and Sawyer; putting his finger to his lips he enjoined silence until he was back in the water.

'There's one standing at the edge above me. We'll wait for the cannon to fire again and I'll pull him over under cover of the smoke. He's standing behind everyone else up there so his disappearance won't be noticed,' and he ascended the stanchion again.

The sound of the loud splash as the man fell into the harbour was covered by the insane noise of the battle and the decreasing rumble of the devil's weapon. Leash followed the shot as it flew across the harbour. Beneath it he glimpsed a longboat making for the quay where they were. Sawyer broke the pirate's neck as the boat nudged its nose beneath the quay alongside the ladder.

'What the hell,' exclaimed Nicholas falling back against a stanchion and knocking his head…he saw stars.

Sawyer, startled, lost his grip and bobbed in the water. He surfaced spluttering, holding his knife in front of him ready for any attack.

Leash, hanging on the foot of the ladder stared silently at the newcomers, every nerve tingling in his body as he and Balar prepared to grab the prow and upend the boat.

'Wait! Do not do anything hasty, we are Connors' men; I am the bo'sun, Tangler. Are you off the Lobos?' asked a tall, thin man standing between the thwarts, holding his cutlass at Nicholas' neck.

'Who else would we be?' asked Sawyer truculently. 'You don't think we'd be down here if we were Lonsdale's, do you?' he asked as he pushed the body of the dead brigand farther beneath the quay.

'What are you doing here?' asked Tangler.

'We're going to capture Lonsdale and throw his cannon into the harbour,' answered Leash. 'So leave my friend be,' he nodded at the cutlass resting against Nicholas' jugular.

'Oh aye, and how do you propose to do all that? Just walk through them and take him,' Tangler smirked.

'Yes,' answered Leash, his face a mask of indifference. 'You can join us if you wish but you follow my instructions.'

'And why should I do that?'

'Because I am telling you.' Balar stared through Leash's eyes and into Tangler's head.

The bo'sun, returning the look, heard a voice in his head telling him to do just that. Tangler had no idea that Balar was in his brain demanding obedience—he only knew that he had to obey the hidden, inner voice.

'Very well. I have ten men, with me, what would you have us do?'

Sawyer and Nicholas looked at Leash astounded—a slave ordering a bo'sun was not the done thing. This Tangler had obviously taken them to be the crew of the Lobos. Sawyer just didn't want to be around when he realized his mistake…he'd kill them himself.

'From what I saw, everyone is staring along the quay at Osvaldo. If we're quiet they won't see us climbing up in this smoke. We can stand at the back and re-assess the situation then,' ordered Leash.

'I've just thought of something,' said Nicholas rubbing at his neck where the cutlass had drawn a little blood. 'Won't they wonder why we're all soaking wet?'

'We'll be standing among Connors' men. No-one will notice us,' said Leash still stony-faced.

Climbing up onto the quay took but moments for the thirteen men. Nicholas touched his heart for luck when he realized the number. They stood a little aback from the commotion in front of them, but Leash stood on a crate to look over their heads and along the quay. Not one of Lonsdale's men peered behind. But if they had they wouldn't have been surprised to see anyone there…one pirate looks much like another. But such was the lure of Osvaldo that no-one took a blind bit of notice of them.

Leash stepped down and huddled to the side with Tangler, Nicholas and Sawyer. 'We're going to have one hell of a job getting through these. We can't all go together, they'll think it very strange all of us pushing through. We'll have to split up. One party make for Lonsdale, Tangler, you and Nicholas can do that; take a couple of men with you. Sawyer you make for the cannon with some others, half a dozen should do it that cannon looks very heavy. I'll take the rest and grab that svartalfar. We'll wait for another shot and move under cover of the smoke.'

At that there was another ear-splitting crash. Leash held on to Tangler's shoulder before moving off. Balar again stared at the man, his voice warning that Lonsdale was not to be killed. He was to be taken hostage. Tangler, glassy-eyed, nodded his head and Leash tapped him on the shoulder in parting.

The Hound's bo'sun and two of his men pushed through the crowd with Nicholas. Three accompanied Leash and with shoulders forward jostled their way to the svartalfar, ignoring the mutterings from Lonsdale's men on either side. The rest followed Sawyer and bulldozed their way to the cannon.

Balar was more intrigued by the southerner than with the monstrous instrument of death on the quay. He dragged Leash's eyes to the svartalfar standing nearby against a warehouse wall, directing operations. *'I haven't seen them for thousands of years.'*

'Who?' asked Leash now studying the carnage in the front of Osvaldo.

'The svartalfar.'

'So?' Leash asked.

'Black elves—weapons masters. I thought they'd all died out with the other elves and the dragons.'

'Balar, shut up. We haven't got time for fairy stories now.'

'Dear God, what's happening over there?' Nicholas asked dumbfounded at the sight that met his eyes in the open space between the two opposing forces. He, Tangler and his two cohorts halted to watch the very strange spectacle that had ensnared the attention of Lonsdale's men. They all stopped pushing their way through the crowd, astounded at the sight of a strange animal prancing about in no-man's land.

Nicholas, who was about to walk up behind Lonsdale, stood, mouth agape staring at the animal dancing grotesquely in front of Osvaldo. It was huge, as tall as two men it had the appearance of a weasel with a gigantic mouth open wide displaying two rows of brown-stained, yellow fangs. It stood on its hind legs and swayed drunkenly, holding a flagon of brandy in one of its front paws and a huge cigar in the other. Singing its heart out in a human voice, it came towards Lonsdale in an erratic line back and forth across the quay.

It mesmerized all those watching. Shouting and baiting of their enemy ceased as all stared motionless at the obscene caricature. At least all those the giant creature faced did. Those behind it, Osvaldo's people, not being in eye contact, only saw a huge weasel moving forward. The illusion, conjured by Karnica, only affected those in front of it and Lonsdale's men never moved a muscle, never made a sound. The Hag's familiar had hypnotized them. It also obscured the advance of the slaves and the Lobos' crew who were now broadside to the leading cannon.

'Stop looking at it Leash. It's a trick...an illusion that's all. But beware,' and Balar licked his lips, panicking, *'do not let the Hag see us. Just do what we came here to do, it's easy now Lonsdale is hypnotized.'*

Balar's words, although puzzling, spurred Leash on and he looked around from where he was standing alongside the svartalfar. Nicholas and Tangler were standing behind Lonsdale. Sawyer and his men were not far away at the cannon. All were as glassy-eyed as Lonsdale's people.

Taking a deep breath he struggled through the awestruck brigands and put his hands over Sawyer's eyes and whispered. 'It's a hallucination,' and he then did the same with the others.

Rousing from the trance, Lonsdale was grabbed by Nicholas supported by Tangler and his two men. Sawyer and his party bent their backs and pushed the cannon across the quay and into the harbour. No-one attempted to stop them. Leash's men took hold of the svartalfar.

At the same time Osvaldo's slaves reached the first cannon and, turning it on its wheels, pushed it into the water. Osvaldo had no trouble disarming each and every one of Lonsdale's men still watching the weasel.

Karnica lifted the spell and the familiar assumed its proper size.

Coming out of their trance, Lonsdale's men were disoriented for moments, but finding themselves unarmed and under the weapons of Osvaldo, some panicked.

There was pandemonium until Leash strode across and shouted in Lonsdale's ear. 'Tell them to stand quiet or you're a dead man,' and he pressed the point of his dagger against the man's windpipe.

'Well done Leash, I'd almost given up on you,' Osvaldo said walking over, a big grin all over his face.

'Thank you Captain, it was a lot easier with the illusion you created,' answered Leash removing the dagger from Lonsdale's throat and bowing.

'You noticed it was an illusion? Strange, she said everyone in front of her familiar would be hypnotized, including you.'

'She...sir?'

'Let me introduce you, Leash. This is my Hag, Karnica,' and he turned and beckoned the witch forward. 'Karnica, meet the brave man who captured my foe.'

She stepped up to Osvaldo and, straightening her stooped back, she looked at Leash—and into him. And she screamed. 'Bala-a-r...!'

Balar erupted within Leash and lunged at the Hag. He grabbed her by the throat; ripping her head from her shoulders he threw it into the harbour to join the cannons. Her torso fell to the floor spouting blood from her open neck. With her death the weasel-like familiar vanished in a puff of evil-smelling, yellow smoke.

Stunned silence met the horrific act until Osvaldo roared. 'You've killed my Hag...you've killed her!' He turned to Cowper. 'Seize him, bind him, I want to know why,' he almost wept. 'She was my Hag,' he raged, spittle running down his chin. 'I needed her. Take him to the Lobos. I will question him before he dies. You like torture, Leash?' he asked. 'You better learn to like it. You are going to suffer the torments of hell before I allow you to die!'

The following morning at sunrise, Leash was brought up from the brig of the Lobos to stand before Jos Osvaldo. The captain was sitting on his quarterdeck at a small table eating his breakfast off solid silver plates and drinking from a silver embossed goblet.

Leash was again in a terrible state. Gunter had not been gentle when he threw him down the ladder and incarcerated him behind the small wooden door of the cell built into the prow behind the sail locker.

Gunter had earlier taken great delight in dragging Leash along the quay, pulling him off his feet and securing him to a bollard in sight of everyone. The manner of the Hag's death had brought back memories of when he was attacked by a vampyrus. Although he didn't recognize Leash as being his assailant, it didn't stop him taking his revenge on him. He beat him with a belaying pin, kicked him and lashed at him with his bullwhip. When Leash asked for water, Gunter hit him in the mouth, breaking his nose and lips. He left him to suffer thirst and starvation until the Lobos was brought into harbour.

Leash had all night to wonder at what Balar had done. One minute he'd been talking and bowing to Osvaldo, relieved at a job well done...the next, all hell had broken loose and he was again being held a prisoner by a sadist. He'd questioned Balar for hours. Why had he killed the old woman? He wouldn't say, wouldn't even admit that the Hag had screamed his name. How had she recognized him? Again he wouldn't admit that she had. He cowered. That was the only word to describe his manner. Balar was petrified because the Hag had said his name. And that was the reason he now found himself standing in front of Osvaldo, the pirate captain with the worst reputation for cruelty amongst all the vicious pirates.

Osvaldo laid down his fork and slowly dabbed at his mouth with a pure white napkin. Leash could see the rage in his eyes, though his temper seemed to have cooled. He waited on tenterhooks. Was this how he was going to die? Was his life to end at the hands of a man curiously besotted with an old woman—a Hag, a witch who practised the black arts?

Osvaldo put down the napkin on the table and leant back in his chair studying Leash standing between Gunter and a huge pirate whose face was covered in tattoos.

'Why did you kill my Hag?' Osvaldo asked, his voice dripping ice.

Leash had also spent the night thinking of an answer to this question. He stared straight ahead over the captain's shoulder and replied in a steady voice, belying his inner tension. 'She frightened me, Captain. It was instinct. She was dead before I realized what I was doing. I'm sorry.'

Osvaldo returned his look, no emotion showing on his face. 'It seems you have a habit of killing those belonging to me.'

'I'm sorry, Captain, I don't follow,' Leash answered, puzzled.

'Vlad… you killed him so I am told.'

'I did, before he could kill me.'

'Is it right you used a chicken bone in the eye?'

'Yes, Captain.'

'You are resourceful it seems…and dangerous to me.'

'No, Captain, why should I harm you? You had already promised me freedom for destroying the cannon and capturing Lonsdale.'

Osvaldo picked up the goblet from the table and supped the red wine slowly, not taking his eyes from the injured man. He wondered why Leash was not cringing. The man was speaking the truth…he knew when a man was lying, could see it in his eyes. No, there was something about this man he'd picked up from an open boat on the ocean. Under torture he hoped he'd find out.

'Why were you in that boat?' Osvaldo asked sniffing the bouquet on his wine.

'I'd escaped from a demon on Sanctity, Captain.'

Osvaldo burst out laughing. 'A demon, hey!' he looked at Gunter grinning his contempt. 'I see. I suppose that demon frightened you as well, did it? Did you manage to kill it before fleeing the island?'

'Yes, Captain.'

Startled, Osvaldo asked. 'Then why didn't you make for Griffin, surely that's a damned sight nearer than where we found you?' 'I couldn't, Captain.'

'Why?'

Leash licked his lips afraid to say the truth but knowing a lie would be seen. 'I killed the Grim's cabin boy and Locklear was sailing for Griffin Town.'

Osvaldo shot to his feet knocking over the table and spilling plates and wine, dropping his goblet to the deck he stood and kicked his chair away. His face was suffused with blood, his eyes starting from his head. 'The Grim…Locklear?' He screamed and Gunter stepped back afraid to be anywhere near him. 'You know Locklear?'

'Yes, Captain, I was his second helmsman on the voyage from Drakka.'

'What is the Grim doing in these waters?' he asked ominously.

'We were sailing for Mantovar taking the princess home when we were blown off course. We called in at Griffin to make repairs but they didn't have masts. We needed to go to Sanctity for those,' Leash answered, even more puzzled at Osvaldo's mien.

'The Grim is dismasted?'

'Aye, Captain, it lost its main and mizzen. Locklear needs them or they'll never survive the voyage to Drakka.'

'And you were carrying Prince Cedric's daughter?'

'Aye, Captain.'

'Why return to Drakka?'

'There is a demon-created storm to the north, between them and Mantovar. It's the only place they can take her to safely. I believe they intend taking the princess home up the Great North Road through the Drikander.

'Cowper!' he shouted and his second in command stepped forward from where he'd been listening behind his captain. 'Cowper I want the Lobos at sea within the hour. We sail for Griffin. We have him at last!'

'The treasure on board we'll never get it off loaded in time,' Cowper warned.

'We'll take it with us. Inform Connors he is to take charge in Armadillo until I return. Years I've waited my chance…years Cowper. Now we kill him and take the Grim.'

'Aye, aye Captain. And this man?' he asked nodding at Leash.

'Throw him back in the brig I haven't finished with him yet. Gunter, take good care of him—I want him fit and well when I put him to the fire.'

Fifty-eight

Anselm woke the following morning feeling woozy. Most of the night he spent thinking over their situation and it had been the early hours of the morning when he had finally fallen asleep. Escape had become imperative. But not just for him and Shadra, they had to take Manon with them. And how on earth do a human and a forest elf rescue a water sprite, imprisoned in a rock cavern, on the other side of what they could sense was an immensely thick limestone wall?

And what would they do with a water sprite in the same cave as they? From all the stories he'd been able to recall from his childhood, sprites were very lively, very mischievous, would they be able to control her? Would they need to control her? From her conversation she seemed highly intelligent, although a little naïve. But there was no question of leaving her—all they needed was a way out, ideally from one cell. Logistically it would be easier than organizing an escape from two. So first they had to figure out a means of bringing Manon into their cell. Without Shadra's magic there was no possibility of entering hers, they could not walk through a wall.

'Shadra,' he turned his head and called across to his friend asleep on his cot.

Shadra pulled the blanket over his head. 'Go away, I refuse to open my eyes, it's too early.'

'Shadra, how do we get Manon in here with us?' he asked, ignoring the elf's reply.

'I'm already in here with you,' Manon said, her voice floating in mid-air.

'Shadra poked his head out of the snug blanket and opened his bleary eyes. 'He means all of you, Manon, not just a little bit like now.'

'Oh! Well I can't join you in there the fountain is too small.'

'Can't we make it bigger,' Anselm asked, 'I mean enlarge the hole so that you can come through?'

'I've been doing that for centuries, water wears away limestone eventually, you know. But I've only made a few cracks around the stream on my side.'

'I don't know, Anselm, what do we do with her if we can get her in here? How do we escape from this cell?'

490

'I can't think of everything … haven't you any ideas?'

They lay down again on their cots when they heard their breakfast arriving. The footsteps were loud in the passageway outside and the door was pushed open with a bang as it rebounded off the wall. Crystal walked in carrying a large tray with two bowls of steaming porridge. She laid the tray on the table with a sigh of relief.

'Oh, that's heavy! You two eat a surprising amount, don't you?' she asked attempting a small smile.

'Yes,' Shadra answered, 'it's all the exercise we get…you know the long hikes over the mountains, climbing the trees in the forest. It's better than being free,' he added sarcastically.

Crystal sucked in her breath and lowered her tear-filled gaze. 'I'm sorry but there's nothing I can do. The Magician says you are to stay locked up until he decides what to do with you.'

'You know he's not liosalfar, don't you?' Shadra said. 'So why do you follow him?'

'What do you mean? Of course he's liosalfar, one of us, otherwise he wouldn't be here. How can you say such things?'

Anselm sat up and swung his legs over the side of his bed. 'Haven't you ever sensed it, even without your magic?'

'Don't be silly! Do you think we'd allow him to have use of our magic if he wasn't one of us?'

'Do you have a choice? I mean can you take your magic back and use it yourself?' Shadra asked trying to catch her eye. It was still very difficult, even after the weeks they'd been imprisoned to get her to look into his face.

'Of course we can, that's why we let him take it in the first place. He must have the collective power of all our abilities to protect us from the Cragga and guard the…guard the…' she couldn't say any more and turned away.

'The eggs—to guard the dragons' eggs?' Shadra asked softly.

She turned back sharply. 'How do you know,' she gulped, 'how do you know of them?'

'You'll be surprised what we've learned in here, Crystal. Now why don't you fetch Roidan and we can tell you what else we know. The liosalfar are in great peril—and it's not from Shadra,' Anselm said lifting her chin and staring into her eyes.

For long moments there was silence until she trembled, she'd never ever met a human before let alone gazed into his eyes. Nervously she looked away and pretended to shiver. 'It's cold in here;

you'd better put some more pellets on that tray but don't add too much water.'

'Will you bring Roidan before it's too late?' Shadra interrupted.

'I'll speak to him, but I can't promise he'll come.'

'Tell him the Magician killed his predecessor,' Anselm said quietly, his tone and the look in his eyes persuading her of the truth. Shocked, she ran from the cell forgetting to lock it behind her.

Anselm and Shadra stared at each other for minutes not believing that escape was now possible. They almost ran to the open door to stare both ways into the corridor, even in the dimness they could see it was empty.

'Come, Shadra, let's find Manon and get out of here,' Anselm grinned.

'No, we can't,' Shadra said his face haggard at the decision he'd made.

'No! What do you mean, the door's open we can get out of here easy, before they return.'

'Aye, but we have to make them understand they are in danger from the Magician. If we run now there's no way they'll believe he's a demon.' Shadra turned back into the cell and sat on his bed. 'If they come back and see us still here…with that door open, then maybe we can persuade them.'

'And if we can't, we'll have missed an easy escape. We could be incarcerated here for years—like Manon,' Anselm stated unequivocally.

'No we won't. I know of a way to get us out of here at any time—and get Manon away.'

'You do? Then why have we been wracking our brains for days?'

'Because it has just come to me,' and Shadra told him.

Roidan paced the floor of his room in the barracks; the only sound that of his light slippers gently skirting the polished wood timbers. His head down, hands clenched behind his head the tidings she brought staggering him.

Xelnor, standing by the window staring out at the town of Alfhime, brooded over Crystal's words. He and Roidan had often thought there was something different about the Magician, had discussed it on numerous occasions. But neither had dreamt their leader was not liosalfar. Even now, admitting the possibility that he had murdered and was a demon, was beyond belief.

Crystal sat in one of the two seats, a straight-backed, plain, wooden chair that Roidan used at the small table. Biting her bottom lip, her head resting in her hands, elbows on the table, she went over in her mind what the prisoners had told her. Little though it was, their news was earth-shattering, enough to turn their lives, and the lives of all mountain elves, upside down. She'd constantly felt uneasy around the Magician but had always put it down to the fact he held her magic and those of every other liosalfar. Nevertheless, looking back over the time since he'd been elected she could never remember actually seeing his face.

She looked up, dropping her hands to her lap. 'Have either of you ever seen him? I mean seen his face—I haven't,' she asked softly, afraid of the answer.

Roidan stopped his pacing and gazed at her thoughtfully. 'I can't remember, his hood is constantly raised.'

Xelnor turned from the window and stared from one to the other of his companions. 'We've all seen it at least once, haven't we? When he took my magic I stared into his eyes. I had to for my magic to pass to him. As you did, or have you forgotten?' he paused and stared at the table top, his mind elsewhere. 'Perhaps…perhaps forgetting was essential if he is a demon. I don't recall his face I was in a trance. I…I do remember his eyes though, they made me tremble. I don't know why.' He walked over to Roidan's bed and sat on the edge. 'But is that enough to doubt him?'

'He has not the manners of a liosalfar,' answered Crystal, 'he is very discourteous. Remember what he said to our forest cousin…and to the human. He showed nothing but contempt for them—and let them know it.'

'Yes, and the way he turned their backs on them when we led them off to the cells, gross discourtesy. God, I don't know what to think. Xelnor, Crystal, we'll have to speak with them. I can't believe we've been duped all these years.'

Crystal suddenly jumped up. 'Oh, my God, I ran out and never locked their cell,' she held her hands to her mouth, all colour drained from her face.

Roidan and Xelnor stared at her, equally white-faced. If the Magician discovered they had allowed the prisoners to escape then not one of the jailers would see another dawn. And that was another reason for doubt. No liosalfar had ever been executed by their own people.

'Well, even if we aren't going to escape quite yet, Shadra, my little elf, we can at least prepare Manon for escape,' Anselm said going to the bag of pellets and putting a handful in his pocket.

'Careful, don't let your pocket get wet, my tall human,' Shadra replied dryly. 'We don't want your britches going up in flames.'

Anselm teetered a moment and considered removing the pellets. If Manon got too close? 'Can you hear me Manon?' he asked.

'Of course. Are you going to burn the lock off my door?' the water sprite asked her young voice full of excitement. She had heard every word when Shadra had explained that if they packed the heating pellets into the lock of their door and added water, they could burn their way through.

'Yes, but we don't want you to flee right away. You must remain in your cell until we say it is safe to run…or in your case, to flow. Understand?' asked Anselm.

'Yes, but the temptation will be great. I want to see my Mama,' she said, nearly crying.

'You will, I promise, Manon,' Shadra said not too sure if he could keep the promise. But he was determined to do all in his power to re-unite water-sprite and hurricane.

Shadra and Anselm crept into the passageway and made their way to the door of Manon's cell. It looked totally different to that of their cell. For a start there was no gap at the top or bottom of the door, it was flush, sealed tight with the roof and floor. Both sides of the door were also sealed, not even room for the point of a knife. There was no keyhole. The door was secured by a latch and a padlock, the screws not penetrating entirely through the timber. It appeared that the screw heads must have been welded to the latch when the liosalfar still had their magic. There was no means of packing any hole with pellets.

'We seem to have a problem, Shadra,' said Anselm scratching his head.

'We'll have to burn down the door, pack as many pallets as we can against the foot…and pray,' the elf answered.

'We can't have it too hot, water boils you know,' Anselm said a bleak look on his face.

'You mean…'

'Aye, I don't want to boil Manon to death.'

'Don't be silly, Anselm. I can turn myself into steam, how do you think I can become a hot water geyser?' Manon said from behind the door.

'I didn't know you could,' he replied.

'Come on, let's grab the bag and tip it all against the door. The quicker we burn our way in the better. We don't want my cousins returning and catching us half way through.' Shadra ran back to his cell.

It didn't take them long to fetch the pellets and pack them against the foot of the door. But when they added the water they had to step back way past their cell for the heat and flames. The pellets burnt white hot and the timbers of the door – although centuries old and damp on the inside from the water-sprite it imprisoned – soon succumbed. But it was a full hour before the pellets burnt to a powder and then finally went cold. All the time the elf and the human expected the liosalfar to return before Manon was released. But their luck held.

Shadra and Anselm looked through the demolished door and their eyes met those of a young child. Manon, in the form of a beautiful, blue-eyed, blonde girl of about ten years of age, was smiling ecstatically. She ran to both of her rescuers and hugged them. 'Thank you, thank you,' she cried. 'Can we get out of here now, my Mama will protect you from the demon,' she pleaded.

'Not yet, Manon,' Anselm said kneeling down in front of her so that his eyes were on a level with hers. 'We must do as Shadra says. We cannot leave the liosalfar to be destroyed by the Magician. We have to help them to escape as well.'

'Do you?' asked Roidan from behind.

Unbeknown to them the three liosalfar, Roidan, Xelnor and Crystal had arrived at the cell door and were now staring in at the elf and the human comforting the little girl.

At the little cottage inhabited by the Cragga, Ryn sat on the snow studying the hurricane unbelievably in the form of an old woman. Her story dumbfounded him. The tales of a long forgotten war fought by wizards and their allies against black sorcerers and demons was breath-taking.

But what unnerved him more than anything was his place in the story.

'I think we had better resume clearing a passage into Alfhime, Helydd, and the sooner the better. Do you really think the dragons are somewhere below the clouds?'

'That is what the liosalfar claim they are guarding—dragons' eggs,' she said, her shifty eyes avoiding his innocent black eyes. It seemed there were still things she hadn't divulged.

Ryn looked at her, wondering if he should push her for an explanation. But he decided against it, there were other pressing matters and dragons were the furthest thing from his mind. Nevertheless, they now had another reason to seek entrance into Alfhime—not only to rescue Manon, Shadra and Anselm, they had now to free the dragons.

'Let us go, Helydd. The ability to heal that Aidan passed to me has succeeded. I no longer have any injury in my body. I am going to dig and not stop until we are in Alfhime.'

Manon involuntarily stepped back farther into the cell; long years of imprisonment had birthed a hatred for her captors. The failure of their escape plan brought on an unassailable fear in her, bringing on a need for violence.

But Shadra sensed the passion building within the dungeon and he guessed its origin. 'Wait, Manon, please. We have to explain, they are not yet convinced of their danger.'

'I will not be kept from my Mama any longer, Shadra. It's not fair,' she cried, 'I love her and she needs me.'

'They will not imprison you again,' said Anselm, 'I give you my word,' and he turned to the liosalfar, placing his body between them and the water-sprite. 'She has told us why you have kept her here all these years. Your sentence is inhuman and cannot in all honesty be justified. I know it was not you personally who imprisoned her, but you are the ones who are maintaining it. Enough is enough!'

Roidan glanced at Crystal and Xelnor and sighing he turned his gaze on Shadra, ignoring for the moment Anselm's words. 'What is this about the Magician not being liosalfar?'

'Manon knows more of him than me. Ask her,' Shadra said.

'Then if you will stand to one side, Anselm, I will. Do not worry we will not harm her,' said Roidan.

'I am not worried—it will take more than three liosalfar to get past me,' he warned. And those listening knew it to be true.

Roidan licked his lips, the only outward sign of fear on his face. He stared at Manon. 'I did not expect to see you in the form of a little human child. Why this shape?'

Manon returned his stare, her eyes cold and deep. Her appearance might be that of a young girl but she was in fact hundreds of years old—and it showed in that look. 'Because I choose to. Why are you liosalfar in that shape?' she sneered.

Taken aback it was Crystal that answered. 'We were born like this,' and she added as an afterthought, 'Manon is a pretty name for a pretty girl.'

'Do not patronize me, liosalfar. Do you wish to see me in my true form? If you do you will not live for much longer, but neither will my friends.' She stood between Anselm and Shadra and held their hands. 'It is lucky for you I do not want to harm them or you would be dead by now.'

The words, coming from such a cherubic face, seemed to sound much more horrific and there was a collective intake of breath within the cell.

'Tell us of this Magician before making more threats, dragon killer,' hissed Xelnor.

The temperature in the room dropped sharply as the threat of violence increased. Roidan pulled Crystal closer as Xelnor gripped the hilt of the dagger in his belt. Not that it could have served any purpose in protecting him from the water-sprite.

'Wait, please,' said Shadra, 'let's talk quietly and sensibly. Manon, we will find it easier to get out of the valley with their help and we won't get that if you kill them. You, Xelnor, are not going to get any information out of her if you call her names. She has been unjustly treated by liosalfar for centuries so her hatred, her lack of trust and unwillingness to help you, is perfectly understandable. Roidan, Crystal shall we start again?'

'Very well,' and Roidan nodded at the others. 'Manon, we understand how you feel…'

'You have no idea how I feel, liosalfar!' Manon spat the words.

'Manon, please, we are not the ones who imprisoned you, it was our ancestors. We can't speak for them—after all you are the one who broke the egg, killed the dragon,' said Crystal.

'It was an empty egg, I killed no dragon.'

'Empty! How can that be? Roidan we must…'

'Quiet Xelnor, we can investigate that later. We have a far more urgent need of answers now. Please, Manon, what do you know of the Magician?' Roidan, licking his lips again, stared at the little girl. Her words had startled him, shocked them all—they had not known the egg held no dragon.

'He is a demon!'

'Oh, come on…'

'Xelnor, shut up,' Crystal ordered and her glare more than anything, brought his silence.

'How do you know he's a demon?' asked Roidan

'I could feel him trying to take my magic and when he failed, he hissed. And then he gloated and told me he had outwitted my mother. He told me she had shown him a way into Alfhime. He was supposed to bring her so she could rescue me but he betrayed her instead. He asked me about the egg I'd smashed. He wanted to know about the others…if they were empty. I told him I didn't know and asked him how he didn't know, after all he was liosalfar.'

'Yes? What else did he say?' asked Roidan equally puzzled.

'He laughed and threw his hood off,' Manon trembled and gripped Anselm's and Shadra's hands tighter. 'I have never ever seen the likes of it before—he was horrible. I…I couldn't tear my eyes away, he…'

Shadra turned to her. 'Manon, what did he look like, you have to tell us.'

'He…his eyes are red, they have no pupils. His ears hang to his neck and his tongue…his tongue is more like a snake. I can't say anymore.' She closed her eyes, paused and took a deep breath. And then with a voice full of hate she shouted. 'If you don't believe me ask him to remove his hood. You look at his face!'

Way above them, on the upper surface of the cloud barrier over the valley, Ryn took a breather. He was standing in the same hole as before, using magic he was enlarging it with his fingers and his beak—going at it as if he was possessed, which he was. He was desperate to break through and rescue his friends—and Manon for Helydd. He looked up at the Cragga watching him from the edge of the clouds, being careful not to touch the swirling vapour and set off the alarms in Alfhime.

'How much more?'

'Not a lot more, Ryn. Another hour and it should be large enough for me to float through and you to fly into the valley. But we must wait until nightfall before you break the lower skin or the cloud cover will dissipate too quickly. We must remain undiscovered as long as possible.'

'How far is it to the dungeons…the cells?'

'I'm not sure which end of the town we will land at. But if it's the farthest it will take me an hour at least to walk around. I daren't use my magic too early or the Magician will detect me,' she said wringing her hands. 'He is truly evil, Ryn my friend, we have to be very wary.'

Ryn smiled. 'You can ride on my back; it'll only take moments then.'

Helydd grinned. 'You know I never thought of that…no-one has ever carried me before.'

'How do we get him to remove his hood?' asked Crystal full of fear.

'I don't know yet. But first we have to get to the surface. We can hide these three in my house,' said Roidan.

'Then you believe us?' asked Shadra.

'Yes, I do. There have been many times in the past that I have doubted him. His lack of civility, his malice…'

'And his solitary lifestyle,' Crystal interrupted, 'none of this is normal behaviour in liosalfar.'

'How about you, Xelnor,' Anselm asked, 'do you believe us?'

'I do not know, but I will go along with it for now. Are you sure that egg was empty, Manon?' he asked visibly shaken by the news.

'Yes!'

'Let us go, Roidan. As you say we cannot do much about anything down here,' and Xelnor was the first through the door.

It didn't take them long to reach the surface where dusk had already fallen. The Magician waited for them to all emerge from the cave before making his move. Before Roidan or anyone could retaliate the demon pointed his skeletal hands at them and they were struck dumb and motionless—including Manon.

'You don't honestly believe that you could hide your intentions from me, do you? With your magic I see everything,' he hissed. 'Take them,' he said turning to the mountain elves standing at his back.

'Take the traitors and the prisoners to the Hall—they will be executed in the morning.'

It was a long line that formed up going down the hillside. Roidan led followed by Crystal and Xelnor, all three unable to speak or move anything but their legs. Shadra and Anselm came after with Manon between them, the Magician bringing up the rear. They were unable to speak to warn the other liosalfar they were following the orders of a demon. They made their way slowly towards the centre of Alfhime and the Moot Hall. None noticed a slight lightening in the darkness of the cloud cover behind them.

Ryn glided down through the hole he'd made carrying Helydd on his back. He landed on green grass and bracken on the mountainside and they watched, puzzled, as the column of liosalfar wended away from them.

Helydd tensed as she stepped down from Ryn's back. 'That is the Magician,' she whispered in the bird's ear.

Ryn trembled; he could feel the evil emanating from the demon. 'What do we do now?'

'I kill him, of course.'

Ryn looked at her, startled at her tone. Now that it had come to it he'd never dreamt he'd have to aid in killing. 'Do you have to?' he gulped.

'Yes, my friend. That is the only way to deal with demons. They must not be allowed to live to pollute the air we breathe. Besides, his death is the only way the liosalfar can retrieve their magic.'

'Do you want them to? They still have Manon somewhere.'

'They cannot beat me in my birth form, Ryn. And I cannot leave them helpless in the mountains. Come the morning when the sun rises the clouds will disappear and a normal climate will prevail. Snow will fall once again in Alfhime and the cold will kill the liosalfar if they are not protected by their magic.'

'I thought you hated them, Helydd.'

'How can I hate these liosalfar? We were once allies. It was their obsession, to protect the dragons' eggs, overwhelming them that led them astray. These are not the ones who imprisoned my daughter. No, these were taught by their ancestors to keep Manon from me. They don't know any different. You and I, my friend,' and she smiled, 'are going to have to teach them. But first you are going to have to fly over them, distract them and land well in front. They are bound to stop when they see a magnificent bird such as you and then I will act. It is possible they may all die but that cannot be helped. It is better I confront these here before they enter the town. There I will do untold damage and kill far more.'

'Can't I stay with you, Helydd? I mean…won't they kill me when they see me?'

'No, Ryn, they won't have time. I will be upon them before they know it. You cannot be close to me or you will die as well. I won't be able to protect you from me.'

'It's only those in that column will be killed?'

'Yes.'

'Now?' Ryn asked and she nodded.

Ryn, a Wandering Albatross of the Giant Albatross family, spread his vast wings, ran and flapped his wings. He soared into the air and flew towards the line of walking figures. In moments he was sailing over the Magician and the column and he landed a hundred yards in front of Roidan.

The column abruptly halted, those behind Roidan closing up on him and bumping each other before they realized the cause.

The Magician, from his place at the rear, could not see Ryn and he hurried forward. 'What is this, why have you halted?' he snarled. And passing the two liosalfar at the rear he saw the bird. Raising his head he peered from below the overhang of his hood and was suddenly afraid. There was huge magic in the bird, he could sense it immediately.

But then he felt magic behind him and a wind grew, fluttering the folds of his robe at first, drawing his look behind. His hood blew from his head. And if there was any doubt left in Xelnor's mind it was dispelled at once. The Magician's face was paler than white and his jowls sagged like soaking wet, dripping cloth. His tongue darted from his mouth and its lizard-like form licked his lips in terror as his blood-red eyes, lacking pupils, stared at the Cragga growing into a hurricane. Helydd blew them all off their feet and they fell in a heap, helpless. She stared at the Magician not noticing that not all in the strung-out column were liosalfar. She never noticed the small green forest elf or the human. And she never saw her daughter, the water-sprite. She increased her speed until the nearest liosalfar was lifted into the air and dashed against a nearby rock, his body rolling away into the distance. A second followed the first in being crushed against the ground by the phenomenal wind she raised. Helydd had to get at the Magician and didn't care who got in her way.

However, Ryn saw his friends behind Roidan and felt the wind coming towards him blowing his feathers all awry. He panicked and screamed at Helydd to stop. But she never heard him—could not over the roar she created. So Ryn bent his neck and stumbled forward pushing against her gale until he passed Roidan, Crystal and Xelnor sprawled on the hard-packed earth of the track. He hunched down over Shadra and Anselm and the little girl and the wind passed over his back. But the power in it was immense and he knew he was going to die—to die a second time with his friends.

And then he saw the Magician, the demon, lifted into the air. Ryn looked up and watched as the demon floated above his head and was abruptly drawn away towards the Cragga at the rear. And the wind lessened on his back. The Magician rotated in the air, his robe torn and streaming from his waist exposing the green scales of a lizard with his face twisted in agony.

'You betrayed me, Jehan, demonkind,' roared the Cragga, her powerful voice sounding even louder over the wind she generated. 'You were supposed to rescue my daughter, evil one, not enslave the liosalfar. Tell me—before you killed Gabriel did he pass on his secret to you?'

Jehan grimaced, the pain unbearable. 'What secret, you useless puff of wind?'

'The secret of the eggs.'

'The fool didn't tell me they were all empty, if that's what you mean. If he had I'd have asked to leave these miserable mortals long ago,' Jehan sneered.

'He told you nothing else?'

'What else was there, crone? I discovered the eggs empty not long after I came here,' he groaned, his chest constricted, his breath taken by the wind. 'There was no need for Gabriel to tell me these elves were guarding nothing.'

'Who were you going to ask?' Helydd asked puzzled.

'What?'

'Whose permission were you going to seek to leave?'

'My master's of course—he made me stay.' I'll never say who he is, cow!'

'Then die.'

The Magician blew apart, bits of him disappearing, blown away by the wind. And with his death the magic returned to the liosalfar and the wind died down. The Cragga regained the form of the old woman.

Helydd looked at the carnage she had wrought and sighing she shuffled forward to see if any remained alive. Her heart turned over when she saw Ryn amongst the bodies and she ran to him. 'Ryn…Ryn, my friend,' she shouted, 'you shouldn't be there. I told you to stay down the path in front of them. Oh, Ryn are you all right? I'll never forgive myself if…' And when Ryn stood her heart nearly did stop as she saw the little girl beneath him.

'Oh no…oh no…please no,' she screamed and dropped to her knees beside Manon. Picking her daughter up in her arms she nestled her close.

'Mama…is it really you…at last?' Manon stirred and opened her eyes. 'It is! Mama let me hold you, let me look at you,' and she lifted her hands and held her mother's face, caressing her cheeks lovingly. 'Oh, I've missed you Mama,' and Manon and Helydd burst into tears. As did Ryn, watching.

Roidan breathed deeply, not knowing what had happened, he felt different, lighter—fuller. He stood up pulling Crystal to her feet as he did and glanced at Xelnor sitting on the ground his head in his hands. He stared into Crystal's sparkling eyes noticing a difference in her. 'What happened?'

'I…I'm not sure, Roidan, but I think we've got our magic back,' and her smile was brighter than the moonlight just peeking through a break in the clouds.

'He was a demon, then,' said Xelnor dejected, 'we have followed a demon all these years. I can't believe it.'

'The demon is dead now, Helydd killed him. You are free to live your lives. And Manon is also free from you at last,' said Ryn.

'Helydd? Who is Helydd?' asked Crystal.

'I am,' said the old woman looking up at them, Manon still cradled in her arms.

'You are? Who are you?' asked Roidan mystified.

'I am the Cragga, Roidan, come for my daughter and my friend's friends. You will never have Manon again.'

Roidan recoiled, stepping back he nearly trod on another mountain elf staring white-faced at the old woman, others scrambled from the ground.

'There is no need to be afraid; she saved your life when she didn't have to.' Ryn said pacifying their fears.

'Ryn, you big wonderful bird, my friend for life,' Anselm said putting his arm around the bird's neck and planting a big kiss on his feathers. 'What took you so long?'

'I came as quick as I could, Helydd showed me the way,' he grinned, his beak twisted this time into a recognizable smile.

'It is a pleasure to meet Manon's mother. We must thank you Cragga. We were about to be executed by the Magician,' said Shadra. 'You have not only saved our lives, but also returned my magic to me.'

'They're my friends Mama. They helped me escape from the nasty dungeon. I want to take them home with us. Can we?'

'Well, for a while I suppose, my darling Manon,' and she hugged her daughter again. 'But I suspect they have their own homes to go to. Come, let us leave, I might have rescued the liosalfar from the demon and returned their magic but that doesn't mean I want to be friends with them. They've hurt us far too much.'

'Cragga, I thank you, on behalf of the liosalfar and…and apologize for the wrong we have done you and your daughter,' said Roidan, bowing almost double.

'Time will heal, Helydd,' said Ryn.

'It will take a long time,' she replied, staring at Roidan. 'Shall we go Ryn?'

'We must check the eggs, Roidan. If Jehan said the truth then we really have wasted our time—our lives,' said Xelnor getting to his feet.

They all turned their separate ways. Anselm and Shadra to follow Helydd and Manon, while Roidan, Crystal and Xelnor moved towards the cave leading to the dungeons. The surviving liosalfar, staring back up the path at the Cragga, shuffled towards the town.
But Ryn stopped them. 'Wait,' he said, 'Helydd have you nothing to say?'

'About what?' she said all of a sudden her eyes had regained its shifty look.

'The dragons' eggs, Helydd…and the secret.'

'Oh…yes…I suppose it's about time you knew.' She licked her lips as everyone stilled and stared at her expectantly.

'The eggs you have been guarding all these centuries are really empty,' she said.

'But you do know where the real eggs are, don't you?' Ryn stated with a big grin all over his face.

'Oh, yes…I know where they are. Not that it will do you, or them, a lot of good.'

'What do you mean?' asked Shadra a dark premonition taking root in his heart. 'Is it the secret you mentioned?'

'You liosalfar have not been wasting your lives protecting the legend of the dragons. Long ago it was decided, by the wizards and the Green People, that I was to be the guardian of the eggs and you were to keep the secret of how to revive them.

'However, it was felt that further protection was needed for the eggs. So a subterfuge was instigated to distract all attention from me, the actual guardian of the physical vessels. It was put about in certain quarters that the liosalfar guarded a legend and that legend was the eggs of dragons. But if anyone was ever to infiltrate the liosalfar and steal the eggs, all they would find were empty receptacles. Only the Magician would know of the true guardian. But in case I was ever coerced into handing over the eggs I was never to know the secret of how to revive them. That secret was the Magician's to keep.

'These are the eggs,' and she held up her necklace of egg-shaped beads that were around her neck. 'We, the liosalfar and me, were to remain allies until the dragons were needed again. As for the secret, each Magician was to pass it on to his successor at his death.' Her face was bleak and she looked down again at Manon in her arms.

'Gabriel never passed it to Jehan, did he?' stated Crystal bluntly. 'The secret is lost.'

In the silence that followed, the first flurries of snow fell on their shoulders, the first in Alfhime for centuries untold.

'I'm sorry, Helydd, I don't understand. If the Magicians have always known that the eggs were empty, why was Manon imprisoned for breaking one?' asked Ryn.

'The subterfuge was all important; it had to be maintained so each Magician in turn has said. I disagreed. But what could I do? I couldn't tell the world, who'd believe me? Besides, the dragons are far too important to be risked. So, I found myself between a rock and a hard place—I fought for her release.'

'We must elect a new leader,' Crystal said, her voice empty of all emotion, 'and make preparations for winter in the valley.'

'Ah, schrat, you really have been the end of us, haven't you?' said Xelnor despairing.

'He's been the end of us living a lie, the end of us upholding a gross injustice,' Roidan said. 'For that we thank him.'

'Someone else must know the secret for God's sake,' said Anselm.

Shadra pulled his eyes from Xelnor's face. Was the man correct? 'Maybe…maybe the shaman knows of someone.'

'You have a shaman, Shadra?' asked Roidan.

'Yes. We must ask him. It may take a bit of time to find him though, at this time of year he wanders in the Drikander. He has friends there, others much like himself. We must seek him with all haste. As Helydd says, the dragons are going to be vital to our survival—and they'll be needed before much longer.'

Fifty-nine

Thaddeus' hands hurt, his nails bleeding as he scrabbled at the hole to clear the iron bar. He and Augusta had not stopped for hours and had cleared the rod to a depth of his arm's length. But still the bar wouldn't pull free.

He scrambled out from beneath the bench and sat up spitting dirt from between his teeth. 'God, it's murder down there. How deep is the bloody thing?' he wiped the sweat from his forehead in his sleeve. I'm sorry; I've got to rest a minute, any water left?'

Augusta passed him the jug that had been left from the morning. They had sat on the floor in front of the bench when they'd heard someone bringing their midday meal, hoping their bodies would hide the pile of earth behind. They needn't have worried. The man who brought their meal didn't even look at them. He just shoved a tray of tepid mutton soup and a jug of water through the door and left it on the floor.

'Do you want me to have a go?' Augusta asked. 'I can feel it loosening.'

'Let me see your hands,' Thaddeus ordered. And seeing the blisters from gripping the rod too hard, he shook his head. 'No, I'll be all right.'

'Come on, you're hands are bleeding, as well,' she said.
He smiled. 'I'll give it a while yet, widen the hole a bit more. Then you can have a go.'

'Well, at least we know something for sure,' she smiled through the grime on her face, 'the roof of the river must be very deep beneath us, so the ground here is stable.'

'Aye, and there's something else, as well,' Thaddeus said, smiling.

'What?'
'That cat! It hasn't visited us today. I wonder why?'

Aidan and Beatrix crouched down in front of Dom sitting, blank-faced, on the floor his back against the wall of the mineshaft. Adler, with Norbert and others stood behind watching their every move.

Norbert, an old green man, a healer of great ability had already examined Dom and announced that he was at a loss. 'I don't know what it is, Milord. I have never seen anything like it before.'

'Anders, can you see anything there with you?'

'Like what?'

'I don't know...his lifeline...anything,' Aidan said anxiously.

'No, Aidan—nothing.'

Beatrix stared at Aidan. She was terrified for Dom and already blaming herself. She'd gone along with Anders in persuading Aidan to transport the green boy through the afterlife. It didn't matter to her that they'd had no alternative. It must have been his sighting of Limbo that had brought on this trauma. And now no-one knew what to do.

Aidan stood and pulled Adler to one side. 'Take him home and get some others to examine him. Ask the Elders if they know of anything like it. Tell Leonid I'll be back with him as soon as possible. We have to rescue Augusta and Thaddeus and the people of Meltwater, first. Tell him...tell him not to worry,' his mouth suddenly dry. 'I will find a cure—if it takes the rest of my life.'

Beatrix stood up, tears in her eyes. 'Let's get this tunnel cleared, quickly. We don't have much time before the Darkness arrives in Meltwater.'

With that Adler lifted Dom in his arms and carried him to the hole in the floor of the mineshaft and he levitated to the floor of the cavern, Halcwyn following.

It didn't take much longer to break through the farthest rock fall but it took time to secure the roof of the mine. It seemed hours later that they all arrived at the adit, the entrance to the mineshaft at the west end of Meltwater. They all looked out on a town prepared for a siege.

Meltwater was a hive of activity behind high fences and makeshift barriers across roads and alleys. Houses, shops, warehouses, ore dumps and workshops – all on the south side – formed one long, armed boundary. The Moot Hall, the tallest building in the town, was the command centre overlooking the defences. On its roof hard men stood or sat with longbows and crossbows behind a low parapet. The boundary guards were similarly armed although most carried an assortment of weapons, a predominance of pikestaffs standing high in anxious hands. All looked south. Even those carrying on their lives behind the barricades kept glancing towards the road leading up from Griffin Town.

Meltwater was bursting at the seams. People had moved in from outlying mines and small farms in search of protection from the marauding Portolans. They had brought in their livestock and wagons, unwilling to leave their expensive possessions to be stolen or damaged. Most of the wagons were piled high with belongings, some with wooden chests filled with clothes, others with crates holding squawking chickens or ducks. Many had goats tied to their rails.

'What on earth is going on?' asked Norbert. 'They look as if they're expecting an attack.

Aidan pursed his lips. 'We're not going to find out from up here. They haven't sealed off this side of the town, Beattie. Fancy a stroll to the shops?'

'What?' startled she stared at him and he winked. 'Oh, I see what you mean. We walk into town as natural as if we lived there.'

'Aye, we're dressed the same as them. Only Razor, and maybe Lewyn if he's there, know us. No-one else does. We'll have to walk slowly through the crowds not to draw attention to ourselves. We'll make our way to the Moot Hall, that's where Anders said Thaddeus and Augusta are being held. Perhaps we can find out what's going on, on the way.'

'Somebody's bound to see us walking down the mountain, Aidan. They'll be suspicious.'

He grinned. 'Not if we're holding hands.'

'What…you mean act us if we're…you know…'

'Canoodling is the word you're looking for, Beatrix,' and he smiled again as he grasped her hand. 'Norbert, will you and the others wait just inside the adit and wait for my signal?'

'Of course, Lord Aidan, but what will be the signal?' The green man looked askance at the answer.

'I have absolutely no idea, but you'll know when you see it. Let's go Beattie,' and he started off down the track. Ten minutes later they'd reached the outskirts and were wending their way towards the centre of Meltwater and the Moot Hall.

The noise was deafening. Although the outskirts of the town resembled an armed camp the interior attempted to carry on business as usual. But the increased numbers of people taking shelter within its environs caused mayhem. Firstly there was not enough accommodation to house the refugees and tents had sprung up in alleyways and in gardens of prosperous residents. Sanitation was an obvious problem, the stink of the overflowing middens attracted bluebottles, unwashed bodies drew bot flies. These in turn enticed clouds of hawker dragonflies and spitting spiders to feed on them.

Shops did a roaring trade and so did the street stalls. Aidan watched as a cutpurse was knocked on the head by a watchman and dragged away. But strangely enough the inns were almost empty—the regulars were either manning the barricades or patrolling the streets in armed gangs. Aidan and Beatrix stayed well away from those.

'Aidan, we're not going to find out anything just wandering around the streets. We have to ask people,' said Beatrix pulling him to a halt. 'There's a milliners over there,' and she pointed across the road, 'I'll go in there pretending to buy fabric and if I can engage her in conversation I'll question her.'

'All right, but take care, I'll nip in this tavern. I can watch the shop front and for you leaving. Who knows the innkeeper may be talkative. At least I've never met one yet that didn't like to talk.'

He pushed his way through the door into the taproom of the Mount Peaceful Arms. It was an apt name, there were only two old men drinking the mediocre ale. With a board between them they were playing fox and geese on a table near the very window Aidan needed.

The host, a tall broad-shouldered man with an apron tied around his chest draping to his knees, looked up at his entrance and frowned. 'Oh, aye, and what's a young man like you doing in here today of all days?' he asked bluntly.

'What do you mean? You serve ale don't you? That's what I need, it's hot out there and I'm too tired to push my way through the crowds.' Aidan answered as belligerent as the innkeeper.

'How you got time to drink? You should be watching for them Portolans same as everybody else.'

'You aren't. I'll have a pint of your best and sit by the window if you don't mind. I've been up all night at them barricades and I can't go to bed yet, my Da's got it,' he said sitting down at the table next to the players and sighing heavily.

The innkeeper brought over a tankard full of the frothing ale. 'Can't you share your Da's bed then?'

'He farts and fidgets, I'd get no rest. I'll wait till he's up,' and he supped the ale. Wiping the foam from his mouth he glanced at the old men. 'I thought everybody was supposed to be on watch.'

The old man with his back to the window, wispy grey hair falling across his eyes, returned his look. 'We're too old, so Razor's mob said…they also said we'd probably kill ourselves 'cos we can't see straight.'

'Aye,' his companion snapped, 'ready for the scrap heap, a waste of space. They say a lot of things that ain't true. If those Portolans do come I'll show them an' all,' and he picked up a large dagger from the seat alongside him.

'Mind if I watch? I do like a game of fox and geese. Maybe you'll let me play the winner?' Aidan asked and at their nod moved over to their table to join them. He now had a clearer view of the milliner's doorway across from him. He licked his lips and hoped Beatrix was safe. 'What did you mean "if the Portolans come"? Don't you think they're on the way?'

'Razor said they are,' the first man said cautiously.

'Don't you believe him?'

The second man shrugged. 'Benjie's had a run in once or twice with him, he don't believe anything Razor says.'

'Neither do you, Paulie! Anyway, you've heard the rumours same as me,' said Benjie jumping his fox into the space the other side of a goose and removing his opponent's piece from the board.

Aidan watched as a goose was moved to hem in the fox. 'What rumours?' he asked quietly studying the board.

'Never mind, boy, your ears blocked are they?' said Paulie.

'You're going to get yourself in trouble again, Paulie, if you're not careful who you're speaking to,' warned the innkeeper listening from the bar. 'Where you from boy, I don't remember seeing you in here before?'

'Out, down south a ways. We came in yesterday, me Da, Ma and my sister. We were told we had to,' answered Aidan before taking a sup of his ale. 'We didn't want to, but Razor's men said we had no choice. I didn't want to listen to them but when we heard that Bazyli had been captured by the Portolans we had no choice—Razor is his deputy after all.'

'You heard that as well did you? Did you hear anything about a prince?' asked Paulie at last taking his turn and moving his fox to the side.

'Sounds a load of bull to me, Bazyli would never be taken by the Portolans; he's too nifty by half. And as for that prince—how are we expected to accept an imbecile for a king and then forget all our troubles with them Portolans,' answered Aidan.

511

'I heard Thaddeus has been cured by that wizard that was staying at the manor,' said the innkeeper.

'Who told you that?' asked Aidan.

'That Lewyn told me. He was in here the other night, drunk again as usual with that damn cat. You know he lets that cat drink from his glass? He's a stinkpig. I threw him out in the end, had enough of him,' added the innkeeper.

'You definitely can't believe a word he says,' said Benjie slamming a goose next to the fox.

'Anything, hey! Don't forget he told us that this prince and his friends brought the plague and this demon filled fog. Don't you believe that?' said the innkeeper crossing the floor and sitting at the table next to them.

'Carlin, you think the same as me, same as Benjie here. You heard the other rumour didn't you, the one where Bazyli is supposed to have told us all to enter the catacombs?' asked Paulie.

'I heard that too. We're all to go and stay with them Green People who live underground,' interrupted Aidan. 'There seemed a lot of sense in that. I saw that green man in Griffin the other day…he seemed all right.'

'Damn, boy, that's dirty play! You've nearly hedged me in,' said Benjie.

Paulie chuckled and sneered when Benjie played a desperate goose. 'Green devils more like it, that's what I've been told. But I don't care, rather the devil you know…if there are demons in that fog I'd rather be underground than up here.'

'Well, we can't. Razor says it's all lies. Bazyli never said to enter them catacombs, it's all a plot by the Portolans to get rid of us. Anyway there's no way we can get there in time now. That fog will be here tomorrow—and maybe Bazyli with it, so Razor says.' Carlin ran his fingers nervously through his long dark hair.

'You don't believe he's a prisoner then?' asked Aidan.

'Nah, its rubbish, none of us believe it,' said Paulie.

'Aye…but he's taking his time getting here,' said Benjie.

Aidan looked out of the window. Benjie was right. Bazyli should have been here this morning, but for his capture by Lyell and his gang. He supped his ale and pretended to study the board again.

'Anders, are you there?'

'Of course, where else would I be?'

'Bazyli… can you see him?'

512

'Yes, he's on his way. He should be with you sometime this afternoon…late afternoon. He's been hurt bad, though. He's in desperate need of you healing him.'

'What if I know of a way to get you into the catacombs before the fog gets here? Would you go?' Aidan asked.

'You don't believe Razor?' asked Carlin.

'No…I believe Bazyli,' the young wizard answered.

Paulie paused, a goose in mid-air. 'Is it far from here? I'd need to collect my family first. I ain't going without them.' He dropped his goose on the board, not caring that he knocked the pieces out of place. 'You with me, Benjie?'

Benjie sat up straight and leaned back in his chair. 'What do you think, Carlin? You believe Razor? I don't…I detest him.'

'I'm with you,' Carlin said abruptly, 'and I know a few more. But how the hell do we get past Razor's mob?'

'I can get you past them as well,' said Aidan softly, his fingers crossed mentally…he had doubts about revealing he was a wizard.

'Oh, aye, a miracle-worker is you?' asked Paulie.

'You could say that,' Aidan asked, abruptly standing up. 'My sister's coming over, wait a minute I'll bring her in.'

All three stared out the window and watched as Beatrix threaded her way through the traffic. 'She's wearing britches!' Carlin said scandalized. 'I'm not having a prozzy on my premises.'

'What?' Aidan looked at him surprised, and then he twigged what he meant. 'She's in disguise, she's no prozzy.'

'In disguise! You've got every man out there looking at her out the corner of his eye,' said Benjie.

'Aye, and some not bothering with the corners either, she's a very attractive woman,' said Paulie.

'Why'd she need a disguise, young man?' asked Carlin thoughtfully.

'I'll tell you before long. Let me go and get her or she'll be accosted out there. He almost ran to the door and met her as she climbed the boardwalk in front of the inn. He wasn't long bringing her through.

'This is my sister, Beatrix, gentlemen. She's thirsty Carlin.'

Taking the hint the innkeeper shifted and Beatrix sat in his place. She studied Paulie, Benjie and Carlin. 'Aidan tells me you want to leave, is that right? Good,' she said when they nodded. 'Do you know that milliner wouldn't speak to me at first because I was wearing

513

britches? She had some very strange notions about me. I soon put her right on that score. But she's been thinking of leaving the same as you. She assures me that more people believe Bazyli wants them out of here, than they believe Razor and his story that the Darkness is just fog.'

'Then why don't they tell him?' asked Aidan.

It was Carlin that answered that. 'Razor has men, hard men, most of them criminals, the dregs of Meltwater, all obeying him. We lack a leader—we need Bazyli here.'

At that moment the door crashed open. It bounced against the wall and rebounded into the shoulder of a short, stocky man carrying a cudgel. He was accompanied by two others, one armed with a pikestaff, the other with an axe. They looked around the taproom, their glances stopping on those sat at the window.

Carlin whispered quickly. 'Say nothing, leave it to me.'

'Carlin, you old bastard, Maggot, Weasel and me need ale, shift yourself,' the first man said.

'All right, Jeddoe, give us a chance…and watch my door. I don't want to have to repair it again.'

'Bugger your door,' said Maggot moving across the room to leer down at Beattie. 'Who are you then, girlie? We saw you walk in here and we thought hallo, hallo, Carlin's changed his mind about who he serves. Haven't seen you before, looking for business are you?' he sniggered. 'Bugger off Benjie and take these two with you,' he said sitting on the bench next to Beattie.

When the three moved, Weasel and Jeddoe sat in their place. Aidan stood behind Beattie his hands on her shoulders. Carlin lifted an axe handle he kept behind the bar for peacekeeping purposes.

'Now boys this lady is the youngster's sister. Leave them be, they've just come off the barricade.' Carlin tapped the bar with the heavy club.

'Shut it, Carlin. Lady, indeed,' and he laughed. 'Put that away, you don't frighten us. And if you don't listen to us, Razor will want to know why you don't obey his men. You won't stay open long, then,' warned Jeddoe.

'He won't let you terrorize women,' Paulie said.

'He won't know, will he? He'll be too busy making his speech afore long,' said Weasel.

'What speech?' asked Benjie strolling to the end of the table and preparing to raise it into the air the moment Carlin made his move.

'Don't you know anything, old man? He's had the town crier running round all morning telling people to gather in front of the hall at noon. He's going to make an important statement then.' Jeddoe stared across at the landlord. 'I'm waiting, Carlin, fetch that ale over and put your silencer down. I'm warning you.' Jeddoe had been at the receiving end of the cudgel, nicknamed the silencer, on two or three occasions. He rapped his own cudgel on the table to emphasize his orders.

And while the three ruffians, the two old men and the landlord bickered, Aidan and Beatrix had their own silent conversation.

'We daren't let them know we're wizards, Beattie. If Razor suspects we're in Meltwater before we get to him, he'll kill Augusta and Thaddeus.'

'I know, but this man is very offensive the way he's leering at me. I wonder…?'

'Wonder what?'

'I wonder what he'd feel like if I chopped off the bit of his body that he seems to think of more than anything else,' she smiled up at Aidan, a wicked twinkle in her eye.

'Beattie!' Aidan was shocked to the core.

'Don't look so surprised. Augusta and I were brought up around horses. We know all about horseflesh and breeding.'

'I know,' he said blushing to the roots of his hair. *'I just never expected to hear you mention…can we change the subject, please? We've got to get to Razor, somehow.'*

'Any plans?' she asked, and she couldn't stop it, she giggled out loud at the embarrassment on Aidan's face.

'Oi, what you laughing at, girlie?' asked Jeddoe leaning across the table and grabbing her hand, hurting her.

She pulled her hand away quickly, his greasy grip easy to escape. 'Nothing much,' and an idea popped into her head. *'Just follow my lead, Aidan.'*

'I was just wondering how Razor's going to deal with you when he finds out what you want to do to me,' she said smugly, staring at all three.

'What do you mean?' asked Jeddoe, sitting up straight.

'We've come all the way from Griffin because Bazyli sent us and you want to stop us seeing him.'

'Bazyli sent you? Bloody hell, Jeddoe, let's go,' said Maggot standing up.

'Wait,' interrupted Aidan, 'you can take us to him.'

'Why would we do that, hey?' asked Jeddoe.

'Because we'll tell him how you greeted us, if you don't,' warned Aidan.

Jeddoe's hands trembled slightly as he gripped his cudgel. 'Nobody gets to him just like that. You have to have a good reason.'

'Just tell him that Bazyli's son and daughter have come to him for protection,' said Beattie.

In the stunned silence that followed, Carlin dropped his silencer and Paulie and Benjie stepped back against the wall. The three villains gaped, Weasel tipping over the table behind him.

'Well, gentlemen, are you going to take us or do we go on our own and tell him you refused,' Aidan again warned.

With Jeddoe leading and his men behind him, Aidan and Beatrix followed them out into the street. As he passed Carlin, Aidan whispered in his ear to organize those who wanted to leave and to make sure they didn't tote too much luggage. Carlin stared silently and nodded.

The crowd in the street parted as if by magic when they saw Jeddoe and his cudgel. Aidan and Beatrix were walking through the front door of the Moot Hall within minutes. The guards on the Hall allowed them past after only a brief explanation, which included naming Bazyli's offspring. The fear on their faces told more than words.

The rumble from the river caught Thaddeus with the upper half of his body lying down in the hole they'd created. He scrambled free in a rush with Augusta pulling him.

'That's frightening me, Thaddeus, it's louder now,' Augusta said.

'We're nearer the roof that's why. I can't understand why we can't pull the bar out. It can't be much longer surely, it's nearly as tall as the mineshaft now. How the hell did they hammer it in?' He wet his lips with a little of the water remaining in the jug. There wasn't much left and his thirst was raging.

'Well, I don't think we'll have to worry about hiding the earth we've dug out, anyway. I've spread it much as I can and flattened it. Unless the guards are blind they're bound to notice it.' She sat on the ground with him, cuddling up she put her arm through his. 'I wish we had our magic.'

'Don't be afraid, we'll think of something,' he said, smiling at her he kissed her.

'Thaddeus!' she exclaimed, and snuggled closer.

They walked into the office on the top floor that was Bazyli's when he was in Meltwater. Now, of course, it was Razor's. The man was fidgeting in his chair and staring out of the window into the large square, noisily filling up with people waiting to hear his statement. Razor was scared. Lyell and his men should have been back ages ago with the news of Bazyli's death. But if something had gone wrong then Lewyn should have returned to tell him. But no-one had and it was a very frightened man tapping the point of his misericorde below his right eye. He turned at the sound of his door opening and Jeddoe walked in followed by Aidan and Beatrix. Behind them Weasel and Maggot stood sentry on the outside of the door.

'What is this?' Razor asked sullenly, his mind and eyes elsewhere, he didn't even look at the youngsters.

'They demanded to see you Razor,' and Jeddoe licked his lips nervously. 'They say their Bazyli's kids and he sent them here for your protection.'

'And you believed them, fool?' Razor pulled his chair over to the desk and it was only then that he looked up at Aidan and Beattie. 'Shite!' he said recognizing both of them.

'Yes, and you'll be happy to know he was not killed on the road here by those men you sent to assassinate him. A friend of ours protected him. Lyell and his men are dead, Razor, as you will be if you do not release our other friends.'

He jumped up from his chair; kicking it back it almost broke the window as it bounced off. 'How do you know…how do you know I have them?' There was no pretence of denial, pure naked fear causing the muscle below his right eye to twitch.

Aidan strolled across to sit on the edge of the desk and Beattie went over to the window. Standing with her back to it, she stared at the three men who had brought them, her fingers idly stroking the wand she had pulled from its hiding place in her shirt.

'The same wizard who saved Bazyli Montetor's life told us. Now take us down to the mineshaft to get them and we might just imprison you there instead of killing you,' Aidan grinned mercilessly.

'What's he on about, Razor? What's this about wizards? Did you really try and kill Bazyli—and failed?' Jeddoe asked and receiving

517

no answer he turned his back on Razor. 'Come on boys, move it. I want no part of this,' and he left hurriedly with Weasel and Maggot.

Razor led them out of the office and down the stairs into the basement. He pulled a large empty barrel from the back wall of the cellar to disclose the doorway. Passing through it they again descended a long, dank stairwell until they reached another door leading into the mineshaft.

Razor turned to them. 'They're in the shed at the end, here's the key. I'll find a lantern.'

'Don't be silly Razor, we're not going in there without you, so lead the way and hurry up,' ordered Aidan.

Razor grumbled to himself, his words not audible to either wizard. Beattie was the last to enter the mineshaft and she created a light at the end of her wand, startling Razor.

About two hundred yards from the shed, dimly seen in the distance, Aidan shouted. 'Thaddeus, Augusta it's us, we're here to get you out. Are you all right?'

'Thank God for that,' shouted Thaddeus, 'we were getting worried.'

They could hear the relief in his voice, but it was short-lived. At that moment there was another rumble, this time followed by Augusta screaming. The floor shook even more and then abruptly the shed and its occupants disappeared as a hole opened up in the ground beneath it.

Thaddeus and Augusta fell into the river below.

'Augusta where are you?' screamed Beatrix, 'Thaddeus answer me.'

Aidan grabbed Razor by the neck and shouted into his face. 'What's happened, tell me or I'll throw you down there.'

'There's a river below here, that's why we abandoned it. The river must have washed away the floor beneath them. It's not my fault!' He grasped at Aidan's hands and tried to pull them from his neck.

'Where does the river come out?' Aidan screamed it at him.

'I…I don't know. I've never seen it and that's the God's honest truth.'

Aidan stared at him and could see no lie in the man. He flung him away and knelt alongside Beatrix staring down into the hole.

'They've gone, Aidan,' she said tears streaming down her face. 'They've gone. This is the river that leads below Griffin Town and comes out in the harbour. If they survive this they'll come out in the Darkness—without their magic! They'll never survive.'

'We don't know that, Beattie,' he said hugging her close, her tears soaking his shoulder. 'We don't know that.' He stood up with her and looked around for Razor. He couldn't see him…the man had used their distraction to escape. 'Come on. Let's get back to the surface. We'll organize a search to find them,' he added though his voice did not evidence any hope.

Climbing the last flight of stairs from the cellar to the hallway, they heard shouts from outside the building. It wasn't until they went out of the front door that they distinguished the name Bazyli being repeated over and over by hundreds of voices.

Bazyli Montetor met them on the front step. He was covered in bandages and blood, very weak he could hardly stand. 'That Anders, that dead friend of yours saved my life.'

'We know, he told us,' said Aidan despair in his eyes.

'He also told us you needed healing,' said Beattie unable to stop her tears.

'What's wrong with you?' Bazyli asked.

'We've lost Thaddeus and Augusta. If they're alive then they'll be in the Darkness before long.' Aidan gazed up at the noon sky and moaned. 'If they're alive? Anders can you see them?'

'No…it's too dark to even see the river.'

'How about their lifelines…can you see them?' asked Beattie.

'No…nothing.'

'Then they're still alive, aren't they?' asked Beattie, a little hope lightening her tears.

'Not necessarily, Beattie. If they have…passed over, then they'll either have gone straight through the Light or, or they'll be in their own Limbo.'

'Or in the Darkness…alive or dead,' said Aidan, clinging to Beattie.

'Oh, my friends, I'm so sorry,' said Bazyli sinking to the boardwalk.

'We must get the townspeople to Bylani, Bazyli. There's not much time,' said Aidan into Beattie's long blonde hair.

It took the rest of the day and all the night to direct the nearly two thousand people of Meltwater into the mineshaft to meet Norbert and his rescuers. At first people were terrified but, having brought his people up from Griffin Town, they were met at the adit by Lodovico Portolan. And at the sight of Bazyli Montetor embracing him in friendship, the trek into Bylani went well.

But, of course, Lodovico had to be told of his son's disappearance. 'I'm sorry, Excellency, but there was nothing we could do. They went before our eyes,' said Aidan.

'Is he dead? Is Augusta dead?' Lodovico asked a catch in his throat. He was nearly at breaking point.

'We don't know,' Beatrix answered, 'they fell into the river. If they survive that then they will be washed into the harbour in Griffin into…into the Darkness.'

'You will search for them?'

'As soon as all these people are in Bylani, we will leave you. You will have to take care of Bazyli for a few days. I have set healing in place but it will still take a time for him to fully recover.' Aidan said holding Beattie's hand tightly. 'We will find Thaddeus and Augusta.' He did not add that he would also look for their bodies if the worst had happened.

Lodovico breathed deeply. 'I have faith in you, both of you. You found him once before in the Darkness, you'll find him again.'

'And when we have found them we will look for Tragen, Aidan. I promise,' said Beattie stroking his tear-stained face.

'I'm sorry to heap more on your shoulders, but there is another search you will have to undertake as soon as possible on behalf of the Elders of Bylani,' said Lodovico.

'What would that be?' Aidan asked staring into Beattie's eyes—he loved her eyes.

'The Elders feel that the salamanders will not be enough to heal all those with the plague. The old remedy must be found urgently—it's believed to be in the Drikander, in the Green People's library there. They can show you the location,' Lodovico paused. 'The Grim is waiting at Moth to take you. The tree sculptors have all but finished stepping the masts.'

'The Drikander, hey,' Aidan said quietly, wallowing in her eyes. 'Well, that's one place we might find the elves as well, I suppose. Elves, dragons, the shadow's bane—we must not forget that, Beattie. The shadow's bane! When will it all end?'

Sixty

Way across the Great Deep on an island in the mouth of the River Mantovar, an island with the watchful name of Sentinel, another abomination was taking place.

Princess Augusta of Mantovar stood in chains before a black altar, a slab of vugocite standing waist high. But this block of the natural, malignant stone did not smoke like the basin on Sanctity, though it did seem to draw all light from within the chamber. Barely enough remained to illuminate the occupants.

Cumbria, the Abbot of Sentinel, sweating despite the chill emanating from the stone, stared soundlessly at the other two captives standing before the altar. Prince Cedric of Mantovar and his wife, Princess Maria, had been given the ultimatum—kill each other or watch as their daughter was ritually disembowelled.

'You will allow her to go free?' asked Princess Maria.

'I will,' Cumbria sneered.

'How can we trust you?' asked Prince Cedric, his voice empty of all but abject despair.

'You can't. But have you any choice? The vugocite you see is made up of tiny nodules with even smaller spaces between. These spaces I must fill to achieve my master's aim. I have told you the only way I can do this. The spaces and the nodules become one when the blood of sacrifices seeps within—blood and the utmost pain. You will be the last of hundreds. Your lives, your blood, your pain is all I need and then it is finished. I could take that of your daughter's first and then yours. But then my master would have a surfeit…he does not require that. So, either your daughter gives up her life needlessly at my hands and then you…or you two can go first and I banish your daughter from Mantovar with her life. Well?'

Cedric and Maria turned their gaze on Augusta. 'I'm sorry, my darling, we cannot let you die in such a manner,' said Maria. 'I hope you survive and discover a safe haven. Leave Mantovar as Cumbria orders, seek the emperor.'

'Goodbye my beautiful one,' said Cedric, 'we'll see you in the Light.'

Princess Maria and Prince Cedric moved to the altar and lay down on it side by side, while Augusta looked on with tears streaming down her face.

'Remember,' Cumbria said, 'the more pain you suffer the better to fill the rock and the more sure you can be that I will not require your daughter's sacrifice. Do as I have said. Plunge the daggers into each other's abdomen, not your own. If you commit suicide then your souls will not become my master's. Murder it has to be. Kill each other, now!'

They did. As they kissed he pushed the dagger into her belly and she did the same to him. It was as they lay screaming in terror and pain that they glanced at their daughter and discovered the ultimate agony. They had been deceived.

The apparition that was Princess Augusta dissolved in a cloud leaving a small conical shaped amulet swinging freely in its place. And Cumbria laughed. His God had needed the pain of their sacrifice and their knowing of the deceit, to accomplish his aims.

Unlike the black rock on Sanctity this block of vugocite, now filled to its brim, cracked asunder on their deaths and the black fog of the Darkness billowed through. The first demon grabbed Cumbria and broke him in half as the abbot gibbered. The others lunged drunkenly for the doorway out of the chamber and exited onto the surface of the island of Sentinel.

The Darkness waited for a favourable wind to carry it across the water and onto the banks of the River Mantovar.

Tragen stirred, the babble outside his cage woke him from his doze again. The incessant noises of the demons passing his prison, their quarrelling erupting often into violence and resulting occasionally in the sounds of murder, was giving him a constant headache. The tension of expecting a demon to bypass Dyfrig and open the cage was giving him nightmares—the lack of sleep making him ill.

His magic had reached a height never before envisaged. One moment he exulted at what his staff could create, the next moment it scared the life out of him. The ability to breach the dimensions between Life and Death had been inconceivable up until now. What he couldn't do with such power if he was free! But he wasn't free, wasn't able to control his magic to do as he wished. The power had been usurped by an unknown God whose ambitions were also as yet unknown. Why on earth would a God as powerful as this want to cross over into Life—to kill all living souls? Surely it would mean his own demise for once all souls were ensnared in the Darkness, their rebirth denied, who would the Gods control? They'd have nothing. All the Gods would eventually enter Oblivion and be no more—existence of all soulful Life would end.

But the One behind the Darkness was surely no fool. He would know the risk he was running by entering Life. So what on earth could be his purpose? He now had a gateway to pass through the Divide. Yet…yet…the God had made no move to cross over. Why not? What was stopping him? Why was he only sending his minions? And what was the search that Zorzecai had mentioned? They were looking for something. But what could possibly be that important to the One?

Another scream interrupted Tragen's thoughts. It was Dyfrig, again renewing his life. How many times had he gone through the metamorphosis—three, four times perhaps? It was getting worse each time Dyfrig hugged the cage. In that Zorzecai had not lied.

On each occasion a roarer arrived to cross over into Life, it made a bee-line for Tragen's prison and Dyfrig had to fight it off. Tragen identified it by that name because of its terrible sound. There were others, one that screeched stridently, another that cackled and yet another that sobbed continually. But it was the roarer that always wanted to open the cage. And the one that always killed Dyfrig before dying itself.

Tragen was almost feeling compassion for Dyfrig, but then he remembered what the abbot had done in life. Did Dyfrig deserve such a sentence—an existence tormented for eternity? Tragen shuddered. That was also his destiny, unless Aidan could rescue him before a roarer succeeded in opening the cage. For once opened Tragen would die. His cage was trapped in the black rock, the vugocite, the prison full of magic protecting him from death. But if that magic was released in the afterlife it would also be released in the rock. Without its protection Tragen would suffocate and his soul would enter the Darkness proper.

Dyfrig ceased his screaming and in the sudden silence Tragen felt his cage settle, released from the manic grip of the compulsion imposed by Zorzecai. But then he felt the cage tremble again as something heavy enough to make the ground shake arrived outside.

'Master,' Dyfrig moaned, 'Master, please, I can't go on like this, the pain…please Master, release me. I'll do anything you want.'

Zorzecai's sibilant laugh pierced Tragen's brain, the sound of his hiss even more menacing because he couldn't see the demon. 'You have no option, Abbot. Your destiny is my God's to control through me. If you wish to be free of the pain you must learn to combat the demons. You see this kazzie I ride? It is a huge beast is it not? It has been bred to outfly the speediest dragon and it can smell out the key. Guard the cage well, Abbot, for I am joining the search.'

'What search, what is it you look for, Master?' Despite his torment Dyfrig's curiosity was nagging him.

'I search for the key! Another gate has been opened, this time in Mantovar. I return to Life to lead them—and the others not yet free, but will be.'

Tragen inadvertently banged his head as the kazzie moved off, jolting the cage. The wizard had listened enthralled to the conversation. What key could a God want? Nevertheless citing dragons was even more unusual. They had not been seen for thousands of years. How did Zorzecai know of them?

And then Tragen realized all. He knew of the connection between vugocite and Zorzecai. He knew who Zorzecai was and also knew which of the Gods was behind the Darkness. And in his way Zorzecai was more dangerous than his God for Tragen knew where he was going and who he was going to lead.

But above all, more important than even the permanent demise of Zorzecai—Leash had to be found and protected.

'Don't open my cage until you know, Aidan,' said Tragen where only his magic could hear. 'Don't you dare!'

THE END

Lightning Source UK Ltd.
Milton Keynes UK
UKOW051827090712

195714UK00001B/231/P